More praise for
Lady's Maid

"Forster has adeptly interwoven fact with fiction into a poignant and compelling novel. . . . The flowing plot revolves around the rich and precise character studies of poet Browning and her selfless and devoted maid, Lily. Forster captivates readers with a glimpse into the intricate and rigid socialization between the classes of the 1800s."

Cape Cod Times

"An authentic representation of the subordinate role of both privileged and impoverished women in Victorian society and a sterling example of historical fiction. . . . The reader is treated to a revealing account of the passionate romance between Elizabeth Barrett and Robert Browning through the eyes of an intimate observer. . . . [A] fascinating portrait."

Booklist

"A truly engrossing tale . . . *Lady's Maid* is a beautifully told story which will hold the reader's interest to the very end, a wonderful blend of fact and fiction."

The Herald (New Britain)

"Top-drawer historical fiction, akin to the TV series *Upstairs, Downstairs*."

Publishers Weekly

By the same author

LADY'S MAID

LADY'S MAID

MARGARET FORSTER

FAWCETT COLUMBINE

New York

A Fawcett Columbine Book
Published by Ballantine Books
Copyright © 1990 by Margaret Forster

All rights reserved under International and Pan-American Copyright Conventions.
Published in the United States by Ballantine Books, a division of Random House, Inc.,
New York.
This edition published by arrangement with Doubleday, a division of Bantam
Doubleday Dell Publishing Group, Inc.

Library of Congress Catalog Card Number: 91-90637
ISBN: 0-449-90715-5

Cover art: Florence Katherine Mayer "The Straw Hat " (detail) reproduced courtesy of
Fine-Lines Fine Art. Shipton-on-Stour, Warks, U.K.

Manufactured in the Unites States of America

First Ballantine Books Edition: May 1992

10 9 8 7 6 5 4 3

*For Valerie Grove, another hardworking lass
from the Northeast*

PART I

1844-1846

CHAPTER ONE

WILSON SAT UP very straight. This was the first letter she had ever written in her life and she wished it to be correct in every particular. The inkwell, Mother's parting gift and purchased with some difficulty, had traveled with her. It was made of glass, with a hinged lid. The ink itself had traveled separately, tightly stoppered in a small bottle and wrapped for extra security in a piece of green felt. The felt was now spread out with the inkwell resting upon it so that, should there be any spillages, no harm would be done. Taking care to allow the surplus ink to drip off her nib, at last she wrote:

Dear Mother,
Dear Mother, we left from the Unicorn Inn at five in the morning in a Coach. I was well wrapped up and though the air was Raw not in the least chilled and by nine when the sun had broken through I removed my heavy shawl the same which you dear Mother knitted for me so you can be assured I did not suffer. At ten we made a stop Mrs. Maria Barrett pronouncing she was

suffering agony from Backache and so we pulled up at an Inn
whereof I have forgot the name—

Wilson paused. It seemed important, so early in her chronicle, to be
exact. Mother had begged her to write down every detail, swearing
nothing was too trivial for her and Ellen and May and Fanny to want
to know. She could see them now in her head, reading this letter,
when it arrived, so many times they would almost memorize it. And
she could not remember the name of that first inn. But with no
difficulty at all she could remember well enough the noise and confusion and her own fear. Mrs. Maria Barrett was shown into a private
room and her sister with her, and both their maids and Wilson did not
know what to do. No one directed her, no one troubled about her.
Mrs. Barrett's maid ignored her timid request as to where she should
go, but then perhaps she had spoken so softly she had not been heard.
So she had stood on the threshold of the parlor, not knowing whether
to enter with the ladies or not, and then she had been pushed out of
the way by a woman bearing a tray of refreshments and the door had
closed in her face. She had not had the courage to open it again. And
so she turned, heart thumping, seeing nothing for it but to return to
the coach and wait. But Mr. Barrett had taken pity on her. He found
her lurking near the coach and gave a great "Hey! What's this? What's
to do? Not eating, miss?" She blushed and lowered her head, desperately confused. He held out his hand, which she had been too shy to
take, and took her back into the inn and seated her in a quiet corner
and ordered the landlord to see to her wants, and chucked her under
the chin before he left, saying she would have to learn to speak up for
herself if she was going to London.

She did not want to write any of this to her mother. The thought
of her own confusion and distress over such a simple thing as entering an inn was painful to her. She had not known what to ask for,
even. The landlord, impatient and irritable, had stood over her and
she could only think to say water and bread. Water and bread were
what she got, the water brackish and the bread hard. But she chewed
and swallowed and tried not to think of her mother's knead cakes, the

warmth of them melting the jam made from their own black currants and the fragrance of the baking still in the air:

—but we Rested and Fed and went on our way Refreshed. We stopped again at midday, I know not where, and again Mrs. Barrett had the Backache and walked about with a deal of groaning, I am sure, and after she had repaired to a bed and lain upon it until two we once more set off. It was a long weary afternoon Mother and though there was much to see I could not look at all the country we passed through without some tears before my eyes for thinking of Home and you dear Mother—

But it was her mother who had wanted her to go, to snatch this opportunity and get away from home. Mother said it might never come again and at twenty-three she had to be thinking of this and not find herself slaving and working her fingers to the bone as Mother had always done. To go to London and into a lady's service was a great thing to poor Mother, who had never done anything but wash and scrub and clean and, most of all, sew and whose ability to read and write had done her little good. Mother, married at seventeen and widowed at twenty-five, for whom nothing had ever gone right. She had kept her cottage only because she was a good worker and the master did not need it, and the mistress valued her as a seamstress, but she had no rights to it, nothing; she was only the widow of an estate worker, she could be turned out at a moment's notice as she never tired of reminding her daughters. All of them must find work so when the time came there was a chance they could fend for themselves. And to this end Mother drove them all on, snatching a place for Wilson as scullery maid when she was thirteen and urging her to work double hard and be noticed and rise in the world. Which she had done, though it was hard to be noticed when she was so shy and quiet and afraid. First she was under maid, then at sixteen took a place as second parlormaid at the Barretts' house until Mrs. Barrett's lady's maid fell ill and she was called to step in and take her place for a month. She had no training to it, nothing, she knew only how to scour pans and sweep floors and open doors and, lately, how to dust and set a table under a housekeeper's direction. But she did not know how to brush clothes or braid hair or any other essential lore for waiting on a lady. Mrs. Barrett taught her. She liked to teach her own maids how to do things as *she* wanted and no other way and preferred them to come to her without knowing any other person's ways. But after a month her own maid was recovered and had not been ill since and Wilson had been encouraged by Mrs. Barrett to look elsewhere for a situation that was worthy of her. She had done better, she had found one for her herself, with old Mrs. Graham-Clarke in Pilgrim Street, and Mother was thrilled. She stayed nearly seven years with Mrs. Graham-Clarke, from 1837 to 1844, until April this year, when Mrs. Barrett had come to see her and told her of this very special situation to a young unmarried lady who was a distant relative by marriage of hers and lived in London. Mother had been ecstatic. The wage was sixteen guineas a year and all found, six more than she was getting in Newcastle.

Wilson could not understand Mother's urgent pleas to take this London situation. Did she want to be rid of her? Did she not want her near? But both these explanations were so patently false that she could only fall back on her mother's given reason, the same she had always given: she wanted all her daughters to do well for themselves. London was, by her standards, doing supremely well, though Mother had never been to London and knew little of it. She said she did not need any firsthand information. London was where the Queen was, London was where the rich and famous were. And, Mrs. Barrett had said, this young lady's family were one of the first families in London, she believed. She gave a guarantee that Wilson would find no better, no more respectable, no kinder household in all of London. The maid whose situation she would take, Mrs. Barrett had said, was leaving in tears and only because she was to be married. Everyone loved the lady for whom Wilson would work. Mrs. Barrett had tears in her own eyes as she described her distant cousin, Miss Elizabeth Moulton Barrett. She told Wilson what a sad, wasted figure Miss Barrett was, an invalid, almost a recluse, so sweet and delicate and gentle, and moreover *a poet* of some acclaim. Mother had started to say it was her duty to go to such a lady and help her but Mrs. Barrett had interrupted to say it was a privilege. But it was so far away and she had never been out of Newcastle, except once to Durham and then she was glad to get home. She would not see her family for a year and yet there was Mother, pushing her to go, not crying at all.

Except at the parting, when everyone cried, Ellen and May and Fanny as well as Mother; but Ellen had cried for jealousy, May because she was frightened and Fanny because everyone else was crying. Ellen knew she would never rise like Wilson. She started out as a scullery maid but did not progress because she was clumsy and had a temper. Both kept her down. Now she was twenty-one and still in the kitchen and never likely to leave it unless she married. May was more likely to follow in Wilson's footsteps, being neat and docile, but then May was twice as timid as Wilson and afraid of any responsibility. She was better as a parlormaid, Mother said, under a butler's eye and guided by a housekeeper. As for Fanny, she was still at home, though fourteen. Mother said she was not strong and should be kept at home longer if it could be managed. Not strong and not bright either. Wilson wondered often if Fanny, born after Mother was widowed, was a little more than merely delicate, but the subject could not be mentioned. Fanny was Mother's baby, sent to console her, born in the middle of great sorrow and grief, and the mark of this seemed always to be on her.

Wilson applied herself. This daydreaming, this rambling in the head, would never do. She wrote on rapidly, describing the rest of the journey and making a good story of the horse that tried to bolt and losing a wheel at Doncaster and finally arriving in the city itself:

—You would cry out to see it dear Mother it is so Fine and there are Such Sights I cannot think to tell you in one letter. Mrs. Barrett has a very Fine House here full of all manner of good stuff such as you would exclaim to see though in truth I was not there above a day and did not see all the rooms. She brought me here and next day between two and three in the afternoon since the lady was so desirous to see me but not the lady Miss Elizabeth Barrett, as I will be maid to it is another, Miss Henrietta, that I saw and a very pretty lady too. She asked me if I was Quiet because her sister, Miss Elizabeth, had great need of Quiet and I said I was and I was Known to be Quiet in all I did and Mrs. Barrett vouched for me. She asked if I understood her sister, Miss Elizabeth, was not strong and needed great care and many things done for her and above all a Kind and Cheerful person about her. I did not know what to make in reply for, dear Mother, I fear I am not naturally Cheerful and what reply was I to make? Miss Henrietta saw my confusion and spared me and said she was sure I was Kind because I looked Kind. Mrs. Barrett said I was Kind and had no temper. Miss Henrietta said she would consult with her sister but she thought I could come the next day and begin to know Miss Elizabeth if that suited. And so today I came Mother and Mrs. Barrett sent me in her carriage with my box which was appreciated as it is heavy with all my winter goods. I make haste to send this dear Mother and have stamped it and will post it when I can and hope it will find you as it leaves me.

    Your loving daughter,
    Lily.

Wilson's name was not Lily or Lilian but Elizabeth, shortened to Lily from Lilabet, as Ellen had called her when a child. She liked to sign her Christian name because she so rarely saw it and now she had left home would rarely hear it either. She was Wilson, without any prefix, and had been pleased when she became known as Wilson in Mrs. Graham-Clarke's household. It put her above Mary and Martha and Eve, who were only under maids. She was Wilson as the house-keeper in this new place, though unmarried, was "Mrs." Robinson and the distinction was clear.

Mrs. Robinson had treated her with some suspicion but with respect. She had looked very searchingly at Wilson when they met that morning. A fine, handsome man had opened the door to her when she plunged down the area steps. She did not dare raise her eyes while she told him who she was. All she had seen as she followed him down a passage were his black-clad legs and the stone of the ground. She knew that as lady's maid she ought not to behave like a scullery hand, that she ought to have presence and speak up and act according to her station but it was not in her to do so. She ought by rights to have gone to the front door but this had not occurred to her. Mrs. Robinson did not seem to hold it against her. "I like modesty," she said and smiled. Wilson stood and blushed until told to take a seat.

Mrs. Robinson, Minnie Robinson, was large and fat, but soft and dimpled, rather than solid and heavy. She had thick, wavy blond hair under her cap, peeping out all around the edges in tiny tendrils, and bright, sharp blue eyes that looked at Wilson shrewdly. This one, she could tell, would be no trouble. No airs and graces here, maybe a deal too soft for many a taste. What would Crow make of her? Minnie pressed Wilson to a cup of tea and wondered if anyone could be more different from the vigorous, lively Crow who was about to depart among so many tears and sighs. They even looked startlingly different, the two of them. Crow was tall and strong with bold coloring and a great energy of movement which she struggled to control in Miss Elizabeth's company. This new one, Wilson, was small and fragile, nearly as small and fragile as Miss Elizabeth herself. She sat there now with her head bowed and her hands clasped tightly, tight enough to turn the knuckles white. Minnie poured her some tea, urged her to remove her coat if she felt the room was warm enough. Hurriedly, Wilson took off her thick cloak, afraid that by not doing so without being bidden she had caused offense. A neat figure, Minnie noted, a good bust in spite of her small stature and air of fragility. But not a flirt, there was no preening, no sign that this young woman knew she had a good figure: there would be no trouble. Minnie asked her about her other positions and watched her carefully as she recited the dates and names. Only occasionally did Wilson look up, little furtive peeps, then down with the eyes again. The master would not like that—"Look me in the face," he always told his servants and frowned if they could not hold his stare. This one would be afraid of the master, it was certain.

Minnie got up, with some difficulty. She was a little lame in one leg. "I'll take you to your room myself," she said, sorting out the keys hanging on the rack. Most of the servants' rooms did not lock but Crow's did, as did Minnie's own. It was a privilege of which she had no need, though Crow had done, of course. She went ahead, telling Wilson to leave her bag for Charles to bring. Slowly, she walked along the passage, Wilson following, and began to climb the stairs, pulling hard on the banister. The first flight, to the hall, was steep but after that it became easier until the last flight of all. She did not talk to Wilson—she had not the breath to do so—until the second floor and then she paused on the landing and indicated a door and whispered, "Miss Elizabeth's—sssh." Another steep flight and then they were there. Minnie opened the door, indicated to Wilson that she should go in. Wilson stepped into the room hesitantly, as though expecting someone to be there. Minnie could smell lemon juice still fresh in the air. Crow, who had only moved out two days ago, used lemon juice on her hands to keep them white. It was pure folly and expensive folly in Minnie's opinion—there would be no more lemons for Crow to waste on her hands now.

Crow had left the room immaculate. Wilson could see the chest of drawers had been freshly polished and the cover on the bed, a pleasant sprigged pink counterpane, freshly laundered. There were pink and white curtains at the window and a pink cushion in an old basket-weave chair beside the bed. If it had not been for a large and ugly mahogany closet, the room would have seemed too pretty to be that of a servant. Minnie opened the closet with some pride, assuring Wilson it would hold a complete wardrobe, winter and summer, with ease. Wilson blushed. Her few things would be lost in that cavernous cupboard. Minnie sat on the bed, said it was a good bed, that the master had good beds throughout the house for servants as well as family. She said she hoped Wilson would be happy here. Wilson said she was sure she would. Still Minnie went on sitting there until Wilson began to feel embarrassed.

"Miss Henrietta told you about Miss Elizabeth, I expect?" Minnie finally said, getting up.

"Yes, ma'am."

"You'll know, then, about her situation?"

"Yes, ma'am."

"She's had a sad life, poor Miss Elizabeth, a lot of illness and disappointment."

"Yes, ma'am."

"Crow could tell you the weeks and weeks she's wept, never sleeping."

"Yes, ma'am."

"Well then, you'll feel for her."

"Oh yes, ma'am."

Minnie nodded, evidently satisfied. She told Wilson that Miss Henrietta would see her presently and meanwhile Charles would bring up her box. She asked Wilson if there was anything she wanted to make her more comfortable and then she left. Wilson flew to the window and pressed her face eagerly to the glass: chimneys. That was all she could see, a field of chimneys of every size and shape and brick color, sticking up from the roofs below like squat trees. No real trees, no greenery. Carefully, Wilson opened the window and peered first to the right and then to the left. She was not quite sure but fancied she saw a hint of green, far, far to the right, as though there might be a tree of some kind on the horizon. She closed the window, stood with her back to it. The room would do very well. Just then there was a knock, making her jump. Her heart thudded a little as she opened the door. A youth was standing there with her box, staring at her boldly. He went on standing there, saying nothing, staring, holding the heavy box, clearly waiting for her to give him an order. Tongue-tied, knowing she was not behaving as she ought, as a lady's maid ought, a London lady's maid, she pointed at the floor. He put the box down, slowly. She thanked him. Still he stood there. She had no idea how to get rid of him. She put her hand on the doorknob and said thank you again and at last he backed out, never smiling, never speaking.

For the next hour she unpacked her box and arranged her things —three dresses, two petticoats, three nightgowns, two chemises, four pairs of drawers, two nightcaps, four pairs of stockings—and then she moved the jug and basin from the washstand and used it as a desk to write to her mother. When that was done, she could not think what to do next. Should she go down? Should she wait until sent for? She dreaded meeting people she did not yet know on the stairs. Should she change her dress to be ready for the summons from Miss Henrietta? She was full of doubt, weak with the strain of not knowing how to behave. All new places and people and routines were an ordeal to her—Mother could not know how she suffered every time she had to face moving. What she loved was the familiar, the well-tried and -tested. There was no pleasure for her in change.

An hour later Wilson stood trembling outside Miss Elizabeth's door, Henrietta beside her. The landing was gloomy on this turn of the stairs. The thick, dark maroon carpet blended into the skirting board and then seemed to continue up the walls in heavily embossed wall-paper of a similar color. There were pictures on the walls, huge things in gold frames, but Wilson could make none of them out. Miss Henrietta had her finger to her lips. Gently, she turned the knob of the door and pushed it open. Wilson's heart beat wildly. She did not know what she expected to see, nor why the idea of a poor invalid lady should frighten her so, but she could hardly bear to enter that room. There was the faintest of growls and she saw the eyes of a dog staring from right across the room at her. A voice said, "Sssh," and the dog lowered its head. Miss Henrietta moved swiftly across the room and was adjusting a blind, saying, "Really, Ba, a little light will not hurt, surely. It is such a beautiful day." There was no reply. Wilson was afraid to move unless bidden and went on standing just inside the door, her hands clasped in front of her to stop them trembling. She could see very little in the room. It seemed crowded with furniture and belongings and the only clear silhouette in the gloom was that of the chaise longue where the dog sat on a coverlet.

Miss Henrietta, a flash of light in her pretty yellow dress, flitted over to the chaise longue and bent over it. "Darling Ba," she whispered, "I have brought someone to see you. Come, sit up and be introduced, do." Wilson saw the coverlet move and a dark head appear over its rim. Miss Henrietta bent over and lifted the reclining figure to a half-sitting position. The pillow fell from behind the head and Wilson saw her chance. She crossed the room, eager now there was a task to be done, and lifted the pillow, shook it, and placed it with great care and tenderness behind the head. She saw a pair of great, black eyes set in a face so thin and wasted that they seemed indecently large and heavy. She dropped her gaze instantly and retreated a step, giving a half curtsy. "This is Wilson, Ba," Miss Henrietta said. Miss Elizabeth said nothing. Wilson kept her eyes lowered. "Wilson," Miss Elizabeth said, "you have come to look after me?" "Yes, miss." Miss Henrietta, who seemed always to move quickly and energetically, was gone in an instant, saying from the door that she would return presently. Wilson half turned, beseechingly, terribly afraid to be left alone, but it was too late. A rustle of silk and Miss Henrietta had gone.

Wilson stood in front of the chaise longue like a penitent, head still bowed, hands still clasped, body shivering very slightly. "Do sit, do rest," Miss Elizabeth said, her voice light and whispery. "On a chair, miss?" Wilson managed to say. "Here, on this stool." Gratefully, Wilson sank down onto the stool at the side of the chaise longue. She noticed the coverlet was not even and deftly put it right. "Thank you. It is Flush, you know, he disarranges everything." Encouraged, Wilson dared to look up again and this time noted the weight of the black hair, thickly ringleted and parted into bunches either side of the pale face. She saw the mouth was wide and generous and, like the eyes, appeared too dominant for the size of the face. Miss Elizabeth sighed and closed her eyes. "You are tired, miss?" Wilson managed to ask. "I am weary, weary," Miss Elizabeth murmured, "always weary." Wilson kept quiet. She tried desperately hard to communicate her sympathy silently. Every muscle in her body now went still, a great calmness took hold of her. The dog, Flush, sensing it first, lifted his head. He inched across the coverlet cautiously and when at last on the very edge extended his tongue and licked Wilson's hand. She patted him on the head respectfully. Flush retreated, satisfied.

"Well, that *is* a miracle," Miss Elizabeth said. "What power do you have, Wilson, to entice Mr. Flush so? He does not easily give his friendship, I assure you."

"None, miss. I like all dumb animals."

"And dumb humans?"

"Pardon, miss?"

"Do you like dumb humans, Wilson?"

"I don't know as I've known any, miss, not properly dumb. If I did, I expect I would feel the same for them."

The silence was so complete and lengthy, Wilson feared she had given offense and was compelled to look at her new mistress, to search her face for reproof. But Miss Elizabeth was smiling, a strange, almost mocking smile, though the eyes were kind. There was no hint of anger. "It is time for my tea, I think," Miss Elizabeth said, and just then there was a knock at the door and Tilly entered bearing a tray. Wilson was on her feet to receive it at once. It seemed to her that Tilly, whom she had not yet met, thrust the tray toward her at an awkward angle, deliberately sloping it down so that the teapot threatened to capsize, and that she knew what she was doing. Wilson saw the jeer in Tilly's eyes and the turn of her lip but she ignored both and concentrated on bending her elbows in such a way that the tray was leveled. Tilly would learn. She might be new and North Country and insignificant but Wilson knew all about impertinent housemaids and how to deal with them.

She set the tray down, taking care not to bang it on the table. Equally carefully, she poured tea into the tiny cup beside the pot. It was such a small cup it was hard not to overfill it but she managed to stop just short of the rim. There was neither milk nor sugar on the tray so Wilson did not need to inquire how much of each was taken. Keeping her eyes on the cup, she took it over but immediately there was a problem: Miss Elizabeth was not sitting up sufficiently to take the cup and Flush was in the way. Wilson blushed and faltered. She ought to have helped her mistress up first and moved Flush. She made to turn back with the cup but Miss Elizabeth stopped her, saying, "I am an expert at taking refreshment lying down with a dog on my stomach, Wilson. Give it to me." The hands that came from under the coverlet to take the cup were delicate, long-fingered and startlingly white—Wilson had never seen such white, spiritlike hands before. They looked as if they did not have the strength even to hold such a tiny cup.

The tea drunk, Miss Elizabeth sank back onto her pillow, stroked Flush and said, "You may go now, Wilson. Until five o'clock. Thank you." Wilson curtsied and left the room as quietly as she could. She stood outside on the landing uncertain what to do. In her hands she had the tea tray, which decided her. It was the housemaid's job to take the tray but at the Graham-Clarkes' she had always taken the tea tray, there had been no strict rules there, and now she found herself with it, it seemed silly not to take it to the kitchen. So she descended, only hesitating again when she heard laughter and voices down below. Both stopped as she entered the kitchen and put the tray down. Wilson kept her eyes lowered but took in that there were two men there—Charles, who had brought her box, and the imposing man who had opened the door—and Tilly. Tilly, who was very pretty, had taken her cap off and her blond curls tumbled about her shoulders. Wilson was gone before any of them could say a word, fairly rushing out of the kitchen to escape interrogation. Tilly giggled as she fled.

Miss Henrietta had told her five o'clock was an important time in the house. At five o'clock Mr. Barrett returned from the City. He would go straight to his room and change his coat and wash his hands and then he would go to see Miss Elizabeth. She, Wilson, should be there, ready. She should have Miss Elizabeth sitting in her chair, composed and comfortable, and when Mr. Barrett entered she should leave, returning precisely half an hour later. Miss Henrietta stressed the importance of good timekeeping over and over. Her papa, she said, was most particular and the sooner Wilson appreciated this the better. Wilson had been surprised to be warned in such a manner when she had not yet had the chance to demonstrate her punctuality or otherwise, but Miss Henrietta had no need to worry, she was never late, she was renowned for her reliability.

She did not look forward to meeting this new Mr. Barrett or indeed any of the men of the house, and yet until she had met them there was no knowing if she would be happy in this new situation. At old Mrs. Graham-Clarke's the men in the house had hardly impinged on her life; they had no power at all and made themselves scarce. And at Mrs. Barrett's the men were nicer than the women and she had no fear of them—but here, at 50 Wimpole Street, there were so many men and she sensed they were dominant from the attention paid to the time when they would all return. As five o'clock approached it seemed to her that there was an air of not entirely pleasant expectancy in the house. The laughter and noise belowstairs stopped, there was much running up and down and she could hear peremptory orders being issued by Mrs. Robinson. Later, writing to her mother yet again before she went to sleep, Wilson tried to describe the change that came over the place:

—and, Mother, no one trifles with him, be sure of that. I was half scared out of my wits when he first came into the house though I did not see him, being with Miss Elizabeth. I only heard his voice, very deep and strong since I could hear it two floors up though I could not make out the words. And Miss Elizabeth sat up straight and took hold of Flush (her little dog, Mother, that is always with her) and said to him that he was to be good, very good, and not bark or dash about and if he behaved there might be a cake at the end. You would have laughed, Mother, to see that animal, how he looked at her and put his paw out and seemed to promise. Then we heard Mr. Barrett's step on the stairs, heavy and slow, and he knocked and came in and I was never so surprised in my life for he is young Mother and handsome and not a fierce old gentleman such as I had thought. He is tall, but not over tall, with a fine noble face and a good head of dark hair and such a carriage as you never saw. I curtsied and made to leave but he ordered me to wait and Miss Elizabeth said as how I was her new maid, come to care for her and he asked my name. I *tried* hard to be Plain and Honest mother and I lifted my eyes and *tried* to meet his mother when I said Wilson sir, though I fear I faltered. He was not angry or unkind but held my gaze steady and—

Wilson was forced to pause. And what? She could not think how to convey what she had felt, the shiver that had passed through her, yet not a shiver of fear, more of knowing, recognizing this man whom she had never known. It was as though he knew it, too, as though he was satisfying himself that she was who he thought. There was complicity in the look he gave her and an instant approval which astonished her.

—and nodded. He said he trusted I would look after his daughter well, that she was most precious to him and her welfare his first concern. I thanked him and left. When I returned, as bidden, he had gone and Miss Elizabeth was right flushed and how her eyes sparkled Mother. She said to look and see what her papa had given her and laid in my hand the smallest book, a tiny thing, prettily covered in red silk. Miss Elizabeth said I should take it up and open it and I did and it was a psalm with pictures on one side and the words on the other and all so Delicate and Cunning. She said her papa was always kind and brought gifts often and that he had brought a cake for Flush too. She was so happy, mother, the change in her was great and I could not help marveling at it. Later, when I had got her ready for sleep, she said her papa would come and pray with her and that it was a great comfort that he did so, no one knew the comfort.

Wilson finished the letter and blew out the candle. She was glad of the lock on her door. She still did not know who was to the right or who was to the left and it was a long way to the other side of the landing and the safety of Mrs. Robinson. She lay for a long time thinking of home but not as miserably as she had expected. She liked Miss Elizabeth and she liked Mrs. Robinson—that was double good fortune, to like both mistress and housekeeper. Her head was full of questions to which she badly wanted answers—what had happened to Mrs. Barrett, why was Miss Elizabeth ill, what was Crow, her predecessor, like—and she found herself looking forward to the next day more than she had thought possible. One thing was certain: there would be a great deal to write home about.

CHAPTER TWO

T̲H̲E̲ ̲D̲A̲I̲L̲Y̲ ̲R̲O̲U̲T̲I̲N̲E̲ was as Miss Henrietta had described. Miss Elizabeth slept late, though in fact she did not actually sleep, only rested. She had her morning coffee brought at eleven and then Wilson helped her to wash and brushed her hair and changed her nightdress for a gown. Until two o'clock Miss Elizabeth wrote and read. Wilson for a long time was not sure exactly what this writing and reading meant, whether it was letters Miss Elizabeth wrote and newspapers she read, because her mistress liked to be alone when she was busy. But gradually, as she became more familiar with the books and papers in the room, she realized this was a more serious occupation than she had thought. Miss Elizabeth did write letters, many letters, but she also worked at her poetry and wrote articles for magazines which made such an impression on Wilson that she could not help rushing to write to Mother about how

—she writes and writes, Mother, on such small pieces of paper, ever so fine and neat until she has a great collection and then she scores through her writing and writes it out again until it is Right.

It is Clever stuff, mother, such as you or I cannot rightly understand but I mean to try presently. All morning up to dinner Miss Elizabeth applies herself and none must interrupt. Then there are the books, mother, so many of them and all so Thick and Heavy she scarce has strength to lift them. There are books in tongues I have never seen but she makes light work of them, never pausing, the pages turning and turning. It is so strange to see a Lady working thus, I cannot believe it. Miss Henrietta scolds her and Miss Arabel, her other sister I told you of, pleads with her not to work so hard but she never heeds them. They say she will injure her health further and never be well. And, Mother, I fear they are right for whatever ails Miss Elizabeth it is not helped by the little she eats and the lying up all day you would not like to see how she lives, hardly stirring from her room which is kept close—

Wilson could hardly bear how close. She sat remembering home and the Graham-Clarkes' where, for different reasons, fires were never lit before noon unless the frost was hard, and even in summer the house never felt warm. In Miss Elizabeth's room it was summer all the time and Wilson found it stifling, found it a relief to step out onto the landing and feel the cooler air. The windows were kept tight shut and in the afternoons, when the sun came through them, the temperature rose even with the blinds down. But Miss Elizabeth never felt the heat. She had a fire on all night unless it was very warm and on the days when it had to be cleaned out she lay under a pile of furs, shivering, until it was laid and lit again. She told Wilson she could not bear the cold and feared winter above all else, for it meant she was entirely confined to her room.

So far as Wilson could tell, she was in any case entirely confined. It was spring, with many sunny, mild days, but Miss Elizabeth did not venture out. Wilson was with her three weeks before she saw her go into the drawing room at all and had almost come to believe this was something of which she was incapable. It had come as a shock to her, the second day she attended Miss Elizabeth, to find she was not a cripple at all—seeing her stand and walk to the worktable of her own accord astonished Wilson and Miss Elizabeth had laughed and asked her if she had seen a ghost. So Wilson knew walking was possible, under certain circumstances, and had wondered why it was not practiced more. But that day her mistress descended to the drawing room for an hour, she was ill in the night. Miss Arabel, who often slept in Miss Elizabeth's room, on a sofa, told Wilson her sister blamed the exertion of the stairs. She said she would not risk it again for a while. Wilson found it hard to explain all this as she continued with her letter:

—and cannot be healthy. You would pity her, Mother, if you could see how thin she is, she is like a child. Her arms and legs are sticks and she is so small, smaller even than I am, and she has no stomach or chest on her but then she does not eat. She has her coffee, black stuff, evil looking stuff, and sips that all day and otherwise pecks at whatever is sent up. A pudding she will try and fruit if it is soft but meat she detests. I have seen her feed it to Flush when she thinks no one looks. So, Mother, she receives little to make her strong and needs medicine to make her sleep. She cannot sleep without it, she says it is her elixir. I measure the drops, it is laudanum, most carefully and collect a new bottle of the tincture each week from the chemist on the corner and he says it is a wonder Miss Barrett is still alive. She has a Cough which troubles her but no worse than our Fanny's and there is no Blood thanks be to God. But it is a sad life she leads and without her family she would be sadder still.

Wilson blotted the letter carefully. She would describe the family in another letter—there were so many of them, her head had ached with learning their names. Miss Henrietta and Miss Arabel of course were easy but the men were different. She knew Master Septimus and Master Octavius first because they were most in the house and the noisiest and came most often to see Miss Elizabeth. They were the youngest of the six sons, both tall and fair, and although twenty and twenty-two years of age seeming very much younger. They smiled a great deal and always had tales to tell and Wilson was not too afraid of them.

Next up from Septimus was Alfred, called Daisy, which puzzled

Wilson hugely, and he was a lazy young man, always yawning and vowing he was done for. He did not visit his sister so often but, when he did, he sketched her. Wilson saw and admired his sketches and thought him clever even if she never felt entirely at ease. Sette and Occy teased her, if they noticed her at all, but Alfred watched her through his half-closed eyes and she wondered if he was critical of her and if so why. He never addressed a direct word to her and neither did Henry, two years older than Alfred. Henry was the rarest visitor of all in Miss Elizabeth's room—Wilson was there a month before he came. She did not take to him. He was peremptory, frowned a lot, appeared discontented and bad tempered. And she was afraid of his dog, an enormous hound called Catiline. This animal was supposed to remain in the yard or below stairs but when the master was out Henry allowed him to wander everywhere and all the servants warned Wilson to watch out and keep away if the beast was roaming the stairs. The other two brothers were much older, or seemed so. George was the image of his father, though not so tall, and sometimes appeared to Wilson even more impressive. He frowned a great deal and always looked worried and serious and she had heard Miss Elizabeth tease him and ask him if he carried *all* the cares of the world on his strong shoulders. George was a lawyer and came and went as regularly as his father. Charles John, the oldest of the brothers, stayed at home all the time and was often in his sister's room. He was known as Stormie but was very unstormlike. Wilson had never seen such a hopelessly tongue-tied and shy young man—he made her feel bold by comparison.

So far, Mother knew only the names of all the family. Wilson was waiting until she could differentiate them all more usefully before she described them to those at home and made them as vivid as she hoped she had made the servants. Mother was well acquainted by the end of the first month with Minnie Robinson and her "Kindness" and knew, among others, of the flighty Tilly and Simon, the bootboy, and of the alarming Charles, the footman, whose passion in life was pigeons (not that he could keep any in Wimpole Street). Then there was the butler, Mr. John, who was respectful and not nearly as powerful as Mrs. Robinson, and Molly Mawson, Miss Henrietta and Miss Arabel's maid, who had been very nice to Wilson from the start and helped her a great deal. Mrs. Tappit was the cook and Amy the scullery maid and that was it. With the exception of Tilly and Charles, Wilson liked them all and felt comfortable remarkably quickly, but it was only to Minnie Robinson that she felt drawn. Mrs. Robinson ruled the house absolutely and yet no one was afraid of her. She was firm but gentle, always gentle, and inspired in the other servants a desire to please. Even Tilly jumped to put right whatever Mrs. Robinson had found wrong and tried not to offend again. Every day, Mrs. Robinson had Wilson into her room for a quarter of an hour in the afternoon when Miss Elizabeth rested and they took tea. Wilson assumed at first that this regular meeting must be for Mrs. Robinson to keep an eye on her and question her to see that she was doing what she ought—though for a housekeeper to interrogate a lady's maid would not, as Wilson knew, be proper. But, on the contrary, Mrs. Robinson, who was soon Minnie to her, never asked a thing beyond inquiring whether she was content.

One afternoon there was another woman there when Wilson entered Minnie's room. She made to leave, but Minnie called her back and said she wanted her to meet Mrs. Treherne, who had been Crow, Miss Elizabeth's maid. Mrs. Treherne excused herself from getting up, saying she was near her time and tired with the walk from Camden Town. Wilson shook her hand and sat down, shy and a little intimidated. As she wrote to her mother:

—it was Crow, Mother, as I have heard so much about. Tilly told me Miss Elizabeth loved her dearly and cried her heart out when Crow left and vowed she wanted no other maid and I believe this to be true. She is a fine looking woman even now though big with child and her face Minnie says somewhat swollen as well as her belly and legs. She has fine dark eyes, eyes like Miss Elizabeth, but her face is square and ruddy and her expression Frank. She said she was pleased to meet me, as I was to meet her, and she asked me if I liked my new place and was glad to hear I did because my mistress was Precious to her, she had been with her through Great Sorrow and had feared often for her Life. I asked if I might be so bold as to enquire about the Great Sorrow but Mrs. Treherne shook her head and there were tears I am sure in her eyes mother and she said she was not able to speak of it today. I begged her pardon and asked after her health. She said she was to go to Caister shortly to be confined and would be glad to rest up there at her mother's house. When she said that, mother, my own eyes filled, I could not help it, thinking suddenly of your house and what an age it will be before I see you and my dear sisters. I wish—

But after some thought Wilson had scored that out. It was no good wishing for letters from home as long and regular as those she dispatched. Mother did not have the time to write nor did she have so much to write about, though Wilson had told her every detail was of interest to her, every scrap of home life. And Ellen and May were worse. Ellen added a line or two to Mother's letters and that was all and most unsatisfactory. May wrote her own notes but they were poor things and Fanny only signed her name with a row of kisses.

Miss Elizabeth knew she wrote many letters home because she had seen her scribbling. Wilson had thought her mistress was asleep and had pulled paper from her workbasket and a pencil to finish off a long letter she wished to post that day. "Why, Wilson," Miss Elizabeth had said, making her jump, "is that a letter?" Wilson had blushed, dropped her pencil in confusion and vowed she had meant no offense and would not do it again only—and then Miss Elizabeth stopped her and laughed and said what nonsense Wilson talked, that she was quite delighted to find her maid had a taste for correspondence. Ever since, she had plied Wilson with paper and envelopes, requesting to know if she preferred small to large sheets, rough to smooth paper, pencil to ink and, if ink, which ink and what kind of pen. Wilson was embarrassed by her mistress's interest but it went further. Miss Elizabeth examined her handwriting and said it was good and clear and better than hers.

"Where did you learn that hand, Wilson?"

"From my mother, miss."

"As I did mine. My dear mother could not abide an untidy hand.

She would make me copy out my letters to my grandmother until she was satisfied I could do no better. And Bro had his knuckles rapped many a time . . . dear Bro." To Wilson's consternation, the tears had coursed down Miss Elizabeth's face and Miss Henrietta, coming in, had been alarmed and rushed to comfort her, asking Wilson whatever had happened.

"Nothing, miss. We were talking of writing and letters and Miss Elizabeth spoke of her mother teaching her and of, I think Bro, or some such name, and how—" Miss Henrietta shushed her and indicated she should leave the room.

Later, Minnie consoled her. It was, she said, only the mention of those dead loved ones, of Miss Elizabeth's mother and brother, that had upset her. Minnie said she never mentioned Bro's name and hardly ever her mother's and when she did she was quite overcome. It was a sad story Minnie told her and Wilson felt guilty because it gave her such drama for another letter.

Dearest Mother,
I am well and glad to receive your letter this day which came in the afternoon and was a great comfort and I was happy to know Fanny is better and Ellen has bought a new hat though I cannot fancy she will wear such a Creation as you describe very often. I have hardly been out to need a hat even though the weather is fine and I miss the air. Presently I hope to walk to the Regents Park which I believe is a great sight and there is a Zoo and a Diorama and all manner of delights, would that I could see them.
Miss Elizabeth has a Cough and is not as well as previously and we are anxious the weather being good and it not being the season for a cough. But she had been brought Low and has wept many a day and I cannot account for it nor can anyone. But I have discovered some of the sorrows she has and sorrows indeed they were Mother such as will make you weep yourself. Her mother was taken right suddenly, all in three days, when none suspected she was mortally ill and Miss Elizabeth did not speak for two months except the bare necessities. But Mother worse was to follow for she had a brother Samuel and he died of the fever in Jamaica when Miss Elizabeth lay ill at Torquay and hardly had

that blow struck Mother before another brother whom she loved dearest of all was drowned in a storm. Minnie says she was not with her then, being in London here, but Crow, as I met last week, was and thought Miss Elizabeth would go insane with grief. It was four years ago Mother, in the summer, but she cannot speak of it, her suffering being too great still. Minnie says Crow swears Miss Elizabeth willed herself to die and when she did not could only think she had been spared to do her work. She has written such poems that they are to appear in two volumes this August Mother—only think of it! I have not seen any of the poems but Minnie says Miss Henrietta tells her their father thinks they are very fine and will make a stir. A man comes sometimes and he reads them—

Wilson was aware her mother might misinterpret this piece of information and hastened to add that this man was a relation, a cousin. She thought him an impressive gentleman, this John Kenyon, though he was not as handsome as Mr. Barrett, whose age he was. He was large, portly, balding, florid-faced but his bearing was dignified and he had a way of peering over his spectacles which Wilson found endearing. She had shown him in each week and could now meet his level, appraising stare on arrival without flinching. He did not engage her in any conversation, for which she was grateful, but he smiled and nodded and told her once, on the way out, that Miss Elizabeth was fortunate to have replaced Crow with someone prepared to look after her so devotedly.

Wilson thought about what Mr. Kenyon had said after he left, pondering over the meaning of "devotedly." She was not sure if she was devoted or not. The word implied an intimacy she could not in all honesty say that she yet felt. It was only right to use that word about her mother—then, it was literally true. But with her mistress she was still, after a month, nervous and unsure. She had picked up the routine tasks of the day quickly enough, there had been no difficulty there, but she had not caught Miss Elizabeth's measure as easily. It seemed to her Miss Elizabeth wanted something she was failing to give and the knowledge troubled her. Miss Elizabeth would say, "Give me another draught of laudanum, Wilson, my head aches so, I shall not sleep," and when Wilson dutifully measured out drops of the tincture and gave it to her mistress she seemed somehow displeased though her order had been precisely obeyed. "You do whatever I ask, Wilson," Miss Elizabeth had said more than once but it had sounded like a complaint. Once, her mistress had said fretfully, "Crow would not have let me have more," and Wilson had felt humiliated. What did Miss Elizabeth want?

Watching her sometimes, when she dozed, Wilson was aware of a growing tenderness. She sat darning a stocking, as near to the window as she could get (though, the blind being down, not much sun struggled through), and looked around the room and found herself shivering. It was like a tomb, a very well appointed tomb, with everything the dead person could want gathered together for their enjoyment in the next world. The white busts of the poets Miss Elizabeth revered glowed eerily in the half-light and the spines of the hundreds of books glittered on the shelves. And there, shrouded in a heavy coverlet, her dark hair spread out on the pillow, her pale hands hanging listless over the side of the chaise longue, lay this tiny creature, smothered and trapped by all the belongings and furniture. It was a sad life, Wilson reflected, for all its ease and security. Weariness lay heavy in the air, lethargy seemed to seep from the walls, and there was a hint of despair over every surface. Wilson darned and thought. Miss Elizabeth's illness, if illness it was, and the deaths of her loved ones, did not seem sufficient to account for her misery. What more was there to know? She was beginning to feel, as everyone in the whole house did, that she would do anything to bring a smile to her poor mistress's face.

Hearing a carriage, Wilson paused and listened. It was the wrong time of day for callers but she heard, faintly, the door knocker bang and then voices and afterward the door closing and the carriage driving off. Sitting as she was at the back of the house, she could not peep out to see what was happening but she would hear later, from Minnie. She completed a fine darn and made the end good. Miss Elizabeth's clothes were not in good order—in that respect at least Crow had not been perfect, which gave Wilson much inward satisfaction, though she would not for the world have remarked on it to a soul. Her mistress had little interest in clothes, wishing daily she could stay in her chemise and wrapper without the trouble of dressing, but she confided in Wilson that if she dared to do so it angered her father, who liked to see her properly attired. So she had two black silk dresses for the summer and two black velvet for winter and they were all much the same, distinguished from one another only by a difference in collar. The effort of donning this costume exhausted Miss Elizabeth every morning of her life. Patiently, Wilson had learned to leave this laborious dressing until after her mistress had done some of her writing, finding she was better-humored less listless, if she had worked. Then she would try to get it over as quickly as possible, provoking the response, "You are very deft, Wilson." This comment made her blush. She was not sure if it was praise or not and merely said, "Yes ma'am," and bobbed her head.

"Was that a carriage, Wilson?" Miss Elizabeth asked, voice drowsy and eyes still closed.

"Yes, miss."

"I wonder who it could be?"

"Shall I find out, miss?"

"No. It is of no consequence. It will be a caller for Henrietta. I do not know how she can abide to visit and be visited so."

Wilson said nothing. She picked up another stocking and began threading a needle. Minnie had made dark hints about Miss Henrietta and a certain soldier who should be nameless. She said the master was no fool and would see through any pretense. Miss Henrietta, Minnie said, was running it very close and should not count on luck forever. Next week the master was to travel out of London for a week and already Miss Henrietta had been to her, wheedling and sweethearting her into a few jellies and biscuits for a squeeze she planned. Minnie swore to Wilson she would not countenance any defiance of the master's orders and that if he were to leave orders that there was to be no company allowed into the house while he was away, then that would be that: no jellies, no biscuits, no sharing in Miss Henrietta's defiance. But if no such order was issued then, why, it would be a pleasure to oblige.

Some evenings, up in her room after Miss Elizabeth had been put to bed, Wilson heard muffled laughter and faint strains of a violin and knew Miss Henrietta had persuaded her father to let them have an entertainment. Minnie had told her Mr. Barrett could be as sociable as any of them, given the right mood, but Wilson, lying in the dark, could not envisage it. There seemed no strain of fun in the master at all. Whenever she saw him in Miss Elizabeth's room he appeared grave and anxious. She was half tempted to creep down and hang over the banisters to see if she could catch a glimpse of the master enjoying himself through the open drawing-room door but so far she had not had the courage. Her curiosity was never greater than her concern to be at all times beyond reproach. Sometimes Mr. Barrett would detain her a moment as she made to leave Miss Elizabeth's room on his arrival—he put up a finger and paused himself and she curtsied hastily, then stood her ground, looking up at him as he liked his servants to do. Occasionally he spoke to her, never more than the most brief inquiry as to either her own health or Miss Elizabeth's, but mostly he simply held her gaze a moment or two before nodding and with his nod dismissing her. Wilson had heard Tilly swear her stomach turned to jelly and even Charles confessing to a tremor or two when he did this to them but Wilson felt no fear. Mr. Barrett's eyes seemed to her not so much frightening as appraising and since she did her work well and conducted herself in a seemly manner she did not flinch as others did. She tried very hard in one letter to explain this to her mother, emphasizing that

—he is not an angry man, Mother, as Mrs. Graham-Clarke's brother who came to visit, do you remember, and made me tremble with his why do you do this and why do you not do that and his rapping on the chair backs with that stick of his. No, Mother, Mr. Barrett has Dignity and does not interfere and I am not afraid of him as others here are. And he loves Miss Elizabeth, Mother, it is a sight to see him with her, him so straight and tall and her so small and weak and he holds her hand and reads to her and in the evening they pray together for he is very religious Mother being a chapel goer and pleased that I am too. I did not know where to go to chapel when first I came and asking Minnie she said why there is a fine chapel in Regent Street which is but a step away and the master goes there. It is a new chapel and many Fashionable folks go there so I feared at first to go myself and be Noticed and looked for somewhere else to go but not finding another Chapel directly I was obliged to go to Regent Street or not go at all and indeed it is a splendid place Mother, all white and clean and the pews of shining wood and the floor too and the folk are not all Fashionable there are modest folk too. I walk there in ten minutes and I have never seen Mr. Barrett yet but he said to Miss Elizabeth *he* had seen me though I know not how and that he was pleased. The sermons are very powerful Mother such as make me shake sometimes with their promise of Hellfire I do not like to think of it and always remember it. But the singing is stirring and a happy thing and a good deal of comfort.

Coming back to Wimpole Street on Sundays after chapel was the worst time of the week for Wilson. The time when she wondered what she was doing here in this big house in this big city when at home Mother would be cooking the Sunday meal and all of them would be gathering around the table and enjoying the baked apples and the other Sunday treats and most of all the talk, the going over of the week and what they had all done. In Wimpole Street she was lonely on Sundays, would even have welcomed spending the extra spare hours she had with Miss Elizabeth, but she was not needed, her sisters did everything for her on Sundays. Minnie Robinson kindly invited her to eat dinner in her room but Wilson knew Minnie's sister and her niece joined her then and did not want to intrude, so she said she was determined to spend Sundays taking walks. She found Regent's Park quickly enough and it delighted her. She sat beside the pond and fed the ducks and watched the families go by and felt lonely still but not so sad. She tried hard to persuade Miss Elizabeth to think of an outing to the park with Flush but her mistress sighed and said she had not the energy, she could not think of it; but Wilson might make inquiries about a chair and she would see, one day. Minnie Robinson said the chair was in the boot room and was in good readiness and that, should Wilson succeed in tempting Miss Elizabeth, then Charles could take it to the front door any time and he and Simon would carry the mistress into it at her command.

The day came toward the beginning of June, when it had been so hot and sunny for two weeks that Miss Elizabeth was gasping for air and had her window thrown open as far as it would go. Wilson watered the nasturtiums in the window box twice a day and even then pronounced the soil bone dry. "As dry as my poor throat," Miss Elizabeth said, "there is no air here at all." "There is in the park," Wilson said cunningly. "Under the trees it is very cool, miss, and the grass being so fresh and green and the water so blue, it seems even more so." "You overdo it, Wilson," said Miss Elizabeth, but smiled. "Yet Flush tells me the same, he talks constantly of that grass and the glinting water. Well, if I had the strength I might go, just to see which of you exaggerates most."

And so she did, at three in the afternoon. Occy and Sette carried her down with so much silliness about the Queen of Sheba that they had to be admonished and told to be sober and careful and then they made such a case of sobriety and carefulness that Miss Elizabeth laughed and threatened to cough and they had to be warned again. But at last Miss Elizabeth was in the chair and a rug, even on that hot day, placed over her knees and Flush placed on top of it, as proud as Punch. It was such a great event that Minnie came to wave them off as though they were to go around the world for a year. But as Wilson wrote that night:

—it was a great Adventure, Mother, you can be sure and for me too since I was not certain I could manage the chair being so small. Charles was directed by Mrs. Robinson to keep me company until I saw how I went on and only turned back when I was accustomed to the gait of the chair. It is a little stiff but with practice I became proficient and Miss Elizabeth said I pushed it very well and a good deal smoother than any of her brothers. I made as much haste as I could till we reached the Park and then I found a pretty path near the pond that lay under the trees and we stayed there a good while Miss Elizabeth being delighted with the shade and it did her good to be cool and have so much to see that was different. She bade me sit on a park bench and she sat beside me in her chair and it was companionable Mother. Then at last she said she thought she might walk a little with my assistance which was a very daring thing Mother and my own heart beat a little faster with anxiety for if she had fallen what would I have done? But she did not fall and we walked up and down a short distance and she was pleased with her progress and only when she was back in the chair said she was very tired. Now was that not encouraging, Mother? If it goes on we will make a well woman of poor Miss Elizabeth yet.

But it did not go on. The weather broke the next day and it rained and was wild and Miss Elizabeth's disappointment was visible. Wilson was surprised to see how low her mistress became, not even picking up a book all that day and leaving her writing untouched. She stared at the busts of her poets and wondered if any of them would have written a word if they led the life she was doomed to lead. Wilson did not know what to say—she thought of all the many spring days her mistress had refused to go out and was confused. She stayed silent, trying with gestures to soothe Miss Elizabeth, aware she did not understand the true cause of her depression. When Miss Arabel came to take Flush for a walk he would not leave his mistress. "Go, Flushie," she commanded, "the rain will not harm you," but the dog was obstinate, stayed resolutely by her side. Wilson sewed quietly, only occasionally rising to fetch the scissors or tuck the coverlet more securely around Miss Elizabeth's feet. She was troubled to see tears running freely down her cheeks—she sobbed as though some tragedy had only just occurred and Wilson was moved to overcome her shyness and put her arms around her mistress's shoulders. "Hush," she whispered, "hush, hush," and stroked the thin back and held her tight. Flush, agitated, stretched up and licked the tears, making little whimpering noises of concern. "Oh, this *is* a nonsense," Miss Elizabeth murmured eventually and the tears stopped, though her eyes were still full. Wilson let her arms fall to her sides, afraid that she had been too fulsome in her response, too embarrassing, and that her gesture would in turn have embarrassed her mistress but Miss Elizabeth smiled a little and took her hand and said, "Thank you, Wilson, you are very kind."

That night she did not see her father, pleading a headache and general indisposition. Mr. Barrett sent for Wilson—Tilly, delivering the message, was breathless with awe but Wilson went quite calmly to the master's study. She had never been in the room before. It was Mr. Barrett's sanctum, as Miss Elizabeth's was hers, and intensely private. He was standing with his back to the fire looking even graver than usual:

—and Mother for a moment I *was* a little nervous for he looked so Stern. But he bade me sit, though in truth I had rather not done, and then he asked me how Miss Elizabeth was and what had caused the headache. I told him I was at a loss and could only think disappointment. Disappointment the master says and why would that be? I said I did not know but that Miss Elizabeth had looked forward to another outing to the park and her spirits seemed to fall as soon as she saw the rain. Mr. Barrett's face cleared somewhat and he asked if that was all and I said I believed it was. I thought he would bid me to go then but he walked about a bit and returned to the fire and said abruptly that his daughter's happiness was the most important thing in the world and that he believed her to be the purest woman that ever lived and I must remember that. I said that I would and he said I might go.

Attending her mistress that night, Wilson found her exhausted, barely able to lift her arms so that her dress could be pulled off and her chemise slipped on. She said again and again that she was tired, oh, so tired, and that she wished she could sleep a hundred years. Wilson, seeking to cheer her up, was bold enough to ask if she would like Prince Charming to wake her up at the end of her century of sleep but Miss Elizabeth shook her head and said she had no thoughts of princes.

"Do you, Wilson?"

"Miss?"

"Do you have thoughts of Prince Charming?"

"Oh, princes are not for the likes of me, miss."

"But you can dream, Wilson, anyone can dream, he does not have to be a prince, exactly. Now come, do you not dream?"

Seeing her mistress more animated, Wilson knew she must humor her and respond and so she said, "Oh yes, miss, I dream, but not of princes. I dream more of children, ma'am, to be serious, and a home."

Miss Elizabeth was quiet and Wilson worried that she had gone too far but in a moment her mistress, much calmer and more serene now, said, "That is a better dream, Wilson. But there ought to be a father for those babies you dream of, ought there not?"

"Yes, miss, but I don't seem to see him."

"Have you tried, tried hard?"

"Sometimes, miss. On Halloween. Where I come from, in the North, ma'am, we have games, they are just silly games, we peel an apple and throw the peel over our shoulder and it is said to fall in the shape of a letter, the first letter of your future husband's name. And if it is done in front of a mirror and there is only a candle in a far corner of the room, then it is said he will come and look over your shoulder at you if you call his name right." Wilson was startled to have her wrist gripped firmly.

"Does it work, Wilson? Have you done this? Did you see anything?"

Wilson hesitated. Was it wise to continue? But Miss Elizabeth's eyes shone and she sat up straight with excitement.

"Not exactly, miss, but once I saw a shadow and felt a presence but when I turned there was no one there."

"Do you believe in ghosts, Wilson?"

Again Wilson hesitated. She had not meant to start this kind of conversation. But before she could reply Miss Elizabeth had said, "For I do, Wilson, I believe in a spirit world, I *feel* it, often, there *is* something there, some actual life beyond the grave. Of that I have no doubt."

Wilson saw her eyes were bright now and her pale cheeks flushed and feared that, though this animation had rescued her mistress from such misery, it was now almost dangerous and would result in a fever. She insisted on bathing Miss Elizabeth's forehead and hands and stayed with her, watching anxiously, long after she had taken the laudanum. She is suffering, Wilson thought, this is suffering I see, and when she was at last in her room, when Miss Arabel had come to prepare for sleep in her sister's room, Wilson found she could not settle to rest. She paced up and down, troubled at Miss Elizabeth's distress, disturbed by her insistence that there was a spirit world. Mother believed there was. Late at night, sitting crouched over the fire, Mother had seen and heard spirits but they had not frightened her. Wilson, sitting with her, straining to see and hear what Mother did, had been disappointed. She saw shadows thrown by the flames but they were not spirits and she heard rustlings and cracklings from the wood that burned but they were not voices, not the voices Mother could hear so distinctly. Mother had a smile on her face and her head was tilted back as though raised to greet someone. When the trance—for it seemed to Wilson a trance—when it was over, Mother's smile faded and her head drooped and sometimes there was a tear or two. Spirits, to Mother, were a comfort and Wilson would have liked that comfort for herself.

Far into the night Wilson lay awake, her curtains open so that she could see the stars. She thought about home, as she always did, and about Mrs. Graham-Clarke's and her life there and how different it was. Here, she was needed in a way she had never expected. Her duties were not so very different but Miss Elizabeth and the household were both dramatically so. Miss Elizabeth seemed to want something from her which she could not yet define—she felt all the time a sense of inadequacy though she knew she gave satisfaction and was meticulous about her tasks. Each morning, when she went in to her mistress and began to help her wake up, she would find, looking into the great dark eyes, an awareness of some strange panic there, a panic she passionately wanted to soothe. Nothing was said. Miss Elizabeth said nothing, and she herself said nothing, but for a moment or two she found she was overwhelmed with pity, moved very near to tears, and yet she did not know precisely why. There was so much she did not know, so much she did not understand, and before she finally drifted off into sleep she vowed that she would try to cast off her crippling reticence and go toward whatever it was about her mistress which stirred her.

CHAPTER THREE

TWICE IN THE FOLLOWING WEEK Wilson pushed Miss Elizabeth to the park and twice her mistress got out of the chair and walked a few yards beside the lake. There were no ill effects. Miss Elizabeth, a little irritated by the exaggerated remarks as to how well she was looking, remarks made by everyone at 50 Wimpole Street from her father to Tilly, told Wilson that doubtless in time her likeness to Hercules would be complete. But she was pleased, Wilson saw that. It was the first indication that her mistress did not positively want to be an invalid but had such a state pushed upon her. She ate better, though in truth better did not mean a great deal more substantially, only that she managed a whole boiled egg instead of a spoonful of the yolk, and did not send away the mutton without toying with it instead of shuddering and averting her eyes.

Wilson felt a great sense of pride, feeling that it could not be denied she had a part in this happy improvement. Success made her a little bolder and in becoming bolder she was astonished to be approved of. "May I have the window closed, Wilson?" Miss Elizabeth would ask and Wilson, with many if-you-please-ma'ams, said she thought it better that it should stay open while the day was so mild since the room felt uncommonly close. Miss Elizabeth merely said, "I expect you are right. Thank you, Wilson." And when, after Miss Elizabeth had worked all day and protested her head ached abominably and she thought she might take a little laudanum, Wilson had said *she* thought that would not be wise, it being the close reading and writing which had brought on the headache so fierce and that if her mistress were to lie still and have eau de cologne pressed on her forehead this might serve a deal better than an extra draught of laudanum. She soaked a soft cloth in cologne and sat beside Miss Elizabeth, holding it firmly against her forehead, and in no time at all was told the headache had all but gone. In such small ways Wilson began to make her mark and worried less about the shadow of Crow. She even ventured to suggest remedies other than laudanum for the various ailments from which her mistress suffered, begging her to try an infusion of chamomile flowers for her dyspepsia. Mother had gathered the small, fragrant flowers herself and prepared an infusion to mask their natural bitter aromatic taste but Wilson, without access to these flowers, purchased powder from the chemist and, mixing thirty grains of it in water, induced Miss Elizabeth to try it. It worked wonders and her stock rose accordingly.

So she had made her mark but Miss Elizabeth made hers too. Wilson slowly became as devoted and anxious about her charge as the rest of the household and was no longer puzzled by their excessive devotion. To hear Miss Elizabeth criticized, or suspected of malingering, or not accorded her due, was painful to her and roused her to an indignation of which she had not thought herself capable. Her lips tightened when Jane, lady's maid to her mistress's great friend Miss Mary Russell Mitford, ventured to remark that some people seemed to think they had *no* legs. Wilson wrote furiously:

—oh Mother how I boiled up to hear it! She is a sly miss, that Jane, never calling anything nor anyone by name but always hinting and if I ask to whom she may be referring sniffing and saying she meant nothing to be sure. But she does mean things Mother and not pleasant things and it was a trial to me to have

her in my company the three days of Miss Mitford's visit. She is
not even civil about her own mistress but forever saying she is a
Fool and her father a Drunkard. Then her sharp tongue turned to
telling me wicked things about Miss Henrietta and her dalliance
and I begged her to stop for I have no wish to hear such evil
gossip. Oh she said it is not gossip and that is not all for I have
heard master Henry is not what he should be and at that I got up
and said I must leave the room if she would not and she said I
could leave if I liked but it was all true and THINGS went on in
this house which everyone knew if I did not. I did not know what
to do, Mother, and thought what would you do and back came the
answer to myself that you would keep your own counsel and no
more. So I tried not to listen to anything this Jane suggested. It is
a pity Tilly did not follow my example. I heard Jane tell Tilly who
loves such things that Miss Mitford was so fat she had burst two
pairs of stays and so stupid she paid a gardener who took some of
her produce and sold it and kept the money and got her last maid
with child into the bargain and Miss Mitford knew nothing. And
she told Tilly such coarse things about Dr. Mitford which I would
not write Mother—

Coarse things which Wilson could not and did not write down
but about which it distressed her to think. She could not quite forget
them, however hard she tried. There had been such shrieks of laughter from the kitchen as Jane described old Dr. Mitford begging her to
hold his hand and do him a service, an intimate service, and how the
voices had dropped and then once more the shrieks, the yelps of
laughter and Tilly saying it was disgusting for an elderly gentleman
to carry on so and Jane saying they were safer elderly, for last night
as she was going up to bed Mr. Henry—and then the voices dropped
again and there was no laughter but sharp intakes of breath and Tilly
with something to add. Minnie Robinson had come out of her room
then and said something sharply, and thankfully that had been an end
to it. But Wilson could not forget what she had heard, especially what
Tilly had said. She had seen Master Henry with Tilly and even then,
knowing nothing, had felt troubled. She had come around the last
bend in the stairs and there was Tilly leaning against the wall and Mr.

Henry in front of her, one hand braced on the wall either side of her, so that she stood trapped between his arms. That was all. Wilson approached, as she had intended to do, as she felt it was right to go on doing, and Mr. Henry took his hands away and clattered down the stairs and Tilly turned and scurried off into her room. But Wilson had seen her face and seen his face and felt disturbed. Tilly was so excited, so flushed, not at all frightened. Her eyes had sparkled and she had tilted her head back so that she looked through her eyelashes at Mr. Henry and her mouth was slack and open and her whole body, lounging against the wall, provocative in the extreme. And Mr. Henry's face as he dashed down the stairs had been contorted with rage at the interruption. He frowned and bit his lip and glared at Wilson as though he hated her. Later, Tilly had even referred to it.

"Spying, was you?"

"Indeed not."

"Creeping up those stairs, quiet as a mouse, hoping to see something you shouldn't, I dare say—"

"I was going to my room, as I am entitled, as I do at that hour every evening."

"Well, you saw him, what do I care, I can't help it if he follows me everywhere, begging me to—"

"I do not wish to hear any more, thank you, Tilly."

"Miss Hoity-Toity, Miss Give-Herself-Airs, Miss Butter-Wouldn't-Melt-In-Her-Mouth, Miss Jealous—"

Wilson had simply walked out of the kitchen, leaving Tilly in possession, though she had not yet taken what she needed from the cupboard. But how her heart had thudded at the monstrous insinuation, so unfounded and vulgar, how deeply she resented Tilly's accusation. Wilson consoled herself with the thought that Minnie Robinson certainly would not believe her, should Tilly be so foolish as to repeat this to her, and that none of the others mattered. They would all, Wilson sensibly reflected, know about Tilly and about Master Henry, if there was anything to know. She was tempted to mention what she had seen to Minnie Robinson but did not—even with Minnie it was better to keep one's own counsel.

But Minnie herself brought the subject up. "How did you find

Jane?" she asked the day after Miss Mitford and her maid had left. Wilson, choosing at that moment to lift her teacup the better to hide any expression of dislike which might creep onto her face, said she had had little to do with her. "All the better," Minnie said, a trifle grimly. "I wish Tilly had the same sense." Wilson said nothing. She liked this hour in Minnie's cozy room, just the two of them, the atmosphere relaxed and friendly. "But then Tilly has no sense," Minnie went on, "none at all, and it will end in dismissal, sooner rather than later if I have my way. Certain people should be spoken to about leading certain other people down the primrose path but then, with certain other people skipping along right merrily of their own accord, what good would it do?" Wilson thought it safe to say none. "Exactly. But if it should come to the attention of the master, then the Lord help them both and I should be in trouble myself." Wilson kept silent. It struck her that Minnie had a need to confide and that she had no one to confide in. "He's always been trouble, that one," Minnie said with what Wilson was surprised to detect was a tinge of unmistakable admiration. "But," she sighed, "what will be will be and it isn't him I worry over." She paused, refilled the teacups, looked Wilson straight in the eye and mouthed that it was Miss Henrietta. "Now there's a tragedy," she whispered, "there's a love match, with that young soldier eating his heart out, real tears in his eyes sometimes, and him not ashamed to show them. 'Minnie,' he says to me once, 'Minnie, on my life I respect her but it is hard to push a fellow so far.'" Wilson was now bewildered but desperately eager to learn more so she gave more than a half nod in encouragement. "They play with fire," Minnie said, "they play with fire. Miss Henrietta knows what she does but does he? Can he? He's never seen the master deal with this kind of proposition, he's never seen him make short shrift. Miss Henrietta has and she's suffered, oh, how the poor darling has suffered. She came to me afterward, after she'd begged him to let her accept a proposal of marriage, and sobbed her heart out and said she would never marry, never, her father had been furious, would never allow it and she would not try again."

Wilson longed to ask several crucial questions but did not dare. She felt Minnie would shut up like a clam if she did, so she ventured only to murmur, "Poor lady." Minnie took this up swiftly—"Poor lady indeed, poor all of them, and poor master too, for he loves them all, he loves them and does what he thinks is right and does not see he is hard. Only Miss Elizabeth causes him no concern, never being troubled with affairs of the heart. 'Marriage,' she says to me once when Crow married, 'marriage is servitude, Minnie, and, make no mistake, lifelong subjection to a man, that is all.' "

Wilson thought about that last remark a great deal afterward. "Marriage is servitude"—was that what her mistress truly believed? Did she think nothing of love? She longed to ask her mistress about it but of course could not. Instead, as she brushed Miss Elizabeth's hair and dressed her she reflected that, if marriage was servitude, spinsterhood was only another kind of slavery, surely. Slowly, coiling up her mistress's hair, pinning it securely, taking care not to pull the delicate tendrils on the neck, Wilson pondered on the institution of marriage. Mother had married and had been happy until she was widowed and she, as a result of marriage, had children she loved and without whom life would have had no meaning. But if Mother had not married? If she had stayed a seamstress? Where was the life there? A far worse servitude, and nothing to show for it, no comfort, no love. Adjusting Miss Elizabeth's collar, Wilson thought about herself. She was no longer young. She was nearly twenty-four and as Mother used to remind her, she had had her chances. Wilson put a shawl around her mistress's shoulders and thought about these "chances." Not one of them had seemed like a chance of anything but disappointment. Alfred Robson, coalman, big and ugly and skin ingrained with coal dust however hard he washed, and two babies with his sister who'd looked after them since his first wife died. Was that a chance? He only asked her because she smiled at him when he delivered coal to the Graham-Clarkes and he needed a wife desperately. Then there was Benjamin Woolf, more presentable, on his way up in the world, or so he said, as clerk in the city office, but she could not abide his hairiness, the hair creeping out under his shirt cuffs and over his collar tops and making her shudder. Stephen Adams, John Topping, Rufus Isaacs—all of them had asked her and with none of them at all could she see any chance of happiness. And none of them had wooed her or spoken of love.

"You are very quiet, Wilson," Miss Elizabeth said, her toilet complete, her book placed in her hand and the pens and paper on the table at her side.

"Yes, miss."

"What were you thinking of as you brushed my hair, Wilson? Each brush stroke seemed alive with meaning today." Wilson said nothing and gave a little apologetic bob of a curtsy.

"Come, Wilson, we are friends, are we not? Were your thoughts so terrible?"

"Oh, indeed no, miss."

"Well then, try me, do." And Miss Elizabeth placed a hand over hers.

"I was only thinking," Wilson stammered, "about marriage, miss."

"Oh, Wilson! Do not tell me you are to marry!"

"No, no, miss—"

"Thank heaven for that—oh, the *shock*, Wilson—only I thought you meant you had accepted a proposal—"

"No, miss, never."

"Has one been put, Wilson?"

"Not here, miss, and none that mattered."

"So why are you thinking so soulfully of marriage, Wilson? Were you sad? Do you long for marriage?"

"I was wondering, miss, whether marriage was a servitude worse than not being married."

"Were you indeed? And what gave rise to this debate?"

"Talk of marriage in general, miss, belowstairs."

"Ah, of course. What else is there so exciting to talk about if you are eighteen, as someone is, and pretty, as someone is, and much admired, as Tilly is. Am I not right, Wilson?"

"No, miss."

"So it was not Tilly talking of marriage?"

"No, miss."

"So who was considering the institution of marriage?"

"No one specially, miss, it was only general talk."

"Well, never mind that, tell me your thoughts, Wilson, the conclusions you came to. I should be very interested and indeed do not mean to mock."

Wilson hesitated. She wished she had been evasive, had insisted she could not remember what she was thinking of no matter how hard she tried, but it was done now. "I think marriage cannot be a contract, miss, though it is made out to be one by some. It is a holy sacrament, is it not, miss, and God joins people together, and so it cannot rightly be called servitude unless there is no love only calculation."

"Wilson, you astonish me, you state the case like the best of advocates. Those are my sentiments exactly. But look around you and where is the love in the marriages before us? I see precious little of it but a great deal of that calculation you and I abhor. We are better unmarried, do you not think, Wilson?"

"I don't know, miss."

"Marriage still tempts you with its pleading tongue?" Wilson was again silent, almost wringing her hands with the dreadful embarrassment she felt. It would be so much easier to lie.

"Not exactly. It is not marriage . . ."

"Then it is love." Miss Elizabeth paused, a curious smile on her pale face. Wilson was struck, as she always was, by the way in which that smile made her mistress look so young and pretty, lighting her eyes and softening the pallor of her cheeks. In repose, her face was drawn and lifeless, a pitiful sight, and then came the smile and the great eyes danced and life was there after all.

"It must be a great blessing to be loved, miss, and to love back."

"You love your mother and your sisters, for you have told me so often and I see it for myself, and they love you back."

"But they love me because I am their daughter and sister, begging your pardon, miss, and a man, a husband—"

"Would love you for yourself and not because you were a wife, a woman?" Wilson nodded. Miss Elizabeth touched her hand again and then took up her book, the signal that Wilson could go.

That afternoon, when once more they went to Regent's Park, they seemed surrounded by lovers. Over the grass they walked, arm in arm, the girls drifting in sweet-pea colors, their gowns only just clearing the grass, their parasols like so many little pretty clouds twirling on their shoulders. How they smiled up at their companions and laughed encouragingly and gazed adoringly and the men, many in soldiers' uniforms all smart in regimental colors, walked proudly, backs straight, mustaches carefully brushed and oiled, arms respectfully steering their precious ladies. Wilson pushed Miss Elizabeth past them humbly, taking care to steer adroitly, closing her ears to the chatter and giggles. She felt wistful, tender, as she helped her mistress out of the chair and onto a bench, she did not like to sense the pity in people's eyes as they took in this frail, black-clad young woman with barely the strength to stand. The yearning that overcame her was not for herself but for her mistress—she wished so passionately, as she took her place beside her, that it was Miss Elizabeth idling along the path in the palest pink or blue, Miss Elizabeth laughing animatedly and at her side a man entranced by her, a man of strength and character, a fine man all of her own.

"Wilson!" Wilson felt her arm clutched tightly and turned to face her mistress, alarmed at the cry of distress, sure some pain had struck and she was ill. But Miss Elizabeth's eyes were huge and bright with excitement, not closed in agony, and she inclined her head, urging Wilson to look where she looked, to take note and see what she saw. And what she saw was Miss Henrietta, way across the lake, arm in arm with a splendid soldier in a blue coat. "Oh my, ma'am," whispered Wilson. "It is Surtees Cook," said Miss Elizabeth, "and if Papa knew . . . unchaperoned, in public—"

"No, miss, look, there is Master Alfred, behind, they are not unchaperoned."

But Master Alfred was well behind, a good five hundred yards behind, dawdling along, running a stick along the railings and yawning and looking everywhere except in the direction of his sister. Wilson and her mistress watched as Henrietta and Surtees turned away from the lake and toward a high hedge where there was an opening into a flower garden. Their pace slowed, they seemed to take forever to reach the hedge, and then they were behind it and although Wilson, with her good eyesight, strained and strained she could not see them emerge into the garden. As for Alfred, he lost them entirely. They both saw him stop and look around, quite unconcerned, and then whistle and take to standing with his hands in his pockets staring vacantly at the water. It took a long time before Henrietta and Surtees came back to join him and, when they did, it did not escape Wilson's notice, in spite of the distance, that Miss Henrietta's bonnet had tipped off her head and hung by its ribbons and that her hair had tumbled down. She took Alfred's arm and hung onto it and walked quickly, looking at her feet, while Surtees Cook hurried to keep abreast and was ignored by her. "Well, Wilson," Miss Elizabeth said quietly, "we have seen something today I had rather not have done, but we will not say a word."

What pleased Wilson was the way in which that "we" was said—flatly, with no emphasis, casually, not querying that she would agree. There was no suggestion that it was in the nature of an order nor any feeling it had been a warning. Her mistress had automatically assumed that they would feel the same and when Wilson wrote to her mother about it she took care to underscore that this was

—a most high compliment Mother such as many a mistress would not have given and I was happy to receive it. We have not talked of it since but I could not help hear Miss Elizabeth say to Miss Henrietta when she came into her room Well Henrietta you have enjoyed your walk in the park I am sure have you not and Miss Henrietta was all confusion and before I left the room I heard her begin to cry. Molly, Miss Henrietta's maid, is a good sort but she is young and Tilly makes short work of her and so when Tilly asked Molly why Miss Henrietta was seen crying before dinner and what ailed her Molly shrugged and did not know only she supposed it was something to do with Surtees Cook who had called and been refused and sent in a note. Oh says Tilly and I bet I know what was in that note did you read it Molly. Molly was angry and said she did not read notes except when they were addressed to her and what had given Tilly such an idea indeed. Tilly sniffed and said some people were not as good as was made out. At any rate, Mother, Miss Henrietta is upset and it is all to do with Surtees Cook who is a second cousin removed I believe and only a poor soldier without means to marry Minnie says so what is to be done nobody knows I am sure. Mr. Barrett does not think of Miss Henrietta as he does of Miss Elizabeth—

No, he did not. Wilson had been perturbed to see the brusqueness with which Mr. Barrett spoke to Miss Henrietta and Miss Arabel. There was neither affection nor respect in his voice, whereas when he addressed Miss Elizabeth there was an abundance of both and something more. She could not understand it since Miss Henrietta was so charming and was turned to by all in the house for advice and help and was said by Minnie Robinson to have taken the place of her mother at a tender age. Miss Arabel fared even worse, if anything, at her father's hands. Wilson was troubled when she heard Mr. Barrett speak to Miss Arabel, his tone harsh and cutting when hers had been soft and hesitant. He did not seem to acknowledge Miss Arabel's goodness, which everyone in the house marveled at. She was like a little gray mouse scurrying up and down the stairs, forever fetching and carrying for her lazy brothers, never too busy or tired to be of service. And she did good work, Wilson knew, for the Ragged Children. It was a wonder the master was not moved by her charitable endeavors to estimate Miss Arabel more highly. Miss Elizabeth's poetry meant more to him. He was pleased with the new volumes which were to come out in August and thought, her mistress told her, that several of the poems were beautiful in their piety.

"My papa likes it best when I write on religious themes, Wilson," Miss Elizabeth explained, "but I cannot always do so."

"No, miss."

"Do you care for poetry, Wilson?"

"I don't know, miss, not having read any."

"Then I will read some to you. It will be my pleasure; you shall hear what no one else in London has yet heard and you must tell me truly what you think."

Wilson steeled herself to find Miss Elizabeth's work incomprehensible and prepared to have to admit, with many an apology, that she was too stupid to understand. But she did understand. In her light,

high voice, Miss Elizabeth read aloud a poem she said would appeal
to her, called "The Lady's Yes":

> " 'Yes,' I answered you last night;
> 'No,' this morning, sir, I say.
> Colours seen by candlelight
> Will not look the same by day.' "

That was how the poem began and Wilson had no difficulty appreci-
ating these sentiments—they were precisely stated and her own
entirely. She was surprised Miss Elizabeth should write so, with such
simplicity and feeling, and as the poem went on the force of the
verses did not escape her. It was true, all true. She herself had never
flirted in her life and yet all around she saw how coquetry on both
sides ruled the day. In the fourth verse she found herself nodding at
the line, "wooing light makes fickle truth"; and the fifth verse was so
exactly right, she clapped her hands.

Wilson felt flushed with pleasure but did not know how to communicate this to Miss Elizabeth except by saying she thought the
poem beautiful. Miss Elizabeth smiled and said she would show
Wilson the verses when they were printed in a book and that if she
wished she might have the volume containing them as a present.
That, said Wilson, would be a fine thing.

Wilson had always revered books, without knowing why. When
she first went to Mrs. Graham-Clarke's, it had been her job to dust the
books on Wednesdays. Each volume had to be taken down and the
spine dusted and the top of the pages dusted and the book opened
carefully before it was replaced to make sure all the dust was gone. It
took a long time and was found tedious by the other maids, who were
glad to relinquish the task to Wilson. Week after week, dusting the
same books, opening them at much the same pages, Wilson developed a growing familiarity with their contents though she did not at
any time sit down and read them. They were not truly of any great
interest to her as reading matter because they were almost all about
natural history, Mr. Graham-Clarke's great passion. Wilson was not
desperate to know the mating habits of the crested grebe or when the

swallow migrated or where to but she liked the very arrangement of the texts, the importance of the chapter headings and the attractive appearance of the print. She was sorry when book dusting was no longer within her domain and had been only too happy in Wimpole Street to take it upon herself again. By rights, it was Tilly's job but Miss Elizabeth found Tilly's method of book dusting irritating and so did Wilson—it was done so hurriedly, so carelessly, each book pulled out roughly and attacked energetically with the duster and slammed back into place all in one jerky movement. So Wilson had offered and her offer was graciously accepted by those concerned and now she dusted books on Wednesdays, just as in the old days.

But the books were different as Wilson discovered very quickly. Miss Elizabeth had so many slim volumes of poetry, each difficult to dust, unlike the big Graham-Clarke natural history volumes, which were an inch or two broad at the top where the dust sat visibly. These poetry books, on the other hand, had to be virtually caressed, they were so thin. And the poems were set out so spaciously that lines leaped out, demanding attention, as she took her duster reverently around them. Wilson learned the names of Shelley and Keats and Wordsworth and knew the titles of *Queen Mab* (a name she loved) and *Endymion* and *The Prelude*. She read snatched lines from all of them, mouthing them as she dusted, looking forward to the following week when she could add some more. She knew that if she had the courage and was prepared to speak out Miss Elizabeth would be most likely to tell her to take down whatever book she wanted and read it in her room but she was not yet bold enough to be so forward. And if she had been, it would not after all have been the poetry she would have borrowed but the books from the other side of the room, the novels. Sometimes she read whole pages of those and she longed to know what happened to Alice Darvil in *Ernest Maltravers* and whether she did or did not have a child by him as seemed likely by the last few pages of Volume One. She could not find Volume Two, however hard she searched, and did not even consider asking for it. Even more absorbing was *Rob Roy*. All three volumes were there but, however assiduously she dusted, Wilson could do no more than take in lines that seemed to leap out at her of their own accord—"I must inform you at once, Mr. Osbaldistone, that compliments are entirely lost on me, do not, therefore, throw away your pretty sayings" was one of these, for it sounded just how her mistress might speak in reply to flattery. She could not link this with another line a little later in the same volume—"My dear Mr. Francis, be patient and quiet, and let me take my own way, for when I take the bit between my teeth, there is no bridle will stop me"—but felt they were excitingly connected. She would have liked to take all of *Rob Roy* to her room for, as she wrote to her mother:

—I have a deal of time on my own Mother more than you would think and more than I ever had so I am not tired as before. Miss Elizabeth likes to be by herself to read and write and she rests many hours besides and has no need of me so long as I am near should she do so. I sew and have fully repaired all her clothes and she exclaims at the neatness of my darns and is well pleased with the freshening I have done. She asks me if I do not think sewing an abomination and was surprised when I said no I did not but liked it and thought it useful and was happy to sew. I have made her a lace collar for her black dress which was drab and in need of some decoration and she thinks it a wonder that my fingers can fashion such a gossamer thing from mere thread as she says. And Miss Elizabeth goes to sleep by nine and sometimes eight in the evening so you see I have extra hours to myself which I might otherwise not have.

And what did she do with those hours? Wilson asked herself and fretted because the answer was not as much as she would have liked. In the daytime, when she was obliged to be near at hand even if not required, the problem was not too pressing. She embroidered and crocheted and was tolerably content. But in the light summer evenings when Miss Elizabeth had retired, or even before then when she had no need of a maid because Arabel was with her, Wilson was restless. Then she would have read, if she could have had free access to the books which filled her mistress's room or been able to afford to buy her own, which was quite out of the question. Newspapers and magazines were easier to come by. Miss Elizabeth took a great many of both and when they were cleared out each month Wilson could have her pick but she found most of them dull reading. Only *Punch*, which at 4d. a month seemed expensive to her, entertained her and she read it from cover to cover, pausing often over the cartoons and wishing she could always work them out.

Miss Elizabeth asked her once if she had been to the Diorama. She did not like to say she could not afford the entrance fee in case it seemed ungrateful but it had been hard to avoid doing so when her mistress urged a visit upon her. Nor had she yet seen any of the sights of London, not even the river, or visited a theater. She had been nowhere but Regent Street chapel and Regent's Park and also along Oxford Street. Often, climbing the stairs to her room when it was still a brilliant June evening outside, she had wished she had a companion to take her out or that it were acceptable for her to go alone. But her only friend among the servants was Minnie and Minnie only went out to visit her sister. With the rest Wilson did not mix and was on the whole too old as well as too senior to do so. If Miss Elizabeth had led a different life, then so would she have done: she would have accompanied her as other lady's maids accompanied their mistresses and had a fine time. It surprised her, after three months in Wimpole Street, to realize how very much more restricted her life actually was than it had been in Newcastle, but of course, as she reminded herself, there she had known so many people with whom she had grown up and also she could wander abroad with confidence on her own, knowing where to go and where not to go.

Miss Elizabeth asked her often and, Wilson felt, anxiously if she missed home.

"Yes, miss, indeed I do."

"What do you miss, Wilson? Besides your mother and sisters of course." Once more Wilson was embarrassed—to be asked to discuss her feelings in such a way was excruciating to her and yet Miss Elizabeth would persist in spite of her surely obvious discomfiture.

"Home itself, miss, the ease of it. And Newcastle. It is not a beautiful place but I have known it all my life."

"But does London not excite you, Wilson?"

Wilson was guarded. "I expect it would, miss, if I saw it as presently I am sure I shall."

But that was the wrong thing to say, for as she wrote to her mother:

—my poor mistress wept to think she held me back as she vowed she held all back who were around her and she would not listen to my denials and indeed Mother it was thoughtless of me to speak so and I was ashamed. But Miss Elizabeth must have spoken to Miss Henrietta for the following afternoon she said to me Wilson you are to go out and see something of London you are to accompany Henrietta to her friend Mrs. Maggs which is a good drive away across the river and you will go in the carriage with her and see some sights. Well Mother I protested of course and said my place was with her and indeed I wished only to be with my own mistress and do what was right but she would not hear of it and said Molly, as is Miss Henrietta's maid, had a pain in her face which was true and could not go and I was needed and would oblige Miss Henrietta and in short it was an Order. How she laughed when she said it was an Order and how happy she was for me and I was excited I confess. We set off at three o'clock and drove down Regent Street at a trot and then round Picadilly and into the square and then oh Mother we went down the Mall for all the world like the Queen herself and St. James's Park was beautiful then we crossed Westminster Bridge and my breath was taken by the sight of that mighty River and the Dome of St. Pauls far away. Miss Henrietta pointed out this and that and was very kind and then we arrived at Mrs. Maggs and stayed until five when we set off to return. But Mother we did not return all the way ALONE. Hardly had we set off than Miss Henrietta leans forward and says Wilson my sister says you are discreet and I hope you are and I said I believed I was and she says good because I am going to ask you to be discreet. And then the carriage stops near the bridge and a soldier got in and it was Surtees Cook Mother!! He bowed to me politely and said good evening Mrs. Wilson and are you well and I said I was and then he took Miss Henrietta's hand and they talked of meeting the next day to go on a picnic to Richmond and whether it could be managed, Miss Henrietta said she thought it could and that if a party of eight or ten should go then there would be no objections from a certain quarter. Then Mr. Cook, for I know not of his rank to call him by it properly, he got out of the carriage and we went home to Wimpole Street. Miss Elizabeth asked me how I had enjoyed the outing and said she could tell even before I spoke that I had enjoyed it because my face showed it and I said I was glad of that because I *had* enjoyed it indeed and I told her what I had seen. Now Wilson you will be able to write to your mother and tell her something of interest and I said I would. Miss Elizabeth then asked me how I had found Mrs. Maggs house and I said what I had seen of it seemed very pleasant but that the housekeeper was not as kindly as Mrs. Robinson nor the Kitchen as comfortable as ours. So this is not such a bad place Wilson she said and I said it was a good place and I would always say so and she seemed relieved. Wilson she said I will be frank and tell you I do not like change and I am glad you think this place satisfactory and I hope you always will.

There were tears in her eyes as she spoke, Wilson saw them clearly and was touched. Only three months and it appeared she had won a place in Miss Elizabeth's heart simply by being herself and trying hard to please. Mrs. Graham-Clarke had not cried or shown any emotion when after seven *years* she had given notice. The old lady had sniffed and said some folk did not know when they were well off and would rue the day. The good reference she gave her was worth a great deal to Wilson but a little show of affection and gratitude would have meant more. Miss Elizabeth knew how to show both. She was not effusive but with those tears in her eyes and that touch of her hand and her thoughtfulness for her maid's pleasure she showed in kind her appreciation. Coming into Miss Elizabeth's room that night, Miss Henrietta saw Wilson painstakingly combing Flush's coat while his mistress held him and said, "Oh, such devotion to duty, Wilson! Why, Ba, you have a treasure of a maid and no mistake." Miss Elizabeth merely smiled and nodded, while Wilson blushed, but after she had gone to her own room she found herself thinking it was true, she *was* literally devoted to her mistress and half in love besides.

CHAPTER FOUR

THERE CAME A DAY in August when Miss Elizabeth placed in Wilson's hands two green-backed books and said, "There, Wilson, I said you should have your own volumes and there they are for you to keep with you, if you wish." Wilson blushed and was incapable of speech (though of late she knew she had become much less tongue-tied and was proud of it). She had never owned any book except the Bible and the Book of Common Prayer.

"Oh, miss," she managed to say at last, "oh, miss." She hugged the books to her chest and smiled and knew that, though it was foolish, she had tears in her eyes. "Well, Wilson," said Miss Elizabeth, "I hope you are as ecstatic when you have read the poems."

The books stood on her washstand in a tin box Wilson had taken, empty, from the kitchen, afraid that the precious volumes might somehow get wet even though she was most careful to remove them from the stand when it was in use. She had told no one of the gift, had smuggled them up the stairs in a workbasket, afraid she might meet someone who would inquire how she came to be carrying books, and such fine-looking books, to her room. She would of course have been quite safe if challenged, for she only had to show the flyleaf to explain all. "For Elizabeth Wilson—Elizabeth Barrett Barrett, August 15th, 1844." Not thinking to find any inscription, not imagining these books would be stamped with such evidence that they were hers personally, Wilson had experienced a slight sense of shock when she came upon the writing. For days now she had watched Miss Elizabeth pore over piles of these books, writing in many of them before they were handed to her to pack and send to the post, but she had never thought hers might be one of them. It was almost too much to be so included when the other names of those honored were so far above her. Wilson felt she ought to remark upon the inscription but could not think how to express her gratitude sufficiently. She longed for her mistress to inquire how she found the poetry but no inquiry came and no reference was made to the gift again. Wilson felt she might burst with the need to say something but her opportunity did not come for almost a month, when Miss Elizabeth laughed out loud at something in a magazine she was reading. "Why, Wilson, do listen to what this gentleman says of my poems: 'This poet had done better to confine herself to those romantic ballads and sonnets which are so becoming to the female pen instead of straying in a subject very near to politics about which she can know nothing.' Well! What do you say to that?"

"I don't know, miss, I'm sure, except the ballads are very beautiful and so are the sonnets and, as for politics, miss, I know not what the writer means."

"Neither do I, except I suppose he means I ought not to write about suffering and injustice and should not include 'The Cry of the Children' and suchlike."

"Oh, if *that* is politics, miss, then indeed the gentleman is wrong, for I cried at it and thought it very true and wondered how you could know, if you will excuse me, being so removed from such dreadful things."

"Newspapers, reports, there is no mystery, Wilson, and novels, which are so wrongly despised, I learn a great deal from novels, I assure you. You cried, you say? You truly cried?"

"Indeed, yes. 'They look up with their pale and sunken faces, And their looks are sad to see'—"

"Why, Wilson—you can recite from it."

"Many a verse, miss, and soon I shall have it all by heart as I want. And, miss, to write in the books for me, naming me, it was too much, miss—"

"Now *I* shall cry if you continue, dear, and that will never do with Mr. Kenyon coming and staring at me through those spectacles of his, just looking for faults. But I am glad you are pleased, Wilson. It makes me happy. And I am more than glad you like my poems enough to have them by heart."

Later that day, when Wilson had shown Mr. Kenyon in, she heard her mistress say as the door closed, "Wilson is quite the critic, you know—she comes on rapidly and is not all the mouse you might take her for, Mr. Kenyon." Climbing the stairs, she wondered about that— was she a critic? What *was* a critic? Someone Miss Elizabeth esteemed, that was certain. Over and over again Wilson heard her mistress pick up a newspaper and say now there was a good critic or throw it down and declare that critic was no critic but a fool. As for being taken for a mouse, she was used to that. Because she was so small and moved about quietly and had a tendency to avert her eyes, and because her coloring was light and she had no distinguishing features and spoke only when spoken to—she was naturally judged a mouse and people could be forgiven for thinking this. It had never worried her. There were advantages, particularly working in a large household such as Wimpole Street, in being thought a mouse. She knew she aroused neither fear nor jealousy and so everyone was pleasant to her. Since she never gossiped she never became party to all the plots and sub-plots raging in the house. She had shown she could stand her ground, if need be, and her quiet demeanor was no longer interpreted as possible weakness. Minnie Robinson congratulated her on gaining everyone's trust. "It is not often," Minnie told her approvingly, "that the master commends a servant, I can tell you, and he said to me only yesterday how satisfied he is. Now that is an important word to the master, Lily, one he rarely uses, for he is very rarely satisfied. You must know as I know, he mostly gives vent to his dissatisfaction."

Indeed Wilson did know. Mr. Barrett, at the moment, was deeply dissatisfied with Miss Henrietta and Mr. Alfred (because they had been on a picnic without permission), and with Mr. Henry (because he had gone to see a friend in Dover) and the whole house knew it. The master was not an evasive man in this respect—his displeasure came straight out and was witnessed by whoever was there. If that person were Tilly or Charles or even Molly, who should have had more loyalty, then the entire staff knew within five minutes. He did not raise his voice but his anger was unmistakable and the whole house felt it, even Miss Elizabeth upstairs in her sanctum. "Oh, Wilson," she whispered on one such occasion, "I do wish Henry would not anger Pa so. He is a most thoughtless boy to cause such displeasure, and all for a trip to Dover. I ask you, can it have been worth it?" Wilson said nothing, only measured out the laudanum with a steady hand. "He ought not to go against Papa, who loves him dearly." Wilson gave her mistress the tincture she had prepared and watched while it was taken, drained to the last drop. Miss Elizabeth lay back, her eyes closed, murmuring, "We ought all to be careful not to hurt poor Papa."

Wilson passed Mr. Barrett on the stairs as she went down to the kitchen carrying Miss Elizabeth's dinner tray, on which the food was barely touched. He frowned and stopped. "You carry trays, Wilson? Can this be right?" "It is to avoid disturbing Miss Elizabeth, sir; it means no one else need enter her room, sir." The frown lifted a little. Wilson stood there uncertainly, not knowing whether to proceed or not. The tray began to tremble a little in her hands with the effort of holding it steady. "Take your tray, Wilson," Mr. Barrett said finally, nodding, "you do well." Relieved, she continued to descend the stairs but was not even to the first level when she clearly heard Miss Henrietta's laughter and the sound of a door banging and feet pattering and she froze, knowing the master would hear them too and, if he came to investigate the hilarity, would see what she saw: Surtees Cook hand in hand with Henrietta in the hall and Simon, popeyed, still holding the knob of the closed door. But fortunately Mr. Barrett continued on his way to see his eldest daughter and, that time, disaster was averted. Wilson was relieved. Her mistress's desire not to be involved was beginning to be hers. Not to know was to avoid

blame, or to go a good way toward doing so. She deposited the tray
and, after Mr. Barrett had gone, returned to Miss Elizabeth's room.
She finished tidying the room and lifted Flush up. The doctor had
been adamant: Flush was not to sleep on his mistress's bed but in his
basket. The moment she lifted the dog he began to struggle and yelp,
desperate to return and snuggle down under the bedcovers. Miss
Elizabeth smiled and murmured that surely one night would not hurt
but Wilson said she had her orders from the doctor and from the
master and she was disposed to obey them. She said she would bring
the little dog back when Charles had taken him into the yard. Miss
Elizabeth roused herself to beg her to make sure Charles watched
over Flush carefully and did not allow Catiline, Henry's bloodhound,
to harass poor Flushie. Wilson said she would do so, though she knew
as everyone else in the house did that it was Flush, a quarter the size
of the other dogs, who terrorized them.

But when she reached the kitchen, carrying the squirming spaniel,
Charles was not there. Instead there was a new young man.

"Oh, Wilson," said Minnie Robinson (who Wilson could see was
flustered and anxious), "this is Timothy. Charles has been sent off."
Wilson did not inquire why. Twice this week she had seen Charles
quaking outside the master's study and heard some talk of his having
been caught drinking wine in the cellar but she had firmly repressed
her desire to know more. In good time, all was always known in this
household.

"This is Mrs. Wilson," Minnie said, "who is lady's maid to Miss
Elizabeth Barrett." Wilson nodded, Timothy smiled. Afterward, Wilson described to her mother how

—there was no cheek or Impudence in his smile Mother or I
assure you he would not have had one back from me and indeed I
was very sparing with my greeting knowing full well as I have
always done how Smiling can be misunderstood and that it is
better to withhold the smiles at first. But he is a pleasant young
man who conducts himself Seriously and appears respectful to all.
He had a place at Mr. Kenyon's in Devonshire Street I think it was
but Mr. Kenyon shutting up his house to go abroad had no need

of him until the spring when he has been told he will be taken on again if he wishes and that is as good a recommendation as any the master has said. He is not tall but he is broad and strong looking and looks well in his uniform better than Charles who wore it untidily and often annoyed Mr. John who took responsibility for him. He is from the Isle of Wight where Mr. Kenyon has a house and came into his service at twelve years old being bootboy. All this I learned from Minnie for you can be sure Mother I did not question him in such a familiar manner myself. Flush tried to bite him of course but he dealt firmly with that naughty animal and said as how Mr. Kenyon had warned him of that Mighty Fierce Hound and had been bitten himself and had told Timothy the way to Flush's heart was with a cake. I said there was some truth in that but that Flush would not take cakes from anyone and Timothy said he had no cake in any case. He stroked Flush cleverly and took him into the yard and caught him again without difficulty and had the decency to wipe the dog's paws before he handed him back for it was raining outside and they were wet. He will do well here I should think if he can keep clear of Tilly who made eyes at him immediately—

Wilson was not in the kitchen long enough to observe how Timothy responded to Tilly's eye flutterings and coquettish smiles. Doubtless he would be flattered, as most men were, but she wondered if he would be smart enough to scent the danger, to appreciate that Tilly could hardly help herself and that her flirting meant nothing. Tilly was flying higher than a mere footman. She had a follower who was butler to a household around the corner and was proud of it and had told Minnie she could not help it, if it came to something sooner rather than later. Minnie told Wilson privately that she only hoped it did and that Tilly would marry her butler and be sent off, and next time she would take care to engage a girl a good deal more humble and docile. But this Timothy would provide Tilly with some sport which she would consider harmless and Wilson feared for him. She watched him carefully over the following weeks and was relieved to find he was more knowing and adept than she had given him credit for. He smiled back at Tilly readily enough but Wilson noticed he never sat beside her at dinner, even when a chair was vacant, and never allowed himself to be alone with her but moved on quickly, inventing, Wilson was sure, some pressing business. It was hard to fathom Timothy who, as she told her mother,

—is not in the ordinary run of young men Mother but is a Curious Fellow. For one thing he reads and I do not only mean newspapers as many a footman does if they are passed down to him but pamphlets which he buys and which he says are about the Condition of the World in which he is much interested. He is quiet about it and does not Flaunt his reading but I have come upon him in corners applying himself and never hearing me pass. And Miss Elizabeth has noticed him too for yesterday she said to me oh Wilson this may be the last warm day of the year for I do not often go out after the end of September and so I think I would like to go to Regents Park if you are willing and I said as I was surely willing and ready and it was Timothy who carried the chair down and placed her in it. When he had left us seeing I managed well Miss Elizabeth said so that is the new footman is it and I have heard he is a good fellow who does not drink and is dutiful and my father says he is an asset and I must write and thank Mr. Kenyon for loaning him to us. I said nothing, except that I believed he was giving satisfaction but that I could not judge since I had little to do with him I was sure. Miss Elizabeth murmured the lady doth protest too much and smiled and since I failed to take her meaning Mother I said nothing. After an hour Timothy came to accompany us back as had been arranged and Miss Elizabeth spoke to him charmingly. She asked if he liked his new place and he said he did and she said she believed he was a Reader and he said he was and he hoped it caused no offense and she said indeed no he had come to the right house to be a Reader and might she inquire what he read and he said all the information as he could get about why the world was as it is. This pulled her up Mother you can imagine. She thought a bit and then she said had he found any answers and he said not yet but he lived in hopes. When we were back in her room, Miss Elizabeth asked me if I did not find Timothy pleasing. I said I did not know. I did not think about him. Well Wilson she says then you are even more extraordinary than I thought. I said nothing. It is not often an attractive young Man who shows he has a Mind comes your way Wilson she said eventually and yet you do not think about him. I knew I colored Mother and indeed I was hurt. Do you have a brother Wilson she asked for I believe you have only told me of sisters. No I said I have no brother. Well she said that explains all for I have had eight brothers and I have been teased within an inch of my life by all of them over such things and in truth my dear that is all I was doing and I see you are not used to it and take it ill and I am sorry for it. Then I said I did not take it ill but that it was ill founded teasing for I had spoken the truth—

But had she? Wilson struggled to assure herself that she had, that she had no interest in Timothy as she had declared. Yet there was no denying she was aware of his presence and that, unlike Charles's, it did not serve only to annoy. Timothy never spoke to her unless there was strict need. He made no attempt at small talk and neither did she. When they passed each other on the stairs, the place they seemed most frequently to meet, he stood aside and was polite and she was polite in return and tried if possible not to raise her eyes. At dinner he rarely sat near her and, when he did so, politeness again ruled the day. He spoke to Minnie deferentially, as he ought, and to Mr. John but did not take part in the banter of the other servants. Once Tilly found he was proof against her charms she quickly branded him a snob and wished he were back in his old place, for he was a wet blanket with his reading and his silences. Wilson saw that no one agreed with her. She watched the other servants and saw clearly that Timothy had become popular without trying. There was something about his solid appearance which inspired confidence. He was always smart and clean and alert and the smile Wilson had admired from the very first proved to be no superficial grin, to be switched on and off at will, but a sign of his warmth and own contentment. Whatever Timothy's worries about the world, he did not let them drag him down. There was no restless talk, no evidence that he wanted to be up and off.

He had become friends, in so far as the term could be applied in such circumstances, with Mr. Octavius. Wilson saw them together going out of the house, Mr. Octavius even putting an arm around Timothy's shoulder and laughing. Timothy, she noted, was not familiar in spite of this; there was the same politeness in his demeanor as always. She wondered what Mr. John would think and if the master had observed the connection. But then it turned out the master had himself appointed Timothy to accompany his youngest son about town, which intrigued Wilson and raised Timothy higher in her estimation. She allowed herself to relax her guard a little and, though still offering no direct encouragement, did not actively ignore the young man. Now, when he offered to relieve her of Flush as she carried the dog up or down the stairs—he had a habit of tearing along and doing his best to trip up anyone also negotiating the stairs—she accepted. She went so far, surprising herself, as to remark one day that he had quite won Flush over. He said he had been brought up with dogs and knew their ways. He said sometimes he thought they were a deal easier to understand than many a human being of his acquaintance and then begged her pardon if that had sounded rude. Wilson said he had not sounded rude and that she thought what he said had some truth in it. Timothy said, "Mr. Flush seems to mean a great deal to Miss Elizabeth."

"Yes indeed," Wilson replied. "She loves him to distraction."

"He is a comfort to her, being confined to her room mostly."

"Oh, he is more than that," Wilson said, smiling. "She teaches him to count, you know, and even to read, though her brothers laugh her to shame. He is a spoiled little dog, is Mr. Flush."

"So people say, but an excess of love never hurt anyone that I have seen."

Wilson did not reply to that, feeling vaguely shocked at such free talking. The sentiments Timothy expressed without any kind of embarrassment alarmed her—this was not the stuff of pleasantries, not the nice-day, are-you-well of normal intercourse. Yet he did not seem to think he had said anything in the least out of the ordinary, and maybe he had not. Alone in her room, Wilson wondered why she recoiled at the very word "love." Miss Elizabeth spoke freely enough of love, though not of romantic love, and her poetry was full of it. But Wilson never did, it was not how she had been brought up nor how she was in herself. She knew she loved her mother and sisters but endearments had barely existed between them and demonstrations of affection were rare. The only expressed love was for God, said in prayers, sung in hymns, chanted in psalms. Watching the master at evening prayers Wilson had been struck by the passion with which he loved God. Through lowered eyelids she had seen Mr. Barrett's face lighten, in a way it never did at any other time, when he spoke of the love he had for God, who saw all and understood all and would redeem all. "Let us love the Lord," he would end and his expression was fervent enough to make Wilson uneasy. At other times, when she met him on the stairs or crossing the hall, the harshness of his face contrasted violently with his praying look—there was no movement in it, it was set and stern and above all closed.

Timothy, Wilson soon saw, was not afraid of Mr. Barrett any more than she was. They were both united in this lack of fear which was so clearly exhibited among the other servants, both higher and lower (for both Minnie and Mr. John had a trace of fear for the master, though it was kept well hidden). Everyone recognized this, of course. Should any servant need to have dealings with the master, the help and advice of Timothy or Wilson was quickly sought. They became the oracles on how Mr. Barrett would react and they were always uncannily right. Timothy in particular, after he had been in the house no more than a month, could predict what Mr. Barrett would say or do and he was regarded with considerable awe because of this unfailing instinct. "The master cannot abide deceit," he explained once to Wilson, "and that is the key to him." Wilson nodded but ventured to add, "It is how he judges deceit that counts." It was Timothy's turn to nod. "There are those," he said, "who would not recognize deceit if you showed it to them and those who would smell it however it was disguised and the master is one of them: he has a nose for it, and so have I." Wilson thought a moment and then said, "I, too." The silence between them afterward, held for a full five minutes, felt precious to her.

She told no one of this bond, this growing bond, with Timothy. It did not do to talk of one servant to another and even Minnie was included in that ban. Nor did she mention it in her letters home, knowing only too well how Mother would latch onto it and imagine things. The only person with whom she was tempted to discuss Timothy was Miss Elizabeth. It became an almost overpowering urge and Wilson found herself opening and closing her mouth like a fish many times in her need to speak. This came upon her either late in the afternoon, at teatime, when there was something particularly cozy about the tableau in the room, or at night, when she was making her mistress ready for bed and the atmosphere in the lamplight was predictably intimate.

Wilson liked Miss Elizabeth's room at night. During the day she found it oppressive, too dark and dismal until the sun struggled through the blind at three o'clock. Often, she wished she could clear away one of the sofas, the heavy maroon silk-covered one for preference, since it took up so much room, and move the claw-legged armchair to a corner instead of allowing it to dominate the center space, and insist some of the books should go to make more space and light. But Miss Elizabeth liked it dim, preferred the crowding, said the busts of the poets looked better perched above so many volumes of their works. Once Wilson tentatively mentioned her worry that the room was not clean enough, with so much to attract dust, but Miss Elizabeth said she was quite comfortable with dust and her lungs were used to it. She was amused at Wilson's irritation, though it was barely expressed. With the lamps lit and the curtains closed, the fire built up and burning merrily, Wilson liked the room better and was always pleased when this stage of the day was reached. It was then, going lovingly through the rituals of hair brushing and washing, that she felt so near to speaking of Timothy. And Miss Elizabeth, as though she had divined this, tempted her by speaking of him first.

"Papa says, Wilson, that Timothy reads newspapers most attentively and is of the same mind as he is about the Chartists."

"Indeed, miss."

"Papa thinks him a most intelligent fellow, quite above his station in life, and wonders at it."

Wilson said nothing, only concentrated hard on brushing hair, forty, forty-one, forty-two strokes, counting softly aloud the better to appear abstracted.

"He must have had some real education to be so informed. I shall ask my cousin Kenyon all about him when he returns. Does Timothy intrigue you yet, Wilson? And I do not seek to tease you this time, dear."

"I have very little to do with him, miss. He seems pleasant enough. But I hardly mix."

"So I hear. Now that is both a good thing and a bad thing, Wilson. I like your discretion, it pleases me, but to carry it to the extent of never mixing is to deprive yourself of friends, is it not?"

"I have no need of friends, miss." When she said this, Miss Elizabeth put up her hand and stayed the hairbrush and twisted around to look up at her maid, who gazed back at her, quite composed, only anxious to continue brushing, to count sixty two, sixty-three until a hundred was reached and the hair glistening in the firelight, crackling with its black energy.

"I hope I am your friend, Wilson? I never could abide those who say they could not be friends with a servant and boast of the distance they keep. I *wish* to be thought of as a friend."

"Very well, miss."

Miss Elizabeth let the hair brushing continue, apparently satisfied, and there was no more such talk that evening. Instead, she complimented Wilson on the success of the recipe she had used to wash her thick black hair, shining now so beautifully. She begged Wilson to tell her once more what she had used and, relieved to return to such mundane matters, Wilson related how she mixed half a dram of rosemary oil and half an ounce of honey and one ounce of proof spirits, then added half a pint of lavender water gradually, finishing with the final addition of an ounce of Belmont glycerine.

"You should market it, dear," Miss Elizabeth said, laughing, "and make your fortune."

But Wilson reflected long and hard on what had been said previously. What did it mean, a mistress telling a maid she hoped she was her friend, that she wished to be thought of in this relation? To her ears, it sounded either false or dangerous or perhaps both. The gap was too wide. To be a friend, her mistress would need to bridge that gap, surely, and Wilson could not think how this could be done.

Certainly *she* could not do it. She saw very plainly that it was her role to respond but not initiate, and even in her response to be at all times guarded and prepared.

She wondered how Timothy managed with Mr. Octavius, whether he too saw this "friendship" as suspect or had means she did not have to measure and judge it. But she would never ask him, never.

CHAPTER FIVE

To Wilson's disappointment, it was as Miss Elizabeth had told her: once September ended, her mistress did not venture forth. The outings to the park, taken only rarely in any case, stopped. Twice in early October Wilson pointed to the deep blue sky, visible from the window over the chimney pots, and exclaimed how mild it was, how like a summer's day, but her mistress shuddered and claimed to feel a nip in the air in spite of being insulated in her room. Instead, she reclined on the sofa, reading French novels, while Wilson sat sewing, wishing they were out in the park admiring the autumn leaves. Sometimes, if Flush was very restless and succeeded in annoying his mistress by constantly pushing his nose into her book, she would be told to "take him out, do, dear Wilson." Then she would get the lead and put on her coat and walk to Regent's Park alone, letting the dog run wild once they had passed the flower garden.

She knew, of course, that she must be careful at all times and hardly needed Miss Elizabeth's reminders to be on the lookout for dog snatchers. Wilson had never seen a dog snatched but tales of how it was done were often repeated by the other servants and Timothy had held them all spellbound describing how he had once foiled an attempt to snatch Mr. Kenyon's pug—the animal had been in the very bag of the snatcher before Timothy caught up with him and knocked him out cold. Well, Wilson knew she could never knock anyone out cold and also that she could never, in her long skirts, chase and catch such a scoundrel as Timothy had, so she was extremely careful with Flush. She always put the chain on *before* she opened the front door and never took it off until she was back inside and the door shut. In the park, she let Flush off the lead only in the wide-open grass area where no dog snatcher would be able to run as fast as he. Luckily, Flush was surprisingly obedient for such a lively, spoiled dog—she had only to shout once and he would come instantly.

On her walks in the park, Wilson never met anyone she knew, though there were people in plenty around. It made her wistful, brought home to her most forcibly that this was the real difference between Newcastle and London. Even after six months she never saw a friendly face, was never hailed with pleasure and called upon to pass the time of day, which she would so have liked to do. Then one mid-October afternoon she did hear her name and wrote of it delightedly to her mother that evening.

Dearest Mother
You will not believe what a happy afternoon I have had and just when I know I had sounded Despondent which I should not have written of and hope did not cause you anxiety for you know I cannot always be Cheerful no more than you can and I do not expect it. Well, I took Flush to the park about two o'clock Miss Elizabeth having said if he did not stop Kissing the pages of her book, for Kissing was what she called it, I should have said licking, she would be driven distracted. It was a very Fine day Mother so warm and sunny as you would not believe up in the dear North and me only wearing a coat for the date's sake and no other. The trees are beautiful all reds and yellows and Flush went near mad with joy rushing among the fallen heaps of leaves and rolling over and over in them as he loves to do and which means a great deal of brushing and combing when we get home before he

is fit for Miss Elizabeth's bed. I sat on a bench and watched him
for you need not fear I dare not take my eye off him and presently
a woman with a baby in her arms comes along and smiles and says
I believe there is room for another and I said there is room for
three never mind two and indeed I was glad of her sitting down
because it is Prominent to sit alone and I try to avoid it for fear of
being importuned though in truth you will be glad to hear it has
never happened yet. Now as the woman spoke I had a feeling I
knew her but reasoned it was impossible knowing no one except
the folk at Wimpole Street and a few visitors there and a few
faces as I see weekly at chapel. So I said nothing. But the woman
turned to me herself and said excuse me but I believe we have met
are you not Mrs. Wilson as is maid to Miss Elizabeth Barrett.
Indeed I am I said and I had a mind I knew you but I cannot recall
how. Oh she says I am Mrs. Treherne, Crow as was. Well, I was
astonished Mother to find someone I knew in any manner of
speaking. I am sure I would have known her at once and said so
only her face was different since we met that once in Minnie's
room and then she was big with child too. She said it was of no
consequence I did not know her and she would not expect I
should. Then she showed me her little baby and oh Mother you
never *saw* such a beautiful child indeed you never did. She is
nearly four months of age and so Rosy and with eyes so Blue as to
take the breath away and the prettiest thatch of yellow hair like
down Mother. Well, I held her and she looked up at me and smiled
as if she knew me and Mrs. Crow I mean Treherne said she smiled
a great deal and was no trouble and she was going to bring her to
see Miss Elizabeth if I thought it fitting and I said indeed I did and
it would gladden Miss Elizabeth's heart to see such a lovely baby.
Then we talked of Miss Elizabeth's health and I said I thought it
seemed moderately good but that her spirits were often low and
it was not always fathomable why and Mrs. Treherne sighed and
said that was always the trouble and she could tell me things that
would explain it somewhat but it was not the time or place. I
asked her how she fared herself and she said very well and her
husband's bakery in Camden Town showed a profit but that she
missed Miss Elizabeth indeed she did and if it had not been for
being away at her mother's at Caistor for her lying in and then,

being ill after, for her own health and only returning to London a month since and having much to do then she would have called at Wimpole Street. I said I was sure she would be welcome and I would tell Minnie and Miss Elizabeth and we would look for her coming as soon as she was able. She said it was not often she could get away but for the good of the baby she tried to get out if the day was fine for soon it would be foggy and too dangerous to expose her to such evil air. It was very pleasant to have a companion Mother as you can imagine and to nurse the baby a little though Flush did not like it. When he saw me holding the Little Creature and smiling at it he barked and jumped up and Mrs. Treherne said Oh Duke Flush you are jealous are you and the dog heard her voice and you can be sure recognized it and jumped on her knee and licked her face and we both laughed. The baby is called Mary Elizabeth, Mary being for Mrs. Treherne's mother and Elizabeth for herself. I said my name was Elizabeth and she commented how strange that Miss Elizabeth should have maids of the same name. I said I was known as Lily at home but had heard it only from Minnie for six months and missed it and she said she knew how it was and was Lizzie to her family but never heard it all the years in Wimpole Street even Minnie addressing her as Crow because she fell into the habit early and could not get rid of it. So I begged her to call me Lily and she begged me to call her Lizzie and that is how we left it. I hope I see her again and have made a friend.

As soon as Wilson got home and had gone through the ordeal, for both of them, of cleaning Flush she hurried to Miss Elizabeth's room with news of her encounter. Her mistress lay in the same position she had been in two hours before, her book still held close to her face, the only difference being that she had nearly finished it. Flush jumped up and was hugged. Wilson pulled up the sofa table Mr. Kenyon had sent before he departed—a pretty piece of furniture with a rail to stop Flush jumping on it—and began to lay out the tea things, telling Miss Elizabeth about Crow as she did so. The news was received with great interest and Wilson subjected to a veritable interrogation. The drift of it was quite clear to her.

"Did Crow, for I cannot call her Treherne, did she look well, Wilson?"

"Indeed, miss, though her face was much thinner."

"Ah yes, with overwork no doubt, poor Crow, it cannot be easy. Her face was never thin here."

"It was after having the baby, I should think, miss, for it does thin the face in women."

"Is the child pretty?"

"She is beautiful, she has eyes as big as ever you saw and so blue—"

"Like her father's. Billy Treherne has big blue eyes, to which Crow succumbed. It was his looks that trapped her and he is good looking, I can see that. Does his business flourish?"

"I believe so. Mrs. Treherne said they were very busy—"

"And she most of all, she will work her fingers to the bone, you can be sure of that. She wept when she left me, Wilson, wept and wept, and it was not just because of me, it was because she knew the life that lay ahead, the hardship that such marriages bring."

Wilson said nothing but felt troubled. Was it something she had said, without realizing, or how she had said it which gave Miss Elizabeth this strange idea that Mrs. Treherne was a miserable, unhappy wretch instead of the blooming mother she had sought to describe? Tilly knocked and handed in the tea tray. Wilson put it down on the table and poured the tea. Miss Elizabeth was not done yet.

"Did Crow mention calling to see me, as promised, Wilson?"

"Oh yes, miss, she said as how she meant to do it the first moment she was able—"

"When *he* would let her, she meant."

"She did not say as—"

"She had no need to, I understand. She is married now and has abrogated all her rights, as women do. Well, I would not, though all that is past now, thank heaven, and does not need thinking of. Poor Crow. She loved me dearly but made her choice, if choice it was, and there is no help for it."

Perturbed, Wilson cleared the tea things away and put more coal

on the fire though the room was stifling hot. Miss Elizabeth complained of feeling cold now that the sun had gone and would only be
placated by the sight of a roaring fire—she lay huddled in a shawl on
the sofa from which she had not now moved for some three hours.
Her face, since speaking of Crow's alleged desertion, was pinched
and her eyes moist with tears that needed only the slightest provocation to fall. Settling down in her corner, Wilson applied herself to her
needle and watched her mistress furtively. It was not her place to
speak out; it would do no good if she advised a turn around the room,
at least. Miss Henrietta, when she came in, might achieve this but
Wilson knew she could not. The misery in the air was thick and sour
and there was little she could do to relieve it except wait. She knew
by now that one of two things would happen: either there would be a
storm of crying resulting in a headache and a call for laudanum which
would in turn induce sleep, or a book would be picked up and slowly
succeed in capturing the reader until all pressing unhappiness was
dulled. Today, to Wilson's relief, it was a book. Miss Elizabeth
reached for a new book lying on the table and turned onto her side.
Though at first tears had to be wiped away as each page turned, soon
they stopped and the pages turned more and more rapidly and the
book was held closer to the face and Wilson knew the battle was won,
for the time being.

The next day was another glorious autumn day but not only was
there no tempting Miss Elizabeth out, there was no escape for Wilson
either. Her mistress had a cold. The sneezing began in the night and
by morning there was a slight fever and Wilson was needed to bathe
her forehead and give hot liquids every half hour. So Arabel took
Flush. The spaniel was reluctant to go. He dug his paws into the
bedcover and sniffled anxiously and whimpered when Wilson forcibly removed him and handed him to Miss Arabel. Wilson held out the
chain and offered to put it on but Miss Arabel said she would wait
until she was about to leave. Wilson said nothing but would have
liked to point out how difficult Flush could be, once outside, if the
chain were not already on—he was always so eager to get to the park
that he could shoot off like an arrow from a bow. But Miss Arabel,
who took him often, must know that.

The afternoon was long. Wilson spent some of it trying to remove a large ink stain made only that morning when Flush had knocked over the inkwell. Miss Elizabeth did not care about it and urged Wilson to leave the mark alone for a housemaid to deal with; but she was determined to try her own treatment. Watched with some irritation by her mistress, she rubbed the stain with salt of sorrel, obtained without Minnie's knowledge from the kitchen, and then scrubbed at it with cold water brought up in a pail. Then she rubbed in some hartshorn, ignoring the advice to "leave it, Wilson, do" and washed it again. To her delight, the stain was visibly paler. Her last trick was to soak the stain in skimmed milk, from which she had taken care to remove every vestige of cream, and then to wipe it with a dry cloth. For an hour she left it and then pronounced triumphantly that it was all but gone and no one would know ink had been spilled.

"What a victory," Miss Elizabeth said sarcastically.

After that diversion, Wilson felt unaccountably restless and had to control her urge to walk about, for fear it disturbed her mistress, who lay dozing and wheezing on the sofa without even the energy to read. Every half hour she applied a fresh cold cloth to the patient's head and tried to persuade her to sip some hot lemon and barley water. Mostly, she failed to get any liquid at all through the cracked and swollen lips. Then, about five o'clock, there occurred a calamity which brought on a real fever. Flush had been stolen by dog snatchers and Arabel was hysterical. A ransom was demanded and finally paid, which brought the safe return of Flush. But the drama, concealed from Mr. Barrett, who would not have sanctioned payment, made Miss Elizabeth truly ill with a raging headache.

Of course, Flush was thereafter spoiled even more than usual for at least a week. Wilson did not begrudge the little dog his extra cakes and the cream from the milk (for Flush preferred milk to water) but she found it hard to go along with giving him best chopped breast of chicken. Though she could have sworn none of this disapproval showed in her expression as she cut up the chicken and fed it to Flush, her mistress commented, "It is not *every* day Flush is returned to us, Wilson, now is it? And he has suffered so, you must not begrudge him a touch of luxury." Wilson protested she did not begrudge the little dog anything and that indeed her mistress was quite mistaken to imagine she did but it came into her head how, when her sister Fanny had a stomach ailment that went on and on until a doctor had to be found and paid, how he had said breast of chicken would be the best nourishment for such a delicate stomach and how the procuring of the chicken every day for a month had been almost beyond their resources. And now Flush gobbled it down and, after all, it was no great thing: chicken was not considered an expensive morsel in this house. Breast of chicken was ordered every day all the next week for Flush and, as she carried the dish up the stairs, preferring to do this job herself rather than entrust it to those whose preserve it was, Wilson marveled inwardly at what she was doing and how she accepted it. She was a servant and did what she was told and that was that. If the mistress's dog wished to have finely chopped breast of chicken with just a *touch* of cayenne pepper on it then, why, she would chop it and pepper it and serve it to his lordship.

"Chicken for the Duke, is it?" Timothy asked her one day, meeting her on the stairs and knowing what she carried in the covered dish. He smiled but she did not. She looked, she supposed, a trifle grim, enough to be remarked on though she said nothing, only nodded politely. That night, when she took Flush down to the yard, Timothy took him out for her and they stood there in the doorway watching the dog relieve himself in the furthermost corner, away from Catiline's kennel.

"He has a good life, for a dog," Timothy observed.

"He has a good life for anyone," Wilson said, more tartly than she had intended.

"Ah well," Timothy said, "there are penalties to be loved so, even for a dog. He does not have much freedom, for all the petting, nor much company."

"He is warm and well fed and safe," Wilson said, "and there are many out there tonight as would settle for that." And then, greatly daring, and wishing, the moment the words were out, that she had held them back, she added, "Have you read Miss Elizabeth's poem as is about poor children starving and cold?" Timothy looked startled, shook his head. "It is a beautiful poem," Wilson said, "but I cannot help thinking, when I read it, as I did again last night, I cannot help thinking of Flush eating breast of chicken." She stopped abruptly, her face hot, glad of the darkness in the yard and the light behind and not in front of her. Timothy coughed. Was he embarrassed? She did not care if he was, but if that was the reason for his coughing, a sound false to her ears, then she had misjudged him and would not do so again.

Timothy stepped out properly into the yard and beckoned her to follow him. Wilson did so, shivering, though it was not yet truly cold. She could not see Timothy's face and he was speaking in a voice so low she had to go right up to him to hear. She felt like a conspirator, bending toward him, straining to catch his words. "It will not always be thus," he whispered, "things will change, they *are* beginning to change. You will see, the poor will have their day." Wilson recoiled, frightened, alarmed that he had misunderstood her harmless reflection for an incitement to some kind of revolution, or so it sounded. She turned and rushed back into the kitchen, not even waiting for Flush to be given to her, and Timothy, following, had to touch her arm to restrain her and hand over the dog. "Now what has offended you?" he asked, his expression, which she could now clearly see, anxious and confused. "For, whatever it was, I do beg your pardon most humbly, Mrs. Wilson, indeed I do so." She said nothing, only turned away and, holding Flush so uncomfortably tightly that he yelped, made for the stairs. Timothy pursued her, repeating that he begged her pardon humbly though he knew not for what. Finally, to get rid of him, she said she accepted his apology and there was no need to speak of it again. Then she fairly rushed up the stairs and into Miss Elizabeth's room, banging the door in her haste in a way she would always take care not to do.

"Why, Wilson!" Miss Elizabeth exclaimed, dropping her book in astonishment. "You run as if followed by the hounds of hell."

"Oh no, miss, the door crashed of its own accord and I know not why." She walked over to her mistress's sofa with Flush, holding him out to receive his good night kiss, but for once this kiss was perfuctory and Wilson herself of far more interest.

"Has someone annoyed you, Wilson dear, for if they have you

must tell me," Miss Elizabeth said quietly. Aware that her face was still flushed and her hands damp with perspiration, Wilson struggled for composure and said with emphasis, "Indeed *no*, miss, no one has annoyed me, I have only annoyed myself and said something as I ought not to have done and it was misunderstood and I would be obliged, miss, if you would ask me no more about it, for it was nothing." Miss Elizabeth raised her eyebrows and held her gaze steadily for a moment but then shrugged and said, "We must all have our private domains, I grant you that."

When Miss Elizabeth had been prepared for bed and Flush put in his basket, Wilson went straight to her room. No sooner had she closed the door and leaned against it with relief than she saw an envelope on the floor at her feet. Cautiously, knowing it could not be a letter delivered through the post at this hour, she bent down and picked it up. The hand was bold and quite unknown to her. Inside was a single piece of paper and on it the words, without any form of address preceding them: "If I spoke as though intending harm it was not meant, nor did I have any seditious action in mind but merely uttered a general prayer and hope for the future. Believe me, Timothy Wright." Wilson tore the letter up into tiny pieces, as though its very existence incriminated her.

She could not understand why she had reacted so violently to Timothy's words which, the more she recalled them, seemed more and more innocent. It was she, as she reminded herself, who had planted the seed by speaking out as she did and why should Timothy not reply as he did? Lying quietly in bed, praying to herself, repeating over and over the Lord's Prayer, she saw everything differently —of course Timothy had merely expressed a hope for the future. He had intended no harm and she had been foolish to assume he did. She would have to make amends the next day.

The thought caused her some apprehension. She had never been easy with the men servants but then, until now, she had not had much opportunity to overcome her intense shyness. Mrs. Barrett in Newcastle had kept only a general manservant and Mrs. Graham-Clarke not even that. She had only a gardener and his boy, called in to lift anything heavy and to drive the carriage. But now, in Wimpole

Street, there seemed almost as many male servants as female and she found it both confusing and embarrassing. The butler, Mr. John, was remote enough not to trouble her by noticing her particularly but with the others she was obliged to have some relationship and she could never decide what it should be nor could she dictate how they treated her. Charles had been well on the way to being impudent, which she had dealt with mainly by keeping out of his way, but the lesser mortals such as the bootboy had been entirely respectful and gradually she had come to feel more comfortable. But Timothy was something new. She was not at all sure she could address him, even now, without at once blushing deeply, which she hated. It was such a curse to blush so. It meant every man understood by your blush that you were smitten by him and fair game. She had tried so hard to conquer this unfortunate habit but, always, she had failed. She knew that if she were to seek Timothy out with the intention of being so brave as to *apologize*, her face would be peony red and any manner of motives deduced forthwith. She would have to steel herself and did not relish the prospect.

But she had no opportunity. The next day Timothy had gone off with Mr. Octavius, she knew not where, and Miss Elizabeth was expecting a new visitor, which put her into a state of such violent agitation that Wilson did not have a minute to herself all day. She forgot entirely about Timothy in her fascination with the spectacle her mistress made of herself. As soon as Wilson went in that morning, even before she had time to say good morning or to comment on the noise the storm had made the night before, she was confronted by a mistress actually in tears. "Oh, Wilson!" she cried, stretching her arms out piteously. "There is no escape, Mrs. Jameson comes today and cannot, *cannot*, be turned away. What am I to do? I cannot pretend to be ill or Papa will be angry, and indeed such deceit is wicked—oh, what can I do?" Wilson began going through the usual tasks mechanically, without replying, knowing that such routines were soothing and had their own effect, and once Miss Elizabeth had been washed and her dressing wrapper put on and her hair brushed she became calmer. But now it was eyes closed and head thrown back and brows furrowed as though in pain. "Have you a pain, miss?" Wilson asked, but the head was shaken and a groan escaped. "Only the pain of having to receive this stranger," she murmured, "for which I have only myself to blame." Safely behind the sofa, adjusting the blind at the window, Wilson permitted herself a smile. Miss Elizabeth had made the first move; *she* had written to Mrs. Jameson, telling Wilson this lady was an eminent critic and writer whose opinion of her poems, which Mr. Kenyon said Mrs. Jameson had admired, she would value. She had expected a letter back and had expressed annoyance at each post which did not include a letter from Mrs. Jameson in reply. And now Mrs. Jameson was coming.

Wilson told her mother in a very long letter what a very curious lady Mrs. Jameson had turned out to be:

—really, Mother, she is most peculiar looking and not as you would fancy a learned lady would look and Miss Elizabeth thinks the same saying did you not wonder Wilson at the lack of eyebrows and the thinness of the lips. Well, I would not say as I noticed either but was taken rather with the shade of Mrs. Jameson's hair which Mother was so pale a red as to be nearly pink and if it were another sort of lady you may imagine what people would think. She is small, as small as I am, and wears a fierce expression though her words were kindly enough. She stood on no ceremony saying as I showed her up now what is your name and I said Wilson ma'am and she said was that all my name for she supposed I had been christened and had not always answered to Wilson only and I told her my name and then as we were at the first landing, for she took the stairs briskly, she asked where I was from and when I said the North she asked what part for she knew the North well having lived at Whitehaven in Cumberland as a child and then at Newcastle on Tyne for a year or two. Well Mother I was so surprised I stopped short and begged leave to ask where in Newcastle Mrs. Jameson had lived and she said over the shop of Mr. Miller, bookseller and publisher. She said her family were very poor, her father being in bad health and only a portrait painter at that which was precarious and they were glad to find rooms above a shop and thought themselves lucky. She said we must talk of Newcastle someday and I said I should like that and then I showed her into Miss Elizabeth's room. Such visits liven her up no end Mother and there is great benefit to be had from them even if they leave her tired. Her father however observes only the tiredness and was solemn about it and frowned and said with Winter coming on she must take care to guard her health. When I put her to bed tonight she sighed over what he had said about the Winter and said she dreaded it and felt walled up in a tomb and wished she could fly England for the Winter and go to some warm country as Mr. Kenyon did and many others she knew of. She said she dreamed of Italy and sitting in the sun and saying goodbye to coughs and colds but that it could not be, she could not break up her father's home again. Then she sighed some more and said let us pretend Wilson dear let us pretend we can go where we like and where would you go. I said I had no desire to travel further than I had already traveled from home and she cried shame on you Wilson you are too timid. That is as may be I said but it is the truth. She became excited which I never like to see at that hour and said had I no soul, did I not wish to view Niagara Falls and all manner of other places of which I had never heard. Before I left her, she clutched me by the hand and said if I were to go abroad to winter would you come with me dear Wilson and Mother I did not have the heart to say indeed not. She is like a child sometimes Mother and puts me in mind of Fanny in her weakness and yet *I know she is not weak*. So I said I would to stop the tears and bring a smile to her lips and settle her for the night and now I live in fear of it coming to pass and then what should I do? But I do not think this is anything but wishful thinking on her part (please God). And I do not think her father would permit it—

It was in this that Wilson placed her real faith. Minnie shook her head and said, when told of Miss Elizabeth's hopes, that Mr. Barrett would as soon see her dead at his feet as send her abroad. Hadn't he sent her to Torquay to winter when the doctor swore she could not survive another London winter some six years ago? And hadn't she been worse there than she ever had been in London? No, he would not hear of it and Wilson need have no fears. But consoled though she was by Minnie's emphatic assurances, Wilson found that, instead of dismissing the idea from her mind and being relieved, on the contrary she thought of it even more and was faintly disappointed that the proposition had little chance of success. She could not understand herself. She did *not* want to go farther away from her mother and she had never in her life daydreamed or nursed visions of going abroad. But now she began wondering what abroad was like, what it looked like, what it felt like living in the sun. One of Mrs. Jameson's books lay on Miss Elizabeth's table—*Visits and Sketches at Home and Abroad* —and Wilson found herself dipping into it whenever her mistress slept. Slowly the idea that abroad might be exciting grew upon her and the notion of travel itself took on a new perspective. It would never be dull, that was for sure. Every day would bring variety and, as the autumn ended and winter began and the first of London's fogs enveloped Wimpole Street, this was what Wilson began to long for and what was sorely lacking: variety.

CHAPTER SIX

THE FOG WAS SO THICK throughout November that Wilson was afraid to go out. She had seen nothing like it before and wrote in awe to her mother:

—the depth of it, Mother, so as you cannot see further than a foot in front of you and that is no exaggeration. Often of a morning lifting Miss Elizabeth's blind I imagine it is still night for the fog presses so close to the windowpane there is no light to be seen and the mistress cries out to let the blind fall again and have the lamps lit all day. We are prisoners, Mother, only the men venturing forth and glad to be back again. Then there is the breathing, Mother, for this fog creeps into the nostrils and is evil smelling stuff and brings on coughing even from those with healthy lungs. Timothy, as I have told you of, came back from lighting the way for Mr. Barrett coughing fit to burst and he is strong and healthy and he had a scarf well wrapped round his mouth and nose but it did no good. Miss Elizabeth comes nowhere near this fog as you may imagine but she swears she can smell it and feel it and she coughs twice as hard as usual. What is strange Mother is how the fog muffles sound. There are few carriages abroad and those that still are on the streets seem to make no sound at all. We are a good way from the river but we hear the foghorns sound and a right mournful noise it is. I wake up to hear it and shiver and I am glad I know no one at sea.

Trapped indoors, Wilson saw that she had after all been accustomed to more life outside 50 Wimpole Street than she had either realized or appreciated. She missed the outings with Flush, the walks to post letters, the visits to the Regent Street chapel and the occasional excursion with Miss Henrietta. Standing one afternoon at the window, desperately trying to convince herself the gloom was lifting and she could make out a chimney pot, she heard her mistress say, "It is a shame, Wilson, that you cannot be out for a while to break the monotony. I well know how time hangs when one is confined indoors." Her voice was weak and sad and Wilson felt guilty that she had provoked the comment with her wistfulness.

"Indeed no, miss," she protested, "I am happy enough inside out of such a fog."

"But you would be happier outside in the sun doubtless and so would Flush."

"The fog will lift soon, I am sure."

"Ah, there you are mistaken, Wilson. There are more fogs than you can imagine. London is swathed like a mummy all winter long sometimes. You will get used to being held prisoner here with me, I am afraid."

"It is too comfortable to be a prison, miss," Wilson said bravely, "and the company too respectable."

Miss Elizabeth smiled. "That is nicely put, Wilson, and I thank you for it. I could not abide a sulk for a maid. Come sit by me, hold Flush on your knee and let me rest from his wriggling awhile."

Wilson sat on the end of the sofa and took Flush. She held him firmly, stroked him the way Timothy did, in long movements beginning between the ears and sweeping down the backbone all the way to the tail. Flush grunted and settled down, resigned. "Look at me, Wilson dear," Miss Elizabeth said, "look at me, full in the face if you please." Wilson looked from her own blue eyes into her mistress's large brown ones and held her gaze as steadily as she could. She was strangely at ease. Staring was rude, especially for a servant, but she had been bidden to stare and she found it curiously satisfying, though she could not have said why. She could see herself reflected in her mistress's pupils and she stared at her own tiny pinpoint reflection. She felt pleasantly relaxed, almost sleepy, and there was the faintest sound of buzzing in her ears. Above it, she heard Miss Elizabeth murmur, "I think I could do it, I think I could, I *feel* I could, do you feel it, Wilson, do you?" Wilson noticed that as she softly replied, "Do what, miss?" the buzzing stopped and that, when she found herself blinking rapidly at the same time, so did the sleepy feeling. Miss Elizabeth let out a small sound of exasperation. "There, it is spoiled, and I do believe we could have managed it. You are most receptive, Wilson, did you not know that? It is quite frightening, it frightens me." Wilson, bewildered, could only continue to stare, but her mistress was no longer staring back. "Oh, it was an experiment," she said. "I hear so much of this mesmerism and, though I would rather not, I *do* believe in it, Wilson, I do believe the power of the mind can be such that it can conquer the mind of another. I did not try to conquer yours, dear, only to see if a rapport might exist, if in certain circumstances it might be possible to mesmerise you, not that *I* should truly try. Did you feel sleepy, Wilson?"

"Indeed yes, miss. And there was a buzzing in my ears which I could not account for."

Miss Elizabeth drew in her breath, "I knew it, I *knew* it," she said. Wilson could not credit her excitement, or the passion with which she recounted the tale of her friend Miss Martineau's experience of mesmerism which had provoked this little experiment of her own, to her friend Miss Mitford, who had again come to stay.

Miss Mitford stayed two nights and, since she did not bring Jane, for which Wilson was thankful, required help with her toilet. Wilson gave it gladly. Miss Mitford talked all the time but hardly paused for answers, so all that was needed was an attentive air and the occasional exclamation. She had the most extraordinary hair style under her strange bonnets and it took all Wilson's expertise (and hair was

not her forte) to curl and plait and twist the wild gray-brown locks
into the shape Miss Mitford demanded. All the time she worked, Miss
Mitford chatted, her plump red face beaming with delight at her own
reflection. "You do very well, Wilson," she said, "and I am grateful,
for I know I do not have hair like your dear mistress, oh, is it not
beautiful like a raven's wing if that were not such an unattractive
cliché as well as inaccurate, for who can deny there is a good deal of
blue in a raven's wing and Miss Elizabeth Barrett's hair has far more
shine to it and is far more lovely than any wing of any raven I have
seen and I have studied a few. But she is a pretty little person
altogether, is she not, Wilson, and ought to have a better fate than she
has and would have if she went abroad as I would like her to and tried
to urge upon her when first I met her, to no avail. Now I was born to
be a spinster, indeed I was, and I do not think I could have taken to
husband or children with a dear father needing me as my poor father
does but Miss Barrett, I will *not* have it that Miss Barrett, one so
pretty, that she was not meant to grace some fortunate man's arm. I
cannot bear to think of her pining away but her cousin Kenyon has
tried too and had no greater success. Come the summer, Wilson, and I
shall move might and main to bring something about, though with
whom I do not know, for no one is worthy enough. Miss Barrett
thinks the game is over and never played in point of fact but I do not,
I do not think it is over for either her or for Miss Henrietta, though of
Miss Arabel I have doubts, she is wedded to her charity work and of
too religious disposition to seek romance."

The bonnet was on and tied, and off Miss Mitford went, pressing
a half guinea into Wilson's hand though she demurred. Wilson had
heard her mistress say Miss Mitford was poor, and Jane had told her
Mr. Mitford drank away any money she had, so she did not want such
largesse, but she saw how pleased Miss Mitford was to give it and
how a refusal to accept would offend. So she kept the half guinea to
send to Mother for Christmas and thought of what a difference it
would make to the season for her. Christmas had not been a festival
very joyously kept in Mother's house. She associated it with her
husband's death, though that was early in December, and all her
childhood Wilson had been more aware of tears at Christmastime

than in any other month in the year. It astonished her, with this as her own particular legacy, to find that Christmas in Wimpole Street was an affair of such importance, with plans being made from the end of November and an atmosphere of excitement present from the first of December itself. She said as much to Minnie and was told she had seen nothing yet and would surely enjoy herself. And she did, finding in all the preparations a warmth she had thought lacking in the household.

Minnie of course took the brunt of the extra work but did not seem to mind. Under her direction the whole house was decorated with garlands of holly and ivy, even the banisters threaded with greenery, and red candles were placed in clusters in every room; and there were three trees, something Wilson had never seen, each hung with silver and gold baubles. At evening prayers the master regularly reminded them all that this was a religious festival and that the birth of Our Lord should not be the excuse for an excess of inappropriate merrymaking but even he seemed pleased with the way in which the house glowed in its Christmas colors. Wilson wished passionately that

—Fanny could see our trees, Mother, for they are the prettiest sight in the world and when it grows dark we clip little candles onto the tips of the branches and light them and put out the lamps and it is enchanting to behold. There is to be a big dinner on Christmas Eve of twenty-four people and twelve more invited to the party afterward and Miss Henrietta is in charge of it and is rehearsing charades with Captain Surtees Cook. Miss Elizabeth commented that she had thought charades by their nature were spontaneous and she cannot help but think any kind of preparation only a form of cheating and something Papa would not approve of were he to come across it but Miss Henrietta for once dismissed this criticism of her sister's and said charades were a form of play and if they were to be done properly required rehearsing like a play and as for their papa he had allowed charades and would remember he had and there was no need to worry him over such a thing. Miss Elizabeth said she would not worry him for the world and that it was Henrietta who did that, more was the pity. Miss Henrietta asked what she meant by that and Miss Elizabeth replied she had only to think of whom she rehearsed with to be able to answer that herself. Miss Henrietta blushed and left the room and I felt sorry for her. I did not let my displeasure with my own mistress show but I made sure when next I encountered Miss Henrietta that she sensed I did not condemn the charade practice. Indeed, I helped Miss Henrietta procure a mat from my room which Captain Cook had need of and carried it down to the drawing room where Captain Cook said it was just the very thing for one syllable he had in mind. Minnie says Miss Henrietta had better be careful for this rehearsing means being alone with Captain Cook and the master would be angry. I mentioned that the door was open and that the drawing room is a public room but Minnie said a great deal can go on behind an open door in a room public or not and that she was not born yesterday even if I was. She declares I am smitten with that young couple which is not true Mother but I do feel for them. Captain Cook is very kind unlike some gentlemen in this house and always passes the time of day and is Considerate and remembers servants have feelings too. The other day he walked with Flush and me and the pavement being thinly coated with ice begged me to take his arm up to the corner where he would turn the other way and I was very grateful for it and thought it gallant.

Wilson was going to Camden Town to visit Lizzie Treherne when Surtees Cook set her on her way. She had the address written on a scrap of paper with a map of sorts sketched on the other side by Lizzie. Always modest, she had not believed the invitation to call and take tea one Sunday was genuine but Lizzie was insistent and the piece of paper proved it. To go into someone's home here in London seemed an event of such enormous significance that Wilson almost dreaded it and had begun to make excuses to Lizzie when last she called, declaring that she did not know if she would be free. "On a Sunday afternoon?" Lizzie asked, reproachful, and Minnie, in whose room they all sat, echoed, "On Sunday, Lily? Now come." So there she was, slipping and skating a little, cutting through Regent's Park toward Bayham Street with Flush pulling at the lead, in danger of tripping her up with every yard. She picked the dog up as she came out of the park and gave him a sharp slap and a warning to be still. She would rather not have brought him but he was her alibi: if asked where she had been, she could rightly say she had been taking Flush for a walk. Why she felt the need of an alibi she did not quite know but she was reluctant to tell her mistress where she was going, to whose house she had been so pressingly invited. Lizzie had not yet seen Miss Elizabeth, though she visited Wimpole Street every three or four weeks. Always, told Lizzie was here and desirous to show her baby, Miss Elizabeth coughed and said she feared she would spread her cold to the darling baby and would Wilson please tell Crow (which was how she continued to address Lizzie) she was heart-broken not to be able to see her and looked forward to next time. Silently, Wilson nodded, wondering why Lizzie, an intimate of so many bygone years, was treated like some dreadful stranger. She said nothing but, discussing the excuse given with Minnie, she expressed the opinion that Miss Elizabeth could not bear to see her old servant blooming and happy, that it was necessary for her to retain the image of Crow as downtrodden and ruined by the marriage for which she had not forgiven her. Minnie thought this quite likely. It was hard on Lizzie, she said, to be spurned when she had been so close and given so much but then, when all was said and done, she was a servant and that was the way of things.

Outside the door of 6 Bayham Street Wilson hesitated. The place was a bakery, with William Treherne's name in white letters on a black board running across the length of it, above the doors. She could see no knocker and when she pushed the big doors experimen-tally she found they were securely locked. She walked past the bakery and found an alley alongside but Flush growled as she began to walk timidly into it, another dog barked in reply and she stopped. The alley was dark, even on an afternoon with a hazy sun still about, and she felt nervous. She hated not knowing her way about, knowing only Wimpole Street and its environs, all so broad and clear and grand. At home, she was familiar with streets like Bayham Street and no alley held any mystery for her but now she felt intimidated by her ignorance and was glad of Flush. She scolded herself, telling herself over and over that she was imagining shadows and noises and that Lizzie would live in a respectable neighborhood and would not invite her where there was any danger. She was behaving like a grand lady, half terrified with tales of the violent poor. She smiled at this thought and as she walked more boldly into the alley a door opened and there was Lizzie, baby in her arms, beaming and welcoming her in.

Wilson did not realize until she entered the Trehernes' home how homesick she had been. She gasped with pleasure at the sight of the wooden table spread with a cloth exactly like Mother's best white starched cloth, even to the pattern of crocheted threads around the edge, and the scones and tea bread sitting on crystal stands that were a copy of Mother's. The room was tiny and too crowded and felt instantly familiar. A fire roared and Lizzie apologized for the sheets airing on the clotheshorse and moved them away and Wilson begged her not to trouble herself, for she was quite at home with sheets airing and indeed loved the smell. There was a battered old settle filling all of one wall and the table and a large armchair took up the rest of the space so that walking about the room was not possible and Wilson had to squeeze her way to the fire as Lizzie insisted. She set Flush on the floor, admonishing him not to move an inch or he would be out in that alley where some other dog still barked. Obediently, Flush lay down and closed his eyes. Lizzie put the baby down too, laying her on the settle with a cushion to stop her falling off, and then she took the kettle from its hook over the fire and poured water into the waiting teapot. Tea was given, and scones offered and taken, and some of Lizzie's mother's raspberry preserve spread on them and Wilson was utterly content.

She stayed an hour and never had time gone so quickly. Her normal reticence seemed to vanish, so much so that afterward she could not believe she had told Lizzie the things she had. But then Lizzie understood, she had been in exactly the same circumstances and nothing had to be explained. It was a relief to talk about Miss Elizabeth, to discuss her with Lizzie, who had been equally close, and to ask questions it had never felt right or decent to ask anyone else. It worried Wilson that her mistress did not seem like other women and yet the subject was of such delicacy, it was impossible to bring up.

Now she brought it up, or rather clutched the line Lizzie threw when she inquired if Miss Elizabeth was still not well in *other* respects, apart from her chest. Wilson said this was something she had not liked to broach: Miss Elizabeth did not bleed and yet did not seem concerned. At first she had thought her mistress dealt with this herself but she knew there was no way in which it could be done without her knowing. Where would she procure and prepare the material and how would she wash it or dispose of it? It was a mystery Lizzie solved. She told Wilson that Miss Elizabeth had ceased to have her monthlies when her brother was drowned and, ever since, she had bled only a little at long intervals. She would never have this told to any doctor, Lizzie said, and called it a blessing. She said she was of an age when regular menses were of no consequence because there was no prospect of bearing children and that was the only importance of such things. But Lizzie had wondered often if this lack of bleeding might be an indication of serious disease and Wilson agreed with her—it might. But how could a doctor be consulted in the face of Miss Elizabeth's obstinacy?

They talked, too, of the other Barretts, of how uncomfortable they felt with George and with Stormie, for very different reasons, and how they positively disliked Henry. Lizzie asked Wilson if Mr. Henry had been a nuisance to Tilly and they both laughed. She told Lizzie how useful Alfred was to Henrietta, and Lizzie said she was glad of it, for Henrietta had been good to Alfred and she liked to hear he had overcome his natural indolence sufficiently to support his sister. In the middle of this discussion as to the rival merits of the brothers, Lizzie's husband came in. Wilson stopped speaking immediately and almost spilled her tea as she hurried to stand up and take her leave, though both Lizzie and Billy Treherne himself urged her to stay.

Afterward, once she was back in 50 Wimpole Street, a wistfulness settled over Wilson which turned into a kind of sadness. Miss Elizabeth asked her if she was quite well and, being told she was, wondered if she had had bad news from home, which Wilson assured her was not the case, but no more was said. It was like a dull ache inside, her memory of Lizzie's living room and the longing to have just such a happy home with a husband as handsome and pleasant as Billy Treherne and a baby as sweet as theirs. She had no doubt that, as her mistress suspected, Lizzie worked too hard but it was all for something, it all went somewhere and such happiness came of it whatever the weariness. As she went through the dull routine of preparing Miss Elizabeth for bed, Wilson felt slight tremors of panic. Three months ago she had been twenty-four, a great age not to be married and without a sweetheart or even a follower in her life. Unplaiting her mistress's hair and beginning the brushing, a task she usually found rewarding, Wilson felt horrified at the thought of doing this forever, leading this kind of life until she was too old and was pensioned off. She did not want it. She wanted what Lizzie had and she wanted it sooner rather than later. Everything her mistress had said to her over the last few months on the subject of marriage suddenly seemed to her absolute nonsense and she felt angry that she had allowed herself to be deluded with fine talk of a freedom from marital servitude which was no freedom at all. Her anger, some of which found its way into the hairbrush she was using, extended to Miss Elizabeth herself. Minnie had told her that next birthday her mistress would enter her fortieth year, her *fortieth*, and Wilson could not bear to think of it. How could this life she led, of reading and writing, immured in this stifling room, how *could* that be preferable to what Lizzie had? That darling baby alone made Lizzie's fate infinitely preferable.

The next day Wilson was her usual placid self but she was aware of looking about her differently. Timothy, encountering her on the turn of the stairs, as he did many times a day, was surprised to find she did not drop her eyes and merely murmur a good morning with clear intention of evading conversation, which was how she usually responded to his greeting. She said good morning but smiled and looked him in the eyes and seemed disposed to chat further. It was the first time since the incident in the yard that she had acknowledged him as a human being and he felt reprieved from a crime he knew he had never committed but for which he had been sentenced. Wilson was not pretty, he found himself thinking, but she had a poise and stillness about her which was far more attractive than mere prettiness and when she smiled, which was rarely, the change in her was far more remarkable than in other women who smiled more often and with greater ease. Dimples appeared and the up-turning corners of her mouth drew attention to the generous lips and the fullness of the cheeks. What Timothy liked best about Wilson was the intelligence that radiated from her—she was not silly, as so many maids were, nor was she proud. There was, he was sure, a great deal more to her than anyone supposed, if only he could find his way through to it. But his time was limited. Soon Mr. Kenyon would return and he would be taken on again in Devonshire Place and would not hesitate to go, vastly preferring the Kenyon establishment to the Barrett one. Except, of course, for the absence of Wilson there.

Her smile gave him hope and on Christmas Eve the hope was justified. First, there was a dinner of some grandeur—certainly Wilson, who had seen nothing like it, thought it fantastic, though to Timothy, who witnessed such dinners almost weekly at Kenyon's, it was nothing spectacular—and then, in accordance with Henrietta's wish, everyone gathered in the drawing room for charades. The servants filed in at the back of the room and stood watching, keeping well toward the wall where there were no lamps, and they were almost invisible in their black and white clothes. Minnie Robinson was the only one seated and Wilson stood behind her, marveling at the richness of the reds and gold reflected in the mirror along the far wall. Miss Henrietta attracted every eye in her red velvet dress and beside her Captain Cook, in full regimental dress, caught the light on his epaulettes and buttons. Admiring the way in which the red of Miss Henrietta's dress set off her dark hair and white skin, Wilson thought of her own mistress, lying alone upstairs, refusing to come down even for Christmas, wearing her dull black gown, the one she wore day in and out, and how magnificently transformed *she* would look in just such a red. Now Miss Henrietta was clapping her hands and calling out excitedly—Wilson saw her father frown—that Captain Cook's party would lead the charades when everyone was still. Mr. Barrett, in full evening dress, sat bolt upright with Miss Trepsack, his dead mother's old companion, on one side and Miss Graham-Clarke, his sister-in-law, on the other. Wilson had heard a great deal about this lady, who was distantly related to the Mrs. Graham-Clarke she had served, and was rather in awe of her, as indeed were all the servants. Minnie had told her how, in Hope End days, her childhood home, this aunt had come to stand in for the dead Mrs. Barrett and had ruled the roost most effectively. There was an air of tension in the room in spite of the chatter and the festive decorations, with everyone waiting to see what Captain Cook would come up with and half dreading a scandal.

There was a sharp "sssh" from Alfred. "Ready?" he asked and there was a chorus of "yes" from within. "Then pray silence," he shouted and silence fell instantly as the door opened and Mr. Septimus entered alone, dressed to look exactly like a boot boy and carrying the mat from Wilson's room. Solemnly, he unrolled the mat as the door opened again and Mr. Octavius, dressed as a postman, walked past him and made a great pantomime of climbing imaginary steps and knocking on an imaginary door and dropping a letter through an imaginary opening. All the time he was doing this, provoking laughter, even from Mr. Barrett, with his winks and suggestive expressions, of boredom, exhaustion, anticipation and the like, Mr. Septimus was shaking the mat. "That is the end of the first syllable," Alfred announced as Septimus and Octavius finally exited. "Post," shouted out Henry, followed by "step" and "door" and "stamp." Mat, thought Wilson, but said nothing. Now Alfred shouted for silence again and on came Henrietta, dressed as a country girl and carrying what looked like heaps of straw. Octavius and Captain Cook followed, dressed to look like farmhands, which caused great mirth, and all three actors began gathering up the straw and tying it into stooks. Once more the little company left the improvised stage and next in was Captain Cook, carrying two big sacks which he put on the table. Meanwhile, Henrietta went past him and stood in a corner eating honey from a jar. Alfred announced that was the third and final syllable. There were calls of "honey" and "bags," but nobody could come up with a whole word. Wilson could not hear what anyone was saying, there was such a hubbub, but Mr. Barrett was smiling and shaking his head and everyone seemed very pleased. "You have failed!" cried Alfred. "And now here is the whole word." He opened the door with a flourish. There stood Octavius in a white tablecloth and a gold and purple scarf, clearly meant to be a clergyman in vestments. He walked across the room and then turned and waited and the strains of the wedding march floated into the now utterly silent room as Henrietta marched in on Septimus's arm, carrying flowers in her arms and with a veil over her head.

"Matrimony!" shouted Henry in the silence and there was a great storm of applause followed by loud accusations again of cheating. Wilson kept her eye on the master, as did all the servants and a good many of the family and guests. He was no longer smiling but he clapped slowly and made no sign of anger. Once everyone saw this, they turned to cheering the performers.

The servants had their own party afterward and the one subject of discussion was the daring of Captain Cook and the impudence of him. "He could have been out in the street for all he knew," Minnie vowed. "I've seen the master turn nasty for less." But none of the other three groups with their "Catastrophe" and "Magnificent" and "Uproarious" had come anywhere near entertaining the company as much. Now, as Mr. John played his fiddle and there was dancing, Timothy presented himself to Wilson and asked her if she would care to hop with him, for hop it would have to be in such confined quarters. A week earlier, Wilson would have said no. When she nodded and smiled she knew she was deliberately choosing to reject all her previous attitudes. She said yes and took Timothy's arm and together they jostled in the space where the big kitchen table usually stood. Above the noise of the fiddle and clapping and talk, they discussed, as everyone was doing, the full implications of Captain Cook's choice of word. Did he intend matrimony this coming year? Would there be a wedding in the house at last? Was 1845 to be the year for the lovers?

CHAPTER SEVEN

Wilson loved the arrival of the post every bit as much as her mistress did, though receiving so few letters herself. But Miss Elizabeth was generous with her larger share and would often beg her maid to "listen, do" as she read out some particularly interesting passage. Gradually, Wilson learned a lot, becoming aware how imperfect was her own epistolary style. It was unnecessary, she soon realized, to use capital letters in the haphazard fashion she did, and she began to appreciate the importance of correct punctuation. She resolved to try harder to emulate Miss Elizabeth's educated correspondents. She had, as usual, studied the day's envelopes as she carried them upstairs one morning in the second week of the new year. Mr. Kenyon's hand she recognized and was fairly sure another was that of Mr. Horne, a literary friend of her mistress's who wrote most amusing letters, but the third envelope was a puzzle. It was postmarked New Cross, an area quite unknown to Wilson, who wondered if it was in or out of London. Normally, such a missive would have been good for at least ten minutes' speculation before the paper knife was called upon to do its work but Miss Elizabeth, after glancing at the postmark, laid the letter aside with far too casual an air, remarking that it was doubtless from some unknown person commenting on a poem and would be left to the afternoon. Other letters arrived that day but Wilson could not fail to notice that the New Cross letter remained unopened. It was also noticeable that Miss Elizabeth was in great good humor in spite of having coughed half the night away. Mr. Barrett, greatly pleased, commented on this to Wilson as he left his daughter's room. "She is very cheerful," he said, "in spite of this wretched affliction, an example to all of us, Wilson, of Christian fortitude." Wilson murmured agreement and hoped the mood would continue. It did. Three days later another New Cross letter arrived. This time her mistress seemed to think an explanation was called for. "It is from the poet Robert Browning," she said, "about my work. I am very pleased to have it."

She was also, Wilson surmised, very pleased to reply. The letter she wrote back seemed to take up a great deal of time for one who usually wrote so swiftly and fluently. Two drafts of this letter were torn up and thrown on the floor, from where Wilson retrieved them to put them on the fire, and there were many clickings of the tongue and other signs of exasperation. Wilson vaguely remembered her mistress speaking of this poet Robert Browning to Mr. Kenyon but could not recall what had been said. There was no one whom she could ask about him, even if she had been bold enough to voice her curiosity, so she stopped thinking about Mr. Browning's letters and turned her attention to the latest one from her mother.

What Mother wrote about during January and February was how she looked forward to her eldest daughter coming home in the spring. It had been agreed when Wilson took up her employment in the Barrett household that every year she would be entitled to two weeks' holiday and the time was approaching to claim it. When Miss Elizabeth, who had begun to show great interest in the weather, asked if it was milder than usual for February, Wilson took the opportunity to remind her that with spring beginning the subject of her holiday was in her mind. "Ah yes," Miss Elizabeth said, "you must go to your family and I shall have to be brave, shall I not?" She asked when Wilson would go and Wilson said the end of April if it was agreeable, so as to be home for Mother's birthday, which fell on May Day. Miss Elizabeth clapped her hands and exclaimed aloud and could not believe that Wilson's mother shared her own beloved dead mother's birthday and said certainly she should be there for it and, counting backward, it would be best if Wilson departed on April 18 and she regarded this as settled. She asked when Wilson's own birthday was and if she set much store by it, for she made little of her own. Wilson said she would be twenty-five on September 14 and that she did not quite like the idea; she did not relish being a quarter of a century with no home of her own. Miss Elizabeth was very quiet after she said that and Wilson feared she had precipitated one of those attacks on the institution of marriage which plunged her into such confusion. But her mistress only said, "Ah yes, a home of one's own is a fine thing."

All thoughts of home, which were constantly with her from the middle of February, made Wilson happy but when the early promise of spring disappeared in a savage frost and a bitter east wind just as the daffodils in the park looked ready to bloom, she was obliged to contain her impatience. There was ice on the pavements and once more she was confined indoors, reduced to standing at the window in the afternoons and peering wistfully into the street. London had taught her she liked to be outside more than she had realized—she disliked intensely being kept in, had come to depend on her walks with Flush to Regent's Park. But it was not just the fresh air and exercise and the change of scene she craved; it was also the possibility, indeed the increasing certainty, of company. Other people were as regular in their park walks as she was, after all. Ten months of leaving 50 Wimpole Street at much the same time every weekday and following much the same route had thrown in her way much the same people, people who now nodded or lifted their hats or smiled in recognition. And then of course there was Timothy, who had gone back to Mr. Kenyon, on the gentleman's return from abroad, and took his pug for a walk at the precise time that Wilson took Flush. It was, she thought, an amazing coincidence.

The moment Timothy left the household in Wimpole Street, Wilson had felt easier with him. She had not liked the scrutiny of the other servants, the eagle-eyed observation of every word and look exchanged. Sometimes it seemed the servants' hall existed only to gossip about the various liaisons in the house, imagined or otherwise, and she was always on the alert to prevent any tittle-tattle about herself, so even after Christmas she was more reserved with Timothy than she had intended to be. But then, at the beginning of February, Mr. Kenyon returned, unexpectedly owing to an illness of a relative, and Timothy joined him almost immediately. Wilson met him every day in Regent's Park for two delightful weeks until the sudden vicious return of winter put a stop to her outings. She was sorry for this and yet, going back over her encounters with Timothy, wondered what there was to be sorry for. It did not amount to much. They met, always pretending their meeting was accidental, at the main gate and walked for twenty minutes in one direction and twenty in the other and during that time talked mostly of their employers. Timothy, of course, had much more to tell than Wilson. He was, she thought, quite boastful in his description of Mr. Kenyon's immense social standing and the magnificence of his dinner parties, as if such things would impress her. "Really," Wilson was moved to say one day, "I wonder your master wishes to spend so much energy on entertaining. My mistress would not think of it even if she were able to. She despises socializing; it is a waste of creative energy." She knew, even as she said it, that she was merely repeating, parrotlike, Miss Elizabeth scolding Miss Henrietta but she could not resist it. Timothy was not put out. He laughed and said he believed his master enjoyed himself and gave others much enjoyment, for certainly even very great literary names were eager enough to come and waste their creative energies at his generous table. Wilson bridled a little, reading into the mention of "very great" literary names a possible reflection of her mistress's lesser one, and then realized how silly she was being. She admitted to Timothy that pleasure and enjoyment of any visible kind were low on the horizon of her mistress's life. "A letter from Mr. Browning the poet," she confessed, "is the highest of joys in her day. It is quite pathetic to me." Timothy nodded and looked serious and said he had not been untouched by Miss Elizabeth's plight when he was in Wimpole Street and that he had wondered how Wilson stood it sometimes when she could have found happier employment with ease. That had turned Wilson's tongue sharp. She told Timothy her employment was quite happy and that she had never wanted a situation where she would be gadding about night and day with some silly empty-headed lady. She insisted the regime in Wimpole Street suited her quiet tastes excellently. Timothy shrugged and said he was glad of it but that he liked a little bustle himself and had found the Barrett household a mite oppressive and had always been glad to be sent off with Mr. Octavius. For reasons she could not understand, this had offended Wilson so much that she had not spoken for the rest of that walk.

It was only this kind of exchange that she was missing by not being able to go to the park while the intense cold weather continued but Wilson was obliged to admit, if only to herself, that it mattered more than she had thought. She felt deprived, lost without her little daily excursion. Her park life was her own life, and all the more precious because of this, and Timothy was her only friend outside the house apart from Lizzie Treherne. Every time she spied Timothy's jaunty figure approaching, her spirits could not help rising and his own broad smile was impossible not to match. She knew he was interested in her and regretted only that her unfortunate response to his earlier attempt at a closer degree of friendship had apparently made him wary of approaching her again. He was always absolutely formal and correct, treating her with dignity and a slightly exaggerated respect which made her uncomfortable. He never came anywhere near suggesting they go for a walk together or indeed that they should meet: the pretense was kept up that even their afternoon walks were purely accidental and not to be counted on. Wilson had begun to fear that the first move would have to come from her and she could not think of making it.

But, deprived of Timothy's company, she was beginning to think she could do so. Miss Elizabeth had almost lost her voice, so there was not even the distraction of talking with her, and life was twice as quiet as it usually was. Miss Henrietta had a cold and stayed in bed and Miss Arabel, never given to much conversation in any case, had a harsh cough of her own which prohibited her from visiting her sister's room although she was not ill enough to take to her bed.

Wilson seemed to live in a gray twilight world, performing all her duties mechanically, feeling time was suspended until the frost should go and the ice melt and the sun bring everyone to life again. She felt restless, unable to settle either to write or read, and disinclined to find comfort with Minnie, with whom she normally spent a good deal of time. It was Minnie, in her wisdom, who assured her that everyone was out of joint because the seasons were. "There is nothing worse than a spring that goes back on itself," said Minnie, "even the master feels it. No one will be right until there is some warmth in the air and then we will see things go too much the other way, I daresay, and that will be trouble in itself." Wilson could not fathom exactly what Minnie meant but was consoled to think that perhaps what she felt was only a seasonal affliction. She told Miss Elizabeth something of what Minnie had said, merely to pass the time, and her mistress smiled and managed to croak that Minnie was a great believer in spring fever and thoughts of love and had made the same obscure prophecy every year for as long as she could remember and, whatever happened, always declared she had been right. She herself, she said, had no hopes of life improving with the spring. She had no hopes of anything. Hearing this, so sadly said, Wilson's heart began to beat a little faster with distress and she was glad when Miss Henrietta scolded her sister and thought of any number of things for her to look forward to and promised her that when the sun came out her spirits would rise and her health improve as it always did. "And there is your poet, Ba," Miss Henrietta teased, endeavoring to be lighthearted. "You have made a new friend and, come the spring, may become acquainted." Miss Elizabeth was not pleased with this and told her sister not to be so foolish, that being approached for a meeting with Mr. Browning was a thing to dread, not hope for. But irritation banished the tears and Wilson was grateful to have another crying fit averted. Sometimes the tears came so thick and fast that her own bodice would be soaked in them as she held her mistress tight and patted her like a child. It was this emotional abandon which made Wilson incapable of judging her poor mistress as she would others and Lizzie had told her to beware of it. "You will not be able to leave her, as I could not for so long, Lily, you must watch this, you must not get pulled in too far."

Once the second, true spring had begun it seemed to hurtle along at a frantic rate. The very first afternoon Wilson rushed so eagerly to the park the heat of the sun seemed tropical in spite of the beads of snow still spotting the grass and the slivers of ice around the rim of the lake. Wilson loosened her coat and pushed her bonnet back from her head and, like Flush, lifted her face up and breathed deeply and felt she had come up from a long way underground. Timothy caught her unawares. "And where have you been, Mrs. Wilson, all these long two weeks?" "Indoors, for sure," said Wilson, but she smiled and made certain he knew she was not reprimanding him. Timothy, it seemed, had still walked forth, swearing the air had been wonderfully bracing and nothing to be feared and that he would have thought Wilson would have been tougher. "Well then," Wilson said lightly, "perhaps I am weaker and more ladylike than you thought, Mr. Timothy." "I would not like you the less for that," Timothy replied swiftly, and she found herself blushing. Pleased, she walked with him the length of the rose garden and he told her of yet another grand dinner party at which he had served. "Your lady's poet was there," he said. "Mr. Browning and a host of other literary grandees." She could not help asking what Mr. Browning was like, though tried to make her inquiry as casual as possible, not wishing Timothy to sense her curiosity and label it vulgar. "A small fellow," Timothy said, "smaller than I am, but a fine head and a strong voice. He talks a great deal and very loudly." Wilson would dearly have loved to press Timothy further but did not dare. Instead, she turned the talk to the subject of the Corn Laws and Miss Elizabeth's wish to write for the Anti-Corn Law League, and Timothy came to life at once. For the next twenty minutes he lectured Wilson on the iniquities perpetrated by the government and was full of information about riots there had already been and those confidently predicted. There was no mistaking his own sentiments. Listening to him, Wilson was dismayed to find how quickly she became bored; she found she had been looking at the daffodils and estimating how long it would take for the tight buds to open and had not in fact heard a quarter of what Timothy was saying.

He did not seem to notice. In full spate, he squired her out of the park, clipping his dog on a lead and attaching Flush for her; then, holding both dogs firmly, he continued to walk with her back to Wimpole Street. Wilson attempted to point out that he was going past his own house but Timothy could not be interrupted and swept along with her, unable to break off his discourse. By the time Wimpole Street was reached, she felt quite exhausted and dreaded any response to the half-hour tirade being called for. But before No. 50 was reached, Timothy broke off suddenly and nudged her:

—and Mother he said Do you see that man on the other side, well it is the poet Mr. Browning as sure as I am standing here. Well you could believe I looked very hard and saw the man clearly. He was walking very slowly along past No. 50 and looking up at the windows as though expecting to see something of interest which at that time of day I could have told him at once was not likely for there would be no one in any of the rooms at the front of the house. I observed he was smartly dressed wearing fine yellow gloves and a well cut coat with a velvet collar and carrying a hat and cane. He is as Timothy had told me small and trim but with something confident about him that belongs to another taller man I fancied. It was something to tell my mistress when I got in but I did not. I cannot say Mother why I held back. It was only that I had a feeling she would not like to be told either that I had seen Mr. Browning or that he appeared to be examining the house. So I said nothing of it and talked of the pleasant walk I had had and Flush too. She got up this afternoon for the first time in two weeks and walked around the room a little vowing she was as unsteady as a child of two and she was. I said practice would make her stronger and that she would be well advised to take regular turns around the room and extend them to the rest of the house and then when I came back from my holiday she might go out again. But at this mention of my going away she began to weep and went back to her bed. It is always the same Mother for she cannot bear any talk of my departure but you may be sure I remind her constantly and will not be put off indeed no. Miss Henrietta's maid Molly will look after her and I have begun to show her what she needs to know and it will do very well. And I am to travel by the stagecoach Mother about which I have made inquiries and I shall do it in three stages and will manage it very well do not fear—

But Mother would of course be very afraid and Wilson was not as sanguine as she sounded. She had almost no experience of travel. Her only journey had been made with the Newcastle Barretts and she did not look forward to traveling alone and having to fend entirely for herself. Miss Elizabeth, sensing her reservations, played upon her doubts and wondered aloud how she could face such an ordeal. Wilson, remembering her mistress's boasts of how she would travel the world if she could, said she expected she would survive as others had done. That day, Miss Elizabeth retired to bed at four in the afternoon and Mrs. Jameson, who had been told she might come at four-thirty, had to be put off. Wilson was embarrassed but Mrs. Jameson was not. She stood in the hall and shook her umbrella—there had been a brief sun shower moments before—and, after she had listened to Wilson's explanation and apologies from her mistress, she shrugged and said what of it, she had been visiting at 51 and was not in the least put out and she supposed there might be somewhere she could sit for a moment and pass the time of day with Wilson herself while she got her breath back. Wilson was alarmed and confused. She stared at the redoubtable Mrs. Jameson helplessly. Did she mean she expected to be taken upstairs to Wilson's attic bedroom? Surely not, such a request had never been heard of and was quite unlikely and improper. What, then? Did Mrs. Jameson expect to be conducted to the *kitchen?* Where on earth did she imagine she could have a conversation with a lady's maid?

Just then, to Wilson's relief, Miss Henrietta came out of the drawing room and down the stairs and saw Mrs. Jameson and greeted her warmly. "Do not keep dear Mrs. Jameson standing, Wilson," Henrietta reprimanded her. "Come, Mrs. Jameson, make do with me since Ba is indisposed," and she led the lady away, leaving Wilson alone in the hall. Her knees felt strangely weak. Later, writing to Mother in her room, she began to feel quite angry:

—for, Mother, what can Mrs. Jameson have expected of me and how could she have spoken so and what should I have said if Miss Henrietta had not come along? Do you not think it was thoughtless of her? She must know I could not take her anywhere and indeed it was not right to embarrass me thus. But it would be a fine thing, would it not Mother, if a maid could entertain a lady and think nothing of it? As it is, a maid can hardly entertain another maid without arousing comment. I would like to give tea to Lizzie but where can I do it and have a measure of privacy? Nowhere, and I feel it when I go to Lizzie's little house and she is so hospitable to *me*. Now, Mother, you will think I have been long enough in London and learning dangerous notions if I come out with such thoughts and really it is only vexation and nothing more.

But when Miss Elizabeth inquired the next morning, with a guilty air, if Mrs. Jameson had called and if she had been displeased Wilson could not resist saying, "Yes, miss, she called and was only sorry you were unwell"—she paused a fraction, lingering on the "unwell," to let her mistress know she doubted the unwellness very much—"and was not in the least displeased but said she might talk to me a little while before leaving."

"And did she, Wilson?"

"Why, no, miss, how could she? I could not keep the lady standing in the hall and I had no rights to take her to any other room and I could not think how she imagined it would be possible. This is not my mother's house where I could have made Mrs. Jameson welcome and indeed would have done so and made her tea."

Miss Elizabeth was silent a moment or two. Wilson plumped up some cushions overenergetically and was aware she blushed as she spoke which was very annoying. She turned away to hide her hot face. "So what did you reply to Mrs. Jameson?" Miss Elizabeth asked, her tone of voice low and careful.

"Miss Henrietta came along and took her off, miss."

"Ah, the insuperable problem was solved."

"In a manner of speaking," Wilson said.

"But you hold the incident against Mrs. Jameson, I can see."

"How could I, miss? Being only a servant."

"More than a servant, dear Wilson—a friend, surely, a friend to *me*."

And there the matter ended, for the moment. Miss Elizabeth smiled so sweetly and held a hand out so pleadingly that Wilson felt her resentment fade, leaving behind only a faint sense of the absurdity of this situation. At every turn she gave way to her mistress and never held on to any grudge. There were many ways in which she could, even as a maid—in some ways, especially as a maid—make her displeasure felt but she never thought of employing them, waged no subtle war with the permanent frown and all-day brusqueness as weapons. She smiled as usual, was gentle as usual, moved around quietly and soothingly as usual. She let Miss Elizabeth sigh and consoled her, she let her weep occasional tears of exhaustion and depression and sought only to cheer and comfort her, she was ever ready with little gestures and remarks designed to lighten the weary hours.

"Is it spring properly, Wilson?" Miss Elizabeth began to ask at the beginning of April with monotonous regularity.

"Indeed it is," Wilson replied, eager to enumerate the proof. "The birds are all back and singing and the daffodils fully out in the park and everything jumping into life." She could not understand why, instead of smiling at such good news, Miss Elizabeth covered her eyes with her hands and groaned. "Why, whatever is the matter, miss? Spring is not winter, there is no need to fear it so."

"I have promised that in the spring I will see Mr. Browning. He insists so and I held out hope that when spring came and I felt better he might come and visit."

"Well then, miss, so much the better. He is a very nice gentleman, I believe, and looks it."

"Looks it? You have seen Mr. Browning?"

"I have seen him several times lately."

"Wilson!"

Aware that she was teasing, Wilson went on sewing, refusing either to lift her head or continue. The "Wilson!" was repeated again, urgently. "Yes, ma'am?" Wilson replied innocently, darning a hole in a stocking with absolute concentration.

"Describe him, at once, and where and how you have seen him." Wilson took her time, dwelling lovingly and unnecessarily on all manner of inconsequential detail before coming to her brief glimpses of the poet. She was particular about the clothes, starting at the boots and working up to the hat, and vague about the features, deliberately. Miss Elizabeth listened without interruption, bearing Wilson's slow delivery well, and was quiet afterward. There were no unseemly giggles or artificial intakes of breath. She said only, "You have a masterly eye for the outline, Wilson, so observant to be sure. How fortunate Mr. Browning is not wanted for some crime or, with your information, the police would have him. Now Miss Mitford and Mrs. Jameson and Mr. Kenyon have not told me half as much. They appear to know nothing of the gloves and the material of the coat and the cut of the trousers and suchlike—they are quite useless. If *you* had been at these dinner parties and heard Mr. Browning speak and watched his face I would have had him through and through, I see."

Wilson shot her an anxious look and was glad to see the smile playing around her lips. It would not do to have seemed to mock. The letters now came and went with great regularity and Mr. Browning was not to be trifled with as a subject of discussion. "I will wait until your return from the North, Wilson," Miss Elizabeth said eventually, appearing very satisfied, "yes, I shall wait until then. I could not endure the strain of such a visit, if it must be made, without you to help me. So that is decided: it cannot be until May and then you must be settled once more and it is likely to be later in May rather than sooner. A meeting is of no consequence after all, it is not something I see any need for, only Mr. Browning presses so."

Wilson noticed that, once this decision as to the date of Mr. Browning's visit was made, Miss Elizabeth seemed to dread her approaching absence less, which she thought very curious. Now, if she mentioned the journey or her packing, Miss Elizabeth took it well and showed some interest. She liked consulting timetables and maps and was most helpful, pointing out connections Wilson had missed and in effect planning her journey for her and doing it so efficiently that a whole overnight stop, which Wilson had been dreading, was saved. She inquired if Wilson had money enough to ride inside the coach all the way and, when told she had not, provided the additional silver herself, begging Wilson to think nothing of it. She had, she assured her, money of her own and little enough to do with it. Wilson, thinking of the forty pounds a year spent on laudanum, reflected that the three guineas given to her were not extravagant.

The master, too, showed himself unexpectedly liberal at the last minute. He called Wilson into his study and told her he was pleased with her, that she had worked well. Wilson thanked him. He said he should like to send a gift to Wilson's mother of some chocolate from Jamaica, newly arrived and of excellent quality. Wilson curtsied and thanked him again. And then he said that, although she was in his daughter's employment, he would like to contribute something to the expenses of her journey home and back, and gave her two guineas. Wilson said he was most kind and prepared to bow out gratefully. But Mr. Barrett had not finished. He looked her straight in the eye, in his usual manner, and said that she of all people must know how his daughter fared. "She has been low lately," he said, "and the winter hard. Is there sign of improvement, do you think?" Wilson made no mistake: the rigid bearing and expressionless face could not conceal Mr. Barrett's anxiety. "I think there is a little improvement, sir, and with the warm weather more to be hoped for." He nodded. "We must work together for that improvement, Wilson, and with God's will we shall see it yet." Then he let her go.

She left on Friday, April 18, weighed down with presents. The chocolate from Mr. Barrett, a piece of lace from Miss Elizabeth and a cake from Minnie—all for Mother. Then there were ribbons for her sisters and embroidered bookmarks and illustrated religious texts from Miss Henrietta and Miss Arabel. Everyone gathered to wish her well and she no longer minded, such was the spirit of kindliness and good will, that the Wimpole Street servants saw Timothy arrive to carry her to the coach point.

"Write to me, Wilson," Miss Elizabeth begged, "one letter at least, to assure me of your safe arrival and good health, and I will write to you, dear, if you would not mind being reminded of

Wimpole Street?" At the last minute the sight of her mistress looking so fragile and forlorn as she struggled to hold back her tears was almost too much for Wilson and she was on the verge of saying she could not desert her post but then the thought of Mother gave her courage and with a last embrace, wholehearted on both sides, she was down the stairs and off.

CHAPTER EIGHT

THE COACH BREASTED Highgate Hill and, as the ride became smoother and the sensation of being about to slip disappeared, Wilson opened her eyes and was prepared to look out of the window she had paid so dearly to be beside. Gradually the excitement of departure faded and was replaced by an acute awareness of her traveling companions. Timothy, who had seemed mercifully experienced in these things and of whom she could not think without the most profound gratitude, had arranged her place and seen to her luggage. She could not have managed without him. The noise and confusion at the first fare stage had been so great she had wanted to go straight back to quiet Wimpole Street and stay there. But Timothy had pushed and shoved and argued with the driver and now she had one of the best places all the way to Grantham and the promise of the same to York—with the help of an additional tip given by Timothy to this driver to pass on to the next (though he had warned her neither driver's honesty could be relied upon). He had done everything he could to ensure her comfort and had said goodbye so warmly and with such a pleasant smile that Wilson had taken his hand and squeezed it and vowed she would never forget his kindness.

Nor would she. He was a good man. She looked out of the window at the green fields beginning to run alongside the road and thought Timothy would get on in life. He was bound to, with such energy and intelligence and with a name already for reliability and initiative. Mr. Kenyon thought highly of him and was a liberal employer. Timothy had hinted only last week that Mr. Kenyon was willing to advance him some capital when the time was right. When Wilson had asked what he meant, Timothy had explained that his employer liked to set his servants up in a business if they had the desire and aptitude and should it prove, upon inspection, a sound venture. One footman had been set up as a publican and had already paid Mr. Kenyon back and another, only an under footman, had had such skill at carving from wood that Mr. Kenyon had set him up in a carpentry business and he had succeeded so well that he now employed people himself. But Timothy had confessed he did not know in which direction he wished to go or what use he wanted to make of such a generous helping hand. He was neither publican nor carpenter in the making, that was sure. He was biding his time and at twenty-four, Wilson's own age, could afford to.

Wilson kept her eyes on the outside view, the better to avoid scrutinizing her companions, though she could see, out of the corner of her eye, that they did not show the same delicacy. The woman opposite stared quite openly and Wilson knew her dress and bonnet were being examined for clues as to her station. Well, this inquisitive creature, far too overdressed herself to fool anyone into thinking she was the lady she would have them believe, would learn very little, unless she was particularly shrewd. The traveling dress Wilson wore, made of a dark navy cloth with piping of lighter blue, had been her Christmas present from Miss Elizabeth, or rather the material had been given to her and she had made it up herself from a pattern lent to her by Lizzie. It was good material, as anyone who knew about such things could tell at a glance, and the design was modern without being the height of fashion. Her bonnet was not new but it could pass for a recent purchase because it had been worn only on Sundays and very carefully looked after. It was a light gray and matched the navy dress reasonably well (though, if she had not decided to treat herself and take an inside window seat, Wilson would have bought a blue bonnet she had seen in Oxford Street which was the precise color of the piping on her dress). She wore gloves, of course, and had a thick cloak of a dark gray, rather rough material, the same one in which she had left Newcastle and which she now heartily detested. She saw this gaper had finished with her clothes and was clearly perturbed by the evidence of the book lying on Wilson's lap. The book was closed and the title visible to anyone with reasonable eyesight. It was *Country Stories* by Mary Russell Mitford, which Miss Mitford had personally given to her, declaring that, though it was not a new volume, it had some value all the same, she hoped, and might be enjoyed by Wilson's mother as well as herself. Wilson was very proud of the gift and carried it now on her lap as a mark of the esteem in which she felt Miss Mitford had held her by choosing to give it. It was, she knew, the sort of book a discerning lady might read on a journey and spoke for itself. She smiled slightly as she continued to gaze at the passing scene: she was being a snob and delighting in it.

The other people in her compartment were all men, one of whom looked ill and the other three decidedly old and frail. No one spoke, though even if they had done so they would have had difficulty being heard since the wheels on the road and the hoofs of the horses made a tremendous noise. Not, Wilson thought, the most amusing of traveling companions, but then she had no wish to be amused. She had her book and she had her thoughts. She could see, in her mind's eye, Mother and her sisters getting ready for her homecoming at this very minute, rushing about cleaning and polishing quite unnecessarily, as though she were a royal personage and not a girl coming home. She had written to Mother quite sharply when informed of these preparations, telling her not to be so foolish, but Mother had replied that her visit coincided with the need to spring-clean and was only being used as the occasion for it. She was, Mother said, to have her own room, to which she was entitled now, and again Wilson had written back objecting and saying she wished to share, as she always had done, with Ellen and would be hurt to be turned out of the bed she had always slept in, sharing with Ellen while May shared with Fanny and Mother had the little room to herself. What Wilson most wanted was the old order back, without change. She was embarrassed to realize how much she was looking forward to the warmth of a shared bed and a crowded bedroom after a year in her lonely attic room. The best talking was at night, whispering, huddled under the covers with Ellen. Things were said then impossible to say in the cold light of day, things either too intimate or too silly for open speech. It would be from Ellen, at night, that she would learn anything of interest that had happened in the past year, all the inconsequential trivia that she missed and that had never been worth committing to paper. And in return she might perhaps bring herself to speak of the strange hold her mistress had on her, and of Timothy.

This time, when the horses were changed at each stage, Wilson was not so timid that she could not seek refreshment at the inn. She followed the more confident passengers and merely copied what they did, and by doing so found herself sitting with a lady and a gentleman who had joined the coach at Derby and were traveling to York. The gentleman was kind enough to offer to order for her and under his wing Wilson ate and drank and felt better. She discovered it was quite easy to attract this kind of helpfulness merely by being dignified and modest and realized her new costume assisted the process.

She had elected not to stay overnight, thereby entailing a journey of some twenty hours, with a cold and agonizing last stage, late at night, which she found hardest to bear. This second coach, which belonged to another company, was not as comfortable or as wind-proof and it seemed full of crying children. There was nothing to see out of the window and no light to read by, even if she had had the energy. Wrapped in her cloak, Wilson greatly regretted her decision and regretted it even more when, arriving in Newcastle and alighting at last, she could not see the trap Mother had engaged to meet her and carry her the last few miles to Fenham. She descended from the coach aching and exhausted, and when her box had been taken down, she collapsed upon it and closed her eyes. It was bliss just to be still, not to be swaying and jolting with the coach, but soon she began to feel very cold and stood up, determined to inquire at the Golden Lion

Inn if a trap had come for her and was perhaps around the back. The coach had arrived nearly an hour late because a horse had fallen lame, and the carter Mother had hired might have gone inside to wait. But hardly was she at the door before he came out, and after that everything fell into place. It gave her great pleasure to write to Miss Elizabeth and tell her so, just as she had promised.

My dear Miss Elizabeth,
I write to keep my word and tell you I arrived safely at my mother's home last night a little before midnight feeling most weary but in good heart and oh miss that heart overflowed and my weariness vanished when the door of my home opened, for they had all been waiting and listening for the trap and had become sure as time went on and it was long past the hour when I ought to have arrived that some misfortune had occurred and were steeling themselves for dreadful news and they all stood in the doorway and held out their arms and cried for joy and I did not know whom to hug first. You may be sure there were many kisses and that it was fully half an hour before I had looked at everyone properly and was surprised to find them all looking rather better than worse after this long year. Mother's hair is a little white and I was anxious when I found she was thinner but she assures me she feels better for having lost a little fat due to her teeth hurting and not being able to eat as heartily. Fanny has grown and may end up the tallest of all of us which will make nonsense of her being our *little* sister and pleases her hugely. Ellen has her hair in a new way which is not exactly to my liking for I find it lengthens her face and gives her a severe expression but I did not say so. May has come out a little and is not quite so shy and quiet and is doing well in her position and will perhaps make a lady's maid after all. They all declare I am *greatly* changed and swore they felt quite nervous of me and that I looked like a different person and when I was indignant and inquired what they could mean they whispered to each other and smiled and I threatened to beat each and every one if they did not stop it at once and make themselves clear which in the end they did by saying I looked like a lady. Well said I you know I am not nor do I try to ape my betters but if by that you mean I have a more confident

air and a little dignity at last then I am glad of it and will forgive you but if you mean I fancy myself as so many ladies' maids do then I will beat you all the same. No beating was necessary I am thankful to report for they all said they had only meant my traveling dress and the way I wore my hair and that they liked both very much and found them becoming and very London like which since none of them have ever been to London you might think a worthless comparison. It is very strange to feel a visitor in my old home, miss. The first day I felt lost since neither my mother nor my sisters would allow me to do so much as lay the table but waited on me hand and foot and I confess the novelty quickly wore off and I did not exactly like it. But today being Sunday we have been to chapel and I feel once more that I belong. You are not to imagine I forget you miss for I think of you constantly and hope your cough is better than it was and Molly is managing what needs to be done. My mother and sisters ask about you and wish to know you in every particular so your ears may burn to be the subject of so much description. Give Flush my love and tell him I have left him on duty I expect him to take care of you for me—

Wilson could not think how to end and pondered over the rival merits of "faithfully" and "sincerely yours" until she decided neither was fitting and simply signed her name. She had tried to make her letter lively but knew it contained none of her real feelings and found herself wondering what it would be like to write freely of her confusion to Miss Elizabeth, who was sensitive to such things. If it had not seemed likely to be a betrayal, she might have attempted to describe how displaced she felt and, even more disturbing, how she so quickly found she had changed and in changing was not so content to be home as she had always been. So many things made her impatient, though she stifled this unworthy impatience. The little cottage, though as cozy as she had remembered, seemed so very much smaller, and its smallness seemed unattractive suddenly. She was horrified to find herself missing the big rooms and wide staircase of 50 Wimpole Street and shocked to notice herself cringing at the noise of people washing in such close proximity. Privacy and solitude had been thrust upon her this last year but she realized after the first week back home that they had grown on her and that she was more suited to both than she could ever have dreamed. She was also more suited to command. At home, Mother was in charge as she had always been and Wilson had never questioned that she should be, had indeed always thought herself fortunate that she had a mother so in control. But in Wimpole Street she had gradually grown used to making decisions and enforcing them. She found it hard not to treat her family as she treated her mistress and was forever telling them they could or could not do things, in a way which at first amused but then annoyed them.

What was even harder to accept was the measure of boredom she experienced each day. She was ashamed of it, denied she felt it, kept telling herself how comfortable and easy everything was. Ellen was out at work and so was May, though she still came home each evening, but Mother and Fanny were always there and she was obliged to witness the dullness of their routine. So much time and energy were spent on simple tasks necessary to run the household, tasks she was no longer much aware of in Wimpole Street. Hours spent heating water and scrubbing clothes and floors, hours gathering vegetables and scraping, peeling and chopping them, hours devoted most of all to the sewing which provided Mother's income. Nobody ever sat and read all day as Miss Elizabeth did, nor did they converse. Listening to Mother and Fanny chattering on about nothing, Wilson found herself craving stronger meat. She realized how much her mistress *did* talk to her and how she involved her in all the topics of the day, whether she was interested or not. Mother and Fanny had heard nothing about O'Connell and Ireland, the one topic on Miss Elizabeth's lips at the moment, and they cared less. Once upon a time Wilson knew she also would have been obliged to admit she did not know of this O'Connell or what he stood for, but now she was disappointed that everyone at home was so ill informed. She asked herself over and over if she could come home and live there permanently and she did not dare consider that the answer might be no, whatever her love for her mother and sisters.

The true pleasures of her holiday were the physical ones. It was pleasant to walk about Newcastle. She liked the chance to chat and say good day to so many familiar faces. She smiled to think she had ever been impressed by the upper reaches of Pilgrim Street or by Grainger's covered market, and as for Bainbridge's being all a department store could hope to be—it was absurd. But the familiarity of Newcastle pleased all the same. It was good to saunter The Side and find it not at all terrifying with its noise and bustle and to think that, if she wished, she felt quite brave enough to go into the Surtees House cocoa rooms. She liked taking short cuts, something she could not aspire to in London, liked knowing she could find her way through the chares, the narrow lanes connecting the main streets, and never feel afraid as she had done when first visiting Lizzie in Camden Town. Even going back to the country, to Fenham, after such an excursion to the town, had its pleasures and she no longer sighed for more bustle and life. She would never, she thought, belong to London as she did to her hometown. It was true that she had had to go away to appreciate her own background but, now that she did, it was only to reject it in part. It would always be there, always comfort her, but now she wanted something more. Instead of making her wishful for a past she had wished to reclaim, her holiday at home was making her long for more change, more adventure. Timothy spoke often of his travels the year before when he had been the one to accompany Mr. Kenyon. London, he told her, was nothing compared to Paris and, as for Venice, it was sublime; until she had seen it she could, he assured her, not consider she had truly lived. She had laughed at the time but now, amazed at the ordinariness of Newcastle compared to the excitement of London, she wondered how much more there was to see and learn and felt sorry for those, like Mother, who had been nowhere and seen nothing, whose whole lives had been circumscribed by lack of opportunity.

She was delighted when, on the tenth day of her holiday, she had a letter from Miss Elizabeth. The mere sight of the tiny envelope and the spidery handwriting threw her into the sort of ecstasy her mistress herself experienced on receipt of such a thing. She hugged it to her chest and wondered where on earth in such a house she could find privacy to read it, away from the expectant faces of Mother and Fanny, who appeared to assume *her* precious letter must also be theirs. At the risk of offending them, she withdrew to the bedroom and, when Fanny immediately followed her, said as gently as possible that she would be down soon. The look of misery on her sister's face at being rejected in so outright a manner so affected her that she instantly regretted her coldness and called Fanny back and let her lie with her on the bed while she read the letter. It was only one sheet but very closely written in Miss Elizabeth's diminutive hand.

My dear Wilson—
You cannot imagine how very pleased I was, and Flush too, for he knew instinctively who had written, to receive your letter and know you had survived the journey and had been greeted with such love. It was worth enduring the discomfort, was it not, to find a mother's arms around your neck and sisters' smiles before your eyes? I know I would travel to the ends of the earth in a rickshaw if necessary to see my dearest sisters should we ever be parted (which God forbid) and were I to be offered an embrace from my poor departed mother there is no journey I would not make. But this is only to show you how envious I am and how I share your joy.

We are trying hard, Flush and I, to be joyful here without you but we confess it is hard work for *nothing is right*. Molly does very well and I am an ungrateful wretch to venture to criticize her but I cannot help it. Who wakens me each morning with such gentleness and kindness, Molly or Wilson? Who brings me my tea at precisely the temperature I like, Molly or Wilson? Who knows when to speak and when not? Who moves around so quietly? Who knows how to tuck a shawl in and plump a pillow and in general see to a most tiresomely particular lady's needs? Why, you, dear Wilson, and I miss you at every turn and grow more sour with the lack of it every minute. I dreamed last night that your mother declared she could not spare you and though I beseeched her in my dream to send you back to me she would not and I woke in tears. Dear Wilson, do not let my dream become reality, will you? I am not ashamed to tell you how I need you.

But before this letter turns into one long complaint let me tell you that everyone in Wimpole Street is well except for Catiline, who has a thorn embedded in his paw which has turned septic.

Naturally, Flush and I feel for the poor animal but it has made life quieter.

Now, do you remember the odious Jane, Miss Mitford's maid who so annoyed you with her disloyalty? Well, *all is found out* and she is dismissed. Poor Miss Mitford discovered wicked Jane opening a parcel to her and pocketing the contents (being a bottle of madeira sent with his compliments from Mr. Kenyon to her father). Now she is maidless again and writes in the most despairing tone that she has not the heart to take on another maid in her life and must shift to manage for herself since her luck with maids is so bad. I feel guilty that mine is so good. *My* maids are the very best and I know it and never cease to marvel at their devotion. With which outrageous but nonetheless deeply sincere piece of flattery—but can flattery be sincere?—I will close and wish you God's speed for your return.

Elizabeth B. Barrett

Wilson blushed as she finished the letter and folded it neatly and replaced it in its envelope. That was what her mistress did, always replaced the letter after the first reading so that the second could seem like the first opening all over again. Fanny asked what it had said and could she read it or have it read to her. Wilson replied that she would find it too dull since it was merely a message from her mistress hoping she was well and wishing her a safe journey back. At the words "journey" and "back" Fanny began to cry a little and asked why she had to go so far away and only come home once a year for such a wretchedly short time. Wilson said she must earn her living and it was earned better in London and Mother had wanted her to go there. "She doesn't anymore," Fanny sniveled, "she wishes you were back home and she said only the day before you came that she had heard of a good place with a nobleman's wife in Durham and she was sure you might get it and be near us and see us every week as Ellen does and Mother said it paid as much as London does." Wilson stiffened and withdrew her arms from around Fanny. "Mother has said nothing of it to me, Fanny, and I do not think she could. She knows I am committed to Miss Barrett and could not forsake her so readily." Then Fanny began to howl in earnest and through her sobs swore her sister loved this Miss Barrett more than her and it was a dreadful thing. Wilson hushed her and told her not to be so foolish and asked how an employer could ever, *ever* be loved more than a mother or a sister and why it was almost blasphemy to say so and Fanny ought to be ashamed and would make *her* cry if she persisted in such untruths. They lay on the bed together, clasped in each other's arms, until Fanny had ceased to cry and Wilson had coaxed a smile from her. She felt exhausted. It was, as she had assured Fanny with such passion, more passion than the denial warranted, a lie that she loved Miss Elizabeth more than her family, and it truly disturbed her to think such an idea could have entered Fanny's head. She did not *love* Miss Elizabeth at all. But nevertheless the mention of Mother finding a good place for her up here in the North had frightened her, not simply because the lure of London was strong. It was more than that, the thought of letting her mistress down was unbearable. She felt needed and depended upon and responded by giving more of herself than strict duty called for.

She said nothing of this to Mother and dreaded the subject of this place, wherever it was, being brought up by her. Under the bed-clothes she asked Ellen, home for the night on Saturday, whether there was any truth in what Fanny had let out and Ellen whispered back that there was and that it was a very good place, paying sixteen guineas, the same as London, and the lady, like Miss Barrett, some-thing of an invalid. Wilson groaned and Ellen asked what was the matter and she confessed she would not know what to say if Mother brought up the subject. Ellen was silent such a long time that she nudged her and asked if she was awake. "I am awake," Ellen said softly. "I am only thinking over what you have said. Mother thinks you will be pleased." "But I have been home ten days," said Wilson, "and nothing has been said. Why does Mother hold back? Why does she not tell me about this place?" Again Ellen was silent and mur-mured, "You must ask her." but that was just what Wilson had no intention of doing and, as the days passed and the date of her departure came near, she began to think both Fanny and Ellen had been mistaken or that Mother had thought better of the suggestion.

Then, two days before she was due to return to London, Wilson found herself alone with Mother in front of the fire, both of them sitting watching the flames die down before they went to bed, and she knew something was about to be said. She thought of getting up and taking herself to bed before a word could be uttered but she did not move in time. "There is a place I have heard of," Mother said, looking all the time into the fire, "with a lady in Durham. I know you can have it." There was a pause and Wilson was painfully aware she ought to break it and sound eager but her tongue seemed tied. "But," Mother now went on, and Wilson was sure she was about to say she knew her daughter did not want this place and was about to cry as Fanny had cried, "but the night before you came, sitting here as I sit now, a lady came to me. She was small, smaller than you, Lily, and dressed all in black and she carried a baby in her arms and she held out the child and said to me, 'Do not take Wilson from me or you take everything I might have.' I could smell the scent of flowers and feel a heat greater than the fire and I could hear from far off the sound of a man's voice, a deep voice, talking. The lady smiled at me and cradled her baby and put a finger to her lips and then she vanished and I was at once cold and shivering and could not at first understand what had happened or who the lady was and then I thought of Miss Barrett and I knew it was her, come from some future time to warn me and to plead for her own happiness. You must go back, Lily, for something very wonderful will happen and you will be a part of it, though I know not how or when. I cannot take that baby from that happy lady, I cannot let you find another place until your work is done."

All the time Mother was speaking, Wilson felt a physical sense of disturbance. She could not see clearly, her hands shook, her heart raced. Mother's face was indistinct and she seemed to hear her voice from a long way off. Her breath came in shallow gasps and she felt a kind of terror seize her. The moment Mother was silent, these symptoms of panic vanished. She went over to Mother, who was weeping softly, and took her in her arms and held her tight. She did not know what to say about this prophecy, whether to refer to it or argue against it or act as though it had never been made. For a long time, until the fire was a dull glow and all warmth gone, she sat close to Mother, feeling her trembling, and then she made some tea and they drank it companionably, calming themselves by doing so. Mother was exhausted. "I do not want to see the future, I am sure, Lily," she said, "I don't look for it, I try to turn away, for it is so much more dreadful than the past." She sipped the hot tea, blowing gently on the steam rising from it. "It is only lately I have begun to see ahead," Mother went on, "and always it is something to do with you, never Ellen or May. Once I saw Fanny"— and she began to weep again— "she was so happy, her cheeks bright and full, and she waved and laughed and told me she was far better off and I must not grieve." To this, Wilson dared to make a response. "Now, Mother," she said, "you know that is because you worry so about Fanny's health and worry brings on imaginings which we all have—" "No," Mother said, "no, these are not imaginings. You would know, Lily, if you saw and heard as I do."

In bed at last, Wilson lay awake for a long time thinking about what Mother had said. It was so impossible that Miss Elizabeth should bear a child that the whole vision, if that was what it had been, seemed the purest nonsense. But Mother had said she would know these were not imaginings "if you saw and heard as I do." Mother had often expressed surprise that none of her daughters had inherited her gift of second sight and had said she thought Lily the most likely to develop it. When Wilson protested that it was a gift she did not want and was glad had not fallen to her, Mother reminded her that she herself had not "seen" until she was twenty-five and that there was no choice in the matter in any case. So long as Mother's visions were confined to the past, Wilson had been able to tolerate her peculiarity but now that she was delving into the future it was a different matter. She realized, lying in the dark, that she was afraid of the future, that she did not wish to see into it, even if she could see happy events. She wanted very much to remain in ignorance. And she would say nothing to Miss Elizabeth who, though irresistibly drawn to such matters, would find such a prophecy ridiculous and would imagine she was being mocked.

Nothing was said, the next morning, of what Mother had told her. It was Sunday and everyone was at home and there was meat roasting in the oven and the sun shone. All five of them went to chapel and then walked on the Town Moor in the afternoon, with Wilson describing the difference between such natural wild country beauty and Regent's Park, which she declared pretty and a miracle, existing as it did in a big city, but a pale imitation of the real thing. Her mother and sisters were pleased she preferred the Moor and, seeing how sensitive they were in her praise of London, she began deliberately to look for more and more to exclaim over and swear she would miss, once back in gray Wimpole Street. She picked pussy willows and catkins, saying how such a thing was impossible in London; she pointed to the fields and said how hemmed in was Wimpole Street; and she drew attention to the peace, broken only by bird song, and said it was music to her ears after the hideous din of the capital. Her affection for her birthplace made all of them proud to be still living there and, as they walked arm in arm through trees just beginning to meld into each other as the delicate new green leaves spread like lace over the black branches, Mother began to sing and all the sisters took up the refrain of "Summer Is Icumen In." I must be mad, Wilson thought, to give up *this* and go back to *that*.

The last few days were painfully sweet. Fanny never left her side. From when she woke up and came straight to her eldest sister until she closed her eyes at night, holding that sister's hand, she clung to her, linking her arm through Wilson's so tightly that she threatened to drag her to the ground. Her huge eyes, reminding Wilson strangely of Miss Elizabeth's for all that they were blue and not brown, gazed into her sister's as though trying to memorize her every feature. She was so utterly frail and dependent that even to free an arm seemed an act of rejection. She tried to encourage Fanny to practice her writing, promising she would have her very own letters if she would write back, but pen and ink work seemed beyond the girl's grasp. She would start to copy the letters Wilson wrote out but gave up before a single row of even one of them was legible and complete. It was exasperating but, curiously, Fanny did not appear depressed by her failure though she apologized sincerely enough. What is to become of her? Wilson wondered, as she observed that it was not only writing skills Fanny lacked. She could not sew without the stitching becoming ragged in a moment, and the simplest of cooking tasks, though she could manage them, held no attraction for her. Halfway through rolling pastry she would simply abandon it and wander off. Mother was endlessly tolerant and seemed to expect nothing better of her youngest child. The same excuses were made for her at fifteen as had been made when she was five and Wilson began to realize that the suspicions she had always had of Fanny's mental inadequacy were correct. She was backward if not totally deficient. There was something seriously lacking, though it could not be readily seen—Fanny looked quite normal and could converse fluently, if in a childish way. But as she appreciated Fanny's true condition, Wilson began to fret over her future. If anything happened to Mother, who would look after Fanny? Not Ellen or May, who were in service, yet who else was there? And so, before she left, she resolved to speak to Mother and set her mind at rest: Fanny would be her responsibility and she would acknowledge this and pledge to support her and guard her. How she would do such a thing she did not know and did not stop to work out. All that mattered was the promise.

Waking on her last morning to the sun flooding through the thin curtains, Wilson turned her head gently and looked in turn at each of her sisters. Through the open door of the adjoining room she could see that the covers were thrown back off Fanny and May and she smiled to see how chubby May looked next to the slender Fanny. May's sturdy arms were flung out over her head and her freckled face frowned in sleep. Whereas Fanny lay so tidily, so primly, her hands clasped on her chest and her expression serene. They were an unlikely pair of sisters but then, thought Wilson as she looked at Ellen beside her, so are we. Ellen had changed both in her looks and in herself. She was heavier and tougher, in every way. Wilson was shocked to hear her boast—it was more in the nature of a boast than a confession—that she was sharing in a fiddle at her place of work. It was all to do with food deliveries and the signing for three hams when four were delivered and suchlike, with proceeds from the sale of the fourth ham split between cook and Ellen and the kitchen maid. When Wilson tried to say it was a dangerous business, that little deceptions could lead to bigger ones and that Ellen should beware, her sister laughed under the bedclothes and said she knew how to look after herself. It seemed to her that Ellen had, on the contrary, no idea at all. There were tales of a gardener who was no better than he ought to be and of meetings with him in the shed and what Ellen described as "fumblings" which she was not going to give in to but which she clearly enjoyed and over which she had little control. It was a life belowstairs quite unlike her own virtuous existence in Wimpole Street. She felt further estranged from her sister by the knowledge that Ellen's conduct was so much more common than her own.

Am I a cut above the general run? Wilson wondered, eyes half closed, savoring the warmth of the bed and the pretty patterns the sunbeams made on the wall. Was I meant to leave all this behind and do something and be someone and go somewhere? Ellen with her hams and gardeners, May with her polishing and awe of the butler, Fanny in a dream, none of them with a speck of ambition beyond the ordinary and all content to stay here forever. London has made me restless, she thought, restless and discontented, unwilling to settle for the humdrum, and yet what could be more humdrum than her daily routine in Wimpole Street, what more uneventful? She had no reason, no possible justification, for feeling excited about her return and yet that was how she did feel—nervous, eager, expectant, quite unlike the poor waif she was when first Mother forced her south. "Something is going to happen," Mother had said and she believed it to be true, in spite of all the evidence to the contrary. She got up quietly, tiptoed to the window and peered out at the beautiful May morning, beautiful for Mother's birthday. In a whisper she said, "Something is going to happen," and then laughed at the absurdity of it.

CHAPTER NINE

WILSON COULD hardly credit the effusiveness of the welcome she was given by Miss Elizabeth. She presented herself, when she arrived in Wimpole Street, with some hesitation, not sure whether she ought to go and change first. The moment she opened the door of her mistress's room, quietly and carefully as she always did, there was a cry of "Wilson! Dear, dear Wilson," and Miss Elizabeth actually rose from her sofa and came toward her, and so did Flush, barking frantically. A second before she was embraced, Wilson drew back, aware of her dust-coated clothes and of a worry that to move into her mistress's outstretched arms was not perhaps quite proper. But Miss Elizabeth's gesture was so sudden and sincere that it could not be spurned and she accepted the welcoming embrace with pleasure. It was she who broke away first, protesting that she was not fit to be touched, and Miss Elizabeth who clung on, half weeping, half laughing. Her relief was so visible, so tangible, that Wilson had never felt more gratified in her life.

It took her very little time to discover that Miss Elizabeth was in a great state of general agitation which had little to do with her own return. Mr. Browning, it seemed, was pressing to be invited to meet Miss Elizabeth and would no longer be put off with excuses about health or weather.

"Well, miss," Wilson said calmly as she went about her old routine, "he must be invited and the thing got over and then you know you will feel the better of it directly." There was a great deal of sighing and pressing of the hands to the heart and a tear or two and a trembling lip but finally it was agreed, a day must be fixed. Mr. Browning should be allowed to call one weekday afternoon.

To Timothy, Wilson confessed she wished this precious Mr. Browning was not coming at all. "It is so very rare," she told him, walking in the park on a beautiful day toward the end of her first week back, "so unusual for her to have a new gentleman calling, and it has quite unhinged her."

"Maybe she has expectations," Timothy said idly, not thinking, looking instead at Wilson's face, which seemed to have filled out and grown rounder and prettier since she had been home and was now faintly flushed with what he failed to identify in time as a rising indignation.

"What *nonsense*," she snapped and, "How *like* a man. It is nothing to do with expectations, it is the fear in her."

"What fear?" said Timothy, genuinely bewildered. "Is Mr. Browning an ogre, then? I cannot see it, I'm sure, him being so small and—"

"Oh, heavens," Wilson swore, "what or who he is has nought to do with it. She dreads *all* new people, she cannot help it, there is no reason for it but it is there, this dreadful nervousness. She has not a shred of confidence and, though I never thought to have any myself, I am a lion compared to her."

"Don't take on so," Timothy begged. "It is not your concern, now is it? *You* getting upset on her behalf does no good that I can see." He kicked a stone and whistled for his dog and felt irritated himself that Wilson appeared to be able to think of nothing but Miss Barrett since he wished to talk of quite other matters, matters mainly to do with arranging for Wilson to go down the river with him for the day. He did not dare ask her now because he knew she would say she could not leave her mistress while she was in such a state.

He was right. Every day for the whole of the next week was dominated by the coming visit of Mr. Browning, and Wilson was as exhausted as her mistress by the time May 20 dawned. She went in to find Miss Elizabeth as white and strained-looking as a woman on her deathbed. Her fingers were bloodless, numb, and she held them up, announcing she had no feeling anywhere but her heart, which was beating wildly. She refused to get dressed, saying she would wait until nearer the time or she would faint with the exertion. The usual tiny cup of strong black coffee was refused—"I will drink and eat this evening if I am still alive." Wilson knew she ought to laugh at such melodrama but instead felt distressed. It was not *right* that one small, frail woman should suffer so over such an unremarkable occurrence as a visitor. She did not attempt to argue Miss Elizabeth out of her exaggerated gloom but was as sympathetic as she could be. This only produced tears of gratitude which at least removed some of the tension.

At midday Wilson helped her mistress to dress. She had wondered if perhaps another dress might be worn, had even suggested the pale gray or the dull green silk which hung in the wardrobe and had never been worn in all the time she had been there; but no, the black silk was called for as usual. The only difference was in the collar chosen to go over it and the jewelery. Instead of the cream crocheted small collar, changed every day, Miss Elizabeth produced a delicate shawllike white lace collar which she said Mr. Kenyon had brought her from Malta and she had never had occasion to wear. Wilson admired it, but not too extravagantly, knowing that too much enthusiasm was almost certain to see the collar rejected, which would be a pity since it both softened the black far more effectively than did the cream and also lightened the wearer's pallor. She had always privately thought that cream was quite the worst color for her mistress to wear. It made her skin appear ashen, whereas white made it look, though still startingly pale, clearer, more translucent. Below the collar, where it divided on the bosom, Miss Elizabeth directed her to fasten a beautiful brooch which Wilson had never seen before. It was an amethyst set in gold filigree, the stone heart-shaped. The moment it was pinned on, Wilson could not help exclaiming at its beauty. Miss Elizabeth looked at her anxiously and said she thought perhaps it was "too overdone," that the brooch was "too rich" for her modest dress and only made her look ridiculous. Wilson vowed it did nothing of the sort but that on the contrary the black and white of dress and collar were the perfect background for the amethyst. Sighing, Miss Elizabeth left it on, murmuring that she could not bear vanity.

Another hour was spent checking the room. The armchair in which Mr. Browning was likely to sit had to be placed at an exact angle to the sofa where Miss Elizabeth half reclined, and then the sofa table had to be moved in case it impeded his passage to the chair or restricted his legs when he was seated. Wilson did what she was told though well aware that, since Mr. Kenyon, who was much taller and heavier than Mr. Browning, sat in the chair with the greatest of ease, it was unlikely the new visitor would have any difficulty. Certain books had to be on display and others removed and there was something not quite right, though only Miss Elizabeth could see it, about the arrangement of the plants. Patiently, Wilson carried out orders, realizing all action, however trivial, was a distraction. And then, at one-thirty, when all was as right as it could be, Miss Elizabeth said she would attempt to sleep for an hour, or at least lie with her eyes closed and the blind down. Wilson was to go away and come back at two-thirty precisely with a glass of very cold water.

Closing the door behind her, Wilson felt quite overcome herself. She had no doubt that her mistress, though she might close her eyes, would not sleep for a moment. She stood at the top of the stairs, leaning against the wall, and could not bring herself to go down. No one knew, as she knew, how Miss Elizabeth suffered. Miss Henrietta had even laughed the day before at the idea of any apprehension about the impending visit. "Why, Ba," she had cried, "how can you be so silly when you know you long to meet your poet?" That was how he was referred to throughout the whole house—"Ba's poet is coming," "Miss Elizabeth's poet is to visit." There was a mocking tone to this which Wilson did not like. She also wondered, as she slowly descended the stairs, whether she was quite prepared to like Mr.

Browning herself, the cause of so much distress in her mistress. Would he come to mock too? Was this visit made in a spirit of vulgar curiosity? The very idea made her feel cold toward him.

Thereafter, Wilson was glad to go for her walks with Flush. She did not know what had happened after Mr. Browning's visit but only that the pleasure it had so plainly given her mistress turned to pain upon the receipt of a letter sent by the new visitor as soon as he reached home. Miss Elizabeth had wept over her reply and been greatly agitated. Now she was asleep, worn out with grieving, and would not be herself until the evening and the need to put a brave face on for her father. For once, Wilson was not eager to meet Timothy in the park, indeed found herself hoping he would not be there; but he was and there was no escape. She would have liked to talk to Lizzie Treherne or even Minnie Robinson but Timothy was the wrong person for such a delicate subject. She was offended when he straight away asked her, "And how did Mr. Browning do? Did your mistress find him agreeable?" She could have slapped his smiling face, which suddenly struck her for the first time as capable of leering. "Quite agreeable, I believe," she replied stiffly. Timothy fell into step and put his arm around her waist. Lately, this was a privilege she had permitted him, though only when they were away from the main path. Today, she flinched as his arm came around her and frowned. "Is something the matter?" Timothy asked. She said no. They walked for a while, admiring the last of the cherry blossom floating down onto the lake. "Lovely day," Timothy said and, because he said it gently and because it was a lovely day, she felt warmer toward him. "I wish," she said, "I could persuade my mistress to come out again and perhaps I will." He was silent for a long time and as they continued their walk he replied only in monosyllables. At the end of the walk he turned to face her directly and said, "All you talk of is Miss Elizabeth, day in and day out." She blushed and said defensively, "Well, what would you have me talk of?" He took her hand and said, "Us." "Us?" she repeated foolishly. "And what is there to talk of, pray?" "There *could* be many a thing," Timothy said, and turned away as he spoke, dropping her hand.

Wilson stood quite still, alerted by Timothy's tone of voice and stance to something out of the ordinary. It was not the time to pretend. She cleared her throat and touched Timothy's sleeve. Flush, who had returned of his own free will, growled at her feet. "Timothy," she said, "you are a good friend. I know I tire you with my anxieties over Miss Elizabeth but who else can I confide in, seeing you every day as I do? If it is a burden, I will stop, though if people do not talk, to those they believe fond of them, of what is in their head, then what can friendship be worth?" She delivered her little speech with her eyes carefully fixed on the ground but then, as she finished, lifted them to meet Timothy's.

He was still grave, "So I am your good friend?" he asked.

"Indeed," she said.

"Well then," he said, "a friend may ask a favor, I believe, and not be misunderstood?"

"He may."

"Come with me on the river to Richmond, Tuesday next. There is a steamer leaves the pier at ten in the morning and if you were to take a day off we could go down the river and picnic in the deer park. Now, will you come with your friend or is your devotion only to Miss Elizabeth Barrett?"

Put like that, she had no option, but though they parted on good terms, Timothy whistling and cheerful, she worried all the way back to Wimpole Street about giving her word for a Tuesday. Tuesday had already become Mr. Browning's day and she was depended upon to open the door and show him in and out. There had been three more visits, in spite of the disastrous letter, each easier than the last, but still her mistress was nervous and in need of support beforehand. But then, while Wilson debated whether to ask permission, fate played into her hands. With flushed cheeks, Miss Elizabeth announced that there was to be an invasion, that her Uncle and Aunt Hedley and three of their children were to come from Paris to stay and all normal life would be at an end. She said it dramatically, despairing aloud of ever having any peace for the entire fortnight, but Wilson judged she was not truly displeased. All she dreaded, she said, was her aunt and uncle bringing up the subject of her brother's drowning, which she could not abide, and yet, since she had not seen them for five years, it was inevitable the memory would emerge in some form or other. She wept a little as she thought of the last time she had seen these relatives but was soothed by Wilson rather more easily than usual. "You will like my Uncle Hedley," she said, "and my aunt, too, but you must expect her to interfere, Wilson dear, and you must remember she was born wanting a finger in every pie. She is my mother's youngest sister and has led a charmed life, the luckiest of all the four sisters." Wilson was then treated to a Graham-Clarke history and a description of all the sisters and their various idiosyncrasies. Miss Elizabeth was in such good humor at the end of the recital that it seemed the ideal moment to ask for a Tuesday off. Permission was granted without details being inquired, though there was a hint of curiosity in the way her mistress said, "I hope you intend to do something special, Wilson?" She said she did, that she had been invited to go to Richmond by boat but gave nothing else away.

The minute the Hedleys arrived, Wilson saw what life in a normal London household might be like. All was noise and confusion and constant calls for assistance of one sort or another and for once she was glad to retreat to the calm of the back room on the second floor, though the bustle penetrated even there. The Hedleys brought their own servants, including a French maid, but seemed to have need of the Barrett ones, too. Minnie hated it but the other Wimpole Street servants enjoyed the chaos and liked the house ringing with shouts and laughter in spite of the extra work. And Wilson quite liked it too, to her own surprise, writing to her mother that

—Mr. Hedley is a hearty kind of man quite unlike Mr. Barrett and dotes on his wife and daughters. He is most genial and generous with his tips and no one can do enough for him. Mrs. Hedley dresses very fine and could not do without her French maid who is called Thérèse. She speaks good English and though at first I found her too voluble for my taste she has grown on me and we are friends. She is driven distracted with all the ironing she has to do especially of the Misses Hedley's frills and flounces of which there are an abundance and Miss Arabella, the eldest, is most particular and likes her hair dressed elaborately too. Miss Elizabeth, seeing her cousin Arabella's French plait, took a notion to try it and bid me imitate it. Well of course I could not do it and was laughed at for my pains though in truth I laughed myself. Then Thérèse said she would teach me and I stood at her elbow and paid attention and afterward made a creditable job of it only to have Miss Elizabeth declare she preferred her old style and that was that. I have plenty of free time since Mrs. Hedley likes to sit with Miss Elizabeth and I am not required at all in the afternoon so Flush and I have very long walks and enjoy them with the weather being so fine. Miss Elizabeth has promised me that when her aunt and uncle are gone she will begin again going out in the chair and I am to see it is ready which I will.

On the day she went down the river with Timothy, Wilson succeeded in putting to the back of her mind everything to do with her mistress, which pleased her companion very much. Everything pleased him, everything was right. The sun shone, the river sparkled (though Timothy wondered darkly how it could when he knew for a fact what awful things went into it) and because it was a weekday the boat was not too crowded. They sat in the prow and, though the wooden seats were hard and uncomfortable, they had room to spread themselves and change position. Wilson was glad she had worn her new gown although she had worried that a boat trip was not the right occasion for such a light blue sprigged cotton and that her dark red stuff would have been better. But Timothy admired it at once and said the color matched her eyes and was his favorite color, one his mother wore when she was younger. They chatted about families all the way to Richmond, with Timothy breaking off every now and again to point out something of interest.

When the boat stopped they got off and climbed Richmond Hill to the deer park and Wilson, who had no idea such country existed near London, exclaimed at the vast expanse of greenery and the huge number of trees. They walked toward a pond and stopped just above it. Timothy took off his jacket and spread it on the grass for her to sit upon and then he opened the bag he had been carrying all this while, producing with a flourish a pie and some cold ham and bread and a bottle of what he said was Mr. Kenyon's cook's elderflower wine. She could not get over the fact of a *man* going to such trouble and, though she did not like wine of any kind, it seemed churlish to refuse to drink a little. It struck her, seated beside Timothy and tucking in to the pie and sipping the wine (Timothy bade her drink first if she was not too proud to drink from a bottle) that it was very comfortable to be so looked after. Never, in her own personal experience, had she seen a man cherish a woman to the extent of preparing food for her. And Timothy, she knew by now, did cherish her and the idea was not unpleasant. But was it anything more? Covertly, still nibbling the pie and wishing it did not have quite such a strong crust, she watched Timothy from under her lashes. He was drinking from the stone bottle now that she had finished. His head was thrown back, his throat working away to swallow the liquid, and she noticed how muscular he was, how powerful his neck and shoulders. She remembered Miss Elizabeth saying once that she did not care for very masculine men. It surprised her, and made her shiver in spite of the heat, to discover as she watched Timothy that she disagreed with her mistress—she did like masculine men, she was attracted to strength and a certain toughness. Men like Mr. Browning the poet, though pleasant, hardly seemed men to her. She had a sudden vision of Timothy picking her up and carrying her with ease, keeping her in his arms however much she struggled, and though she wanted to be at no man's mercy the image gratified her. She doubted if Mr. Browning would be able even to lift her off the ground, small though she was. But then, as Timothy put the stopper in the bottle and turned to eat the bread and ham, there was a certain wolfishness in his eating that faintly repelled her. She liked manners, and men of Timothy's class were not famous for elegant manners. Such speculation and reflection tired her. She wanted her response to be instinctive. As Timothy finished and smiled at her and lay back in the sun, patting his jacket to indicate she should do the same, she allowed her real feelings to take hold of her.

She lay beside him and did not refuse his hand and allowed her own to be squeezed and was quite breathless waiting for the next approach, knowing what it would be and resolving to do nothing to prevent it. For a powerful man, his kiss was gentle, a mere flutter on the lips, and instead of being masterful he was hesitant. Slowly, he raised himself onto his elbow and, looking down at her, he smiled and said, "We suit, don't we?"

The rest of the day passed in a daze. To Wilson's relief, Timothy did not seek further intimacies, seeming content to kiss and hold her hand and be beside her. She could sense this was not what he wanted to do but what his intelligence dictated and dictated correctly. If he had attempted to press himself upon her or engage in one of those embraces she could see others enjoying farther off in the bushes, then she would have been obliged to get up and request to be taken home. Nobody needed to tell her the importance of respect and she knew that, however severely she was put to the test, however strong her desires, she would never sacrifice it. Any man who presumed to overwhelm her would be given short shrift. But there was no need for such a struggle. Timothy made himself content with the minimum of contact and she relaxed as she realized he was no threat. They talked, they walked, they idled the afternoon away and by the time they caught the last boat back she was willing to admit she had a sweetheart. It was dark when she let herself into 50 Wimpole Street and she was glad to get to her room without seeing anyone, though she had nothing to be guilty about—it had been arranged by Miss Elizabeth herself that, in order to make her day off complete, Arabel would act as her maid at bedtime—she felt as though she had somehow deserted her post. Lying in her bed, unable to sleep, she wondered what she had started and where it would end. Not in this house, of that she was sure.

It was difficult, next morning, to hide the true state of her emotions from her mistress, whose perceptions were so quick. "Why, Wilson," she said at once, "how pretty you look this morning. The river air has given quite a bloom to your cheeks."

Wilson blushed. "The weather was fine, miss," she said hurriedly, "and the breeze strong. I fear I have burned a little and ought to have worn a bonnet."

"It suits you very well," Miss Elizabeth said, staring at her. "And did you enjoy the deer park, Wilson?"

"Oh, indeed, ma'am. It is very pleasant out there, almost like the real country."

"I have never been, though invited to make an expedition by Mr. Kenyon often enough. Perhaps I should go and see if the Richmond air can do for me what it has clearly done for you." The tone of voice was light and teasing but Wilson did not mistake the underlying meaning. Miss Elizabeth had not asked with whom she had gone to Richmond but the very fact that this information had not been volunteered had been noted as significant. She would have liked to tell her mistress that discretion was not merely one of her characteristics, one from which Miss Elizabeth knew she herself benefited, but a part of her nature. Under no circumstances did she wish to share that part of her personal life. If this caused offense, then so it must. She would describe the park and tell of the boat trip and in general give her mistress some amusement from her day out but she would not widen this account to speak of Timothy. That was private and, for the time being, would remain so.

She mentioned Timothy only to Lizzie Treherne, and Lizzie immediately warned her of what she already knew. "Miss Elizabeth dislikes servants' followers," Lizzie said. "She is always afraid of them, for they are a rival to her. She may wish you well, indeed she *does* wish us well, and she may declare herself your friend and intimate that confidences can be safely given but on that subject, Lily, do not trust her. She will seek by all manner of cunning ways to discredit Timothy and half the time you will not even know she is doing it, I know." Lizzie finished, nodding her head. Wilson at once agreed she was right. "It is nothing as yet in any case," she protested, "there is nothing to it. I like him, I am sure, as he does me but I see no further." "I do," said Lizzie, smiling. "One thing will lead to another and then what will you do? What Billy and I did, without a doubt, and it was the best thing I ever did in my life. To think I nearly told my mistress, not wishing to deceive her. How foolish that would have been and, oh, the scenes it would have led to. As it was, Billy begged and pleaded with me to keep it quiet and he was right. She could not have abided knowing I was to be married to him and she will not be able to abide you marrying Timothy." "Oh, heavens!" exclaimed Wilson. "No one has said anything about marrying, Lizzie. You jump ahead. Marriage is not part of any of my plans." But Lizzie would not leave the subject alone and it gave her such clear delight to talk of it that Wilson gave up, only swearing her to absolute secrecy.

But things moved swiftly. The walks in the park were no longer enough after that day in Richmond. Timothy urged her to meet him in the evenings, too, and though at first she swore it was impossible she found herself conceding that on certain evenings, when Miss Elizabeth retired early, she would walk down Devonshire Place at ten o'clock precisely and if Timothy would always, on the off chance, do the same, then sometimes they might meet. The uncertainty as to whether it could be managed only added to the excitement and on many a light summer's night Wilson slipped out of Wimpole Street with her heart thudding at the prospect of finding Timothy waiting. The nights she did not go, and these were the majority, seemed dull. She was no longer content to sit in her room sewing or writing to Mother. Indeed, her letters home grew less regular and shorter and, though Mother never complained, Wilson was ashamed. It was not the time Timothy took which prevented her writing so much as her dislike of concealing what he was rapidly coming to mean to her. She did not want to tell her mother any more than she wished to tell her mistress. If it came to anything, then Mother at least would be overjoyed but, if not, she would be worried.

Of course, there were those in Wimpole Street who had strong suspicions that Wilson was romantically involved. Minnie Robinson knew of Wilson's evening excursions but said nothing. She liked and trusted Wilson and what she did outside the house was her own affair so long as it did not get back to the master. Wilson so far had met with his entire approval and she did not like to think of this being forfeited. So long as no one saw anything and reported it, then Wilson would be safe but, if she were seen walking with a follower in the vicinity of Wimpole Street after ten at night, then there would be trouble, the kind of trouble which in this house led to instant dismissal. So Minnie watched and waited and kept her own counsel but apprehensively, fearing what the summer would bring before its end.

CHAPTER TEN

EVERYONE VOWED it was the hottest summer in London for years. Wilson could well believe it. Every June day began with a blue sky and by sunset, splendid sunsets, not a cloud had been seen. She walked to Regent's Park in the thinnest of dresses and without even thinking of carrying a wrap of any sort and, once there, she and Timothy sat at the water's edge trying to feel cool just by looking at the lake and wishing they could swim in it. Flush hated the heat and was bad-tempered but Wilson thrived. Used as she was to the North, she had never expected to enjoy a hot climate but she found it greatly to her liking and felt twice as lively. Timothy, remarking on it, suggested they go at once to live in Italy and to hang with England. Wilson laughed and asked if they could eat the sun for food and sleep under it for shelter and Timothy said he did not see why not. Life, he swore, was easier abroad and both of them would find employment— Wilson stopped him by putting a hand over his mouth, a hand that was at once grabbed and kissed, and then a tussle began and she told him to desist at once, for someone might see. "Someone might see, someone might see," Timothy chanted and would not listen to her rebuke and the reminder that this was a public place. "Tomorrow," Wilson swore, "I will not even hold your hand if you will not behave."

But there was no opportunity to deny that privilege which Timothy now took as a right. Miss Elizabeth, of her own volition, said she thought she might try the chair if tomorrow was as warm and lovely as today. Tomorrow was. Professing delight, she hoped convincingly, Wilson got her mistress ready and two of the Barrett brothers carried their sister down to the chair and off went mistress and maid. A hundred yards away Wilson saw Timothy waiting and began to frown and shake her head when she was still a long way off. To her relief, she saw Timothy slowly begin to walk in the other direction. The wheelchair had, after all, made them prominent enough for him to spot and act accordingly and she was glad he did not choose to make a fight of it. By now, she knew Mr. Timothy well enough to be acquainted with the strong streak of stubbornness in him. It would have been perfectly conceivable that Timothy, out of sheer rebellion, would choose to stand his ground and greet her and her mistress as though there were nothing to hide. Miss Elizabeth would need only to see Timothy look at her and, no matter how distantly she returned his greeting, all would be obvious.

So there was no meeting that day or that evening. The Hedleys were still staying and were entertaining and Wilson's help was required. As she dressed her mistress for the rare event of receiving visitors after dinner Wilson felt a faint resentment, realizing that she would not get out by ten o'clock. She was far from being a free agent, that was the trouble. Her whole life, as Timothy never tired of pointing out, was circumscribed by the code laid down for servants. What she wanted was so simple and innocent, only to meet her sweetheart and enjoy his company—but she had no right to claim this. Thinking about this as she adjusted Miss Elizabeth's collar, she qualified it: it was not only being a servant which hampered her freedom of conduct but being a woman. Earlier in the day she had passed Miss Henrietta rushing upstairs in tears and Molly had told her that Surtees Cook was not allowed in the house at the moment because the master was displeased with Miss Henrietta. She had gone to visit a female friend, unchaperoned, while Surtees Cook was also visiting and her father had called this outrageous. She was to stay in her room during this evening's socializing and was not to leave the house without her father's express permission hereafter. It was, Wilson decided, very little better to be a lady than a servant.

All of that last week in June and the first two weeks in July Wilson did not once meet Timothy in the park. Miss Elizabeth, from sitting in the chair, progressed to a few faltering steps unaided and, though feeling her own loss acutely, Wilson was delighted to see such evidence of recovery. Everyone in Wimpole Street exclaimed at Miss Elizabeth's progress, commenting freely on the weight she was gaining and the beginnings of some color creeping into her cheeks and the increase in her appetite. Another extraordinary thing had happened but of so private and intimate a nature that only Wilson knew of it. One morning she went in to her mistress and found her looking confused and alarmed. "Wilson, my regular health has returned," she whispered and when Wilson did not immediately understand she repeated, "My *regular* health, my *womanly* health." Wilson nodded and went off to procure the necessary cloths. Her mistress seemed pleased and, though all that day and the next she remained prostrate, she was not depressed. The bleeding was slight but definite and Wilson wondered what the connection with an improvement in general health could be. Even then, during the days Miss Elizabeth stayed in her room, she could not escape to meet Timothy, for her mistress did not wish to rely on anyone else in her delicate condition.

By the end of July, when the daily habit of meeting Timothy had been so completely broken that he no longer waited by the gate, Wilson was quite desperate. She had managed to slip out on a few evenings but never for long and always with an increased feeling of apprehension. "This is no way to carry on," Timothy protested and she knew it was not. She had to decline his pressing invitation to go down the river again nor could she get away to visit other places with him. As her mistress grew healthier, so she grew more demanding and Wilson could hardly remember the long, long hours spent sewing for the sake of something to do. This at least was a suitable topic to write of to Mother, who loved to hear

—How adventurous she is getting too. All the time I have been with her, Mother, she has never so much as been near a shop nor paid a visit but now we do both. We went in a carriage to Oxford Street at a quiet time and though she walked only from the carriage to the shop and through the door and then sat down Miss Elizabeth did more than she has done in years. She chose some pretty material for a dress and it is *not* black but a pleasant green and will suit her. She said that when she was young and cared about such things she always wore green since it is her favorite color, the color of nature. Only afterward, once home, did Miss Elizabeth pronounce herself worn out though she looked well enough and has not had a single fainting fit for the whole time since I returned which is remarkable.

It was only writing to her mother that made Wilson see how remarkable this really was. She paused as she wrote, considering whether what she had written was strictly true. It was. No fainting fits, no headaches so severe the blinds had to remain drawn all day, no attacks of palpitations so alarming a double daytime draught of laudanum was called for. This new, improved health of her mistress was no illusion, and with it went a more cheerful disposition, fewer hours spent steeped in melancholy. In fact, Wilson herself was accused of just such a thing. "Why, Wilson," Miss Elizabeth said to her one morning, when she had first gloried in another lovely day and confirmed she would be going out to the park again, "you look quite downcast of a sudden. Are you unwell? Is there bad news from home? Come, tell." Wilson blushed deeply and insisted there was nothing the matter, claiming merely to have slept badly owing to the heat. The excuse was accepted but she knew she was watched closely and tried hard for the rest of the day to be more animated, but it was difficult. The only day she felt truly herself was Sunday when it was almost certain she would meet Timothy.

The third Sunday in July it was Timothy's turn to have bad news. He was to leave London the following week for an extended visit with Mr. Kenyon to Hampshire. "When?" cried Wilson. "Thursday, I think," said Timothy gloomily, "and there is nothing to be done about it, for it will always be thus. I am not my own master nor you your own mistress unless we strike out for ourselves." Wilson was silent. Again and again Timothy would refer to "striking out" and it made her impatient. He did not know how or when to strike and was no nearer realizing any of his grand but vague plans. "That is that, then, for the summer," she said. "By the time you return it may be winter and then where will we be? How can we meet when it is cold and wet?" Timothy made a noise of exasperation, swearing September and October in London were nothing to fear, and then, after some hesitation, said that he had been thinking and had a plan. Wilson waited, though he seemed to think she should speak. "I know a man," said Timothy, "who wants a partner in the printing business, a partner with some capital of his own and a will to work hard to build the business up. Now, if I were to say to my master I wished to be that partner and if he were to make inquiries and see this business to be the sound venture I know it to be, then he might set me up as promised and we could marry." Wilson flinched as though struck. It was the first time marriage had been mentioned and to have it part and parcel of a business deal, mentioned in literally the same breath, offended her. She had to struggle not to let tears appear in her eyes and to answer in a level voice, "There are a lot of 'ifs,' Timothy." This seemed to cheer him, to act as a spur to a tumble of plans that now came rushing from his lips and produced an animation she liked to see. He even said, at the end of an outline to do with the printing process which she did not understand, that he could not bear to be apart from her for another minute and would do anything that they might be together.

Once home, she had plenty to reflect on. Would she, like Timothy, do "anything" to be with *him?* She thought not. It depressed her that she was not so carried away. Did it mean she was not so much in love? Perhaps. What was love, in any case? She was attracted to him, too attracted, she sometimes thought. If she had not had a cool head on her shoulders, it was easy to see how she could be carried away were he to put sufficient pressure upon her. And she liked Timothy, liked to be with him, to hear him talk. She believed him to be a good, kind man who would always do his best, but it was that best which bothered her. What were Timothy's true prospects? He could not know. How could a footman, even a footman of charm and intelligence, become a printer? And what of printing? She knew no printers, had no idea how profitable or secure such an occupation would be. Timothy assured her that printing belonged to the future, that soon there would be more and more need for it, but what did he know? If she married Timothy for richer, for poorer, she did not want it to be for poorer. Her horror of being dragged down was so great, she could not contemplate willfully bringing such disaster on herself. Perhaps, if Timothy went ahead and became a printer and was taken into a business, then after a year in which he had proved himself she would marry him. But if she could reason thus, so calmly and shrewdly, could she be in love?

The very next afternoon, knowing nothing, Miss Elizabeth pondered aloud herself. "My cousin Arabella is contemplating an engagement, Wilson," she said, "and she asks me when I think she ought to become engaged. How long should she leave between engagement and marriage?"

"Six months," Wilson said, abstracted.

"Six months, ten months, a year, it is not of the slightest interest to me, it is all artificial and such nonsense. If people are in love, then it is an absurdity to be bound by such conventions. Do you not agree?"

"Well, miss, some declaration and some waiting might be for the best."

"In what way?"

"Oh, so as to be sure."

"Sure of what? Of what the world thinks of you? *I* should not care for its judgment."

"It is a big step," Wilson added, knowing how lame this sounded but wishing, in a way that surprised her, to keep the conversation going.

"*Marriage* is, but not love. Love is no step at all." Miss Elizabeth said this so vehemently that Wilson, who was watering the flowers in the window boxes, turned around to stare. "Now, dear, do not give me, that look my Aunt Hedley and Mrs. Jameson give me, for I cannot bear it. I do not mean I am *in love,* to put it as vulgarly as they do, but only that I know by instinct that if love is there it declares itself and cannot be denied and has nothing to do with engagements and marriage. When the time comes for you, if not me, Wilson, you will *know.*"

Then I do not know, Wilson thought sadly. I do not know. That is precisely the agony. Yet does *she* know? Does Miss Elizabeth? And if not, how can she speak with such authority and why do I bow before her verdict? Showing Mr. Browning in the next afternoon, she gave him the kind of searching look she usually took care to avoid. "Good afternoon, Wilson," he said, "and it is a good afternoon too. Is Miss Barrett well? Is she enjoying this weather?"

"Indeed, sir, she has been out every day and shows the benefit."

He smiled and nodded his head in delight and Wilson found herself smiling back. He was a nice man, she thought as she led the way up the stairs, nice friendly eyes, nothing cold or haughty about him but a general warmth. Miss Elizabeth greeted him now like an old friend and Wilson was not encouraged to linger. Lately, Flush had begun to take a dislike to Mr. Browning, which was unfortunate. He made a nuisance of himself by rushing for the poor man's ankles and attempting to nip them. Today, for that reason, he was banished and skulked in the yard outside. Miss Elizabeth said he could be brought back for the next Tuesday visit when she hoped he would have learned his lesson. The idea of Flush being penalized in any way for Mr. Browning's sake was the clearest indication there could be that his status was changing: Mr. Browning was being preferred to Flush, in a manner of speaking.

After these Tuesday visits, Miss Elizabeth was always animated. Wilson tried to catch her mood in her letter to her mother, describing how

—she is trying to prepare herself for a different life as all can see. Tomorrow she is going to spend the day at Mr. Kenyon's house and I with her. Mr. Kenyon has often suggested a change of indoor scene would benefit her and since the day after he goes to

Hampshire and the house is to be shut up it is the last opportunity
till the autumn. I was surprised when she told me—

So surprised she dropped the jug she was carrying and was
mortified to have to apologize and make up a story about her hands
being wet. Fortunately, she had not yet filled the jug with water nor
did it break in falling but her confusion was noted and wondered at.
"You have not been yourself of late, dear," Miss Elizabeth said. "I
have said it before and now I say it again. Will you not tell me if
anything is amiss?" She protested that there was nothing amiss, that
she had foolishly not dried her hands properly and now they were dry
and it would not happen again. "Well then, I repeat, I am to pass the
day, or the greater part of it, at Mr. Kenyon's house tomorrow and he
is kindly sending his carriage for us. Will you take anything I may
need, Wilson, for I should not like to bother any of Mr. Kenyon's
household." Wilson promised she would and went out of the room to
fetch water to put in the jug and the flowers Mr. Browning had
brought the day before. She had trimmed the stems and now arranged
them in the fresh water. Looked after carefully, they would survive
until the following Tuesday. Her mind was racing ahead. She would
see Timothy without a doubt but though this made her glad it made
her anxious too. They had parted on Sunday without her making a
direct answer and she had not managed to see him since. He needed,
she knew, some reassurance that she approved his plan and that she
would stand by him. Any coldness on her part would be interpreted as
a refusal of marriage, but how could she be anything else but cool in
front of Miss Elizabeth?

The coach came at midday and they were ready. It was a very
short distance from Wimpole Street to Devonshire Place but Miss
Elizabeth treated the journey with great seriousness and made much
of feeling so well at the end of it. "You see, Wilson," she said, "I am a
traveler in the making, would you not agree?" Wilson, remembering
the ordeal of her journey from London to Newcastle, could not
forbear to say, "This is hardly traveling ma'am," and was told, though
with a smile, not to be discouraging. They stopped outside Mr.
Kenyon's lovely house and Timothy came out directly. "Why, it is

Timothy, is it not?" Miss Elizabeth cried. "Do you remember Timothy, Wilson?"

"Of course, miss. Now do take care with your gown or it will catch in the door again." Bending down, Wilson fussed over the dress, neatly covering her own embarrassment. But Timothy was being wicked.

"And I remember Mrs. Wilson, Miss Barrett," he said as he carried their basket up the steps, "for how could I forget when she kept us all in order?"

"Good gracious, Timothy," Miss Elizabeth said lightly, "I have never seen Wilson as a tartar."

"Oh, I did not mean *that,* miss, she is too pretty to be a tartar."

It was outrageous and Wilson was furious. Timothy was laughing and smiling but Miss Elizabeth was not. She went quiet and held her head a little higher; if Timothy only had the wit to see, this was a sign that she thought he was being impertinent, as indeed he was. He showed them into the drawing room, a magnificent room which overlooked the park and was as full of light and sun as the Wimpole Street drawing room was always dark and gloomy.

"How strange it seems," her mistress mused aloud, "to stand in another room instead of my own."

"The change will do you good," Wilson said.

"It may, though I have never before been a friend to change, have you, Wilson?"

"Me, miss?" said Wilson, unpleasantly aware of Timothy still finding ridiculous things to do in the vicinity of the fireplace, still straightening perfectly straight fenders and the like.

"Do you care for change for its own sake, Wilson?"

"No, miss, I do not. I have never welcomed change, though sometimes afterward I can see it was for the best." She knew Timothy was listening intently, and not just because it surprised him, she was sure, to hear a mistress and a maid converse so. Half of her wanted to give him something to think about and she was also not unaware of being proud to be thought worthy of engaging in abstract discussion.

"Precisely, Wilson. That is what I think myself. But why, in that case, do you suppose we are so reluctant to make changes? Why do we cling to the old ways and routines even though we do not necessarily like them?" By now Miss Elizabeth was seated on the sofa and Wilson on a chair in front of her. She took her sewing out and began to hem a border, feeling more comfortable with her hands occupied.

"I expect it is fear, miss," she said, neatly clipping off some thread and concentrating hard on threading a new needle. "We like what we know and fear what we do not." To her relief, she realized Timothy had gone.

"It is very timid of us," her mistress said. "I am ashamed of my own timidity, Wilson, I must confess."

"And I of mine."

"What do you think it will take to make us brave, dear?"

Wilson shook her head. Sometimes she grew secretly exasperated at this kind of talk, for which her mistress had a great taste. Often she would become so confused as question after question and hypothesis after hypothesis were presented to her that she was hardly aware of what she was saying and yet Miss Elizabeth drove her on relentlessly to say something.

But today she was rescued by Mr. Kenyon himself, who came to inquire if there was anything he could do for them. Wilson stood, giving her mistress a quick interrogative look, and at the slightest inclination of her head curtsied and absented herself as Mr. Kenyon sat down. Once out of the drawing room, she hesitated. She did not know the house. Below, she had no doubt, Timothy lurked, awaiting her wrath, which he must be aware would be released the moment she was alone with him. But she did not want to be alone with him. Quietly, she began tiptoeing down the beautiful curved staircase, pausing every three or four steps to listen. It would not be proper for her to go into any room in the house except the housekeeper's but she knew that once she ventured belowstairs Timothy would pounce. It was her intention to hover around the hall, if possible to find a cloakroom or suchlike in which to hide. Mr. Kenyon had said he would be only a few minutes since he had much to do before departing for the Isle of Wight, and in any case part of his success in persuading his cousin to spend the day in his house had been his assurance that she would have the place to herself. But the hall was not empty. The butler was opening the door and a maid was crossing it, carrying a tray. Wilson froze on the last bend of the stairs. She could not possibly sneak into any anteroom while the Kenyon servants were watching. It would be beneath her dignity and remarked upon. The accepted behavior for a servant of her standing, as she well knew, was to introduce herself to the housekeeper, who would invite her to sit down in her room. There was no option. Slowly, she continued to descend the stairs, praying for some miracle before she was obliged to go through the door leading below. There was no miracle. The butler preceded her, opening the door for her himself, and she heard Timothy's voice as she followed.

Still, there were others present; the housekeeper came forward and the butler introduced her. A young girl, presumably the kitchen maid, stared openly and was told to get on with her work. It was, Wilson saw, while trying not to appear inquisitive, a kitchen as pleasant in its own way as the drawing room and equally bright. The housekeeper offered her tea and she accepted, hoping thus to avoid being alone with Timothy. But clearly some agreement had been reached and the housekeeper was in his confidence because, the minute the tea was brewed, she disappeared, smiling all over her face and saying she knew when two was company, especially a certain two. Timothy pounced at once, trying to grab her hands. She snatched them away and said fiercely, though keeping her voice low, "How dare you speak like that in front of Miss Elizabeth, how dare you shame me so?"

"Shame you? Oh, come, Lily, not I—it was only a piece of wit—"

"Wit? It was cheek and recognized as such."

"Then I am sorry for it."

"Sorry does no good."

"What does any good, then?"

"I don't know, I'm sure. Nothing does any good—to speak so, when, you know it to be dangerous."

"I am going away tomorrow, Lily, and nothing will be dangerous anymore, I will not be near you, and I must have an answer."

"To what?"

"To *what*? Now *you* shame *me*, for sure. A man asks you to marry and you cannot remember and do not think it requires an answer?"

"You did not ask me to marry, Timothy, you mentioned marrying, that is all, and it is different."

"Very well, Lily, will you be my wife?"

Again, even though it was properly phrased, Wilson had to fight back tears, tears she would not in the world have her suitor see. It was so ordinary, here among the teacups down in the kitchen. As he asked her, Timothy actually sugared his tea, stirred it and swallowed. But it was a proposal and needed a reply. "Well, Timothy," she said, breathing deeply and taking hold of her own teacup, "you honor me. I wish I could give you the answer you want." He put his cup down quickly at that and looked so shocked she instantly softened toward him. "I am not saying no," she went on, touched as relief flooded his features and his smile reappeared, "but I cannot say yes, not yet, not with your future so uncertain. I care for you deeply, oh, I do, you may be sure, you know that, but I am afraid of the future. I do not want poverty, Timothy, I want a secure home for my children and a chance to be happy together, and I ask myself if I am right to risk that chance on so slender a promise."

"Slender?" Timothy echoed. "What I promise is far from slender, Lily. If my master advances the capital, then I am as good as made. In a short time I will pay back his loan and be in profit and a fine future will be ours."

"Well then, what I say is let us wait until it comes to pass."

"Wait?"

"You said 'in a short time,' Timothy. Let us wait that short time until your printing business is in profit and then marry if you will."

He was silent, searching her face, weighing his words. She looked at him without flinching and ready to be judged. "A short time," he said slowly, "was a manner of speaking. I do not know how long it will take to prove myself in this printing business. It may take one year, two years, even three, though I will work my back off to make it shorter."

"Very well," she said, "one, two, three years, what of it?"

"What of it? That you can ask? All that time when we might be together, working together?"

"I, work as a printer?"

"No, no, you know I did not mean that, I meant living together, me working and you—"

"Yes, me what?"

"Why, supporting me as a wife and—"

"Bearing children?"

"If God willed it, in time."

"And if the printing business were to fail?"

"Well, then, I can always return to this work."

"With a wife and those children God wills?"

"Lily, you are hard on me."

"I am hard on myself, hardheaded for both our sakes, and you will thank me for it."

"Do you not love me?"

"I may do, who can tell? If I do, I will find out. It will stand the test of time."

"So the answer is no."

"The answer is the one I have given you, honestly, and it has cost me dear to pain you, believe me."

At that, he came around the table and put his hands on her shoulders and sighed. "Nothing is ever simple," he said, "and I thought at least this was, a man loving a woman and wanting to marry."

"Why, Wilson, my dear, you are as white as a ghost!" Miss Elizabeth cried the moment she returned to the drawing room. She half rose from the sofa, her face anxious and her arms outstretched. Wilson sat down quickly, embarrassment and distress turning her complexion from white to red, which at least reassured her mistress. "Then you are not ill," Miss Elizabeth said, "it is something else or someone else, am I not right?" Wilson had not the energy to put up a pretense. She nodded, busied herself once more with the sewing. "It is Timothy?" Again she nodded, feeling too helpless to resist. "Well, I thought as much," Miss Elizabeth said indignantly. "He has been importuning you and must be spoken to. I will *not* have my maid treated so. I will speak to Mr. Kenyon—" "Oh no," she interrupted, "begging your pardon, miss, but there is no need to do that, it is not at all necessary. Timothy is a good man and kind. Nothing is his fault. There was a misunderstanding. It is all sorted out now and tomorrow he goes with Mr. Kenyon to the Isle of Wight for heaven knows how long." She bent her head but could not this time help a tear escaping, and this tear dropped onto the red silk she was sewing and spread like a stain. She dabbed at it frantically but her mistress took the silk away and held her hand and said, "I can guess, my dear, I can guess what transpired and I am sure, sure, you have made the right decision. It has been in front of you for some weeks, has it not? Whether to say yes or no? I felt it in the air and in your looks. And now you have said no? And he has taken it badly? But of course he has, who would not? You must not weep, Wilson, for you did right. You are too intelligent to be overcome by flattery, too honest to admit to a love you do not feel."

"I do not know what I feel," Wilson burst out.

"But that is an answer in itself," Miss Elizabeth insisted. "If you loved him, you would not need to ask whether or not you did, do you not see?"

All day spent in that pretty room Wilson marveled at how much she had allowed her mistress to suppose. She had let her think Timothy had been refused and the affair was at an end when it was not and she might still marry him. Before they parted in the kitchen, Timothy had earned her admiration by saying she spoke sense and even though he hated hearing it he would accept her terms. He would ask his master to fulfill his promise and see how he made out and in a year he would come to her again and lay before her his progress. He even acknowledged the virtue of a complete separation since he found seeing so little of her a terribly frustrating business. He requested permission to write, which she leaped upon as what she had hoped for. But Miss Elizabeth supposed all was at an end and so straight away deceit was being entered into it. Whom did it harm? No one, she decided; she could have her secret and if necessary, in a year, divulge it. Meanwhile, not knowing it made Miss Elizabeth happy. She had thought she might lose Wilson as she had lost Crow, and, knowing she was not going to do so made her quite triumphant. There was nothing she liked better, she said, than seeing women apply common sense to affairs of the heart.

For a long time afterward she was particularly solicitous to Wilson, who was grateful though plagued by feelings of guilt. Timothy's letters did not arrive as regularly as Mr. Browning's but they came far more frequently than she had anticipated and gave her such pleasure. Wilson went to great lengths to conceal this correspondence, but her mistress was not suspicious since she was far too occupied by the end of August with a plan of her own, a plan of which she had told Wilson, with many requests that she tell nobody else. The plan was to do at last something she had intended for many a year and from which she had held back: to winter abroad, in the sun. She asked, with shining eyes, what Wilson thought and, when Wilson said she thought it an excellent idea, she clapped her hands. "You will come with me, will you not, dear? And not be afraid to leave your own country and your family behind for a few months?" Wilson said that, far from being afraid, she was now so far different from her former self that she positively yearned to go abroad and she ventured to ask where, if the plan came to fruition, they might go. When her mistress said she hoped Italy, her heart leaped. Timothy had only just written that his plan to become a printer was delayed because he was to accompany Mr. Kenyon to Rome in the coming winter and the effect of this news had been to make her instantly regret that he would be so far away. Still cautious, still reluctant to recognize love, she nevertheless had begun to think of the absent Timothy in a way that suggested she might well have been mistaken in doubting her own feelings. "When will we go, miss?" she asked and was thrilled rather than alarmed with the reply: "In a month or so, if it can be arranged."

CHAPTER ELEVEN

ONE MORNING in late August, when the weather had broken and rain streamed against the windows for the first time in months, Miss Elizabeth said she saw nothing for it but to call the doctor and seek his help. As she spoke, she was standing near the windows in her room, watching the ivy in the window box gleam in the heavy shower, its dark green leaves suddenly glossy after weeks of hanging limp and dusty against the wall. She had a shawl around her shoulders but she shivered, though in spite of the sudden drop in temperature it was still not really cold. Wilson, busy pouring out coffee for her mistress, did not see her tremble and pull the shawl closer around her as she came to take the cup but, looking up as she handed it over, she saw the misery on her face. "Why, miss, whatever is the matter? Are you not well?"

"I am well enough but for how long? Oh, it will be the same story, Wilson, another month and I shall start to cough and be unable to move from this room. I am tired of it, tired, tired." Wilson waited, knowing it was not for her to bring up the subject of going abroad for the sun. Again and again during the last month mention had been made of this intention but never had it come to anything so far as she knew. Now, with the rain and the change in temperature, winter approaching gave an urgency to the secret project.

"There is nothing for it," Miss Elizabeth said, sipping her coffee, "I must do what everyone advises and call in Dr. Chambers." She shuddered as she said the name, as though evoking an ogre. "I must tell Papa tonight that I wish to consult him and then it will be done." She drank a second tiny cup of coffee and then said, "You have not met Dr. Chambers, Wilson. He is perfectly pleasant but he terrifies me. All doctors do. I cannot revere the medical profession except for dear Dr. Scully in Torquay, who died and left me, his patient, alive. For the rest, I have no confidence. They poke and prod and peer and end up telling me what I know and do not need to hear. But Papa will heed Dr. Chambers, who is the Queen's physician, you know. If Dr. Chambers were to tell him it is imperative I winter in the sun, then he would listen, so the ordeal must be gone through and that is all there is to it."

An ordeal it was. Miss Elizabeth told her papa she felt unwell and wished to see the doctor. By all accounts Mr. Barrett was not pleased. Minnie vowed his face was dark as thunder when he came down from Miss Elizabeth's room and Simon, who was sent with the note requesting a call from the doctor, said the master seemed reluctant to send him at all. The answer he brought back was that Dr. Chambers would be pleased to attend Miss Barrett at three o'clock the following afternoon. From the moment this news was received Miss Elizabeth was agitated and quite unable to sleep, "Oh, I do so hate these examinations," she complained to Wilson, "and yet it is not through any foolish false modesty. I do not want to be touched by a stranger's hands, doctor or not. I feel so at a disadvantage, half undressed and bound to be still and obedient while I am observed. It is horrid, is it not, Wilson?"

"I don't know, I'm sure, miss," Wilson said, "never having had a doctor nor seen one except when Mrs. Graham-Clarke was visited and I saw no examination then. Mother often wanted a doctor for Fanny but we only once had one. We had to make do with an apothecary other times and he was a rough fellow none of us cared for."

"Then I am fortunate to have a skilled doctor to call and you tell me so very nicely, Wilson, and I am ashamed not to be more grateful. I will try to be calm and not make such an unseemly fuss."

Minnie insisted that Miss Elizabeth's room should be cleaned extra well, in so far as it was possible with her in it (and her protests loud at the invasion of maids). No doctor, Minnie said, should be able to say that any room under her charge was anything less than immaculate; and she personally supervised the dusting that morning and came along to check that the brass fender gleamed satisfactorily and that there was not a speck of coal dust anywhere. Wilson, to her embarrassment, had not realized until the cleaning operation was over how very necessary it proved to have been. She swore that from now on she would insist on Miss Elizabeth vacating her room one day a week so that a proper job could be made of it. Minnie, flushed with indignation at the state of the room, said she would hold her to that.

Dr. Chambers arrived promptly. Wilson met him at the foot of the stairs, all resplendent in a sparkling new apron over her dress, starched white and stiff. Miss Elizabeth said it was a nonsense to dress up for a doctor but all the servants who might remotely come into contact with the Queen's doctor had been reminded by Minnie not to disgrace the house. In the event, Dr. Chambers hardly seemed to look at her. He gave his hat and cloak to Simon, picked up his bag and stood waiting to be guided to his patient with an air of deep boredom. He was neither as tall nor as imposing as she had expected and did not inspire the awe his position merited. As they ascended the stairs he did not speak. His tread was slow and heavy and Wilson was sure she heard him wheeze on the first landing and sigh as he saw yet more stairs. By the time they reached Miss Elizabeth's room she noticed his face was very red. As she put her hand on the doorknob to open it he motioned her to wait. They both stood there a moment or two until he nodded and she showed him in.

Miss Elizabeth was in a nightgown and wrapper, lying on the sofa. Wilson thought how pretty she looked in the soft white garments, so much more flattering than the dark daytime clothes she habitually wore. She was not even too shockingly pale and indeed was not ill at all but some sort of pretense had been necessary to justify calling the doctor. Dr. Chambers stood looking down at Miss Elizabeth with an air of doubt, his thumbs stuck in his waistcoat pockets and his spectacles slipping down his nose. Wilson, standing to one side ready to help her mistress remove her wrapper and open her nightdress, felt the tension as, in a faltering voice, Miss Elizabeth related how weak she felt in the chest since the good weather had departed and how she could feel the old lassitude overwhelming her and was afraid all the good of the summer was about to be undone. Dr. Chambers did not speak. After what seemed an eternity, he turned from scrutinizing his patient, who had grown increasingly flushed, to open his bag. Wilson's eyes were riveted on the contents. He drew out a strange-looking contraption with a long rubber tube attached to what looked like a silver disc. It divided at the other end into two parts. Her heart began to thud unpleasantly loud as her imagination went to work on what this implement might be used for. Then Dr. Chambers asked Miss Elizabeth if she would be so kind as to remove her wrapper and open her nightdress. Wilson stepped forward and swiftly took the wrapper off, then undid the lacing at the front of the nightgown. Dr. Chambers asked that it should be undone further to make his work easier. When Miss Elizabeth was open to the waist, her breasts partially exposed, Dr. Chambers sat down beside her and put into his ears the ends of the tube, then picked up the silver disc and applied it to Miss Elizabeth's chest, tapping with his fingers as he did so. Watching his face, Wilson saw he was completely absorbed and did not even notice Miss Elizabeth's appearance. The moment he had finished he turned aside while the nightdress was done up again and the wrapper replaced. Then, his bag repacked and closed, he stood up and resumed his former stance.

No one spoke. Miss Elizabeth looked frightened, Wilson thought. The doctor had not yet spoken and, as she wrote immediately afterward to her mother:

—I did not know what to do but stood uneasy wondering if I should go out though Miss Elizabeth had directed I should stay in attendance throughout the visit. At last Dr. Chambers spoke and said he had used the stethoscope, for that is what they call the instrument I told you of, and it had proved there was not absolute disease of the lungs only a congestion which was not as yet severe. In the matter of wintering abroad in the sun this was something he would recommend to any patient with a chest complaint such as hers but it would not be right to say such a thing was a matter of life or death. When Dr. Chambers had departed Miss Elizabeth wept and would not be consoled, vowing all was lost and there was no hope of going abroad. I soothed her as best I could but she was as yet distressed still when her father came to see her. I made to leave but she clung to me and Mr. Barrett did not bid me to go so I remained and heard him say he was relieved that Dr. Chambers saw no cause for immediate concern. Miss Elizabeth made a great effort and said so I am not to winter abroad and her father said she could surely answer that herself and left the room. Well, then there was a storm of crying and in the middle of it she called for pen and paper and I said you are not going to write in the condition you are in and she said she must, she must write at once to Mr. Browning and tell him all her hopes were dashed. It was as I thought, Mother, it is not only for the pleasure and ease of the sun that she wishes to winter abroad but to be out of her father's house and near Mr. Browning. And now she cannot go though her brother George is to plead with the master for her.

At last, after taking a double laudanum draught, Miss Elizabeth was asleep and Wilson free to go to her room. On the way up, she met Molly, who had been sent to find her and ask her if she would step into Mr. Barrett's study as soon as Miss Elizabeth was asleep. It was only the second time she had ever been sent for and, at nine in the evening, unusual enough to be doubly alarming. Wilson smoothed her dress down and turned about. Doubtless an inquisition was to follow in which the master would seek the truth about what Dr. Chambers had said; but since she knew he had spoken to the doctor himself, what harm could she do that was not already done? As she crossed the hall, dim in the light of a single lamp, she was startled by Mr. Barrett's door opening suddenly and Mr. George stepping out. He did not speak to her but stalked past her, angry-looking and clenching his fists, which only increased her nervousness. She hesitated in front of the door Mr. George had just closed with what was nearly a slam. It seemed wise to leave the master on his own for a moment or two, wise not to follow upon Mr. George's heels too closely. She shivered slightly as she stood there in the half-light, her face only inches away from the solid door. Though she was still not afraid of Mr. Barrett she was more wary than when she had first come into his house. She had by now learned his humors too well, knew quite how peremptory and even brutal he could be, even if inherently fair. He was, she knew, dangerous and though she had never had cause to suffer at his hands she had seen others do so, both family and servants.

Finally, she knocked and was told instantly to enter. The master was standing by the fire, his back to her. He wheeled around and she saw he was very flushed. It crossed her mind that he had deliberately let himself be seen facing a roaring fire so that she would think his face was red because of it, when that was not the reason at all. She stood a good few yards from him and yet could feel him tensing, could sense his jaw clenching, his foot tapping, his arms straining as he locked them together behind him. It seemed to cost him a great effort to speak.

"You were present, I believe, when Dr. Chambers examined Miss Barrett?"

"Yes, sir."

"And you heard him say what? What precisely?"

"As Miss Elizabeth has told you, sir."

"What was that?"

"Dr. Chambers said wintering abroad would help her chest."

"But that she was in moderate health and this abroad business was not absolutely essential? Am I correct?"

"I did not hear everything, sir."

"Then you are even more discreet than given credit for. Well, I spoke to the doctor myself and tomorrow my own doctor will see Miss Elizabeth. I will have this straight once and for all, is that understood?"

"Yes, sir."

"Please tell my daughter Mr. Elliotson will attend at 3 P.M."

"Tomorrow, sir?"

"That is what I said."

"Tomorrow is—"

"Tuesday. And on a Tuesday, you were about to say, my daughter has a visitor, the man of the pomegranates, the poet. I am aware of that. She has time to inform Mr. Browning his visit is impossible."

"Yes, sir."

Still she stood there. Still Mr. Barrett kept her there. She wondered what else he had to say.

"You would go with your mistress abroad, would you, Wilson?"

"Yes, sir."

"And are you hoping to go abroad?"

"Whatever my mistress wishes, sir."

"That is commendable. You may yet be put to the test, though at my behest and not hers. You may go."

Wilson went, perturbed by the emphasis with which he had spoken of a test, rather than by the words themselves. There was nothing she had said which she regretted yet she felt that in some indefinable way she had failed her mistress. She had not spoken strongly and ought to have done so and the master had sensed this. It was a comfort to write to Timothy:

—how caught I feel my dearest Timothy for in truth I am confused and hardly know my own mind. My mistress plays a game of her own with stealth, and I am not privy to the rules. But I fear my mistress has lost the game and we rest here and I envy you your travels with Mr. Kenyon. So now I suppose it is goodbye for the winter if, as you intimate, you are to leave this next Sunday and I wish you well and would appreciate news of you before too long and I will write from time to time if you have an address to hand though I will be starved of news to match yours. I cannot say I relish the thought of winter any more than my mistress though I do not suffer as she does with the lungs. I miss our walks in the park and to give you satisfaction I must confess I miss you too in a manner of speaking not having any other such good friend—

The minute she had written that, Wilson felt she had betrayed Lizzie Treherne, to whom she could tell even more than to Timothy. Lizzie knew all about the yearning to go abroad and had kept pace with the growing passion to be where Mr. Browning was. "It was the same with Mr. Boyd, the blind scholar who was her teacher in Hope End days," Lizzie vowed. "Ask Minnie, and she will tell you how, when the family had to leave Hope End, Miss Elizabeth wished only to go to Bath where Mr. Boyd was. But you must not let her distress and agitation pull you down, Lily, or there will be no end to the misery. Once she has resigned herself to not going anywhere she will settle and all will be well, you will see. It is no good making yourself ill over it as I see you do. Keep calm and cheerful and rise above all the plannings and mutterings in that house or you will go mad."

Lizzie was right and Wilson knew it. She tried to detach herself, though distraction was hard to find without Timothy. She walked in the park feeling sulky and was bad-tempered with Flush when he would not stop straining on the leash. Mr. Elliotson had been quite different from Dr. Chambers. A thin, gaunt man who moved in short, jerky steps, as though on the balls of his feet, he had not applied the stethoscope. He had felt Miss Elizabeth's pulse, talking all the while of the importance of good food, and felt her forehead and looked at her tongue and asked three times as many questions as Dr. Chambers had done, most of them about the state of his patient's bowels. Wilson, who was well acquainted with her mistress's condition, was yet again surprised at some of her answers but would have been too nervous to contest them even if she had not been too embarrassed. If the doctor had talked to her he might have heard a different story, one of almost constant constipation and mighty efforts to relieve it. She had prevailed upon Miss Elizabeth to try another of Mother's cures with some success, one in which small green walnuts were placed in salt and water for nine days, then sieved and left until turned black, when she put them in a jug and poured boiling water on them. Her mistress had vowed the water enclosing them looked poisonous but had agreed to sip some of it after it had been boiled and appeared more of a syrup. Her bowels had at least opened partially the next day but she would take no more of the walnut water though Wilson assured her that, with brandy added, the mixture lasted years. The constipation continued but the doctor was not told. He would have heard too how that regular health of which Miss Elizabeth was so proud was now very irregular and caused concern. She was not concerned but Miss Elizabeth was, waiting each month with anxiety for evidence that she was a normal, healthy woman. Wilson could not understand the fuss or see such a nuisance, one she herself found a dreary inconvenience, as significant. If Miss Elizabeth were married, it would be different but since she was not the absence of her "regular health" hardly mattered. Let Tilly grow white-faced with terror every now and again, having good cause, but not Miss Elizabeth surely.

Wilson knew, as she wandered in the park, keeping her eye on the clouds, that part of her restlessness was to do with her birthday. Tomorrow, September 14, she would be twenty-five. A quarter of a century, and what to show for it? A good dress on her back, a few savings under her bed in the tin box with Miss Elizabeth's poetry, a safe and secure job, but no home of her own, no husband, no children, no foreseeable future other than work and work again. London had made her discontented—no, she corrected that in her mind as she corrected the direction in which Flush was heading. It had not made her discontented so much as more *aware*. In Newcastle, her expectations had been so low. Now, thanks partly to Timothy and partly to Miss Elizabeth, she thought of things that had never crossed her mind before. She was ashamed at how covetous she was becoming, an unpleasant trait she had never thought to see in herself and one which Mother had frowned upon in others. She worked hard and had so little. It had once angered her to hear from that dreadful Jane, Miss Mitford's maid, that Miss Elizabeth had referred to her as "desperately dear" at sixteen guineas a year. She had not, of course, let Jane see her fury but it had lain within her all this time and was only now beginning to boil over. Did Miss Elizabeth realize how little sixteen guineas was? She tried to save half each week but it could not be done without a self-denial so demanding it made her wretched. She could walk in the park for free but precious little else. To go to a play with Minnie was a rare treat but she relished it and would not give it up. And she liked pretty things, had more taste for them than she had ever supposed, so Oxford Street, near and tempting, made her still more discontented. Miss Elizabeth bought her two dresses a year but everything else she had to find for herself and London was full of delectable boots and hats and gloves. She bought a pair of shoes as a birthday present to herself which cost six whole shillings—such exquisite shoes of a leather so soft and fine they caressed her feet when she put them on and were quite irresistible. But she knew she ought to have resisted them since at six shillings they fell only a shilling short of her weekly wage. It was wicked, sinful—but such shoes were too great a temptation.

At chapel, the minister preached regularly against the sins of pride and vanity, so much so that she often thought he had her in mind—for, having bought the shoes, had she not been daydreaming of a sprigged muslin she longed to buy but for which she knew she had no use? It was a beautiful blue and brought out the color of her eyes famously: lately she had come to realize her eyes were her best feature and should be made more of. It was silly to wear gray and black and brown when those neutral shades only made her more insignificant than she already was, whereas a deep, sky blue worn near her face brought up her eyes and made her almost pretty. Mr. Henry had said as much, not that she set any store by what that young man said and not that he had dared to be impertinent. It was only that as she was coming out of Miss Elizabeth's room once and he was going in he had jumped back as though startled and claimed not to recognize her "because you look so different, Wilson, in that blue blouse." One or two of the servants had made remarks about a follower being surely in the running but she had put a stop to that sharply. She had no follower nor wanted none and she would thank them to remember that. Minnie, who had guessed the truth about Timothy, saw to it that no one else made the same mistake again.

Turning back for home, Wilson tried to be honest with herself. She was, she dared to think, as sensitive to atmosphere as her mistress, who had often herself commented on this. "Ah, Wilson, what do we suspect?" she would often say when a visitor had left and they would discuss together whether some member of the family was or was not pretending to be happy when both of them could feel the depression or anxiety seeping through. They had each only to look at a face to feel they knew the mood of the person behind it and prided themselves on their perception. And now Wilson confessed to herself that what was really troubling her was neither her age nor the failure of the plan to winter abroad but something both deeper and more subtle. It was all to do with the change in her mistress and that change was all to do with Mr. Browning. When she took his letters in these days Miss Elizabeth seemed to vibrate, to grow vivacious without saying a word, to become altogether lighter and warmer. The old languor would pass and in the instant that the precious letter was put into her hand a cloud lifted from her. The letter would be pressed to her heart, even to her lips, and her smile was not simply of pleasure but of rapture. When she was writing her reply, Wilson was now sent out of the room and her last glimpse of her mistress showed her to be totally absorbed, head bent protectively over her paper, her left arm shielding it. Closing the door, Wilson felt excluded and also, she realized, envious.

This unseemly envy persisted and grew more troublesome before and after Mr. Browning's visits. Wilson found the eagerness, the open hunger, with which Miss Elizabeth now waited for Mr. Browning almost unbearable. At first, she had smiled to herself and been happy for her mistress, even worried anxiously that she showed too much need, but recently, since the failure of the plan to go abroad, the evidence that Miss Elizabeth yearned so for her Tuesday visitor had begun to unnerve her. It made her feel cold and lonely to witness such emotion. Was this how she should have felt about Timothy? How she should feel now? And then, when she showed Mr. Browning in, the alacrity, the confidence, with which he crossed the floor and the joy in her voice when she returned his greeting were all too much. Bitterly she reproached herself for that pang of jealousy and reminded herself over and over again of how she had hoped and prayed just such a happiness would come the way of poor Miss Elizabeth. But now that it had, her delight was tempered by this wretched envy. She saw quite clearly that here was love in all its simple splendor. Flush saw it too, and hated it. Hearing frenzied barking the week before, while Mr. Browning was there, she had gone down to Miss Elizabeth's room to take the dog out and one look at both their faces had told her what had caused Flush to bark. Unless she was very much mistaken, Mr. Browning had kissed or at least embraced Miss Elizabeth. For no other reason, except a bodily contact he would not permit, would Flush bark so. Miss Elizabeth, asking her to remove the dog and banish him once more to the yard on Tuesday afternoons, told all in her averted downward gaze and Mr. Browning, fidgeting with his collar, was no less revealing. Wilson thought she ought to smile at their innocence but instead was particularly grave.

Lizzie, told the tale, had thrilled to it but could hardly believe it. During the following weeks, as Wilson made the walk to the Trehernes' her highlight of the week, Lizzie became bound to acknowledge that she was right and a love affair was in progress. "She has said nothing," Wilson always reminded Lizzie, "nothing direct at all."

"But that is how it would be," said Lizzie. "She is afraid it cannot be true and dare not trust that it is." Wilson nodded, though mildly annoyed at having to give Lizzie credit for divining anything at all now that she was the expert herself. But, expert or not, when Lizzie asked, "Where will it end?" she could not answer. "Where do such things usually end?" she replied with the lift of an eyebrow, and they both looked at each other and then laughed a little at their own relish. "Ah well," Lizzie said, groaning at the weight of the second child she was carrying and stretching her back where it pained her, "then we will see. Maybe it is a year for wedding bells and soon she will be in the state I am in now." Wilson could not imagine it; looking at Lizzie's vast size—the baby was due on Christmas Day—she found it quite impossible to envisage Miss Elizabeth swollen with child. Contemplating this, she found it equally impossible to imagine her in bed with a man and blushed as such an image flashed briefly through her mind. What was happening to her that she could indulge in such gross speculation? There was speculation too, in December, about Miss

Henrietta's future. Crossing the hall one day, Wilson came on Surtees Cook folding Miss Henrietta in his arms. She broke away and cried, "Captain Cook has been promoted, only think!" Wilson gave a little bob, embarrassed now to be caught with a tray like any common scullery maid, but Miss Henrietta was so flushed with pleasure that she noticed nothing. "I cannot stay, even if I were welcome," Captain Cook was saying. "I only came that you should be the first to hear before it appears in the *Gazette*." As Wilson went down the last flight of stairs she heard Miss Henrietta clap her hands and then the door opening and shutting.

Minnie Robinson, of course, knew all about Captain Cook's promotion, so did everyone belowstairs, where Tilly was speculating heavily. "Now they'll get married for sure," she breathed, eyes bright with excitement as she conjured up visions of the fun a wedding in the house would be. "Don't talk nonsense, Tilly," snapped Minnie, "we'll have no silly talk of weddings if you please." Afterward she told Wilson she doubted if any promotion of Captain Cook would make the slightest bit of difference to Miss Henrietta's marriage prospects. "The master is set against all weddings," she said, "no matter who the suitor, he don't hold with them. And poor Miss Henrietta hasn't a penny to her name, nor has my Miss Arabel. 'Tis only Miss Elizabeth got the legacies from her grandmother and her uncle and it is no use to her either. 'Tisn't fair, never was, but there you are, when are these things ever fair and there's nothing can be done about it."

Next day Miss Elizabeth herself said much the same. She showed Wilson the two lines announcing Captain Cook's promotion but sighed as she did so. "I fear dear Henrietta exaggerates the effect of it," she said, "but it is very little more money, certainly not sufficient to marry on, Papa would say. Money should not have anything to do with marriage, or that is what I believe, but when it comes to the managing of it, why then Papa's viewpoint has some strength. If Henrietta had but a hundred or so of her own all might be different, but she has not." Wilson, sensing her mistress's distress, folded the newspaper with even greater gentleness than usual and placed it on the table. "Have you seen him, Wilson?" her mistress suddenly asked.

"Yes, ma'am."

"Is he very fine?"

"He is tall, ma'am, and well built and looks splendid in his uniform."

"So Henrietta says. How she does love his regimentals. But is he handsome, Wilson? Would you say?"

Wilson hesitated. Here was another instance when she was caught by her inability to be ready with the quick meaningless response. "He has a kind face, ma'am, very kind, and gentle too, but he is not what I would call rightly handsome, as I think you mean."

"Well, that is good to hear. I like kindness and gentleness in a man better than good looks. I should not have liked to hear you say Captain Cook was full of bluster, a swaggering soldier who preened himself."

"Indeed no, ma'am."

"Henrietta longs to present Captain Cook for my inspection but I could not bear it."

Wilson still could not bring herself to ask direct questions, however much her mistress encouraged her to break with formality and do so. All she could manage was, "He is a fine gentleman, ma'am, and I am sure would be glad to meet you."

"Oh, I have no doubt of that, but then think what might come of it, think of the position I might find myself in should anything transpire."

"I beg your pardon, ma'am?"

"With Papa, Wilson. It is best that I do not know and have never spoken to Captain Cook, do you see?" Wilson did.

She had told her mistress that Lizzie was expecting again and the reply had been "Poor woman." Wilson had felt indignant about this. Why "poor woman" when little Mary was nearly eighteen months old? It was a decent interval, more than many a woman had, and the new baby was wanted and welcome though Lizzie had been heard to say she hoped that would be an end to it, God willing.

When Lizzie was brought to bed of a boy ten days late and Miss

Elizabeth was told, she asked if Wilson had seen the baby and when assured only briefly, and this said with a casual air, she seemed relieved. No further questions were asked about Lizzie's son and she had no idea Wilson had walked to Bayham Street almost every day, where it was perfectly true she hardly saw the baby but saw a great deal of Mary, whose nurse she almost became. Every afternoon she and Flush took the little girl out and Lizzie slept. The weather, which had been mild all winter, was still fine, with neither snow nor ice on the ground and a complete absence of cutting east winds. Watching Mary stagger along the paths in Regent's Park, Wilson felt a great longing to have just such a cheerful little creature of her own. She picked Mary up when the child grew tired. All the way back to Bayham Street Wilson breathed in the curious scent of Mary's cheeks and hair and felt her warmth and, though the weight seemed heavier with each step and Flush's lead became tangled, she was sorry to reach the child's home. Who could resist the task of peeling off Mary's mittens to reveal the fat, dimpled hands or pulling off her boots, of which she was so proud, and rubbing the stockinged toes to warm them? There was nothing, Wilson felt, that she would not do for a child.

She was silent that day when she returned to Wimpole Street and performed all her duties mechanically but Miss Elizabeth made no comment. When once she would have asked if anything was amiss she now seemed not to notice Wilson's existence. She was in a trance half the time, constantly pausing in the middle of writing or reading to stare into space, a half smile on her lips. Wilson would ask her once, twice, even thrice if she was ready to take coffee or have her hair brushed and there would be no answer. On Wednesdays, the day after Mr. Browning's visits, she was particularly removed from all everyday concerns and sometimes did not speak at all. Minnie shuddered when Wilson commented on this and vowed there was danger in the air and it would all end badly. She was even more convinced of this when Wilson reported that Mr. Barrett no longer came to his daughter's room to pray with her before bed. "What a deal has changed in a year," said Minnie.

Minnie's words reminded Wilson that it was indeed a year since

Miss Elizabeth had first received a letter from Mr. Browning. When her mistress smiled, looking up with shining eyes, and said that today was an anniversary of some importance, she was able to say she knew what it was. "To think, Wilson, that a year ago I was such a deprived person and now I feel blessed by all my letters." Wilson could think of no response. Since she had read none of these precious letters, what her mistress said seemed faintly ridiculous and almost irritated her. "They are very special letters, dear," Miss Elizabeth said softly, as though appearing to realize her mistake, "very tender and true, increasingly so. Will you not believe me and be happy for me?"

"Indeed yes, ma'am," Wilson said hastily, "I am very glad for you, truly."

"And I dare to be glad for myself." But then a great sigh followed. "Glad but frightened all the same, Wilson, frightened of what is to come and the courage needed to achieve happiness." Wilson stayed quite still, her hands folded in her lap, her head slightly bent. She struggled to interpret the nuances of every word spoken, every small movement and expression of face and body. Every time she sneaked a quick look at her mistress she saw something different—pride, joy, alarm, hope all chased each other in her eyes. "Do I have the courage, Wilson, do you think?"

"For what, miss?"

"For life, for choosing life."

"Why, yes, miss. You are alive, miss."

"I am now, half alive at least, but not fully, gloriously alive, not fully wakened in every sense. And I could be, I *will* be, if I have the courage." Again, Wilson could think of no reply to make, though by now she had no doubt what was being said. I spend my time, she thought, not knowing what to say when something most needs to be said.

"Well, I will have my coffee now," Miss Elizabeth said finally, "and drop such fanciful talk until another time when I can take you into my confidence with some meaning, for I talk in riddles and you are very good to listen so carefully, dear. Now, let us talk of spring and your holiday."

CHAPTER TWELVE

B<small>UT</small> <small>SPRING</small> again double-crossed everyone that year. Daffodils well above the ground in late January, buds opening in early February, and then when it seemed they were to have no winter at all in London that year the backlash came, just as Minnie always predicted. Snow hung on the blossom in March so thickly that it was impossible to separate the white pear tree blooms from the crystallized flakes. The effect was pretty but the result cruel. It seemed to Wilson that her mistress, instead of bewailing the setback of the seasons, welcomed it. The whole household expressed their amazement at how Miss Elizabeth flourished and, in expressing it, seemed to suspect some secret to which only Wilson was privy. Writing to her mother, Wilson confessed she felt

—my mistress is happy it is true, and it is all to do with Mr. Browning, but nothing has gone further that I have been told. Except for what she is writing which she shows no one and does not talk of and cannot be like her other work which she is open about. On afternoons lately when I have brought in the tea she has been lost to the world in her writing hearing neither my footstep nor my voice and when the cup is put in front of her coming to with a start and coloring and hiding her paper under a book. It is not a letter which so absorbs her, that I do know, because my eye is quick enough to see it is set in lines like poetry. There is nothing untoward in Miss Elizabeth writing her verse but her manner over this makes me think it is very special poetry and others might conclude of some intimate nature but what it is I cannot say. She talks constantly of Italy and was found with timetables spread out yesterday but they were only to help a friend who contemplates going abroad she said. I hear Pisa and Rome and Naples mentioned in a most familiar fashion and grow to like them—

In fact Wilson grew to yearn for them. Only one letter from Timothy the whole winter and that was a poor thing but it was posted in Rome and had a magic of its own. It arrived after Christmas with news that he would be back in London by March but March came and went and no Timothy had appeared. Wilson was ever alert to hear Mr. Kenyon's name, for Miss Elizabeth expected his return soon, but she failed to hear it. As her mistress blossomed she felt herself fade. She let her mistress's clothes out and took her own in. She watched her mistress's color turn from an absolute pallor to a healthier paleness and her own robust complexion fade to an unattractive sallow. And yet she was not ill, nothing specific ailed her.

Minnie said she needed a tonic and would pick up when she went home. The very word made Wilson shudder. Last year she had looked forward with such longing to going north but this year the thought had no attraction. She did not know if she even wanted to go at all. When Miss Elizabeth suggested she could name a day, she said it was early yet and the time need not be fixed. Her mistress queried this, asking if her mother would not like to know when she was to come, and Wilson was obliged to admit that she would. Finally, the same two weeks as the year before were fixed and this time there was no attempt to put her off or exert any kind of emotional blackmail. It seemed to Wilson that her mistress was, on the contrary, pushing her to go. "Now, Wilson dear," Miss Elizabeth said the night before, "enjoy your holiday, for next year, perhaps—I cannot say precisely why, but next year it may be that a visit to your loved ones will prove —difficult to arrange. I cannot say more. Or it may be your holiday will come at a different time and you must prepare your mother for this. Will you do that, dear?" Wilson said she would and prepared to take her leave. Miss Elizabeth seemed to look at her more closely than she had done for a long time and to be startled by what she saw, for she said, "Why, Wilson, I had not noticed how thin you have become until just then or is it your new traveling coat? Your mother will say I have worked you too hard—have I, dear?"

"Indeed no, miss."

"I am glad to hear it. You must tell me if you find the chair too heavy to push, for you have pushed it a great deal lately."

"The chair is not too heavy, miss, and I like to be out."

"I know you do and so do I and at last I can be. It does me good but I cannot say, looking at you, Wilson, that anyone would think it does *you* much good. Now go and this year I will be brave as befits my new cheerfulness, and not force you to write to me. The time will fly."

For Wilson, it dragged. She could hardly believe how long two weeks could be and how much of a strain on her nerves was the effort of appearing to be delighted. Every night she had a headache from all the unnatural laughing and chattering she forced herself to do and was glad to get to bed, away from Mother's eye. Only to Ellen on her weekly night at home did she confide that she did not know what was the matter with her. "I feel low," she whispered, "and have the heart for nothing." Ellen asked her how long she had felt pulled down and, thinking back, Wilson decided it was since the plan for Miss Elizabeth to winter abroad had come to nothing. "It seemed such a blow," she murmured, "as much to me as Miss Elizabeth and yet I cannot think why." Ellen laughed under the bedclothes and pinched her. "Ah," she whispered, "but then ask yourself who *is* abroad as you might see if you went and then ask yourself again why you feel so low." Wilson was cross and pinched Ellen hard in return. "It is nothing to do with Timothy Wright," she muttered. "I was glad he went, wasn't I? I told

you I was. I wanted free of his pestering and he was nothing to me."
Ellen snorted and had to be pinched again. "Absence maketh the heart
grow fonder," Ellen recited and added, "How long is it since he went?
Six months? Longer? You fool yourself, Lily. You are in love, that's
what all this feeling low is." "In love with a man that writes once?"
Wilson flashed back. "Oh, men don't go in for letter writing," Ellen
said. "Mr. Browning does," Wilson argued. "But he's a gentleman,"
said Ellen. "Their ways are different, and even so I bet not many men
do as he does. Our sort of men don't rate letter writing, that's the
point. You wait till you see this Timothy and if your inside turns to
water and you feel an itch down there, then——"

But she got no further. Wilson slapped her once for vulgarity and
again for impertinence and Ellen was so annoyed at being beaten, for
what she had said was only a bit of fun, that she left their bed and
went to sleep with May, vowing she would not come home again
while Wilson was there if she was to be treated so. But she did come
again, the next week, and Wilson heard all about her new young man
who was an apprentice nearly out of his time at the glassworks. "We'll
get wed next spring," Ellen said confidently, "but don't tell Mother,
for she doesn't like Albert, she says he is after one thing and has no
manners, as if I cared for manners, but you will like him, Lily, and I
want you to meet him before you go and I will see to it that you do."
Wilson wished she had not bothered because she liked Albert Cole no
more than Mother did. He was rough and cocky and had an insolent,
challenging air. She could not see what Ellen liked about him, beyond
a certain rough handsomeness, and that made *her* even more wary.

"Isn't he manly?" Ellen breathed, and Wilson was obliged to agree
that, if manly meant big and heavy and tough, then yes, Albert was
manly but not in the way Timothy was. Timothy, in being manly, had
an air of strength, of confidence. Albert, on the other hand, reeked of
brutality and of stupidity. Unlike Ellen, she would not feel protected
by such a man but threatened. It alarmed her greatly and shocked her
to be told by Ellen that she had given herself wholly to Albert some
weeks past. "I couldn't resist it," Ellen whispered. "I wanted it so bad
and so did he. I was scarce in control of myself, I tell you." Wilson

made an exclamation of disgust. "Now why do you click your tongue?" Ellen said. "God made us so and I see no cause for shame."

"God has not joined you together in his house," Wilson said, "and that is cause for shame enough, I think."

"Oh, that's chapel talk," Ellen said, "and I don't care for it."

"And I don't care for the fool you're making of yourself. What will you do if he doesn't keep his word and marry you? What will you do if you get with child?"

"He will keep his word," Ellen whispered back fiercely, "and I am careful."

"Others have been careful, or so they thought, and lived to see there is no such thing."

"But there is, and I know of it but since you are so unkind I shan't tell you even if you beg me."

"Fine talk," said Wilson scornfully, "and I don't want to hear of it. We will just see how all this ends. Mother will never forgive you."

"Mother will never know unless you tell her and if you do I will never forgive *you*."

She did not, of course, mention a word to Mother, who seemed too much preoccupied with work she was doing for a Mr. Conroy, a druggist who had opened an apothecary's shop in Newcastle. He came out to Fenham to gather the plants and herbs and berries he needed to make his powders and, hearing of Mrs. Wilson's reputation, had sought her out and suggested she might help him. He brought out glass specie jars for her to fill, first checking that she could indeed discern the difference between the many plants he needed. Wilson could see how happy Mother was collecting the specimens and knowing to what good use they were put. Fanny went with her to the Town Moor and the woods near Fenham and enjoyed the open air, even if she was no real help to Mother and could not tell a dandelion from a cowslip. Mr. Conroy's new shop was imposing and, when taken to see it, Mother had blushed to think she had helped to stock such an impressive array of storage shelves. "If I had my time again, Lily," she confided, "I should like to have become an apothecary, if women were able."

Ellen, Wilson saw, was far from Mother's thoughts but, watching her sister, she decided Mother must surely guess. Ellen was quite transformed and came in from seeing Albert flushed and defiant and triumphant. She was not a pretty young woman but she had suddenly taken on a glow that made her attractive. She acted as though she had won some coveted prize and the victory intoxicated her. It maddened Wilson but she was at the same time fascinated by Ellen's clear enjoyment of her carnal relationship with Albert. The mere thought of Ellen and Albert coupling made her nauseous but, if it could make Ellen so happy and lively, then it could not be the thing of horror she had always imagined, something to be endured for the sake of love and marital duty or the procreation of children. She would rather have died than ask Ellen what it was like but when, at night, Ellen boasted of how she felt, her sister did not silence her. "The minute he touches me," Ellen murmured, "I am on fire and pulling him to me and I can hardly bear the time it takes to loosen our clothes and feel each other and then when we are joined and he is thrusting and thrusting it is never hard enough and I feel I might burst with all the running toward him in me until I catch him and then I leave this world, I do, I leave it and know not where I am." Wilson turned on her side, away from Ellen. "Oh, it is sweet, Lily, and exciting, and I don't care who knows it, I can think of nothing else."

On her return, when Miss Elizabeth asked how her mother was and then, naming each one, her sisters, Wilson found to her fury that she blushed as Ellen was mentioned. Her mistress smiled and looked inquiring. "Is there some news about Ellen?" she asked. "Are we to hear wedding bells?"

"In a year, miss. She thinks."

"Then it is not settled?"

"She says it is settled."

"But you do not believe her?"

"A year is a long time and the man in question is—"

"You falter, Wilson. Out with it, is what? Untrustworthy?"

"I do not know, but I met him and I cannot say as I would trust him, no."

"Ah, but you are out of the ordinary run, dear. Perhaps your sister Ellen lacks your discernment."

"Perhaps she does," said Wilson a little bitterly.

Leaving Mother had been hard, even harder than before, now that she felt guilty about her own desire to go, which she had to struggle to hide, and guilty too because she could not pretend that Ellen was an adequate substitute for herself. Ellen was selfish, her head filled, on her own admission, with thoughts of Albert and nothing else. All her free time was spent with him, leaving May to help Mother with Fanny, who was not well at the time Wilson left. Her mother said nothing to make her think she was worried but she read in her eyes a sorrow and even a fear that had not been there before. Some of this Wilson tried to tell Miss Elizabeth, who was sympathetic but inclined to wander off into predictable memories of her own mother which ended in a certain tearfulness. "Mothers are our best friends," Miss Elizabeth murmured. Wilson, paying lip service to this, thought how in her case it was no longer true. Lizzie had become the nearest thing she had ever had to a best friend, one to whom she could talk about Ellen and her distress about Timothy Wright.

Mr. Kenyon, it seemed, had been back in London two months and Timothy with him. When first she heard this, Wilson felt a great rush of excitement and began immediately looking out for the post as eagerly as did her mistress. Mr. Browning's letters arrived daily as usual, sometimes twice a day, but there was nothing from Timothy. Despondent, Wilson brought herself to believe he would call rather than write and took to grooming herself with extra care each afternoon and making sure everyone in the house knew she was in. But then, in a flash of inspiration so obvious that she laughed aloud, she realized that of course Timothy would expect to meet her in the park. When she said this to Lizzie, her friend looked grave. "Now, Lily," Lizzie said gently, "remember you sent him off, won't you? You promised nothing, only said you would think about it if he proved himself. Well, a man might get tired of that, for all your letters, if he got them. A man, on travels such as Timothy's, may see things differently. So you must be prepared, Lily, and not expect to start again where you left off."

Afterward Wilson was grateful for Lizzie's warning. If it had not been for her words, she had no doubt she would have made a fool of herself, and if there was one thing she could not bear to see publicly damaged, it was her pride. As it was, she was able to conduct herself admirably when one day toward the end of May she and Miss Elizabeth met Timothy Wright in Regent's Park with a young woman on his arm. Miss Elizabeth was walking at the time, holding on with one hand to the chair which Wilson pushed, though it was rarely used now. Timothy was coming straight toward them and, even if she had wished to avoid him, Wilson could not have done so. She gripped the chair handle tightly and arranged a smile on her face. As Timothy came abreast she blazed the smile in his direction and he nodded, his face a fiery red, and she nodded and they were past. Her mistress turned to say, "Is that not—" and then stopped. She put her hand tightly over Wilson's and squeezed it. "I think we will go home now, dear," she said, "I am tired after all." Once home and tea prepared, she said she felt she wanted to be alone for an hour and Wilson might go. No reference was made to Timothy.

As Wilson toiled up to her room feeling sick and numb, Molly called that there was a note come for her and that it was downstairs. Dully, Wilson trailed down and picked up the note, seeing at once who it was from. In her room, where the strong afternoon sun flooded in to mock her misery, she first lay down on the bed and wondered if she might cry. No tears came. Sighing, she contemplated Timothy Wright's note. Should she even open it? It would only add to her humiliation, she was sure, and yet she could not prevent herself. Slowly she drew the single sheet of paper out of its envelope. The information on it was minimal. Timothy said he was sorry not to have told her he was married but it had happened quickly and he had not had the opportunity to let her know. He had married a Mrs. Oliphant's maid in Rome in February by special license at the British Embassy. He had left Mr. Kenyon's employ and with his help was running a boardinghouse with his new wife, who was expecting, in Cheapside. He hoped she "would not feel bad" about it.

It was that last phrase which helped her recover. Contempt braced her and she took up her pen in a rush of furious energy and wrote:

Dear Mr. Wright

I thank you for your note which indeed it was not necessary for you to send since I had no claim on you nor you on me as I know of. My good wishes to you and your wife.

Yours faithfully,

Elizabeth Wilson.

She took the note out immediately and ran with it to the post box and dropped it through as though it were a live coal. There. That was at an end, and she had been right all along. Love, he had called it, and here he was no better than Ellen's Albert. Mrs. Oliphant's maid, whoever she might be, had provided what he wanted and long might they rot in their boardinghouse. So much for fine ideas of being a printer. How clever she had been to see that as a ploy. Printer indeed. If she had gone along with him, it would be her now, toiling away in a boardinghouse and expecting a child. But there was no pleasure in her self-righteousness and she was too honest to falsify the record even to herself. For another hour she lay on her bed, going over what had happened and castigating herself too. She might have had a proper understanding with Timothy and, once committed, she knew he would not have let her down. She had asked too much, been too honest, given him too little encouragement and not enough hope. She had only herself to blame and even now did not dare reckon how much. Perhaps, after all, she had done the right thing, perhaps she had never loved Timothy and that slow growth of feeling she had felt when he went away had been mere loneliness. She had never felt that lurch of the stomach Ellen spoke of or any leap of the heart. Maybe she never would and must settle for a Timothy in the future.

She moped and slept badly and feared Miss Elizabeth would worry about her and seek to find out what was wrong, which she dreaded, but there was neither comment nor interrogation. As the sun shone brilliantly throughout June, Miss Elizabeth grew happier and happier and more oblivious to all around her. Everything was touched by her happiness, and if Wilson had not been so despondent she would have laughed to observe the more absurd aspects of this transformation. Miss Elizabeth waxed ecstatic over a quite ordinary patch of grass in the park, plucking handfuls of it and smelling it and throwing it over herself, declaring it was nature's most ordinary but most wonderful bounty. She looked out of the carriage window—for they went for many a ride now—and exclaimed in rapture at the lights in the shopwindows, swearing she was in fairyland all at once. At first Wilson was irritated but then her mistress's delight, if ridiculous, was infectious and she smiled in spite of herself and Flush barked and the three of them hugged each other. Such joy found its own response and as the glorious summer continued Wilson found herself comforted and cheered by it until she was nearly her old self again.

Only then, toward the end of July, did Miss Elizabeth speak of noticing her depression. They visited Mr. Kenyon before he went to the Isle of Wight and Timothy came to mind as they entered the house. A new footman showed them up to the drawing room and then out again at the end of the visit, and once they were in the carriage Miss Elizabeth said, "I hope no unhappy memories were revived in that house, Wilson."

"Indeed no, miss, none at all," Wilson said cheerfully, though she had expected to feel a pang or two of regret.

"I hear the boardinghouse is in trouble," Miss Elizabeth said, prefacing her statement with no reference to Timothy. "Mr. Kenyon does not expect to recoup his investment."

"I am sorry for that."

"When the child comes it will be even harder for them."

"It is always the way."

"So you were wise, Wilson. I should not like it to have been you struggling in a boardinghouse, weighed down with the child."

Wilson was silent for a while and then could not help saying, as mildly as possible, she hoped, "Lizzie Treherne is not pulled down, for all the second child. It does not always happen, ma'am."

"Oh, Crow," Miss Elizabeth said, "she works hard enough for ten."

"As I should have done, though I have no regrets."

"I am glad to hear it. It made me sorry, to see you suffer, dear, but now you have grown back into yourself and it is all over."

It was perhaps mild rebellion against the complacency with which this was said that made Wilson more open to interest than she would otherwise have been. Lately, Miss Elizabeth had taken to regular shopping and in one shop where she bought a pair of fur-lined boots, though outside the sun scorched the pavements, there was a most attentive young man who fitted the boots and dealt with the purchase—attentive to Wilson as well as to his client. He was smartly dressed and had an open countenance of such honesty that Wilson was much struck and he was respectful without being obsequious. "What a pleasant young man," Miss Elizabeth commented on leaving the shop. "We will go there again, Wilson, when I buy a lighter shoe." And they did, twice. Miss Elizabeth tried on the entire stock, it seemed, and finally bought a pair of the prettiest green kid slippers, which she said made her feel as vain as Henrietta. But the bow on one of them was a fraction loose and the young male assistant promised to have it attended to and then delivered to Wimpole Street. He delivered it himself. It was pure chance that Wilson was leaving the house with Flush as he did so and chance again, or so she thought, that he was walking in her direction (she did not admit to herself that, knowing where his shop lay, she changed her direction). He introduced himself most properly as Reginald Pomfret and in the brief five minutes they walked together managed to impart a great deal of information. His uncle owned the shop and, though a mere assistant at the moment, Reginald had been promised a partnership. He lived with his widowed mother out at Barnet and was a churchgoer. As they parted, he hoped they would meet again.

Wilson saw little chance of this. Wandering in the park, she reflected how impossible it was for a woman to make any kind of headway in this situation. If she went to the shoe shop on any pretext it would be seen through and her interest advertised, which would not do. Whom she met was entirely dictated by the life she led and always, always she had to wait for the first and even second move or sacrifice her dignity. Outsiders like Reginald Pomfret were beyond the pale, and she did not really care. But chance again brought him before her and with such speed she began to think it was "meant." The Hedleys once more descended on Wimpole Street for their daughter Arabella's wedding and after the bride-to-be had seen Ba's darling slippers nothing would satisfy her but that she should have a pair in white. Wilson took Mrs. Hedley and Arabella to the shop, where the charming Reginald sold them not only the slippers but two other pairs of shoes each. The resulting parcel was so large that Mrs. Hedley would not hear of it being taken in the carriage and, as Wilson wrote to her mother,

—positively ordered the assistant to carry it around without delay. I never thought shopping could be so tiring, and wished Miss Elizabeth had kept me with her, but she said I was to guide her aunt and cousin around the shops though believe me they need no guidance and I am the lost one. Mrs. Hedley said to me in the carriage that she knew her niece and could tell there was something afoot and doubtless I knew what but she would not demean herself by plaguing me to tell her. I said I did not know what she meant and needed no plaguing to say so. Well Mrs. Hedley said it is that poet and he means something to her and I shall have it out with her before I go. Miss Arabella Hedley had kept silent but then she said she felt sorry for her poor cousin and that it must be embarrassing to have such speculation when it was all so ridiculous. Ridiculous says her mother and why pray and Miss Arabella tosses her pretty head (she is very pretty) and says oh come now Mother for you know dear Ba is old and ill. Old, old repeats her mother very angrily, I'll thank you to watch your tongue, miss. Ba is only just forty and that is not old I hope and as for ill she has never looked less ill and I never did believe this illness was anything but unhappiness. Miss Arabella laughed and her mother was even angrier and bade her explain herself further and Miss Arabella said it was only that to talk of love and marriage, which was what her mother hinted at she knew and of Cousin Ba in the same breath was silly. It made her feel nauseous, she swore. Oh said her mother so you are the only person in the world entitled to talk of love are you and Miss Arabella colored and said she believed she never had talked of love and her mother said very quietly so that it was quite unpleasant then maybe you should, maybe you should, and maybe your cousin Ba knows something you do not and ought to and I will thank you to hold your peace. I wished I were not in that carriage for the next ten minutes so great was the hostility between them. I looked out of the window, remembering how scornful my mistress is of this marriage and how she told me she feared her cousin Arabella would regret it though she might never admit it because she could see no sign of her being in love. Then all was forgotten in the buying of lace for the wedding dress which took hours and hours and cost more than I earn in five years Mother though I do not wish to sound complaining—

Wilson and Miss Elizabeth had many a discussion about the wedding of Arabella Hedley and Mr. James Johnstone Bevan, whom she was to marry on August 4, both of them scandalized at the price not just of the wedding gown, which, as Wilson had told her mother, cost forty guineas merely for the lace trimming, but of the six dress pocket handkerchiefs at four guineas each and the reception for fifty people estimated at £1000. Henrietta, coming in when they were deep in scorn of such ostentatious show, was cross with them. She flared up and accused her sister of being a spoilsport.

Wilson noted that her mistress was unrepentant. She even smiled at Henrietta's noisy exit. "Henrietta hankers after the distinction herself," she murmured. "She would so love to be the center of attention for a while, as a bride must be. She cannot understand why this holds no attraction for me, indeed she does not believe I speak the truth. What would you say to a wedding, Wilson?"

"Yours, miss?"

"Oh no. Heavens, it was but a generalization."

"I enjoy a wedding, though I cannot say I have been to many and none of Miss Hedley's grandness."

"I shall not go to the church."

Wilson, even after two years, could not presume to ask why not but, as ever, her silence and the sudden, stiff resumption of whatever task on which she was engaged spoke volumes that were not lost on her mistress.

"It is not from pique or anything like it, you know, Wilson," she said. "It is that I could not bear the church. It would be too much for me. I should faint."

"Is a church so fearful, miss?"

"Not fearful so much as overwhelming. I could not trust myself to stand with others and hear the music and feel the emotion. It would be too much."

But the outings to shops continued. A warm cloak was bought and joined the fur-lined boots in the closet. "They will be warm for the winter," Miss Elizabeth said and Wilson risked rejoining, "I am glad you intend to go out this winter, miss, and not shut yourself up in here." This brought a smile she could not quite interpret, a roguish, ironic smile that demanded but did not get a reaction. Putting the new cloak away, Wilson found herself hoping all the nonsense about wintering abroad was not to be gone through again, only to end in nothing. Already, Mrs. Jameson had started urging another attempt and Wilson wished she would desist. It seemed Mrs. Jameson was offering to accompany Miss Elizabeth and that this was to be an inducement for her to proposition her father once more. It would be like her luck, Wilson reflected, if, after all, this was the autumn she was called upon to leave London just as it had become attractive once more.

She had walked out with Reginald Pomfret twice. He had been very correct and proper. One Sunday afternoon he had walked in Regent's Park with her for half an hour and another Sunday had met her out of chapel and accompanied her home. She quickly discovered he was very different from Timothy Wright, even allowing for the difference in station, which was not after all so very great. With Timothy, of course, there had been joint interests since he had worked within Wimpole Street. Wilson did not know what to talk about with Reginald. Certainly not about her mistress—it would have been quite improper to discuss her with someone like Reginald, who did not know her. But looking after Miss Elizabeth was very nearly her whole life: if she did not talk about her and the Barrett family, this left a great gap. Nor did Reginald seem interested, as Timothy had been, in current affairs. Because Miss Elizabeth had been discussing them, Wilson threw out a rather grand reference to the revised Corn

Laws but Reginald hardly seemed to know what she was talking about. She wondered if perhaps he was not rather ignorant, then rebuked herself for putting on airs. Reginald was pleasant and easy and it was a relief to have someone with whom to walk. She was also obliged to admit that he was attractive, far more attractive, more of the gentleman, than Timothy. Her stomach still did not lurch but she did experience a surprising sense of pleasure when he took her arm to guide her across the street and, though she did not know how the image had come into her head, she had a momentary vision of being kissed by Reginald and enjoying it. He was so clean-looking in his smart coat and highly polished boots and he had such faultless manners that all her innate caution began to weaken. When he asked her to the theater one evening in late August she did not even think about refusing and was taken aback when Miss Elizabeth did not seem pleased. She would rather not have mentioned her invitation at all but since she needed to leave the house as soon as her mistress had dined, and was in effect asking for an evening off, there was no way around this.

"Oh, so you have another follower, Wilson," Miss Elizabeth said, with an edge of coldness to her tone. "I hope he is respectable."

"As I am, miss," Wilson said quietly.

"I did not mean to offend you, Wilson."

"I am not offended, miss."

"Good. You may of course go and I hope you enjoy the play, though it is not one I would wish to see."

"Thank you, miss."

Thank you, but some of the anticipation had gone. It seemed to her unfair that Miss Elizabeth should resent any attention being paid to her maid. Why, Wilson thought, cannot she be glad for me? It took Lizzie Treherne to enlighten her. "Why, Lily? Because she needs you too much, goose. She is jealous and don't ever forget it." But what, Wilson wondered, was there to be jealous of? There was nothing there, nothing to make anyone jealous, no intimacy whatsoever between herself and Reginald Pomfret. He seemed to like to squire her about and even to spend money on her, which, deducing he could not have much, she thought generous; but they made no headway at all.

Conversation between them, wherever they were, continued to be extremely limited and yet this lack of discourse was not due to shyness. The truth was that Reginald was not a talking man. He spoke when there was something to say and had no love of talk for its own sake. As I now have, Wilson thought. It was Miss Elizabeth's fault. She had been brought out of her simple yeses and noes and had grown used to fulsome explanations. She could not be doing with Reginald's pleasantries and little else. Yet, knowing this, she still allowed him to walk out with her and knew he would presume she must feel some affection for him. There was little affection and what there was waned rather than grew, but he did not seem to be aware of this. Instead, he began to talk of taking her home to meet his mother and to intimate that he considered their walking out would soon be put on a different footing, which alarmed her. She had the feeling he might soon propose and was overcome with embarrassment at the prospect, knowing he did not love her nor she him. It was Miss Elizabeth's fault again. She now looked for love and that was ridiculous. Reginald was a good match and she ought to accept him. He could give her security, unlike Timothy, and was that not the most important thing a suitor could offer? Observing her mistress and Mr. Browning, she wondered.

All thoughts of Reginald Pomfret were banished the next day when Flush was stolen yet again and her mistress's hysteria brought Wilson out of her state of reverie. The two sisters, Miss Elizabeth and Miss Arabel, had taken the little dog shopping with them—which Wilson had thought very foolish but, since it freed her for the afternoon, had said nothing. Flush disappeared between shop and carriage and Mr. Henry was sent to negotiate with the Fancy immediately. Unfortunately, Taylor, the head of the Fancy, chose to come and make his demands in person and was thrown out by Mr. Barrett, who loudly forbade anyone to pay the ransom for the dog. Once he had done so, not a brother could be found who would defy him. "Very well," Miss Elizabeth said, "we will go to Taylor ourselves, Wilson. *We* are not so cowardly."

Writing late that night to her mother, Wilson vowed:

—my heart has still not ceased pounding Mother for I admit I was half terrified and did all I could to dissuade my mistress from venturing into Shoreditch this being a most disreputable district worse than Pandon, worse than any Newcastle has to offer. But she would not be held back and there was nothing to do but go with her and try to hold her back from any foolishness. She had the idea, Mother, that because she is a lady she would be treated as such which only proves her innocence of the world. The moment we had left respectability behind and had entered on dark and narrow streets I did not know, like the worst chares at Butchers Brook, I was afraid of what would happen should she seek to alight from the carriage in her finery knowing it was quite likely she could be spat upon and even have her shawl snatched. She said I talked nonsense but when the cab driver lost his way she had taken heed enough of my words to send him to ask at a public house where Taylor lodged. While he was gone we were alone and quite unprotected but she would not let me close the curtains and therefore as I expected we were soon peered in upon and a crowd of rough people gathered. Give us a shilling, missus one old crone begged and even stretching in her hand which was all scabby touched my mistress's sleeve and I saw she would have her bracelet off in a trice so I said right sharply hold off there or there will be trouble for you which caused horrid laughter but at that moment our cabman returned and we continued. You were savage to that poor woman Wilson my mistress says reproach-fully and I could have given her sixpence at least to buy bread for her children. Bread says I she would buy no bread but gin you can be sure and moreover the moment she was given so much as a farthing the rest would be upon us and no hope but we would have been overwhelmed. She was not inclined to believe me but by then we were deep into Shoreditch and arrived at Taylor's home. Our carriage had difficulty getting down his alley being crowded with filthy urchins fighting and rolling on the ground and we all but ran over several. Once we halted the carriage was surrounded and almost rocked by the press of people attracted to it. Two pretty ones someone shouts and another asks who shall pluck them for they will be tasty morsels which bit of wit earned screams of joy. I do not know that Miss Elizabeth heard half of the swearing which followed but Mother I hope not. Taylor being out his wife if such she is which I doubt came from the building and my mistress made to get out to greet her saying she did not wish to be thought superior. I on the other hand locked the door, praying it would hold and urged her to forget thoughts of offending and talk through the window. This Mrs. Taylor was huge, like a washerwoman, with greasy hair and a rank smell coming off her which if we had been closer would have overpowered us but she was willing enough to be civil and said she would tell her husband we had called and had the money for the dog. Then she said all insolent would we not step down and take a dish of tea which impertinence produced ribald laughter. At last we were on our way home and my mistress took me to task for my fears saying these people were more to be pitied and that I ought to sympathize with their poverty which was not their fault. I told her I had no need of instruction on poverty having seen plenty of it and that she was mistaken if she judged poverty made savages of us all. Then she was quiet and we spoke no more. Taylor turned up at the house again and after another altercation, this time with Mr. Alfred, we had Flush back eventually and my mistress is excited rather than otherwise by her adventure talking of nothing else.

Wilson, on the contrary, was depressed. Shoreditch seemed to her a terrible warning of what lay beneath her, of what she might have come to if she had not, under Mother's guidance, made something of herself. To her mistress, it was another world far removed from her own, but to Wilson it was the nightmare always at the back of her mind. She shivered at the memory of those ravaged faces which had peered into the carriage and Reginald Pomfret seemed more attractive than she had ever thought him. Marry Reginald and she would be respectable, respectable and safe and far removed from Shoreditch.

CHAPTER THIRTEEN

WILSON KNEW as soon as she began to descend the stairs at six o'clock in the morning that something was up. She saw Tilly ahead of her, coming out of the drawing room with the ashes, and her air of excitement was unmistakable. She looked up eagerly at Wilson, mouthing, "Have you heard?" and when Wilson composed her face into an expression of aloofness—she never encouraged or indulged in gossip—would not be put off. She clutched Wilson's arm as she passed the turn in the stairs and said, "The master is closing the house up and sending nearly all of us to the country."

She heard the same startling news when she went into her mistress's room, to find her at her desk scribbling away.

"Wilson, have you heard? George has been sent to find a house in the country."

"Yes, miss, I have heard."

"Then you will understand my alarm. The moment I finish this note you must take it yourself and post it so that it will reach Mr. Browning this afternoon."

"Yes, miss." Of course, thought Wilson as she put the cup of coffee down in front of her mistress, if they went to the country, then no more Tuesday visits, and even daily letters might present difficulties. Quietly, as Miss Elizabeth wrote furiously, the paper screened by her disheveled hair, Wilson stripped the covers from the sofa that was really a bed and began throwing them over chairs to air. She had hardly finished before her mistress was pressing an envelope into her hand. "There, Wilson, go now, if you please, without delay, and you will catch the first post." Looking at her, startled at such urgency, Wilson saw how bright her face was, how alive and strong. If the news of going to the country had appalled her, it was not horror that showed but rather the same sort of excitement Tilly had exhibited. It intrigued her. As she left the house a few minutes later to post the letter to Mr. Browning, she pondered the significance of such animation. How could Miss Elizabeth greet such news in that kind of way, almost as though she relished it? Surely the country meant no Mr. Browning, and yet Mr. Browning was the only person about whom she seemed to care. By that evening, when she was writing to her mother, Wilson had suspicions impossible to voice but which it was a relief to put on paper:

—she does not seem to think she will go to the country Mother for all her father has been and told her so and very grim about it too. I was quite frightened by his expression, for he commanded me to stay and I was embarrassed to witness what followed. His tone was abrupt and his countenance stern when he addressed Miss Elizabeth and I could not help but think he was holding himself rigid as I have seen him do before and struggling for composure and it was this bearing that was remarkable more than what he said which was only what we already knew that the house needed decorating and must be emptied directly. Miss Elizabeth was perfectly cool and said she understood and she thanked her father and said she hoped he would be able to enjoy some of the country air from which he had just hoped she would benefit. Afterward when he had taken his leave she said to me that she could not think what ailed her father but that there was more to this sudden edict than decorating the house and she wondered what it was. I longed to ask her why she was not distraught but of course could not. After Mr. Browning's reply had come by the evening post she was even livelier and smiled and kissed the letter and took deep breaths. I was bold and asked if Mr. Browning was not very, very disappointed to hear we were off to the country and she laughed such a strange false laugh and said no Mr. Browning is not disappointed, on the contrary he thinks it is time I left London. I said nothing but felt uncomfortable. All day I felt as if something was brewing but could not guess what other than the proposed exodus—

Watching her mistress closely, Wilson waited for the inevitable reaction to set in, for despair at the thought of being banished to the country to overcome her, but her mood of high good humor continued. Her brothers and sisters were all out, at a picnic near Richmond —the very word caused Wilson to smile sadly at the memory of herself and Timothy—and, most unusually, Mr. Browning was to call, although he had already been on Tuesday and this was a Friday, a day he never visited.

Letting him in, Wilson was struck at once by his eagerness. He always was eager, always did look bright and lively, and was in the habit of climbing the stairs quickly, but that day he positively rushed, so much so that by the turn of the stair he was ahead of Wilson and when he reached Miss Elizabeth's door had to wait for her to catch up. She looked askance at him and he smiled and begged her pardon and at the sound of his voice the door flew open and Miss Elizabeth stood there. Wilson distinctly heard him say, "Oh, my love!" as her mistress said, "My own!" and then he was in the room and the door closed all in a flash. She knew without any doubt that they were in each other's arms and the realization stunned her. She went slowly downstairs, thinking how stupid she had been. All the signs had been there and, though she had recognized them, she had not made them into anything significant. What she had known was that Mr. Browning cared for Miss Elizabeth and Miss Elizabeth cared for Mr. Browning but what she had not reckoned on was that this caring could ever come to anything.

By the time Mr. Browning left, Wilson had come to the conclusion that he could only have come on a Friday and in the state he was if he had urgent reasons for doing so. What could these be? Was he thinking of asking for Miss Elizabeth's hand? The very thought made her tremble and feel faint—what a scene there would surely be. But when she went in to her mistress with the tea things she found her so happy and even relaxed that she could not believe such drama was in the offing. She put the tray down carefully and suddenly felt Miss Elizabeth's fingers around her wrist.

"Wilson, you care for me, dear, do you not?"

"Why, yes, miss, I believe you know I do."

"And you would see me happy. Would you not?"

"Indeed yes."

"Well, I may be about to be very happy indeed, if only I can find the courage and I believe I can."

"I am glad, miss."

"But I will need your help, dear, when the time comes and I will ask a great deal of you and you must be prepared. Can you guess, Wilson?" Wilson, her wrist still imprisoned by the cool, slim fingers, hesitated. It was precisely the kind of invitation she dreaded. So many mistakes could be made and, once made, would be impossible to retrieve.

"I have an idea," she said slowly, "but I hardly think I can be right."

"Tell me your idea."

"Indeed I dare not, it is too fantastical."

Miss Elizabeth laughed and released her wrist. "Then you have almost certainly guessed, Wilson, for I grant you it is fantastical and will be called so and not believed till proved and we will say no more."

But when it came to bedtime Wilson observed that the pleasant ease which had seemed to overcome her mistress after Mr. Browning's visit had been replaced by a general agitation so marked that she automatically measured out a double dose of laudanum without being asked to do so. "Here, miss, take this draught which I have made strong and calm yourself, do, or you will not sleep tonight."

"I will not sleep in any case, I could not, but I will not take the laudanum, Wilson, for fear it numbs my brain and renders me too feeble to act. Oh, Wilson, come, come, sit down, dear, sit near me and hold me."

Alarmed, Wilson sat on the sofa and put her arm around her mistress's shoulder. "Why, miss, you tremble so, what is it? What troubles you?"

"Wilson, nothing troubles me except fear, fear of myself, fear that I will prove a coward tomorrow when so much is to be asked of me." Her voice dropped to such a low whisper that Wilson had to bend so close that her cheek almost touched her mistress's. She could feel the heat that came from it and tendrils of hair brushed her own skin, making her shiver. "Wilson, tomorrow I am to be married to Mr. Browning at Marylebone parish church." It was said in a rush, all on one note, quite expressionlessly, but once the news was out, she seemed to give a great gasp and then she laughed, half hysterically, and clutched Wilson to her and rocked her. Then she pushed her away and scrutinized her face. "Why, Wilson, you look as if you have seen a ghost. Had you not guessed after all?"

"No, miss," Wilson managed to stammer, "not that it was to be done secretly, so sudden like and without the master's—" A hand came swiftly over her mouth and her mistress's expression changed to one of alarm. "Do not say his name, do not mention it to me, do not tell me it is a terrible and dangerous thing I do, for I know it and cannot help it and it must be so." Silent, Wilson watched her. The room, lit only by one bedside candle, was full of shadows. The busts of the poets loomed enormously above her head and by the dying light of the fire she could see her mistress's great eyes reflecting the candlelight. Flush, crouched at her feet, whimpered and Wilson picked him up and stroked him. Her head was full of practicalities but she could not bring herself to deal with them. Miss Elizabeth sighed and lay back. "I will not sleep but leave me now, dear, and in the morning come in early."

Wilson stood up, holding Flush. She felt unable to leave. Her mistress looked so forlorn, lying there in her white shift like a child. She blew out the candle but still did not leave and again Flush let out the smallest of sounds. "Good night, miss," Wilson said, her voice strangely rough and uncertain, "good night and God bless."

She did not sleep herself. All night she shifted in her bed restlessly, obsessed with questions to which there was no answer and all of them trivial. What should she put out for Miss Elizabeth to wear on her wedding day? She could not wear black, surely she was not thinking of it, but then if she did not wear black what was there in readiness for her to wear? The green, the green silk? But although quite recently purchased it would need letting out, now that she had put on some weight, and the last time she had worn it she had complained that the trimming was shabby and needed renewing. Was there time to renew it? Could she dash out to Oxford Street and find a matching trim and have it back and sewn on before the wedding? But there would be so many other things to do, it did not bear thinking about. And how would she want her hair dressed? In ringlets? But the ringlets only took well if her hair was freshly washed and if it was washed it took hours to dry and she never went out after washing her hair. Perhaps she would just twist it back and wear a bonnet. Of course she would wear a bonnet but she had no bonnet suitable to be married in. At the thought of how shabby Miss Elizabeth's bonnets were, Wilson had to get up. She paced the floor, clutching herself, almost weeping at her mental picture of this pathetic bride, and feeling it to be her fault. If only she had had more notice, if only a day's more, she could have worked wonders but now, now, it was too late. Cautiously, Wilson opened the window and leaned out. The cool night air calmed her. She closed her eyes and thought how foolish she was being when there were so many more important matters to be decided. How would they leave the house? They could pretend to go for a walk, she supposed. But everyone knew they would never go for a walk without Flush and if they took Flush what would they do with him at the church? No, they could not take Flush. So it would be better if they acted as though they were going to visit someone. But who? Had Miss Elizabeth thought of whom they might say they were visiting? She visited so few people apart from her old teacher, Mr. Boyd, and Miss Trepsack.

Just before dawn Wilson fell into a light doze, which did her more harm than good. She woke at six o'clock with a blinding headache and a feeling of nausea. Dressing herself, she felt stiff and awkward and wondered at first if she were ill. Grimly doing up her boots, she scolded herself for such feebleness. She must be strong for Miss Elizabeth's sake. Taking the coffee, she was not surprised to find her mistress in tears. So great was her compassion that she needed no bidding to embrace her, knowing exactly how she felt, what she had been through during the night. She wept in Wilson's arms and then smiled and murmured that today of all days she must not bear the marks of tears on her face. Then she managed to stop and to raise herself up and begin her toilet. After she had drunk the coffee she appeared restored and was able to answer Wilson's many queries.

They would leave the house a little after eleven, as though going for a walk, and Mr. Browning would be waiting with his cousin at the church. Afterward—her voice faltered as she said the word—afterward they would take a carriage to St. John's Wood where her friend Mr. Boyd lived. Then Wilson would return to Wimpole Street and Miss Elizabeth would rest at Mr. Boyd's until Henrietta and Arabel came to fetch her home in the afternoon. All this was imparted in a breathless monotone, hard for Wilson to catch. When it was finished, there was a pause. Miss Elizabeth closed her eyes and lay back on the sofa bed, as though exhausted by the recital, and Wilson stood transfixed beside the table. It was the mention of the hour which had rendered her almost incapable of speech—eleven o'clock, barely four hours away, and so much to be done. She let out a groan at the hopelessness of performing any kind of miracle with costume or appearance, whereupon her mistress's eyes flew open and she asked what was the matter. "You will not fail me, Wilson?" she asked, sitting up and throwing off the covers and holding out her hands beseechingly.

"Why, no miss, but eleven in the morning—it is so soon, I thought it would not be until the afternoon—and so much to be done."

"So little, dear," Miss Elizabeth said gently. "It is not a case like my cousin Arabella's. I shall put on a clean dress and that will suffice."

"But which dress, miss?" Wilson almost wailed.

"Whichever you say. I am happy to be in your hands."

For an hour Wilson was entirely preoccupied in choosing a dress and doing what she could with it. The green silk was the only possible choice but, as she had suspected, it was too tight at the waist and the white lace trim at the neck was dingy. Rapidly Wilson opened the seams at either side—fortunately she had made them generous in the first place—and then stitched them back up, praying that there was just enough material to hold. There was. Next she cut away the lace entirely and transferred another collar from one of the black velvet dresses, doing it so well that the new collar looked as though it had always been part of that dress. Throughout this frenzied sewing, Miss Elizabeth read. Neither she nor Wilson spoke. Flush trotted around the room sniffing and scuttling and, as both looked up at the same time to watch him, Wilson and her mistress smiled at each other tremulously.

At nine-thirty the bride began to dress, still professing lack of interest in what she was to wear, but when Wilson put out a taffeta petticoat it was firmly discarded in favor of a fine lawn one "because taffeta will rustle in the church." They both froze when the green silk dress only just slipped on and Henrietta came into the room and exclaimed at how grand her sister was looking this morning. "Quite dressed up, Ba," she remarked "and where are you going?" Wilson, who was at that moment doing up the side-seam fasteners, could feel Miss Elizabeth's heart pounding though outwardly, even to the trained eye, she appeared cool. "To see Mr. Boyd," she said, "and Wilson thought I ought to get out of black more, even though it is hardly worth it for a blind man." Henrietta seemed satisfied with this explanation. She stayed awhile longer, complaining how dull life seemed now the picnic was over. When she had taken herself off Wilson thought it permissible for her to ask, "Miss Henrietta does not know then, miss? Nor Miss Arabel either?"

"Indeed no, and they must not, they must not be part of it. Only you know, Wilson. I can trust no one else nor implicate them for fear they suffer if all is discovered. As it must be, sometime." She shivered and said she thought the silk dress not warm enough and that she needed a shawl.

From nine-thirty to eleven seemed an eternity. Miss Elizabeth sat not on her sofa but near the window on a straight-backed chair, motionless. Her coat lay in front of the fire, warming. Wilson, ready in her own coat, hovered near her, wishing she could think of something to say. Later, looking back on the day, she wrote to her mother that

—it was a solemn hour, Mother, between ten and eleven for can you imagine my feelings as I was obliged to watch this poor creature suffer so? She was white, so white, whiter than I had ever seen her and held herself as though she might snap if touched. At eleven o'clock she stood up and said it is time and we must go and we left her room with a backward look at Flush who had been told he was not to come and consoled with a cake bought specially for the purpose. Now Wilson says Miss Elizabeth if we meet anyone I rely on you to address them for I do not trust myself to speak. We got to the bottom of the stairs and were about to cross the hall when the master's door opened and I thought my mistress would surely collapse with fright but it was only Tilly finished doing the brass fender and we were out of the house without difficulty. At first Miss Elizabeth seemed revived by the air but then after we had gone a few yards along the street she clutched my arm harder and I felt her weight increase on me and I knew the worst had happened and she was about to faint so I began talking to her, all manner of nonsense about weather and flowers and anything that came into my head and all the time I was steadying her and encouraging her along until we reached the corner where there is a chemist. I go there regularly for the laudanum and the man knows me and indeed saw through his window that we were in difficulties and had left his counter before we reached the door and had a chair ready. Miss Elizabeth sank down onto it and I saw her lips were blue. I spoke quickly saying I was sure a whiff of sal volatile would be sufficient to bring my mistress to herself and if that did not work then I would indeed go for help so the chemist brought us sal volatile and I pressed the salts to my poor mistress's nose and she took a deep breath and straightway some color returned and she pronounced herself better. We made our way from the shop, Miss Elizabeth walking stronger. But no sooner were we in Marylebone High Street than the attack comes on again and she says Wilson I think I am done for. I could see the fly stand only a few yards down the street and I raised my arm and one of the cab drivers sitting on his box mercifully saw me and brought his cab to us and helped Miss Elizabeth in and took us the short distance to the church. The moment the cab stopped I saw Mr. Browning on the steps of the church with another gentleman and I said to my mistress who was lying back against the cushions with her eyes closed why miss there is Mr. Browning waiting for you and Mother you never saw such a transformation. Mr. Browning ran down the steps and she gave her hand into his and from that moment I had no fears Mother. She smiled and looked up at him so trustingly and her eyes shone. We went into the church, which was empty as you would expect on a Saturday morning and we seemed very small in it and every sound we made echoed. I stood with Mr. Silverthorne, Mr. Browning's cousin, who was the other witness. The minister read the marriage service in a low voice, so low that even though I stood directly behind Miss Elizabeth I had difficulty hearing it. Her response was very faint though she swore afterward she had never shouted so gladly in her life but his was loud and clear and seemed to boom and echo around the church. Then it was deathly quiet while the ring was put on Miss Elizabeth's finger and she became all at once Mrs. Browning. When it was done and she turned to walk back down the aisle there were tears in her eyes but she smiled too and it was like sun and showers together. I did not know whether it was fitting for me to embrace her in public but she stepped forward and hugged me and Mr. Browning took my hand and looked very directly into my eyes and thanked me for my part in all this and said he would never forget, never, and that if it were not for knowing his wife were in my hands he could not allow her to leave his sight. Well Mother I was in a fair way to being overcome again but rallied and we went out and Mr. Browning hailed two cabs and put his wife and myself into one and himself and his cousin into another and we went our separate ways. We went to St. John's Wood to Mr. Boyd's house and on the way my mistress took off her ring and held it in the palm of her hand where the diamond glittered and said it grieved her to

remove it but she must. At Mr. Boyd's house the cab was kept
waiting while I took Mrs. Browning in and made her comfortable
for suddenly all energy had gone again and she was trembling
with fatigue. The housekeeper promised to see that she ate some
bread and butter and drank some water and on that understanding
I left. The cab took me back to Wimpole Street but not to our
house it being agreed previously that it would look odd if I
returned alone. I got out at the top of the street and walked
straight away through the park to Lizzie's where I had a bite to
eat and played with little Mary. Miss Elizabeth, I mean Mrs.
Browning, had made me swear I would tell no one so I could not
tell Lizzie and it was agony to stay silent when I burst to tell—

At three o'clock, when Wilson entered the house and began
writing this letter to her mother, she thought what a relief it would be
to share her knowledge with Miss Henrietta and Miss Arabel at least
but the new Mrs. Browning had been adamant that they were not to
know even now. How such an event was to be concealed she could
not imagine—one look at their sister and surely they would guess.
But no. If they guessed, they did not admit it. Both seemed grave
when they returned with their sister (who, Wilson thought, was far
too suspiciously lively and talkative) but nothing was said. It appeared Arabel had forgotten what Miss Elizabeth had said and had
been alarmed to find Flush on his own and had even said she had
wondered if—but she was cut off sharply.

When they were alone together that evening, Mrs. Browning
sank back onto her sofa totally exhausted. "Oh, Wilson," she whispered, "what a day, what a day. I am more dead than alive." She
pressed a hand to her forehead and sighed and Wilson hurried to
prepare the tincture of laudanum.

"Now, ma'am, tonight you will surely take this draft, for I fear the
worst if you have another night like last night."

"Oh, indeed I will and I would hope to sleep for a week until this
nightmare separation is over."

"You will feel differently, ma'am, when Mr. Browning comes on
Tuesday."

"He will not come, not at all. My husband refuses to demean himself by disclaiming our new status, and besides, it would be too dangerous. It is better we do not see each other until—" She stopped. She opened her eyes and sat up and motioned to Wilson to sit down beside her and took both her hands as she always did when she had something of importance to say. "Wilson, I have not told all, not yet finished asking far too much of you. Soon, as soon as it can be arranged, within the week, I fancy, Mr. Browning and I are going to Italy and, dear, we beg you to accompany us. Will you? Will you stay faithful and true? Will you leave your family and your country to risk all with us?"

Wilson took a deep breath. She seemed to see Reginald receding in a mist but then he had been insubstantial in any case, more in the nature of a fantasy than a real thing, unlike Timothy. She felt no regret. And then to go to Italy, at last, was not the same as going with the Barretts to the country, which she had dreaded as a kind of banishment. Nor did thoughts of her mother and sisters hold her back as once they would have done, for she had felt remote from them for more than a year and the feeling had nothing to do with distance. So she nodded her head and said she would go and her mistress cried with relief and then laughed with delight and Flush barked distractedly, whereupon Mrs. Browning said he was to come too. Then she made Wilson promise again to tell no one, not even her mother in a letter, at which Wilson did demur respectfully, saying her mother would suffer such shock if not told until after her daughter had left the country. Mrs. Browning wept and said she was the cause of much suffering and she knew it and would be the cause of much more before she was done and it was dreadful, dreadful, but she had to ask for this sacrifice or all would be lost. So Wilson, with tears in her own eyes, agreed, and agreed too that she would not even post the letter about the marriage until they were ready to leave.

The following week was such a strain that Wilson was twice late in rising out of pure fatigue. Her head ached with all that was to be accomplished once the following Saturday was fixed for the day of departure and she was tempted to take laudanum herself. The only support she had was the certainty that Minnie Robinson knew and commended her. She knew because Miss Elizabeth had borrowed money from her, an occurrence so extraordinary it could not but indicate some dramatic cause. "She said it was to cover a temporary embarrassment," Minnie told Wilson, smiling strangely, "and I know what that is likely to be but I played my part and asked no questions and needed no assurances my savings would be returned to me in a short while, for I know they will and I know what will happen in that short while and was not born yesterday." She nodded energetically and then eyed Wilson challengingly. "So you are a close one, Wilson, saying nothing, eh? Well, it is as well you will not be here with the rest of us when the master finds out, God help him. He would have you through that door with no reference to follow in a trice and then where would you be, eh? Have you thought of that? Has she?" Wilson, who was washing lace collars at the time, made a great deal of noise with the water and avoided answering. "Well, she is a lucky one, having you, and I hope she knows it and I think she does. I want the poor love to be happy and you do right to help her, Wilson, even if you do not trust old Minnie enough to tell her how, eh? And wise too. I mean no offense, I know the risks and would rather be able to look the master in the eye and swear to God I knew nothing."

But since Minnie had guessed all, except the time and place and what had already happened, she was a valuable help. Caught carrying a box down the back stairs, Wilson blushed but Minnie only said, "Not that one, there's a stronger one in the second attic and I will have Simon up there this afternoon putting things away and it will be left by the back door as though to throw out." And it was, and Wilson transferred the clothing to it. Mrs. Browning had stressed they must travel light, only a box and a carpetbag between them, and then had produced books. Aghast, Wilson had found the courage to say that with four dresses, two pairs of boots, three chemises, a cloak and two bonnets, not to mention smaller items, there was not room for a single volume, no, not one. Mrs. Browning had bid her reduce the number of dresses and throw out the bonnets but Wilson had refused. She had said, in a show of anger, surprising herself, that perhaps her mistress would prefer her to go stark naked herself that she might have books to read, and then there had been an apology and tears of contrition and no more was said. But then, packing the dresses, Wilson had felt something solid in the folds and had opened out the thickest dress, which her mistress had folded herself, and there was a small volume of Mr. Browning's verse and inside a package, quite bulky, of papers, wrapped in oilskin. Annoyed, Wilson almost put them aside but then found a gap down the side of the box and slipped them in. But three other books, furtively concealed in the boots, she firmly removed and paraded in front of her mistress, telling her she needed that space for stockings and all manner of such small necessities. Shamefaced, Mrs. Browning took them back but when she said she would pack her carpetbag herself Wilson knew what would happen.

All the way through that terrible week, when the house was upside down in preparation for the exodus to the country, both Mrs. Browning and Wilson struggled to write letters. Always, there were tears at night from both of them, from Wilson just as much as her mistress, for now that she had come to the point of bidding farewell to her mother she was overcome with the enormity of the step she was taking. Such a panic rose in her as she returned to the letter she had begun on the wedding day that she was unable to see the paper clearly and, when eventually she had written down, in wild-looking writing, where she was going and why, she found herself incapable of composing a farewell. Who knew when she would see Mother again or poor Fanny? She would be across the sea from them, unable to go to them immediately should she be needed, perhaps not even knowing she was needed. This last thought almost brought her to the point of speaking out against going after all but then Minnie, finding her red-eyed as she came into the kitchen in the middle of the week, took her aside and was sympathetic, asking whether it was thoughts of her family which depressed her. When Wilson nodded, Minnie said she could be depended on to write and, if Wilson were to tell her mother to remember that Minnie Robinson would always find her, it might set her mind at rest a little. "I will know where you are," Minnie said, "because Miss Arabel will always know, once you are gone, and where she is I will be. And I will write to you, Wilson, you may depend on it." This proved such comfort that Wilson at last finished her letter. It lay for three days beside her bed and each time she looked at it, waking and before going to sleep, she shuddered, hardly knowing whether with fear or excitement. It was such a jump into the unknown. All safety, all security, would vanish. Her mistress would be her responsibility, however good her husband. And what of him, what if he were not good? What if her mistress were unhappy? To whom would they turn, in a foreign land? On those last three nights, Wilson succumbed and took a sleeping draught, unable to bear the strain any longer.

PART II

1846–1857

CHAPTER FOURTEEN

THE SEA was not rough but nor was it calm. The waves swelled without crashing into each other and the boat went with them, dipping and climbing in a smooth but ever changing motion which some of the passengers found soothing and others more upsetting to the stomach than a storm. Wilson was in a cabin with her mistress and twelve other ladies and maids, all with enamel bowls placed at their sides. When one vomited, as someone did even before they were out of the harbor, the mere sound set off the others and within the half hour not a bowl had remained unused.

There was no hope of sleep. Both she and her mistress had loosened their stays and made an attempt to compose themselves for sleep but the noise of those being violently ill and the moans of others, sure they were about to die, made such a luxury impossible. Every time Wilson looked at her charge she saw that, though her eyes were closed, tears seeped from underneath the lids and the very sight of them released her own. She pressed a handkerchief to her mouth and screwed up her face and cried as silently as she could, half from exhaustion and half from fear. What a day it had been, what a strange and terrifying day with so much that was new in it! Such excitement she had felt when they reached Vauxhall Station and boarded the shrieking train and then such exhilaration as it started and the countryside passed them on either side at what seemed a frightening speed; and there, in front of her, was this smiling creature lying protected in the arms of her husband. But then the mood had changed at Southampton. Only once had her mistress said, "By now, they will know all at home," but it had been enough. Mr. Browning had kissed her fingers gently and whispered soothing words which Wilson could not quite catch, but the glow had gone from his wife's face and the mouth drooped. They rested at an inn while Mr. Browning saw their luggage onto the boat, and tried and failed to secure a private cabin for them, but this rest was fatal. Mrs. Browning wept throughout and wondered aloud how she could have done what she had done and the violence of the weeping wore her out. Wilson had applied cloths rung out in cold water to her mistress's eyes but she was still bearing the marks of tears when they rejoined Mr. Browning. At once he insisted they should change their plans and stay overnight at the inn until his wife had recovered but she became distraught at the idea. She swore she would not be able to rest until across the sea. So they had boarded at once and now here they were halfway to France, suffering as much from sorrow as the sea.

Searching in her bag, Wilson found the tablets the apothecary had recommended for seasickness and took two more. She had tried to urge them on her mistress but they had been spurned when Wilson had been unable to say of what they were made. Mr. Browning, it seemed, disliked all medicines and had extracted a promise from his wife that she would take none without his knowledge. It was a pity, Wilson thought, for whatever was in them seemed to be doing some good. As well as suppressing nausea, they made her feel less agitated. She was lying on a pallet, side by side with Mrs. Browning, the wretched Flush cowering at their feet, asleep after a terrible bout of sickness. There were two storm lamps suspended from the low beam which ran from end to end of the cabin but these gave little light. All Wilson could make out were the shadows of the other women, most tossing and turning and every now and again half rising, and the wooden slats of the cabin walls. The portholes were closed, since it was night. She thought of her room in Wimpole Street and of how comfortable the bed was, how fond she had become of her own quarters. She would never see it again, most likely never be allowed into No. 50 Wimpole Street again. Inside that room she had left her own letters, already stamped, and in her note to Minnie had begged her to see they were posted. There was one for her mother, one for Lizzie Treherne, one for Reginald. She had pleaded with all of them to write to her, giving as an address the *poste restante* office in Orleans which her mistress had said would be best. She imagined Mother reading her news and letting out a great cry of shock, and for a moment she felt a flash of resentment toward the figure beside her, toward the person who had been responsible for such an act of cruelty. Why could she not have been allowed to warn poor Mother, who was hundreds of miles away and never likely to be near a Barrett or able to reveal the secret? She should have disobeyed and written to Mother a week ago, as she had intended. Then Mrs. Browning gave a sob, and felt for Wilson's hand, and instantly the resentment vanished. Holding hands, the two of them drifted, toward dawn, into a restless doze.

At Le Havre all was hopeless confusion. Wilson stood supporting her mistress, who was barely able to stand, while Mr. Browning struggled through the mob to secure a place in the diligence destined for Rouen and then Paris. The air was raw, slightly misty, though Wilson could tell that soon it would lift. All around the yelling and shouting increased in volume and not a word of it was distinguishable. Suddenly she felt isolated, in spite of Mrs. Browning's arm through hers, and wondered why the thought of not knowing a word of the language had not scared her till now. How would she shop? How would she make her way with other servants? How would she speak to chemists and doctors and those other people she might be obliged to communicate with on her mistress's behalf? She would be dependent on her for every syllable. But the sight of Mr. Browning pushing his way through the crowds restored her to her duty. He had taken a room in an inn and there they would rest for several hours. "If you take my wife's left arm, Wilson," Mr. Browning was saying, "and

I take the other, then we will manage. *Excusez-moi, s'il vous plaît . . .*" Slowly, Mr. Browning shouting out this phrase all the while, they pushed through the throng. It was strange being a three-some, stranger still not to be in charge. But she had more power than she knew. That evening, when they climbed into the diligence, she was touched when, half fainting, her mistress sank into her seat and, turning to her husband, assured him, "Wilson knows how to make me comfortable, Robert," and he stood aside humbly and begged her to arrange things. With the greatest satisfaction Wilson took the cushion Mr. Browning had attempted to prop behind his wife's head, pushing it instead into the small of her back. Then she took a rug and wrapped it adroitly around her mistress's knees and a shawl which she fastened around her neck and chest in such a way that it could not work loose. All this time Mrs. Browning smiled up at her trustingly and Mr. Browning watched intently and said he *thought* he saw how it was done.

It took an age before they were off and then the jolting was severe, worse than any coach Wilson had been in—she saw her mistress's forehead crease with pain and immediately Mr. Browning was distraught, and sprang up and appealed to Wilson to think of some way of protecting his poor, fragile wife from being bruised to death. "Perhaps, sir," Wilson said, "I can cradle my mistress in my arms and that way save some of her limbs from a buffeting," and she got up, putting Flush down, to set about doing this. But Mr. Browning had seized her idea for himself and had half lifted his wife onto his knee so that only her legs lay on the seat. "Oh, Robert, how comfortable I am now," she murmured. Wilson smiled to see his look of pride and tenderness. She readjusted the rug and then sat back, closing her eyes, but seeing from beneath the only partly closed lids the sweetness of the picture before her. Heaven knew, Mr. Browning was no strong, powerful man but he looked convincingly protective and his wife was so very small that a man would have had to be a real dwarf not to appear huge beside her. She saw how his hand caressed her cheek and his arm tightened around her breast and her own heart beat a little faster. Here was a bride who had not yet truly been claimed by her bridegroom and, though she despised herself for such thoughts and would have been disgusted and outraged if anyone else had voiced them, Wilson could not help speculating with some sense of alarm on the consummation that was soon to follow. It had never, of course, been spoken of, but she could sense no apprehension in her mistress. "I want to be with my husband heart and soul and body," she had said last week, and her voice had strengthened rather than faltered on that last word.

The diligence stopped at Rouen, where Mr. Browning carried his wife into the inn, Wilson following with Flush. She noticed people staring at her mistress, whose body seemed to hang lifeless from her husband's arms. Though no one knew it, her eyes were closed through embarrassment, not unconsciousness, and as soon as they were alone she opened them and laughed to think what a picture Robert had made. She drank some coffee, making a face and saying it was not nearly as good as the coffee Wilson made, and ate some bread and Mr. Browning was pleased. The ride from Rouen to Paris was completed in the dark. "Look at the stars, Wilson," Mrs. Browning whispered and Wilson peered out of the window and saw how brilliant indeed the stars were and how the moonlight caught the metal bits on the horses' harness and glittered against their flying manes like jewels. In spite of the ordeal behind them, she had never seen her mistress so wide awake at night. Excitement made her eyes seem even more huge than they already were and happiness gave them a liveliness they so rarely had. "Pinch me, Wilson," she murmured, "I cannot believe this is real."

"It is real enough, ma'am," Wilson replied, clutching Flush, who had fully recovered and was desperate to run around, "only look who is beside you." Mr. Browning smiled and squeezed her hand and looked a little less anxious than he had done all that day.

But when they reached their hotel in Paris the anxiety returned. He stood appalled in the room where he had just laid his wife on the bed. It was small and dingy with bed linen that had given off a cloud of dust when her body was put upon it. There was an odor with which Wilson felt uncomfortable but did not dare mention in case it was merely foreign cooking drifting upward. While she began to unpack night things from their bag, Mr. Browning went to the window and opened it. Immediately the volume of noise made him close it. "Oh, Ba," he said, "this is not what I intended." His wife stretched out her hand and said, "It is perfect, Robert, do not distress yourself. Wilson will make me very comfortable." Oh, will I, thought Wilson, at that very moment deciding she was in for a night of coughing and choking. The dust, she had had time to see, lay thickly everywhere and indignation, suppressed for Mr. Browning's sake, made her cheeks burn. This was no place for a lady with a delicate chest, but she supposed she would have to find a rag and clean the room herself before sleep was even thought of. At least a good fire burned and there was coal in plenty beside it. Mr. Browning had already said he would take the single room for tonight, wishing her to stay with her mistress until she was over the journey. His wife had demurred, but he had been insistent. So now he bade her good night, while Wilson tactfully turned her back and shushed Flush, who was still inclined to growl at such contact. She dreaded either ringing the bell for service or going in search of it herself, but she needed hot water and towels and a cup or glass in which to mix the laudanum and she knew she ought to be taking charge and seeing to these things. She was so grateful when Mr. Browning said, as he left, that he had ordered hot water to be sent and that it was to be brought by someone who spoke a little English.

Wilson had never slept with her mistress before though she had spent many a night sitting up with her. She felt shy about climbing into the same bed, where by rights Mr. Browning ought to be, and delayed the moment as long as possible, hoping her mistress would fall asleep first. But she did not. When Wilson at last slipped between the covers, thinking how strange to lie beside someone other than Ellen, her mistress spoke at once.

"I hardly wish to sleep," she said, "when there is so much to see and do."

"If you don't sleep, ma'am," Wilson said, a little sternly, "you won't be fit to see or do anything. And Mr. Browning has told me, he has said, you are not to move from this bed for two days at least, he is so afraid for you."

"What nonsense. You must tell him it is nonsense, that I am

perfectly well." But even as she said this, a small cough escaped her and, in attempting to choke it back, a bigger one erupted. Wilson was out of bed in a trice and at her side with a glass of water. The coughing over, her mistress subsided back onto her pillow and she once more got into bed.

"Now, ma'am, if you will allow me to know what is best, no more talking. Sleep is what you need—what you must have, or else Mr. Browning will be frantic and never let you out of this room."

"I should not mind," came a last murmur, "if he were only in it with me." But he was not in it the next night either, though he had barely left it the whole day. No matter how much his wife swore she was well and wished to get up he would not allow her to do more than sit up. Wilson, watching him, was at first amused and then impressed. He was absolutely firm and yet there was nothing domineering about his insistence. She saw at once that this was the firmness of concern and that her own mistress was in reality the stronger should she choose to exert her will. Today, she did not, but sank back laughing against her pillows, content to have her husband at her side, holding her hand and sharing the grapes he had brought her.

"Go out, do, Wilson," she urged, "take Flushie to meet some French dogs and give yourself some air."

Wilson hesitated. "I should like to, ma'am, sir, but . . ." and she stopped, blushing.

"You forget, Ba," Mr. Browning said, "Wilson is a stranger to Paris without an idea of where to go and unable to ask. Now, Wilson, look, I will direct you and you will do very well, do not fear." And he leaned out of the window with her and pointed this way and that and showed her where to walk to find some greenery and space for Flush and then for good measure he took a pencil and drew a simple map.

Wilson clutched it all the time she was out, terrified she would lose it and be stranded forever. She had Flush on the lead of course, the handle of it wrapped twice around her hand for safety. The woman sitting at the desk in the lobby of the hotel said something to her as she passed through but she got away with a curt nod. She did so hate it when people spoke and she had not the faintest idea what they were saying. Once out, she took a deep breath and walked slowly down the street, repeating Mr. Browning's directions in her head—left, left, right, cross the road, right again and, yes, there was a gate and the entrance to a rather scorched, bare patch of grass, more of a square than a park, but with children playing on some swings and benches where mothers sat. She walked Flush around the grass twice, not daring to let him off the lead, though he strained frantically, not daring to sit down herself in case anyone spoke to her. Then she headed back to the hotel, looking furtively at her map all the time and relaxing only when she recognized the street. She walked up and down it several times, feeling safe at last, and then realized she could walk right around the block without crossing any roads and without losing her bearings. So she walked round and round, examining the buildings and looking at the other passersby and coming to the conclusion that their foreignness was limited to certain articles of clothing and that their faces looked like faces anywhere. When she came back into the hotel the woman in the lobby spoke again and this time Wilson could tell from the interrogative lift in her voice that she was asking a question. She blushed, and smiled, and nodded, and hurried past as quickly as possible, feeling humiliated. This could not go on, she must endeavor to learn, parrot fashion, some simple words.

The Brownings were in each other's arms as she entered, though she had been careful to knock and then wait.

"Did you enjoy your promenade, Wilson?" Mr. Browning asked.

Wilson noticed he made a move to release himself from his wife's arms but that she clung to him. "Yes, sir. It was pleasant to get some air, sir."

"My sentiments entirely," her mistress said. "When am I to be allowed to breathe the air of Paris?"

"If all is well, in another day or two, but I cannot guarantee it, Ba, for it depends how you are."

"Really, Robert, you make such an exaggerated case of it, to be sure, and it is not necessary, is it, Wilson? Do tell him I am not china and likely to break."

"Well, ma'am, I don't know about china, but I think Mr. Browning is right to be careful of you."

"There you are, Ba, I am right all along."

"Wilson, you are a conspirator. Shame on you."

And at that minute, as they all laughed, there was a clatter of footsteps on the stairs outside and then a frenzied knocking at the door, a knocking so violent they all started and Mrs. Browning clutched her heart. Wilson rushed to open the door and was almost pushed aside by the woman who burst in.

"Why, Miss Barrett! Mr. Browning! Why, you poets! How you amazed me! How your note surprised me! How delighted I am! And in Paris! Here! Safe and well and *married!* It is hardly to be believed! I cannot credit it!"

On and on Mrs. Jameson exclaimed while the Brownings smiled. Wilson stood watching, feeling an enormous sense of relief for no reason at all. In a moment Mrs. Jameson whirled around and confronted her too. "Wilson! And you said not a word! My dear, how loyal! How true!" And to her embarrassment but pleasure she was seized and embraced, too, and even Flush, of whom Mrs. Jameson was not over-fond, received a squeeze and wagged his tail appreciatively. "But *this* will not do," Mrs. Jameson announced next, making a sweeping gesture with her expressive hands around the room. "Whatever can you have been thinking of, Mr. Browning? Shame on you. Such a noisy situation and no view besides. Come, you must join my niece and me at the Hôtel de la Ville de Paris. They have rooms, I know it. I shall go ahead and see everything is prepared and you must pay your bill and follow within the hour. I will not brook a refusal, indeed I could not. It is my duty to see you properly housed and cared for, indeed it is."

The difference was marked. Wilson, unpacking once more, was impressed with their new quarters and could find no fault. The Hôtel de la Ville de Paris was in a quiet street with a fine aspect and the rooms they were given were charming. There was even a narrow balcony in Mrs. Browning's room with double doors opening onto it, and flower boxes along the iron rails full of cascading pink geraniums. The linen was clean and smelled of lavender and the furniture was like pretty country furniture. After a day there, it surprised Wilson to find her mistress allowed to get up and stand on the balcony and, after another, she was visibly so restored that she was allowed to go

out. It was on that night that her honeymoon truly began. Courte-
ously, Mr. Browning took Wilson aside in the afternoon and said he
thought she might move to a room he had taken for her on the top
floor. "You will be glad, I am sure," he said, "of a little time to
yourself." It was so delicately put that she almost demurred, ready to
protest that she was happy to continue as they were, but stopped
herself just in time. And she was glad to be on her own that night
since it gave her the opportunity to write to Mother for the first time
since she had left Wimpole Street. She found it a great pleasure to
describe the journey and then to give her family a sketch of Paris of
which she had by then seen something and could state authoritatively
that

—the streets are much livelier than in London, Mother, full of
Punch & Judy shows and the like, and the clothes the women
wear much more spectacular so that it is hard sometimes not to
turn and stare especially at the hats which are great creations at
the moment with fruit on them. Then it is very countrified for all
it is the capital city with so many flowers growing everywhere,
boxes and boxes on window sills and steps and my mistress likes
that very much. Mr. Browning continues very careful of her and
would not even consider claiming his place beside her at night
until now when she is much rested and showing no ill effects from
the journey. I left her waiting for him tonight looking very pretty
in a blue nightgown I kept back for the occasion though she
laughed at me for it and would almost have been annoyed if she
had not been so happy. She never wears blue but this was some
very fine lawn given to her by her Aunt Jane and I smocked it and
edged the sleeves and neck with lace, and really it is a lovely
garment and she looks better in it than in white which makes her
look like a ghost. I brushed her hair even more than usual until it
gave off great sparks of light and sprang away from her face with
a life of its own, which is a good sign as I told Mr. Browning, for
when she is ill her hair shows it and does nothing but hang limp. It
is very curious, Mother, but when I left her she was not at all
nervous but quite composed and happy and unworried and I did

wonder for a moment if she was fully aware of what was to happen. I know I should not be so calm—

But Wilson tore that page up, stopping at the end of her remarks about Mrs. Browning's hair. It was not seemly to discuss such feelings with her mother and she was surprised at herself. Instead, she wrote the next night to Lizzie, to whom she could be freer. Again she began with the journey and a mention of the sights of Paris, but then quickly got down to confiding more private happenings, telling Lizzie, after many reminders of how she was not to mention any of this to a soul, that

—their *true* wedding night made her very happy, Lizzie, and it was no idle boast. When I went in the next morning, taking care to keep my eyes modest and acting as I always act, Mr. Browning was not there but had got up and washed and was out for a walk. I thought this a little remarkable but said nothing and averted my gaze so that she would not think I was looking for any signs of how the night had gone. As I helped her off with her nightgown I could not help but remark to myself that it looked very fresh and not as though it had been worn and it was perfectly unmarked, if you take my meaning. Nor did she complain of any soreness or betray any signs of such, but on the contrary was more lively than she ever is in the morning. She smiled at me and said Wilson you are discreet as ever but I sense your anxiety and would only have you know I am *very* well and you are not to listen to tales other brides tell you and which I have heard myself. Well, it was I who blushed, Lizzie. At that moment Mr. Browning came back looking energetic after his walk and she held out her arms to him and I disappeared at once to see to the ironing of her dress. So, Lizzie, our fears were quite unfounded and she has taken to marriage better than we hoped and may yet take to more than that. I do not think she even entertains a thought of motherhood believing herself incapable of it but I will be on the lookout, I can tell you, and I have marked down when her last monthly was for she is very forgetful and constantly surprised since they began again that time I told you of. She is not well sometimes when it occurs and I am fearful of this event happening while we are traveling for she would have to lie up and no mistake, but it is possible we may get to our first stopping place on the route, being Orleans, before it happens. We leave the day after tomorrow with Mrs. Jameson and her niece Gerardine, who is seventeen. Mrs. Jameson is an experienced traveler and of course a woman besides so you may imagine how glad I am to be under her wing. Gerardine is very pretty but very young and given to thoughtless remarks, I find. Seeing me the other day attending to the trimming on my mistress's bonnet she says is Mrs. Browning very old and when I replied indeed no, implying by my manner I hope a reprimand for asking such a thing which you will admit was rude of her, she said she thought she must be to have such a dreary old-fashioned bonnet and her a bride. I said pretty sharply that to Mrs. Browning there were things more important than *bonnets* and that quietened her. I had not thought I could be so fierce, but I was angry. She must have said something to her aunt for Mrs. Jameson came to speak to me shortly afterward and begged pardon for her niece. Indeed Wilson, she said, I am concerned that traveling with a pair of lovers may have a bad effect on Gerardine and put ideas into her head which her parents would not thank me for. She is very impressionable and if she sees a great deal of loving before her very eyes she will want to turn to it herself. I assured her Mr. and Mrs. Browning were unlikely to make an exhibition of themselves before Gerardine and she laughed and said I was right—

But although she was right and there were no embraces in front of Gerardine or anyone else, Wilson privately thought that the girl would have to be very unobservant not to see scores of instances every day which spoke of the passionate love her master and mistress had for each other. Throughout their journey to Orleans, by train and coach, it was there in every look they exchanged, in every word they spoke to each other, in every polite handing in and out of carriages. Mrs. Jameson smiled to see it and then tried to hide her smile but she would catch Wilson's eye and it would break out again. It was only as they neared Orleans that a certain tension replaced the ever growing tenderness between them. The night before they were to arrive there, Wilson found her mistress weeping when she went to make her ready for bed. "My letters, Wilson," she murmured, the tears falling fast, "my letters—they wait for me like poison darts ready to strike my heart."

"Now come, ma'am, they are only letters, whatever is in them, and it is wrong to upset yourself so over pieces of paper, and Mr. Browning will not be pleased."

"He does not understand, and you ought. Papa—oh, Papa will—oh, he will have . . ."

"There will be other letters, ma'am, from Miss Henrietta and Miss Arabel, and I cannot believe all your brothers will be angry. Now come, you must not weep and upset yourself or it will be the worse for you."

"As I have told you myself, Ba," said Mr. Browning, who had come in very quietly. "Thank you, Wilson, you are very sensible and I wish your good sense did not fall on deaf ears."

So, with a good deal of placating, Mrs. Browning was lulled to sleep and the final part of the journey faced with a resolute air. Wilson could not help feeling excited at the thought of letters of her own waiting for her, too, and hoped passionately that she would not be disappointed. Surely Minnie would have kept her promise? And it would not have been beyond Mother to post a letter to Orleans? But when Mr. Browning came into their room in the inn where they had elected to stay in Orleans, the package he was bearing carried no letters for her at all. At least, she supposed not, since he held them all out to his wife and she took them, hands trembling, murmuring, "The weight of joy or sorrow?" Mr. Browning, though pleading earnestly to be allowed to stay to support her through the ordeal of discovering how her marriage and flight had been received, was sent away, but he would not allow Wilson to be banished too. "I wish to be alone," her mistress said, but Mr. Browning was adamant—there must be someone at hand in case the shock was too great. So Wilson retreated to the little dressing room and made a show of hanging up clothes: in that way Mrs. Browning was, and yet was not, by herself.

The rooms were so still that it was impossible not to hear envelopes being opened and paper unfolded. The slit of the paper knife seemed a most sinister sound and Wilson shivered involuntarily. Very, very quietly she smoothed out a dress and picked bits of fluff and Flush's hairs off it, all the while conscious of the absolute silence which had replaced the crackle of paper. For such a long time it seemed there was no sound at all, not the smallest cough or clearing of the throat, not a hint of any kind of exclamation, and then she heard a little gasp, no more than a sharp intake of breath, and the words, "Oh no, no, it is too much." Hesitantly, she put the dress down and went to the door. Her mistress was sitting straight-backed, staring out of the window, and down her cheeks the tears ran so thick and fast, her whole face was awash. She made not the slightest attempt to stem them but merely allowed them to cascade even down to the collar of her dress without appearing to notice. But, though this deluge of tears showed her distress, her body and the expression on her face did not. She did not shake with sorrow, there was nothing of helplessness in her bearing but rather an almost military compo- sure and in the tilt of her chin and the set of her mouth pride rather than despair.

Standing in the doorway, half fearful, Wilson waited. At last, without turning around, her mistress said, "You may tell Robert to come in, Wilson, but first wipe my face, dear." Eager to be allowed to do so, Wilson came forward with a soft handkerchief and gently dabbed the tears which still fell remorselessly.

"There, ma'am, there," she found herself saying, soothingly, "it is over now, all over."

Her mistress smiled wearily and said, "Not over, dear, but just beginning and what a long story it will be." Then she took the handkerchief herself and in a determined fashion blotted her eyes and closed them and then when she opened them again the tears had all but stopped.

Wilson, standing anxiously beside her, could not help seeing the strong, bold handwriting of Mr. Barrett scrawled across the paper lying in her mistress's lap and, noticing her eyes take this in, Mrs. Browning took the letter up and said, "Yes, it is as I thought, cast off into outer darkness, but that is not the worst—see, here and here, from my brothers, *all* my brothers, all the same, full of fury, full of unkindness and not a hint of love between them."

"Not Mr. Septimus, ma'am? Not Mr. Octavius?"

"Both, all of them, George speaks for all of them, they wish to disown me. Only my sisters"—and here her voice broke as it had not done when cataloguing her brothers' cruelty "—only my dear sisters love me and forgive me and pray for me and are everything to me that I could wish."

Then she did dissolve a little and embraced Wilson, who patted her shoulder and tried to offer some comfort before going for Mr. Browning. She left them together and took Flush for a walk, pleased that as she left the inn and was saluted by the concierge she was able to say, *"Au revoir,"* without a tremor. She did not go far but was glad to be out and better able to hide her own bitter disappointment that no one had thought fit to write to her. Tears came into her own eyes to think she had not been worth a line from anyone and she had to scold herself hard for such vanity. Perhaps, once they were settled in Italy with a permanent address, perhaps then she would get letters. And if she wrote, setting out her address clearly, surely there would be a response. It upset her to discover how important letters already seemed to be and she felt for the first time how hard it had been for Mother to have her so far away and quite dependent on pieces of fragile paper for any contact. She would write every week, she vowed to herself as she made her way back to the inn, even if Mother never wrote to her.

But when she had brushed Flush and carried him upstairs, Mr. Browning was waiting for her and in his hand had two letters. He begged her pardon and said he had not at first seen them, since he was so anxious to find those he knew would be certainly there for his wife and himself. Wilson blushed with pleasure and dropped Flush so suddenly that he yelped with indignation. Mr. Browning said she should retire for half an hour and enjoy her letters and she fairly rushed to her little room, barely larger than a cubbyhole, where she sat on her bed and first savored the envelopes. One from Mother, one from Minnie Robinson. She held Mother's, imagining the fuss to get the right postage and the very post box in which it would have been deposited with many a parting kiss. She could see Mother now, touching the seal with her lips, sending it on its way with a prayer for its safety. It made her so nostalgic she could hardly open the letter and, when she did, her eyes were misted over so that the words were not clear. She blinked several times and then read Mother's neat hand. The letter was short but full of concern with not a hint of rebuke. It spoke of Mother's delight for Mrs. Browning and endorsed the part her daughter had played and wished them all good luck and longed to have news of them before long. Wilson cried a little, partly with relief, partly with pride in her mother's generosity. Then she opened Minnie's letter, which was longer and mostly concerned with how Mrs. Browning's news had been received. Wilson could see exactly the scene Minnie described (with considerable relish). She shuddered as she imagined Mr. Barrett receiving the news of his daughter's flight and did not wonder that even Minnie had trembled a little when the master addressed all the servants and forbade them to speak of Miss Elizabeth ever again.

Wilson sighed as she finished Minnie's epistle for the third time. She had felt herself back in Wimpole Street and the weight of that oppressive atmosphere had her by the throat. Here she was, in the sun and light of France, and back there it was gloom and dark. Her mistress said these were her sentiments exactly when Wilson confessed her guilt. "Well, we must be happy, dear," she said that night, "for it is a happiness bought at great cost and we must be worthy of it." Wilson nodded, pleased to hear her so resolute. "Tomorrow we leave for Italy," her mistress said, "and then it will be a new beginning." For me, Wilson, reflected, it already is. She had felt disorientated the moment she left English soil. Every day increased her sense of isolation, her strange feeling of not existing at all. Through the windows of carriages and inns she looked on scene after scene which bewildered her. Nothing was the same, not the trees or the buildings, not even the colors, and yet she could not precisely put her finger on the foreignness of anything except the language. Only by sticking grimly to the set routines of her mistress's toilet and the methodical supervision of her welfare could she steady herself. It was as though she were on a merry-go-round, everything whirling and the excitement of the ride tinged with a desire that it should stop. In Italy, it surely must.

CHAPTER FIFTEEN

WILSON STOOD in the doorway, rigid with fright. All morning she had put off the expedition and now it could be put off no longer. At noon the shops would close and before then it was imperative that she procure the essentials needed. Stiffly, a basket on her arm, she left the shelter of the Collegio di Fernandez and walked slowly down the street. It was nearly the end of October but the sun was fierce and she screwed up her eyes. In her hand she had a list, neatly written out in Italian by her mistress, and if in difficulties had resolved simply to thrust it in each shopkeeper's hand. She had practiced saying, *"Buongiorno"* and *"Quanto fa?"* over and over again. If only the shopkeepers would stick to this interchange she would fare well enough, but she greatly feared a torrent of voluble Italian would accompany every attempt at a purchase. It was just so. No sooner had she managed her greeting, followed by her simple request, before a flood of language assailed her. She could only repeat the one phrase she knew and blush and stand her ground and proffer money and hope for the best.

She was not always sure that she received it. The people seemed kind, smiling and nodding at her, but when she was handed change she found it impossible to reckon up quickly, and occasionally, she would discover afterward, on painfully working out what she should have left, that she could have been cheated. Feeling obliged to report this to the Brownings, she was a little hurt to be laughed at. Italy, they said, was not England and things were not so exact and a few *lire* here and there would not worry them. In time, they assured her, she would get the hang of it and she was not to distress herself. But it did distress her. She resented being thought of as a fool instead of being respected for her astuteness. And she did not altogether like the way she was looked at, either. Italian men were very forward and verged on the insolent, she decided. They had a way of examining her, with a rapid head-to-toe scrutiny, which left her uneasy. Her skin prickled when her palm appeared to be caressed as money changed hands and she cringed before the wide, wide smiles. Twice she came home so near to tears that her mistress could not fail to notice and be concerned. Wilson heard her say to Mr. Browning that it was hard for her and she wished dear Wilson had a friend.

That was the trouble. She had not even a semblance of a friend in Pisa. Never for one moment had she thought she would miss the servants in Wimpole Street to any great degree (though she had known she would miss Lizzie), but now she was desolate without them. She had kept herself to herself, it was true, but though her privacy had been respected she had, over the two years she was there, established a good relationship with everyone in the house and was never in want of someone with whom to pass the time of day. If she had wished a closer contact, there had always been Minnie. Now she had no one. The landlady seemed aloof and she felt that even if there had been no language difficulty she was decidedly not a friend in the making. The housemaid seemed barely able to speak at all and Wilson had heard but not seen the others in the building. She still seemed to live in a frighteningly silent world, dependent on her employers for any conversation at all, and what made this situation worse was the realization that she was excluded from their intimacy. Always, they seemed to stop speaking when she entered the room and, although they would resume again quickly and never fail to draw her into their dialogue, she felt she had interrupted something private and precious. Even alone with her mistress she felt her presence was only endured until Mr. Browning reappeared and was acutely conscious that the old freedom between them had gone. She had never, she knew, overstepped the bounds of correct conduct and become familiar, the undoing of so many maids, but there had been a connection that had almost gone.

Mrs. Browning, of course, noticed it herself. Wilson saw herself being observed and waited for the inquiry which was inevitable. "Wilson, dear, you seem low in spirits." She went on brushing her mistress's hair and said nothing. "Am I right, dear? Are you unhappy?"

"Indeed no, ma'am."

"Then you are ill?"

"My stomach is a little upset, ma'am, with all the foreign food, but it is nothing."

"And yet you *are* dispirited. Do you miss England, is that it?"

"A little, but not overmuch. Really, ma'am, do not concern yourself if I appear a trifle out of sorts. I will soon pick up."

"Well, if you do not, dear, and wish to go home, then you must speak out and I will arrange it. I would not hold you here against your will, nor keep your services if you are unhappy and find it all too much."

To her own alarm, this assurance made Wilson feel worse than ever. She suddenly saw how dispensable she was now thought to be. The journey was over, the dramatic transition made, and her mistress fondly imagined she could manage without her. Though she knew this had not been the intention, and that she was being foolish even to consider it, she could not help feeling there had been a hint that she *should* go home. But what would there be for her if she did? Perhaps a gift of money to tide her over? She doubted that since both Brownings spoke constantly of their poverty. But otherwise the immediate, desperate need to find another situation. And where would she go to in order to find this new place? Not Wimpole Street. It would be back to uncertainty and confusion and over it all the terrible disappointment of having somehow failed.

It was the thought of this failure which made her take herself firmly in hand. One thing she had was time, too much of it. Mr. Browning was ever with his wife and she was not needed for long stretches of the day. There was no Lizzie to visit, no Minnie to chat to, and though she walked with Flush beside the Arno she was not as enamored of this promenade as she had been of her turns in Regent's Park. It seemed to her that she could make no progress in this country until she could speak its language and so she resolved to teach herself from a book. It was a book their landlady produced one day during a confusion over the word for mist (a mist which had suddenly descended in the middle of November). She had opened this book and pointed to *"misiera"* at the back of it and Wilson had seen it was a kind of dictionary but also a grammar book. The landlady had urged it on her, making it clear after a good deal of sign language and general pantomime that it had been left behind by two English gentlemen and that she was welcome to it. Gratefully, Wilson took the book and thereafter applied herself for an hour every day to studying it. Since her bed was in a tiny slot of a room so dark she could not make out the print, she took to sitting out on the landing in the afternoons while Mr. Browning tore himself away for his daily stroll and her mistress slept soundly. The book was simply laid out in twenty lessons, with vocabulary to learn at the end of each, and written exercises to do. These she found troublesome but persevered since she liked the action of writing and took some pleasure from covering sheets of paper—a commodity always made generously available by her mistress—with these strange new words.

The loneliness receded a little toward Christmas, by which time she had begun not only to recognize words said to her but to put them together herself. Her head did not ache so violently at the end of each day, assaulted on all sides by the incessant babble. And as she grew more proficient, so she grew more adventurous, taking to walking around the city until she had its layout completely and twice was able to direct Mr. Browning to an address he had not been able to find. She discovered it was a quiet, safe place and that the stares of the men did not after all lead to unpleasantness. Flush, of course, was delighted with Pisa since, in the absence of dog snatchers, he had so much freedom. She did not need to have him very often on the lead and he became well known, running the length and breadth of the city every day but always returning home by nightfall. Watching him, Wilson wished she had half his daring but even so was pleased with herself for not moping and for doing the best she could, though this still had not brought her companionship. But the Brownings were forever discussing when to move on and where to, so she drew some consolation from this. "Pisa *is* a little dull, Ba, is it not?" she heard Mr. Browning say, and at once her mistress was all anxiety lest he was bored, which he strenuously denied. "Not bored, Ba, how could I be bored with you, my heart? I spoke only of Pisa in general and see no shame in admitting it is a dull place. It will not do to make our home in and get down to hard, regular work."

It seemed to Wilson every place in the world was mentioned as a possible destination and all of them found wanting for one reason or another. She knew none of them so could not pass judgment on whether Venice was preferable to Rome or Florence to both of them. What she did venture to contribute to the daily discussion was a suggestion that, if a move were to be made, then it would be as well to make it sooner rather than later. "Now why is that, Wilson?" her mistress asked, smiling. Wilson stared at her steadily, thinking it impossible that she could have no real idea, but her stare brought no response at first and then the wrong one. "I suppose you mean because of the winter," Mrs. Browning said. "But it is hardly worthy of the name here and nothing to fear."

"I was not thinking of the winter," Wilson said, and left it at that. She was quick to notice a change in Mr. Browning's expression and not surprised when, later, he waylaid her on the stairs and pressed her to say more. As ever, he was a master of tactful suggestion. "Am I to understand, Wilson, that you would wish my wife to be kept quiet in the next months?"

"Indeed yes, sir."

"More than ordinarily quiet?"

"Yes, sir."

"And is this because you think her more than ordinarily vulnerable?"

"It is."

"Due to new circumstances?"

"I think so, sir."

"Yet she does not?"

"No, sir. If I mention my suspicions she dismisses them as nonsense."

"Might they be?"

"It is always possible, sir, but when I look at her and observe how much plumper she is and when I know what I know . . ."

"You are certain."

"Yes, sir."

He went off thoughtful, his brow furrowed, and that evening, at bedtime, Mrs. Browning took her to task for upsetting her husband. "Really, Wilson, you should not have spoken so."

"Someone must speak," Wilson muttered, hurt at being so openly criticized.

"And for why? Where, pray, is the urgency?"

"In what you might lose."

"How can I lose what I do not know I have?"

"*I* know. It is four months since anything happened, ma'am, and before that for nearly eighteen months you were as regular as any woman . . ."

"Wilson! Stop, do. You know quite well that a change of air, of food, and the traveling itself can all alter the mechanism. It was always so with me and now it is again and I think nothing of it and would thank you not to plant such ideas in Mr. Browning's head. As it is, he will hardly let me walk around the room without worrying that I will overtire myself."

Reprimanded with such vehemence, Wilson said no more but with each month, as she wrote to Minnie:

—I am more convinced. Say nothing to her sisters, Minnie, but if there is no announcement soon I will be surprised. She continues very well though not as well as she would have us believe. She eats well and takes to the food here better than I do. Oh, Minnie, what I would give for a mutton pie! At first we were in a quandary, not knowing what to do about our meals for none are provided, and between us we were ignorant of the art of cooking, myself as much as them, but then the landlady said it was customary to have meals sent in and that is what we have and my mistress is greatly taken with it. She relishes all manner of strange food and so does he and both swear they are glad to give up the roast beef of old England dinners but *I am not*. My stomach troubles me as it never did and if I had not brought with me, thanks to *you*, the cream of tartar and Dr. Driver's Efficacious Pills I do not know what I should do. I take them at night and presently the pains subside but then the next day when I am once more obliged to eat the same spiced food or starve they return. It has turned cold, though my mistress will not have it that it is real cold, by which I do not understand what she means, I am sure, for when we went to church on Christmas Eve it seemed colder than it ever did in London and I thought my nose would freeze on my face. Nor is our apartment well appointed, Minnie. Indeed, it is downright shabby and I sometimes think my mistress is blind for she appears not to notice the bare floorboards hardly covered with one poor quality mat such as you might not think good enough for the kitchen. Nothing is comfortable. There is not a curtain to be seen, and as for the furniture it would not grace a servant's room in Wimpole Street and that is the truth. The church we went to as I was telling you of was not a church such as you know, Minnie, but Catholic and full of ritual. It made me feel queer to stand there listening to that chanting and with gold seeming to flash everywhere and the air full of incense and, indeed, I felt giddy and had to steady myself, and everywhere I looked were pictures and statues of shocking nudity and I thought I might faint at the grossness of it. Would that everything was as plain and simple as at home where the senses are not deliberately inflamed.

Some days she felt that all of her was inflamed. Her head, her stomach, even her eyes seemed to burn; she had difficulty containing her discomfort. She wished desperately she had Mother near at hand with her herbs and concoctions, knowing exactly how to treat almost any ailment. Even thinking of Mother made her eyes fill with tears.

One more letter only since the one which had awaited her at Orleans, and then nothing, though she herself had written every week without fail. She had written to Minnie begging her to forward one of her letters, thinking it might somehow give it a better chance of being delivered, and Minnie had assured her it had been sent. But it had brought no reply and now it was two whole months since she had had a line from her family, whereas though her mistress complained constantly that she did not get half as many letters from her sisters as she sent, nevertheless it seemed to the letter-starved Wilson that she received something by every post. Only Minnie wrote to her, and that was a fact. Lizzie had sent nothing, not a single word, which grieved her greatly. Minnie mentioned that she had called with her children and had said she was writing but no letter had appeared. And as for Reginald, well, she had expected nothing there. She could hardly remember he had existed.

One day in early January all her misery seemed to come to a head. She had woken with the stomach pains she normally was not troubled by until after supper and then suffered the mortification of diarrhea. Her skin felt cold and clammy and yet she could not bear to put on her shawl over her dress. She went in to her mistress barely able to stagger through her duties and yet was aware that she dissembled so successfully that nothing was noticed. But then Mrs. Browning was in a permanent dream these mornings, sleepy and smiling, languorous but not with the old, deadly languor but rather a catlike satisfaction. Immediately she had finished dressing her mistress, Wilson rushed to her cubbyhole and lay down with relief. In Wimpole Street there would always have been someone to observe and report the state she was in, but here she could lie until midday if she so wished and no one would be the wiser. Flush did not even need to be walked, being a gentleman-at-large in Pisa without need of escort. She wept into her pillow and wondered what all this was for—the loneliness, the anxiety, the constant struggle to make her own way in this foreign city. Whom did she hope to please? Not herself. She had tried so hard to make a new and better life but it seemed without reward. Both Mr. and Mrs. Browning had praised her only the other day for her new facility with the Italian language and she had been momentarily proud but now she saw the absurdity of her pride. She wanted only to be home, among people who knew and cared for her. At midday she dragged herself up and bathed her sweating forehead and went to supervise dinner, none of which she could eat herself. The mere sight of the veal stewed in peppers, over which both Brownings exclaimed with delight, made her nauseous and she always rejected outright the mess of garlicky vegetation they called a salad. The afternoon passed in another daze of misery and discomfort. She supposed she must have slept a little, for when she came to her arm was numb where she had been lying awkwardly and she could tell by the decrease of light that it was evening. She sat up and was immediately struck by a pain in her left side so savage she cried out. No one heard, or, if they did, they did not investigate. The thought of such neglect made her weep again and she had the greatest difficulty controlling her desire to lie down and never get up.

But she did. At nine o'clock, when she was required to prepare her mistress for bed, she was there, pale and dark-eyed but upright and apparently as composed and efficient as ever. But she could not speak. Several times Mrs. Browning addressed remarks to her but she was unable to reply for fear the facade she was so carefully maintaining would crumble. Fortunately, these remarks were of so general a nature and of such small importance that they hardly required an answer. And then Flush was being particularly demanding, yelping and barking, leaping annoyingly about the room, so that all was distraction. All the usual tasks done—the endless hair brushing, the hanging up and folding of clothes, the laudanum mixed—Wilson was just thinking she had successfully survived and might now retire to bed once more when the pain struck again. She could not suppress a groan, or prevent herself collapsing on the floor, her hands pressed to her stomach. Even as she lay huddled there she was gasping her apologies, saying over and over she could not help it and was sorry, and then she was engulfed in pain and unable to reply to her mistress's frenzied inquiries. She heard her say, as if from a long way off, and as though with an echo, that she would go at once for help and then she must have fainted because she heard nothing more till Mr. Browning spoke to her. "Wilson? Wilson? Are you unwell? What has happened?" She tried to raise herself up but only succeeded in increasing the pain and fell back, crying out. "Oh, Robert, go for Dr. Cook quickly, dear, go at once," she heard her mistress plead, and then the sharp rejoinder, "I will go nowhere, Ba, while you stand in a shift and bare feet—you will catch your death of cold." Both voices swam around Wilson's head and she could not make sense of either but she was aware of gentle hands lifting her and of being carried across the room and laid on the bed and the next thing she knew was her mistress holding her hand and whispering soothing words. She opened her eyes and saw Mrs. Browning's face close to her own, wet with tears and tense with anxiety. She tried to say she was sorry but was hushed at once and told to lie still and not disturb herself until the doctor came.

Dr. Cook was brisk. Wilson was in too much pain to notice how brusque his examination was or to observe the slight air of impatience with which he turned to the Brownings at the end. Her greatest anxiety was the certain knowledge that she was in the Brownings' own bed and must get out of it as soon as possible. She lay still, conscious that the pain was at last receding. Before she could get up, her mistress appeared once more at her side, a cloth wrung out in water in her hand, and applied it to her maid's forehead.

"Oh, ma'am," Wilson murmured, "you must not."

"Now, dear, listen," her mistress was saying, "Dr. Cook says you have inflammation of the stomach and that with rest and a bland diet you will be as well as ever in a few days, but you must take no more of those pills Minnie gave you nor any cream of tartar. Weak tea and a little toast is all you must eat. Your poor stomach has been assaulted with the seasickness at first and then the change of food and climate, and it is nothing more, thank God."

"I beg pardon, ma'am," she whispered, "I will return to my room directly if . . ." and she raised herself up satisfactorily this time and swung her legs down onto the ground just as Mr. Browning returned from seeing the doctor out. He rushed forward and supported her as she began stumbling across the room.

"Well done, Wilson," he said, "with such determination you will recover all the better."

"Yes, sir. I beg pardon, sir, for . . ."

"There is no need, Wilson. We are all human and liable to sickness and must help each other. Ba! *Still* barefooted. Will you play with your life? Will you torture me so?"

Lying at last in her own bed, feeling weak and weepy though free from all pain, Wilson could not help dwelling on his sole concern for his wife. It was only natural, she did not contest that, but it reminded her that she herself was no one's first concern. She could run around in bare feet and a thin shift in the snow if she wished and no one would be distraught or feel their own life threatened. She could lie here and die and her death be a mere inconvenience until she was replaced with another maid. She cried again at that, great racking sobs heard by no one, and then wiped her face with the coverlet and chided herself for self-pity. But she had planted in her own mind a thought that greatly troubled her: who *would* replace her and what would the consequences be? If she were to lie in bed and eat slops for a week, how would her mistress manage, she who had never so much as put up her own hair? It would be an impossibility. Some other maid would have to be brought in, at such cost, and there would be no end to the trouble it would cause. Perhaps the new maid would be preferred and then what? Sent back to England after all? It was only complete exhaustion which put her to sleep once such a possibility had entered her head.

In the week that followed, Wilson was surprised and gratified several times over each day. Nothing was as she imagined. When she woke the very first morning it was to find her mistress standing at her side proffering a cup of camomile tea with a smile of pride and pleasure—her mistress, who never put a foot out of bed before eleven and had no more idea of how to make tea than a child of two. Wilson was so shocked she could not speak and stared at the tea as though it were poison, but Mrs. Browning urged her to drink and watched her so eagerly that she was obliged to sample the tea.

"Is it good? Have I brewed it well? Robert said to let the kettle boil fully before pouring it on the leaves and I truly did."

"It is delicious, ma'am, but I cannot let you wait upon me, I must . . ."

"You must stay in bed, dear," her mistress said firmly, "and I shall be an angel of mercy and do all that is necessary and I daresay it will be very good for me. You shall see, I shall reveal hidden qualities and no doubt be given a medal."

Five days later, writing to Minnie, Wilson marveled at what her mistress had accomplished, swearing:

—I never would have thought it Minnie, and nor would you, for she has been as kind as a person ever could be, and if I had been her sister I could not have been more tenderly treated. I lie on her own sofa, which is not, to tell you the truth, so comfortable as it has looked when she has been upon it, and I eat from her own hand and great is Mr. Browning's mirth at the charred toast I am offered, but to me it is as precious as caviar and as strange. The landlady helps out and otherwise she sees to herself and the result is comical if only I were not too much to blame to laugh. Her dresses are done up all wrong and her hair a sight to behold and though she does not care and professes herself perfectly content Mr. Browning is not pleased and gave great sighs of approval when today for the first time I was able to put his wife to rights. He likes her at all times to look neat and tidy and takes careless-ness in appearance very ill.

The very first day Wilson resumed her normal duties she was instantly aware that it was her mistress's turn not to be well. Coming into the bedroom, beaming to be once more active, she found her white-faced and tense, clutching the coverlet to her chest. "Why, ma'am . . ." Wilson began, alarmed, but was hastily shushed.

"Do not let Mr. Browning hear," her mistress whispered, "he is in his dressing room and knows nothing. I have had a pain, that is all, a pain such as I have never had before, but it is quite gone and was nothing."

"Stomach pains, ma'am?"

"No, and yet in the region of the stomach."

"Cramps, ma'am?"

"A little like cramps. Perhaps it is that, perhaps I am about to have my monthly health after all, Wilson."

"And perhaps something else, not health at all."

"Sssh! You are determined to make a fool of me, Wilson, and it is not kind. Now say nothing, I beg you. I will rest in bed a little, to be safe, and nothing need be said."

But that night Wilson was awakened at three in the morning by a frightened Mr. Browning and hurried into the bedroom with him. Her mistress lay there making no sound but with her brow creased in pain. Surreptitiously, Wilson peeped beneath the bedcovers, under the pretense of straightening them, expecting to see blood, but there was none. She placed her hand lightly on her mistress's stomach to try to locate the pain but was told it resided nowhere specific. Raising her mistress up, she asked Mr. Browning to fetch her a small glass of brandy and managed to force it through the clenched lips. A little color came into her mistress's cheeks and she began to relax and within a quarter of an hour announced the pain had entirely gone. Mr. Browning meanwhile had pulled some clothes on and said he was going to get Dr. Cook. Then followed a scene such as Wilson had never witnessed before and which she described a trifle breathlessly, later in the day, in a letter to Minnie:

—so strong, you will remember how strong she can be when she is determined and out came the "I will not" and "I shall not" and "I tell you this" and "I tell you that," and Mr. Browning was quite dumbfounded at her passion and begged her not to upset herself and asked only to say one word more in favor of his argument but she would not hear even that and said the matter was settled and she would thank him not to mention it again. He was in low spirits all day and I think she was sorry to have spoken so and was very tender toward him. All this week she has been careful not to walk too far and has slept in the afternoon which she had vowed she had given up. There have been no more pains but of a morning I have noticed she is very white and when I have asked her if she is feeling nauseous she has said No, very sharply, and that she knows my meaning and will not have it, but, Minnie, I swear she pretends, even to herself and now I think Mr. Browning shares my suspicions for I catch him looking at her when she does not know and his eyes wander over her as though searching for evidence. It should not be long in coming for by my reckoning she is now four months gone and will soon show and feel movement and then we shall see.

Throughout February, Wilson watched and waited but never again mentioned her suspicions. Several times she saw her mistress place a hand lightly on her belly, as though exploring it, but she said nothing and when, dressing and undressing her, she saw unmistakably that her breasts were swollen and fuller than usual, she bit her lip in order not to comment. Often, watching her mistress set off with her husband, followed by an excited Flush, for a walk along the Arno, it was all she could do not to call after her to take care, in her condition. It disturbed her that in another way Mrs. Browning was not taking care but carrying on with normal relations regardless. It had never been Wilson's task in Wimpole Street to change the bed linen but here it was and, though she disdained to acknowledge such things even to herself, she could not help but be aware that if there was not already a child conceived there soon would be or it would not be for want of trying.

She thought it significant that when at last, on the first of March, to her great joy, she received a letter from Lizzie Treherne, it contained the news that she was expecting again. Mrs. Browning, told this news, was not as contemptuous of Billy Treherne as she had previously been. "And how old are the first two?" she asked. Wilson told her almost three and fifteen months. "Well, that is not so bad," Mrs. Browning said, "though still too close for comfort. But then what can Lizzie do? Precious little. Please God, after the third she will have a longer rest." And then, as Wilson tidied away the breakfast things when Mr. Browning had gone to dress, she asked, "Crow had a difficult delivery the first time, did she not, Wilson?"

"I believe so, ma'am. Though she is big and strong, she was not built well for it, as some women are."

"Upon what does it depend, do you think?"

"The hips, ma'am. My mother is small and fine-boned but she has the hips for childbearing and had no trouble."

There was a pause. Wilson, knowing full well what game was being played, waited.

"Have you attended a birth, Wilson?"

"Yes, ma'am, long ago, when I was barely sixteen. It was one of the housemaids, ma'am, where I was first employed. She had told no one and was taken with the pains in the night. I was sharing a room with her and there was no time to fetch anyone. She put a gag around her own mouth so her screams would not be heard and held my hand so tight I had the nail marks for weeks. But it was all over in half an hour and she was at work in the kitchen only a little late."

"Wilson . . . you speak so calmly . . . I am breathless . . ."

"It was nearly ten years ago, ma'am."

"Even so . . . to have witnessed such a thing . . . to have known what to do . . ."

"Oh, I did not know what to do, not in the least, it was Leah who knew what to do, for it was her third. The minute the baby shot out she snatches the gag off and tells me to pick it up by the heels and slap it and poke my finger in its mouth to clear it and then she had the scissors ready to cut the cord and I did it though I nearly fainted and then she had newspaper ready for when—begging your pardon, ma'am—the afterbirth came away. Everything was taken care of by Leah."

"And the baby, what happened to the baby?"

"He was wrapped in a shawl and that afternoon I took him to the address Leah gave me. 'Ask no questions,' she said and I asked none."

"It makes me faint to hear such a story, Wilson, even though Leah means nothing to me."

"She was small, ma'am, like you. She had another child after I left but then the mistress found out and she was sent off."

"Where did she go?"

"I cannot say. I heard the master gave her money."

"The master? Were they his?"

"Why, yes, ma'am, she had the first at fifteen and everyone knew except for me and I soon knew afterward, after that third."

"No more, Wilson, I cannot bear it."

Wilson could not help smiling as she left the room. All her

mistress had wanted to know was that someone in her household had experience and with the perfectly true story of Leah she had put her mind at rest. There was, Wilson reflected as she let Flush out, no comparison of course. Mrs. Browning would be unlikely to share Leah's luck and have a first baby slide out so naturally. There would need to be a doctor and midwife in attendance for such a case, when it was a woman of over forty giving birth. She supposed Dr. Cook, who had attended her, would come and bring with him the best midwife he could find. He really should be in attendance now, right from the start, guiding Mrs. Browning as to what she should and should not do. Wilson tried to do this herself, but every suggestion she made was rejected throughout March. She told her mistress the room was too hot, that she was walking too far, that she should not eat such spicy meals, but since she could never back up her advice with the information that all these things were said to be bad for pregnant women she had no defense when she was derided. Where, she wondered in despair, would it end?

It ended on March 21, the first day of spring and a glorious one, quite belying the events inside the Brownings' apartment. The day before Mrs. Browning had gone out in the spring sunshine to walk not along the flat paths beside the Arno but up into the pinewoods behind Pisa. She and her husband had taken a carriage there and then climbed in the woods. It was agony for Wilson to let her go, knowing her intention, and even worse to see her return so unusually flushed and excited. The talk that evening was of moving to Florence the next week, and before she retired Wilson was given instructions to begin packing at once. There was no nighttime disturbance, though she half listened for it, but the next morning her mistress announced she would stay in bed. Seeing Wilson's inquiring look, she said, almost crossly, "Yes, I have pains, but they are nothing, do *not* say a word." Wilson did not. All morning she stayed close and observed from her mistress's face that there was a sinister rhythm to these pains and that it was a rhythm which increased in strength as the day wore on. Mr. Browning was so agitated he could not keep still and then, at midday, when a groan escaped his wife's lips, the first she had uttered, he grabbed his coat and, shouting that he would wait no longer, he went for Dr. Cook. There were no more protestations from the bed.

Wilson stood at the bedside, obeying Dr. Cook's instructions. She pulled back the covers to the top of her mistress's legs and carefully lifted her shift. The doctor placed his hands on her belly, none too gently in her opinion, and prodded and pushed and grunted at what he found. He asked Mrs. Browning if she would oblige him with the date of her last bleeding and when she said she had no idea but believed several weeks ago Wilson could not help a sharp intake of breath at the lie. Hearing it, the doctor turned abruptly and stared at her. He really was, Wilson thought, a most unpleasant fellow and she was glad she had not been well enough that night he attended her to notice this. But he asked her civilly enough if she was better aware of her mistress's regularity and she said she was and that it had last been almost five months ago. This seemed to make the doctor more bad-tempered than ever. He snapped his bag shut quite ferociously and asked for patience, though from whom it was not clear. Mrs. Browning stared up at him with pleading eyes, which he ignored. Turning on his heel, after a curt good day and the promise to return the next day, Dr. Cook left the room. Two minutes later, as Wilson finished tidying the bed and putting a fresh coverlet on top, Mr. Browning hurtled into it. "Oh, Ba!" he shouted, and seized her in his arms, crushing her against him. About to absent herself, Wilson was stopped at the door and told on no account to go. "You were right, Wilson," Mr. Browning said, "my wife *is* to have a child and we ought to have listened to you and now we will and perhaps if God is good all will yet be well."

Long before the next day ended, Wilson knew it would not be. That evening, after hours of excruciating pain, written so clearly on the poor sufferer's face, the bleeding started. She knew from her sudden startled expression that something had happened and begged Mr. Browning to leave the room for a moment. The blood was dark red and coming away in small clots. "Don't let me see, Wilson," Mrs. Browning whispered, and turned away while Wilson stanched the flow of blood with a towel she had already prepared. In no time at all it was soaked through and her own heart began to beat faster in panic.

She rushed to the door and sent Mr. Browning for Dr. Cook, telling him to make all speed. He was back with the doctor within ten minutes but before then Wilson had changed the towel three times and by now the clots were huge and the blood unstoppable. Mr. Browning was sent both for ice and for hot water, which seemed to confuse him hopelessly, and meanwhile Wilson was instructed to lift her mistress high on the pillows and give her some laudanum. Dr. Cook worked quickly and silently. Mesmerized, Wilson stared at his hands, which suddenly seemed deft and confident, first pressing and then holding. He took an instrument from his bag and held Mrs. Browning's legs open, or so it seemed, and then appeared to delve inside her and the next moment a hideous mess of blue-black matter oozed out of her. The doctor lifted it clear and put it onto a silver dish and examined it briefly before returning his attention to the patient. More blood was flowing, but not so fast and without clots. He checked inside —Wilson winced as she felt her mistress shudder and grip her hand—and then he motioned for Wilson to use the hot water to wash the blood away and told her to put another towel there and observe it closely for the next hour.

"Well, madam," he said at last, "I am sorry to tell you you have had a miscarriage of five months' duration and had you called me earlier you need not have had it at all, in my opinion."

Hearing this, Wilson raged at the cruelty of it, but her mistress merely opened her eyes and murmured, "Five months! Only imagine!"

But Mr. Browning, who came in as the disgruntled doctor left, was inconsolable. He threw himself on the bed and wept as though his heart would break and Wilson found tears streaming down her own face at the sight of his devastation. She left them together for a moment while she disposed of the bloodstained towels and carried the covered dish with the fetus in it outside. It should, the doctor had said, be burned at once, but where? She could not burn it on their own fire. Slowly, she walked down the stairs, her pitiful burden filling her hands, and at the bottom turned into the landlady's kitchen where a great fire roared. There was no one about. She uncovered the dish and looked at the slimy, bulbous lump of what reminded her of liver. Her eyes went over it, seeing all too clearly the fronds that were arms and legs and the wobbly sac that was a head, and then she took in the fact that it would have been a girl. The fire spat and stung as she slid the unborn child into it and she watched, repelled, as it was devoured. She would never tell anyone, not even her mistress herself. If asked, she would say she had not looked or that it was too early to discern the sex, and she was sure Dr. Cook would hardly have been interested enough to notice.

The landlady, coming into her kitchen, was avid for news but Wilson gave her none. "My mistress has miscarried," she said stiffly. "I would thank you to be considerate." The only satisfaction was being able to say it in Italian.

CHAPTER SIXTEEN

WILSON WRAPPED the watermelon in a net and attached it to a thin rope and then slowly lowered it into the well, keeping it away from the rough stone sides. She let it go just under the water and then secured the rope on the handle of the winding mechanism. Everyone had drawn their water for the day and she had no fear the melon would be tampered with. This was the only way to get it cool as it should be, as her mistress liked it, and today being the Brownings' wedding anniversary she wished to present them with slices of the pink fruit as iced as she could make it. Back in the kitchen she prepared the knead cakes for tea, another treat, though in the hot weather not so appropriate. She perspired freely as she struggled to get the oven to the right heat and her hands were slippy as she turned out and shaped the dough. A raw, northeastern day was needed for knead cakes and an appetite all the sharper for battling with a keen wind. She cooked the cakes on top of the oven, flipping them over with a knife when they sizzled. The young Italian girl who now helped her watched fascinated and Wilson lectured her all the time in a mixture of Italian and English, instructing her as to the niceties of a perfect knead cake. The girl was slow but willing and, though there was hardly room for two of them in the tiny corner called a kitchen, Wilson enjoyed her company. She sang and laughed a lot and was cheerful.

Wilson herself felt cheerful. As she changed her dress, ready for the little ceremony she planned to make of the presentation to her employers of melon and knead cakes, she naturally thought back over the year. Only a year since that day she had crept out of 50 Wimpole Street and made her way to Marylebone Street with Miss Elizabeth as she then was—only a year and yet it seemed a century. Smoothing her hair, she reflected how changed she was, and for the better. That restlessness which had plagued her, that sense of something missing, had gone. "You will soon get over the hump," Minnie had written when, back in January, she had been low enough to think she had made a mistake. Right from the day they had arrived in Florence she had begun to think she might make a go of her new life and not need to be so brave. For a start, she had company. Florence was lively and full of English and in no time at all she had been greeting other young Englishwomen, also ladies' maids, whom she saw day after day in the course of her shopping and walks with Flush. She had not even had to brace herself to make the first move but had been approached directly in the button shop by Sarah Allen, maid to a Mrs. Loftus, whose husband was "something" in the diplomatic service. Sarah was unmistakably English with her very white skin and yellow hair, the yellow of a strong cheese and not exactly attractive. But even had her looks not marked her out, Sarah's loud voice would have done so. She was a Londoner and had an accent Wilson could tell she had tried to work on and failed. Listening to her, as she sorted through a tray of pearl shirt buttons—Mr. Browning was very particular about buttons matching—Wilson felt rather shocked that this Englishwoman hardly made an attempt at Italian. A few words from Wilson procured what she was after in the shop, and their friendship was made (though Wilson was not sure she wanted it). Sarah Allen latched onto her and would not let go, that was the truth. But she was bold and talkative and at her side Wilson had seen more of Florentine life than her own mistress, who commented, not without envy, on her social life. Each

day now she was rushing through her work in order to meet Sarah
and together they promenaded through the streets and squares, endlessly engaged in gossip and congratulating themselves on their own
luck at having such desirable situations. "I would not go back to
London for all the tea in China," Sarah declared, and although not so
vehement, Wilson was inclined to share her enthusiasm for Florence,
where the sun shone every day and the vitality of the city invigorated
every inhabitant.

Ready at last, she went for the melon and prepared the feast on a
tray. Butter for the still hot knead cakes and honey and some figs and
grapes as well as the melon. The minute she heard the bell tinkling in
the drawing room she picked up the tray and walked in, smiling
broadly. "Happy anniversary, madam, sir," she said, blushing, and
Mrs. Browning clapped her hands and looked at her husband and they
both burst out laughing. "We had a bet, Wilson, as to whether you
would realize it was our day," her mistress said.

"As if I could forget, ma'am."

"Do you remember how I almost fainted . . ."

". . . I thought we would never reach the church . . ."

"Oh, how terrified I was and how strong you were, dear." And at
the endearment, Mrs. Browning held out her hand and went on, "It
would please us both, Wilson, if you would join us for tea this once."

Blushing even more deeply, Wilson went for another cup and
saucer and when she returned Mrs. Browning waited for her to sit
before handing her a small package. "It is from both of us, dear, as a
memorial of that day you stood by us, for without your help we
would not be here."

"And what a sin that would be," Mr. Browning murmured.

Wilson felt close to tears. She had to take a deep breath before
opening the box in which lay a turquoise brooch on a bed of red
velvet. Staring at it for several seconds before daring to touch it, she
at last picked it up and turned it over and over. It was such a lovely
thing, bright but delicate, the turquoise in the shape of a star and the
gold setting making the star into a circle.

"Will you not pin it on, dear?" Mrs. Browning asked and leaned forward to do it herself. "There, it looks very well and brings out the blue in your eyes."

All that evening, while Florence exploded in a grand display of fireworks and the streets were thronged with dancing crowds—the celebration to mark the Grand Duke's gift of certain civil liberties had coincided with the Brownings' wedding anniversary—Wilson felt an inner elation that matched the festive mood of the city. She had not the faintest idea why there was such jubilation but hardly cared. With Sarah holding her hand so that they would not be separated in the dense crowds, she found herself singing and chanting with the best of them and when flowers were offered she took them and threaded them in her hair like everyone else and marveled at how happy everyone was. Up above, she caught a brief glimpse of her mistress sitting on the balcony of the Casa Guidi watching, and then she and Sarah were whirled away toward the Piazza Pitti and lost sight of home. But she had not a tremor of fear; as she realized this, there flashed into her mind a vision of her mistress and herself, in Shoreditch, when they were jostled by that other terrifying crowd and she knew the difference was more than mere circumstance. Italian men no longer seemed threatening nor did she interpret their curiosity as she once had done. There was a courtesy present, even in a street crowd, which impressed her.

Breathless, she and Sarah managed to detach themselves from the throng near the Ponte Santa Trinità and collapsed laughing onto a stone seat. "It is like this every festival," Sarah gasped. "Oh, they know how to enjoy themselves, no one back home would believe it."

"What is it for?" Wilson shouted above the noise of drums and trumpets and cheers.

"It hardly matters," Sarah screamed back. "It's their Grand Duke letting them do something or other, heaven knows, but it must be good news."

At that minute a splendid procession began to pass over the bridge with a carriage in its midst in which a magnificently dressed man was waving to right and left. Wilson stared in awe at the tall, heavy guards who walked in front, each bearing a flaming brand. "The Grand Duke!" Sarah yelled and, pulling Wilson up, pushed her way to the front, but Wilson had eyes only for the guard and hardly looked at the Duke. She had never seen such impressive men, so straight-backed and broad-shouldered, and could hardly wait to be back in her room so that she could tell Mother how

—thrilling it was, Mother, to see the Grand Duke's guard for you never saw such specimens of manhood, all hand-picked for the Duke's service, and I am told educated men all of them as well as so tall. They are taken from all over Tuscany, the very best the country has to offer, and once in the guard you may not marry nor lead any but a most proper life, and the competition to join is great as you may expect, it being a high honor. Sarah Allen, the maid to Mrs. Loftus as I told you of, has been introduced to one of the guard and thinks highly of him and is to receive an invitation for herself and one other to pass through the public rooms at the next audience held by the Duke and I am to be that one. Well, Wilson, my mistress says to me, I envy you for I have never been in the Duke's palace and would like to go and have no chance of it. I will write and tell you of it when it happens, Mother, but would *beg* of you before that date to *write to me* and tell me how you fare and if Fanny is recovered and every scrap of news, for when one is so far from home the craving for news is a terrible thing, as I am sure it is for you, but only think how I oblige, Mother, and it cannot in truth be said the same of you and I mean no criticism. It is two months again since I heard from you and that a very short letter, and I cannot tell if another has gone astray as I fear. Tell Ellen to write the address very plain.

The address was in fact always written very plain but she needed to imagine all manner of excuses for the lack of letters from Mother. In a whole year she had had only four and none that satisfied. Granted, Mother did not have much to write of, except to describe the new station that was being built or relate how a cholera epidemic raged, which was not pleasant to hear. The last, in July, had said Fanny was laid low with a fever and had driven her frantic with fear that Fanny had succumbed to the epidemic. Her mistress, entirely sympathetic to her distress, had known of an English lady about to depart for York and had asked her to take Wilson's reply home with her and see it on its very short way from York to Newcastle. The lady had written since to Mrs. Browning saying it had been done, so Wilson waited daily for a response to her anguished plea for immediate news of Fanny's condition. None had come and her agitation had subsided only through sheer exhaustion. Mrs. Browning had assured her that, if the *worst* had happened, then a communication of some kind would never have been delayed. For a while Wilson watched out for black-edged envelopes but when none appeared was compelled to become philosophical. There was no doubt that the new fullness of her life helped her to quieten her anxiety. Whereas in the early days in Pisa time had hung so heavily that the arrival of letters was a momentous event, now, though letters were still a cause of great joy, the wait for Mr. Browning to come back from the post office was not a desperate affair.

Minnie had proved her most reliable and frequent correspondent, Lizzie falling by the wayside after a single apologetic letter written in reply to her own third. Minnie wrote fortnightly and at some length, which pleased and surprised Wilson. Naturally, Minnie wrote of Wimpole Street and from her Wilson learned a great deal she was able to censor judiciously before relaying to her mistress. She did not think it fitting to tell her what Minnie had written of Arabel, who was reported to be in tears daily over her father's command that she should not go so regularly to her work with the Ragged Children's Charity. Instead, she passed on the news of Arabel's delight in letters from Italy and her joy at her sister's happiness.

Her mistress rewarded her with a smile and a few tears. She spoke often of her guilt at what she had left her beloved sisters to bear, of how she had condemned them to endure what she referred to as the "unbridled masculine rampancy" of the Barrett household, so that to hear they rejoiced in her escape and were not further cast down by it was a great relief. She could not, she said, enjoy her own happiness knowing they were wretched on her account.

It seemed to Wilson that Mrs. Browning missed her sisters more and not less as time went on. All that autumn, when they were obliged to leave the spacious rented rooms in the Casa Guidi and cram into what seemed a doll's house by comparison in the Piazza Pitti, she spoke of them longingly and, though she was back to old Wimpole Street habits, writing industriously for several hours every day, she was dreamy and nostalgic, sighing often for their company. She liked to talk of them and, since it was almost entirely talk full of memories, Wilson provided a better audience than her husband. She reminisced about Henrietta's squeezes, her impromptu dances where she loved to do the polka, and it was Wilson who could pick up the "do-you-remembers" and add onto them with memories of her own. Then, after such a session, invariably ending in smiles that changed to tears, Mrs. Browning would take Wilson's hand and hold it tenderly for a moment and say that at least she was not quite bereft of old friends.

Telling Sarah Allen how touched she was by this and other evidence of the regard in which she was held, Wilson was shocked at her new friend's response. "Well," Sarah said sharply, "you *are* a fool to be paid in soft words. This mistress of yours is getting three for the price of one from what I see you do and are to her. What is it you are? Cook or lady's maid? Seamstress or lady's maid? Housekeeper or lady's maid? *You* may think you are treasured, but I for one do not and am glad to be part of a proper establishment and not constantly asked to lower myself."

"There is no lowering," Wilson replied indignantly.

"There is lowering and lowering," Sarah said mysteriously, "and you would be wise to mark the difference before it is too late and you live to regret it."

"I have a girl under me," Wilson said, "I do not do everything."

"A girl under you?" Sarah laughed derisively. "That child? Fit for what? Sweeping a floor? Taking the washing? And even that under your direction. It is not who is *under* you, Lily, it is who is *with* you. And you have no one, you carry too much. But who am I to point it out if you are so adoring of this mistress of yours? I do not adore mine, nor want her to hold my hand, but I see she does right by me and if she were not to, why, Florence is full of those who would and she knows it. A good English lady's maid is much in demand, Lily, and you would do well not to forget it. I wonder your precious mistress has not noticed for herself how rare you are and how she ought to take steps to keep you."

How could she, Wilson wondered later, turning over and over in her mind what the outspoken Sarah had said, how could *my* mistress know of any other household when she never left her own? It was an impossibility, she had no point of comparison. And as for striving to keep her maid, why, that too was to misunderstand the nature of their relationship. Sarah spoke so often with contempt of Mrs. Loftus and was as full of ways in which she, Sarah, could get the better of her as Ellen, poor foolish Ellen, had been. It sickened Wilson to hear the pathetic record of cheating and trickery, the lack of respect and trust, the complete absence of true regard. Instead of making her discontented, Sarah only made her happier to be on the footing she was with her employers. She would never let them down, they would never betray her. This knowledge made her smile with pride and able to spot the jealousy which prompted Sarah Allen to speak so. She knew her well enough now to know that she was no Lizzie Treherne, faithful and compassionate, but was always on the lookout for her own advantage. As a companion Sarah was excellent but as an intimate, Wilson knew, she would not do. Moved to tell her mistress something of Sarah, after she had been to the Grand Duke's assembly, she found herself instantly understood. Mrs. Browning confessed that even a perfect husband could not give her what her sisters did and her husband, hearing only the first part, that he could not give her whatever it was, lifted his head from his book and expressed alarm to fail her in any department. When told his failing was the ability to relish and impart the slipslop of feminine gossip he laughed.

All that sunny winter, mild beyond belief, Wilson was often moved to observe how surprised those back home would be to hear so much laughter among the three of them. She even saw new lines on her mistress's face made through constant laughter (but knew better than to point them out). And she knew that on her own face there was more often than not a smile, replacing the look of bland composure she had previously cultivated. If her mistress had changed in appearance as well as demeanor, then so had she. Her own slightness had become more rounded, her own dresses needed more generous measurements. As she wrote to Minnie:

—you would wonder to see me nigh to *buxom* and as for my complexion though I have taken care to wear a bonnet at all times against this fierce sun and to use a parasol whenever I may, I have turned a brown color and am mortified though I am told it becomes me. You will want to know who told me and I dare hardly tell you for it is one of the Grand Duke's guard! Now you must not think Minnie that I am a sadly changed person and have become loose with my favors for I never would, but when a woman is approached in the most proper fashion by a most respectable intermediary and humbly beseeched to notice an individual as august as one of the Grand Duke's guard, then it is impossible to be dismissive. His name is Leonardo Righi and he of course being one of the guard, very tall, some six feet and two inches if you can imagine, and with dark hair and eyes. He is very formal and correct and did little more than present his credentials when first he made my acquaintance and was most anxious I should know his background which is that he is from a place, a small town, called Prato and his father is a medical man and his brother a prosperous haberdasher. He has a high opinion of Englishwomen and has heard they make the best wives! Well, of course, that is nonsense to talk of wives when we have met but twice and always with others, but I liked him the better for making the seriousness of his intentions plain though it amused me when I think how little I know him and yet *he* seems to have made his mind up. I am I assure you, Minnie, in no hurry to choose or to marry though my mistress is as good an advertisement for marriage as you can see and may soon be an advertisement for something else which she says I may tell you. There is no doubt this time and I had no need to point it out that she is expecting an interesting event in late summer, God willing. This time she is taking great care and Mr. Browning even greater. We have begun to sew and knit the little clothes and I never thought to see her so content over a needle. Dr. Harding has been called in and we like him very much and much more than the doctor in Pisa. Mr. Browning asked him if it would not be wiser for his wife to break off entirely the habit of laudanum but the doctor said he knew it to have little effect on her condition and it might be more material to stop the port wine which Dr. Cook prescribed, so it is no more port wine which my mistress is glad of for though she finds the Chianti her husband urges on her very pleasant, she has never liked the other. So we wait and this time will make no mistakes.

It made no difference. Though Mrs. Browning looked and sounded well as the new year of 1848 was brought in, and there were no pains or bleeding throughout January and February, in the middle of March Wilson was obliged to inform Minnie that her mistress had once more miscarried. Mr. Browning had again been almost too tender for a man. Wilson marveled at his solicitude and was annoyed with the cynical Sarah Allen, who only asked, "How long have they been wed?" with the corners of her thin mouth already turned down derisively.

"Eighteen months," Wilson said, "it is not nothing, after all."

"And it is not *much*," Sarah alleged, shaking her head, "not much at all, barely out of the honeymoon, and if as you tell me she has had two miscarriages in that time he will still be eager in that department."

"Whatever do you mean? I told you, he has said he cares little for a child but only . . ."

"Oh, I did not mean *that*, I meant his rights and her favors. If she has been expecting twice, and her frail, and had two miscarryings, and been ill, then it stands to reason Mr. Browning will not be tired of her yet, for he has had weeks and months, I daresay, of deprivation in bed."

"Sarah Allen!" Wilson exclaimed and got up from the seat in the Boboli Gardens where they were enjoying the sun. She turned and faced her friend, who was openly laughing at her discomfiture, and told her she did not understand true love and that was all there was to it—and she would thank her not to discuss the Brownings in such lewd terms.

"Oh, sit down, Lily, do," Sarah said. "You are so easily offended, as though that mistress of yours was all angel."

"I like respect for her."

"Well, you shall have it, I shall be as respectful as you like, but you can't stop me or anyone else from thinking what we think."

Nor could she. There was speculation in plenty among all the servants, in and out of the house where they had their lodgings, and Wilson grew tired of denying her mistress was either about to die or that she had vowed she would never risk becoming pregnant again. She hated the gossip, but ignoring it in Florence was not as effective as it once was in London. And she knew there was gossip about herself too, once Signor Righi had been seen bringing her a bouquet at Easter. It was a flamboyant bouquet, a violent mixture of scarlet tulips and crimson carnations buried in a cloud of yellow mimosa, and the whole lot tied with a pink satin ribbon. Wilson had stared at it when the servant girl, eyes wide with excitement, carried it in, and then there had been an unfortunate moment when Mrs. Browning had thought it was for her and had exclaimed in disbelief "From *Robert?* Such as these?" until she had read the card and laughed and said to Wilson they were from her follower. Wilson had not missed the hint of mockery. The flowers were vulgar, if ever flowers can be said to be such a thing (which she doubted). Separating them, she thought how lovely the tulips and the carnations looked on their own and put each variety in a separate jug. At least the card had been restrained, merely wishing Mrs. Wilson a Happy Easter, and happy it had indeed been. With the inquisitive Sarah as chaperone, she had walked out with Signor Righi twice and twice more lined the square to see him march at the very head of the Duke's procession to church. Then the Brownings, on Dr. Harding's advice, took to going for long carriage rides in the country around Florence, and these coinciding with a minor indisposition of the Grand Duke's so that Signor Righi's duties were lighter, she enjoyed a pleasant outing herself to Fiesole— without Sarah Allen.

Signor Righi was nothing if not correct. He did not, of course, wear his full dress uniform for such an occasion, but Wilson was relieved to discover that if anything he looked even more splendid in his ordinary uniform which, in her eyes, was anything but ordinary. Walking by his side, she worried only faintly that they might look incongruous and cause mirth since Signor Righi was so tall and she was so very small but she quickly realized nobody would be given to the slightest smile when faced with such a fellow. On all sides they met with admiration and Wilson, shy to the point of extinction, was amazed to find herself responding to it. She knew she looked pretty in a new dress of a very pale turquoise cut away at the neck in a fashion she had never worn before and with the Brownings' brooch pinning the most delicious of lace shawls around her shoulders. She was treated with such deference, it was almost an embarrassment and when she saw a boy scurry to bring her a more comfortable chair at Signor Righi's peremptory bidding she wondered what was happening to her. Her Italian was quite good enough to understand the general drift of her suitor's conversation though she was not proficient in answering fluently (and not above taking advantage of her supposed ignorance of the Italian language when it came to replying to questions about her feelings for him). She knew that after such a speedy beginning to their relationship Signor Righi was not likely to wait indefinitely for her to commit herself but she was enjoying the experience of being courted so much, she hardly wanted it to come to any conclusion.

"Will you marry him, then?" Sarah Allen asked, and would not be put off with a shrug. "He is a good catch, Lily, and if he's willing to leave the Grand Duke's guard to wed, then he is truly smitten."

"It is far too early to think of marrying," Wilson said.

"Too early? How is that? What age are you, Lily? Over five and twenty if I'm not mistaken."

"Just," Wilson lied, annoyed with herself.

"And have you had other offers?"

"Certainly I have."

"Then you ought to know how good this one is," Sarah said smartly. "What can you see that is wrong with it?"

Wilson did not reply but silently answered herself. It was the old query: was she in love? And the old riposte: what is love? She liked to be with Signor Righi and was flattered by his attentions. She even thought he would make a good husband, if being courteous and respectful meant the same thing. She was attracted to him, in that when his hand touched her elbow to guide her across the street she felt a frisson of what might prove to be desire, but the thought of anything more intimate rather appalled her. Then she had not met his family, or seen Prato, nor did she know what manner of life she would be leading if she left the Brownings' service—which was another thing. How could she leave when her mistress was once more pregnant, though none knew it but the two of them, not even Mr. Browning, and was quite desperate that this time she would bear the child? The utmost care must be taken and only she could see that it was. Only a month after they had moved back into the Casa Guidi, at the end of their short lease in the Piazza Pitti, Wilson had felt instinctively that her mistress had conceived and yet had no reason to. Writing to her mother, to whom she still wrote regularly, though a full winter had gone by without a line in return, Wilson tried to describe how

—there was the oddest feeling, Mother, when I went in to her that morning, the morning after Midsummer's Night. She was lying half in, half out of the bed, with everything disarrayed, and the shutters being still closed and the room dark in any case, it was difficult to make her out. I opened the shutters and turned to say good morning ma'am and another beautiful morning it is, when she lifted herself up and smiled and held out her arms as though in joy and I went to her and she embraced me. I am so happy, dear, she said, and for nothing in particular. She seemed secret in herself and it crossed my mind that something might have so transformed her but I said nothing there being nothing but ridiculous fancy to say. All the next month she was especially lively and well, and by the time Mr. Browning took her off on an excursion at the end of July when this city burned like a furnace and he wanted her out of it, I was sure she was expecting again. I spoke of my conviction and she put a finger to my lips and nodded but said I was not to speak of it yet for she hardly dared to believe she was given another chance. Well, Mother, I was uneasy knowing that rattling about in a carriage and on these roads, which are very poor once outside the city, was quite the worst thing for her delicate condition but when I said so she told me I was being presentimental and that it was too early in her pregnancy to do any harm. I begged her to tell her husband but she would not, saying he would cancel their holiday and wrap her in cotton wool at once which she could not abide. I wondered if I should not defy my mistress for the first time and do what I thought right and not what I was bid, but she saw the look in my eye, I daresay, and said, now Wilson, you must not tell my husband for that would be cruel and I will tell him myself upon our return. Which she did and it was as she said, him being determined to keep her in her bed though she is only a few weeks gone. By our reckoning it will be the end of February and it is only August, but it is not too soon to be cautious in the extreme. Dr. Harding was brought in and has spoken in private to Mr. Browning. He came to me the morning after the doctor's visit and was very grave and said, Wilson, only you will understand the care that must be taken and I will need your help as never before, saving once. Then he said he planned to wean my mistress, his wife, from the laudanum which he had a conviction whatever the doctors said was the cause of the miscarrying, and she had promised to let him have his way being determined nothing this time should even be suspected to be her fault. So I am mixing half the quantity of the tincture with water and she takes that and in another week I am to reduce it further which frightens me for I have seen her once when she could not get it, the bottle being knocked over and broken by Flush that night, and it was a dreadful sight. She could not be still and became near demented and I was at the chemist's when he opened, and rushed to her with the correct mixture and only then was she calm. So now we are holding our breath and there is a pause, very welcome after this busy time furnishing these rooms, which formerly were furnished by the owner who has now removed his things. And Mother, we have a manservant, a cook by the name of Alessandro and do not think I am pleased for I am *not*, decidedly. He is a most boastful man and believes himself to be a genius and furthermore his quarters are so cramped and intrude on mine which are also cramped and altogether I find the new arrangement not at all to my liking and have said so. The dinners Alessandro prepares are all very well and I do not find fault with his cooking though you would laugh at his idea of a good stew, but the man himself I cannot abide. He is forever presuming to know more than anyone else and to hear him talk you might imagine he had been everywhere in the world and cooked for Kings which cannot be the truth or he would not be here. He is not old but so fat it ages him and he has eyebrows so thick they make me think of apes and I find myself quite ill and unable to look at him. Furthermore, though I cannot yet be sure, I fancy he is a cheat of the first order and fools my master into believing he has spent on food what he has not in fact spent and if so he will in time be found out for he has not yet guessed how careful my master is with money.

Alessandro looked at her and if she had not known he had a wife and three children elsewhere in the city, to whom he returned on Sundays for the night, Wilson would have felt uneasy. As it was, she tried hard to absent herself from the miserable hole called a kitchen, though with her room so near to it there was no hope of escaping the knowledge of Alessandro's noisy presence. He was, she thought, the noisiest, messiest cook she had ever seen at work but neither of the Brownings, secluded in their huge rooms at the front of the apartment, ever seemed to hear or see him. At night, when he climbed the ladder to his bed above the kitchen, Wilson could hear him snoring and the sound unnerved her. She lay imagining Signor Righi in bed and wondering if he snored in such a heavy, masculine way. Mr. Browning did not, of that she was sure. He had a delicacy and modesty remarkable to behold and in his person was as fastidious as any woman. Alessandro was not. He was crude and clumsy and it outraged her that he did not attempt to protect her from his ablutions and worse, whereas she took care both to wash and to perform all natural functions with a regard for what others could see and hear. What she suffered from the company of Alessandro made marriage to Signor Righi all the more attractive and she resolved to speak to her mistress as soon as an opportunity arose—let her be safely over the miscarrying months and then she would speak out and say she intended to marry after the baby was born.

Before she could make such an announcement a disaster of such magnitude overcame her that all thoughts of engagements and marriage and other happinesses were swept away. One afternoon in September Mr. Browning came back from the post office with a fat-looking letter for Wilson. He presented it to her with a smile and hoped she enjoyed whatever was in it and suggested she should give up combing Flush for the fleas that plagued him and retreat at once to her room. Instead, quite breathless with excitement and the promise of such pleasure at last—for she could see the envelope was in Mother's own hand—Wilson begged leave to take herself off to the Boboli Gardens where she could sit in the sunshine and make a festival of her letter. All the way there, she clutched her letter to herself, the very weight of it pleasing her, and even once she was seated just inside the entrance on her favorite seat in a pretty arbor she turned the precious letter over and over, pressing it first to her cheek and then to her lips, caressing it with her fingertips and squeezing it fondly. Inside was all the news of almost a year and she wished to savor every morsel wrapped up so enticingly in it. At last, drawing a deep breath, she opened it and spread out the sheets of thick paper, counting them before she began to read. There were four large sheets, all so closely written it would be difficult to decipher Mother's wavering script, but never would a labor be more lovingly performed.

"My dearest Lily" (the letter began, and even reading those simple, obvious words, Wilson's eyes misted over and she had to wait a moment before continuing),

> I thank you first for your many letters which have been like manna from heaven and much loved. It has torn at my heart that you will have wondered and fretted at my silence but when you know all you will understand I was not mistress of myself and unable to compose a letter . . .

A cold hand seemed to grip her heart as she read those words and she felt herself shiver. Looking up, she watched a child bowl a wheel along, laughing and shrieking, and tried to reassure herself that Mother's words were not necessarily ominous. Almost reluctantly now, she returned to the letter, holding the first sheet a little way from her as though, after all, to distance herself from whatever news was to come.

. . . which made any sense and was not cruel to you being so far away. I cannot even remember when I last wrote nor can Ellen but we told you, I am sure, of Fanny's illness, her first illness. She was taken very bad in the summer with what we thought was a fever such as she has had before which you will recall witnessing and I dealt with it as before with herbs and medicines and nursed her carefully and she seemed to get better, but then two months after the onset of this fever and one month after it lifted she fell ill again and burned so hot a cold cloth was warm against her head in a moment and she was delirious not knowing who I was. I sent at once for Mr. Conroy, who as you know is expert at fevers, and he took one look at her and said he thought this was no ordinary fever but like a plague. The very word threatened to throw me into strong hysterics but I struggled and gained control and asked Mr. Conroy what should be done. He said nothing could be done except for watching closely how the fever progressed and if any sores broke out when we would know for sure that he was right and this was a strange infectious fever previously not endured. We took turns, Ellen and May and I, and no sores appeared but the fever never lifted and Fanny was unable to swallow even so much as a teaspoon of water. Mr. Conroy returned and said he believed now it was diphtheria and the throat must be lanced. I near fainted at this but he forced my poor baby's lips open and showed me the pus and I saw it was as he said. He said there was a clever young doctor newly started whom he knew of, but he was costly and could I stand the expense of having him perform the operation necessary. I said cost did not come into it where Fanny's life was concerned and that between us my daughters and I would pay this doctor whatever he charged. He was sent for immediately and came and everything was made ready on the morning of Midsummer's Day. Dearest Lily, I will spare you what took place, there being no use in harrowing you, though indeed I wrote a wild letter to you immediately after telling you all but thank God had the mercy to tear it up. And it has been like that ever since—I write, I destroy and never get nearer breaking this terrible news. Dearest Lily, poor Fanny bled to death on the table here. The young doctor was not so clever and in operating severed an artery without knowing and continuing to say afterward that Fanny's artery was awkwardly placed and her neck thin, and it could not have been otherwise. You will wonder and perhaps be angry that two long months have passed and only now are you told this news and not with a black-edged envelope or seal to warn you and as there properly ought to be, but I could not bear to frighten you so at the very beginning. Dearest Lily, if I have acted wrongly, forgive me, it was for your sake, truly. And as to the immense delay I have been afflicted with other troubles though beside Fanny's death nothing else touches me. Ellen is with child and the father whose name you well know and with which I will not sully this page which bears real sorrow will not marry her nor stand by her and she has been sent off from her place. She is neither ashamed nor cowed but defiant and likely to humiliate us even further than she has already done by throwing herself before this worthless man and begging him to notice her. The child is to be born at Michaelmas and how we will manage I do not know for I have not finished this weary catalogue of woe. Dearest Lily, we have to leave this house. The fate I always dreaded has befallen us since Sir Richard Robson has died and his estate passed to his son who has sold the house and estate with all its holdings and buildings and we are evicted without appeal as from the New Year. It has been pointed out to us how fortunate we are to be given time to prepare but it is hard to see any fortune in it. I have been frantic with thinking where we might go and how we might manage and have spent many nights between weeping and praying and seeing us all on the parish but the kindness of Mr. Conroy has saved me from true despair. He has a brother in Sheffield, who has done well for himself and runs two apothecary businesses and is in need of some steady person to help him prepare medicines and the like. Now I have no training as you know, but I have helped Mr. Conroy often and he has been much impressed with my poor skills and with my neatness and has told his brother and explained the circumstances and there is a house available. I am to help this other Mr. Conroy and May is to be maid to his wife and if Ellen sees sense and leaves her child here with whoever can be found to take it she too is to be found a place and we will earn our keep and have a roof over our heads if in a strange place. You will see now, Lily, why this letter took so long to form itself and I am truly sorry for what it contains. It is an unspeakable relief to me that you at least are happy and doing well and you are not to do anything foolish which I fear you might knowing your kind heart and true feeling. Stay where you are, Lily, for the storm is passed and you can do nothing. Brighter days are ahead, I have a certainty of it. The other night I sat by the fire, weeping a little, I confess, and all of a sudden I saw Fanny laughing and running about and throwing kisses to me and felt much lightened. And then I saw a house I did not recognize and myself baking in it and everything neat and well appointed. And, finally, I saw you dearest Lily in such a pretty frock of the palest turquoise and at your side a man of immense height who squired you about with great finesse. Now, Lily you have not spoken of a man and I ask you if there is such a one to tell me of him, for we all must have hope and trust to God, who knows all and does what He does for our sakes.

The last words of endearment read, Wilson folded up the letter with stiff fingers and replaced it in its envelope. She would burn it, the moment she reached home. Such a document did not bear keeping. Every line was cruelly embedded in her mind and would never be forgotten. Where, she wondered as she rose and began to walk slowly back to the Casa Guidi, where were her tears? There were none now the letter was done. Everything about her felt dry—her throat, her eyes, her mouth. She swallowed repeatedly, licked her lips, tried to create saliva and failed. Entering the dark hall of the Casa Guidi building, she stumbled and put out a hand to steady herself, a hand that met the cold, moist stone with relief. She stood leaning her forehead against the wall for a moment before wearily climbing the stairs. As quietly as possible she opened the heavy door into the Brownings' apartment, hoping to slip into her room and lie down but Flush met her in a frenzy of welcome and Mr. Browning followed behind, smiling. She blessed him for his discretion. He saw her face and said nothing at all, only took her arm and led her into the drawing room, calling on his wife to come at once, but not in a voice to cause her alarm. She came, smiling too, and also saw her maid's stricken face and knelt down beside her chair and took her hand. "My sister Fanny is dead," Wilson said dully, and then at last began to weep.

CHAPTER SEVENTEEN

I N OCTOBER, just as she was beginning to think there might after all
still be some happiness in life, Wilson heard from Leonardo Righi—
she did not like the slightly derisive way in which her employers
always referred to him as "Mr." Righi, which was not even correct—
that the Grand Duke, under pressure from the city fathers, was
disbanding his personal guard. Leonardo was going home to Prato
where he would take employment with either his father the medical
man or his brother-in-law the merchant. But he could not go without
the answer to his proposal of marriage and it must be definite. When
he said this, his eyes were full of reproach and Wilson knew she had
been remiss. It was not fair to have kept Leonardo dangling all
summer and she was a little ashamed. He seemed to require so little of
her, claiming no favors even after months of walking out, and yet she
did not think for one moment he was a cold fish (which she had
always suspected Reginald Pomfret to have been). When he kissed
her hand at the end of each occasion upon which he had taken her out,
his eyes conveyed messages of unmistakably passionate intent. But
he did not presume to do more than kiss her hand and, though she was

pleased to be so honored, she was puzzled. Leonardo was courting her in such a strictly formal manner, she could hardly credit it and could not quite decide what to make of it. Daily, Sarah Allen, of whom she was growing tired, pointed out to her what might happen. "There are other pebbles on the beach, Lily, and you are not that special." It was altogether better to discuss what she should do with her mistress who, since the devastating news from home, had been truly tender and solicitous.

Because she was now undeniably pregnant and at what was pronounced by Dr. Harding to be the most dangerous stage, Mrs. Browning spent almost the whole day prone once more, rising only from her bed to walk to her sofa, very like the old days in Wimpole Street. And as in those days, which in all other respects were so different and felt as if they belonged to another age, Wilson sat beside her mistress for many hours, keeping her company and being on hand to save her the effort of moving. She sewed baby clothes to add to the layette wrapped up in tissue paper after the last miscarriage, and as she sewed she felt so troubled that it was not surprising her mistress should ask her, very gently, if she was still grieving for Fanny or was there another burden pressing heavy. So Wilson told her of Leonardo's imminent departure and of how she was committed to replying the next day.

"How long have you been walking out, dear?" Mrs. Browning asked, her voice low and almost caressing in its concern.

"Since Easter, ma'am."

"And now it is autumn. A long time, but some loves are slow."

"I do not know if it *is* love, which is always the trouble with me. He is very attractive, I feel his attraction, if I am to confess freely, ma'am."

"But of course you are, and why should women be ashamed of feeling that physical attraction men exhibit so carelessly and are rather praised for than otherwise? I am glad you are attracted. And for the rest?"

"He is a good man, honest and respectful and reliable, which I like. He is courteous, treating me as a princess, however absurd."

"It is not at all absurd and makes me like the sound of Mr. Righi more and more."

"I would trust him as to his prospects. He is not likely to turn out a wastrel. But Prato, where he lives, is, they say, a very small place up in the mountains and I have always preferred cities. I should be very isolated, knowing no one but him."

"That is the key, Wilson—do you *need* anyone else, dear?"

Wilson looked up from the tiny dress she was sewing and held her needle suspended. Her mistress's meaning was unmistakable: *she* needed no one but Robert. If Leonardo was not sufficient for Wilson, then the conclusion was meant to be that she could not be in love. She hesitated, feeling somehow tricked. It was true, Mr. and Mrs. Browning were everything to each other but it was not the whole truth. Many an afternoon, especially of late, Mrs. Browning had pined, and even wept, for her sisters and, though she was not close with any of the Englishwomen in Florence who paid visits, she enjoyed the distraction they occasionally provided. And only the day before, when told a young woman by the name of Ogilvy had moved into the apartment above them in the Casa Guidi, and that she had a new baby and was something of a poet and had a pleasant husband, Mrs. Browning had been thrilled and suggested she might have a friend at last. It was not honest to pretend that, if she had been Wilson, Leonardo would be enough.

"Yes, ma'am," Wilson replied, stitching once more and her eyes lowered conveniently, "I fear I do. It would be very lonely with only a husband and no friend or family and I unable to speak the language as fluently as I would like. I would be very dependent on Signor Righi and I have learned to value my independence, which you may not think is very great, having no home of my own and little income, but which feels so to me."

There was silence. Wilson felt herself tremble a little and she felt hot about the face. She hoped she had not caused offense with the mention of income. It was another of Sarah Allen's refrains: "What they pay for what you do, Lily, is a scandal and they should be told so. Why, I have twice as much and do half the work and I would not stand for it." Hearing from a reluctant Wilson that she had not had an increase in salary in all the four years she had worked for the Brownings, Sarah called her a fool. "Every year I claim an increase, even if it is only a shilling or two, and I am given it gladly. Mrs. Loftus knows it is an English maid's market here in Florence, and were she to lose me she would have difficulty replacing me whereas *I*—I could go anywhere, there being Americans in the city most desirous of such a maid as I. Look at you, Lily, you are comely and neat and expert and you speak the language very well, which is unusual in a maid and more than I can manage. You could go where you wished if you were turned off." Wilson had ignored her, but since Mother's letter the thought of being able to send more money home had begun to obsess her. She would buy no more new dresses or bonnets nor waste money buying ices to eat with Sarah Allen and she would send Mother a money order every month with Mr. Browning's help. But if she married, there would be no money of her own.

At last her mistress spoke. To Wilson's relief, she did not pick up any reference to money either way. "You are uncertain, dear," she said, "and if I were you I should be guided by your uncertainty. Would it not be wise to wait? And do not think I speak only from self-interest, though I do not deny it is there. In my condition . . ." And she made a gesture of such pathos and looked so forlorn, Wilson found herself saying hurriedly, "Oh, ma'am, do not think I would desert you until the baby is safely born—I could not be so cruel." Once she had said it, it seemed the answer she had looked for. The next day she met Leonardo and they walked over the Ponte Santa Trinità and along the Arno and she told him that if he were willing to wait until the spring, until Mrs. Browning's baby was born, then she would be glad to marry him and gave her word now that she would. He appeared overjoyed and kissed her hand and to her amazement wept a little. It gave her the most curious sensation to think she meant so much to him and that there was evidence of such deep feeling. He did not seem to resent the six months' interval, once she had reaffirmed the engagement was official, saying it would give him time to prepare a home fitting for her. For the first time he embraced her before he left her—though not before requesting permission to do so—and, enfolded in his arms, Wilson felt happy and relieved. His excitement and joy were so evident, she herself was infected by them and returned to the Casa Guidi quite radiant to tell her mistress of her decision. It was greeted with a measured enthusiasm and a restraint she rather resented but nevertheless her health and "Mr." Righi's was drunk that night and when, before he departed, Leonardo presented her with a beautiful ring he said had been his mother's, this was admired with a more genuine pleasure.

She wore the ring not on her finger, except at night, but around her neck. All day as she worked she could feel the cold little bump of it between her breasts, lying there like a tiny egg, and it made her smile. A ring was something. It made it safe to write to Mother:

—I hope it will not be too great a shock, my dearest mother, for you have suffered enough this past year but I am engaged to be married. I have not told you of my suitor, wondering not only if anything would come of it but also being unsure of my own feelings and not wishing to startle you unnecessarily. He is called Leonardo Righi and as you will easily deduce from that is Italian and has been until this week one of the Grand Duke's personal guard but this guard being disbanded for reasons that I do not rightly understand he has returned home to Prato, a village in the mountains. His family is good, and he has some money and may start a business of his own. He is tall and handsome and most courteous and as you see I'm more than a little in love with him . . .

The moment she had written this, Wilson felt she *was* in love, as though the mere act of writing the words had settled her doubts. She felt warm and happy toward Leonardo and had quickly found since his departure that his face haunted her and she looked constantly for his imposing figure striding toward her.

. . . but we have agreed to wait until March before we marry and oh, Mother I would that you could come though I know it to be impossible, and weep at the hopelessness of such a wish. But I have extracted a promise from Leonardo that when the Brownings go to England which they intend to do someday he will release me for some months and I will travel to England with them and see you in your new home. So that is something to hold on to for me, Mother, and I hope for you, and now that you have written that letter you dreaded I pray you will continue to write that I might not be shut away from your concerns being tragedies or not. I am vexed with Ellen and wish she could be brought to see the error of her ways and the harm she does you. To abandon the child when it is born is a dreadful thing but if it were possible some kind family might take it and keep it until such time as Ellen had a home for it, but if she sticks with this cruel man what hope is there of that. Ellen is not bad but she is easily led into bad ways and I fear for her. Is there no hope Albert can be shamed into at least providing something for what is his child? Or is he beyond shame, as my poor sister Ellen seems to be. I am glad May stays staunch and true and looks to being a help to you in the difficult days ahead. Would that I were at your side, Mother. My life here is easy, were it not for our cook, the disagreeable Alessandro, who however may not be with us much longer, and I have plenty of hours strolling in the sunshine which I would wish to spend with you. Mrs. Browning continues very well. She felt the child quicken yesterday morning and Dr. Harding says that is early, being only, it is estimated, fourteen weeks and means it is a strong child for which we are all thankful. The laudanum is reduced to ten daily drops only which if you will remember it was once forty is astonishing. Sometimes, it is true, when Mr. Browning is not there my mistress begs for a little more, but I only pretend to oblige and so far it has satisfied her. By the next month we are to be down to six drops and Mr. Browning has hopes to be off it entirely in the last crucial months. If she carries this baby past next week it will be longer than she has ever done and Dr. Harding says we are now in the most critical period.

Mr. Browning, of course, as Wilson was well aware, held that every minute of every hour of every day was critical and was beside himself with anxiety if his wife confessed to the smallest ache, pain or sensation of discomfort. She soon grew so tired of his alarm that it was only to Wilson she spoke, in whispers, of any ailment. Together they pondered the significance of a burning feeling high in the abdomen after meals and the sudden cramp at night in her right leg. But at least Wilson had a new confidante and one who seemed most expert in all matters to do with maternity. This was Jeannie, maid to Mrs. Ogilvy, the new tenant on the floor above the Brownings'. Jeannie, a straightforward Scottish girl from Dunoon, had been with the Ogilvys three years, during which time she had witnessed the birth of Louisa, now two, and Alexander, born only that September. For the slight morning sickness Mrs. Browning was experiencing Jeannie confidently recommended five grains of ginger and five of baking soda to be mixed with thirty drops of sal volatile and taken with a small glass of water. This remedy worked and Wilson began to place as much faith in Jeannie as she always had done in Mother. The burning feeling, Jeannie informed Wilson, who promptly informed her mistress, was merely indigestion occasioned by the weight of the baby in the womb pushing against the stomach and it would get worse but was of no consequence. And as for the cramp, this was another unavoidable hazard of approaching motherhood but might be alleviated by rubbing the legs before retiring with oil of primrose. Oil of primrose was purchased and rubbed into Mrs. Browning's legs by Wilson and there were no more cramps. Jeannie was at once hailed as a genius.

"Och, I'm nae a genius," Jeannie smiled, "but I've taken Mrs. Ogilvy thro' twa bairns and I've listened to the doctors, that's a'. You larn as ye go." What she wanted to learn herself was Italian, for though she'd been in Italy, off and on, these three years with the Ogilvys she had never picked up more than a smattering. Wilson helpfully dug out her old grammar book and gave it to Jeannie and together they began at the beginning, Wilson acting the part of the Italian in the conversational exercises.

Jeannie Black intrigued her highly. She was not in the normal run of lady's maids, and was indeed not so much Mrs. Ogilvy's maid as her general help. An Italian girl was employed as nursemaid and there was another woman to do the rough work, but Jeannie ruled the roost and seemed to lend her hand to everything. She was, Wilson observed, an object of great curiosity to the Italians, who could not get over her bright red hair and endless stream of chatter and her loud, raucous laugh. Though only twenty-six, Jeannie appeared much older, partly through her stoutness. But what fascinated Wilson most was how she treated, and was treated by, pretty young Mrs. Ogilvy. Jeannie was maternal toward her mistress but not in the least deferential, sometimes startling Wilson with what sounded like impudence but appeared to be accepted, with a smile, as "just Jeannie's way." She had always thought her own relationship with her mistress extraordinarily free and had been proud of the friendship between them but now, as she watched and listened to Jeannie and Mrs. Ogilvy, she wondered how she could have been deluded and described amusingly to Minnie how

—you would blush, Minnie, to hear this Jeannie talk back to her mistress as we would call it and all in an accent so thick I could not attempt to reproduce it on this page for fear you would tear it up as gibberish. She is so sure of the regard in which she is held that she thinks nothing of calling her mistress a *nuisance* if you can believe it for forgetting to tell her that a dress is torn until it is to be worn again and only then discovered. How can I keep your things in good order if you do not tell me you ripped it, this Jeannie says and adds, I do not know what you were doing and you a mother with a young baby climbing in those woods like a boy, and would have thought you had more sense. Well! Could I speak thus? And you may ask if I would want to. But the Ogilvys are devoted to their Jeannie and if she is annoyed and talks of returning to Dunoon they are distraught.

Would the Brownings be distraught, Wilson had to ask herself, if she talked of returning to England, or of going to Prato forthwith? Somehow she imagined not. Sorry, even worried as to how they would manage without her, but no longer, not for a long time, distraught. The difference saddened her and, since her mood was always so quickly reflected in her demeanor, the reason for her downcast air was inquired into. Was it Mr. Righi? No, because he wrote beautiful letters of continuing devotion of which she was very proud. What then? On a sudden inspiration Wilson said it was Alessandro and, once she had named him as the source of her melancholy, she came to believe it. She was tired, she told Mrs. Browning, of his boasting and of his untidiness, and was certain her early suspicions of his dishonesty were true. There was a silence, during which she had the strange sensation of feeling she had the upper hand. "Dear Wilson," her mistress pleaded, "try to be patient, as I know you can, and in a while we will replace Alessandro which, you know, is not easy and cannot be done in a moment. Will you bear it, dear, on a promise of resolving the problem as soon as we can?" Graciously, Wilson said she would. Only afterward did she see she had missed the perfect opportunity to ask for an increase in her salary.

As it was, even with the small amount she earned, she sent Mother money in November and January and had the satisfaction of receiving prompt thanks. The move to Sheffield was made comfortable because of the extra pounds, through which a place in the coach was secured for Mother while Ellen and May traveled by cart with the few sticks of furniture the family had. It was, Mother related to Wilson, a long and weary journey made more distressing by Ellen's grieving not for her baby, who had been stillborn, but the disappearance of her lover. She was "utterly broken and without hope," Mother wrote, and all who looked on her pitied her for a poor dejected creature. Wilson, upon reading this, felt a twinge of guilt. She had not been sorry enough for Ellen, blaming her for adding to Mother's woes, and now she felt a rush of compassion. Poor, silly Ellen—her baby dead and its father proved worthless. When she remembered Albert and compared him to her Leonardo a sense of her own good fortune made her dash off at once a letter to Ellen in which she offered her love, her prayers and strength to endure the ordeal ahead.

She would much rather write to Leonardo, to whom she poured out a long account of Ellen's history, managing in the process to confess how fortunate she felt in having a fiancé like him, so respectable and honorable and trustworthy. Perhaps it was this effusiveness, she often felt afterward, which prompted Leonardo to pause before replying, as if she had given him too much to digest. In December his weekly letters stopped. Eight she had had since his departure, all posted on a Monday, all four pages long, all full of the building and furnishing of a house for them both. Told there was snow in the mountains, Wilson waited patiently, convinced this was the explanation for the lack of letters. Probably Leonardo had not even received hers and was fretting at the lack of news, as she was. When the new year of 1849 dawned, all Wilson wished from it was a letter from Prato. None came. Each day, concerned at her agitation, Mr. Browning redoubled his inquiries at the post office which, he was the first to agree, resembled chaos. But there was no mistake: no letters for Wilson, c/o Browning. She hardly knew what to do. Alessandro, to whom she had unwisely boasted of Leonardo, feeling it was time she returned boasts on one subject at least (she had had quite enough of his wife, whom he described as a beauty but who Wilson had been reliably informed was a slattern), was openly derisive, telling her Signor Righi had doubtless found himself a good Italian woman. Furious, Wilson ignored him but cried tears of rage as much as misery in private. Though she imagined it ought to be beneath what dignity she had left, she composed a short note to Leonardo, asking only to be informed of any change of heart. Mr. Browning sent it for her, arranging for its delivery to be signed for and a reply paid. The letter was duly recorded as delivered but no reply was forthcoming. That, it seemed, was that. Shaken, Wilson had to write to her mother at the beginning of February that

—I am no longer engaged, Mother, but do not distress yourself for who knows if it is not for the best, and though I have wept a little it is more from a strong mortification than an upset heart. Mrs. Browning tells me I am fortunate to have found Leonardo out before it was too late but though it would be a comfort to think like that I cannot in justice do so but rather fear I asked too much of him, first keeping him waiting for my answer the whole long summer and then making it a condition that I could not marry for another six months which since he was obliged to go home was hard. I believe him still to be a good man who had no desire to trick me and who cared for me truly. I do not know what to do with his ring, which is very precious and beautiful and was his mother's. Mrs. Browning says it would not be right to send it through the post and that it will be sufficient to write once more asking for it to be collected if he wishes and this I will do. Well, Mother, I do not know if this will disappoint you or not for it is true that if I had become the wife of an Italian in Prato, for all I had the promise of a future journey to England, I would have been in a sense lost to you. Now I can tell you for certain that next year I will travel to London with the Brownings and, God willing, their child, and be there several weeks at least and have already had the assurance from them that I may take my holidays then and be with you. I will be thankful by then, I do not doubt, to be in England for all I am happy with Italy. There is much disturbance here with talk of war with the Austrians and I do not like to think of such violence though my mistress laughs at my anxiety and vows she is untroubled and indeed desirous that war should begin and the Austrians be driven out and the Italians have what is theirs. It is not good for her to read accounts of what is happening for she becomes greatly excited and flushed and might cause her child to be born prematurely in which case it is not likely to survive. Her husband begs her to remain calm and swears he will bring her no more newspapers if the contents result in such agitation. Many people have left Florence, among them Mr. & Mrs. Loftus with their children and maid, Sarah Allen, with whom I have been friendly. My mistress says scornfully that they are cowards all. I do not know that I am not a coward myself and given the chance would flee too but with my mistress in the condition she is in it would be impossible even if she wished it. She is nearly full term and Dr. Harding is most pleased with her.

This was true, but it was not the whole story. Dr. Harding, after his visit on February 10, took Wilson aside. He had examined and left Mrs. Browning in her bedroom attended by her anxious husband, whom he had just assured all was as well as could be. They stood together, doctor and maid, outside the door of the Brownings' apartment, the doctor's head dropped in thought, and Wilson was hardly able to see the expression on his face in the gloom. His voice, kept low, seemed to echo; the echo made his words sinister.

"Now, Mrs. Wilson," Dr. Harding said, and coughed before starting again, "Mrs. Wilson, you are a woman of good sense, as I have seen, and reliable in every way but you must be aware, as I am, that Mrs. Browning's case is very particular."

"Oh yes, sir, I am indeed, sir."

"Very particular, and because it is so particular I must, as her medical man, take most particular measures. There may, Mrs. Wilson, though I would thank you not to breathe a word of this, for alarm can be contagious and cause panic, which would be injurious, there may be cause for skilled nursing and even the use of instruments. Should this be the case, I would wish to have the services of another person as well as yourself and I do not mean an ordinary midwife. There is an Italian woman, Signora Romalfi, with whom I have worked on some desperate cases where more than a cool head and a steady hand are called for. Do you take my meaning?"

"Yes, sir."

"I intend to inform Signora Romalfi tomorrow that the birth is imminent . . ."

"Indeed, sir? So soon?"

"I do not think it is soon, though these things know no rules and the best estimate is only a guess. The head is engaged and the child feels full grown and large, very large."

"Oh, sir!"

"Now come, Mrs. Wilson, that is not necessarily a disaster. Mrs. Browning is small but I have seen small women give birth easily to large babies and large women suffer torment bringing forth tiny ones, so all is not lost. But it is of the utmost importance that all the signs of labor beginning should be accurately noted and for that I would rather depend on you than Mrs. Browning. Do you know what a show is, Mrs. Wilson?"

"I believe so, sir. It is the coming away of liquid that lies in front of the baby, I have been told."

"Very good, that is near enough. Now your mistress may think nothing of a show, or may on the other hand think too much, but either way I wish you to send for me at once and get her to bed even before I come. And any pains, *any* pains, from this day forward *must* be reported. Is that understood?"

"Yes, sir."

"Well, I will bid you good day, Mrs. Wilson, and trust I leave my patient in capable hands, as I know I do."

Wilson was not so sure. These days, as she helped her mistress dress and undress, she was rather alarmed by the immense size of her belly. The rest of her had hardly fattened at all, making the mound seem even more enormous than it actually was. She would stand, as her shift was slipped on, with her hands on her stomach and when the baby kicked she smiled and looked at Wilson proudly. But then on other days, when there was no movement, she was tense and looked down in despair at herself and wondered aloud if she had harmed her child with the laudanum. Then Wilson would soothe her and remind her she had all but ceased to take any laudanum this past two months, that the couple of drops she still liked smuggled into her glass last thing at night were of no consequence. She was not always successful in setting her mistress's mind at rest. Once, as she wrote to Minnie,

—I could do nothing with her. She lay and wept and looked at the portrait of her father which hangs opposite her bed and said she did not want to die without his forgiveness. Her distress became so great that I vowed I would have to go for her husband at which she made a great effort and stopped, saying she could not cry before him nor wound him by talking of death. I said thinking to brace her up that it was wrong to talk of dying when it would mean leaving Mr. Browning bereft and she smiled a little and said she could not indeed afford to leave this world when there was a Robert in it and him the most perfect man in the world which she did not deserve.

Sitting sewing pink twilled muslin for the lining of the wicker-work cradle throughout the February afternoons, Wilson had plenty of time to ponder on this adoration of her mistress's. She had known Mr. Browning now two and a half years and was still not used to him. He was everything his wife said—patient, tender, full of feeling, entirely lacking in masculine traits of the more unpleasant and common variety—and yet she could not agree he was a perfect husband. He was not the husband she wished for, even if the fault was in herself. She knew quite well that her mistress was the stronger-willed and though Mr. Browning was not weak he was given to bowing before his wife's wishes, in a way Wilson found suspect. She would not wish to lead her own husband but felt in herself the need to obey.

Mrs. Browning sighed and asked for a glass of water, closing the book she had been reading. "Well, such a fuss," she said, "and now I discover it is not for so very much."

"About what, ma'am?"

"*Jane Eyre*, the sensation of London last summer, or so everyone writes to me. I see no reason why you may not read it, Wilson. It is about a poor governess, of good family but in reduced circumstances, as so many are." Mrs. Browning looking at her curiously, then said, "Wilson, do you remember first coming to Wimpole Street? And were you very afraid of us all? Did we make you suffer, like poor Jane Eyre, and were you very lonely?"

Wilson smiled. It was typical that one question should follow another without pause for reply. "I remember it very well and thought everyone kind but I *was* lonely and lost, as you might expect."

"Of course I might. Was I heartless, dear?"

"No, ma'am. You were sad and not well then and I wished very much to help you."

"As you have." The eyes filled with tears but a smile came too and then another question. "Do you regret coming with us, Wilson? Tell me truly."

"No, I do not. It has benefited me."

"Indeed it has. All can see. When we go back to London it will be *you* who draw the compliments now you have flourished and grown into yourself and blossom so."

It was with such chitchat that they whiled away the long afternoons while Mr. Browning walked the crowded streets where almost every day there was a commotion and rumors of an Austrian invasion rife. Wilson did not like to go out partly because she was so fearful of her mistress's health, taking too literally Dr. Harding's words that he relied on her, and partly because she was afraid she would be caught up in some insurrection. Sarah Allen, who was her most reliable companion, had in any case gone and there was no Leonardo to squire her around. The dreadful Alessandro, coming and going, took a delight in breathless stories of violence erupting all over Florence and though she did not believe him Wilson had no desire to put him to the test. Her sole recreation was with Jeannie, who occasionally invited her to ride in the carriage with her and Louisa when they went for a ride arranged by the Ogilvys. A reliable driver took them and another man was engaged to sit on the box as guard and Wilson felt very safe.

Knowing the redoubtable Jeannie was only overhead helped Wilson sleep at night as February ended and March, when Mrs. Browning would certainly be confined, came in. If there was a sudden crisis, Jeannie would come, even before Dr. Harding, to advise her. On March 6, her own birthday, Mrs. Browning was uncharacteristically irritable, even snapping at her husband, who had only wished her happy birthday. No celebration was allowed nor any mention of her birthday welcomed. While admitting that she never had seen her mistress in the four birthdays she had been with her acknowledge the day with any joy, Wilson nevertheless was sufficiently disturbed by her crossness to mention it to Jeannie, who at once saw significance in it. "Dogs are a' the same," she pronounced. "Aye twitching when their time is nigh coming and canna stay in the one place."

Putting her mistress to bed that night, Wilson could not help examining her undergarments carefully for fear there was evidence of a show either not noticed or thought insignificant. It was a distasteful task and she did it furtively before placing the pantaloons in the laundry bag. Similarly, every time Mrs. Browning went to relieve herself Wilson felt the uncomfortable need to hover near at hand and could not refrain from asking, "All is well, ma'am?"

The atmosphere in the apartment throughout the next two days was unpleasantly tense. Mr. Browning would not go out, Flush would not go out and Wilson felt worried if she only went so far as the kitchen. They were all glad that Alessandro had two days' holiday since he alone was impervious to the sense of imminent danger and annoyed all of them with his crashing and banging and lusty singing. Mrs. Browning no longer read in the afternoons. She slept, without benefit of laudanum, and otherwise lay on her bed staring ahead at the side of San Felice church. A hundred times Wilson had checked that all was ready and there was no more to be done. She still sewed, a pink muslin pillowslip for the tiny down pillow lying in the cradle, but every stitch took immense concentration. She had just finished a seam when, without the slightest sound or merest indication of movement, she felt a change in the air and looked up, alarmed. Her mistress was lying perfectly still but her eyes had widened and she held her breath. Wilson, putting her sewing down, said, "You have a pain?" but the moment had already passed and Mrs. Browning smiled languidly and denied she had. Though she watched attentively the rest of the day, Wilson could detect nothing amiss and came to the conclusion she had imagined her mistress's discomfort. But when she went to bed that night she took off only her shoes and her dress and laid them out on the chair at her side, all ready to slip on.

She was awake in an instant, hearing Mr. Browning coming down the passage before ever he reached her door and knocked, and had her dress on while she replied at once to his query that she was awake and ready. Her own heart beat with the excitement of it as she followed him into the bedroom where, since it was not quite dawn, a lamp burned at the bedside. Her mistress lay propped up with pillows, serene and smiling, and held out her hand. "Well, Wilson," she murmured, "March is a month of birthdays, is it not?" Wilson, barely able to speak, could only nod dumbly. "Now, dear, do not look so frightened—why, two white faces peering at me will do me no good at all and I am cross with Robert for waking you, only he would do it."

"You have had pains all this last hour, Ba, you know you have."

"They are not much, but I believe something else has happened which Wilson can attend to, Robert, if you go and dress or walk about, my love."

Investigating, with none of the embarrassment she had expected, Wilson found clear evidence of a show and quickly cleared away the sheet. "The doctor must be sent for," she announced and silenced protests at once by stepping next door and telling Mr. Browning to send the porter for Dr. Harding. Then she took a clean sheet from the drawer and made the bed neat and helped her mistress back into it. All was ready long before Dr. Harding appeared at half past six to find Wilson agitated and her mistress quite calm. He examined his patient, took her pulse, sounded her heart and pronounced her in excellent health. To Wilson's horror, he then snapped his bag shut and got up to go. She could not help saying, "You are not leaving us, sir?"

"Indeed I am, Mrs. Wilson, since this is likely to be a long affair, and I will only be a nuisance. You have a timepiece? I wish you to observe it and when the pains are regular, coming every ten minutes, send for me. Signora Romalfi is on her way and will be here by mid-afternoon. Now, Mrs. Browning, you must keep your strength up with nourishing food, nothing heavy of course, and plenty of liquid. If you could sleep it would be so much the better, for it will be a slow day. But by the end of it we will have this child in our world and all well."

Nobody shared his confidence. Signora Romalfi appeared at three in the afternoon, and two hours later told Wilson that Dr. Harding must be sent for since the pains were regular and strong. Off went Mr. Browning again to fetch Dr. Harding. He took off his coat, exchanging it for another he carried in a bag, and settled down by the bedside, observing his patient and smiling. "So we make progress," he said, "and you are bearing the pain admirably, Mrs. Browning. Now if you will tell me when a pain next grips you I will take the opportunity to do my bit." After a few minutes his patient stiffened and turned her head aside and whispered that the pains had returned. Wilson watched the doctor turn back the bedclothes and gently feel all around the mound that was the baby. He seemed surprised and said, "Strong contractions, Mrs. Browning, and yet you do not cry out—well done, well done." Then he had Wilson light a lamp, though it was not yet dark, and hold it high over her mistress's legs, and she saw him slip his hand inside, his face abstracted. The lamp wobbled a little in her grip as her own insides seemed to contract with the sight of this shocking interference and she was as relieved as her mistress when the doctor had done. "Well, my dear," he said, "you are well dilated and I shall stay the night."

Mr. Browning offered to have a meal sent in, apologizing for the absence of Alessandro. The doctor thought that a good idea, but only if Mr. Browning joined him, and so, though it was clear to Wilson Mr. Browning would have difficulty forcing anything past his lips, it was agreed. She and Signora Romalfi ate from a tray and sat on either side of Mrs. Browning, who only drank a little water from time to time. Taking the tray away, Wilson was followed to the kitchen by Dr. Harding and with the door shut he requested a pan of hot water. Fascinated, she watched him take out of his case a gleaming metal instrument resembling nothing so much as a giant, awkward pair of pincers. "Never fear," he said, seeing her terror, "we may not need them but it is as well to be prepared. I only heat them for cleansing purposes though I am sneered at for it and told it is not necessary. Well, I like to do it and have everything clean as may be." Wilson was impressed and in the course of the next few hours grew even more admiring of the doctor. He had such great patience, talking to Mrs. Browning of Italian politics and of books and of mutual friends in Florence but ever sensitive to her pain, knowing when to desist and wait. He allowed Mr. Browning in at intervals and showed him how to rub his wife's back, the better to alleviate the pain, and encouraged him to stroke her brow and comfort her.

But at midnight Wilson later related to her mother how

—Mr. Browning was turned out and how sorry I felt for him, Mother, for it was agony for him to leave her and there were tears in his eyes. But it was necessary for the pains became very fast, one after the other, and very strong and the doctor examining her found her fully dilated and the crisis reached and he could not have seen her as she then became without much suffering himself. The doctor put aside the bed coverings and had her turn on her side and raise her knees. I thought of those wicked instruments in the hot water and could hardly keep still for fright. But nothing was done and in half an hour Dr. Harding told her to push. Then the most extraordinary change took place, Mother, for hitherto though nigh silent she had been almost wild and thrashing about and now she became still and gave great gasps as she pushed all rhythmic as though to some strange music and in a moment Dr. Harding cried out that he had the head and she must hold back a moment then push once more and it would be done, which she did perfectly and the next thing I saw was the baby held up by his heels and *roaring*, Mother, like you never heard. It is a fine boy, Dr. Harding said. Signora Romalfi brought the baby to her then, all wrapped tightly, but she would not look at him until her husband should be allowed in. But I looked and, oh Mother, such a beautiful child as you never saw with a face so rosy and tufts of dark hair and every feature perfect. He made little noises and turned his head and Signora Romalfi said, she had never seen such energy in a newborn babe. But still Dr. Harding would not let Mr. Browning in saying there was some bleeding he was concerned with though it was not serious and wished it to have ceased before allowing her to receive him. In an hour or so it stopped and Dr. Harding pronounced the flow quite normal now. But he preferred one of us to stay when Mr. Browning came in and I elected to be that one while the nurse went for some sleep. Mr. Browning made straight for the bedside never looking into the cradle and he was trembling and the tears streaming down his face and he clasped her hand and gazed into her face. He could not believe she had come through the ordeal so safely, Dr. Harding having told him that he had never seen a natural function so well performed, and once his joy had abated it was replaced by pride and at last he looked at his son. Mrs. Browning asked him if they had not been overendowed with happiness and how had they come to deserve it and he kissed her and said God was good. Then he left as instructed by the doctor and although it was morning by then we left the shutters closed and she prepared to sleep for she was truly exhausted. And so, Mother, it has all ended happily and I look to our journey to England to show off this child before too long.

CHAPTER EIGHTEEN

THE RUSHING of the stream over the rocks quieted the baby, as it never failed to do, and Wilson was at last able to perch on a boulder and rest. She gave Flush, who had followed her, a warning look which told him clearly he must not bark and set the baby crying again. Flush wagged his tail, a little mournfully. Though he no longer sulked, because this newcomer claimed so much of the attention that had been his he was still far from enamored of the baby. Cautiously, Wilson lowered little Wiedemann from her shoulder and into the crook of her right arm and looked down on him. His eyes, huge like his mother's, stared back at her, still bright with unshed tears, and as she talked to him, a prattle of nothing making no sense even to herself, he began to smile, his fat cheeks breaking into the dimples which so delighted his adoring mother. He began to "sing," to make those birdlike sounds which his parents declared were the sweetest music in the world, and to kick himself free of the shawl in which he was wrapped. His legs were chubby and strong and though he had been protected from too much sun had turned brown, the color of an autumn leaf. Wilson propped him up so that he could see as well as hear the water and he pointed and gurgled and jumped in her arms. All day he had been wildly excited and she and the *balia*, Dolorosa, were worn out with carrying him around. It was, they both knew, the effect of yesterday's trip to the top of Mount Prato Fiorito. How could such a young baby, a mere six months old, be calm and tranquil, as he ought, when, as she had written to Minnie,

—he is exposed to such adventures? Really Minnie you would wonder at it as I did but my opinion counts for nothing in the bringing up of this child. We set off on donkeys if you please at eight-thirty in the morning when since it is now September it is not yet too hot and we traveled up the most steep and dreadful path sometimes with the donkey almost standing on its hind legs it seemed and slipping often so that stones went crashing down the mountain. First I carried our precious babe with him securely lashed to my chest and then Dolorosa who is the wet nurse took him but she was so afraid she prayed and cried the whole way and blessed herself at every corner. We got to the top before noon and a cloth was spread and we had a picnic of chicken and ham and cheese and figs and strawberries and my mistress was in raptures. Even then the baby was not placed in some quiet shady corner but she would have him *naked* Minnie naked as the day he was born and laid out on the ground to roll and kick as he willed. Mr. Browning I am pleased to say did demur a little but she would not have it that there was any fault in allowing their child to display himself thus and merely said it would do him good. Eventually he grew red in the face and began to cry and Dolorosa was allowed to take him and feed him and afterward he slept in a basket we have and I was relieved. The way down was if anything worse than the way up and I felt I might crush our baby if I fell forward over the donkey's head since I had him the whole way Dolorosa needing to be blindfolded to persuade her to go down at all and not being in a fit state to carry the boy I was exhausted with the worry and the fatigue of attempting to keep straight-backed. We got down safely and Mrs. Browning declared she had never had such a wonderful day and would write to her sisters and describe the glories of the views but my legs shook and today they ache and indeed Minnie I confess I will be glad when we are gone from here which I trust we soon will be.

From the moment they had arrived at the end of June Wilson had been disenchanted. The house the Brownings had rented this year was so remote Wilson could hardly believe it was civilized and for once was in agreement with Alessandro, who called upon God to help him as they installed themselves in the tiny rooms. Meanwhile her mistress was in ecstasies, enchanted with the shade the trees gave, thrilled with the silence, constantly counting her luck that no house could be seen from theirs. There was nothing at all to do or see and by the end of the first week Wilson was in despair. She looked at Dolorosa, ever content merely to sit in the shade with her feet up, feeding the baby or dozing, and not even appearing to miss her own child, left behind in Florence with her mother. She seemed to count herself privileged to get out of the heat and be paid for it and her cheerfulness put Wilson to shame. If it had not been for Jeannie, staying with the Ogilvys a short distance away, she felt she would go mad.

As it was, she felt permanently irritable. If the baby was asleep and the work done she was free in the afternoons but hardly relished her freedom. She wanted to get away from Dolorosa and Alessandro, with whom she felt little in common and who were becoming too friendly for her taste and clearly wanted to be rid of her as much as she wanted to go. All there was to do was trudge along the stream with Flush at her heels and back again, or scramble up the mountain paths and into the woods as her mistress did with her husband. She had heard Mrs. Browning tell Mrs. Ogilvy that "Nature restores Robert," and that the beauty and peace of the scenery healed his grief for his mother, who had died soon after his son was born, but it did not soothe her own discontent. It was restful and cool, of course, but dull beyond belief. The only benefit isolation brought that she could think of was that it showed her how unsuited she was for country life. If she had married Leonardo Righi and gone to Prato she was sure she would have regretted it. And that was another thing . . .

There had been a letter, brought on from Florence by a friend of the Ogilvys. The letter addressed to Wilson was in a hand she knew only too well and had thought never to see again. Mrs. Browning recognized it too, as she handed it to her, and stared at her hard. Wilson felt quite composed, even uninterested, as she took the letter, but after she had read it she was thrown into a state of bewilderment. Leonardo wrote, in a shaky hand, to say he had been ill, very ill, nigh unto death, with a recurring fever which had lasted the whole year until now when he was much recovered. He said her letters had been kept from him when he was ill and he had only read them and been much distressed by them some weeks ago. He vowed he would come to Florence in October to make her his own.

Mrs. Browning said at once that it was all nonsense. She pointed out that Mr. Righi's letters had stopped before Christmas and that an illness such as he had described could never have been responsible for a weakness so great he could not have managed a line before now. Wilson herself was only confused. What confused her was not so much Leonardo's explanation but her own desire to believe he had not been false and she had not been duped. She had once heard her mistress tell Mrs. Ogilvy how pleased she was that "dear, sensible Wilson got over her disappointment with the faithless Mr. Righi very well and quickly and really does not care." It was not true, and she had burned to hear her misery so lightly described. What she *had* done was accept Leonardo's defection as something which had to be endured but she had not stopped thinking about him. It was the same as, only worse than, after Timothy disappeared from her life. She remembered the attraction, the comfort of being loved by someone, the satisfaction of being a pair. And she had missed it. No other man had taken her eye, and the birth of Wiedemann together with another birthday passing had depressed her utterly.

The child was fast asleep. She cuddled him close, loving the softness and warmth of his body, loving the way it seemed to fit so naturally the contours of her own. Often, watching Dolorosa bare her huge breast and slip the nipple into the baby's mouth, she had felt an answering spasm in her own breast and as the child sucked and fed and the surplus milk trickled down Dolorosa's skin and stained her dress she had been struck with awe at the sight and became weak with the longing to perform this maternal function. And then, when she picked Wiedemann up sometimes from his cradle and he clung to her, she had experienced the same yearning to produce such a miracle. Over and over her mistress called him—"our little miracle"—and never stopped congratulating herself on her own blessed luck. Hearing her, Wilson wanted to cry out that her own luck was cruel, that at twenty-nine she ought to be married and have a child of her own, but then she would remember the long, long years her mistress had served as a spinster before "the miracle" had happened and feel guilty at such unworthy thoughts. But she worried, as she had never done, about her own future. Once having doubted whether marriage was for her, she now positively looked for it. If Leonardo arrived in October and if her feelings for him were rekindled, then who knew what she might do?

Except that she did not want to go and live in a mountain village. She wanted to live in Florence, or at least some fair-sized town, and not be withdrawn from the vitality and gaiety of city life which she had learned to love and which suited her. It was odd, she knew, that someone such as herself, thought of as so quiet and demure even now, should prefer the city but she did. She felt less conspicuous, less thrown on her own resources. The silence of Bagni Caldi this summer had almost driven her mad, it had made her question the purpose of her life, and no amount of praying had stopped this introspection. It was not enough to tell herself that God decided all, that it was not for her to make her own path. She felt it was and, since she could not think how to do so, was plunged into despair and a strange fearfulness. And she could no longer truly remember how she felt about Leonardo. She half dreaded the sight of him.

Slowly, she walked back down the stream and across the bank toward their rented house. She could see, from a distance, her mistress lying on a wickerwork chaise longue under the shade of the trees, reading. That morning she had been sick and had returned to bed, declaring it was merely the aftereffects of the excursion to Mount Prato the day before. "I daresay you will tell me it is my own fault, Wilson," she had said, quite sharply, and Wilson had said nothing. She thought the reason for the nausea quite other. Her mistress ought to know that she was likely to be pregnant once more and, if she did not, then this time she would not remind her. The baby would be born in April, a mere thirteen months after the birth of the little love she held in her arms. Coming into the garden, she could not help noticing how well Mrs. Browning looked, in spite of the morning sickness and the fatigue from yesterday. All July and August it had been hot, with only the slightest of breezes, but she had thrived on it. The arms that held the book were quite rounded and the body on the chair not nearly as insubstantial as once it had been. But the greatest change since the birth of her baby was in the face. The eyes did not dominate it entirely now that the cheeks were filled out and the ghastly pallor which had so often given it the appearance of a mask had given way to a healthier, creamy complexion not untinged with a little color.

She approached the chaise longue and her mistress looked up and smiled and held out her arms. A little reluctantly, for his mother had a way of holding the child awkwardly and if he sensed any discomfort he would waken, Wilson handed over her charge. But he slept on and his mother gazed down at him, letting her book slide to the ground. Wilson picked it up, looking at the title as she did so. It was *The Count of Monte Cristo*.

"I have a fancy you have read this before, in Wimpole Street," she could not resist saying as she handed it back.

"Well, of course I have read it," Mrs. Browning said, lightly stroking her son's cheek with a finger, "but what is to be done when new novels are so hard to get? You of all people ought to know the deprivation, Wilson. Why, I have not yet even had a copy of Mrs. Gaskell's *Mary Barton* and it has been out almost a year. It is too bad."

"I heard Mrs. Ogilvy speak of it," Wilson said, wishing she had the courage, as Jeannie would have, to beg her mistress not to run the risk of disturbing the sleeping child with that irritating stroking. "It is about a poor woman and how she is wronged by the son of an employer. Mrs. Ogilvy says it is much admired by Mr. Dickens and thought a very brave book for speaking out."

Mrs. Browning looked at Wilson, a little astonished. "Yes," she said, "and that is why I wish to read it. I have had a mind for years to speak out myself, though not in the manner of Mrs. Gaskell. There *is* injustice for women in the world and we, who are so fortunate, must not forget it."

Wilson could not think exactly why, but for the whole of the next month, until the return to Florence put it out of her mind, she felt a kind of vague disgust at what her mistress had said. Later, she had heard her question Mrs. Ogilvy closely about *Mary Barton* and express her concern for all the poor and exploited women in the world and yet, leading a life such as hers, how could she know of them? She thought of Mother and Ellen and May, eking out a perilous existence in Sheffield, so far from their real home and dependent on the charity and word of one man for their livelihood—let Mrs. Browning experience *that* and she might know what she was talking of. Then Jeannie had just been given her annual rise, without the least need to ask for it, and Wilson was painfully aware that she, who had still never had a rise, was being left behind. It did not need a Sarah Allen to point out that she was now a nursemaid as well as all the other roles she filled. But each time she thought of casually mentioning the subject the words dried in her throat, seeming too greedy and ungrateful. Mrs. Browning had only to smile at her and call her "dear" for all resolution to speak out to leave her.

Yet mid-October, when once more they were all installed in the Casa Guidi, would have been the time to make a stand since no sooner were they back than, as Wilson wrote to Minnie:

—we are expecting another interesting event next April but do not speak of it to anyone Minnie not even Miss Arabel for Mrs. Browning is very desirous to keep the news secret a little longer the better to be safe. Naturally, this time she hopes for a daughter and counts herself lucky to be given the chance. Would that I had it myself. I tell you Minnie this darling of ours brings out in me feelings I did not own up to having and I can hardly bear to think of not having a baby of my own before too long so you will see this little angel has put me in a dangerous way. But do not think from this that I am about to take the plunge for it is quite the reverse. Signor Righi did not after all appear as promised and now I have written him off entirely. My hopes though raised last month were not high so the disappointment has been less. I am resolved not exactly to look elsewhere never having been driven to looking before but not to close my eyes to the approaches that are made for it will not do to ignore every sign of interest men being only human.

But now that there was Wiedemann to care for, she found she was not much in the kind of situation or among the kind of company where it was possible to attract any male attention. Her day was spent with other nursemaids and babies and there were no more long peregrinations of the exciting sort she had made with Sarah Allen. It seemed an eternity since the two of them had sat eating ices outside cafés watching and being watched furtively by interested parties. Wiedemann demanded all her attention and it was always more sensible to take him to the Boboli Gardens, even though it exhausted her, than into the city squares. Nor did she have the free time she had once had, confessing to her mother as Christmas approached:

—I have hardly a minute to myself and you must not imagine me any longer a lady of leisure but quite the reverse. At nine months our precious baby wriggles like an eel in my arms and is nigh to jumping out of them in the street so much so I have told his father I cannot safely carry him in any place where it is crowded. In the house he is ever on the carpet rolling over and over and dragging himself from one end to another tormenting Flush who bears it well while all the time his mother claps and praises him and though his father intervenes to say he is not convinced such freedom is wise he is ignored. And Mother it is not too soon to say he is spoiled indeed he is. I love him not a whit less than they I do believe but I can hardly bear to watch the level of indulgence. He has more toys than he knows what to do with yet they are forever buying more. There is no weaning attempted—Dolorosa feeds him still and is glad to keep the job on and his mother loves to think of him at the breast. When this other baby comes it is hoped Dolorosa will serve and Wiedemann be weaned accordingly but I foresee trouble.

It never came. In mid-December Mrs. Browning started to bleed. She remained in bed from then onward but another bleeding followed and the pregnancy pronounced at an end. It was without drama, so much so that within the week Mrs. Browning was as well as ever and, though chastened, not plunged into misery. "At least," she said, "now we are certain to go to England in the summer, Wilson, and you may write and tell your mother so. We will go in May and stay until it turns cold, so you will have plenty of time to visit your family, dear. Is that not exciting?"

Immediately Christmas was over—made memorable by Wiedemann crawling on the Day itself—plans began. Maps and guidebooks littered the drawing room and there was no other topic for discussion which held the interest more. Mr. Browning, Wilson noticed, seemed a little harassed over the route, constantly begging his wife to remember the cost and to look for ways of cutting the expenses down. One way was to take Wilson and no other servant, so Wiedemann must be weaned and Alessandro paid off. Wilson heard this with satisfaction, on both counts. Wiedemann was now standing and about to walk, it was not, in her opinion, seemly to have him chasing after Dolorosa to be fed. And as for Alessandro, once paid off he might never come back and that would be so much the better.

Spring, when it arrived in March, was so particularly lovely that year that Wilson felt an ache in her chest. She could not understand what was upsetting her and did not dare confess, when questioned, that she had a sense of foreboding. She had no faith in this long-desired trip to England even though plans were firmer than ever now Miss Henrietta was married. She could not decide whether this might mean she was at heart reluctant to go, or whether she was in some way ill. Jeannie, forthright as ever, said she was more likely to be exhausted with all she was doing and vowed she was wearing away into a shadow. Wiedemann kept her running after him all day long and in addition she fulfilled not only her normal duties but those of seamstress since her mistress wanted a whole new wardrobe made for London "so they will not think me shabby and decidedly the worse for married life."

The plan was to leave not in May, as originally intended, but in

June, before it became too hot. The Ogilvys and Jeannie departed before them, for Naples, and instantly the Casa Guidi seemed a lonelier place. Wilson realized how shut in she had become since little Wiedemann was born and how dependent on Jeannie for any company, and yet she did not have the energy to go out on her own and pick up the contacts she had once had. In the afternoons, trudging up the stone stairs with the baby in her arms, she felt exhausted and likely to collapse with fatigue but the moment they entered the apartment Wiedemann was off, racing to the balcony, which his father had been obliged to cordon off, so dangerous was it. Sometimes she felt tears come into her eyes, tears of self-pity, and she had to be stern with herself. It even entered her head that, once back in England, she might just as well stay there for all the happiness being in Italy was now bringing her. Better to be with Mother, helping her after such a long desertion.

"Do you long to be in England, now that April's there?" Mrs. Browning asked her, laughing at the words she had just quoted. "Do you, Wilson?"

"It will be pleasant to be home, ma'am," Wilson said. "I think it will be refreshing."

"*I* think it will be terrifying," her mistress said, and shuddered. "Were it not for seeing my sisters, I would not go. And of course there is my baby to show off."

Wilson, who at the time had only begun to suspect, went on folding clothes and kept her thoughts to herself.

"You are in one of your quiet moods, dear."

"Oh no, ma'am."

"Then it must be because you have a secret."

"Perhaps."

"And that secret is to do with me?"

"I do not rightly know."

"I think I do. You are quick, Wilson, but by now I am experienced in these things and not the innocent I once was. You think I may be with child again, that is it, is it not?"

"Yes, ma'am."

"And if I am, we cannot go to England."

"Indeed not."

"Well, it is only just possible. Let us wait another month and say nothing to my husband."

It was a foolish warning, for as Wilson wrote to her mother at the end of May:

—her husband was always on the lookout and guessed almost as soon as we did. It appeared to me, Mother, that he was far from truly regretful at canceling our trip to England but did it as though freeing himself of a burden. I alone was desolate, knowing it means I will not see you for another long year and I have vowed never again to promise I am coming until such time as bags are packed and carriages taken. The baby will be a Christmas baby and Mrs. Browning is determined to keep it, not moving from her bed more than an hour each day in an attempt to be tranquil. It is strange but I have observed this time she is growing big with great speed and it is possible now, when she is barely two months gone only, to know she is carrying a child. She is of a mind to believe this means it is a girl but I am skeptical and think it not wise that she should get into the habit of having a daughter. So we are to be here all the hot summer and Mr. Browning is to try to find a villa somewhere near but cool.

Mr. Browning failed in his task. He looked here, there and everywhere and could not find any place cheap enough or near enough or attractive enough to take for the high summer. Meanwhile, the thermometer in June climbed to over eighty degrees and his wife lay clad only in a white wrap on her bed, longing for the cool of the evening. Wiedemann ran around all day long until his blond curls were plastered to his hot forehead and he cried with the heat. Wilson was demented with the effort of keeping him cool and suddenly longed for the stream at Bagni Caldi, though she had so detested the last summer there. Early in July, Mr. Browning heard of a villa at Siena and went to look at it. Wilson asked Alessandro, who was still with them, where Siena was and what sort of place and he rolled his eyes to heaven and sighed and said it was inland, on a high plateau, but nowhere near sea or water of any kind. In the event, and rather to

Wilson's relief, Mr. Browning was back that same night, declaring both villa and situation impossible.

Afterward Wilson dreaded to think what would have happened if that isolated villa outside Siena had been taken. Surely, her mistress, as she told Minnie:

—would have died and I do not exaggerate. Never, Minnie, was she like this before. In the middle of the night I heard my name called in a frantic tone and got up to find Mr. Browning going for the doctor and when I got to the bedside I saw at once the sheets were already drenched in blood and more and more coming away and oh Minnie I almost fainted at the sight. Then Dr. Harding arrives and takes one look and tells Mr. Browning to go at once and wake Alessandro and between them to bring as much ice as they could procure. When Mr. Browning and Alessandro had brought the ice Dr. Harding wrapped the blocks in muslin which fortunately was to hand being newly bought in lengths to make new curtains and packed them all around my mistress's body. Minnie, she lay like that for two whole days. It was terrible to look at her, so deathly white and her lips almost blue, and I cried Minnie when she smiled at me and said dear Wilson the trouble I put you to. At length, the dreadful bleeding stopped. That was a month ago Minnie and her lack of progress is frightening. It is pitiful to see her drag herself around, there is not an ounce of flesh on her anywhere and as if she did not have enough to bear with this miscarriage which Dr. Harding has said not one in five thousand women would have survived our dear baby was taken ill two days ago. It was we now think a touch of sunstroke for he had been out in very hot sun with Dolorosa. By nightfall he was almost delirious and in a great fright we sent for Dr. Harding who said that there did not seem anything materially wrong and that in the morning he would be well which to our joy he was, to all intents and purposes. But he is pale and I am worn out Minnie. I was glad when I heard Dr. Harding tell Mr. Browning that it was imperative his wife and child were got out of this city where the sun now makes it into a cauldron. Indeed, since it is nearly the end of August, it could be said the worst is over but September can be uncomfortable too so we are to leave tomorrow for Siena, the very place we were to have gone in July and thank God we did not. I will not write from Siena Minnie since the posts will be variable it being a remote place.

It was remote. The house had seven rooms and stood on a hill, Poggio dei Venti, the Hill of Winds, two miles from Siena. In some ways it was even more remote than the house they had taken the year before at Bagni Caldi since there was no settlement near it, but to her own surprise Wilson found it more congenial. Coming toward the house at the end of a long and exhausting journey from Florence, she had been much struck by the English feel to the countryside. There were hedges that bore a resemblance to English hedges and lanes which were strikingly similar and the vineyards from a distance looked like English fields. The views from the house were extensive, the eye stretching across the high plain to the mountains beyond, and there was a sense of space she had never felt before in Italy. In front of the house was a little flower garden, full of flowers quite recognizably English, and at the back a vineyard and an olive grove perfect for Wiedemann to run around in. All that worried Wilson as they settled in was the cold. The breeze blew strong and fresh through all the open windows and she found herself shivering in such an obvious fashion that her mistress grew quite annoyed and insisted on showing her that, whatever her belief, the temperature stood at seventy degrees. All the same, Wilson pointedly donned a shawl.

Within a week she had grown used to the climate and had benefited as much as her mistress. In the morning when she got up she felt fitter than she had done for a year and had the energy to run with Wiedemann in pursuit of the pigeons he adored. Together they raced around the garden and played with a ball and Wilson enjoyed herself more than she would have thought possible. Now that Wiedemann was eighteen months old, he was fun as a companion and she was absorbed in teaching him so many things. He did not yet talk, though his mother swore he was capable of it but simply did not choose to demonstrate his capabilities, and she spent hours encouraging him to say "Mama" and "Papa." She spent other hours persuading his mother to have him weaned and at last, after they had been in Siena a month, she capitulated. Aloes were smeared on Dolorosa's breasts and Wiedemann duly made an expression of disgust as he took the nipple into his mouth. To the astonishment of all except Wilson, there was no screaming. As she had insisted, the child was ready to leave extreme babyhood behind. It was his mother who was sad when he was weaned, not Wiedemann. Wilson, when expressing satisfaction at the transition, was reprimanded.

"Do not wish his life away, Wilson, I beg you," Mrs. Browning said and Wilson to her astonishment saw tears in her mistress's eyes.

"His *life*, ma'am?" she queried, shocked.

"The faster he grows, the quicker his childhood passes and I would not have that for the world."

"But he could not have sucked at Dolorosa until he was a great lad."

"He is not a great lad yet but a very small, rosy cherub still."

"A cherub with a will to grow and have his hair cut."

"Cut? Oh, Wilson, you frighten me, how can you say such a wicked thing and indeed he cannot have asked for it to be cut when he does not talk."

"He pushes his curls away and pulls at them and makes himself plain. And when his father trimmed Flush last week he all but snatched the scissors to do the same with his own hair. Which may be a good idea, though I say it as shouldn't."

"You most certainly should not. The darling's curls are one of his chief glories and must not be touched, not for many a year. Never speak to me of cutting Wiedemann's hair, Wilson, if you do not wish to provoke me, dear."

Wilson put down the washed grapes and nodded, not trusting herself to speak, but the minute she was in her room and Wiedemann sleeping—sleeping far better than he ever did in the Casa Guidi, thanks to all the fresh air and exercise from which he was now benefiting—she began a letter of outrage to Minnie, telling her how

—it does not make sense Minnie to keep the boy's hair so thick when it cries out for trimming and would not spoil his looks in the least. Likewise she will have him dressed in silks and satins which are not suitable for the running around he does when these same flimsy materials catch on bushes and get torn so completely I cannot mend them. As for his appetite, she is not a bit concerned that presently he will eat only *prosciutto* a kind of spicy ham Minnie and grapes and will not take anything more substantial not even bread. Heaven knows how this precious child will be brought up if the lack of rules we have now is anything to judge by. She says she wishes him to be happy and that children should be trusted to know what is best for them which you will agree is the most manifest nonsense Minnie. How we will contain the child when he is back in Florence in the Casa Guidi I do not know.

The answer was, with difficulty, which his mother was the first to admit. Wiedemann's new habit was to snatch his hand free of Wilson's and to attempt to dart across streets without her. This was so clearly dangerous, she brought herself to speak out. She did it quietly, taking care only to make sure Mr. Browning was present with her mistress.

"Ma'am, sir," she said, her voice even, "I cannot any longer take Wiedemann in the streets. He is too heavy to carry and is determined to break free and run."

"Then let him run," Mrs. Browning said at once, to be followed by her husband remonstrating and saying, "Now, come, Ba, you do not think. If he runs in the streets he will get knocked down. He must have a rein, do you think, Wilson?"

Before Wilson could reply her mistress jumped in to object, saying, "He is not a horse, Robert, for shame."

"Then what do you suggest, my love?"

"Dolorosa can carry Wiedemann. Why else do we keep her on but to be useful a little longer? And then, when he is stronger and walks steadier and sees for himself streets full of people and carriages are dangerous places, then he will submit and walk properly with Wilson."

She made all to do with her child so easy, Wilson reflected. And yet it was not easy. He was turning, day by day, into a tyrant, if one so greatly adored and in himself so loving could be termed a tyrant. Everything within the Casa Guidi had to be done *his* way, and it was wearing. When she was alone with him, Wilson imposed her own conditions which the child seemed happy to abide by, seeing them as a game. "Hands!" she would say before she let him feed himself and he would hold them out, knowing that if he did not allow them to be wiped there would be no food. But the moment he was with his parents all hope of restraining influences vanished. He knew, instinctively, that he was out of her jurisdiction and made the most of it, smiling wickedly at her as he indulged in some particular bit of mischief, as she wrote to Minnie:

—you will see at once what I mean when you have witnessed it which I believe, though I do not tell my poor mother yet, will be in the summer.

CHAPTER NINETEEN

T HE EXCITEMENT had precisely the effect she had anticipated and dreaded. Knowing her expression would betray her disapproval and provoke the kind of caustic comment which was all the more hurtful for being sweetly said, Wilson turned aside as soon as she had taken the child from his mother's arms. He clung to her, his face red, his eyes over-bright, and bounded up and down so that it was all she could do to restrain him. "Lily!" he said, over and over again. "Lily! Lily! Lily!" Where had he got her name from since no one used it, but then where had he got his own? For two months now he had begun to speak, if the strange mixture of English and Italian words he came out with could be called speech. "Pen," he called himself and she found that easier than the "Penini" he had begun with. But then, as Jeannie had remarked, given an outlandish name like Wiedemann, to honor his dead paternal grandmother, what could the poor bairn do?

So Pen wriggled and fidgeted and clung to her neck, kissing her behind the ear and licking her cheek, chattering all the time she carried him to the room they shared. It was at the back of the guest-house, away from the noise of the Grand Canal, for which she was thankful. It would be nearly midnight in any case before the child would sleep and if their room had been at the front, where all night long, it seemed, gondoliers shouted to each other, there would be no settling him at all. And the dark water frightened him as much as it did her. She shivered as much as her mistress exclaimed with delight at the sight of the moon rippling on the black, black streets of water and could hardly bear to go near the front balcony. Even in the daytime, when the same water was blue and bubbling with colorful life, she felt uncomfortable, seasick, unbalanced just to be so close to it. Venice did not suit her. She saw no beauty in what her mistress called the "divine floating sea-pavements" and shuddered at the marble palaces admired as mysterious. To her, they were sinister, unfriendly, the very facades harsh and overpowering. The whole of Venice felt alien in a way neither Pisa nor Florence had ever done and when she was left alone, as she had been this day when his parents took Pen to the play (much against her wishes), she retreated to her room, closed the shutters, lit a candle and tried to pretend she was back in the Casa Guidi.

Next door she could hear, very faintly, both Mr. and Mrs. Browning laughing as they ate their late supper. The play, they said, had been most entertaining and their tiny son's behavior exemplary. "Except, Ba," Mr. Browning had added, "for the chains." Looking askance at her mistress, Wilson had seen her put her finger to her lips and then, when caught out, she murmured that it was nothing, her husband had only referred to one very *small* incident when an actor had been too convincingly put into chains. . . . Grimly, Wilson tucked up the child and sat at his side, knowing that she was in for a night of it. He was only just two years old and there he was, watching scenes that could do nothing but inflame his already overactive imagination. It was scandalous. But strangely enough, Pen fell asleep at once and did not waken that night at all. Instead, Wilson herself lay awake, wishing she was either back in Florence or already in England —anything but this traveling which made her feel displaced and anxious. Flush, crouched at her feet, seemed to feel the same and had been unlike himself ever since they left Florence.

One day she heard her mistress swear she could live in Venice forever, that it was her natural home, that she had never felt so well. The mere thought of this made Wilson feel giddy and if it had not been for Mr. Browning immediately saying *he* certainly could not stay in Venice, that he had been feeling bilious ever since they arrived, she would have given notice there and then and somehow got herself home. As it was, they left Venice the next week and traveled to Milan by way of Verona, sixteen hours by train and coach with Pen in near hysterics all the way. Stoically, Wilson endured his violent dancing about, relieved that at last they were away from water and land looked like land.

Her relief was short-lived. From Milan—of which she saw nothing since Pen had a cold and she was confined indoors—they journeyed on to the Italian lakes. Then came the passage of the St. Gotthard the next day, and if the canals of Venice had seemed ominous to her the snowy crags of the Alps almost made her swoon with fright. She cowered in the corner of the carriage, a shawl over her eyes, clutching Pen frantically to her, convinced the icy rocks would at any moment crash down and kill them all. It did not make sense to her that her frail and delicate mistress was sitting, swathed in shawls, on the *outside* of this coach, glorying in the magnificence of the scenery.

Of course, she was teased for it. All the way to Paris, a journey of such discomfort and tedium she thought of it as yet another possible death before it was over, Wilson had to endure the sly smiles and the remarks as to how strange it was the things some people, who were brave really, were frightened of, and she blushed and then rallied and said she was sorry for it but she could not help being frightened on that perilous route and believed there was not one woman in three who would not have felt the same. Then her mistress laughed and patted her knee and said she was quite right and that she was merely glorying in her own fearlessness by which she had been amazed herself. A little mollified, Wilson tried to put the experience behind her and hoped she would never have to repeat it.

Things improved rapidly once they were in Paris, where they stayed three weeks. Mr. Browning was very preoccupied with business affairs and there was much talk of financial embarrassment.

Wilson was familiar with the tensions to which this gave rise—her mistress being unconcerned and disdainful, her master worried and intense. From her point of view, efforts at economy were always beneficial. It meant the Brownings stayed in and kept quiet and Pen was therefore more likely to follow a soothing routine. Amusing him in the daytime was easy. At every street corner, as she knew from before, there seemed to be a Punch and Judy show and she had a delightful rest of it, merely walking him there and holding his hand. As she watched over Pen, she daydreamed about going home. It would be strange, with her old home gone. Mother had written that the house they had was "neat enough," which had a reluctant ring to it, and she could not in fact imagine going home to anywhere but the cottage where she had been born. Mother's new house was a town house in a street, a different thing altogether, and as to Sheffield it meant nothing at all to her.

"Are you glad to be going home, Wilson?" her mistress asked her the day before they were to leave, at the beginning of the last week in July.

"I am, ma'am. Though I wish it *was* home."

"Is home a place, then?"

"Partly. I was born in Newcastle and . . ."

". . . it will not mean the same to be with your family in Shef-field. Yes, I understand. But where your mother is, dear, is always your home." Mrs. Browning sighed and took Wilson's hand, in one of those tender, impulsive gestures for which she was forgiven so much. "I dread it, Wilson, dread London, dread my old home with its old sorrows. If it were not for seeing my sisters . . ."

"Well, you *will* see them, and they will see Pen and that will be worth anything, you will see."

What Wilson saw instead, after three weeks in London, was that she had been wrong. No matter the unfeigned delight with which Miss Arabel greeted her sister, no matter that her brothers came around, no matter the admiration Pen aroused—none of it balanced the misery of being so near to her father, knowing she was still unforgiven. Day by day Wilson felt the sadness grow in her mistress, saw her features droop, heard the cough begin. It was as though there was a shadow over everything and nothing would lift it. Visits to Wimpole Street were agonizing in the unhappiness they aroused. "So near, Wilson, so near," her mistress murmured, intensely distressed every time they went in and out of the front door. Her room was now Miss Arabel's and they stood in it almost awed by the flood of memories, and every time a door banged or a window rattled Mrs. Browning clutched at her throat and her eyes grew wide with fear, even though she knew her father was safely in the City.

Wilson herself found it difficult enough returning to No. 50 Wimpole Street and did not quite like to be there. She wondered how she could have been impressed by the house, finding it dark and dreary and not the grand, luxurious place she had thought on coming down from the North. She would never return to such a place, she was sure, or belong once more to a servants' hierarchy. Sitting with Minnie—a much aged Minnie, whose leg was stiffer than ever and clearly pained her more—she was uneasy and ventured to suggest it might be as well if she did not come again for fear of offending Mr. Barrett.

"It is all nonsense. You are as bad as your mistress, who frightens her child with tales of her father," Minnie said crossly to Wilson. "He is only a poor, unhappy man and she has the child himself thinking some monster comes here every night. It makes my blood boil."

The next day Wilson went, by train, to Sheffield, sorry to miss seeing Miss Henrietta and her baby son, who were due to arrive from Somerset. There had been a strange scene before she left, a dialogue full of misunderstandings which she pondered for the first half of the journey. It seemed she had been expected to want to take Pen with her for the two-week holiday and that this was to be graciously granted to her, as a privilege. Shocked, she had turned down the suggestion, the assumption, with an emphasis which had surprised the Brownings only a little less than herself. There had been hurt looks, a coldness in the atmosphere, a distinct hint of accusation in the way Pen had been told. "Lily does not want you, darling." She had blushed furiously to hear it. Naturally, the child had screamed and clung to her and she had difficulty prising his arms from around her neck. He began to scream, "Lily stay! Lily stay!" and it took all his father's strength to take him from her. Remembering his piteous cries, tears came to her eyes and the countryside was blurred. She felt guilty at leaving her darling and then angry at her own guilt. Surely she was entitled to two weeks with Mother and Ellen and May without being made to feel somehow mean and unkind? "We would have thought you would wish to show Pen to your family," her mistress had said sorrowfully, "and had been disposed to bear the separation bravely for your sake, Wilson." This announcement had rendered her speechless in its hypocrisy. They had wanted her to take Pen for their *own* sakes, she was sure of it. Even with her there, in constant attendance, Pen was unhappy in the dismal rooms Miss Arabel had rented for them in Devonshire Street. He cried often and asked on the hour when they were going home. And now, with her gone, his plight would be infinitely worse. His mother had declared she would look after her son entirely on her own and really she did not understand the half of what that meant. Wilson wiped away her tears surreptitiously and smiled, not without a little malice, of which she was immediately ashamed.

She arrived in Sheffield at six in the evening, a fine, sunny evening, though it would not have been thought much of in Florence. She was relieved to discover Sheffield was not, on first impression at least, the raging inferno she had anticipated but that it was surrounded by gentle green hills which gave it more of an air of the country than she had thought possible. Neither Mother nor either of her sisters was at the station to meet her. It struck her, as she waited, how assured she had become since her last trip north when she had thought herself so supremely confident. Five years in Italy had given her a poise which transformed her and she was aware of it every time anyone glanced her way. She could never look haughty, nor did she wish to, but nor could she any longer look hesitant and ready to be cowed. She held her head high, as Italian women did, and had quite given up the modest lowering of the eyes which, in England, befitted her station. She was not, of course, bold or coquettish in her carriage but in the sweep of her skirt and the tilt of her hat she signaled a knowledge of the world which brought her respect. The stationmaster himself came into the waiting room and doffed his hat, inquiring if he could be of service. When, after half an hour, none of her family had appeared, she asked him to order a cab for her. It was only when she gave the address, King's Head Yard, that his expression changed from the respectful to one a great deal less deferential.

Riding through Sheffield's streets, the horses' hoofs ringing on the cobbles, Wilson saw that the houses were becoming smaller and blacker and altogether less salubrious. Her mind flashed back to Mother's cottage in Fenham and her garden and the grounds of the big house which lay adjacent, and it was suddenly borne in upon her what Mother had suffered and how this suffering had not found its way into the pages of her letters. Not a word had escaped her of how dingy her new environment was nor had there been a single complaint as to the lack of a garden. When the cab pulled up at the end of a dark alley, she could no longer delude herself: Mother had come down in the world. The cab driver would not leave Norfolk Street, saying she must make her own way into the alley and find the yard. She walked down it hesitantly, carrying her box with difficulty. She felt she was in a maze, a rabbit run of dirty lanes with high brick walls on either side. She was perspiring freely before she came on the yard and the nine cottages Mother had described. She knew she had been followed; women came from nowhere, it seemed, and stared. She stood at the door of the cottage she had identified as Mother's and banged the knocker. Nobody answered. Uncertain, she went on standing there, wondering what she should do, but even then, in her distress, noticing how much greater her command was over herself. She did not break down, nor did her heart pound. She knew how to conduct herself and if, in another moment, the door did not open she would turn and address these leering women in terms they would understand.

But even as she lifted her gloved hand—gloves bought in Paris and quite distinctive—there was a great shout of "Lily! Oh, Lily!" and, turning, she saw running around the corner where two alleys met her mother with her sisters following. They seemed to fly toward her, shawls billowing, skirts flapping, as she stood with her arms outstretched; the onlookers were silenced by the wave of emotion sweeping before the three running women. And then they were all together, in a huddle, and the door was opened somehow, and they all fell in, laughing and crying at the absurdity of it. Explanations flew through the air—how they had been kept past the proper hour, how they had raged, how they had been unable to do anything—and were ignored. "You're here," Wilson kept saying, "you're here, you're here now." It seemed a long time before she looked at any of them properly, though even in the midst of the hugging and kissing it had registered that Mother's hair was now entirely white and that Ellen had become painfully thin. Mother brewed tea and there were knead cakes made and Wilson drank and ate and regaled them all with the fame of these same knead cakes throughout Florence, and all the time she realized she was looking for Fanny. She began to cry, choking on her knead cake, and Mother had no need to ask why. She wept too, and Fanny's name was spoken and a lock of her hair produced, twisted into a ring inside a silver locket. Wilson hung the locket at once around her neck and felt comforted and was better able to ask all the questions crowding her head.

By the time these were answered it was midnight and they were all weary. Mother blew out the lamp and raked the fire—the house was cold even on an August night—and they all went up to bed. Wilson dreaded being put in with Mother and was embarrassed by this dread but May went in with Mother and she slept with Ellen. The room was as tiny as the cubicle she occupied in Casa Guidi, with one bed in it and no room for anything else, and as she undressed and laid her clothes carefully on the bedstead rail she thought longingly of the old bedroom at home with its cupboard and chest and the pear tree outside the window. Then she was in with Ellen and, though exhausted, had another ordeal to overcome before there was any possibility of sleep. She knew she had to get Ellen to talk of her dead baby or leave a barrier between them and so she kissed her and said, "Tell me, Ellen," and without pretending she did not know what was meant, Ellen began to describe her baby and the horror of the still, blue-white face and her despair and they wept themselves to sleep.

In the morning everyone had gone. Wilson sat up in the strange bed and could not believe she had heard nothing. Dressing, she went downstairs into the cold back kitchen and found a note hastily scribbled by Mother. It said they could not miss work, not for anything, and that they would be back as soon after six as possible. Reading it, Wilson felt a stab of irritation—was she not worth taking a holiday for?—and then pulled herself up quickly. It was her mistress's attitude which had brushed off on her, the attitude that did not take into account the needs of others. Would Mother *choose* to work if she could be at home with her eldest daughter? Of course not. To doubt that was ridiculous. And then, looking around the kitchen, wandering around the cramped house, poking into the few drawers and cupboards, Wilson realized how poor Mother had become. She appeared to have nothing except this doubtful roof over her head and yet she and May and Ellen worked long shop hours. Everything was as clean as it had always been, the fireplace was freshly black-leaded and the brass jug glittered as it always had done, but the house had no soul. In no time at all Wilson felt oppressed by it and longed to be out, but when she looked through the window at the slate-gray rain falling, all desire to wander the streets left her.

But she did in fact stir herself to go out in the afternoon when the rain had all but stopped. She had no clue as to the lie of the land but stepped out boldly, resolved to go in the direction from which her family had come the day before. The street she came upon was called Fargate. It was as unlike a Florentine street as it was possible to imagine. She drew her cape about her and shivered as much from distaste as from the fresh easterly wind which had begun to blow. As she breasted the hill she struggled to silence the loathing she was beginning to feel for this place but then, when she saw ahead wave after wave of similar streets and houses and chimneys, she could not contain her horror. Her senses, so finely attuned in Italy to light and color, so released by sun and warmth that they had blossomed and flourished, shrank from the sheer dreariness of what she saw. And in this, somewhere, Mother and May and Ellen slaved away and were grateful that they were privileged to earn a living and inhabit a house. Slowly, a great resentment beginning to build up within her, Wilson carried on down the hill, without the least idea where she was going, numb with misery. She wanted to take Mother back at once to the cottage, put her down among the people and life she knew, and have her once more treated with the respect due to her. There life had been hard but not barren. It was made rich through a hundred associations, made happy through knowing and being known in the area she had been born and brought up in. All that was swept away. The big house sold, the owners impervious to the fate of "good Mrs. Wilson" in her tied cottage. Had they even inquired for her? Had anyone belonging to them looked out for her? No. She had been served notice and that was that.

Turning a corner uncertainly, Wilson was splashed by a horse and cab going through a puddle. She shook her wet skirts in exasperation, annoyed to see the ugly black stains on her blue dress, and remembered just in time that she was no great lady to fly into a tantrum about a spoiled gown. Proceeding more slowly, she reflected she was no one at all, had no position of any value, whatever she might think and however she might look. She could do nothing for Mother beyond give her the pathetically small amount of money she could spare. For the first time in her life she found herself wishing she were a man, with a man's greater ability to earn. As a butler, she would have had money worth talking about and certainly enough to pay Mother's rent. It seemed to her that coming to Sheffield had only served to remind her of how useless she was, useless yet lucky. She was out of this. Whatever happened to her, she did not believe she could ever be doomed, as Mother and May and Ellen were, to passing her days as they did. She was secure in the Browning household, she had a cherished place and always would have, she was protected from the harshness of true poverty and thanked God for it.

Utterly lost, she came at last, though she knew not how, to the Market Place and the High Street where she saw a different Sheffield. There were several fine buildings and the shops on either side had windows full of fashionable clothes. The trade in and out of them was brisk, though her trained eye took in the general dowdiness of the customers. More settled, she inspected several of the shops, comparing them with those in London, and in James Burgin's and Co., drapers, she bought a lace collar for Mother's dress. She would go back and fix it as a surprise for her return. In her box, which she had unpacked before she left and then repacked because there was nowhere to put anything, she had presents from Italy, but this lace collar would add a little extra to Mother's. She spent on it some of the £5 Mr. Browning had given her as a present before she left, £5 she had nearly returned to him, knowing, since the subject had been constantly mentioned, how hard pressed he was for cash. Taking the change, she almost laughed aloud at how stupid it would have been to be so carried away by the supposed poverty of her employers that she refused the only present of money they had ever made her. She would buy treats for tea with the rest: strawberries and cream and some honey and a joint of beef for Sunday dinner. There was no point in hoarding such a miserable amount with which nothing worthwhile could be done. Defiantly, she went about her purchases and was almost glad when every last penny was gone. The role of Lady Bountiful, she decided, did not suit her—it smacked too much of the kind of charity Mother had always been too proud to accept.

She never did find the place where Mother and her sisters worked. She asked for directions but was never given them. She even got up one morning resolved to accompany them, but they were all gone before she was ready. It was plain that, for whatever reason, they did not wish her to visit the premises where they labored such long hours. She tried questioning Ellen and met only with noncommittal answers and her idea of what they all did and in what surroundings grew stranger every day. Mother said she worked "behind the shop" but Wilson did not understand the term. She had in her head an old image of Mother mixing herbs, pounding them in a pestle and mortar in their cottage kitchen, but knew that was not the right description of what she did now. In her letters, Mother had made her tasks sound so pleasant but one look at her tired face at the end of a long day told a different story. Her hands told another. Wilson was shocked to see how stained they were, dull red up to the elbows and the nails yellow and the skin puckered. She scrubbed them fiercely every night but the color never faded. She said only that Mr. Conroy made his own perfumes and was experimenting with various natural dyes to color them and that sometimes he was not successful in his ideas and the dyes were too strong. More alarming than anything to Wilson were the small burns running up the inside of Mother's arms. She pointed them out, with concern, but Mother snatched her arms away and pulled down her sleeves and said she had been careless and spilled some of the hot glycerine and gelatine when pouring it into the molds in the making of suppositories. Ellen helped her but sometimes also worked at the counter and complained constantly of the ache in her legs. The owner of the pharmacy worked there himself, though he had a stool to sit on when trade was slack, and she did not. She was not allowed to sit, not ever, and was continually reminded she had her place, a place more usually taken by a man, and there were plenty of men wanting it, on sufferance. Ellen said being in the shop itself was a rest compared to her more usual task of preparing plasters, which she hated. She mixed lead oxide and olive oil and water into a thick paste, then spread it, with a special hot iron plaster, on pieces of sheepskin or swansdown. But at least Ellen, whatever she was doing, seemed to prefer her Sheffield work to being in service in Newcastle. She met people, she said, and was not forever hidden away and a shop assistant had more status than a kitchen maid.

May was maid to the wife of the owner but did not call herself lady's maid. She was, she said, maid-of-all work though hastened to add she did nothing truly dirty since she had a girl under her. Her employment was unusual. She came home every night when the shop shut and had Sunday off. Wilson thought this indicated a thoughtful mistress but soon learned otherwise. She was allowed home each night, May said, so as she could be paid less and forced to work twice as hard for the privilege. There were four young children in the house in Cheney Row where she worked and, though a nurse was employed, May spent half her day guarding them and was paid exactly the same as if she were indeed only a parlormaid with nothing to do but show people in and out and twirl a duster. But for Mother's sake, she told her sister, she was resolved to stay and endure the coarseness and meanness of her mistress. She much preferred her old in-service job in Newcastle, where she had been among truly gentle folk, but touched Wilson by her understanding of how important she was to Mother now that Fanny had gone to rest. Wilson saw May was developing a dignity and sense of responsibility entirely lacking in Ellen and was glad of it. At twenty, May was more mature than Ellen and also far more attractive. She was the tallest of the three sisters and the only one with brown eyes and dark hair. Already she had had what Mother called "good offers" and Wilson did not doubt marriage would come sooner rather than later. There was a young doctor, Mother said, much smitten with May and if he made a proposal she would be pleased. May only smiled and said, "Where I go, Mother goes."

There had been no offers for Ellen, and Wilson was not surprised. Her sister bore all the marks of what she had suffered in both her appearance and her manner. From being so heavy, Ellen had shrunk to nothing and the loss of weight did not suit her. She looked all bone, angular and awkward, and her face, which when full-cheeked had had a certain plump prettiness, was haggard. Her hair, never her best feature—May had the best hair in the family and Wilson's own, though mousy colored, was curly and thick—had become lank. Scraped back from her forehead, it gave her the look of an old woman. And the jolly if empty laugh had gone. Ellen no longer giggled at every possible joke and she had developed a habitual frown which made a marked crease between her eyes even when she was not in fact frowning. Wilson felt desperately sorry for her, especially when, in one bedtime conversation, Ellen confessed she still loved the man who had deserted her. Albert had been, she said, her life, and as she came out with it Wilson knew it was a statement of fact, not a melodramatic gesture made for effect.

Wilson in her turn was questioned. Mother touched lightly on Signor Righi and what had happened but Ellen probed deeper. She seemed to wish her sister to confess to a passionate love affair and a heartbreaking betrayal and, when Wilson did neither, was confused and dissatisfied. "Did you not love him?" she asked suspiciously, and when Wilson shrugged she said, "Well then, you were a fine one to tell me only to marry for love, Lily, not that I had the chance. What would you have married for, I should like to know?" Wilson said something about there being different kinds of love and Ellen made an expression of disgust and said she was fudging it. "But you look well on it, Lily," she ended grudgingly. "To look at you, anyone would declare you led a fine life and when I think where you have been and what you have seen I wish I could change places and that's the honest truth." Knowing it was indeed the truth, for who would be Ellen, and Ellen in Sheffield, Wilson tried to paint a darker picture of her life but failed dismally. It was no good, as the rain pelted down, pointing out that the heat of an Italian summer was a dreadful thing, no good, as mother and sisters sank down at the end of the day with weariness, saying she was on the run morning to night with Pen, and no good, when at the end of the week their pitifully small combined wages were spread out on the table, saying she was grossly underpaid.

So she returned to London, at the end of the two weeks, more saddened than otherwise. Not even Pen's rapturous greeting—a great shout of "Oh, my Lily, I love you, darling!"—and her mistress's hardly less fervent relief—"I thought I should die, Wilson dear, if there was one more day of this slavery!"—could lift her depression totally. Mrs. Browning asked her gently if all had been well at home and to her surprise tears came into her eyes and were noticed. She managed to say that all was well but, when pressed, squeezed Pen tighter to hide her distress and could only murmur, "Their life is so hard, ma'am, you cannot imagine." Pen stroked her face and said, "Poor things," and his mother then became quite distracted by the child's sensitivity. "Is he not caring, Wilson? Only listen to him, the dear, kind boy." Wilson kissed Pen again, as he snuggled down so comfortably in her arms, and nodded. No inquiry followed as to what exactly had been hard about her family's life in Sheffield and the next day, when still the memory of it hung over her and her low spirits did not revive sufficiently to satisfy, there was the faintest hint of reproof in the air. "Come now, Wilson," Mrs. Browning said, lightly enough but with intent, "brooding will not help, will it, dear? Can you not be happy to be with us again? For *we* are happy to have you." And then it seemed churlish not to smile and attempt pleasantries and try to forget her unhappiness.

But in all the bustle of preparing to leave London for Paris, where they were to winter, Wilson did not forget to write home and was able to express in words feelings she had been unable to voice while she was with her family. To her mother she wrote with some passion:

> I wish I had known Mother what you were going to when you left your home for that stranger's house in Sheffield and though I could have done nothing substantial to help being in Italy and without means to do so I should have encouraged you to try all other ways of staying in Newcastle. It grieves me to think of you in that house which is a mean place and not fit for you and no more yours after all than our cottage ever was and all of you dependent on the whim of the one employer and his wife. I am set to save harder than before to endeavor to rescue you from that place and return you to Newcastle and am resolved that when we have returned from Paris which I believe will be next June or July for a return visit is absolutely to be depended on I am glad to say why then I will put my case for a rise to 20 Guineas which is the sum I have been advised I warrant for the many services I perform. Then, Mother, half of that can be yours, for I have been good to myself and need not be as extravagant as living in Italy has made me. And I am likewise resolved to see if I cannot find places for Ellen and May in good families in the North and bring you all together again there. I know this to be an ambitious proposal, but it is up to us all to use our talents and not always bow our heads meekly before what is wished upon us. And now Mother I must close for we leave tomorrow evening and in my absence many things have been neglected which must be attended to before we leave. My mistress is in poor health and has been much pulled down by the increase in coughing and the strain on her strength through caring for the child which as you can believe has made me better appreciated. The child himself is fretful and pale and wishes to be free of the constraints he lives under in these three small cramped rooms and so we are all impatient to go though where exactly we are going to nobody seems clear.

It made Wilson tight-lipped to endure the uncertainties of the Brownings' plans during the next few days. Mr. Browning, as ever, scurried around with a distracted air inspecting lodgings and Mrs.

Browning, as ever, criticized everything he found and Pen would not settle until some stability was achieved. Eventually, an apartment was found in the Champs Elysées and some order restored to their days. There was a maid, Désirée, who went with the apartment they rented and she relieved Wilson of some of her more onerous duties, leaving her freer for Pen. But once more the old battle began. Paris was a sociable place and invitations to this and that poured in, invitations which surprisingly often included Pen and were accepted. At first Wilson rather relished being in attendance at parties, but the effects on her charge were so marked, she soon grew to dread them. At the parties she could hardly bear to watch the little boy simpering before a crowd of adults ogling but also sometimes subtly mocking him. As he grew more and more overwrought she tensed and waited for the explosion of one sort or another which inevitably came. There would be a sudden outburst of exhausted tears or a tantrum in which he hurled himself on the floor and it was her task to take him away and soothe him. It was no way to treat an infant.

Often, when finally Pen had fallen into an exhausted sleep in her arms in the quiet of their room, she would look down at him and think how she would change things if he were her little boy. No silks and satins then, but serviceable wool and cotton, no blacks and grays but cheerful blue and red; no early-hours-of-the-morning parties but a proper bedtime at six o'clock; no groups of grown-ups talking way above his head but the company of other children. She would be loving and kind but strict. She would even slap, though never viciously. And she would not pander to him, there would be no bid to be popular. He was a dear, sweet child, but he was spoiled and it did not help that his parents were the first to say so. "Love never spoiled a child," his mother said defiantly, but set Wilson wondering where love ended and worship began. They had differences almost every day now on points of Pen's upbringing and she was growing tired of the battle. She was also not as enamored of Paris as her mistress, though greatly preferring it to every other place they had stayed except Florence. It was lively enough and with always something to see, but she had no entrée into any kind of congenial society. Exist it must, as she had found it did in Florence, a whole network of

connections between maids, but she failed to discover how it oper-
ated. Désirée taught her some French but her will to learn seemed to
have vanished—she was stupid at absorbing French in a way she had
never been with Italian. She felt more and more, as the winter gave
way to spring, as though she was at a crossroads with no idea which
way to go, only knowing that it was no longer enough to let fate
decide. What had she written to Mother? That it was not always
enough to bow down and be meek. Precisely. Her time, she fancied,
was coming, a time to bargain and gamble on her future.

CHAPTER TWENTY

THE ROOM was very still, so quiet it was difficult to believe this was London. Wilson, without meaning to, realized she was holding her breath and that her heart was beating with uncomfortable speed. She was standing, hands clasped in front of her, and in a mirror on the far wall she could dimly see her reflection. I look like a penitent, she thought, about to bow my head and pray. This so annoyed her, she jerked her head up and parted her hands, letting them hang instead by her sides, the fists clenched.

Her mistress had still not replied. She sat at her desk, pen in her hand, poised to write but frozen in midair. "Wilson" she said at last, quietly, almost tremulous. "Wilson dear, I do not think I can have heard you aright. Say I did not?"

"I cannot, ma'am, when I know not what you heard. But what I said I can say again if you like, which is that my salary has remained at sixteen guineas for some eight years' service and I am advised it ought to be more for what I do and would hope you would think likewise, ma'am."

The words were fine enough but in the practicing of them, while they were all still in Paris, she had not taken account of Mrs. Browning's eyes and the shock in them and the frown of pain across her forehead and the exhausted droop of her shoulders. Astonishment she had anticipated, though there was nothing to be astonished about, and even coldness, for her mistress frequently used coldness as a weapon, but distress was so very hard to bear—distress and herself the cause of it. All her instincts were to cross the carpet between them, to bridge the gap she had been careful to create before she began, and embrace the dejected figure opposite. But she did not. She stood her ground, clenching and unclenching her fists, knowing her own color was high and that when she spoke again her voice would tremble. She tried to remember the words of Lizzie Treherne, whom she had at last visited the day before, as soon as she arrived back in London. Lizzie, mother now of three children, had been overcome at first with guilt and shame at her failure to correspond all these years but, reassured that no accusations of infidelity were to be made or any rebuke contemplated, she had quickly opened her old self to Wilson and they had continued their friendship as though it had never left off. Lizzie told of how well the bakery was doing, with another shop opened and Billy helped by two partners and a move planned that very month to a better house in a more salubrious district near the fields north of Kentish Town, and Wilson told of the years in Italy and then, inevitably, for it was the real reason for seeking Lizzie out, of the coming conflict in which she felt bound to engage. Lizzie had warned her that to be resolute she must keep her distance and had recollected, as though it were yesterday, how she herself had melted at her mistress's tears and if she had not already been married would without doubt have given up all idea of it rather than inflict such hurt. "She cares for you, Lily, as once she cared for me," Lizzie said, "but she cares for herself most, as people do. She likes the old order to continue, as you know by now better than I, and hates the threat of change, but that will be your trump card and mind you play it. And if you shrink from leaving her service if need be, then don't start the game or you will lose."

Well, she had started the game and there was no going back. And she had chosen her time well, she knew. All July, since they arrived back in London on the sixth, the Brownings had depended on her more than ever. Pen had been with her almost constantly, so much so that she never had a free hour, but she had not so much as murmured against the domestic tyranny. She had taken him together with Flush to the park, to her old haunt, every afternoon, leaving his parents free to visit a seemingly endless horde of literary folk who claimed their attention, and in the evenings she had stayed with him while they went to the theater and made the most of being in London. Even in the mornings, when Pen was used to crawling into bed with his mother, she had taken him out, the better to give her mistress the chance to rest since she vowed she was exhausted with all the socializing.

And now, if necessary, she was preparing to withdraw all that. Still she waited. At last Mrs. Browning, who had attempted all this time to stare her out, the great eyes tear-filled, lowered her head. "Well, Wilson," she said, her voice low and indistinct, "I will speak to my husband if you are determined as I see you are. But I hold out no great hope that we can oblige you with extra wages. We are hard pressed ourselves, as indeed you know, and it is not within our limited means to be more generous than we already are." There was a pause, a quick look up, and then "I had thought you loved us more than this request would seem to indicate, dear, and even that you felt yourself amply rewarded in love if not guineas, for indeed we do love you, greatly, and think of you as a friend more than a servant. I hope and pray you have never felt any unkindness from us in all these long years."

"No, ma'am, and I hope you have never felt any from me as I know I have tried at every turn to help. But servant I am, ma'am, when all is said and done and several sorts of servant though it is not recognized in my wage. And though you are hard pressed, ma'am, and I am sorry for it and would that you were not, think how much harder I am pressed and with my mother suffering great hardship and growing older and I being unable to relieve her as I ought. It is not for myself I wish more money but for her and because I am told I ought to be better rewarded."

"Indeed, and by whom?"

"By everyone, ma'am."

"You tell *everyone* how poorly we pay you?"

"I tell no one, ma'am, but those that ask and I have never yet said I was poorly paid, always taking care to express no opinion. It is others who are surprised and think my services undervalued."

"But they are not undervalued, Wilson. Do we not tell you, my husband and I, at every turn, how we are grateful and love you and count our blessings in having you every day? Grant that we do."

"I grant it readily but gratitude and love and blessings cannot pay bills or increase my savings beyond their pitiable state. And if you are not extravagant, ma'am, as you believe yourself not to be, no more am I, hardly spending a penny on myself."

She paused. Though her voice had grown stronger, she sensed she was being sucked into an argument where, if it persisted, she would inevitably lose out. She had vowed *not* to argue, merely to state her case and leave it at that, and now here she was, on the very threshold of battling it out. It would not do. She had almost, when claiming not to spend money on herself, pointed out that the only money she had spent on pleasure this past six months had been on a birthday present for Pen in March. A whole month's wages spent on a magnetic swan which the child had seen in a shopwindow in Paris and craved. And the very day she bought it for him, secretly, her mistress had bought a hat for herself for twice the price. But she knew she must not bring forth such evidence to show she was ill done by, for if she did she would emerge as shrill and mean and grasping. She must maintain her dignity and, if that meant not being provoked into a quarrel, then she must hold her peace and resist the temptation.

So she stopped short and waited yet again. The tears had gone from Mrs. Browning's eyes. Instead, the eyes were clear and full and held an expression approaching wonder. Wilson was dismissed and left the room, her legs feeling weak. Nevertheless, she took Pen to the park and sat on a bench watching him play with Flush who, though such an old dog now, cavorted around as though a puppy. When they returned in the late afternoon both Brownings were waiting and Miss Arabel had come to take Pen for an hour. There was a solemn air about them and from the moment she was called in

Wilson feared the worst, but Mr. Browning's first words were promising enough. "Come and sit with us, Wilson," he said, "and take some tea."

"Thank you, sir, but I have just taken some and do very well as I am."

"Well, no matter. At least sit, I beg you, and let us be friends."

Wilson sat, though on the very edge of the chair positioned for her in front of the sofa where the Brownings sat together. Mr. Browning looked at her directly, but with an attempt at a smile. "Now, Wilson, I am told you consider sixteen guineas insufficient for the duties you perform for us and I am sure you are right and that you are worth whatever the market price is. But we are not a market, we are a family and you, my dear, are a much-valued member of it. All the members of a family, you will agree, can only benefit from the prosperity of the whole and, if that whole is not too prosperous, why then the members all suffer. I am afraid you, as our servant, suffer as we do, in proportion to your position in this family, and there is at the moment little we can do about it beyond hold out the certain promise that should our circumstances improve financially, as I sincerely hope they will, you will be the first to know and to share in our increased fortune. Will that do, Wilson?"

Wilson saw her mistress smile and pat her husband's hand admiringly and all at once she was jolted out of the state of placid acceptance Mr. Browning's soothing and reasonable words had induced in her. "No, sir," she managed to say, though her voice would hardly bring out the words. "No, it will not do. I must have twenty guineas, as others do, or I am a fool and a poor one."

"I cannot believe this!" her mistress gasped.

"Hush, Ba," her husband said, and stood up. He paced the floor a little, thumbs in waistcoat pockets, and stopping in front of Wilson pulled up another chair and sat down very close to her. "Wilson, perhaps you do not understand—it is that we do not have twenty guineas a year to give you and that is the truth."

"Then I am sorry, sir."

"Sorry?"

"I must give in my notice."

And with that she got up immediately and left the room. Strangely, for she was well aware she had not won any kind of victory but rather the reverse, she felt a curious sense of triumph. *She had spoken up,* said what had been in her mind for many a year, and she had not failed, when challenged, to play what Lizzie had called her trump. And yet, as she put Pen to bed and he clung, as he always did, so very tightly to her, she began to see what she was doing in a different light. Where would she go and find such attachment, such unquestioning adoration? No other child except her own, a thing not looked for at the moment because there was so little chance of it, could ever mean to her what Pen Browning meant. Hadn't she seen him born? Hadn't she been the first, even before his mother, to hold him in her arms? And now, if she left, she would never find such an attachment again. Even if she went into a household with children the nurse and the governess would claim them. Sitting beside Pen as he lay chattering away, desperately staving off sleep, she never thought of winning, she never imagined the Brownings would pay her the four extra miserable guineas she wanted. She smiled slightly to herself and thought how well she knew them. It would be what they called "a matter of principle" and not of poverty. When her mistress said she had thought she was paid in love, that was a precise statement of her case—she really did believe the coinage of love was worth more than gold.

Nothing was said that evening. They all three bade each other a polite good night. But in the morning Mr. Browning spoke to her on his own and said, very gently, that they were obliged, with the greatest regret, to accept her notice because they were truly unable to meet her conditions. Wilson found herself blushing deeply as she replied in that case there was nothing for it but for her to go and find a place that would pay her the going wage to which she believed she was entitled and she noted his hesitancy, most unusual in the man. Emboldened by it, she said she hoped she could still take her holiday —and he said of course—and that she could expect a character reference, if she had given satisfaction in some respects. Mr. Browning shook his head sorrowfully and said, "Wilson, Wilson," and that she surely had no need to ask. He would write a reference such as no servant would ever have been able to show and the only danger might be the impossibility of anyone believing in it. But for all these flattering words, Wilson felt the steel in him: he would not think of backing down but would let her go, however reluctantly. Eight years with all that had happened in it and she was not worth four guineas.

Dressing her mistress that morning, she was unable to speak. Her throat felt closed with the effort of suppressing emotion and she was not even sure what emotion it was. Grief was there somewhere but also anger and a kind of shame. This last she dimly discerned but did not understand. She had nothing to be ashamed of but *they* made her feel she had, they acted as though she had done something shabby, as though she had let them down, and this she resented. Once the resentment had taken hold of her she began to be incapacitated. She dropped the hairbrush, found her fingers would not plait hair, and was incapable of selecting and picking up the right pins. Watching her unaccustomed fumbling, her mistress put a hand on her wrist and said, "Wilson, dear, will you not think again? We love you very much." If Pen had not at that minute staggered in bearing a purse he had found and if he had not succeeded in opening that purse and if a handful of guineas had not, to his delight, come tumbling out and rolled in all directions, then she did not know what she might have replied. But the purse did snap open and the guineas did roll and she was able to say, "I have thought enough, ma'am, and I must earn what I am worth while I am able."

She made no attempt, during the week that remained before her holiday was due, to look for another situation. She knew there were agencies with whom she could register and that *The Times* had column after column advertising for superior ladies' maids, but she had no inclination to try to place herself. Perhaps she would find something in Sheffield, though even as the thought went through her head she knew the idea horrified her and that she would have to be in a bad way indeed before it came to pass. But she had no energy to think. She felt spurned and humiliated and it was all she could do to drag herself through each day. That fleeting, delicious sense of triumph, because of bringing herself to the sticking point, had quite vanished. Instead, it seemed that the Brownings were triumphant.

They did not flaunt it but it was there in subtle ways, in looks exchanged and heads held high. Only Pen was himself, telling her every day he loved, loved, loved her and would marry her when he was a man if he could not marry Mama.

Lizzie, whom she visited almost every day, chided her for her dejection. "Come, Lily," she said, "you will feel better after your holiday and see you have done the best thing."

Wilson, nursing Lizzie's youngest, a girl of fourteen months, said, "I don't know as anything feels best, not when it will mean leaving Pen," and she hugged little Jane harder. "How he will manage without me I do not know and that is no boast. You do not know how it is with us, Lizzie, me having care of him since the hour he was born. He is like my own child, and such a curious child with more than normal needs. He took one look at the girl who was interviewed to be my replacement and screamed—he would have only his darling Lily, he said, and his mama and papa would not be his best friends anymore if they sent Lily away. Well, of course they said, with many a meaningful look at me, that they were not sending Lily away, it was Lily who wished to go, and then it was as though he had been struck and he hurled himself at me and really, Lizzie, I could not move an inch for the arms around my knees, the strength of the child, you would not believe it. And now every night he tries to make me promise never, never to leave him and sometimes to get him to sleep at last, I confess, I half promise though whether he understands it is only a *half* promise I do not know." Lizzie listened and clucked her tongue sympathetically and urged her to be strong but she felt far from strong. The distress and bewilderment crept into every corner of her being and she longed for some solution.

It came unexpectedly and in such a roundabout way that she was never sure she had read the signals correctly. There had been a succession of girls interviewed, each proving worse than the last. Wilson had shown some of them in and could not believe such slatterns and silly misses were getting past the door.

"Personal recommendation is the only way, Robert," she heard her mistress say with a sigh.

Her husband appeared irritated. "The point is, Ba," he said impatiently, "you will not get a nurse if you request a lady's maid and vice versa. The issue is ridiculously confused and ought to be cleared up— what is it we want, nurse for Pen or maid for you?"

"Wilson," his wife said simply. "What we want is Wilson."

Then the door closed and she could hear no more. But immediately afterward, when she went in to take the tea things, Mrs. Browning said, "I believe you have not had your new dress, Wilson, and indeed you ought to have it for your holiday. It is too late to have it made so you must go and buy yourself something pretty, dear. I have been remiss in not mentioning it before."

Wilson, in spite of the smile on her mistress's face, felt wary. She had had the two summer dresses she was entitled to, both made in Paris that spring. Her mistress could not have forgotten since they had bought the material together and there had been much discussion on the relevant merits of a cream poplin and a rose-tinted cotton. So what was this? Slowly, she looked at, but did not take, the two guineas lying on the table, put there this moment by their owner. "I have had my summer dresses, ma'am, if you remember. This is one and the other, the pink, for best." It crossed her mind that she had been subjected to a test of honesty but this was dismissed when her mistress quickly said, "No, I had not forgotten, nor did I think you had, but two dresses are not enough these days with Pen ruining them for you. I should like you to have another summer dress and another winter from now on, though of course you will not be staying." And at that Mrs. Browning's face fell.

"I would not stay for more dresses, ma'am," Wilson said, tight-lipped, "for indeed dresses mean little to me. If I stayed it would be because I would not leave when a certain person needs me so."

But afterward Wilson found herself wondering if she had missed a subtle shift of ground. What was being offered in the guise of dresses? A compromise? A way out? And she had foolishly rejected it. Money had been offered *for a dress* but who was to comment if no dress materialized and the money was taken? She had only to say, in the unlikely event of being challenged, that she had not yet found what she wanted and meanwhile the sovereigns could go to Mother. It would be a cheat and she still would not appear to win but she would know, and her employers would know, that she had. So that same day she took a deep breath and said, in the evening, as she prepared her mistress for bed, "I beg your pardon, ma'am, but after all I think you are right about the dress. I have only just now discovered a tear in this skirt which Pen made with a branch he would wave in the park and I think I had better accept the money for another dress in lieu and it would be very kind to increase my clothes allowance by four guineas a year." The joy on Mrs. Browning's face as she whirled around could not have been feigned. "Oh, Wilson *dear!*" she cried. "Then you will stay? These misunderstandings are over? Oh, Wilson, I cannot tell you how relieved I am. How I have hated every last one of those daring to think they could replace you. Never, never, let us go through that again. And now Pen will be happy, for you know yourself he has suspected the worst and been inconsolable."

But Pen was not happy just then, for of course it was time for Wilson to go on holiday and he had to be told. His mother tried to placate the screams by saying she would look after him herself, morning, noon and night, and he need fear no strangers. Wilson herself was more adept. "Do you want Lily to come back from her mother's to you?" she asked, and when assured this was the case told him, "Then be brave and trust her and she will come back, but if you scream and do not believe your Lily, then she will not want to leave her mother and come home to such a boy." Pen was instantly silent, only snuggling up to her and putting his thumb in his mouth. "I will go on my holiday and then I will come home and we will go back to Italy," she promised, returning into her own persona. Then it was endless cuddles and kisses and finally he fell asleep in her arms, his blond curls still damp with the fever of alarm he had worked himself into. Knowing it was the only way to save him further anguish, Wilson crept out of the house as soon as she had laid the child in his cot and Billy Treherne kindly took her to the station. "Beaten, eh?" he said to her, but smiled and without waiting for a reply said, "The Barretts are hard to leave, Lily, and don't I know it. I near enough never thought I'd get Lizzie out."

"It is not a case of the Barretts," Wilson replied, a little stiffly, for she was never quite at ease with Billy. "It's the child that holds me. Every day I am gone he will weep for me and that is no lie."

Nevertheless, she stayed three and not two weeks in Sheffield, though she knew it prolonged Pen's agony and was sorry for it. As soon as she arrived at that dismal little back-street house she sensed a difference in the atmosphere, a lightening of the exhaustion which had filled it the year before. On the surface, nothing had changed. It was still claustrophobic and poorly furnished, the cold was still intense for all it was summer and the whole place as dark as a coal hole with a smell of damp which nothing Mother could do would lift. But the inhabitants were different, markedly so. There were smiles on all three faces and smiles deeper than those of welcome. There was a relief and happiness present and Wilson soon knew why: both May and Ellen were to be married. They hardly knew how to tell her and it was hard to say who was more excited. May's, as might be expected, was the better match. The young doctor had proposed and been accepted and the marriage was to take place in six months when he had established himself in his uncle's practice. There would be a house to live in, a very pleasant house on the outskirts of the city with a garden for Mother, who would of course go with May. Mother cried when she told Wilson, in private, how Dr. Burnham was everything she could have wished for May—kind, gentle, clever and above all a gentleman.

But it was Ellen's match that startled. Ellen was to marry that very month and it was to be at the wedding that Wilson stayed her third week, writing:

—I am sorry, ma'am, to prolong my visit, but you will understand that it would be a cruel thing to miss my sister's wedding by a few days only when the likelihood is I may not see her for years and having sisters yourself and knowing too of Ellen's history you will sympathize with my desire I trust. It is all a great surprise and it was not until I had spoken with my mother that I was assured all was well. Ellen's husband-to-be is a widower and a farmer from

East Retford a village near Sheffield. He was in Sheffield in the spring to bring his two small children to his sister's after the death of his wife and while here came to the pharmacy where my sister works and made her acquaintance while buying pills for his younger child who was afflicted with a skin disease. He is forty years of age but my mother says in no way elderly but instead a fine, strong man, very blunt and direct. It is true she says that in appearance he is not unlike Albert Cole, who caused Ellen her former misfortune, but that there the resemblance ends for he has been in all ways honorable speaking first to my mother of his intentions before proceeding to divulge them to Ellen. Mother says he was frank, confessing he had sore need of a wife and that this had been in his mind ever since he came to Sheffield but that he would not take anyone since he judged a marriage without genuine affection and regard worse than useless. He said Ellen's modesty and simplicity had impressed him and that he liked her concern for the child she did not even know, this being his sick child for whom he collected the pills. Mother was afraid Ellen would scorn the offer though it was a good one and none better likely to come and was determined not to press her. But Ellen was at first thunderstruck not having thought herself worthy of any man's attention for a long time and then delighted because she had noticed and liked Mr. Wilson as he is called. This coincidence of the surname being the same as ours, though it is a common enough name, struck us all as propitious though I do not rightly know why. At any rate, Ellen accepted and they marry this Tuesday week and leave for East Retford the next day. All is bustle and confusion as you may imagine and we are determined to give Ellen the best wedding we can.

It was not after all a very splendid wedding but Wilson saw that Ellen hardly noticed its deficiencies. She was quite transformed by her luck, or what she saw as her luck, and had regained the old cheerfulness which had been her only real asset. She laughed again, that irritating giggle which irritated no longer, and her smile banished the haggard lines on her face (except for the crease of misery between her brows which was too ingrained ever to lift). Naturally, there was a new dress called for and Wilson made it, buying the material with the dress money Mrs. Browning had given her for herself. She firmly guided Ellen toward a blue stripe and away from a sprigged yellow which made her look jaundiced and was far too young for her. In the matter of hair she was authoritative, insisting Ellen's lank locks should be braided into a French plait, the very style she had once cursed for the difficulty it caused her but which she now approved above all others and could turn out like the best hairdressers in Paris. Mother had a pearl brooch and a pair of earrings and when these were worn Ellen suddenly looked elegant and her homeliness was for the moment banished. She made a very touching bride, sweet in her simplicity, affecting because she was demure and yet so clearly eager.

About the bridegroom Wilson was not so sure, though when Mother anxiously sought her opinion she found no difficulty stressing his finer points. It was true he was handsome in a countrified way and that he did not look a day over thirty for all the weather-beaten skin. It was also true he was not afraid to meet a direct look and that there was not a hint of hypocrisy about him. He was not, Wilson calculated, a mean man or a cruel one. She watched him cradle his younger child, a frail little boy of two, and saw his tenderness and was greatly heartened to see the respect with which he treated her mother. Yet as she watched Ellen pledge herself to honor and obey William Henry Wilson until death did them part there was something in the set of those broad shoulders in front of her which she did not altogether like. The last wedding she had witnessed had been the Brownings' and then she had felt no such misgivings. What was the difference? She sang the hymn Ellen had chosen and wondered. It was, she decided, Ellen's ignorance. Ellen did not know this man, could not claim to know him after half a dozen brief meetings over a month. She was *attracted* to him, that she had made too plain for her sister's liking, but she did not *know* him as Elizabeth Barrett had known Robert Browning and even, Wilson saw, as May already knew Dr. Burnham.

The married couple went off in a horse and cart with Ellen not in the least tearful. Wilson marveled at the ease with which her sister went off to an unknown destination with a man who would that night become as intimate with her as ever a man could be. William had been told, of course, about Ellen's dead baby and the circumstances of the birth. There had been no need to tell him, and Ellen herself had wished at least to wait until after she was married, but Mother had insisted, saying it was no way to start a new life, she wanted no deceit practiced. Ellen was dreadfully afraid William would no longer want her but he had merely thanked Mother for her honesty and said everyone made mistakes. More important to him had been Ellen's meeting with his children and this had gone well. The children were with them now, the boy asleep in Ellen's arms and the girl sitting beside her, happy to have a new mother. Ellen said she would write as soon as she was able.

Before Wilson returned to London there was indeed one short note from Ellen, saying only that they had arrived safely and there was a lot to be done in Mr. Wilson's house in Carol Gate. All of them read easily behind those lines. "A wife ill two years, dead these six months, I should think there would be a lot to do in any house," Mother said and then, "I ought to go to her, she will need me with two children to care for, one of them sickly, and a house to scour from top to bottom." But even before Wilson could say anything, May stepped in and said Mother was too tired to think about going anywhere and would do well to take care of herself rather than Ellen. "When I am married, Mother," May said, "you will stop working, as it has been agreed. You will become a fine lady of leisure and take tea with Arthur's better patients." Mother laughed but looked pleased and Wilson felt a pang of envy at May's ability to do what she had failed to do—give Mother a home and care for her. But it was a foolish envy and she scolded herself for it. The security of May's imminent future made it possible to leave Mother with a lighter heart than she had ever been able to do. "When I next see you," she whispered as she gave Mother a last embrace, "I expect to see you dangling a grandchild or two on your knee."

Mother's happy laughter was the nicest of sounds to bring back from Yorkshire and kept a smile on her own face all the weary way back to the Welbeck Street lodgings. But once there, it vanished at once. Her mistress looked and sounded worse than she had ever done since Wimpole Street days and Wilson could not help saying so. "That cough, ma'am! Where has it come from? And your eyes! Buried again, as they used to be. It is shocking, you ought not to be up and dressed at all and would not have been if *I* had been here."

"But you were not, dear Wilson," Mrs. Browning murmured in a wheezy voice, "and now you see the consequence, you see how I need you, and always will." She sank back on the sofa, luxuriating in Wilson's return, sighing with relief as the room was put to rights and Pen, half mad with joy, forcibly removed by his darling Lily. Within a day, Wilson had restored order, though driven distracted by her charge's insistence that she should sing with him every one of the many nursery rhymes he had learned with his mother during her absence. It was too much, she was sure, for his three-year-old brain and she said as much, only to be laughed at. There was no point in her protesting and she knew it. What Pen needed was a simple, regular routine in familiar surroundings and until they were back in the Casa Guidi that was impossible.

They were not there for another six weeks after she returned to London. First there was the christening of the poet Tennyson's son to delay for and then, once in Paris, which they had planned only to pass through, a matter of a lost traveling desk which had to be sent on from London before they could proceed. Once they were on their way again, leaving Paris on October 23, the final part of the journey back to Florence proved a nightmare. Never had Wilson known arrangements go so wrong and she could not but blame the Brownings themselves, both of them. How *could* they have chosen, at that time of the year, a route which led over Mont Cenis? It was bitterly cold and the inns had not all been properly booked and once they were obliged to travel on throughout the night in search of accommodation. She slept with Pen, as she always did when they traveled, and could not decide which was the greater ordeal—his chattering or her mistress's prolonged bouts of coughing which literally, on several nights, shook the thin walls between their rooms. Wilson was convinced her mistress was more seriously ill than she had ever been in Wimpole Street and Mr. Browning was convinced she was dying.

Hearing the coughing reach bed-shaking proportions one night, the last night before they estimated they would arrive in Italy, Wilson got up and crept out of the small room she shared with Pen. She stood in the passageway listening, a shawl over her nightdress. On and on it went, first the raw whooping sound, then the rasp of the breath at last caught. Every time the rasping stage was reached, she held her own breath. She knew the poor sufferer's face would be contorted with pain. How Mr. Browning stood it she did not know. She could hear him saying, "Ba, try to take a sip of water, do, only a sip." She leaned against the wall, tired herself, but unable to rest while this dreadful attack continued. Her own heart beat steadily, her lungs functioned perfectly and she found herself thinking she would not change places with any soul afflicted with such health whatever they had and whoever they were. It was more of a comfort than she had ever found such thinking before.

The door opened gently. Mr. Browning gave a start when he saw her and she put a finger to her lips. "Pen is asleep, sir," she whispered.

"I would that his poor mother was," Mr. Browning whispered back. "What can be done for her, Wilson? I cannot bear this agony. She has no strength left and the coughs tear her apart and she brings up—she discharges—I cannot help but see that she . . ."

"I know sir, I know. But the doctor once said if the blood— begging your pardon, sir—the blood, if it is only threads, and bright, is not from the lung and nothing to be feared."

"She has said so herself, but I fear, I fear." Wilson saw tears in his eyes and put out a hand to touch his arm. "Now, sir," she said, very softly, "do not despair. I promise you she has been like this before. Listen, we must make all speed to Genoa and then rest up. The warmth will restore her. We could start now, sir. She does not sleep and neither do we and Pen sleeps so soundly he can be carried to the carriage. Come, sir, let us leave this place and get to Italy."

They did so. At four in the morning they set off on the last lap and arrived in Turin by midday. Wilson urged no further delay, pointing out how cold it was in the city. So they traveled on, in a rush, to Genoa, as being the warmest place they could quickly reach, and they were just in time. On the very outskirts of the city the coughing took over entirely and the invalid almost choked. Mr. Browning was terrified, Pen screamed and Wilson herself, though outwardly calm, was very much afraid her mistress had burst a blood vessel and injured herself fatally. But Genoa was safely reached, bathed in sunshine though it was November, and it was perfectly true that, as Wilson wrote to Minnie that evening:

—it was like magic, Minnie, when that sun flooded through the windows of our carriage and fell on our poor sufferer's closed eyes. She felt the heat of it and struggled to open her eyelids and was almost blinded by it and said where are we and when her husband said in Genoa, Ba, and nearly home she smiled. We found rooms in a clean inn and Minnie some inns we have been reduced to have been far from clean and there we put my mistress's bed before the window and she lies there in the sun and it has done her the power of good already. We will stay here until the coughing or the worst of it has subsided entirely and then continue to Florence which we will all be relieved to see for never has there been a more ill-starred journey.

By the end of November that journey was only a shudder in all their memories. Mrs. Browning's recovery was so complete that only Wilson and her husband knew how near to total collapse she had been. It was like watching someone come back from the brink of the grave, Wilson reflected, and would have liked to say so if it had not sounded so false. Not only did the coughing stop, except for the merest eruption from time to time which could not be mentioned in the same breath as what had gone before, but her mistress gained weight rapidly and her eyes were no longer entirely sunken. With her returning health came a desire to write and to Wilson's unfeigned delight a new and rigid regime began in the Casa Guidi.

She never thought it would last, confessing to her mother in her first letter from Florence that

—I have seen this before, Mother, and it has not lasted above a week before the old order has been restored and we are back to being in bed until noon and playing with Pen when we are up. Mr.

Browning has always been less inclined to work than she has and indeed I have heard her often take him to task and berate him for wasting his talent. It is not for me to say, but I have often thought it odd when listening to those who visit this house and speak so kindly of him and praise him so very highly to know that Mr. Browning seems to set little store by any writing at all. But at any rate he is applying himself diligently now though I know not to what effect. All morning they write, both of them, and I remove Pen which is a great shock to him but will do him no harm. And what has aided this happy state of affairs is the efficiency of our new manservant, Vincenzo. I told you of how Alessandro was conveniently paid off when we left for England to my satisfaction you may be sure and now we have this new fellow. I confess I was taken aback when first I saw him for he is the very opposite of presentable, Mother, and my mistress complained to me that her husband cannot have had his eyeglass on when he engaged him or that it must at least have been in a poor light. Not to put too fine a point on it Mother and I would not say this except to you, but the man looks as if he might *smell* and there is indeed a whiff of the stable about him. I feared the worst but he is well able to do his job with the minimum of fuss unlike Alessandro to whom the simplest task was a production and we get on well enough. He is respectful and very quiet and causes me no bother for which I am grateful. So we are well settled in again Mother and Pen sleeps better and is altogether easier now that his day is regular. We have been out in the gardens a good deal and I cannot tell you how warm it is though we are nearly in December. Florence is full of visitors here for the winter and I daresay I shall make some new acquaintances before long.

Strangely, she did not, but this did not depress her as once it had. Sitting once more in the Boboli Gardens watching Pen play, Wilson wondered what kind of change had come over her. Instead of the sense of frustration and restlessness which had plagued her before the trip to England she felt a curious relief in simply being back in Florence. Her prospects on every front were no better and in some ways worse, for she had tried and failed to obtain an increase in salary, but there was a contentment that came from her daily round that had not been there before. She felt sure, now, that she would be with the Brownings all her life and this did not fill her with the dismay it had once done. Pen was hers as well as his parents', her child, and she never doubted his loyalty. And Italy, increasingly, seemed more attractive than England though she could not, as her mistress could, quite throw off her patriotism. But to compare Florence with Sheffield was an absurdity and even to compare it with London was to find her home country's capital wanting. She had become addicted to the warmth, to the light, to the expansiveness of Italian life, and to think of ever being reduced to Mother's circumstances in Sheffield made her shudder. Thinking of her married and about-to-be-married sisters, she felt not a twinge of envy. She would rather be single and have her life.

But in spite of the gratification which came from such reflection, Wilson was still aware of that deeper hunger which had begun to rise in her that summer before last in Bagni Caldi. What her mistress had been heard to refer to as her "female nature" troubled her, though on the surface she appeared perfectly calm. She saw no man who attracted her that winter, but knew that men in the abstract did. She dreamed of being crushed in a man's arms, of being kissed by a man's lips, of being pressed to a man's body. The man had no identity. He was just A Man, who sometimes fleetingly would have the characteristics of someone she knew and sometimes not. They were not dreams she could relate to anyone and she was pleased to find that when she woke up they had not left her anxious or unhappy. On the contrary, there was a comfort in the dreams. She wondered how Mother would interpret this, guessing she would judge any dream that gave happiness was sure to signify luck. Where the luck would come from Wilson had no idea or even if it ever would come, but she was not disposed to destroy her own harmless fantasies. There was nothing wicked in them. She was not, at thirty-three, an old woman to whom such visions might smack of indecency, but still young and healthy enough to have expectations. She knew she was prettier and more attractive than she had ever been and, if time was going to run out, then it had not yet begun. Ellen, at thirty, looked years older than she, and May, for all her youth, had the ways of a middle-aged woman. So Wilson took care of her looks and as her mistress worked in one room and her master in the other she sat in the sun and smiled to herself and bided her time.

CHAPTER TWENTY-ONE

Vincenzo was an odd little man. Nobody could have been more different from Alessandro in both appearance and temperament and Wilson was grateful for it. And he was honest, which Wilson had always known Alessandro was not, as well as efficient. Before very long she had discovered he was also a great worrier and what he worried about most was his health. He was slight and had a stoop to his thin shoulders which increased his aged look (though, at thirty-eight, he was barely older than Wilson). First thing in the morning he looked hardly capable of lasting the day and last thing at night ready to collapse. Wilson felt sorry for him and a little irritated. He seemed to her to have no pleasure at all in life except possibly the bottle (though he never overstepped the bounds of propriety except on a Saturday night when she could hear him singing in his loft). When her mistress sighed over Vincenzo and wondered how her husband could have been so misguided as to employ such a pathetic, unsavory individual, Wilson was surprised to find herself defending him. "He is tidy, ma'am," she said, "and does his job without fuss and keeps himself to himself. He is better than some." By which, of course, she meant Alessandro.

Certainly Vincenzo enabled Wilson to feel very much in control in the household. Things were once more done *her* way and she enjoyed the power. Vincenzo was particularly cooperative over preparing plain, wholesome food for Pen and allowed her to (was even eager to let her) prepare the menus. Scotch broth once more steamed in the tiny kitchen during the wet days of January and February and there was no Alessandro to sneer and hold his horrible bulbous nose and do his best to spoil it if she left the pan unattended. By March, Wilson was fairly certain Vincenzo was a little afraid of her, which she could not reconcile with her own perception of herself. He almost cringed when she came upon him, as though according her the same respect as the Brownings, and he was beside himself with apologies if he accidentally got in her way. It was a strange feeling, to arouse such alarm in others, but one not altogether distasteful. She remembered vividly, spying Vincenzo about to go down a corridor, then hold back because he saw her coming, how she had been wont to do that very thing when a young housemaid. The memory of the agony of it all made her reflect how far she had come. Not, perhaps, as far as Jeannie, who had verged on the altogether too familiar, but far enough to make her status as servant infinitely more complicated than she had ever thought it. She would never cringe again before anyone. Wait, delay, be respectful: but always with dignity and in expectation that she had some standing too. Nobody any longer had the power to intimidate her. She knew herself to be perfectly *au fait* with the customs of the drawing room as well as the kitchen and could, and did, carry off her duties before any of the Brownings' guests with aplomb.

The night Vincenzo was taken ill there had been quite a gathering of such guests in the Casa Guidi. It was early summer by then, with the sky as blue as her own best dress, and the Brownings had entertained their three favorite visitors until almost ten o'clock, an event unusual enough to cause comment. When told Mr. Tennyson, Mr. Powers, and Mr. Lytton would partake of a light supper, Wilson had expressed surprise, since the more common invitation was to have those three gentlemen to tea. "It is a special day," her mistress told her, "an anniversary, Wilson, surely you remember?" But Wilson did not. Birthdays and weddings she had no doubt of but the significance of May 20 had passed her by and she had to be reminded it was the date Mr. Browning had first called some eight years since. Vincenzo prepared an excellent supper but was in such a torment of nerves that long before it was served he was groaning in anguish for the state of his *pollo coi funghi secchi,* a special favorite of his employers. Afterward, when the guests had gone, Wilson saw him press a handkerchief to his forehead in a gesture of such theatrical despair she almost laughed. But instead she scolded herself and inquired kindly if she could get the poor man a drink to soothe his nerves. The drink was declined. Vincenzo staggered off to bed, his face blotchy and red, and Wilson took to her own.

At two in the morning she was woken by Flush growling and heard a loud and prolonged moan. She took a candle and went to the foot of the ladder by which Vincenzo ascended to his sleeping quarters. She called his name but received only a gasp in reply. Hesitating, for she had no desire to see the man in his bed, she heard another cry of such pain that she turned at once and went to rouse Mr. Browning. He immediately ordered Wilson to tell the porter to go for a doctor. She fled down the stairs and the porter for once took his cue from her flying feet and was willing to go for the doctor. Vincenzo was bled, with Wilson acting as nurse, a task she did not enjoy. The man looked dreadful, his eyes glazed and his face running with perspiration. The verdict was that Vincenzo was suffering from acute indigestion and ought to rest. But where? Hearing the Brownings discuss this, Wilson was again aware of a distinction between herself and any other servant. Not for a moment was it suggested that Vincenzo should be looked after in the Casa Guidi until he was well. On the contrary, there was an indecent haste in the way he was moved to a cheap lodging house that very morning, clutching a month's wages and an additional gift of money. The air of relief when he had been removed was palpable and to Wilson both distressing and threatening—such was the fate of a servant and for all her own sense of security it made her shiver.

She went to inquire after Vincenzo, taking an egg custard she had made, the following day and returned with dramatic news, that he was in hospital with miliary fever.

What happened to the man when he left hospital Wilson never knew. He had his wages a month ahead but after that, what? It disturbed her to think of him, weak and wretched, with no one to care for him, and if she had had less fear of carrying disease she would have attempted to help him. As it was, energies in the Casa Guidi were concentrated on selecting a new servant before the exodus for the summer to Bagni di Lucca. Mrs. Browning wanted no more mistakes: applicants must be interviewed during the day and have a minimum of three references which would be carefully scrutinized and checked. "And, Robert," Wilson hear her plead, "*health* is of the utmost concern. You cannot have looked at Vincenzo, dear, and judged him bursting with health. I defy you to say so. Look carefully, Robert, appraise a man's strength and vigor first and foremost." There followed a spirited defense of his interviewing technique by Mr. Browning, who roundly condemned strength and vigor as the most important aspects of a servant's character. "Now, Ba," he remonstrated, "where should we be if we took on a great oaf who could fell a tree with one blow and carry me in one hand downstairs if the fellow was so stupid and so inexperienced that he could only burn the dinner and did not know how to lay out clothes and could not for the life of him work out the formula for opening the door and showing people in? Health yes, but strength no."

There were six other applicants but none to compare with the seventh. Wilson, seeing Ferdinando Romagnoli for the first time, felt that quickening of the heartbeat, that tremor of the nerves, which she had been waiting for all her adult life. It surprised and even shocked her. What had Ellen said of her Albert? That her stomach turned to water and she could not gainsay him. What had her mistress said of her husband on that far-off day they had recently celebrated? That she took one look and knew she was irresistibly attracted. And what a fool I was, Wilson thought, to imagine Timothy of Reginald or Leonardo meant anything to me. But she was quick to hide her own confusion, not by one flicker of expression betraying any interest but rather the reverse. The more attracted she felt the more important it seemed to be careful, not to blush, not to smile too invitingly, not to suggest in any way that she was smitten. She kept her eyes down and her ears open and served the Brownings their tea on the day Ferdinando was engaged as though nothing could interest her less. But writing to Lizzie, all caution was allowed to disappear, though she warned her friend:

—you must not tell anyone of my foolishness Lizzie only I need to share my excitement with someone and indeed you are the safest recipient by far of my confession which verges on the downright silly. It was as other women have said and I have scorned them for it and in truth I *am* dazzled by his looks which is not wise. Signor Righi, if you remember, though you may not as I hardly do myself, Leonardo Righi, then, was tall and handsome but always in a military way if you take my meaning. He was correct and impressive but did not yield and so there was a formality in all he did which I often judged might signify a coldness. Ferdinando Romagnoli is quite otherwise. He too is tall and handsome but with no rigidity in his bearing at all. Instead he is easy and bent at once to lift Pen and enslaved him immediately. He has thick black hair, worn shorter than most, and a broad face upon which there is almost always a smile showing good teeth as my mistress noted. His eyebrows are thick and bushy and he has a mustache of the same variety. He is thirty-six years old, which you know is near to my own age, and served as a volunteer in the 1848 Rising which has greatly endeared him to his new employers. His family live in a village beyond Fiesole and he seems fond of them so he is not a solitary character. You will ask Lizzie and I will not beat about the bush but tell you at once that by some miracle he is *not* married. Mrs. Browning thought this odd and wondered why and hoped it did not mean he was of a bad character with women which Mr. Browning took exception to and said he hoped that since he himself was unmarried at the age of thirty-four she had never deduced it meant *he* had such a character. There are many reasons a man may not have married he said and one may be he has never found the right woman and has wisely waited as I did for you. Not that I think of marriage,

Lizzie, being not so foolish as to judge a man on his appearance but to *you* I will not deny my relief at Ferdinando's single state. Meanwhile he fits in very easily being somewhere between Alessandro and Vincenzo and having the better part of each without the worst which is to say he is cheerful but not insufferably so and attentive without being servile. He is perhaps less of a cook than Alessandro was but infinitely more of a valet and butler than poor Vincenzo. We shall better see how he fares when we go to Lucca, a place as you know Lizzie I do not have much fondness for but there is no denying it is at least cool and good for the child and may not prove so inhospitable upon this occasion.

She did not add that her hopes of a livelier time rested on the new manservant's charms rather than on the place itself, which once more was the quieter of the hill villages at Lucca. At least the house taken from the middle of July was large and they were not, as they had been before, squashed into small rooms. She slept with Pen at one end of the house and Ferdinando slept at the other next to the kitchen with the Brownings and the living quarters in between. If she had wished, it would in those circumstances have been possible for Wilson to avoid seeing much of her fellow servant but, as it was, she rather regretted the distance between them and so did Pen. Ferdinando was quickly his most intimate friend with whom he wished to spend every minute of the day. Hardly had he woken before he was listening for Ferdinando's whistle outside his window, the signal that he was ready and waiting to take Pen to the stream. Naturally, Wilson had to go with him—how could she leave a four-year-old child? Why, anything might happen, since men were known not to take the care a woman did. Her mistress, told this, stared at her strangely and smiled and said doubtless she was right, anything could happen. . . .

So each morning, before either of the Brownings was astir, Pen and Ferdinando and Wilson made their way through the gardens to the field leading to the stream. Even at eight the sun, though low in the sky still, was hot and a haze rose off the grasses waving almost imperceptibly in the smallest of breezes, which would soon disappear. A cock crowed and was answered by another and a donkey brayed exhaustingly from across the stream. Ferdinando carried Pen on his shoulders and sang as he walked, a song he had learned in '48, which he was teaching Pen. His old gun was slung on his arm and every now and again Pen would lean down and touch the muzzle and shiver and Wilson would check for the thousandth time that it was not loaded and only carried to remind Ferdinando of his rabbit- and not his man-killing days. Once at the stream, Wilson spread a blanket she had brought and made herself comfortable while Pen gathered sticks and bigger bits of wood and Ferdinando whittled away with his knife and fashioned them into boats and then both of them ran up and down the bank shrieking and jumping as these "boats" raced down the stream. Then Ferdinando would repair the stepping-stone ford he had made and encourage Pen to go from one rock to another and back again, making the small boy feel a hero for successfully negotiating the rushing cataracts that to him were like Niagara Falls.

There was little for Wilson to do, that morning hour, except daydream. She pulled a grass and sucked the end and watched the man and the boy through half-closed eyes. They were so very different, one so dark and strong and powerful, the other so fair and fragile and slender. Ferdinando as a boy must have looked very striking. Tall, he would have been, even as a child, with always that look of confidence that comes from strength. He would have had the man he was to be stamped on him in a way Pen did not. With Ferdinando all that had to happen was growth whereas with a child like Pen the transition from boy to man needed a transformation so complete it was impossible to imagine the finished product. When Ferdinando took his shoes off and rolled up his breeches to wade into the stream after an escaped boat, or when he threw off his jacket and opened his shirt toward the end of their morning hour as the sun turned fierce already, Wilson could hardly avoid a sharp intake of breath at the sight of his muscular brown legs and the glimpse of the hollow at the base of his throat. She blushed even though neither man nor child looked her way and turned aside for a moment to hide her confusion, which deepened every day. Ferdinando had an attractiveness everyone felt. In his company both men and women smiled and felt the better for being with him. But the pull toward him which Wilson felt went far beyond this. She wanted Ferdinando not only to be with her but to touch her and yet she felt if he did she would die of pleasure.

There was no sign of such an impending death. Ferdinando was respect itself. He still called her Mrs. Wilson and was deferential, though not in Vincenzo's way. There was not the faintest inkling that he was interested in her or admired her or wished to know her on another footing and Wilson did not know how to interpret his attitude. He was not cold toward her—he was not cold toward anyone— but in the glances he gave her she could discern no message. She did not know what to do beyond being as pleasant and amiable as possible and taking every opportunity, whether he knew it or not, to be in his company. She used Pen shamelessly, but began to wonder by the middle of September whether this was as clever as she had thought. While Pen was with her, how, after all, could Ferdinando see her as anything but a nurse? And since he was genuinely fond of the boy he would never neglect him to prefer her. They were never alone, not until one day when Pen went to spend the day with the Storys at the next village.

If Pen doted on Ferdinando he was hardly less enamored of Edith and Joe, the nine- and six-year-old children of William Wetmore Story, an American sculptor who also lived in Florence. When first they had arrived in Lucca, Wilson had taken one look at Mrs. Story and decided she would not do as a friend for her own mistress, being too obviously flirtatious and gushing. But whether it was because of a need for the companionship of women or that Emelyn Story had hidden qualities, the two mothers became good friends and so therefore did the families. Wilson approved of the friendship, while secretly preserving reservations as to Mrs. Story's true character, because it brought Pen into the company of other children. She was happy to have Edith and Joe in her charge, upon occasion; as well, Pen and she and Ferdinando took them all off on picnics while the parents sat and talked poetry and politics. Surrounded by all of them, Wilson felt she was head of a ready-made family, with Ferdinando the robust father. It was play-acting of the most ridiculous sort but, since none knew of it, harmless. Edith and Joe, quite delightful children with none of that spoiled nature Wilson had seen too much of in children of their station in life, adored Ferdinando as much as Pen did. He was their hero, breathing fire and adventure with his tales of his exploits in the '48, and he could do all the things their own fathers never thought of doing. Ferdinando climbed trees for them and made rope swings and built tree houses and was at every turn energetic and daring. It was hard for them, and harder for him, when he returned to cook or appeared to wait upon them in the house in his capacity as servant—they would hardly accept him in that role.

For weeks Edith and Joe came to visit Pen but at last, when there was just beginning to be a chill in the air at night, Pen agreed to go to them if Ferdinando as well as Wilson would take and collect him. His excitement was terrible. Clutching him to her heart, his mother murmured that she understood because she had felt exactly the same as a child. When the moment came to wave her goodbye, Pen, perched on his pony, cried piteously, as though going to the North Pole for a year, and it was only Ferdinando's inspiration in giving him his empty old gun to hold, so he might pretend he was a soldier, that saved the day. But once at the Storys', his fear evaporated and Wilson left him running happily after a pig with Edith and Joe. She and Ferdinando left together, promising to return in eight hours, when the sun was beginning to set. They walked slowly back down the hill, the pony left grazing in the Storys' orchard. It was odd not to have Pen between them, endlessly claiming every moment of their attention. Ferdinando remarked how good it would be for Pen to have such a day and Wilson agreed. Then there was silence for another quarter of a mile until at last Ferdinando said quietly, "What will you do with yourself, Mrs. Wilson, without the boy tied to you?"

Afterward Wilson confessed she had never thought to say anything so bold in her life to such an innocent inquiry. When once she would have assured him she had plenty of work, or outlined in detail a routine of sewing and mending, or vowed her mistress had every claim on her attention still, now she heard herself say, "I am fancy-free and wondering how best to celebrate." It was astonishing and her blush, once the words were out, so violent even her eyes burned. Ferdinando laughed and slapped his thigh and said so was he, free as a bird for the day, and with all manner of plans to make the most of it.

What Wilson then loved most was how he instantly assumed the lead. They both went back to the Casa Tolomei to report Pen's safe arrival and happiness and to check that they were not wanted until late afternoon and then, with what Wilson supposed must be described as some cunning though she did not like to think of it as such, they went their separate ways and met in the tiny village square. Ferdinando had a basket with him, covered with a cloth, and was mysterious about its contents. He said he would take Wilson to a secret place she would much admire and so they set off up a track, with Ferdinando every now and again taking Wilson's elbow to help her over a rough bit. Soon they came to a narrower track which branched off the main one and here Ferdinando slashed through the undergrowth so that nothing would catch on her gown. She was panting a little with the exertion and was relieved to find they were now on the level, with no more climbing. Suddenly the thick bushes parted and they came to a glade where the stream widened into a pool. All around the trees closed in but, where the pool was, the grass was clear and short, as though it were a lawn, and the sun directly overhead shone upon it like a spotlight. Wilson was dazzled by the brilliant light and drew back into the bushes but Ferdinando pointed to a spot the other side of the pool where the branches of a huge elder tree shaded a flat-topped rock.

There they sat and picnicked. Cold chicken came out of the basket and cheese and bread and a perfect watermelon and a flagon of white wine which was set to cool in the water. Ferdinando whistled as he laid out the food and smiled at Wilson and did not know that in her answering smile was the memory of another picnic in Richmond Park and the determination that came from it not to lose another God-given chance.

"Well, Mrs. Wilson . . ." Ferdinando began but she stopped him.

"Why do you address me so?" she asked. "I am Lily to Pen and to my friends."

"Then I can count myself as a friend?"

"What else? Would I follow an enemy and eat with him?"

"Well then, Lily, I was going to say it is a long time since I had such pleasure as this."

"And a long time since I did, likewise."

"When I was young I wanted only to be a soldier."

"And when I was young I wanted only to be a bride."

"A bride!"

"A bride, in white with orange blossom in my hair."

He picked a yellow flower from the grass, as like to an English buttercup as ever she had seen, and gently threaded it into her hair. For a man so large, his touch was gentle and his strong fingers nimble. It crossed her mind he had done this before and so there was some asperity in her tone when she added, "Yes, a bride, how foolish I was, to be sure."

"Why foolish?"

"There are better things in life to want than being a bride."

"You say so? What things, then?"

"Oh, I like my independence." Then she laughed and, leaning back against the rock, shaded her eyes to look up at the sun. "In a manner of speaking, of course, not really in my circumstances having such a fine thing as independence. But my mother and sisters . . ." She stopped. Sheffield seemed so far away. A year ago its wet, gray, cold streets and the deprivation of Mother's life had made her shudder and now, in the sun, she shuddered again.

"Your mother and sisters?" he pressed her.

"Oh, I was going to say they had all been or were to be brides and I would not change my life with any of them."

He was lost. He smiled, but his eyes were troubled. She was being foolish, this was not talk for a picnic, she was putting him off with her attempt at philosophizing. So she took a bite of onion tart and praised his cooking though indeed the pastry was not nearly as light as her own. As he leaned forward to cut a piece for himself she saw the long, ugly scar on the inside of his arm, stretching from his elbow into the sleeve of his blouse, and wondered that she had not noticed it before.

"Is that a battle wound?" she asked, touching the beginning of the scar with her fingers.

He laughed derisively. "A rout wound, that is what it is," he said. "Nothing more. We turned tail and ran before the Austrians when all our lines had been cut to shreds. It was flee or die, and the brave died."

"Nothing brave about dying when you can live to fight another day."

"If it comes, and if it does not come soon I shall be too old to be of use."

She felt sorry for him. He hung his head and spoke so sorrowfully and seemed ashamed. "Well, we are a fine pair," she said lightly, "to talk of disappointments and lost hopes on such a day. We need Pen to chatter us out of our sighing."

"No," he said and looked at her with an unusually serious expression. "It is good not to have Penini. I would rather have you to myself when I can."

By the end of the first week in October, when the weather turned cool and cloudy at Bagni di Lucca and the return to Florence was made, Wilson and Ferdinando had managed to be alone many more times, though never for as long as that day they picnicked. There were endless stratagems for managing it and never a day went by without at least half an hour's indulgence in each other's company without benefit of Pen's chaperoning. "You two mine fwends," he would lisp and join their hands together across him, little knowing the pleasure it gave them. Aware how observant her mistress's eyes were, and fearing above all else attention drawn to her growing love for Ferdinando, Wilson worked hard to dissemble effectively. Ferdinando was not so astute. She scolded him in private for smiling at her too knowingly and for seeking her out with his eyes every time he came into a room where she was with the Brownings. Her caution puzzled him. He could see no reason for it and took it at first to mean that she thought she was doing wrong. Patiently, she explained that she did not like people to know her business until there was proper business to know and that she wanted no smirks and hints and teasings at her age. So Ferdinando had tried hard to respect her dignity though it did not come naturally.

What did come naturally, too naturally, was his urge to make love to her. They had progressed from hand holding to kissing and then to embracing but it was thus far and no further—Wilson drew back whenever his ardor led him to stray beyond the most innocent boundaries. And yet she was, he sensed, neither frigid nor a tease. He could feel her wishing to respond as he held her in his arms and her body followed his until he pressed her too far. He could tell that refusing him distressed her as much as being refused distressed him. Trembling, they would both pause and disentangle themselves and he would tell her he loved her and wanted only to make her happy. They must marry at once, he said, and then there would be no bar to their proper union. But she became sharp with him and told him they were not in a position to marry and did he not see how penury and disaster would follow if they did? She would be dismissed instantly and they would be obliged to part. What kind of married life would that be? Ferdinando shook his head and confessed himself beaten: if they were not to marry, what were they to do? Wilson replied that they must wait, they must start saving and bide their time, but as she wrote to Lizzie:

—oh Lizzie only you know how hard that waiting is for I have no doubts anymore and love him truly and no longer ponder what that word means. But think, Lizzie, of our situation! He has no income but what he earns and neither have I and were we to marry mine, which is the greater, would stop and if I were to be in the family way I would be unable to go and look for employment elsewhere. Ferdinando protests our master and mistress would be happy to have us as a married pair and swears I am thought so highly of that they would not let me go, but I know them better Lizzie and so do you. For a while it might be well but if I should fall and be with child why then the tolerance would stop as it always does and she would say as most would that I could not blame her and had brought dismissal on myself. So what is there to do? I find it hard to deny him for I am denying myself and it is not wise to continue with this frustration. He has healthy appetites and so I am bound to say and to my own astonishment do I and would no longer condemn my sister Ellen as once I did. Then I think of how it would kill Mother should anything happen as it happened with Ellen and *I cannot do it.* I am near mad with it all Lizzie, and though Ferdinando neither forces me nor turns angry

but is only sad I fear for the future if this continues. Write to me
Lizzie for God's sake and give me some direction.

Surprisingly, Lizzie did write and by return. The Casa Guidi was
all in uproar when the letter came because the entire household was
moving to Rome to winter and Wilson was diverted from her personal anguish by the need to pack and organize all their belongings.
But she found a moment to read Lizzie's letter and it calmed her, for
her friend pointed out that, since she was undoubtedly in love with
this Ferdinando and he with her, there was no point in waiting—they
should marry at once before, as Lizzie put it, "the need arises as it did
for me."

Ferdinando did love her and he *was* a good man, but what Wilson
found herself thinking all the long eight-day journey to Rome was
that, though good, her lover was neither clever nor enterprising. He
had no ambition, was at a loss when she attempted to discuss the
future. He had a situation and merely saw himself continuing in it, for
that was his lot in life. She had already discovered that his whole
existence hitherto had been one of such acceptance. From a boy, he
had taken what was on offer, counting himself lucky that he was
wanted anywhere. And, in his own eyes, he had indeed been lucky,
working in good households and always so easy and popular his days
were never made a misery. People employed him for his personality
and not his skills, which were minimal. If he had bread to eat and a
wage it had never troubled him that he had nothing else. Only on the
subject of his country did he show any fire, and even then he would
always be of the kind that rallies to, but never raises, the flag. So, as
Wilson saw all too clearly, it was useless to look to Ferdinando to see
a way out of their dilemma. She must do it herself. She must think of a
way of using their combined talents to support themselves in a life
together outside the Browning household.

In Rome she and Ferdinando were at first so busy settling into the
rooms taken in the Via Bocca di Leone that they had not a moment to
themselves and hardly saw each other and then, with frightening
speed, a calamity of such proportions overshadowed their lodgings
that all thought of themselves was banished. Joe Story, only six years

old, whom they had last seen sitting on Ferdinando's shoulders and screaming with delight as his head touched the trees, died suddenly. Wilson was with her mistress when the message came and was hardly less affected. Ferdinando was distraught, crying openly and wishing he could have given his own life to save the child's. Throughout the awful days that followed her own romance was the last thing in Wilson's mind and yet the tragedy had a direct bearing upon it. She and Ferdinando as well as Mr. Browning went to the funeral and as she stood there in the gloomy church looking in horror at the tiny coffin before the altar the meaning of the solemnly intoned words, "In the midst of life we are in death," sounded over and over again in her head. Poor little Joe had been struck down by a strange fever nobody could diagnose. Who knew when it would strike again? Who knew if one among the weeping congregation already carried the same seed of destruction? And here she was, her life span more than likely half over, *waiting*, with deliberate effort, to give herself to the man she loved. It was folly.

On Christmas morning a month later, when Wilson went with Ferdinando and the Brownings to attend mass at St. Peter's, she had come to a decision. The next time the opportunity presented itself she would follow her desires and become Ferdinando's wife in all except name. The music soared and Ferdinando at her side held up Pen to see the procession down the main aisle and Wilson's heart soared with it until she found herself crying with the emotion. She shut her eyes tight and wiped away the tears she was too late to control and thought how happy she was to have made the decision. She had to take risks or lose everything. And so that very evening, when the Brownings had gone with Pen to eat turkey and plum pudding with the still grieving Storys, she went to Ferdinando in the kitchen and surprised him with an open show of her affection. Feeling her arms around his neck and her body pressed to his, he was the one to pull back and look at her, a little confused. The question was in his eyes, as it always was, and she answered it by leading him by the hand to her room where a fire burned brightly. Still he did not understand the change that had come over her and stood bewildered as she sat down on her bed and held out her arms. A groan escaped him and he backed away, announcing he would not be master of himself if he held her, and when she whispered that he did not need to be, still he hesitated, unsure and trembling. But he came to her at last and they lay down together still fully clothed, and when she kissed and caressed him without thought of the consequences his sudden joy made him frantic. She had thought the act itself would terrify her but as one by one she was stripped of her garments and as one by one Ferdinando divested himself of his own she felt only her heart beat wildly and a thrill sweep through her limbs until she was all on fire for him.

Whatever he was in other ways, Ferdinando was sure and certain in lovemaking. Wilson was awed by his mastery, his control, his great care for her own pleasure—it was as unlike the fumbling brutalities she had imagined as grace was unlike clumsiness. There was a pace and pattern to the act she had never guessed at and she became a part of it with unlooked-for ease. They had only two hours, but into it crammed months of yearning now given its satisfaction. But almost immediately the deceit began. Flush barked, as though he understood the importance of being a watchdog, and then the noise of the carriage outside and Pen's high voice had Ferdinando leaping for his garments, knowing he ought to be at the door to carry the child up the stairs. Wilson herself, though with equal need to be swift and even more cause to be fearful, found herself languid. As Ferdinando rushed from the room, she dressed slowly and looked at herself in the gilt-edged mirror which hung over the chest of drawers. She ought to look different, transformed, but apart from the flush on her cheeks and the disheveled state of her hair she looked exactly the same. When she went to take Pen from Ferdinando's arms she was glad to find him asleep so that he could be attended to the quicker. She wished to be alone to savor what had happened to her and the thought of next attending to her mistress dismayed her. But when Pen was safely tucked up and she went into Mrs. Browning's bedroom to help her disrobe she found her mistress so taken up with her own misery that she paid Wilson no attention at all. Sitting on the edge of the bed, she was exhausted and weak as much from the emotional strain of a day spent with the Storys, a day in which the fact of Joe's death had constantly to be faced on this happiest of days, as from the fatigue of being sociable for so long. "The agony of it," she kept repeating, her eyes shut, "oh, the *agony* of being with them." Wilson made sympathetic noises and was as deft and soothing as possible in her ministrations. "Life is so short," her mistress murmured as she lay back on her pillows, "so very short, but then death can only be a transition, Wilson, with all our loved ones waiting on the other side."

Back in her room once more, Wilson made ready for bed and thought on what she had done. It gave her a strange feeling of satisfaction to have taken such a momentous step as she had done, on Christmas Day, no ordinary drab weekday, but a special day, already marked for joy. Nor did it affect her mood to share her mistress's mournful reflection that life *was* short. That was what had influenced her most. Life was short and, though her mistress seemed to take that as a reason for concentrating on death and what happened after it, she felt no inclination to do so. Life *was* short and she wanted to enjoy it to the full, to waste none of it. And she felt more alive, more full of hope than she had ever done, whatever the future held. If she became pregnant, then so be it—it had been foolish to try to plan ahead. But she would say nothing to Mrs. Browning, would endeavor to keep secret the true situation between herself and Ferdinando. The only person she told was Lizzie, who could be relied upon to keep quiet and who indeed had no temptation to tell. She was shy about what she wrote, vowing:

—I cannot bring myself to write of it, Lizzie, but you will know to what I refer when I say I was made a most happy woman on this Christmas Day! Indeed, it was not deliberate but happened as you had sensed it would and I have no cause to regret it. The coming together since is not as difficult as it was in your time in Wimpole Street for it is not at all the same here and there is a freedom which we take advantage of with no harm to anyone that I can see. Mr. Browning, who might be more of a danger than my mistress (though she is more astute) simply in being in need of Ferdinando at unpredictable times is out a great deal and has less use for him than in Florence. He goes everywhere to dinners and balls with his wife's encouragement and blessing you may be sure though many do not believe it. Only the other day Isa Blagden's maid, Miss Blagden being a friend from Florence I may not have mentioned to you, said to me I suppose your poor mistress is demented with her husband roving so and her an invalid. I looked askance at her and assured her my mistress far from being demented was pleased and greatly liked to hear her husband telling where he had been and enjoyed at second hand what through feeble health she is unable to enjoy with him. And it is true Lizzie for whatever else she may be my mistress is not nor never has been or will be a jealous woman, and I for one believe her faith to be justified. When Mr. Browning is out we have our own amusement and I do not mean myself and Ferdinando for that concourse is kept for when we are alone here. My mistress is much taken with spiritualism to which as you will remember she has always had leanings. There is at present a great vogue for it in both Florence and Rome and there are seances the length and breadth of both cities. Mr. Browning is loud in his protestations that it is all nonsense but my mistress ignores him and carries on her own way. Now you know how I have told you my mother sees into the future and I have told my mistress the same in the past and she has been greatly taken with Mother's gift and often plagued me with requests to try my own luck though I have told her I do not know myself to have the gift. But lately, such is the strength of the craze, I have been unable to resist her plea to experiment and so we have drawn the curtains tight and put out all the lamps and by the light of one candle only sat at a table together. It makes me nervous even to sit there but though we have concentrated hard neither voice nor hand from the other world has materialized. But with a pencil we have had some experience of an outside force which I am tempted to put down to the agitation of our fingers resulting from scaring ourselves out of our wits. Last night, Mr. Browning being out, we settled ourselves soon after ten o'clock at the table and waited. It was all dark, Lizzie, with not even a candle lit and the only light the dull glow of the small fire across the room. My mistress had taken a double dose of laudanum which if her husband knew he would be very angry and was in a trance before we had half sat down. After a while she bid me take up the pencil for she could feel a presence and I did so and held the pencil tight and waited. I have seen spirit writing done at Miss Blagden's for her maid is famous for it and knew what should happen only nothing did. Then through clutching the pencil too tight I swear I made a mark on the paper and my mistress drew in her breath and waited and the pencil jumped again. After a while my mistress said she could feel the presence had gone and I lit a lamp, whereupon she took the paper we had had before us and declared you have written a K Wilson, who do you know who is a K. Why I said only my mother who is Katherine and not dead thank God. And then I looked at the marks I had made and saw it might indeed be a K and now I await assurance in her next letter that Mother is well which I confidently expect.

Mother had turned excellent correspondent since the summer before, which had made her very happy. Even her mistress had remarked how regularly the envelopes from Sheffield came, professing jealousy since her own letters from home never flowed fast enough for her liking. And the content of the letters had been buoyant and cheerful with news of May's marriage and her happiness with Arthur and the excitement of moving house and once more being a true housekeeper and no longer working for the pharmacist. Only when it was over did Mother confess how weary she had been and how distasteful the work. Ellen, too, was content though Mother implied by the use of the word that things did not go as well with Ellen as they did with May, which did not surprise Wilson. Mother had ended her last letter before Christmas with a hint that in her next she might have some interesting news and so Wilson waited with a certain anticipation for what she guessed would be an announcement that either Ellen or May was expecting.

When, on the seventh of January, the black-edged envelope came for her addressed in a strange hand she did not know, Wilson fainted. Ferdinando, finding her in a crumpled heap on the stone floor of the entrance to the house where they lodged, picked her up bodily and rushed upstairs, wailing as he went. Mr. Browning came out and, seeing the envelope lying on Wilson's bosom to which she had clutched it, hastened to prepare the sofa for her and then to fetch some brandy. Ferdinando kept up a babble of Italian, alternately chafing Wilson's hands and stroking her forehead and, if Mr. Browning had not been so concerned himself, his agitation would have told all. Eventually, the brandy forced through her lips, Wilson's eyes opened, though her ghastly pallor remained. Her fingers grasped the hideous letter and she held it out piteously to her master. "Please," she whispered, "please." Hesitating, wishing desperately that his wife had not gone to visit Isa Blagden, taking Pen with her, Mr. Browning took the letter and said, "My poor Wilson, you wish me to open it?" and when she nodded, "I had rather not, my dear, it is not something anyone but your good self should do."

"I cannot," she wept, "I cannot, I dare not, I beg you, sir, if you have any pity, do it quickly and tell me." Ferdinando held her and she shuddered and closed her eyes again and turned her face into his chest.

Mr. Browning fetched a paper knife and slit the letter open. He read it first, to the end, then put his own arms around Wilson too so that she lay between him and Ferdinando, almost smothered by their weight. "Look at me, Wilson," he begged, "or you will not believe and it will be worse in the end. Your mother and your sister May have gone to—to—they have gone to meet their beloved Maker, my dear."

Wilson stopped crying and sat up. There were no screams, nor did the shock release any indication that she had understood. She was perfectly still, perfectly quiet, and it was far more disturbing to the two men.

"Shall I read your brother-in-law's letter to you? Can you bear it yet?" There was no response but Mr. Browning began to read the sad tale of the fever which poor Arthur had unwittingly brought home with him from a patient's house, a fever which he had survived himself only to have his wife and their unborn child taken instead and, shortly after, his mother-in-law. The funeral, of necessity, had already been held and he begged her forgiveness for the pain he inflicted with his unlooked-for news.

Mrs. Browning behaved perfectly. Returning to the sight of Wilson rigid and catatonic with grief, she at once assumed control. The men were banished and Pen returned to Isa's from whence they had just come. She shut herself in with Wilson and talked to her and prayed with her and held her against her breast. Little by little the tears began to flow again and when Wilson was incapable of seeing or hearing, so great was the misery, she gave vent to her feelings and her mistress wiped her tears for her and held her close. "Cry," she urged, "cry on, cry, my dear, cry for your loved ones or a stone will grow in your heart." Mr. Browning, looking in upon them after several hours had gone by, muttered uneasily, "You will be ill, Ba, this cannot go on," but was sent away. Only as night came and Wilson could cry no more did Mrs. Browning call for a lamp to be lit and food and drink brought and afterward she took her maid to her bed herself.

In the small hours Ferdinando crept in beside her and held her tight, kissing her hands and whispering endearments. The comfort his presence gave her was inexpressible. "Life is short," she sighed, and held him tight.

CHAPTER TWENTY-TWO

WILSON COULD NOT afterward remember anything about the rest of that winter in Rome. When her mistress shuddered as they left the celestial city behind in May and expressed the belief it was forever damned in her eyes because of little Joe Story's death, she was inclined to agree. The thought of Mother *dead* was inconceivable and then, because she had been only able to think of Mother for weeks and weeks, the loss of May suddenly struck her afresh long afterward—May, who was so young and happy and good. The dark thought crept into her head that if it had been Ellen she could have borne it better and then she wept at her own cruelty, for hadn't Ellen suffered enough and didn't she deserve a little happiness? Not that she sounded happy in the two letters that had come since January. The shock of the double death was as great for her as for Wilson and then, in March, she lost the baby she was carrying and her misery was complete. Everywhere Wilson looked in her family she saw only wretchedness. Instead of it growing, with the marriages of both sisters, instead of it multiplying, as a family should, it was shrinking to nothing.

Her mistress was entirely sympathetic and most forbearing when she was tearful and dazed and doing even the simplest tasks with difficulty, but she urged acceptance in a way Wilson found hard to take. Religion was no longer to her (if it ever had been) the comfort it was to Mrs. Browning nor was the assurance that death was but a stage in life. Even the death of Flush, at the age of fourteen, was brought into these general assurances that there *was* life after death. She felt little distress herself at the dog's death—there had been something cruel about the sight of such a very old dog staggering around the Casa Guidi, barely able to see or hear and smelling to high heaven however carefully he was groomed. Pen, of course, was grief-stricken but Mrs. Browning less so. It seemed almost to satisfy her that when Flush was discovered dead she could bear it so well. "It was a natural end," she said, and encouraged Pen to see it as such. A little funeral ceremony was allowed in the Casa Guidi yard where Flush was buried but Mrs. Browning did not go down to watch nor did her husband. Wilson, Pen and Ferdinando, who alone of the adults had wept, buried the dog and said a prayer and planted a small wooden cross upon which Pen had laboriously written Flush's name and dates.

Afterward, back in the drawing room, Wilson was obliged to listen to a description of a young, silken-coated dog cavorting around the fields of heaven, thankful to leave behind his ugly, mangy earthly self. While skeptical, Wilson did find herself drawn more and more into attempts at spirit writing, though she knew it was a dangerous kind of game she was playing. She even, for only the second time in her life, took some of her mistress's laudanum when urged—"It will relax you, dear, and help us along"—and came to love the sensation of lightheadedness it induced. She was almost happy sitting in that dim room with outlines of furniture and fabrics swirling before her and only her partner's heavy breathing disturbing the air. When the pencil jumped in her hand and wrote her mother's name she half knew and half did not where the guiding spirit came from. Ferdinando, who did not like her to indulge Mrs. Browning in this fashion, shook his head sorrowfully when she confessed she hardly knew what she was doing and therefore it could not all be a true deceit. (Not, for example, as Isa Blagden's maid's performance was a sham and that was for sure.) She told him that apart from when she was in his arms those sessions with her mistress were the only times she was at peace. She felt Mother was near, even came to believe that now Mother was dead she might have handed on her gift to her.

She was in Ferdinando's embrace more and more often, no longer caring about any consequences. She had even confessed to her mistress that yes, she was much smitten with him and that they might soon become engaged. The news was taken well. "He is a good man, Wilson," Mrs. Browning said, "and you know him well." Thinking she could not guess how well, Wilson said nothing. All that concerned her was that there was no mention of dismissal. "Ferdinando is already one of our family," her mistress said graciously, "and nothing need change." That was, as Wilson well understood, the key to her attitude: nothing would change, the Browning way of life was unthreatened.

All that long summer, when they did not even escape Florence to go to Bagni di Lucca since there was some financial difficulty to which she was not privy, Wilson gave thanks that by some miracle she did not fall for a child. At the back of her mind there was some anxiety that her failure to become pregnant in spite of repeated lovemaking might mean she was barren and so, though every month she was relieved, she was also a little dismayed. Ferdinando, for his part, more and more frequently urged marriage, confessing himself tired of all the subterfuge. He wanted to have her on his arm as a wife for all the world to see and resented her insistence that appearances should be maintained at all costs. But by the autumn she was wavering. Twice her monthly health had been late and she had seen, as Lizzie Treherne had pointed out, how foolish it was to delay, but then the temptation to continue as they were for just a little longer, saving hard all the while, overcame her.

That winter her mistress suffered the worst congestion of the chest since she had left England to live in Italy and both her husband and Wilson were back to nursing her all night. In these circumstances, it seemed to Wilson heartless to say she was going to marry Ferdinando. This would inevitably give rise to worry over the future and so she delayed the already long-postponed announcement of her engagement even though she had promised Ferdinando on New Year's Day that she would make it. It was unfortunate that she did so, for by the time her mistress was sufficiently recovered to be going out for short drives in the sun it was April and Wilson knew she was without doubt pregnant. Ferdinando was ecstatic and so, she could not deny, was she. Instead of being filled with terror at the prospect before her she could feel only immense satisfaction and joy which was difficult to hide. Fortunately, her mistress was diverted by the visit of two lady friends from Rome and not given to scrutinizing her maid too closely. When Wilson told her, in May, that she had accepted Ferdinando's proposal and was now engaged her news was greeted with a good show of pleasure and she was commended, as she wrote to Lizzie,

—for my honesty, Lizzie, she was much pleased I had been truthful and confided in her and that the trust between us had not been broken which would have grieved her sorely. Well, Lizzie, you can be sure I knew of whom she was thinking when she added that others she had loved dearly had not been so open and that I smiled to myself and thought neither am I ma'am and for good reason. She has from time to time spoken to me on the subject of the power of love and what it can lead to and she is right proud that she understands the forces at work even going so far as to acknowledge the power in some circumstances cannot always be withstood and a wedding ceremony is not in some exceptional cases everything. But I am no fool Lizzie and do not need your warning for were I to admit I give myself regularly to Ferdinando without as yet benefit of clergy it would be a different story, for then it would be a sin. We are so placed here in the Casa Guidi that I would need to be a saint to resist the man I love and I am glad to have found I am not and that womanly impulses I thought to be lacking in me have overwhelmed me. Yet nothing of that sort is suspected and we are careful to act at all times with decorum especially in front of the child. Often he seems like our child for we are a family within a family and he eats and walks and sings with us and is very close. What will happen when our own child comes I cannot imagine but strangely Lizzie and contrary to my previous anxieties I have no fear. But we have announced our engagement and my mistress is much occupied in ways and means we can marry. She is adamant that I as a Protestant and Ferdinando as a Catholic, should have our marriage recognized in both Churches, saying it is her duty to see that this is done. This bewilders us for neither of us, if the truth be told, much care as to the niceties of the marriage service so long as it is performed and quickly, but since we cannot reveal the need for speed no heed is taken of our desire for it. Meanwhile we are all to journey to England in a month or so stopping off in Paris to see Mr. Browning's father and sister. I am nervous of it, Lizzie, on many counts. I will be five months gone by the date of our departure and since already I have difficulty lacing myself I dread to think what state I will be in and how I will bear the traveling having a dread of seasickness and its effect. Then I have no home to go to in England which distresses me more than I can say. My old home in Newcastle being long since gone I had fixed my thoughts on Sheffield though I have no liking for it but now that too is pulled away as an anchor. I have only Ellen in East Retford and though she writes to make me welcome I dread seeing her with all that has befallen us in the interval. Nor do I know if her husband and his children will welcome me as she does and why should they since I am nothing to them. As for Ferdinando, he has never traveled and has a fear of it and will be dependent on me just when I have a mind to be dependent on him. All in all, Lizzie, I wish we were not going and that is the truth.

But there was no escape. They all took ship at the end of June from Leghorn to Marseilles via Corsica. Pen was wild with excitement, flinging his arms alternately around Wilson's neck and then Ferdinando's in a torrent of delighted kisses as they set sail. Fortunately, Mrs. Browning had a slight cough and Wilson was able, under cover of being strict with her, to rest with her in her cabin. To her relief, she was not sick and felt well rather than otherwise. Ferdinando took sole charge of Pen and she was able to conserve her energies most conveniently. While she sat in the cabin, her mistress lectured her on the folly of not marrying with sufficient regard to the laws of both churches and boasted of having obtained a dispensation from the necessary banns. The Archbishop of Florence had provided it and once a clergyman had been found who would accept them and have no objections to a religiously mixed marriage they could proceed. . . . "Perhaps, Wilson," she ended complacently, "you would like to marry at your sister's in September, when you go for your holiday?" Wilson immediately busied herself with some sewing the better to appear composed when she replied. "I think not, ma'am. Ferdinando is a proud man and would rather appear before my sister as my husband."

"Then it is very awkward, dear, for where can you be married?"

"Anywhere, ma'am, for I do not care about the place any more than you did."

Mrs. Browning stiffened and gave a little cough. "It is hardly the same, Wilson. Should I have been able to have my sisters with me in the church I would have chosen it."

"It is a long time to September in any case," Wilson said, "and Ferdinando says he has waited long enough."

Mrs. Browning raised her eyebrows a little and said, "Then if he has waited long enough, another two months is nothing. I really think it would be best to wait until England."

In the event, it was Ferdinando who succeeded in bringing the happy event forward. As they traveled through France it became harder and harder for him to be alone with Wilson and by Lyons he had not slept with her for fully three weeks. At each inn Wilson slept with Pen or sometimes with both her mistress and Pen, and there was not the slightest chance of even an hour together. He could not, he said, endure this foolish separation and so he went to his employers and begged them to allow him to marry their maid with all dispatch. If it could not be arranged because they were traveling, then he vowed he would leave their service and so would Wilson and they would find someone to marry them in Lyons where he was prepared to set up a *fiacre* to support himself. It was an impassioned plea which nevertheless brought a smile to Mrs. Browning's face, a smile she tried to hide but which Wilson saw. She looked at poor Ferdinando and though she loved him dearly could see how absurd he seemed to her employers with his talk of becoming of all things a cab driver in Lyons. Yet she blushed with anger and not, as they doubtless thought, with embarrassment as she witnessed this scene. Who were they to conjure up such difficulties? She was sure that, left to their own devices, she and Ferdinando would have been married long before now. It hurt her to see a fine man like her lover reduced to coming cap in hand to plead for something that was his by right. And so when her mistress hid her smile of amusement Wilson stepped forward and took Ferdinando's hand openly and said quietly, "And I would be happy to be a cab driver's wife, if so be it."

After that, things moved swiftly. Mr. Browning arranged their wedding for July 11 in Paris at the British Embassy and every effort was made to make it a happy event. Mrs. Browning, whose cough, though not serious, was again troublesome, did not attend the ceremony, but Mr. Browning did. It was all modest and humble, a very long way from the wedding day of Wilson's girlish dreams, and the ghost of Mother haunted her throughout, but there were moments of great feeling which she never forgot. Her mistress's embrace, as she left the hotel where they lodged, was one of them, given woman to woman without trace of condescension. "I am happy for you, dear Wilson," she whispered, and her eyes were full of tears. And then, as she smoothed down her blue dress, uncomfortably aware that even though every seam had been opened out it looked too tight, Pen appeared with a bouquet of tiny lilies and wild orchids and presented it to her. That time, she was the one with tears in her eyes. Mr. Browning took her in a carriage to the embassy and made her feel like a queen and when they arrived and saw Ferdinando waiting he looked so handsome and serious that she had the greatest moment of all, a moment as she alighted and he rushed forward to take her hand when she was quite certain of his love and of her own. There was nothing shabby or pitiful about being only three people at a wedding, just as there had been nothing sad or pathetic about her mistress's own. And afterward, when they enjoyed the breakfast she and Ferdinando had managed to prepare, there was a good deal more merrymaking than on the Brownings' own day.

Waking next morning, Ferdinando at her side, Wilson said aloud, "I am a married woman," for the pleasure of hearing the words. She lay looking at the ceiling, keeping perfectly still so that Ferdinando would not wake and interrupt her hour of reverie. It had been achieved. She was married, and happily married, and neither her mistress nor her master had said anything about either her or Ferdinando leaving their employment. All was well. But then she felt the quickening in her womb, the sudden shivering spasms that told her her child was alive and growing, and her thoughts turned to the future. How long could she delay breaking this other news? Over and over she had tried to estimate the date her baby would be born but without any doctor to guide her the estimate was of necessity crude. It might be as early as the middle of October or as late as the end of November. Only one thing was certain: she could not travel back either to Paris or to Florence at the end of September. By then her condition would be glaringly obvious and she would need to take care. But she felt calm and relatively untroubled by it all now she was married. She was respectable, had done the respectable thing.

As soon as they reached London, with lodgings taken this time in Dorset Street, she wrote to Ellen in East Retford begging her

—to excuse the lack of letters Ellen for I have been sore pressed with the traveling we have done and besides much affected at the thought of coming to a place Mother no longer occupies which thought has dragged me down as I daresay it still does you. But I have happier news Ellen and can tell you I was married last week to Ferdinando Romagnoli my fellow servant this last two years. We are here now until September at least and look forward to visiting you in East Retford if we are welcome. My mistress is loath to lose both Ferdinando and myself at the same time having much to do helping her husband see his latest volume through the press and I am bidden to take my holiday first but it is agreed he may come to fetch me so you will have the opportunity to meet with him. He knows as yet very little English for we have always conversed in Italian in which as you know I am proficient but now we are in England he must make more progress. Our weather has shocked him and he fancies this must be January and not July not only because it has not ceased raining since we arrived but for the bitter cold. It makes him value his own country all the more which is no bad thing. He is entitled to his holiday too but has declined the favor except for bringing me from East Retford. Write, Ellen, and direct me as to your exact whereabouts and say if I am welcome.

Deliberately, she said nothing about the expected baby and was glad, when she had had Ellen's reply, that she had thought to conceal her condition. Ellen was not a good hand at letters but even in the few sentences she penned with such apparent difficulty Wilson sensed the misery her own failure to conceive since her miscarriage caused her. The company of her sister, she wrote, might do her the world of good and bring about the miracle she longed for. Telling her mistress this, including what Ellen had also said as to the best dates, Wilson was treated to a look heavy with meaning. "It is rare," Mrs. Browning said as her hair was dressed, "for married women to find conceiving difficult. Certainly, it was not so for me and may not prove so for you, Wilson." There was a pause. Wilson knew she had been presented with the perfect opportunity to tell all but she rejected it. Her mouth full of pins, she merely raised her eyebrows and shrugged her shoulders. "Wilson dear," Mrs. Browning went on, watching her carefully, "you must not be too relaxed about these things. It would be very difficult if you became a mother too quickly when all is said and done—very difficult for all of us, situated as we are. I really do not know how we would manage. There is Pen to care for and myself and, all things considered, we should be greatly inconvenienced, especially while not at home."

Wilson's mouth now free, she felt an answer was expected of her and knew that if it was not the truth it had better not be a lie. "I am only married lately," she said in a low voice, "but I should like a child, I cannot deny, and would welcome one if God blessed me, unlike my poor sister who He has visited with such an affliction as barrenness."

"But of course, dear," her mistress said quickly, "I should like to see you with your own child, how could I not, when you have been a second mother to Pen? But it needs deep thought, Wilson, and a great consideration of the circumstances you are in before it can be properly managed, you will agree."

This was said with the air of making a statement but had the faintest hint of query in it so what Wilson chose to say, as she prepared to leave the room, was "What God wills, He wills, ma'am." Her heart was beating a little wildly and the child inside her kicked its pleasure at her reply. She had to sit down for a while to recover her equilibrium and ponder on the significance of what had been said.

It occurred to her for the first time (though afterward Mrs. Browning could not believe she had not realized this was inevitable) that she might have to leave the household in order to have her baby. She would have to find somewhere to go to lie up and the only place she had was Ellen's, though Lizzie Treherne was quick to offer shelter. "If it comes to it, Lily," she said when Wilson went to see her in her new home in Kentish Town, near the fields, "you may come here where there is always room for you now we are no longer so crowded."

Wilson's eyes filled with tears at the generosity of this proposal but she shook her head. "I could not impose, Lizzie, when you have three young children. I must be with my sister since I no longer have a mother." She wept a little, then steadied herself. Tears, she had been told, were bad for the baby.

Gently, Lizzie pressed her to a cup of tea and said, "You cannot imagine, Lily, that Mrs. Browning will allow you to give birth in her lodgings, now can you, dear? In all honesty, she could not be thought to allow it."

"No," Wilson said, drinking the tea gratefully, "no, I did not fancy she would nor would I ask her to let me stay in my own bed for the lying-in, but afterward I had never thought of being *turned off*, not then, I really had not. My mistress has spoken strong words on the subject often, she cannot abide those who do not treat servants as friends, and if she is a friend, which I do believe her to be, however foolish it makes me, she will not turn me off in my hour of need."

"But, Lily, how would you manage, being in need of being looked after yourself? It is not reasonable, dear."

"There is Ferdinando, who is a genius with Pen, and . . ."

"But he cannot dress your mistress or do her hair! What are you thinking of, Lily?"

"Another girl could be engaged for those intimate services, only for a week or so . . ."

"But the expense—you say yourself the talk is all of economy."

"They need not pay me for that time. And then, when I am on my feet, another child is nothing when there is Pen already. He longs for a brother or sister, begs and pleads to have one, and my mistress often sighs and wishes she could oblige."

"You expect too much, Lily, though it pains me to say it. Your mistress is only as other women of her class and could not countenance such an extraordinary scheme."

"Then what shall I do?" Wilson said, and this time wept without restraint.

She saw, without Lizzie's help, how foolishly optimistic happiness had made her. She had put her faith in her mistress's open rejection of the conventional but now saw she had been wrong. She would become, instantly, the moment her confession was made, a troublesome object to be got rid of. And yet she could not quite bring herself to believe all these years and all the closeness they had bred would count for nothing. When she thought back on the many, many times her mistress had whispered her thanks and acknowledged her gratitude and debt, she could *not* believe that she would not be valued more. Pen would be distraught if she were to disappear and if Ferdinando, his best friend, were to go too, the sheer power of the boy's screaming distress would have his parents pleading for an amnesty. They were, as Mrs. Browning so often fondly remarked, a family within a family and another baby would only, surely, produce rejoicing. By cheering herself thus, Wilson was able to keep going throughout August but then, as the time to go to Ellen's approached, the fear and doubt returned and she knew she must speak out.

She consciously chose her time with the greatest care. Ferdinando, who liked London no better now a little sun had broken through, finding it dirty and too big, had taken Pen to Regent's Park. Mr. Browning was in New Cross, visiting some old friends of his family, and would then go on to dinner with several literary friends at the Garrick Club. He would not be back until very late. Mrs. Browning stayed in bed all morning, relishing the empty apartment and confessing she was all but done in with the socializing to which she had been subjected.

"Just you and me, Wilson," she sighed as her coffee was brought in, "quite like the old days, is it not?"

It was exactly the introduction Wilson needed. "Yes, ma'am," she agreed, plumping up the pillows, "like the old days. Do you remember how long and empty the hours seemed? We sat and sighed for some excitement and now it is excitement all day long and too much of it."

Mrs. Browning smiled and nodded. "How fortunate we have been, Wilson, for I confess I shudder at the memory for all the peacefulness of it. Who could have told how life would turn out?"

"Who can tell how it will turn out still?"

"Ah, we are enigmatic this morning, are we not?" Mrs. Browning said.

"No, ma'am, only truthful. None of us *can* tell what is around the next corner, though we may think we can."

"True, and I for one am glad these days. Too many dreadful surprises are sprung on us for me to have a taste to know what they shall be. Now sit a moment, Wilson, do, for you have been looking weary yourself, dear, and I know Pen has been tiresome and not sleeping with the excitement. Mr. Browning said only this morning he feared you and Ferdinando could not have had a good night's rest since we came and he thought you less blooming than usual."

"Thank you, ma'am. I will fetch my sewing and get on with it." She went and got Pen's jacket which she was repairing and sat at the foot of her mistress's bed and darned. Mrs. Browning read *The Times* and drank her coffee, making some comment from the news every now and again. Is now the time, shall I speak now? Wilson asked herself, but delayed. The sun came into the room in fits and starts and her mistress's mood grew more receptive every minute. It was she who spoke first again.

"Do you look forward to your holiday next week, Wilson?"

"Indeed, ma'am, though I dread it, too, not having seen my sister since my mother and May were taken."

"Of course." Mrs. Browning's voice was at its most gentle. "That has to be got over."

"And I will miss my husband, not having been apart from him yet."

"Then, however cruel, I am glad of it, for it will bring you back to us all the sooner. We could not do without you, Wilson, and that is a fact. It has been terrible before and would be worse this year if it were not for Ferdinando, who will have a time of it."

"I would never wish to stay away, being every bit as attached to Pen as he is to me."

"Thank God for it."

There would never be another moment as perfect. "Ma'am," Wilson began, hesitantly, clutching the jacket she had been darning close to her, "ma'am?"

"Yes, dear?" her mistress replied, absent-mindedly, with the rumble of a cough beginning in her chest. She looked so comfortable there, resting on the pillows with her coffee cup perched dangerously on the coverlet and the newspaper sheets spread wide. It seemed a pity to spoil her morning. But Wilson took a deep breath and began again. "Ma'am, there is something I must speak to you of."

"Mm?" Mrs. Browning murmured.

"I am afraid you will not be pleased."

At that, Mrs. Browning looked up and smiled, though Wilson could see the smile had no meaning in it, that it was merely a politeness and that the smiler was still far away in her own thoughts.

"You may be angry, but I cannot help it."

"Angry, dear? With you? Now is that likely, is it at *all* likely? You speak like Pen when he knows he has been naughty. Did you hear him yesterday, Wilson, speaking to his father? 'Papa,' he began, 'when you love someone velly much it does not matter *what* they do, does it, for if you love them you love *all* they do.' I had to struggle not to laugh. And did you hear Robert's reply? Oh, it was masterly, he said— Wilson, dear, you look distressed."

"It is only I have something I must tell you, ma'am."

"Why, yes, you said so, and here I am prattling on with no thought. Forgive me, dear, and tell away—I am listening with my whole heart."

And she was. Wilson could see she now had her mistress's absolute concentration and was so alarmed by it she found herself wondering if it would not have been better to have told all when her listener was in a vague and dreamy state.

"I am glad you listen with your heart," Wilson said, smiling slightly, "for I have need of it—of your heart and its kindness. Ma'am, I am to have a child."

The response was all she could have hoped for. Mrs. Browning smiled and cried, "Oh, Wilson!" and held out her arms, sending the coffee cup flying. "Now why, dear, did you think I would be angry? Am I so cruel, to greet news such as yours with anger? Am I so selfish?"

"No, ma'am, no, but—how will you manage when I am lying in?"

"Oh, I shall manage as I have done before and there is always little Rosa you know, even if she is only a kitchen maid—she can be trained to take your place for a while and then we must see what can be done."

Wilson picked up the coffee cup, fortunately not broken. How to take the next step? "Little Rosa is in Florence, ma'am, and I will have the baby before our return, before even Paris, if you are set on wintering there."

It was out. The change in her mistress's expression was immediate. "Before Paris?" she echoed. "But we go to Paris in a few weeks, in October. Wilson, you cannot be thinking what you are saying, surely." Her eyes dropped to Wilson's stomach, then lifted swiftly to scan her face. "*Before* October? Can this be right?"

Stiffly, Wilson stood at the side of the bed, almost at attention. Her face burned. She managed to keep her voice steady as she replied, "I do not know precisely when, ma'am, but I last had my regular health in February and so I must suppose October the likeliest month, not having seen any medical man."

Distaste crossed Mrs. Browning's face and she pulled her wrap tightly around her shoulders. "I do not want the intimate details,

Wilson, spare me such things, please." There was a tense pause and then suddenly she got out of bed and walked toward the window. With her back to Wilson, she said, "I thought there was perfect trust between us. I have boasted of it. I have to your face congratulated you on your honesty. And now to find such deceit, of every sort. I cannot believe it. Well, you had better get yourself gone to your sister's, for you will be no use here." Almost immediately the harsh words were spoken she turned around.

Wilson, struggling to keep her composure, was shocked to see tears running down her mistress's white, set face, tears she must suppose of regret and betrayal, her betrayal. "Ma'am," she said, "ma'am, it was not possible to take you into our confidence, for you would have been obliged to dismiss us and then where would we have been, cast out on the streets of Florence?"

"And did you not think of that before practicing your deceit?"

"Indeed I did. I have had to think of how to earn my living since I was a child and the loss of employment terrifies me as you well know, ma'am. There was no wrong . . ."

"No wrong? And you a Christian, Wilson? You speak of there being no wrong? It was all wrong, all of it, from start to finish. You gave in to carnal desires without thought of it being right or wrong and you did so under our roof while in a position of some trust."

"I beg your pardon, ma'am, but that trust has been sacred to me if you mean the care of your child."

She began to weep, unable any longer to maintain the dignity she had striven for, and then to shiver so that she had to clutch at the bedpost. No longer wishing to look at her mistress, no longer able to endure her look of fury and even disgust, she stared at the swirling reds and browns of the carpet and wondered how she could get out of the room before she collapsed completely. Not until her mistress put out a hand to touch her did she realize she had crossed the room and that her voice, if not kind, was considerate. "Sit down, Wilson, rest a moment. I have no wish to quarrel. You will understand this has been a shock to me and I may have said things I would not wish to have said. I must speak to my husband, I must think more on what you have told me, but it is not my intention to hurt you. Go now and lie down. You look wretched and I am the cause of it, I suppose."

If it had not been for the "I suppose" Wilson thought how consoled she would have felt but those last two words were spoken with something akin to contempt. They made it plain that her mistress found her a nuisance and resented it. She was now a trouble and in a flash it seemed that the years and years during which she had been a support had vanished. That brief moment when Mrs. Browning had smiled upon her announcement had been so sweet—her own heart had leaped at the promise of the understanding and sympathy and she had even, in that short time span, heard herself telling Lizzie triumphantly that she had been wrong to predict she would be treated as any maid-servant. Lying on her bed, she tried hard to put herself in her mistress's position, to feel cheated and tricked, but she could not. She, as a married woman who loved and was attracted to her husband, would have understood and been compassionate. As to the inconvenience, it could always be got around, should a mistress so desire it. But clearly she was not going to desire it and had implied there was no obligation that she should. All that comforted her, as she lay there silently, was the knowledge that she was still glad—glad to love Ferdinando, glad to have married, glad even that she had given herself to him when she needed and wanted to and had not insisted on marriage and respectability first. They had some money saved and with judicious handling it would tide them over this crisis.

Throughout the rest of that now unpleasantly long and empty day Wilson appeared punctually to perform her duties. No words beyond the necessary were exchanged. She knew her red eyes showed she had cried for hours but did not care who saw them. There was at least the relief, now the truth was known, of letting her seams out further and undoing the fasteners halfway down her back. She saw her mistress looking and estimating and instead of hunching herself in shame she carried herself proudly. When the baby inside her kicked she did not grit her teeth and ignore the sharp movement as she had done up to now, but instead stood still and held the place where she felt the kick. This did not please her mistress, who frowned and said, "I would ask you not to tell Penini as yet, if you please,

Wilson. It will be most disturbing and I wish to plan how it can be done most harmlessly with my husband." Wilson inclined her head in assent but seethed. Disturbing, indeed. Why, Pen would be ecstatic and his mother knew it.

Ferdinando was relieved their secret was out and that he could begin to take some pride in his approaching fatherhood, but she cautioned him to be restrained. It was impossible to know which way the wind would blow until Mr. Browning had been told and he as well as his wife had reacted to the news. Wilson slept fitfully that night and was up early, anticipating the summons which came after break-fast. Ferdinando was not summoned. He was sent out once more with Pen and it was only the three of them in the rather small and dismal drawing room of the rented apartment. She saw at once that any hopes of Mr. Browning being more indulgent than his wife were going to be unfulfilled, but his first words were tolerant enough.

"So you are to be a mother, Wilson," he said, and even smiled though she saw he was irritable, "and soon, I hear."

"Yes, sir."

"Well then, it is fortunate you have your sister to go to, though not so fortunate for us that this will be no two-week holiday."

"Sir?"

"Clearly, Wilson, you cannot return with your lying-in so near."

"No, sir."

"And then with our imminent return to Paris we will find our-selves in considerable difficulties which we would rather resolve now if it were possible. What are your plans, Wilson?"

"Plans, sir?"

"For after the birth of your child."

"I have not thought, sir."

"Then, without any wish to be unkind, my dear, you had better do so. There have to be plans in these situations." He took a turn around the room and came back to his original position, but still she had not replied. "Let me help you, Wilson. It is quite a simple matter, really. What it comes down to is: do you and Ferdinando intend to return to Florence?"

"Why, yes, sir, of course, sir, it is our home, Ferdinando is a

Florentine and as you know loves his city. We had never thought otherwise, we long to be back in Italy." Relief that she could be so certain about something made her speak all in a rush and Mr. Browning held up a hand to halt her flow.

"And how do you plan to return?"

"Sir?"

"You and Ferdinando and the child—how do you propose to return to Florence?"

"Why, as we would, sir, as we came, whichever route you preferred, we . . ."

"I am not talking of routes, Wilson. You are confused again. Let me enlighten you. We are not returning to Italy this autumn but instead renting an apartment and wintering in Paris. Now, this being so, how can we accommodate you with a baby?"

Stunned, Wilson stared at him.

"Do not look so stricken, Wilson. You must see the problem, surely. How can you care for my wife, who needs so much care, and for my son if you have a baby of your own? It is not possible. And even if it were to be considered, which I do not rightly think it could, nor would anyone expect that it should be, we have not the means to engage a servant to look after you, *our* servant. Indeed, even if we were to return directly to Florence I doubt that you would be fit to travel with us and, once there, the Casa Guidi, as you are aware, is not big enough to house another child nor could we feed one. Everywhere, you see, Wilson, there are very real difficulties."

As he said the last few words, Mr. Browning spread his arms wide, in a gesture of helplessness, and shook his head regretfully. Wilson felt her mouth so dry that it almost choked her to whisper, "Then I am dismissed forever, sir?"

"Oh, now come, Wilson," said Mrs. Browning, speaking for the first time, "nobody dismisses you or mentions forever. You dismiss yourself by your circumstances and, as for forever, that is surely your decision."

"Ma'am?" She was bewildered, she felt a game was being played and the rules had not been explained to her. The mistress who sat opposite her, so aloof and remote, was not the woman who had wept on her breast or the woman whose hand she had held as she gave birth.

"We do not wish to dismiss you, Wilson," Mrs. Browning explained patiently, "but for several months you will be unable to work for us. Is that not so?" Wilson nodded, afraid the tears might start at any moment. "So you are dismissing yourself. As to the future, it is in your own hands. You may of course return and continue to work for us." Wilson looked up, suddenly hopeful, but saw nothing had changed in Mrs. Browning's expression and hope waned. "But you must consider: what would you do with your child?"

"Do?"

"Well, Wilson, you could hardly bring it with you to Paris. Be reasonable, dear." There was a fraction of a pause before the endearment and it was said without affection. "We are not a circus, Wilson, it would be impossible to travel all the way to Paris and then back to London and finally to Florence, all with a new baby."

"Jeannie traveled . . ." and then Wilson stopped. It was too humiliating and would achieve nothing to remind her mistress, even if she dared, that the Ogilvys had regularly traveled the length and breadth of Europe with new babies and Jeannie had vowed it was far easier than with a two-year-old. She tried to take a deep breath but only succeeded in tightening her chest until it hurt.

"We have not inquired yet," said Mr. Browning gently, "of Ferdinando."

"Sir?" She wondered for one wild moment if the paternity of her child was to be contested.

"Does he wish to stay in England with you?"

"He wishes not to leave me, sir, at this time—it is natural, I think."

"Of course it is. Do I take it, then, that he has other employment here in view?"

She was so shocked that she could not reply at all. Feeling behind her, she located a chair and gripped it but Mr. Browning had already leaped forward to help her onto it, and at the same time Mrs. Browning rose to approach her. Their concern was evident and the speed with which a glass of water was brought and her feet put on a stool consoled her, but even in the midst of these attentions she sensed the difference yet again. This was common or garden human kindness, the sort that might be extended to a stranger who collapsed in the street. The Brownings *were* kind but she knew they could be tenderness itself when such feeling overwhelmed them and it did not do so now.

She could not sit there suppressing tears forever. She struggled to get up but was persuaded to rest longer. Already she could hardly remember what it was that had made her feel faint and when Mr. Browning repeated that they needed to know Ferdinando's plans she was overcome all over again. "Why, he has no plans, how should he have," she managed to say, "he did not know he would have need of them."

"Nor would he, if he is to stay with us."

"Why would he not, sir?"

"To be with you and your child, Wilson. You are upset, you are not thinking clearly. If you are to stay in England with your child and Ferdinando is to stay with you, then how can he remain in our employment? He cannot be in two places at once."

"He speaks no English of any consequence," Wilson said, "and he is not happy here. He expects to stay with you and return to Florence when you go."

"Then we would be delighted," Mr. Browning said. "You know how we value Ferdinando almost as much as yourself." The compliment was not lost on her but it rang hollow. "But if he stays with us— I am sorry to press this argument to its conclusion, Wilson, but now we have started it must be done—he cannot stay with you and that is all there is to it."

"He will stay with you, sir," she said dully. "There is no choice. He cannot earn his living otherwise and one of us must or we will be in the workhouse."

There was an uncomfortable silence. Mrs. Browning returned to her chair, her dress rustling. Mr. Browning walked to the window again and stood tapping absent-mindedly on the windowpane.

"It is not our fault, dear," Mrs. Browning murmured, "and there is no need to talk of workhouses."

"Is it my fault, ma'am?"

"I do not wish to be cruel, Wilson, but a woman who acts as you have acted must inevitably expect what has happened. It takes no great mind to assess the hazards of marriage."

"What should I have done?" She was weeping now, but no longer cared.

"That is not for me to say. It is what you ought to do now that is more important and I do not think you are in any fit state to decide. We must leave the decision open until after the child is born and then, if you feel you are able, you may wish to return. Rest assured, Wilson, no one else could ever take your place."

And yet the very next day girls began to arrive to be interviewed for her situation and the speed with which one of them was engaged made Wilson wonder if she was held in any regard at all. Mrs. Browning pronounced herself much pleased with the new maid, one Harriet White. "She is pleasant, is she not, Wilson, and quick?" she said when the selection had been made and Wilson had felt upset out of all proportion.

"Quite pleasant, ma'am, though as to quick she was only quick to state the salary was insufficient in the first instance." Mrs. Browning blushed. Harriet was offered the same wage as Wilson but had only agreed to come for a guinea a month more and had made it plain that, should she stay beyond the six months for which she was contracted, then she would expect a more handsome remuneration. "And Pen was not much taken with her."

Pen had hated her on sight. One look at the rather pretty blond woman who smiled so dazzlingly at him and he had run into Wilson's arms and buried his face in her bosom.

"Pen no want Lily go," he shouted and, turning around, yelled, "Go away!" to Harriet.

"My!" Harriet said. "We have a temper here, I see."

"No," Wilson said quietly, "not a temper. He is distressed. I have been with him since the moment of his birth. It is natural he should resent you. You must be patient with him."

"Oh, I have the patience of a saint," Harriet said airily, "he'll be eating out of my hand in no time, don't you worry."

It almost made Wilson smile to hear such an absurd boast but she held her peace then and throughout the next week when Harriet came to be instructed. The girl would not do, not ever, for all her prettiness and smiles. She was not even truly pleasant. Her manner was quite artificial, a drawing-room performance. In the kitchen and nursery she was sharp and sulky. Ferdinando as well as Pen detested her and the thought of having to work with her drove him to despair. At night it was he and not Wilson who wept and groaned at the trap they were in, wailing constantly that their situation was an insult to his manhood and he wished to shoot himself forthwith. Wilson soothed him and told him to take heart and for her sake and his child's endure these next months as best he could. One day they would all be together in Italy.

He did not come to East Retford after all. Her own departure was delayed until the first week in October, though it made the Brownings nervous to have her still with them. But she had seen a doctor and he had estimated she had another month to go and, in the face of her plea to stay as long as possible with her husband before such a long parting, her employers had given way. Now suddenly huge, she dragged herself around seeing to Pen, and trying to train Harriet to her ways, knowing all the time her mistress wished her gone. In her look there was resentment and impatience and once Wilson overheard her say to a visitor that, yes, it was most depressing having her around.

Finally, on October 7, she packed her trunk and Ferdinando took her to the station. He stood on the platform proclaiming his Italian nature by weeping so hard that his jacket became sodden and yet no one laughed. She herself was composed, because otherwise she could not have left him at all. She had not said goodbye to Pen. His father had taken him to the zoo and there had been a stiff and painful farewell from his mother. But a gift of money had been given to her to help with her lying-in expenses and she was kissed on the cheek and wished well.

She was glad to get out of the house and if Ferdinando and Pen had been with her would not have wished to return. Ferdinando had been given leave—indeed, urged—to accompany her and see her safely to Ellen's but she had not wished him to go with her. Circumstances had changed. She was afraid, now, that once in East Retford she would be unable to persuade him to go back to London. She was the stronger of the two and must do the leave-taking. So she kissed his wet cheeks and vowed her eternal love and got into the train, negotiating the steps with difficulty. Her last sight of him was of him running along the platform to the very end, keeping pace with the train, and he looked such a fine, handsome, strong man, she felt a sudden spasm of fear at the thought of leaving him fair game for the likes of Harriet. But there was no alternative. She had to go somewhere to have her child and Ellen's was the only place she had. The misery of the parting with her husband over, her mind became preoccupied with Ellen's household. If her position proved unendurable, what would she do?

CHAPTER TWENTY-THREE

Long before the day her child was born Wilson knew how grave was the mistake she had made. She blamed herself bitterly for not questioning Ellen more closely, for not attempting to make her sister describe her circumstances in some detail. The two or three ill-written notes she had received in the last year could never have prepared her for how Ellen lived and she did not know whether to accuse her poor sister of deliberate deceit or to praise her for being so forbearing. Again and again she asked herself how Ellen could have allowed her to come, knowing what she knew. Why had she not said outright it was impossible for her to be accommodated? But then she in turn had not been honest and she felt shamefaced to remember the shock she had given Ellen by arriving huge with her unborn child.

Yet in this respect her condition was the one factor which bound them all together—her, Ellen and the insufferable William Wilson. They all loved children and would forgive much for their presence. Wilson realized very quickly that half the trouble she found in the household arose from the deaths of William's two children from fever that summer (of which she had known nothing, Ellen being too distressed to communicate the dreadful news), and from Ellen's own barrenness since her miscarriage. William was murderous in grief, violent with misery, and Ellen was rightly afraid of the storms of weeping which ended in drinking and then in smashing the furniture. Appalled when she first witnessed it, Wilson could only watch William's unhappiness express itself in this ugly way and calculate how long he could endure it before he did himself or Ellen a serious injury. It was more likely he would injure Ellen. Though she felt disloyal, it was some release to write of this to Lizzie—since Ferdinando could not read. (To him, she wrote in Italian, though her knowledge that her husband must suffer the humiliation of having the letter read to him by Mr. Browning acted as the most agonizing form of censorship.) To Lizzie she described the regular end of William's working day:

When he comes home, exhausted in his body from his labors in the fields, and Lizzie if nothing else it is plain he is a hard worker, he is still alive in his grief and begins at once to roar against God for taking away his son and daughter who were wont to wait for him at the gate and were worth more to him than all his land. Ellen, though I say this full of pity and in no spirit of condemnation, Ellen flinches from his voice which indeed is loud and threatening and cowers away from him so that when he strikes her it comes as no surprise. When he has eaten, which he seems to do as a blind man with no evidence of purpose or enjoyment, he begins at once to call for brandy and is capable of drinking himself stupid when we then have the unedifying sight of him stumbling about the room knocking over whatever gets in the way and breaking what there is left to break which is precious little. When at last he has been coaxed to bed he cries many hours and falls asleep at last worn out. In the morning he is silent and morose saying not a word until he leaves the house and then we breathe more easily for the hours he is gone. Upon his return, it is the same performance every day. How we pray for Sundays! For then he attends Chapel and does not drink and that tenderness which I thought to see in him at his wedding can be caught sight of briefly. I thank God my mother has not lived to see how low Ellen has been brought. She knows that only the birth of a child can heal her husband's deep wounds but though she has tried everything to conceive it has been to no avail and now she says he begins to spurn her and to talk of taking other women. It is in these circumstances I am to have my child Lizzie and I am not comfortable with it. Ellen says it will be the saving of them to have a baby in the house and I do not doubt it will soothe her husband and may effect a temporary cure but what of when I leave? It will make their plight worse. So I am unhappy and fearful here Lizzie but I have made my bed and must lie on it until after I am delivered which if the pains I have been having this past week are anything to go by will be soon. There is a midwife who lives in Carol Gate where I am and she has been engaged to come on call and there is besides a young woman who is something in the way of being a monthly nurse and charges but one guinea a month and has experience and with the gift my mistress gave me I have enough to pay for both so I am well served unless things go badly and a doctor is needed which would outstretch my purse. This is a life as unlike any I have led Lizzie and I am faint with longing to be with Ferdinando. How he manages without me I do not rightly know it being impossible to tell from the weekly notes penned for him by Mr. Browning. They are all I believe to go to Paris this next week and then the distance between us will be even greater and will give me more cause for concern. Harriet White goes with them in my place and I am thankful I have seen with my own eyes that she is not to my husband's taste and there is no danger there.

That there would be danger in Paris Wilson had no doubt. She had lived in Paris, if briefly, and knew it held far more temptations for the likes of Ferdinando than London. He was afraid of London and not given to wandering abroad, but in Paris he would feel more familiar and find his way to companions of his own nationality. Once that was done, once he had haunts to visit and friends with whom to visit them, she had less hope of his sworn loyalty. He was only human, only a man. He would succumb. How foolish she had been not to accept Lizzie's offer, how stupid not to have found a way to stay near her attractive husband. All the time she lumbered around Ellen's house, trying to make herself useful and failing, she was plotting and planning her return, her speedy return, to Ferdinando.

Already Ellen had made the offer, tentatively, trying unsuccessfully to keep the longing out of her voice. She could leave her baby here in East Retford for the winter, returning in the summer to collect it before setting off for Florence. A baby so small would not miss its mother if a wet nurse could be found from the beginning. And she would be doing Ellen and William a favor in return for their hospitality. She had seen how things were between them: did she not have a duty to do what she could? And so, as the day of her confinement drew nearer, she stifled all thoughts, once so clear in her mind, of the dangers hidden in such a convenient arrangement. Once she had been safely delivered and the child seen to thrive she would return without delay to the Brownings' household.

It was all quite different from how she had imagined and she many times laughed bitterly at herself for her naïveté in the days following the birth of her son. The birth itself was painfully different. Hadn't she seen Mrs. Browning lie there without a murmur and bring forth a large child with what seemed ease? And there *she* lay, when her time came, screaming incessantly for hour after hour with no hope in her mind of surviving such agony. Long before it was over she knew she could not go on and yet the horror of it was that there was no escape—the pain had to continue, she could not walk away from it. She pleaded and shouted to be put out of her misery but all she got in reply was the instruction to be patient. The more searing the vicious cramps, the more frantic she became until the midwife vowed she would tie her down if she did not cease to thrash around. And then, when it came to the time to push, the pain seemed to swallow her with each effort to obey and she wept as well as screamed and begged and begged for laudanum, for anything to put her to sleep.

Ellen, at her side throughout and in almost as great a state of distress, asked the midwife if nothing could be given to ease the suffering but was ignored. The midwife, who had seen all this before, was contemptuous—this was childbirth, this was women's fate. She said the baby's feet were coming first, hence the difficulty, and that a mother given laudanum or gin or any other opiate would be a sleepy mother and one who might endanger the baby's life. Nothing could be done, she said, except to pray.

They prayed, Ellen and Wilson, and at last, at two in the morning, the baby was born, feet first as the midwife had said. Wilson heard the cry but was so taken up with the instant removal of pain that she could think of nothing else. How still she felt, how calm her body, how peaceful it suddenly was lying there, released from torture. It was Ellen who rushed to see the child, Ellen who held him first, Ellen who cried with joy. Wilson heard, as if from a long way off, her sister tell her it was a boy, a fine big boy, perfect in every detail, with black hair and long legs and a beautiful olive skin, but she had no interest and was content to wait until the afterbirth came away, cleanly, and the midwife pronounced the bleeding all but stopped.

Then Ellen put her son in her arms and again it was different from her expectations. She had thought she would recognize her child, that she would look at him and by some curious natural process *know* him. But the tiny face looking up into hers, the eyes momentarily wide open as if in equal astonishment, was a complete surprise. She did not know it, she had never seen it before, never seen a face like it. As she stared, devouring each feature, exclaiming at how handsome he was, she felt herself shiver with excitement: he was hers, her son, her own. She cuddled him to her and the feel of him, the warmth and trembling weight, bound him to her all in an instant. Without thinking, she fumbled with her shift and put him to her breast and, with the first pull on her nipple and the pain that once more shot through her, she was devoted to him. Any thought of parting with him even for an hour was unthinkable. And yet, in preparation for handing him to the wet nurse, so that she might leave him and rejoin her husband, she rubbed her breasts the morning after the delivery with equal parts of spirit and oil and used the glass tube she had bought to suck her own milk away. She cried while she did so and became so upset that Ellen had to assist and she remembered doing the same for her mistress when Pen was born, only then the doctor had brought an India rubber pump that was far more efficient.

Writing to tell Ferdinando he had a splendid son more like him than like her, more Italian than English, Wilson for once swept aside all inhibitions created by knowing her letter would be read to him. With pride she began:

—On this day the thirteenth of October in the year of our Lord eighteen-hundred-and-fifty-five I gave birth to your son who is a fine healthy boy born feet first. I cannot tell you the love I feel for him Ferdinando and only weep that you cannot be here to see him and hold him and wonder with me that we have created such a splendid child. He has dark hair and eyes and strong limbs and a lusty cry and all is well though I suffered sorely in the having of him, worse than I had anticipated. But I am well and happy the ordeal is over and I have come through. I pray for you and for our reunion that I may present you with your son and see you share my joy.

Then she wept, overcome with misery at wondering when that would be. Any moment, Ferdinando would be taken off to Paris, if he had not already been obliged to go, and it struck her suddenly that she ought to write to her mistress and make plain her desire to return to her service. By the next post she wrote:

—I am already decided, ma'am, that I cannot live without my dear husband no more than you could and my sister Ellen being more than willing to care for my son I am resolved to leave him with her while he is young and return to claim him when we come to England on the next summer visit. This being mid-October I consider I can travel to join you in a month from now and therefore will not have inconvenienced you much I hope. Pray give me directions and I will manage to see to the rest. Kiss Penini for me and tell him my baby is nearly as beautiful as he was.

More tears followed until her baby's head was wet with them and Ellen scolded her. She lay huddled in the bed, watching the wet nurse suckling her son, and the hopelessness of her dilemma depressed her utterly. She had not bargained for the force of her love for her child, for the pull he would exert on her heart. The horror of what she was proposing to do—go, leave him, not see him, not hold him, desert him, abandon him—froze her movements. She lay for hours unable to speak or eat, her eyes following Ellen crooning to her son, cuddling him, carrying him about. And when William came in, that big man tiptoeing, and took the baby and smiled down at him she could not bear it and turned her face to the wall.

She had neither energy nor will to get herself up and no one seemed to care—the baby was the center of all attention. She told herself repeatedly how fortunate she was to have the luxury of lying in bed, warm and comfortable, with food and drink brought generously to her when many a woman in her position had to rise the next day after giving birth and shift for herself, but she did not feel fortunate. She felt trapped, she *was* trapped, and far more securely than she had ever envisaged. The steel jaws of the trap bit her breast and she could not escape without tearing it from her and with it would drain her life and happiness. Yet she could not stay here in East Retford with her child—all the compulsion in her was toward Ferdinando and her life with him. If she could return next summer, then surely ways and means could be found to take her son back to Italy. Feverishly, she ran over the possibilities in her mind, calling in all the friends she had ever had and deluding herself that among them would be one who could travel with a child not yet one year old. Burying her head in the pillow, pulling the covers over herself, she willed herself into the next year, conjuring up pictures of herself and Ferdinando and their son all smiling under an Italian sun.

Outside, it rained. All the rest of October it rained and an east wind blew, and everyone shivered and cursed winter for coming so early. Wilson, on her feet once more, lived for the post, though it brought her nothing but bad news. Ferdinando was with the Brownings in Paris where they had traveled four days after Oreste's birth. There was trouble finding an apartment and then, when one was found, more trouble moving out when it did not satisfy Mrs. Browning—the sofas were hard and ugly and the sun never came in because the windows faced the wrong way. No one had time to write to her. All she had had was a letter of congratulation written by Mr. Browning on Ferdinando's behalf and another by her mistress saying she was happy and relieved for her. But by November 11, when Oreste was christened, she had not had a single other communication in response to her application to return. In the church, with Ellen as godmother holding Oreste and William as godfather standing at her side, Wilson felt already displaced. She had left them in spirit but here she was in body, dull and restless, frantic to get the parting she dreaded over.

On November 20 she received a letter from the Brownings with, enclosed inside, another from Ferdinando not in any hand she knew. She went to her bedroom, already in her mind packing her trunk and giving Ellen last instructions for Oreste's welfare. With trembling hands she smoothed out the Brownings' letter first and prepared to absorb what she supposed would be detailed directions. It was written by Mrs. Browning but signed by them both. Her eyes skimmed the first page, which was full of the tribulations involved in finally settling themselves in the Rue du Colisée near the Champs Elysées, and then the second which gave an account of how much of their post had been misdirected and they had only last week

—received the letter you sent at the end of October Wilson dear (though since you did not date it I cannot be sure when it left your hand, the postmark also being indistinct). I must confess my husband and I were startled by its contents, not having imagined that one who had so recently given birth would contemplate a journey from East Retford to Paris and in all seriousness, Wilson, I fear it would be too much for you. But in any event, it is a journey you will not be called upon to make for it is unfortunately not within our power to receive you back as and when you wish. You will surely understand that in engaging Harriet and bringing her here far from her home we were obliged, if we had any decency at all, to guarantee the length of her employment and her safe passage back to London and we accordingly assured her that she would hold her position with us until next June when we make another summer visit to London. You cannot hold this against us, Wilson, nor can you expect us to cast aside Harriet upon being informed you see your way to returning. You would do far better to stay with your sister and care for your child until next June when we would be happy—indeed overjoyed—to have you back (and will regard that as certain unless in the meantime informed otherwise). We are sorry for any disappointment this causes you but feel sure that upon reflection you will agree we are bound to Harriet.

There were three more pages but she did not then read them. The words "we are bound to Harriet" filled her with rage and she pushed her fists in her eyes to block out the sudden vision of her smirking substitute. Why "bound" to Harriet? What pretense was this? What contract had been entered into of such a secure nature that they were "bound" to a servant engaged temporarily? She had never heard the like of it, she did not believe it. There was more to this than any supposed obligation: they *preferred* Harriet, that was the truth. She was young and pretty and did not burden them with the worries of a married woman. By next summer doubtless they would discover they were "bound" to keep Harriet after all, and at this thought panic filled her. She would never see Ferdinando again, never return to Italy, be stranded forever in East Retford . . .

It was quite half an hour before she could compose herself sufficiently to read Ferdinando's own letter but when she did it cheered her considerably. He had dictated it to a fellow Italian who, just as she had predicted, he had met at a café where exiled Italians gathered. In a great burst of feeling he assured her he wept nightly for her and could not bear being apart from her or their son. She need have no foolish worries that he had become a philanderer, for nothing could be further from the truth. He had not even lifted his eyes off the ground to look at a Frenchwoman and, as for Harriet White,

—she is a thorn in my side which I feel more every day. Penini detests her and cries for you morning noon and night and will not be quietened though his mother and father plead with him to stop. He will not sleep with Harriet and so sleeps with his parents nor will he let her dress him or feed him which I am called upon to do. Every day he asks if his Lily is back and I say No and we cry together for you. Nor is your mistress in reality much happier for this Harriet is not dependable and forgets all manner of things and consequently there is no order in our household which is not the happy place it was formerly. As to not allowing you to return I am devastated by the decision and do not understand it except it were to do with expense for there can be no other explanation. I stood openmouthed when told they felt bound to Harriet and a bird could have flown into it. They were as embarrassed as I have ever seen them and glad when I left the room. And now Lily I am desolate all over again what with the hope that had sprung up in me being so cruelly dashed and I would that I were not a feeble fellow unable to gather you and my son up into my arms and keep you there.

Wilson smiled wearily at that. Ferdinando was quite strong enough to do what he said, if only he were with them, but he could do nothing materially toward bringing them together. There was no alternative: for the next six months she must stay here and find some employment to support herself and save toward the bleak future. Ellen and William were happy to have her and no mention of payment had been made nor, since if nothing else they were not exactly poor, did it need to be. But she could not stay in this house day after day with nothing to do but watch Ellen drool over her baby nor could she compete with her. All Ellen wished to do was act nursemaid and, watching her blossom, Wilson could not deny her the chance. The only pleasure of the day was to see how the birth of Oreste had transformed his aunt and uncle. There were no more drunken rages from William. He returned to being the hard-working, sober citizen he had formerly been and the change in his demeanor was noted by all. "You need not fear, Sister," he said one evening to Wilson as he noted her expression seeing him kissing Oreste, "I know he is not my own flesh and blood and that his father will one day claim him. I know it, I know he is not my dead son and I shan't pretend he is. But the power of holding him, hearing him . . . it heals, it heals. It is as everyone says. It sets me straight."

He was a beautiful, good baby. When she was alone with him, which was rarely, Wilson gloried in her son's looks and in his sweet nature. Memories of Pen were all she had with which to compare him and he excelled them in every particular. Though Pen had been big at birth, with a strong chest, he had lacked Oreste's perfection of form and under the care of Dolorosa quickly became, for a while, fat. Oreste was much better proportioned and his skin infinitely smoother. His black hair thickened rapidly just at the stage when Pen had lost his blond wisps, and his eyes were huge and a dark, dark brown. He smiled continually, never shrieking as Pen had been capable of doing, and slept long hours whereas Pen had woken repeatedly between feeds. All who saw him remarked on the baby's tranquillity and contentment and yet he was as spoiled by Ellen and William as Pen had been by his parents. There was no baby in the world more suited to travel or one less likely to cause disruption in any household. So easy and comfortable was this child of hers that Wilson began to entertain the notion of presenting him to the Brownings and convincing them it would not be out of the question either to take him back to Italy or, once there, to allow him to live in the Casa Guidi. She knew it was madness but it was an insanity she willfully indulged in, to make the East Retford winter days more bearable.

She knew she must find work but lacked the energy to go in search of it. Where, in East Retford, within reach of Carol Gate, could she find suitable employment? She would not live in and thereby throw away the chance to be with her baby, the only advantage of being stuck in England, and so limited her opportunities. Ellen had heard of a vicar's wife who was looking for a parlormaid and might be willing to take someone not living in, but Wilson could not bring herself to go seeking such a job. "Beggars can't be choosers," William murmured, but when she flashed back at him, "I am no beggar and if need be will take my son and go," he hastily pulled back, swearing it had been an idle remark not intended to offend. But, in the event, work came to her. While with Ellen she had taken to reworking her sister's clothes, partly to be useful, partly to keep herself busy and partly because she liked the work. This was one talent of Mother's, at least, which she had inherited and developed. She pulled to pieces a brown dress some eight years old and, by altering the skirt entirely and fashioning a new collar from yet another abandoned garment, she produced a most attractive creation which improved Ellen's sallow looks so much, it was noticed in chapel. Inquiries followed compliments and before long Wilson was in demand as a seamstress. The work suited her homebound circumstances perfectly and soon she had more than she could handle. She hand-sewed beautifully, finishing seams and trimmings so expertly that the dresses looked new. It pleased the few ladies of East Retford who had heard of Paris fashions to have Wilson incorporate little touches here and there which were "all the rage in Paris, ma'am, when I was there last summer and I did not think you would mind if I copied what I saw." No, the ladies did not mind and were quite willing to pay the extra Wilson charged for the unusually tucked bodice or the most originally shaped sleeves. Her fame spread to Sheffield and twice carriages arrived at the door to bring extremely smart clients, all eager to avail themselves of the services this rustic wonder was said to offer. Wilson gave half of everything she earned to William for her keep and the other half she saved. It was surprising how these savings accumulated but then, greatly daring, she had risked charging London prices from the beginning. There was not much to make on the alterations but once she had begun to make new garments she made a real profit. She charged fifteen shillings for a dress, for the making only, because that was what Mrs. Browning had paid for her last new dress over and above the cost of the material and trimmings. Ellen thought it scandalous but her customer hardly murmured, she was so thrilled with the originality of the dress. All the time she stitched, Wilson smiled a little grimly to think how all these years her entire income a week had been half what she could get from making a dress.

But long before spring came she was sick and weary of her life. While she stitched, working in her bedroom for the privacy of it, though the ice was often on the inside of the window and it was foolish to desert Ellen's hearth, she seemed to pass the time in a daze of bewilderment. How had she come to this? What was she doing here, so far from her husband? She had never felt more dead, more cut off from everything she had learned to love. Only Oreste gave her joy and that was a strange, muted pleasure. Knowing she might have to leave him if there was no other way of getting out of East Retford, she tried to keep herself separate from him even when cuddling him —he must not gain power over her head as well as her heart. She yearned for Ferdinando, for his life and vigor, for the completeness she felt with him, whereas here she felt so alone. She could not talk to Ellen, who in any case only wished to talk of the baby, and she had no other friends, except by letter. She wrote long screeds to Lizzie Treherne and Minnie Robinson and even to Jeannie, the Ogilvys' maid, who was now back in Dundee. Nothing she ever received in return was satisfactory, but then Lizzie had three children and Minnie was getting too arthritic to write with ease, and Jeannie found corresponding a strain. She would have liked to pour out her heart to her old mistress, to Mrs. Browning, but did not dare. Her last letter had been chilling.

News from Paris, the only place from which she really craved news, remained sparse. Notes from Ferdinando came regularly enough but they were short and repetitive and became like a formula. Indeed, sometimes she suspected that was what they were—letters paid for and written by a scribe according to an agreed recipe. Mrs. Browning wrote only twice between November and April, saying each time that she was pushed to finish *Aurora Leigh*, her verse poem, and hardly had time to think of writing to her own sisters. Wilson, reading the breathless account of days too short to fit everything into, could not help but contrast this pace with her own weary struggle to get to each bedtime and oblivion. She thought constantly of what she would be doing in Paris at each hour, of what she would be seeing and doing and hearing. At eight in the morning she woke to her cold room and had no Ferdinando to warm her before she touched the icy floorboards and went to Oreste, seeking what he could not give her. She picked him up from the lined drawer in which he slept and, though she kissed him and he smiled and gurgled, all she felt was his helplessness. In Paris they would be making a play out of breakfast, with Ferdinando singing and Pen joining in and the coffee bubbling on the stove and then Harriet—oh, that Harriet—would take Pen out into all the color and variety of the Parisian streets. She would meet other maids and gossip, buy hot chestnuts from a stall and watch a Punch and Judy show, then return home to lunch with all the talk that went with it in the Browning household. Visitors would call, there would be laughter and more talk and the satisfaction of feeling at the hub of things. If she was there, and not Harriet, there would be time off and she and Ferdinando would make good use of it walking along the Seine and sitting in cafés and feeling far less like servants than they ever did in England.

In Ellen's house, though peace now reigned, there was neither talk nor laughter nor conviviality of any sort. William went out soon after dawn, returned for his dinner (eaten in silence) at noon, and came home again at dusk, whenever that fell. He worked hard and in the evening sat by the fire smoking his pipe before retiring to bed early. His Sundays were distinguished by a later start and going to church but otherwise held no distraction. He was civil, played with the baby, treated both Ellen and her sister respectfully now, but offered nothing in the way of fellowship. Ellen was hardly better. She rose with her husband and spent her day cleaning and washing and baking. Her entertainment was caring for Oreste. Wilson remembered her as loquacious but came to the conclusion she had imagined it. Ellen spoke as little as William, appearing to have no interest in anything outside her own house. The world at large was of no consequence to either of them and Wilson, who had never thought it was of much to her, discovered she missed knowing of wars and prices and iniquitous laws and who had written, acted or painted a masterpiece, all ordinary topics of conversation in the Browning household. It stunned her that people could be so self-sufficient when their self-sufficiency was clearly so sterile. She would rather die, she thought, than endure this forever. Watching the evenings lengthen, feeling in April a little heat coming from a still rare sun in the sky, she longed not just for Ferdinando but for Italy. She looked at her son and wished she could see him basking in the heat, as he surely would, in his father's homeland. Only then would everything seem right in her world.

By May she was almost ill with waiting, as she had done all winter, for the post. Soon, soon it *must* bring a letter with a date in it, a date telling her when to rejoin her true family. But May went by and there was no letter saying anything at all. Unable to restrain herself, she wrote three times to the Brownings, repeating over and over that she was *ready* and *waiting* and that they *must not fail* to inform her of their arrival. She even reminded them, though it humiliated her to feel the need to do so, of their *promise* to take her back, and then she trembled to think she might have gone too far. Still no response came and it was June when surely their plans would be made. In desperation, terribly afraid there was something sinister in this silence from Paris, she wrote to Minnie Robinson, begging her

—to tell me Minnie please if Miss Arabel has heard from her sister as to this summer's plans for I had expected before now to be told and I am sore afraid in case I am not included in them though I cannot believe it since I was assured otherwise. Oh Minnie it has been a long weary winter here in East Retford than which there is to me no more godforsaken place. My sister and her husband have been kind and I have much to be grateful for in having their home to shelter me and am not unaware of what I owe to them and how fortunate I have been where others are not but nevertheless Minnie it has been a sore trial and were it not for my precious baby I could not have stood it. He is a fine child never ailing anything nor troubling anyone and is much admired. He begins to crawl and can stand unaided except for holding the tip of a finger and that you know is well advanced for his young age. My brother-in-law treats him as his own which since the poor babe is deprived of his father means much. It is not right Ferdinando my husband has not seen his own child and breaks my heart, so write dearest Minnie and tell me of any plans which have been made known of the Brownings' arrival.

All in a flurry, three letters came in the middle of June, each with the same news, but then Wilson could not have it repeated often enough: the Brownings were to arrive on June 30 and she was bidden to make her way on the twenty-ninth to Mr. Kenyon's house in Devonshire Place to await their arrival. Over and over she read this, checking the date, checking the place, before ever she proceeded to absorb any of the instructions. It seemed Mr. Kenyon was mortally ill at his summer residence in the Isle of Wight and had begged the Brownings to stay in his London home. She would make ready for them and might if she wished have her baby brought down to show off, before leaving for the Isle of Wight, which the Brownings intended to visit partly as a holiday and partly to pay their last respects to their benefactor. She would go with them but should be warned that Ferdinando would not: he would stay in London since there was not room for him or any need of his services in the Isle of Wight. If this did not suit, she should say so immediately and Harriet might be retained. Swiftly, Wilson replied, stating in unequivocal terms that she was ready to go to Devonshire Place, ready to go to the Isle of Wight, and that she quite understood that parting from her husband would be necessary. "There is no need," she ended, "for Harriet."

Minnie told her the same news, adding that Miss Arabel feared her father would order her out of London as soon as her sister arrived; and so did Ferdinando, in a note quite unlike the usual "formula," ecstatically reiterating the concession about Oreste. Suddenly, there was so much to do, the days flew past, and Wilson found herself singing as she sewed. But she was careful to restrain her enthusiasm for leaving in front of Ellen and William, neither of whom seemed to have taken in the significance of her departure. What concerned them both, naturally, was how long Oreste would be gone and, as to this, Wilson knew she must be very careful. She might need her sister more than she yet was in a position to tell, though she had begun to hope, even though she knew it was foolish, that she might not need her at all. All she told them was that she was going to London to meet with her husband and the Brownings to discuss her future. She was taking Oreste to show him off though he could not of course stay with her in the Devonshire Place house—Lizzie Treherne would have him.

The day she left Carol Gate it rained heavily. As she bounced along in William's cart, clutching Oreste, who was swathed in shawls, it seemed to Wilson that was all she would remember of East Retford, the rain, the interminable rain. To a place already gray in her mind it added another depth of shadow and she was vowing all the way to Sheffield that she would never, never live there again.

"Come back soon!" Ellen had cried, opening her arms wide as she ran several hundred yards alongside the cart, the rain soaking her as the wheels threw up spray from the puddles. "Come back soon!" Poor bedraggled Ellen, her arms empty, the miracle she had hoped Oreste's birth would work now only a dream.

Wilson tried to talk to William about Ellen but, without knowing if she had removed Oreste from her forever, it was hard. "William," she ventured, "Ellen will be low, with us gone. Do not be hard on her, I beg you." For answer William whipped the horse and was silent. "And yourself," Wilson went on hesitantly, "you have been good to us, like a father to my child, and I thank you for it."

"I am father to none of my own," William muttered above the noise of the cart, "nor ever will be by the looks of it, so I'd better get used to it."

Wilson could not think how to reply. His tone had not been the bitter thing his words implied but instead had about it a touch of resignation. "It is a dreadful business," she said, not knowing precisely what she meant, wishing only to be sympathetic and not to make William angry.

He alarmed her, just before Sheffield was reached, by suddenly asking, "The boy, when will you be bringing him back?" She did not know how to answer and took refuge in "It depends on my husband."

Once she had left him, she spent the journey to London thinking how nothing depended on Ferdinando, nothing. William, so much the master in his own house and work, would not be able to imagine how little depended on her own husband. He had the power neither of the purse nor of place. The Brownings had all the power. She saw it more clearly than she had ever done, though she had never been blind to the realities of her position. The nine months in East Retford had been like a prison sentence, and while serving it she had had many hours to reflect on the hopelessness of trying to rise above her station. She saw she had to accept it, to be obliging and humble and not act as though she had her own life to lead and could do as she wished. If she wished to be with Ferdinando, if she wished to return to Italy, if she wished to employ herself in the manner she enjoyed, then there was no room for maneuver. Realizing this made her as nervous as the day she had traveled to London for the first time. Now, as then, her anxiety was to please and she had even more to lose. If Oreste could please also, then the whole game would alter. Looking down at him, asleep in her aching arms, she could not see how he could fail to enchant. Surely, once the Brownings had seen him, their hearts would melt and a small corner could be found for him?

So it was an optimistic Wilson who waited in Devonshire Place on June 30, wearing the blue dress in which she had been married and with the brooch the Brownings had given her on their first anniversary pinned to her collar. She stood motionless in the hall when the time of arrival came near, her hands clasped in front of her. Mr. Kenyon had taken his staff with him, except for the housekeeper and a maid, and it had been readily agreed by them that Wilson should act footman when the carriage arrived. She had time, standing there, to brace herself and so successfully that when she heard the carriage stop she was able to open the door calmly and descend the steps with dignity. The first to see her was Pen. He gave a great shriek of "Lily! Oh, my Lily!" and then the door of the carriage fairly shot open and the child catapulted out of his father's arms and into hers. He had his legs wound around her waist and his arms throttling her neck and he smothered her with kisses of such violence, she knew her lips would bruise. She laughed and cried, almost shocked by such demonstration of passion, and tried to calm him down by talking to him but not a single sentence escaped without the kisses cutting it to pieces. "You have grown so . . ." she began and was silenced and, coming up for air, breathed, "I would never have thought you . . ." and lost that too. It was hopeless. She hugged him back and stroked his hair and was enjoying this reunion thoroughly until she heard Mr. Browning say, "Well, Wilson, you will be in no doubt you have been missed." Hastily, she removed Pen from her neck and, still holding him, said, "And I have missed him, sir, and indeed all of you." She tried to curtsy but it was impossible and it began to worry her that Pen's extravagant affection might do her more harm than good. Over his head, her eyes scanned the carriage, where Mrs. Browning still sat. Thinking she was looking for her husband, Mr. Browning said, "Ferdinando follows with the luggage. He will be here presently." She finally detached Pen, who ran off into the house, and went down the last step toward the carriage. Peering in, she was shocked again. "Oh, ma'am," she murmured, aghast at the pinched white face staring back at her, a face so wasted since she had last seen it that it hurt her to look at it. And the face had grown all of a sudden old, without doubt—*old*. The lines had deepened, the skin shriveled. Mrs. Browning smiled and stretched out her hand, but there was a new weariness underneath the general fatigue of traveling.

That evening Wilson lavished all the care and tenderness she had in her on her mistress, who by the time she was in bed was sighing with contentment and vowing she felt heaps better. "Everything is as it should be, dear," she murmured, "and how it has not been for this last year." Quietly, so that she could hardly be heard, Wilson followed the old routine, folding clothes, mixing laudanum, pulling curtains and extinguishing lamps in the familiar way. She liked to do it. There was comfort in assuming her old role and pride in clearly being appreciated for doing so. Only once did she think of Oreste being put to bed by Lizzie and firmly shut the image out of her head. That way, she would undo herself. There must be no tears of nostalgia or any other sort. She must be cheerful and soothing and not for one moment allow any of her own worries to intrude on Mrs. Browning's own. Even when she had been asked how her baby fared she had been careful to restrict herself to a short and favorable answer, then to turn at once to more queries about Pen. When she was asked if she saw a change in the child she was clever. "Yes, ma'am," she began, "he is greatly grown but still a young child for all that, still a baby in his ways and looks." It was an answer that pleased, as she had known it would, and once more she had proved her worth. The first day of the reunion, the first day of what she felt was a trial period, ended satisfactorily.

Not so the second. It began well and ended badly. She was reunited with Ferdinando at dawn after he had been on the road from Dover all night, owing to a series of mishaps. Again, it was she who answered the door, though it was the side entrance this time. She had not been asleep but had sat shivering on the stairs worrying about her husband's late arrival. She had been so anxious about seeing her employers that she had had no time to fret over Ferdinando but, sitting there in the early hours of the morning, she began to feel tense and unsure. Suppose he no longer loved her? Suppose she took one look at him and thought him changed and no longer loved him? He would seem strange, he would be awkward and so would she. But nothing could have been less true: the moment Ferdinando came out of the cab and rushed toward her, her body responded without any doubts. It was so *good* to be held by him, to feel his strength and hunger, and she laughed to think she could have thought otherwise. They went to bed as soon as they had deposited the luggage in the hall, and made love and only afterward did she see how exhausted her husband was.

He wanted Oreste immediately and was dismayed to hear the child was not even in the house. "It is better so," Wilson said firmly, "while I regain my position. I must not seem claimed by my baby or I will be thought no good to them and then what? Then we will never be together and never get back to Italy. Later you can see him and go whenever you like to Lizzie's." He slept and then, that afternoon, went with her to Lizzie's and saw Oreste for the first time. His pride was almost indecent. She was made to strip the child completely and at the sight of his muscular little legs and the broad chest and most of all the prominent genitals Ferdinando was ecstatic, raving at what a fine Italian he was. Wilson was glad Lizzie could not understand a word as the predictions of Oreste's future glory grew wilder and wilder, but she loved to hear the torrent of Italian and, from his antics, so did Oreste. He was not in the least afraid of this big, dark man who had suddenly appeared to fondle and caress him but laughed all the time and was pleased to be shown off. "He is like my father," Ferdinando declared, and then wept because his father was dead and would never see his namesake. "He is a Romagnoli, there is no doubt."

They took Oreste back with them to Devonshire Place for his formal introduction to the Brownings. Ferdinando carried him and seemed oblivious to his wife's repeated instructions as to how he should behave. "No boasting in front of them," Wilson pleaded. "No excessive pride, Ferdinando, I beg you. Let the child speak for himself, do not appear enslaved. And remember Penini's feelings, he may well be jealous if you pay too much regard to Oreste. Keep with Pen, show where your allegiance lies, or we have no future as a family."

None of this had any effect. No sooner had they entered the drawing room, where the Brownings sat together on a sofa with Pen expectant between them, than Ferdinando was off, rushing forward with his son and demonstrating his prowess. Wilson stood back, all the time watching the Brownings' faces carefully. Mr. Browning seemed merely amused but on her mistress's face was a peculiar expression she could not fathom. It was as though she were deliberately holding herself back from the admiration required, distancing herself from involvement with the baby. When Oreste, urged on by his father, put out a hand and touched her knee she seemed to flinch even though she took it. Pen had no such inhibitions—he was Oreste's slave and Wilson saw his adoration might prove her strongest hope. He lay on his back and begged the baby to sit on him and offered his curls to be pulled and his face to be licked, all the time calling on his parents to watch. Here at last was the little brother he had begged for.

Perhaps that was it. Perhaps, Wilson thought afterward, it was Pen who unwittingly did the damage by calling attention to his mother's failure to bear another child, by reminding her that her child-bearing days were over. Perhaps she could not stand the thought of a baby in the house. Whatever it was, after Oreste had been taken back to Lizzie's by his reluctant father, Mrs. Browning said to her, "He is a fine child, Wilson. You will miss him if you are resolved to come with us." It was like a deathknell, no mistake in the message of doom. "I am resolved, ma'am," Wilson replied calmly, "quite resolved."

CHAPTER TWENTY-FOUR

THERE WERE TIMES in the next few weeks when Wilson found herself wondering if she had ever married or borne a child, times when she felt herself to have slipped so effortlessly back into her old life that her new status as wife and mother had no reality. The momentum of each day was so compulsive, she was simply carried along with it and only at night, with Pen often in her arms, did she feel disturbed. Then she would slip out of bed, taking care not to waken Pen, and, lighting a candle, write to Ellen even though she had little hope of a reply. She listed things she wanted to know about Oreste and begged Ellen to reply:

—if you do not Ellen I will become a prey to all kinds of evil fancies which will return to plague me at night. I see my darling's face before me so soon as I close my eyes and sometimes he cries which makes me imagine something bad may have happened. Ellen you are to tell me if it has for otherwise I would not know since Ferdinando cannot tell me being unable to write. And I cannot write to him because there is no one to read the Italian. We are in a sorry fix situated thus and I am dependent on Lizzie Treherne for news of him. She writes Ferdinando is sad and gloomy and in way of despairing separated as he is from both wife and child and hardly knowing which is worse. I am well enough here and have much to keep me occupied, so my thoughts do not stray too much until nightfall. Pen has been in a state of great excitement since his uncles have been here. They declared their nephew was in need of some toughening up and though his mother's protestations were loud they have been teaching him to defend himself. It is comical to watch. He stands with his little legs apart as they have instructed and squares his fists quite red in the face with determination and when Mr. Octavius makes a swing at him but you may be sure only in pretense the little lad darts in and hits his uncle on the nose and we all clap. His mother calling him to her said she did not like to see her baby so warlike he puts his hands on his hips and declares, "I am not a baby, Mama, I am a *man* and men must fight." She pretended to be distressed but her pride was evident. Certain it is that the child gives her all the pleasure she has in life at this time for otherwise she is low what with a cough as of old and the fear her cousin Mr. Kenyon may die at any moment. We are to go to Cowes which is in another part of this island tomorrow to see him and she is dreading it as we all are. I have been warned to keep Pen very quiet, which will be no easy matter after the frolics of this last two weeks. Then we are to journey to Somerset to Miss Henrietta's home and I beg you Ellen *send me news* of my child there to await me. I enclose a money order which I hope to do each time I write.

That had been the agreement: Oreste would be looked after by Ellen and William but maintained by his mother and father. It was a point of honor and one dictated by Wilson, not Ellen, who protested she had no need of money. Oreste would cost nothing to keep as yet. But Wilson had felt instinctively that a business transaction, though it might appear soulless, would strike a bargain more effectively. She did not want her sister to perform an act of charity which might lead her to feel she owned her nephew, that he was hers because of what she had lavished on him. He was merely to be a boarder—that way the contract would be terminated more easily. She had stressed over and over that Oreste would be collected and brought out to Italy just as soon as it could be arranged. This might be a matter of weeks or of months but it would happen. Ellen had nodded and William grunted agreement but Wilson knew neither of them had listened properly— all they wanted was to have the child back. It made it in one way easier to leave him, seeing him so adored and cosseted, but a deep disquiet accompanied her back to London and she was short with Ferdinando, who did nothing but weep. Was anything worth such a separation? Wearily, she had asked the question of herself repeatedly and was half ashamed at the speed of her answer: yes, it was worth it to escape East Retford, to return to Italy, to make something of her marriage.

At all times she was careful to be cheerful, as she had seen she must be. No one caught her moping, no one could have known she was pining for husband and son. She smiled rather more than she had ever done and when it was noted and commented on said she was happy to be back. This was accepted as the truth without her mistress probing deeper. Writing to Lizzie, Wilson could not help remarking:

> —no one cares Lizzie how I feel and I am glad of it for were I to be shown any sympathy I fear I should not be able to compose myself. But they are wrapped in their own affairs and see only that I perform my old duties as well as ever. Upon occasion Pen has caught me sad and has begged to be told why his Lily does not laugh and then I have to work hard to persuade him he is mistaken for if his mother thought I in any way brought sorrow into her beloved son's life then all would be over with me. As it is we have reached the happy stage of my mistress declaring she does not know how she stood that Harriet so long and she no longer hides her belief in my superiority.

At Cowes, Wilson had need of all her patience, since the situation there was even more desperate than had been suspected. The house where Mr. Kenyon struggled to overcome the pain of his cancer was utterly silent and gloomy and terrified Pen, so she spent each day walking with him along the quiet roads, seeking distraction in reaching the sea and watching the boats. For all the amusement this lively scene afforded him, the child could not leave the subject of Mr. Kenyon and his suffering alone. Again and again he asked if Mr. Kenyon was going to God soon and whether he was happy that he would soon be an angel and whether he could be asked to take a message to Joe Story.

It was a dreadful atmosphere for a seven-year-old sensitive child and she was relieved when at last, at the end of September, they went to Somerset. Her mistress was apprehensive about the arrangements they would find at her sister's house but had no need. Henrietta had put them in a cottage in the grounds of her house and nothing could have been more delightful. Wilson's spirits lifted as soon as they saw the Surtees Cooks standing on the steps of their home to greet them —such a happy family they looked, all beaming and welcoming, with no constraint in their bearing. And at last Pen had children to play with. Altham was only two years younger and Mary three, but both of them were such robust children and Pen himself so slight that they all seemed of an age. There was a swing on the apple tree in the garden and a dog to play with and a camp in the bushes and a stream to wade in and all manner of diversions if the cousins themselves had not been diversion enough. The Surtees Cooks' nursemaid, Anne, was a pleasant girl with whom Wilson got on famously and she was only too willing to pass over the latest baby, Edward, only six months old, to the visitor. Wilson cradled the child and though this increased her longing for Oreste it also, in a curious way, made her feel nearer to him. To her great relief, there was a letter from Ellen, short and hurried, but with news that Oreste was healthy and happy and standing without aid.

Sitting in the garden with Anne while both of them kept an eye on the children, Wilson sighed with something near to genuine contentment. "It is very pleasant here," she murmured, looking at the leaves of the giant chestnut tree just beginning to turn yellow and brown.

"Yes," Anne admitted, "but there's nothing here for me."

"Nothing?"

"Oh, the place is well enough and the master and mistress kind and the children good, but I can't be stuck here all my days."

"Where would you go?"

"London, o' course. Get some excitement while I can, see the world." Wilson smiled and, seeing her smile, Anne was offended. " 'Tis all right for you," she said, "you've been to London and Paris and Florence and have seen everything." She shifted on the bench and put her head in her hands, her elbows on her knees.

Looking at her, Wilson saw how restless the girl was and suddenly felt old. "Well, I am an old married maid," she said lightly, "and though I have traveled a bit, I grant you, I cannot think of a nicer place than this."

Her mistress agreed with her. "This is a happy place, is it not, Wilson?" she remarked as her hair was brushed in the evening. "Do you feel it, dear?"

Thinking how much more frequent the "dear" was, Wilson replied at once that she did. "It comes from the top," she added. "Miss Henrietta, or I should say Mrs. Surtees Cook, being so happy herself and her husband too."

"Exactly," Mrs. Browning said, but thoughtfully. "I never thought to see my sister so happily married though it reflects on me to admit it. And with *three* children to her credit, though I would not swop my Penini for all of them together, not even for Mary."

"She is a pretty little thing with quite something of you about her, ma'am."

"Do you fancy so?"

"I do, in the eyes. Miss Henrietta has not given her those dark eyes nor her father. They are like yours."

"Well, they are as well with Mary when no daughter of mine will ever emerge to have them." Acutely attentive, Wilson caught the faintest flicker of a question there but was too wise to leap in and say that perhaps one day . . . Instead, she changed the subject expertly to Pen's friendship with Altham.

"He is good for Pen," she said, "being a steady child given to careful thought. He told Anne yesterday he thought his cousin Pen a genius."

Mrs. Browning laughed. "And he was right, Pen is a genius, though what fate awaits him as such I would not like to guess. He is liable, do you not think, Wilson, to do mad things in his genius?"

"He will grow out of the madness."

"Or into it. Lord, to think of him as a man!"

When the time came to go back to London, the house was awash with tears and on cue it began to rain. Wilson's last view of the Surtees Cooks was of them clustered under umbrellas at the gate, all waving and weeping, even the father of the family. Pen bawled his head off and was inconsolable while, in a corner of the carriage taking them to the station, his mother hunched into herself and spoke not a word. Only Mr. Browning was cheerful, talking of whom he was to visit in London before they left for Italy and running over the plays he would like to see and the things he would like to do before their departure. In response, his wife closed her eyes and seemed to be suffering more. Wilson did not dare betray by the slightest expression either of face or in voice that she was excited at the prospect of their return to Italy. She was even more solicitous in her ministrations to her mistress than usual, matching her sighs with sighs of her own and putting all the sympathy she had into each gesture.

Ferdinando had a feast prepared for them when they reached Devonshire Place but, though Mr. Browning sat down to dine heartily off the splendid ham, his wife climbed the stairs wearily and begged Wilson to make her ready for bed immediately. She wept, with bowed head, while she was divested of her clothes and shivered, though it was not cold. Wilson made comforting little clicking noises with her tongue and pleaded with her to take heart, for soon she would be back in the warmth of Italy and would feel better. At this, her mistress only wept harder, saying, "In Italy I will be further than ever from my sisters. Who knows when I will see them again? With every parting it grows worse, Wilson. I hate the sadness of these good-byes." Wilson, tucking her up in bed after she had finished one sustaining cup of tea, thought of Oreste and his laugh and his little fists waving in the air and it was impossible to restrain a tear. "Do not *you* cry, dear," her mistress murmured, "or you will encourage me and I shall never stop. Do not let my grief affect you so." As if, Wilson thought, drawing the curtains, I cry only for her grief when I have more than enough of my own and cannot afford to give vent to it except under cover of another's.

The next month was wearisome. Though it was only October, the city was swathed in fog and with the fog Mrs. Browning's cough reached what she herself always called housebreaking proportions. Wilson was almost as weary as the invalid herself, what with sitting up with her and rubbing her back with liniment and dosing her with laudanum. Mr. Browning took his turn but, at his wife's insistence, went out frequently and did not return until the early hours of the morning, by which time the coughing had become less harsh and some snatched sleep was possible. He would come into the bedroom to relieve Wilson and she was struck by the energy and vitality he displayed. He crossed the room with such quick strides and threw off his cloak impatiently and his eyes were bright and his whole being alert and vigorous. And there, in the bed, lay this poor creature half dead with coughing, pale and drawn and listless. Leaving the room to go to Ferdinando, Wilson wondered how he could bear it. It was hard for a man in the prime of life to be saddled with such a broken wife and nothing to be done about it. Since her return to their service, she had been obliged to notice that things were different between the Brownings. Their bed more often held a woman alone, suffering, than a couple rejoicing. Her mistress never spoke of the misery this caused her but sometimes, when, after a night of making love, Wilson came into her room unable to suppress that satisfaction which Ferdinando gave her, not knowing it was written into her whole bearing, she would look at her and smile, tremulously, and say, "I forget you are a married woman sometimes, Wilson." The meaning was unmistakable.

Each day was dominated by the necessity of correcting more sheets of *Aurora Leigh*. Dragging herself from bed with the greatest reluctance, Mrs. Browning sat at her desk, coughing away and scanning the proofs for errors. There were so many sheets, Wilson could hardly believe they were all of the one poem and, as she collected up the corrected pages and made them ready to return to the printer, she could not resist peering at the lines. Some shocked her, with descriptions she could not credit her mistress had written. Reading of Marian Earle's pitiful room, so like many a servant girl's attic she had known, Wilson could not think where her mistress had gleaned such knowledge. From her novels, she supposed. And then, skipping pages and reading of Marian Earle's brutal rape, she could not believe this too had come from novels. Wilson's heart beat faster as she tied those sheets and parceled them up and she could not help saying when next her mistress paused for coffee, "It is a story of a poor girl then, ma'am?" Mrs. Browning smiled. "Among other things, Wilson. It tells a sorry tale of life for some women and will be vilified for it." Thoughtfully, Wilson put down the cup. "I should like to read it, ma'am." "Then of course you must, Wilson. I think you will find it authentic."

Before she left England, on the last day of October, Wilson wrote a last strong letter to Ellen and William, going over everything she had already said and urging them to take note:

—that as soon as I can find a way Oreste will be brought to us and you *must not* think he is your own. I know that is plain speaking and may be in the way of offending you but I cannot help it. He is *my son* and only desperation keeps me from him. I would ask you Ellen to speak to him often of his mother and father and not to let him address you as such, shaking your head and saying no when he calls you Mama as he surely will. Say often Mama loves you and will come for you soon and if he is brought up with this it will not come as quite the shock it otherwise would to be taken from you. I fear that will not be until the spring, when many people travel to Florence and I will have no difficulty finding a courier if I or Ferdinando cannot come. By such time Oreste will be walking and beginning to talk and I would not leave him longer even if to come to him I must leave my employment again. Money will be sent every month and you are to use it Ellen to feed him and buy him clothes so he is not a beggar in your house. Please God, he being so young these months apart will in time be lost in his memory and I will be forgiven them. Should he be ill Ellen I beg you to send word with all haste and I will come to him. And I cannot end before setting out on this long journey without saying that should misfortune befall myself and Ferdinando and we are, God forbid, taken from this earth by sudden fever or like calamity you, in bringing up Oreste as your own, which I find true comfort in knowing you would, must not let him forget who his parents were and that they loved him and had no choice in what they did.

She was quite exhausted with emotion by the time she had finished. Death seemed to loom before her eyes, the death of her baby, the death of herself, and it was agony to smile and be pleasant and hide her sense of panic and fear. It was not until Marseilles was left behind and Italy appeared on the horizon that she began to recover and drag herself out of the half-dazed state she had been in. Her mistress seemed similarly affected, announcing her cough seemed to have "dropped off," and, as for Ferdinando, he sang and shouted and grew more exhilarated with every mile they covered. Only Mr. Browning seemed subdued and remained so while his wife declared herself the happiest woman in the world on re-entering the Casa Guidi and finding it looking better than ever after her long absence. While she flitted from one beloved room to another, exclaiming over reclaimed treasures, Mr. Browning stood looking out of the window onto the side of the San Felice church and Wilson was sure she saw in his expression a sense of utter boredom.

She herself did not know exactly how she felt. On the whole, up to Christmas, she felt suspended in time, unsure whether she was happy or not. Ferdinando's unequivocal delight in being back home almost offended her—it seemed to be so simple for him to forget Oreste and what she suffered in leaving him. But saying this was a mistake and did no good; Ferdinando was indignant, calling Heaven to witness her lack of charity and swearing he had wept himself dry for his son. Ashamed, Wilson left the subject alone, recognizing that she only made a burden for her back by accusing her husband of forgetting. It was better to have him cheerful than depressed and he had, after all, endured enough misery in his temporary exile. Only one thing alarmed her and that was his lighthearted assurance that soon they would have other sons. The thought horrified her. Wasn't she doing all she could to prevent this? Hadn't she sought Lizzie's advice and wasn't she following it? Leaping up and douching with vinegar and water as soon as they had had relations and trying to get Ferdinando to leave her alone when she knew she was at a dangerous time. Only immediately after her monthlies did she feel relaxed and even then did not give up the douching. Another pregnancy would spell disaster and she had had enough of that.

All the time she schemed as to how Oreste could be brought over and where he could be put when he was. Sometimes, though she was careful not to be the one to raise the subject, her mistress indulged her and discussed what could be done, but nothing ever came of the vague promises to ask this person or that if they could accommodate an infant in their party traveling out to Florence. "I am too selfish to want to lose you again," Mrs. Browning smiled, "and I fear I would if you had your child near you. What would you do with him, Wilson?"

"Why, board him out, ma'am. It is not the dreadful business it is in London. I know of many a kindly woman who will look after a child for far less than we remit to Ellen now."

"It is no sort of family life, however," her mistress said.

"Having Oreste near would be a beginning, ma'am."

"But what would be the end, since you would have no prospect of setting up house together?"

"In time, we may."

"How, Wilson? You intrigue me."

"Ferdinando must stay with you, ma'am. If I am to speak frankly, you know we must hold between us one steady position and in the way of things, as I have seen, a man's is steadier than a woman's. But I can do other work and yet be a wife and mother besides. I can sew and cook and could take in work."

"But where would you live, in this grand design?"

"Oh, it is not grand, it is humble if nothing else, and dependent on finding a cheap house to rent."

"There are such houses in Florence?"

"Not of this kind, but there are places, Ferdinando says."

"He is no businessman, your husband."

"No, he is not. But he is known as trustworthy and looks it and so do I and if between us we could raise a loan we might get a start and make something of ourselves."

"Ah, a loan," repeated Mrs. Browning with a very deep and long sigh, "how we would all welcome a loan."

That was that. Flushed, Wilson hid her agitation by leaving the room. She knew, for how could she not when she heard so many bits of conversation, that Mr. Kenyon had died early in December and that only last week, just before Christmas, the Brownings had both received a legacy. Minnie Robinson, who wrote rarely now but had made a special effort, having such a good piece of gossip to relate, had written to tell her how the rest of the family had been disappointed in their expectations and the Brownings alone had benefited. Minnie knew for certain that Mr. Browning had got £6,000 and Mrs. Browning £5,000.

Folding up Minnie's letter, Wilson smiled to herself a little bitterly. There had been no mention of the Kenyon legacies, though she had heard her employers discussing some investment in Tuscan bonds which she knew could not be possible if there had not suddenly been money available. Otherwise there was not at first any indication that their financial situation was easier. Not, that is, until the carnival came around the following February when, to his astonishment, Ferdinando was ordered to start preparing a grand entertainment because Mr. Browning was hiring a box at the Grand Ball and would wish his guests to be wined and dined in style. Immediately he heard this, Pen was beside himself to have a proper domino costume and kept up a nonstop barrage of pleading and cajoling until in the end his mother gave way and Wilson was sent to buy material. Pen stood at her knee watching every stitch she put in the blue satin, hopping from foot to foot in his agitation that it should be finished. When the carnival started and the streets of Florence began to fill with costumed revelers he was everywhere among them, convinced that his mask rendered him quite invisible. Wilson grew exhausted chasing after him but laughed all the same—it was rare to be truly in the Florentine spirit and while she was weaving in and out of the colorful, jostling crowds with Pen she felt lighthearted and optimistic.

She assumed that her mistress would not go to the ball and was resigned to missing it herself in order to stay with her. All winter she had coughed, in spite of staying snugly in her bedroom, which had been made out of the drawing room and became her quarters. Her fatigue seemed more than physical. Watching her closely, Wilson saw how the books slipped out of her hands and the sheets of paper remained virgin white at her side. Even letter writing seemed to have palled. She lay, hour after hour, staring into the fire which Wilson kept stoked at all times whatever the external temperature, and only revived temporarily if Pen ran in. Even then she could not match his enthusiasm and was more inclined simply to hug him than talk to him or listen properly to what he said. It was a pathetic sight and one which, as ever, softened Wilson's resentment. Who could hold any-thing against such a wasted, troubled creature? She was ill and in the worst kind of way. Only Mr. Browning knew, as Wilson knew, how dreadfully thin her body had become, how the rib cage could clearly be seen and the breastbone stood out in sharp relief. Against her master's wishes, Wilson had given in to demands for laudanum twice during the day as well as at night, given in because the requests were so urgent and heartbreaking and Mr. Browning was not always there to deal with them. He was out at his drawing class during the day and at dinner, often at Isa Blagden's, whenever company that might amuse could be found. It was easy for him to decree there should be no extra laudanum when he was not there to see the tears and the outstretched hand and the trembling.

But as the whole of Florence took on the aspect of a pantomine during carnival week Mrs. Browning seemed to recover a little. The improvement was due partly to the weather: the sun had come out and the cold wind, which had plagued the city all that winter, dropped. "Wilson," she said on the morning of the ball itself, "I think I might venture as far as the box we have taken and sit there an hour to see the spectacle." Delighted, not making the mistake of even a token discouragement, Wilson brought up the question of dress. What would her mistress wear? Everyone would be in costume and it was not possible to go unless suitably attired. There was no time for even her speedy needle to make a domino—one must be hired. Off

Wilson went, knowing there would be unlikely to be a spare domino in the whole of Florence, and fortunately, as she wrote to Minnie:

—I was blessed and found a woman Ferdinando knows who had a black domino left from last year which had been given to her by a lady of means in payment of a debt this woman being a seamstress. It did not fit exactly but it was not to be expected I would find any that did with my mistress being so small and now so thin. I took it home and made a good job of pinning and tucking it and with the aid of a black lace shawl it was very presentable. And Minnie you will well remember how with animation my mistress can quite transform herself in an hour and so it seemed and Mr. Browning was quite charmed and pronounced her his *bella mascherina* which is to say his beautiful masked lady. She wore her pearl necklace that was her mother's and the diamond brooch that was her grandmother's and was altogether lovely such as she has not been for a long while. I of course had to play my part and improvised a costume for myself out of that old blue dress as was once my best and I had a mask too. It is a strange thing, to go out at night in a mask. We sat opposite each other, my mistress and I, in the carriage taking us to the ball and we could not help but giggle at the sight we made, a foolishness that Mr. Browning could not rightly understand. It is certain everyone masked feels the same for by virtue of hiding one's features Minnie and being in costume and therefore further hidden a boldness is induced. You would not have recognized me in the ballroom where I moved freely among the highest in the city no one knowing my status nor caring and I danced near to the Grand Duke himself and thought nothing of it. This freedom was granted to me on account of my mistress far from staying in our box going out into the furthermost corners of the theater feeling suddenly well and strong. Her husband was beside himself with joy and her happiness to be at his side in the revelry complete. At one in the morning—only imagine Minnie, at one!—Ferdinando served supper in our box and you never saw such a spread. He had made a galantine of chicken which was as light and delicate as any woman could make and sandwiches of salmon and ham all cut artistically because you know presentation is everything to him and then sponge cakes and ices of three flavors and champagne throughout. All that is missing says my mistress is my darling boy and would have sent Ferdinando for him if her husband had not remonstrated and pointed out that the child would be asleep and the nursemaid we engaged with him. We all ate together, maids as well as masters and mistresses, and never was there a warmer feeling. Afterward my mistress did not again leave the box but I was sent out with Ferdinando and we danced and really Minnie I never remember such a happy night.

It ended at two-thirty, when she took her exhausted mistress home, leaving Mr. Browning behind to continue celebrating. The life had gone out of Mrs. Browning as abruptly as it had entered her, and Wilson felt she had a rag doll in her arms as she helped her to bed. It was nearly four when she went to her own bed and she knew there was no point in trying to go to sleep. Ferdinando would return soon. Dancing with him, she had been left in no doubt that he was excited and aroused by the glamour of the evening and as she had bid him good night he had pressed her to him and whispered in her ear and she knew his passion must be answered. Lying there, waiting in their narrow bed, she could not deny to herself that she wanted him to come in a way her mistress no longer was able to want *her* husband to come. But the danger terrified her. Half drunk with champagne, she tried to remember when her last monthly had been and felt some relief that it was surely almost upon her again and she would be safe. Ferdinando, coming in half an hour later, was troubled by no such calculations. He tore his clothes off and rushed into bed and even if she had wanted to discourage him she could not have managed it. Not since their reunion after Oreste's birth had she found such pleasure and they fell asleep in each other's arms satisfied and complete.

Almost immediately the penalty was apparent. In the cool light of day Wilson remembered with none of the difficulty of the previous night when her monthly was due: in two weeks' time. At first the knowledge cheered her and she went about her daily routine humming in spite of her headache. Her mistress was prostrate, a pale shadow on a pillow, and neither spoke nor opened her eyes all day.

Her condition seemed a reprimand and Wilson fell silent and moved about on tiptoe. Two weeks later, as Mrs. Browning was beginning to revive, she herself was full of foreboding. She had not bled on time and she was always as regular as could be. By the end of the week she had no doubt she had been caught and hardly knew what to do with herself. Ferdinando smiled when she shared her suspicions and his smile goaded her to shout that he was stupid. They had one child they could not keep and now here would be another and what would they do? She did not dare cry or appear low in front of her mistress and the strain of once more dissembling exhausted her. It was with the greatest relief that she heard that Mr. Barrett had died on April 17 because then she could weep openly and no one would guess she was crying with all the pent-up force of several weeks of worrying which grew greater every day.

Mrs. Browning, watching her sob, told her she envied her. As ever, she could not find release in tears, not at first. She lay on the sofa, composed, eyes staring, as Wilson shielded her face with a damp handkerchief and apologized for being overcome with grief.

"I had not thought you cared for my father as much, Wilson," Mrs. Browning murmured, though without hint of criticism. "You had little to thank him for, I think."

In reply, Wilson wept some more and managed to say, "I know what it is to lose a parent, ma'am, and be hundreds of miles away and not even at the funeral."

"I doubt if I should have gone to the funeral. I would not have been capable. And he would not have spoken to me, even on his deathbed, had there been time. That is the true pity of it, dear. Now, dry your tears, do not continue to distress yourself, for I envy you too much."

But later, when with painful slowness a tear or two began to trickle from under her mistress's closed eyelids, a trickle that within the hour had turned into a torrent, the torrent she had longed for, Wilson was able to weep freely again. Together, they cried in each other's arms and, had it not been for having learned the wisdom of secrecy, Wilson would there and then have thrown herself on Mrs. Browning's mercy. As it was, the tears for both of them came to an exhausted end. "We must be brave," Mrs. Browning said and Wilson could only echo her.

She did not feel well. Before May was out, she was troubled with morning sickness which she had the greatest difficulty concealing. Pen was always acutely aware of his beloved Lily's spirits and was quicker than anyone else in the household to note and worry about any silence or lack of cheerfulness on her part so, every morning, though she had just vomited into the chamber pot and had not had time to dispose of the contents, Wilson was obliged to smile and sing and try to be as she usually was. Ferdinando did his part, tempting Pen into the kitchen where the smell of an omelet frying would make his wife heave again. Once they were outside, in the Boboli Gardens or walking by the Arno, she felt better but even then she had aches and pains she never had while carrying Oreste. Worse still was the intermittent bleeding. When first she saw the spotting on her under-clothes her heart leaped and she was convinced she was going to miscarry and have done with it. But the bleeding did not increase, though she made sure she was particularly energetic to help it along, and soon ceased, only to return in June. It made her faint to wonder what this could mean. Was there something amiss with the baby? Would she give birth to a monster? Or did it mean she was carrying a girl, as Ferdinando vowed?

There was no doubt, by July, that her pregnancy showed, though only, by her reckoning, some four months gone, at which stage she had been only a little thick around the waist and a little full in the bosom the last time. The mound in her belly was quite prominent and, though she wore her clothes loose and took to wearing an apron on far more occasions than usual, she knew that a discerning eye could tell her condition. But no eye chose to discern. Her mistress remained wrapped in misery, scarcely ever leaving her bedroom, and never seemed to look at her at all. Mr. Browning spent hours at Isa Blagden's and was forever rushing in and out, too busy to notice anything. Only Pen remained a danger and terrified her with his "My Lily is getting fat and fatter and fattest," and cuddling her stomach fiercely. But if the child told this to his mother she either heard nothing or ignored it.

The last thing Wilson could bear the thought of was holidays, but inevitably the subject came up. "We must get away, Ba, we really must," she heard Mr. Browning say one raging hot day toward the end of June. "This inferno is intolerable and everyone makes preparations to leave." His wife only sighed. Wilson, hovering near the door, heard the reply. "If nowhere else, Ba, it will have to be Lucca where at least boredom will be cool. What do you say?" Say no, Wilson pleaded silently, say no, say you have been three times and it is duller upon each occasion and not to be endured. But her mistress said she really could not care and had no opinions and it was all the same to her. "Very well," Mr. Browning said, with some irritation, "Lucca it shall be and there's an end to it." Wretched, Wilson crept away. How would she manage up there? They would all be on top of each other and she would not escape scrutiny, yet were she to confess now she would be dismissed instantly and then what? Better at least to be with them at Lucca where they would be obliged to keep her for lack of a suitable substitute.

On the train to Lucca, Wilson saw Mrs. Browning's eyes light on her swollen stomach for the first time and the question she had dreaded flash into her eyes. That very evening, though they were all worn out with the journey and the heat, her mistress spoke to her once they were alone. Her voice was cold and angry. "Well, Wilson, I see you once more have a secret from me." Wilson hesitated, brush poised to begin. "There is no use denying it, I have eyes when I care to use them, which I should have done by now, but it is remarkable how I persist in believing I am worthy of respect and trust."

"Indeed you are, ma'am . . ."

"Indeed I patently am *not* since I swear you have known of your condition some months?"

"Not precisely. There was some bleeding . . ."

"I do not wish to hear the details, Wilson. Spare me, please. When is this child expected?"

"November, I think."

"And we are in August tomorrow. Do you see yourself giving birth here, might I ask?"

"No, ma'am."

"No, ma'am. Quite. Then what are we to do, since it is our intention to stay until the end of October if we can?"

"I do not know."

"You do not know. Neither do I. Yet it seems I am expected to know, to think for you. I do not take this kindly, Wilson, and my husband will be angry."

Wilson put the brush down. Her hand trembled too much to use it. "I could not help it, ma'am," she whispered, "being a married woman, though I tried to avoid it."

An expression of absolute distaste flitted across her mistress's face. "Well, you did not succeed and now we must all suffer. I had better speak to my husband before we discuss this further."

There was never another discussion. The next day Mr. Browning, though a good deal kinder than his wife had been, summoned Wilson and told her she must return to Florence on September 1, by which time a replacement would be found. He said, gently enough, that though he knew it was hard for her to be parted from her husband at such a time it was not possible that she should risk the last months of pregnancy up here in Lucca. She listened with bowed head, no fight in her, no energy even to cry, and looked up only when he said he and his wife proposed to make her a present of money to mark the end of her service with them. The word "money" did not penetrate her consciousness so much as "the end of your service," but Mr. Browning obviously thought otherwise. "Yes, money," he repeated, "enough, Wilson, for you to rent a house for a year and, I imagine, fill it with paying boarders. It is the best we can do. What do you say?" She said what she was expected to say, the only thing she could say: she said thank you and half curtsied.

When she told Ferdinando her fate he appeared overjoyed and could not understand her fears. He thought all their problems solved and began excitedly to calculate how good a living they could make once the baby was born. "I will be alone," Wilson said in reply. "Who will take care of me? Where shall I turn?" Ferdinando brushed this aside—he knew women in Florence who would come to her for virtually nothing. "Women," Wilson said, "women I do not know and who do not know me? And in an empty house, which I have yet to find." Again, her husband could not see the difficulty. All of Florence had emptied for the summer and a house would be easy to come by when she had the money in her hand to secure it. While she stared at him, seeing only a vision of herself trudging from door to door in search of shelter, he gazed at her with shining eyes, blessing his employers for their generosity. Unlike her, he had already worked out what could be got for the sum promised and reckoned there would even be a little over after the year's rent. This made her laugh. "Oh, Ferdinando," she said wearily, "a house is more than rent and a household does not run on nothing. There will be expense beyond imagining and our only income, until I am in a position to care for boarders, your salary. What can we do on that, with my own gone?"

But nothing could depress him. While she wandered through the Casa Betti sick at heart, he sang and whistled and was plainly relieved. Hearing him, her mistress raised an eyebrow and said, "Ferdinando is cheerful, at least." She knew the "at least" was directed at her and flushed. "I am sorry, ma'am," she said quietly, averting her face, "but the prospect before me does not incline me to cheerfulness." There was no reply. Mrs. Browning went on to give her instructions for the arrival of Isa Blagden and Robert Lytton, who had come, at the Brownings' behest, to stay nearby and were to be entertained to supper. At the Casa Betti, where space was restricted, there was no room for a housemaid or skivvy, so Wilson was expected to share the work with Ferdinando. She noticed that evening as she brought the chicken dish to the table that there was a lull in the conversation until she had left the room and her ears burned. Later, Isa Blagden sought her out and put an arm around her shoulders and spoke to her kindly. The kindness was Wilson's undoing. She wept in spite of herself and said she did not know how she would manage in Florence on her own. Isa consoled her and said she would be there herself in September and would be sure to come to her aid. "I am not wanted here, at any rate," Wilson said miserably, "my mistress cannot abide the sight of me." Isa squeezed her hand and said there were reasons for this and they would pass.

What reasons? Throughout the next week Wilson tried to think of any. Why was her mistress so remote, so unfeeling toward her?

Why did she treat her as though she had committed a crime? It could only be because she was about to be inconvenienced and that seemed such a small burden for her to bear. Yet Wilson saw it was probably the truth. Inconvenience was detested by Mrs. Browning. Currently, she found her husband's devotion to Mr. Lytton inconvenient. Mr. Lytton had fallen ill the very day after he dined with them on his arrival and was pronounced to have succumbed to the fever prevalent in Lucca that year. Mr. Browning hastened to his side and nursed him and Wilson heard her mistress tell him it was "inconvenient, Robert, to have you there so much and not wise, for what if you carry this dreadful fever to Pen?"

Before ever he did, Wilson herself fell ill. She woke one morning to find herself incapable of standing on her own two feet. Her hands shook, her head swirled and sweat filmed her entire body. She vomited, had loose bowels, and cramplike pains incapacitated her. Knowing nothing of the consternation which the worried Ferdinando caused when he reported this, she lay clutching her stomach, sure she was about to give birth prematurely. A doctor was brought and said he thought this not an immediate danger but that in view of her pregnancy she should stay in bed for a week or until all symptoms disappeared. He gave her a draught which sent her to sleep and when she awoke the pains at least had gone, only the profound weakness remaining. She could hear Pen shouting and laughing in the garden where he was playing with Doady Eckley, the son of his parents' new friends, but otherwise it was peaceful. She felt no temptation to try to get up. All day she remained still in the darkened room, watching the slats of light change in direction as the sun moved outside, and finding in the hum of insects and the spinning of dust motes something soothing. She was not surprised when Ferdinando came in to her and, sitting on the end of their truckle bed, told her she was to go back to Florence as soon as she could get up. Annunciata, a new maid, was arriving in three days' time from Florence.

She supposed she could just have gone on lying there forever. Why not? Who could do anything? The Brownings had not so far forgotten their previous devotion to her that they would cast her out, would lift her from her sickbed and hurl her down the mountain. But it was not in her nature to exploit her illness. Before the three days were over, she was up and walking about, though hardly with the strength of a kitten. At least, when she went in to her mistress to attend to her morning toilet for the first time since she had collapsed, she was sent away promptly with instructions to rest some more and not think of doing anything. That comforted her a little. But all comfort was banished when the new maid, Annunciata, arrived. She was a slip of a girl, pretty, with a mass of dark curls tied in a bunch and dimples in her cheeks when she smiled, which seemed to be constantly. Wilson stared at her and hated her at once. The contrast with her cumbersome, depressed self was painful and humiliated her. She saw looks of delighted appraisal everywhere—from Mrs. Browning, from her husband and most of all from her own Ferdinando. Only Pen resisted the girl's gaiety and charm and clung to his Lily.

On August 29 she left the Casa Betti, blind with the tears she had vowed she would not mortify herself by shedding. Her mistress seemed embarrassed by her utter dejection. She kissed her and said, "Poor Wilson, poor dear," and Mr. Browning said, "I would this could be otherwise, Wilson," in a worried tone. He had arranged for a trap to take her to the station and Ferdinando was to go as far as the train with her and see her safely on board. She did not attempt to say anything, only allowed herself to be put in the trap. She did not wave, did not even look to see if anyone waved to her, but sat, slumped, wretched and devoid of dignity. Parting from Ferdinando was over in a second since they had misjudged the time and the train was about to leave. She had only a moment to settle herself and be kissed by him and then he had gone. It crossed her mind he seemed relieved to go.

And now she was alone, starting, she supposed, yet another new life. Her service with the Brownings had ended, they had said so. There was no mention, this time, of her returning. Thirteen years as maid, nurse, housekeeper, seamstress—what had she not been at one time or another and sometimes all of them together? Over. Ended. And her marriage, what of that? A wife living apart from her husband, a woman managing a boardinghouse on her own. A new life.

She had not the energy for it, for anything.

PART III

1857-1861

CHAPTER TWENTY-FIVE

THE HOUSE frightened her, which, she repeatedly told herself, was foolish. It was not even a large house, only tall, with long flights of steep stairs, and had two rooms on each of the four floors. None of them were in a good state of decoration. The paintwork, a dark brown, was peeling and the walls, unusually, had been hurriedly and superficially covered with an ugly beige paper which did not cling properly to the plaster. The floors were for the most part tiled, large-patterned tiles, not unattractive, but in need of thorough cleaning. Wilson could see that when scrubbed the red and white patterns upon them might be pretty. But not even scrubbing would alter the fact that the scullery was dark and ill equipped and one look at the ancient stove made her glad it was still high summer and heating was not necessary. She did not even need to cook since she lived on bread and melon and tomatoes, lacking the energy and appetite to bother with anything else and having only herself to consider. She had engaged a young girl, only fourteen years of age, called Maria, brought to her by the caretaker of the house, and vouched for as "good and obedient." It was a strange experience, to be hiring a servant, but Wilson

was in too confused a state to relish this evidence of her change in
status. It had been all she could do, as she wrote to Ellen,

—to get myself to Florence. I lay on my bed in a cheap lodging
house and cried and I tell you Ellen I wished I was with you and
receiving your kindness which was great to me. There is no one
here who cares for me or will look out for me and I must shift for
myself in everything which is not easy now I am big with child
and not well as I was with my firstborn. It was only the thought of
this poor baby in me that made me stir at all and get myself to a
friend of Ferdinando's who is in the way of knowing all the
business of the street being a wine merchant and visited by all. He
knew at once of a house to let for a whole year, the owners being
abroad and failing to let it before they left last month and seeing
my condition he took pity and had the caretaker prevailed upon
to come to me at his premises. I had no interest in what this house
should be like wishing only for a place and quickly to lay my head
and could hardly rouse myself to inspect it. It is a poor house
Ellen and not clean but it is cheap and furnished after a fashion
and best of all lies next to the Casa Guidi which raised my spirits.
I am now installed and with a maid of all work with me named
Maria. She is near the age we were Ellen when we first went into
service and has no idea how things should be done. I set her the
first day to clean the floors starting at the top and expecting her
to reach the bottom at the end of the day or at least the last floor,
but Ellen she had not managed more than two rooms in eight
hours and those not well done. She said carrying the water up
from the well had taken a great deal of time which, when I saw
her filling the bucket, I was not surprised since she lowered the
rope slow enough to make me fall asleep watching. Then she
must sit in the sun before hauling it back up and altogether I was
enraged and wished I was in a condition to show her how it
should be done. I am at her mercy at the moment though I keep
her and pay her well and might look with justice for harder work
from her, but when I am over my lying-in I will be behind her you
can be sure. She is pleasant enough but how reliable I cannot say
and I am not depending on her for the birth. A woman I know has
given me the name of a midwife who will come and otherwise I

shall have to engage a nurse for the shortest time possible since I cannot be without assistance when my time comes. Ferdinando will return with the Brownings toward the end of October and I pray my delivery will not be before the middle of November. I do little but rest and try to put this house into some sort of order but as yet there is neither pleasure nor profit in it. By next week there will be two rooms ready for occupation but whether I will find takers I do not know or if I will be up to providing the services required. I think of Oreste day and night and weep to think he will be two years of age when this second child is born and of those two years I have had so little. But I feel that I am now in the way of bringing him to me since I have a house and am no longer in service and need only to arrange to have him brought over. Tell him often Ellen that he is to go to Italy soon where his mother and father who love him greatly await him. Tell him Ellen that he might grow accustomed to it.

But would Ellen tell him? She wished desperately that Ellen were in London that she might send Lizzie to judge how Oreste fared and what he understood, but as it was she had no means of knowing. Nothing could be more unsatisfactory than Ellen's barely decipherable notes, which came rarely and only after money had been remitted. On September 1, as soon as she was back in Florence, she had sent £12, almost ten months' wages, to Ellen and had stressed the importance of letting her know such a large sum of money had arrived. A note duly came at the end of September, hurtful in its brevity, frustrating in its lack of information:

—thank you for the money Sister which is put to good use your son being in need of shoes and all manner of apparel since he grows apace. We are well. I hope you are well. The summer has been poor. You need have no worry your son is well cared for as I trust you believe.

Again and again Wilson read it, trying to read some comforting significance into Ellen's twice referring to Oreste as "your son." It was no more than the truth but showed, surely, that her sister was not forgetting the fact. And if Oreste was growing so fast it could only mean he was healthy. But she thought of how, if the positions had been reversed, she would have written pages full of detail to Ellen, would have described a child in such a way as to make him spring from the writing, alive and visible. Oreste, in Ellen's notes, remained hidden from her. He was lost, only the memory of the baby he no longer was having any reality in her mind.

Isa Blagden found her weeping over this one afternoon and took the time to console her, pointing out that soon, in her new position, Oreste would join her and at two years of age would quickly become hers again. Wilson nodded and dried her tears yet again and made some effort to smile. She asked, with some apprehension, how Miss Blagden had left Ferdinando and was told he was well but anxious about her and eager to return to Florence. She also added, without being asked, that Annunciata was not, in Pen's opinion, found to be a substitute for his Lily and that the maid had fallen ill with fever soon after Wilson left and had been useless to anyone. But what Miss Blagden had sought her out for was not only to ask after her welfare or bring news from Lucca but to offer her two lady boarders for three months. The ladies, sisters, were English and looking for somewhere cheap but clean while they stayed on in Florence to attend art classes. Wilson was immediately worried that the rooms she had ready would not be thought adequate, that indeed she did not know if she herself thought they were adequate, and that she would be unable to prepare meals in her feeble condition, but Miss Blagden laid to rest all her anxieties. She inspected the rooms and found them perfectly tolerable and assured Wilson the ladies would require only coffee in the morning and would otherwise dine elsewhere. If Wilson's maid could be guaranteed to clean the rooms each day and deal with washing, which could be sent out, and empty the slops and bring up hot water, then that would suffice.

It was with some excitement that Wilson greeted the Misses Wynne on October 1 and she was aware that the challenge of preparing for them had in some curious way made her feel better. They were younger than she had expected and seemed shy and reticent, emphasizing frequently, all the way up the stairs, that they wanted only a bolt hole and must not be thought of as real boarders. When Wilson was obliged to rest on the stairs, they both begged her not to continue and when she insisted went either side of her, helping her along. The rooms were pronounced charming, which made her smile with amusement, for charming they were not. They were bare and shabby and, if it had not been for the pretty yellow cloths she had made for the tables and the yellow and orange cushions she had covered for the chairs and the blue vase full of roses she had asked Maria to place on the chest of drawers, then they would have been dismal indeed. The Misses Wynne flew to the window and exclaimed in ecstasy over the view of rooftops and more rooftops, and then exclaimed again at their luck in finding somewhere so peaceful and perfect.

Wilson quickly realized how lucky she had been to have the Misses Wynne directed to her by kind Miss Blagden. They could not have been less trouble, leaving the house at ten in the morning and not returning until nine in the evening, having already dined. She hardly saw them, but their presence at night made her feel easier than did Maria's and she slept better. They paid their rent every Friday (the money was put straight into a jar for Oreste's journey) and always inquired if there was any way in which they could be of use to their landlady in her circumstances. They were polite and concerned but only once betrayed any real curiosity. The younger of the two, Miss Violet, said one Friday, with some hesitation, "You were maid, I believe, to Mrs. Browning?"

"Indeed yes, miss."

"And before her marriage, I think?"

"Oh, well before. I went to her in 1844, before ever Mr. Browning appeared on the scene."

Miss Violet clasped her hands together in an anguish of delight and exclaimed, "How romantic! Oh, how I should have liked to be you!"

"To be me?"

"To be near such poets and part of that adventure!"

Wilson was silent. The elder Miss Wynne, Miss Millicent, frowned a little at her sister and was embarrassed. "Violet reads poetry," she offered by way of explanation, "especially Mrs. Browning's. She has whole passages of *Aurora Leigh* by heart, or so it often seems."

"Do you think," Miss Violet said, leaning forward excitedly, "do you think, Signora Romagnoli, *do* you think that one day I might meet Mrs. Browning in this house?"

"Violet!" her sister remonstrated.

"Mrs. Browning does not like visitors," Wilson said, "and as to meeting her, I could not say."

"Of course you could not," Miss Millicent agreed, "and Violet is silly to expect an introduction. Let us forget it at once."

But Wilson did not forget it. On the contrary, the question she saw hovering behind Miss Violet's innocent query remained at the forefront of her mind right up to the day the Brownings returned to the Casa Guidi. The question was, on what footing would she now be with her old mistress? The more she thought about this, the more uncertain she became. Were they to be friends? And if so, how was the friendship between maid and ex-mistress to be defined? She did not know what assumptions she could make. Would she be free to come and go in the Casa Guidi as she liked? Would Pen be allowed to visit her as and when he liked? And what of Ferdinando, her husband? How would they succeed in living together? What would be allowed? Everywhere she looked there were areas of doubt and her apprehension grew.

In every way except one her worries proved unjustified. Both Pen and Ferdinando rushed in immediately the carriage drew up at the door and wonderful was the reunion; then within the hour the kindest of notes came from Mrs. Browning begging her to find the time and energy to visit whenever she was able. Wilson was able straight away. Pausing only to change her dress and smooth her hair, she went into the Casa Guidi, laboriously climbed the stairs and, arriving in the drawing room in some distress through lack of breath, was hastily urged to sit down and put up her feet and take a dish of tea. It was only when the tea came that her pleasure in such a welcome, in being given such evidence of the continuing affection in which she was held, abruptly waned. The tea was brought in by Annunciata. Looking at her, Wilson felt an actual spasm of pain. The girl was not only twice as pretty as she had remembered but graceful and vivacious with the most beautiful smile. But it was not the face or the manner which struck Wilson most so much as the lithesome body. Perhaps because her own was at that time lumpen and awkward she seemed to feel the contrast painfully—such high, generous breasts, such a neat waist, such slender wrists and ankles! Wilson instinctively tucked her own swollen legs more securely under her gown and covered her enormous belly protectively with her arms. Annunciata turned to her, as she put the tea down, and respectfully inquired for her health. The girl's skin glowed, her eyes were bright. It was all Wilson could do to thank her for her concern. And then to watch Annunciata trip back to the kitchen, where her own Ferdinando was preparing supper, was too much. She had difficulty attending to Mrs. Browning's questions and replied in a strained voice. Looking up, she saw her old mistress understood perfectly her misery and confusion and was sorry for it but there was also an air of what looked remarkably like satisfaction about her. It seemed to say that all this inconvenience had ended well and she, Mrs. Browning, had after all gained more than she had lost. Wilson could hardly bear it.

With Pen, there were no such changes in allegiance. If he had had his way, he would have stayed in Wilson's house all day long and, as it was, managed to be there a good half of it. But Wilson played fair— she did not encourage him. Whenever Annunciata came to fetch the child she was firm: he must go at once or otherwise his mother would be displeased and might not allow him to come at all. And this was not simply because she wished to be above reproach: it was also because, nearing her time, she found the eight-year-old boy exhaust-ing. He had not quietened down at all as he had grown older—far from it—and could not now be still for a single moment. He was still pretty, still was obliged to wear his hair in long curls and was attired in the same silks and satins, but underneath all this there was a tougher character emerging. Wilson saw Henry Barrett in him and even a flash of his Grandfather Barrett. Mentioning this once to his mother, she was speedily put right: Pen was *all* his father, lacked entirely the characteristics of those other Barrett males. But when he was with her alone Wilson watched him kicking a ball down her stairs and fight with Ferdinando in her kitchen and knew the time would come when his mother must face facts.

Pen wished, above all else, to see a baby born. To Wilson's embarrassment, he would not leave the subject alone. He cuddled her and felt the bump in a way that made her uneasy as to the propriety of it and asked constantly how this baby was to climb out. What should she say? The normally so frank Mrs. Browning was no help when asked to suggest what should be said. "Birth is a natural event," was all she offered, "and I will tell Pen so." She may have told him but it did not stop the questions. "When the baby is ready," Wilson said, "it will find a way out and if you wish to know more you must ask your mother and father." Whether they explained further she did not know but the questions changed in direction. "*When* will it be born, Lily?" was the next refrain and here she could be truthful. "Nobody knows, only God," she told him, only to be asked if God would divulge the information if prayed to very hard. He wanted a promise that as soon as the baby appeared he should be sent for, "even in the dead of night," so that he might be the first to kiss it. In the event, he very nearly was. This birth was so quick and easy, Wilson could not think it the same process as Oreste's. One moment she was directing Maria in the making of knead cakes, the next she was taken with a sensation of wishing to bear down, no pains preceding it, and had a struggle to get herself to bed and to have Ferdinando and the midwife sent for. Half an hour later her second son emerged, as strong and healthy as the first, and Pen Browning arrived two hours later to go into paroxysms of delight.

Lying in bed that November day, Wilson looked at the baby cradled in her arms and felt dizzy at the sight of his uncanny resemblance to his brother. Only the room she was in and the company she was among marked the difference. All around her were the smiling faces so lacking at Oreste's birth, for Ellen and William could not match the pride of Ferdinando or the ecstasy of Pen, and she felt loved and treasured, not pitifully alone and bereft. Yet the baby, in looking and seeming the same, distressed her. Tears ran down her cheeks as she thought of her firstborn, of how he ought to be here, a part of the family circle. Writing to Ellen as soon as she could manage it, she could not help confessing:

—holding this second baby Ellen puts me in mind more and more of Oreste and I grieve to have him. It is not right we should be parted. In no manner does the birth of this child put the other out of my mind nor can I accept he is a substitute but rather a reminder as if God wished to show me what I have lost and reprimand me for my carelessness. When you tell Oreste that he has been blessed with a brother I beg you to remind him that he is his mother's *firstborn* and as such has pride of place in her heart. We are to christen this child Pilade, being the name of Ferdinando's maternal grandfather whom he wishes to honor. Teach Oreste how to say it. It is pronounced "Pil" as in pill "a" as in the exclamation "ah!" and "de" as in day. The whole together is three syllables and pleasing I think to the tongue.

Mrs. Browning at least thought so. Wilson took the baby in to see her as soon as she was about and he was admired but, she fancied, with some sense of distancing. Mrs. Browning did not wish to hold him, saying she feared her arms were not strong enough and that her cough might disturb him. She coughed, Wilson noticed, all the time, not the hacking, tearing, deep coughs of a bad attack but persistent little coughs, as though trying and failing to clear her throat.

"So are you well, Wilson?" she asked, lying back on the sofa, white and drained-looking.

"I am fair, ma'am."

"Better than I, at any rate."

"Is it the old trouble, ma'am?"

"Oh yes, nothing more. Except the life has gone out of me and in some curious way I hardly care."

"And do you write, ma'am?"

"Write? Good heavens, Wilson, I have nothing to write now, only lines here and there that add up to precious little. If I could take up my pen again and find some hard, satisfying work it would be the better for me."

"Only there is a young lady as lodges with me, who asks me every day what Mrs. Browning writes and is eager to know, for she announces she lives for your poetry."

This produced a laugh which unfortunately brought on such a fit of coughing that Wilson was obliged to put Pilade down and attend to the invalid as though she were still her maid. Relieved, Mrs. Browning did at least say, "You are the best of nurses, dear, and I miss your skill."

"It is nothing, ma'am, and I am glad to assist you. If ever you should need me I will come, night or day, and gladly."

Then she saw Mrs. Browning's eyes fill with tears and her hand was pressed. Annunciata, coming in singing with coffee, was reprimanded for causing a headache to begin on that instant and Wilson could not help feeling triumphant.

But she knew perfectly well it was a foolish and misplaced sense of petty triumph, for the old order had changed irrevocably. Though she might be an ever welcome visitor in the Casa Guidi, though the traffic between the two houses might be unrestricted, she saw all too clearly by the start of that New Year of 1858 that her part in the Brownings' life was peripheral. She felt excluded from their world even though she could not have been better informed; the trouble was, Ferdinando still belonged to that world. He came to spend the night, by agreement, twice a week and she saw him every day but there was no denying that he seemed a visitor and never a member of her household. What concerned her did not truly concern him, however much she sought to involve him. He did not want to be bothered with the problems she encountered, with water that seemed brackish or ceilings that had cracked—they were her concerns and, as she complained in a letter to Minnie:

—I am driven to distraction with those household concerns with which you will be familiar Minnie but then in your case you have but to report them for them to be seen to by the master who will instruct the butler to bring in workmen and I am obliged to go out and seek my own help which is no easy thing. The landlord is abroad and the caretaker seems to have no power to maintain these dilapidated premises. In other ways I suppose I could be said to prosper tolerably well. I have this day bid farewell to the Misses Wynne, two English ladies who have been as friends to me and I am sorry to see them go, and have taken in Miss Hawarth, an old friend of Mr. Browning's together with two other ladies who will stay until Easter. I am pleased to have ladies since they are more comfortable to be with and understand better the difficulties I labor under with a young baby and poor help and no husband constantly at my elbow. But I tell you Minnie, for all the independence, *I had rather have my old job back and be in service with Mrs. Browning.* I daresay you find this strange and may think I am ungrateful when after all I have been given the chance to set up for myself which is not given to many of our station but it is a surprise to me too. I have upon my shoulders so many cares as a landlady that I feel bowed down whereas, and I do not think my memory faults me, I was freer as a maid. It would be otherwise if I had my husband with me and my firstborn but as it is I feel neither one thing or the other. There is more to running a boardinghouse than ever you would think Minnie and hardest of all is the impossibility of finding reliable and trustworthy staff who are not forever thinking of themselves first in a way we would not have dared.

But bit by bit Wilson became aware that she had some small skill in the matter of keeping a boardinghouse and that her future, and her family's, might indeed lie in that direction. She seemed, at any rate, to satisfy lodgers. The Misses Wynne sent two other ladies, rather considerably older than themselves, with a heavy recommendation and they in turn sent a widow and her daughter. Miss Hawarth likewise procured several paying guests, moving Wilson to declare she could not imagine why any lady would wish to lodge in her poorly decorated and furnished house when they might find themselves a place a good deal more attractive and comfortable. "Ah, Wilson," Miss Hawarth had said with a smile, "the keeper is more important than the house and then there are your connections, you know." "Connections?" she had echoed, entirely bewildered. "Why, yes, dear, you *are* the good friend of the Brownings." And so it seemed. Lady after lady breathed heavier when Pen dashed in and out, and on the days when Wilson was a little late with the supper—which she now undertook to provide—on account of having been delayed taking tea with Mrs. Browning there was not a word of complaint but only a diffident inquiry as to how the venerable poetess had seemed. If it had not been for the shamelessness of it, Wilson felt she might have been sorely tempted to exploit this extraordinary advantage.

As it was, she concentrated on organizing her household to better effect. Her days were very full. She now had a girl to watch over Pilade and, as well as the still indolent Maria, another young woman, rather more energetic, who fulfilled the combined roles of house- and parlormaid. Wilson sent the washing out and did the cooking and marketing herself. It gave her great satisfaction that after a couple of months she proved as expert as Ferdinando, learning rapidly how to drive a hard bargain. Ferdinando, she came to see, had never done that, however much the Brownings were convinced he did. Watching him in the market, she saw how popular he was, and certainly he had an eye for the best produce on offer, but when it came to the exchange of cash he parted with it too readily. She saw women, old gnarled Italian housewives, who did not care about popularity, who were quite composed in the face of sour looks, getting fruit and vegetables and even meat at a quarter the price paid by her affable husband and she resolved to become one of these women. She let Ferdinando teach her how to judge an aubergine ripe and a chicken fresh and then she copied those older women she had seen for the rest. She learned to keep her face absolutely still, not to smile, and to look as if, on the brink of completing a bargain, she was going to walk away in disgust. At first her face burned and she was often defeated in her purpose but within a few weeks she was indistinguishable from the seasoned bargainers. Ferdinando did not like it. The market people passed comments on his wife and, he said, threw doubt on his ability to better her. He frowned when reporting this and said it was not good that she should be so hard. He preferred her, he said, to be the gentle creature he had married.

Wilson, telling Mrs. Browning of this, laughed. "Gentle, indeed!"

she said. "And if I were as gentle in the market as I have been for him at home, how does he think I would manage?"

"All men wish all women to be gentle," Mrs. Browning commented, "just as all women wish men to be strong, and to alter this we must first start with our sons and what they are brought up to. We ought not to admire them when they put up their fists and fight or mock them when they are afraid and tell them they must be a *man.*" Wilson looked doubtful. It was not at all the response she wanted, but Mrs. Browning was again in full flow. "Penini knows I think it good that he is considerate and sensitive—he has been brought up to see no merit in violence, and when he is a man he will be as his father, entirely lacking in those so-called manly virtues of domination and arrogance toward women." There was a pause and before Wilson could think how to reply, she added, "But I may never see him as a man," in a low voice.

"Oh, now come, ma'am, do not speak so. You are stronger than you were and, with summer arriving, you will once more pick up."

"Pick up? Perhaps." There was no confidence in her answer. Wilson saw the doubt in her eyes and the droop of her body and felt a shiver pass through her own. It was easy to keep promising that some sun and heat would work its usual miracle but it had been a hard, cold winter and almost everyone had suffered from influenza, Mrs. Browning worst of all. It seemed a long time since she had been out of her apartment, longer still since she had taken a walk. Wilson knew that some visiting Americans had let it be widely known in Florence that they considered Mrs. Browning little more than a ghost and though she had laughed such gossip to scorn she now saw there was perhaps real cause for alarm. "What you need, ma'am," she suddenly said, "is a holiday, a proper holiday."

"I know, and I have plans to have it, if I can but gather the energy in a month or two."

It was awhile before these plans were divulged and, when they were, Wilson's first reaction was one of alarm. The Brownings, it appeared were going to France, to some seaside place, in Brittany perhaps, where they would be joined by members of both their families, somewhere new, somewhere stimulating away from the tired attractions of Lucca. All very well, but did it mean Ferdinando would be taken with them, together with Annunciata? It was all she wanted to know and did not dare ask directly. What wounded her was her husband's indifference. When she pointed out that this might mean she would be on her own yet again throughout another summer he shrugged and said it could not be helped and he had no choice. She boiled at his lack of thought for her and replied, louder than she had intended, that indeed he had, that, unlike last year, there was a choice. Then she brought him her account book, which she had kept faithfully from the first day of opening her house, and showed him the state of things. Since the Brownings' present had paid the year's rent and since she had managed the household so economically there was an actual income, growing monthly, from the boarders, upon which they could live. If Ferdinando left the Brownings' service and came in with her, adopting his rightful position, then she could manage even better and take more boarders and they would be self-supporting besides living together always.

No one could have mistaken the hesitation in his manner. She could see his brain struggling to find an escape route and that he should want one hurt and shocked her. She watched him, waited scornfully and yet was taken unawares when he blurted out, "And Oreste? The money we remit to England, to your sister? It would not be possible." It would not indeed. All of Ferdinando's wages went to Ellen, save for the smallest amount he kept for his personal pleasure. Often, she had felt for him as they both stood in front of Mr. Browning as the money order was made. "All, Ferdinando?" Mr. Browning would ask him and he would nod, but squeeze her hand and hang his head. She had always told him how proud she was of him, that he should work so hard to support his son in a far-off country, and how one day she would tell Oreste it was due to his father's efforts that he had been so well looked after. Now, if he left service, it was true they would no longer be able to afford to remit the regular payments. What was she asking him to do? To throw over that stability she had insisted they must have. It was too soon to do so. In September another year's rent must be paid and the money for that would not this time come from the Brownings. Writing to Ellen, she could not help but be bitter, remarking:

all life seems a trap again Ellen and I expect it has too often seemed so to you and will yet. However hard I work and struggle for the future there are ever snares to catch me and sometimes I see no end to it and think myself doomed to pass my days in toil and nothing else. All of which you will be tired of hearing but it has been brought about by my great fear that my husband will be taken off by the Brownings once more, this time to France and there is nothing we can do to prevent it they being the masters of our fate. But I am resolved that if it must be so I will obtain permission from the Brownings to have my husband journey to England at the end of the holiday and bring his son back with him. He would not need above four days' leave from them and since Oreste is now or will be by then nearly three which is the age Pen first traveled at I cannot see any reason why he need inconvenience the party. The more I think on it the more I see that this cruel sentence may yet be turned to advantage and may be God's way of effecting what I most desire and have been unable to bring about. I will write again as soon as Ferdinando hears he is to go and when I do you must prepare Oreste for the change Ellen so that it is not sprung on him.

But before the decision had been made Wilson was astonished to receive the speediest reply she had ever had from Ellen and quite the longest. She wrote, with an unaccustomed fluency, which made her sister wonder if the words had been thought up by her alone, that

—it would not be good for Oreste to leave here at this moment since he has been ill and though he is making a good recovery the doctor who you can be sure I was quick to call and no expense being spared but your money put to good use has said it would injure his general well-being to travel in his weakened state. He has said the change in diet and water would be calamitous and that he ought to rest where all is familiar for six months or more. I tell you this sister only that you may be warned and not endanger your dear son's health or put your husband to an unnecessary and useless journey.

Wilson was certainly warned—warned instantly by the absurd nature of the letter, of Ellen's sense of panic. It was all too obvious what her plot was and she went straight away to see Mrs. Browning, resolved to ask outright if Ferdinando was to go to France and if so to plead her case. She was at first misunderstood.

"Why, Wilson," Mrs. Browning said, opening her eyes wide, "it had not occurred to me, nor I am sure to my husband, to think Ferdinando might not go with us. How would we manage, dear? He is our servant, we depend upon him."

"Ma'am, I wish only to know."

"Then I think you must take it that you do know."

To Mrs. Browning's clear surprise, Wilson smiled and looked pleased. "Then, ma'am, I beg of you, let Ferdinando go to England and bring home our son." Rapidly, she outlined her plan, stressing the ease of it all and the perfect opportunity it represented to right what she must surely agree was a manifest wrong. "And if those four days he will need to collect Oreste were to come off Ferdinando's own holiday, which he would not take again, then you would lose nothing, ma'am, if you please."

There was a dead silence. Mrs. Browning put down her teacup and cleared her throat. Wilson waited, not sure how to interpret the sudden change of atmosphere. Carefully, Mrs. Browning dabbed at the corners of her mouth with a handkerchief. Still she said nothing.

Desperately, Wilson burst out, "I hope I have not spoken out of turn, ma'am, I hope I have not given offense?"

"I am admittedly a little taken aback, Wilson," Mrs. Browning finally said, her eyes lowered and concentrating on the empty cup. "There is a great deal to take in in what you have said, too much to be done all in a moment. I will have to speak to my husband and consider carefully with him. Such an agreement could not be undertaken lightly."

"No, ma'am. When might I look for an answer? Only I would wish to tell my sister as soon as possible and put paid to her nonsense."

"I really cannot say, Wilson. All is confusion as to our precise plans as yet. I only wish I was clear as to what we will do myself, you may be sure."

Yet the answer came speedily, the very next day, and was a shock. The party would leave for France at the beginning of July and Ferdinando would not be of it. He was told this and not Wilson. When he came to tell her, thinking she would be pleased (though, as he knew she suspected, he was not exactly pleased himself), she stared at him in disbelief and said over and over, "Not go? Not go?" like a parrot. He spread his hands wide in a gesture of incomprehension and invited her to make of this unexpected turn of events what she could. To his dismay, she wept and only then did he hear of the plan with which she had gone to Mrs. Browning. Then he too was distressed, seeing how it would all have fitted in. "Now I must write to Ellen," Wilson sobbed, "and she will think I have bowed to her wishes and feel even more the mistress of the situation." Wiping her tears with the corner of her apron and clutching the baby to her, she searched for the reasons for this *volte-face*. What had she done? What had she said? Over and over she asked the questions and became so demented by them that, though she trembled with indignation, she once more went into the Casa Guidi and, controlling herself as best she could, asked to see her old mistress. Annunciata, with evident enjoyment, said Mrs. Browning had the headache and could see no one. "I have *nursed* her with the headache," Wilson said, "it is nothing to me or to her." Back the maid went, only to reappear shaking her head sorrowfully and saying this headache was so very bad as to quite incapacitate the invalid and render her unfit even for Wilson. Just as she was turning to go, shaking with mortification, Mr. Browning came out of his room and said, "Ah, Wilson," and she turned, her face working with the effort of trying to calm herself. He saw her state at once and without another word took her arm and led her into the little sitting room.

"Now come, Wilson," he said, "sit down and let us talk about this sensibly."

They talked sensibly, for full half an hour, but at the end of it Wilson felt neither clearer nor happier, only numb. Mr. Browning had expressed himself surprised that she had failed to recognize and acknowledge the consideration for herself and her well-being which had influenced their decision about Ferdinando. Had they not remembered her misery at being in Florence alone, without him, the previous summer? Of course they had, and remembering had made them examine their arrangements more closely to see if they could not do without their manservant. They had known it was not right to separate a man from his wife for several months when she had a young baby and a business, in a manner of speaking, to care for. And now this was the thanks they got, these tears of hers, this dismay at what they had trusted would be hailed as good news.

"I ask you, Wilson," Mr. Browning said, gentle but aggrieved, "what did you expect of us?"

She sat with bowed head for a moment, then looked directly at him and replied, "It is only my child, sir, the wanting of my child, and suddenly seeing a way to get him, and then it being taken away. I am confused, sir."

Mr. Browning shifted uncomfortably. "Certainly," he said, "it is hard to be separated from your first child. I have often thought so. But you could not in all honesty, Wilson, expect us to make that our first consideration."

"No, sir. But it seemed, sir, when first I talked to Mrs. Browning, before ever I mentioned my plan, or else I would not have mentioned it, it seemed Ferdinando *was* to go, that there was no choice, that he was nigh essential to your comfort, and then, having spoken out, to find he was not and therefore he would not go and my plan was to come to nothing—it is hard to understand, sir."

"Our plans changed, Wilson, and my wife had not kept pace with them. We need to be as small a party as possible in order to accommodate in one house, one holiday house we shall rent, all of us and members of our respective families, do you see?"

"Yes, sir."

"Well, then, there is no mystery after all. And to look on the bright side, you will have your husband with you throughout the summer and I daresay you will enjoy it very much."

She could not say, at the end of it, that she had. She could not even say she truly felt she had had Ferdinando with her those four months. What precisely he did with himself all day long she never could fathom, but he was not in her company above two hours or so each day. He made great play of all the tasks in the Casa Guidi he had been left to do—furniture to repair, decorations to see to—but to Wilson's experienced eye they would not have occupied an energetic person more than a month at the most. But then Ferdinando was no longer energetic. The fearful heat of the city seemed to encourage him to sleep half his time away and she had never felt more English than when she observed his devotion that summer to the long siesta. And he drank. Living with the Brownings, his intake had been modest but, living with her, it rapidly increased. She did not provide him with wine, to be sure, but he took it in the *caffè* he frequented, a *caffè* where politics were argued over far into the night and the arguers fell asleep at the table. Often he came home exhausted at dawn and slept the whole of the day away. Her anger grew and with it she became shrewish. It horrified her to hear her own voice screaming at her husband for his indolence but she could not help herself. At least Ferdinando's reaction was to be penitent and vow he would not visit the *caffè* again.

Only with Pilade did he act as she would wish a husband and father to act. With the baby, he was gentleness itself, playing with him and caring for him with true devotion. On the evenings when the three of them went abroad together, the worst of the heat over, Wilson felt more content than at any other time, more part of a family. Ferdinando, a clean white blouse on and freshly shaved, looked the handsome fellow who had first attracted her, and the way he carried his son, with ease and pride, made her feel warm toward him. No Englishman, she fancied, would bear his child in quite such a way. And she knew herself to look better, clad in what passed for finery these days, than she did in the house where, with so much work to do, she had not a moment to spare for her appearance. Those evenings were the good times, when she did not question so fiercely what she was making of her life. Otherwise, day after day, a restlessness had seized her again, a restlessness she remembered of old and of which she had learned to be afraid. It was harder than ever to face up to its cause. Did she not now have a husband, a child, a home? So why should she be plagued once more with feelings of frustration? What did she want, apart from Oreste?

Always, she came back to that, with some relief: everything could be explained by her yearning for her other child, the root of all her discontent. But even as she was citing this as the reason, citing it only to herself, she was wondering whether it were true. Suppose, by some miracle, Oreste was brought to her—would she then be happy? Was that all it would take to banish the feeling of gloom which so often half incapacitated her? It was no good confiding in Ferdinando, who merely stared at her as though she were mad, should she even begin to confess her inner dissatisfaction. Life to him was simple: food, wine, sleep, love, and as little work as decently possible. Of the love, she knew he was growing tired but since her own ardor had considerably diminished after Pilade's birth she was not disposed to criticize him for this. They were now an old married couple and it was to be expected. But she did not like the way his eye followed a pretty girl, or the way theirs could sometimes follow him. His appetite for all the other necessities of life had increased and she suspected his carnal instincts were merely turned in another direction. This seemed, more than anything, to symbolize the difference between them. It made her grow cold to think what her marriage might become.

And then, in September, three weeks before the Brownings returned, she received a letter which changed everything. It was black-edged and addressed in Ellen's hand, the very communication she had always dreaded and feared. Terror gripped her so completely that she was incapable of opening it and let it fall to the floor where she very nearly followed it in a faint. She remembered Mother's compassion in saving her from the certain shock of such evil envelopes. But though the blood was pounding in her head and her vision was blurred she managed to take up the envelope again and lie down with it on her bed. It was midmorning, the sun not quite at its highest, the rooms still bearable, with every shutter and curtain now closed ready for the afternoon glare. Pilade was asleep, Ferdinando in the Casa Guidi supervising the painting of Mr. Browning's study. She could hear Maria clattering about with her water buckets in the yard and far off church bells ringing somewhere north of the Arno. She found herself thinking that when she had forced herself to read how and when Oreste had died she would take her sleeping baby and drown both him and herself forthwith. She would do it at night when it would be the easiest thing in the world. All her agitation of the summer she suddenly saw as moving toward this end—she had known, without knowing it, of this tragedy, she had been what her old mistress had called "pre-sentimental." And now she was quite prepared and calm and ready to end it all. Opening the letter carefully, her hands were quite steady and her eyes focused on Ellen's words without difficulty. Only they were not the words she had expected: it was William who had died. Oreste was well.

It was a sign and she accepted it as such. She got off her bed resolute and determined. Life, her life, the lives of Oreste and Pilade and Ferdinando, must be valued. Oreste had been spared and it could only be for a purpose. Swiftly, she wrote to Ellen, exclaiming at

—the cruelty of this my poor sister when you have had so much to bear. I weep to hear of this latest affliction and so unexpected with him in the prime of his life and never an illness and being a big strong man. I do not rightly understand how the medical men could not save him after the accident since you say the cut seemed small and did not appear to trouble him but I have heard that for the blood to be poisoned it takes only a pinprick and that a cut where there is manure about can have this effect if not noticed. Ellen, I would that you could come to me now that you are alone and would ask you to consider it seriously. What is there to keep you in that sorry place? It is not your real home, you have no family together. We are only two of us now and we ought to be closer. Think, Ellen, what Mother would have advised. Why not, dear, sell the house and come with Oreste to us?

It was the perfect solution. Eagerly, Wilson waited for an answer, quite convinced of what it would be.

CHAPTER TWENTY-SIX

The moment the Brownings returned—Mrs. Browning looking, Wilson thought, rather worse than better after her French holiday—Ferdinando reformed. It was galling to her to observe his change in demeanor. There were no more sustained bouts of drinking, no more hanging around the *caffè*, and he was altogether brisker and more efficient. At least when he was not with her she now knew where he was but the comfort this brought her was not as complete as it might have been because he was also with Annunciata during those times. The girl had changed. Four months in France had quietened her down and at the same time given her a veneer of sophistication quite lacking before. Wilson smiled to see it, a trifle grimly. Hadn't it happened to her, in her own day? Annunciata had eyes and ears and both had been busy conveying subtle messages. Whereas before she had been a rough-and-ready Italian peasant, flashing with high spirits, now she thought a little about how she seemed to others and tempered her boisterous good humor. She walked rather than ran, smiled rather than laughed out loud, dropped her eyes instead of staring frankly. The effect was extraordinary. All the natural grace in her now flowed through her body, unspoiled by her bursts of youthful energy. She was quite beautiful.

Mrs. Browning was as aware of this as Wilson and indeed appeared to find nothing hurtful in mentioning it. Watching Annunciata remove her coffee cup, she remarked to Wilson, "You will hardly recognize Annunciata, Wilson. Has she not improved out of all recognition?"

"Indeed she has."

"We have tamed her on our travels, I think, and yet not taken from her that which is precious."

"Precious?"

"Her youth, Wilson, the most precious thing of all, you will agree."

Wilson hesitated only a moment. "Why, no, ma'am, I don't know that it is the most precious thing of all, if I understand you rightly. There are things dearer to me, at any rate, than lost youth."

Mrs. Browning was amused. "Are you sure, Wilson? What can be more precious than life itself, and if one is youthful there is more of it."

"I had rather have the certainties of middle age, ma'am."

"You are *not* middle aged, so how can you know this? And it is a loathsome term, I detest it. One is young or one is mature and that is all there is to it."

She spoke with such vehemence, Wilson thought it better not to risk a reply, though in her head she practiced saying what nonsense she thought Mrs. Browning spoke. But then she had always reacted strangely to the subject of aging, had always feared it. As if reading her thoughts, Mrs. Browning then said, "It is not that I am afraid of dying, you know. I have no fear, knowing it is but a passing from one world to another. But the mask of age is ugly to me. I like to have young people about me."

"Children, ma'am?"

"Especially children. Your own Pilade is a pleasure to me, Wilson. Such a fine child, so like his father."

"I hope he will grow to be finer than his father, may God bless him."

"You say that with some feeling, Wilson? Finer than his father? What can that mean? I wish nothing more for Pen than that he should be *as* fine as his father."

"It is different, ma'am."

"In what way?"

"You are satisfied Mr. Browning *is* fine. I wish I were satisfied my Ferdinando is."

"Wilson! What disloyalty is this? What cause can you have for such doubt?"

"Oh, cause enough."

"But Ferdinando is the very model of a servant."

"He is not the very model of a husband."

"Ought you to be saying this, dear? Will you not regret it?"

"There is nothing to regret. I have said nothing, only that my husband is lacking in perfection, I believe."

How they had got onto this Wilson could not remember, but Mrs. Browning was the more worried. If it had not been for a visitor arriving then and her being obliged to leave instantly, she had no doubt they would have waded into deeper waters and she knew she would not have been sorry. But as it was, Mrs. Eckley was announced and Wilson stood up. She was not quick enough to be out of the room before Mrs. Eckley was in it and found herself trapped by her between chair and door. She dropped a curtsy and was waiting to be allowed through the door when Mrs. Eckley said, "Is this not Wilson, whom I have heard so much about, Ba?" The use of "Ba" registered with Wilson more than her own name—she had not realized Mrs. Eckley was on such familiar terms.

"Why, yes," Mrs. Browning said from her sofa, "but surely you are acquainted?"

"I believe not," Mrs. Eckley said and to Wilson's surprise held out her hand. "How do you do, Wilson?"

"Well, ma'am, thank you."

Her hand was retained and to her astonishment given the slightest but most certain squeeze. Wilson did not presume to squeeze back. She suddenly felt in a great hurry to escape, instinctively disliking this pretty, richly dressed young American. But it seemed

Mrs. Eckley had no intention of allowing her to take her leave yet. "Ba," she said, "did you not say Wilson was in the way of being in touch?"

Bewildered, Wilson turned and saw Mrs. Browning had colored and seemed embarrassed.

"We had some success, one winter, in Rome and that is all," she said.

"More success than we have had?"

"No, no. It was not at all the same thing. You must let Wilson go, Sophie, she has much to do."

So that was the attraction of this unlikely friendship. Pondering what she had just heard, Wilson went home, wondering if Mr. Browning felt the same distrust of Mrs. Eckley as she did. Questioning Ferdinando when next she saw him, she grew exasperated with his inability to notice anything at all. He had no idea how often Mrs. Eckley came or how long she stayed or what Mr. Browning thought. It was, he said, his job to cook and see to his master's clothes and open the door and go marketing, not to be a spy. All he knew was that the Eckleys were lending the Brownings their best carriage so they might travel the more comfortably to Rome for the winter. Wilson froze. All speculation about Mrs. Eckley disappeared from her mind. "Rome?" she echoed. Ferdinando obligingly repeated his piece of news without seeming to think it was either of interest or importance. "Rome," he said, "for the winter. My master is anxious to take my mistress south as soon as possible."

"And you? What of you? Is it to be as before? Does Annunciata go and you stay?" He shrugged, spread his hands in the usual gesture, did not seem to care. But Wilson knew the answer without inquiring any further. Of course Ferdinando would be taken to Rome. Rome was not France, he would be essential in Rome, and if they took him with Annunciata she knew what would happen in no time at all and how it would leave her.

She had not had an answer from Ellen but she could not wait. That very evening, leaving Pilade asleep, she went into the Casa Guidi and formally requested an interview with Mr. and Mrs. Browning.

Ferdinando stared at her as though she had gone mad. "What am I to say?" he whispered.

"What I have just told you," she answered sharply. "Go, ask." She took care to remain on the threshold while he did so.

After a moment Mr. Browning came out of the drawing room. "Wilson? What is this? You stand on such ceremony, at this hour?"

"I wish to speak with you, sir."

"Then speak. Come, come through. My wife is already prepared for bed but then you are no stranger to that."

She followed him through the drawing room and into the bedroom where Mrs. Browning, a thick shawl around her shoulders, sat up in bed. She was relieved to see no sign of Pen, before whom she would not have wished to speak freely. Mr. Browning drew up a chair for her, as nice as could be, and sat down himself. He folded his arms, yawned, begged their pardon and smiled. "Do begin, Wilson," he encouraged her, as though she had promised an entertainment. She felt awkward sitting down but, since she had been bidden to do so, could not choose to stand. Twisting her handkerchief in her lap, she began straight away by saying, "I believe you are to go to Rome soon, sir, ma'am?"

Mr. Browning, with an expression on his face that said he guessed what this was about and it did not please him, nodded. "Go on, Wilson, though it may not be of any use."

"No, sir. It is, sir, ma'am, that I would wish to return to your service and come with you."

Mrs. Browning gave an exclamation of astonishment—a great breathing-out and almost a groan that came with it—and Mr. Browning simply stared at her in disbelief.

"Come with us? But your child, Wilson, and your house. Do you hear what you are saying? Are you *thinking*?"

"Yes, sir, I have thought deeply and I have a plan. My sister Ellen, sir, who has had charge of my firstborn this three long years, her husband William died of blood poisoning in September and she is now alone and I have written even before I heard of the plan to go to Rome to beg her to come out here to me with Oreste and if she does, as I think she will, having no other family or ties, then she might look after my house and other child for the winter and we would all profit without further trouble."

There was a silence so complete she could hear the slight rasp in Mrs. Browning's chest, a rasp that broke into a cough she seemed to welcome. Her husband leaped to give her a glass of water and Wilson to help her sit upright. When the fit was over none of them knew how to act.

"It was the shock," Mrs. Browning murmured. "Such a plan, Wilson!"

Mr. Browning paced about and then said, "You place us in a difficult position, Wilson, and one we can hardly approve. To take you, a married woman and mother, away from your child when you have grieved so sorely for the other does not make sense. If, as you say, your sister will come and bring Oreste, then surely you have achieved your dearest wish? How could you then leave, leave *both* children?"

"Only for the winter, sir."

"Robert," Mrs. Browning broke in, "that has little to do with it, you are forgetting Annunciata, dear. How could we set her aside? We are not even able to consider this extraordinary offer."

But Mr. Browning had become fascinated and ignored his wife's point. "Wilson," he said firmly, "what lies behind this? Why should you choose, if you could, and I do not say that you could, to leave your children? And why would you wish to become a maid once more when you have risen higher? It does not seem sensible."

"It is not, sir," she said calmly, "but I am driven to it. If my husband goes to Rome, then it is all up with me."

"Up with you? I miss your meaning entirely."

"He will succumb to temptation, sir."

"Oh, come, Wilson—think better of the man than that. Why, Ferdinando is the most dutiful, most loyal . . ."

"He is a man, sir, and Annunciata is a beautiful young woman."

"Take care, Wilson, these are serious accusations."

"I accuse no one, sir. I only say he is a man and will act like a man, given the chance. He is human and so is she and all the marriage certificates in the world would not keep him faithful if he were tempted in those circumstances."

"It is a simple case of jealousy," Mrs. Browning said quietly, "and we can have nothing to do with it. And since you push the issue, Wilson, my husband is a man too—no, Robert, let me finish—he is a man too and subject to like temptation and to the charge of masculine appetites and yet I do not doubt his fidelity, wherever he goes. Cannot you have the same faith, Wilson? Cannot your love conquer this jealousy? You are Ferdinando's wife, he is the father of your sons, is that not enough to make you trust in him?"

Wilson smiled, pityingly, and folded her arms. How superior she suddenly felt to that woman in the bed, the woman whom she had so long admired, even idolized, but who knew little of human nature after all. It hardly mattered what her own husband did or did not do when his wife languished in bed, an invalid. Perhaps Mr. Browning was entirely above reproach, though there were those who saw him constantly at Isa Blagden's and thought that friendship promised more; perhaps he was able to subdue the desires of a healthy man in his prime, but Ferdinando would not be able to if temptation was set in his way. And consider, as Mrs. Browning had never done, the close proximity in which servants lived in these rented apartments—it was very often more than flesh could stand. So she smiled on and stood there and in exasperation Mrs. Browning said, "I do not know that we should continue this discussion, Wilson. I think it better if you leave us now."

"Then there is no hope?"

"That is a touch melodramatic, surely. If you mean will we consider your desire to return to our service, then I am afraid not. It is impossible."

"Ferdinando could leave us," Mr. Browning said suddenly. "He would have no difficulty finding another situation in Florence."

"Must you show such generosity, Robert? Is there any need for self-denial of this order?"

"He will not leave, ma'am," Wilson broke in, quite matter-of-fact. "He is devoted, as all of us are. He must go and I must lose my husband and that is all there is to it. That is the way of things, the way the world works."

She saw a look of real dislike cross Mrs. Browning's face, quickly followed by an expression of exasperation. Mr. Browning motioned his wife to be quiet and, taking Wilson's arm, conducted her to the door, saying something to the effect that she must not give way to gloomy thoughts and that doubtless she was tired with a young baby still nursing and a house to run. She might even, he suggested, as they went to the stairs, benefit from a quiet winter with her sister to help and think what joy lay ahead with Oreste brought to her at last. She allowed herself to be shown out, allowed herself to be talked to but said not a word. It was her old mistress from whom she had hoped for much, woman to woman, and none of his soothing phrases meant anything to her. As she descended the stairs, she appreciated for the first time how far she had fallen from grace. She had suspected in Lucca, all those months ago, that Mrs. Browning no longer cared for her as once she had done but she saw that it was worse than that: she was a nuisance, plain and simple. Someone who annoyed with her need for sympathy, who irritated with her shameless display of pathos. They wanted to be rid of her, would be glad to go to Rome and leave her miserable face behind. And as for Ferdinando, he would do what he was told, always. Lacking in initiative, he would be obedient and obedience to employers came before that to his wife. Besides, Florence was dull in the winter, even for a Florentine. Who would forgo the chance of a winter in Rome, the center of things? No, there was no hope of her husband exploding with rage at the thought of leaving her and swearing that he would find a way to remain. She did not even expect it.

And then the letter came from Ellen and her world seemed to darken further. Ellen was emphatic:

—I could not take myself to a Foreign Land as you did Lily and never wanted such a thing and though you would be there that alone would in no way satisfy me and I should be afraid. I will end my days in my own country and that is certain. Nor could I contemplate the journey which fills me with fear near to fainting.

As for Oreste, he talks fluently now and it is of course English and there would be much confusion for him. We are well and have no worries being happy together and not in need William leaving me better provided for than ever I had expected. Your money is spent only on Oreste you can be assured for I have enough. I work at the big house taking Oreste with me it is kitchen work and not difficult and gives me extra. So do not look for us coming Lily but think rather of you coming home if you have a mind.

Wilson's disappointment was matched only by her horror at Ellen's suggestion—never would she return to East Retford. But what alarmed and frightened her most and had her leaping for her pen was this talk of "us," of Oreste and Ellen being a pair who were "happy together" and would never come to Italy. In anger she wrote:

—whatever *you* have a mind to do Ellen it is not for you to dictate Oreste's future and I confess I was disturbed to have you write as though he were your son and not mine, *which he is and you know you cannot keep him* and that it would be wrong. Next summer when Pilade is weaned which I will do long before then I am determined to come myself to England if there is no other way and bring my son back here and I have started saving toward it. As for the English speaking, a child of far more than three has no difficulty learning Italian and is so far from being wedded to the tongue he has begun with that he forgets it within a few months so do not say to me that is an obstacle. You will perhaps be affronted by my frankness Ellen but I am distressed and if you were to think on it you would understand. I am besides about to be deserted by my husband, who is to go this next week to Rome to prepare the way for the Brownings. That would be loss enough if I watched him go with only longing for him in my heart but there is instead a bitterness because he is happy to go life there being preferable to here where there is only his tired wife for company. I do not know how I shall manage this winter and dread it not for the weather which is rarely fierce, but for the loneliness. There will be no one to speak with except Miss Blagden for a month or two when she comes to inspect the Casa Guidi before leaving Florence herself and otherwise not a solitary congenial soul. I have only two boarders, both of whom leave before Christmas, and I am not likely to replace them easily. It is a struggle Ellen and no mistake and though I have been thrifty as Mother brought us all up to be and the rent is paid for the next year I am hard put to pay wages and still eat and keep warm.

At least warmth was no trouble. The moment Ferdinando left, with only the most cursory of farewells, to go by train and boat to Rome in advance of the main party, the icy wind which had swept through the city most unexpectedly throughout October suddenly dropped and it was as if it were summer again. On the morning of November 18, when Wilson stood in the street to wave goodbye to the Brownings, it was hot enough for her to want to move into the shade as soon as they had gone. And that was what it was, a move altogether into the shade. She trailed back into her house, carrying Pilade, and felt the shadows of the entrance hall which greeted her were merciful. She sought out the darkest room and even then closed the shutters, though it was only early morning, and lay on her bed without energy even to feed her son. Meanwhile, in her mind, she had visions of the Brownings rattling along in high good humor with all manner of beautiful vistas to right and left as they trotted to Arezzo and she could hear the conversation and Pen's excited laughter. In another moment she saw Ferdinando waiting in Rome, standing on the doorstep, his arms open in welcome and a welcome most of all for Annunciata. How thrilled the girl had been to be going to the Holy City, how lovely she had looked in a jacket of scarlet silk, a birthday present given only the day before by Mrs. Browning, how she had glowed and shivered with anticipation. . . . All that was over for her. This was her place now, alone in a darkened room with no one to care what became of her. What had she done to deserve such punishment?

The idea that she was being punished began to obsess her and she could think of nothing else the whole winter. She *must* have done something for which she was now being made to pay. Spending most of each day in the house, she had no one except Maria to talk to and Maria was not worth the effort. She would rather talk to Pilade, though she knew this was only a sophisticated way of talking to herself. The child at least seemed to listen. As she bathed him, soaping the fat little limbs with a slow, caressing movement almost hypnotic in nature, she told him how lost she felt, how she no longer knew who she was or where she was and how all that mattered to her was him. He was her sole reason for getting up at all, the only incentive to clothe and feed herself and drag herself from her bedroom where she would much prefer to stay. Pilade did not even splash in reply. He gazed up at her, huge brown eyes unblinking, and made little, soft, dovelike noises she believed designed to encourage her. When she breast-fed him, which she still did though he was now a year old, the comfort of it made her weep and in weeping she felt happier. She would let him stay at the breast long after the milk had gone and the gentle, pulling movement as he continued to suck, though he was no longer hungry, was soothing. He was a quiet baby, watchful, with a stillness about him which, if he had not been able to crawl and stand and almost walk, would have been a cause for concern. "He is an angel," people told her and that winter she began to think he really might be.

An angel. Sent down from heaven for what purpose? To show her the evil of her ways, the evil for which she was being punished. Never an assiduous Bible reader, though while Mother was alive she used to read a few verses for her sake, she now began to turn to it more and more in search of enlightenment but her head swam when she tried to read. Her eyes leaped from Abraham begat Isaac and Isaac begat Jacob to verse 25 of the first chapter of the Gospel According to St. Matthew, to which she had turned simply because it began the New Testament and she had been unable to make anything of the Old. "Firstborn" was the word that caught her attention, "And knew her not till she had brought forth her firstborn son." She read on, about Jesus being born in Bethlehem and about King Herod, and did not stop until she came to the line about Rachel weeping for her children. She read some verses and not others, understood some lines and not others, and stopped at every mention of angels or children or weeping or suffering. Sometimes she would hear some commandment being spoken—"Give not that which is holy unto the dogs"—and others echoed in her head until it ached. As she read on, day after day, often by candlelight, through St. Matthew and St. Mark and on to St. Luke and St. John, it seemed to her a message was reaching her and that message was that she must face her own wickedness. She had been wicked. She had given herself, a virgin, to Ferdinando without benefit of holy matrimony and her firstborn was being withheld from her as payment for her crime. "Servants, be obedient to them that are your masters," she read in Ephesians 6—and she had not been obedient. "Let nothing be done through strife or vainglory," she was told in Philippians 2—and she had striven and been vainglorious. James 1 terrified her most with "Then when lust hath conceived, it bringeth forth sin: and sin, when it is finished, bringeth forth death." Oreste would die, she saw that now, for what was it she had felt for Ferdinando if not lust?

Isa Blagden, arriving one day to look over the Casa Guidi, called on Wilson and found her lying in a dark room, huddled under the covers of her bed, the Bible in her hand and tears streaming down her face. Maria, who showed her in, was frightened and stood at the door shivering. It was all Isa could do to persuade Wilson to let some light in and dry her tears and tell her what ailed her; and when she did so, it made little sense. Disturbed, Isa proposed that Wilson and Pilade should come with her up to Bellosguardo for the afternoon and, since no protest was made, she hustled the two of them into her waiting carriage and whisked them off at once, leaving Maria with instructions to be there upon their return.

Wilson felt only dimly aware of Miss Blagden's kindness but later came to realize that this sign and evidence of human concern had most probably saved her that time from real madness. When she got home, she felt for the first time in months the need to write a letter, to commit her thoughts and feelings to paper and communicate through the medium of paper and pen with someone. But with whom? Her correspondence was in sad disarray. Writing to Ellen, never her most sympathetic correspondent, was dreary work since all she could think of were frantic pleas to tell her of Oreste and she grew tired of begging long before she reached the end of the first sheet. And Ellen never replied now, not even with a note, though money was sent to her as regularly as ever. Minnie Robinson still sent the occasional line but, now Wimpole Street had been sold and she no longer had the doings of all the Barretts to catalogue, her letters were empty things and difficult to respond to. As for Lizzie Treherne, to whom Wilson still felt drawn, she had done her best but, with four children now, she truly had no time to spare for letters, never having found them easy.

There was of course Ferdinando, but she hesitated over opening her heart to her husband, who would in any case need her letter read to him and would be unable to answer of his own accord. She tried, but was not pleased with what came out, with the stilted words:

—I have been unwell though not of anything infectious but rather a serious lowering of the spirits which I struggle to overcome. The days are long and the nights worse. I have presently one boarder only, a gentleman for a change, but see little of him. Pilade goes on well. I am attempting to wean him but it is I and not the child who is loath to finish the business.

Did she want to write such weary stuff? Did Ferdinando wish to read it? No. The thought of it being read aloud was an embarrassment to her. But still the urge to express her feelings tormented her and at last, in defiance of that dislike she had felt on their last meeting, she sat down and wrote to the person to whom she had once been most close, to Mrs. Browning. She begged pardon at once for

—being so free as to presume I will be read but then, ma'am, you must blame yourself for encouraging in me that letter-writing soul. It is a relief to me to take up this pen and sit at a table and endeavor to sort out what I feel pressing in upon me and to know that if sense can be made of it you will make it. But I am mindful in the midst of my own troubles ma'am that you are not in good health for Miss Blagden has told me so and I am sorry to hear it and to think of you unable to leave your room and I am sorry too that the Rome winter does not prove as gentle as you had hoped. I trust that with spring just around the corner you will feel better. I would hope it could work some miracle for myself also but I fear the burden I feel upon my back will not be helped by fine weather. Ma'am, I have been reading my Bible and am left in no doubt that I have sinned and am paying the just penalty for sin and I repent strongly but to no avail as yet. Ferdinando and I being both your servants when we sinned were like unto brother and sister and broke a commandment which was made clear to me on reading the Scriptures. Oreste was the fruit of this sin and is kept from me because of it. Last night I opened my eyes when it was dark and feeling a sudden want of air opened the window when to my astonishment I was in time to see Oreste carried past in the arms of an angel and I wept and called out to him but there was no reply and soon they were gone up to the heavens and lost sight of. I knelt at once to pray and prayed most dutifully till morning when I expected a letter telling me Oreste had been taken. None has arrived but if his death took place as I saw the angel pass I would not hear from my sister Ellen for some time. Oh ma'am if only I had shown myself strong in the face of temptation! When the last trump sounds and I stand before the Lord our God and am judged I will be found wanting and know not what to do. I am like unto a leper here with all faces turned against me except your kind friend Miss Blagden and now she is gone too. The sin is recognized in me and people are afraid. Ma'am, what would you have me do to atone for my sin? Write and tell me and I will do as you say.

But Mrs. Browning did not write. Instead came a letter from her husband enclosed in a note from Mr. Browning. Ferdinando's was kind enough. He bade her to rest and eat well and soon she would feel better. He vowed that when they returned in the summer he would take her for a holiday. He even went so far as to say he missed her and Pilade, and would be glad to be home. Mr. Browning was no less solicitous but she read exasperation in his advice to turn from the gospels to the psalms, "which may have a calming influence." He did not mention his wife.

She duly turned to the psalms but found them equally disturbing. "O Lord my God, if I have done this, if there be iniquity in my hands, if I have rewarded evil unto him that was at peace with me" leaped out from Psalm 7 and so did "Let the wickedness of the wicked come to an end." That was a plain reference to herself. Psalm 13 put her own question well—"How long shall I take counsel in my soul, having sorrow in my heart daily?"—without seeking to answer it. When she read how the Lord looked down and saw His people were "all together become filthy" she trembled. Only the sudden arrival of three new boarders saved her from succumbing to the terror which filled her. One of the boarders was a clergyman, the Reverend Mr. Baron from Cheshire, and he, finding her at every turn with the Bible open, praised her devotion, which released from her such loud protestations of her unworthiness that he was stopped in his tracks. But he was a kind man and took the trouble to sit with her and show her the hope in the Bible, the comfort and joy as well as the gloom. Their Lord was a merciful Lord and, if she had sinned as she believed, He existed to forgive sinners. She should come with him to the United Reform Church in Florence and hear messages not of vengeance but of forgiveness.

Wilson went and it was more the going that helped her than the services themselves. She went with the Reverend Mr. Baron and his wife and daughter and was consoled to be among such a party of cheerful worshipers. She was consoled, too, to have them in her house where they made an uncommon amount of noise and were certainly not easy guests but their beaming countenances and determination to look on the bright side of everything lightened the atmosphere immensely. Because she had to provide for the Barons and for her other gentleman who was still with her she was obliged to go out daily to market and this quite ordinary transaction restored some of her spirits. And there had been a few lines from Ellen, proving that Oreste, so far from being carried to heaven by an angel, was firmly rooted in East Retford and had grown another two inches. She still woke often in the night full of strange forebodings, but with the Reverend Mr. Baron to confide in and laugh at her wilder interpretations of what she had dreamed, she survived better. By May, when a note from Rome told her the Brownings' party was about to come back to Florence, she felt much more stable.

It was the Reverend Mr. Baron who pointed out to his landlady that her husband and his employers, about whom he had heard a great deal, would be lucky to get back to Florence "before war really takes hold." Wilson, shut up in her own world all winter, was astonished to learn what everyone else in Florence had known for many a month—French troops had poured into Piedmont and 1848 was to be repeated all over again. Instantly, she thought of Ferdinando and whether he would go off to fight now as he had fought then. But he was eleven years older and a father of two—surely he would not take up arms? Her anxiety became pressing and now, every day, she had a new and urgent need to go out. In the market, she was told that it was Mrs. Browning's old hero, the French Emperor Louis Napoleon, who had landed at Genoa and pledged himself to help the Italians drive out the Austrians. Almost at once there seemed to be a series of victories reported with which Wilson could not keep up. Nor could the Reverend Mr. Baron but he left immediately he heard in May that the Grand Duke of Tuscany had abdicated: that, he vowed, was the clearest possible indication of open war and he wanted to be away. He left the day Napoleon and Victor Emmanuel entered Milan in triumph. Wilson had no time to miss him and his family or her other gentleman, who had joined their party, before the Brownings were back, similarly propelled by the fear that they might be trapped because of war.

As soon as she saw Annunciata, Wilson felt safe. What had happened to the girl? It took time for her to find out, but she needed no other evidence than her eyes to tell her Ferdinando had lost interest in the pretty maid. (It seemed Annunciata had fallen in love with one of the Papal Guard and was pining for him.) Ferdinando came to his wife in such an open way that she was reminded of the first advances he had ever made and she was stirred in a way she believed no longer possible. There was such relief to be found too in his physical presence—to be held by him, to feel his strength, reassured her. And he seemed more alert than when he had left, less inclined to shrug and yawn and leave everything to her. Gradually it emerged that his concern for his country was the decisive factor in his changed attitude. This, he told her, was Italy's great chance, far greater than in '48, to rid herself of the foreign oppressor and unite to form a great power. If he had been young, nothing would have kept him from joining the Tuscan troops but, as it was, he felt an old man and useless. She needed to console him and assure him he was far from old and found remarkable pleasure in restoring his self-esteem.

Mrs. Browning was hardly less excited than Ferdinando. Paying her first visit to the Casa Guidi, Wilson was moved to exclaim, "Why, ma'am, you look so well!"

Mrs. Browning laughed and made a gesture of dismissal. "Oh, I am tired of being told so, Wilson."

"It is only I had heard from Miss Blagden that . . ."

"Isa has not seen me since the happy news and it is that which restores me to near my old self."

"News, ma'am?"

"Italy, Wilson, Italy! You, with *your* husband, and you ask what news? The news that makes every Italian heart sing, the news that liberty and freedom are abroad once more and this time we shall not fail!"

"Oh, the war, ma'am."

"Yes, the war, the war of right against might."

She found it all extraordinary. It was as though her old mistress were drunk, or lightheaded with laudanum, so intense was her delight. The heat was fierce that June—102 degrees in the shade at one time— but Mrs. Browning went out in it and seemed to have forgotten such scorching sun had once enervated her to the point of collapse. Pen had hung flags on the balcony of the Casa Guidi—one French, one Italian—and told her that he was paid in *scudi* to give to the war if he did his lessons well. To Wilson, they all seemed to be in a fever and, like any good nurse, she waited anxiously for the point of crisis, more concerned about the fate of Mrs. Browning than about that of Italy. It came on July 9. As she went to the market with Ferdinando, each shopping for their respective households—though since hers had shrunk to nothing Wilson had no real need to make the daily pilgrimage—the excitement was unmistakable and so was its nature. There were wailings and tears, and everywhere men sat dejected in front of their stalls while the women looked on, silent and shocked. Bells rang as though for a funeral and the first rumor was that both Napoleon and Victor Emmanuel had been killed. But then Ferdinando made sense of another rumor, that Napoleon had reneged, that he had made peace with the Austrians at Villafranca the day before and all was now over for Italian hopes. All she asked when he came back to tell her was, "Who will tell Mrs. Browning?"

It fell to her. Ferdinando was beside himself, alternately cursing and crying with such violence that he frightened Pilade. He was in no state to break such news to a woman like Mrs. Browning, whose sensibilities were tender at the best of times. So she must do it. If she had known of how the Greeks slaughtered the bearers of bad tidings she might have taken longer to decide it was her duty, but, as it was, she saw no need to fear for herself, only for the person to whom she would relate the devastating news. Shown in to the Casa Guidi by Annunciata, she did wonder if it might be wise to tell Mr. Browning first but he was not about. He had gone early, before it was too unbearably hot, to see if he could obtain a newspaper which might tell him what was happening. Mrs. Browning was still in bed while Pen dashed in and out when he was not feeding his rabbits on the balcony.

Wilson waited until he had gone and then spoke directly. "Ma'am, I have just come from the market. There is bad news of the war."

"*Bad* news? For us? For our cause?"

"Yes, ma'am. There is talk of an armistice."

"Between whom?"

"The French and the Austrians."

Mrs. Browning raised herself from her pillows and, unable to speak, her hand at her throat, waited.

"The French Emperor has signed a treaty at Villafranca and withdrawn. It is all over for the present."

Had she spoken with anything but sympathy? Was she not married to an Italian, with Italian sons? And yet Mrs. Browning looked at her with hatred, her pale face growing steadily darker, and said, "Leave me." But Wilson was afraid to and advanced instead toward the bed, thinking to offer a drink or make a compress for her forehead. Again, she was told to leave and with such venom she recoiled. Miserably, she backed out of the room, not wanting to desert Mrs. Browning and be held responsible for her collapse, if collapse there was to be. Pen, coming once more at a run to see his mother, was stopped and held by her and persuaded to come instead and play with Pilade. Mr. Browning should be sent for and, with Ferdinando still convulsed with grief and rage, there was no one to send but herself or Annunciata. Taking Pen into her own house, Wilson set off, hurrying through streets that told their own tale. Everywhere French flags were ripped in half and trampled on and great gangs of young soldiers joined together to shout and curse the very name of France. All the time she dashed through the streets, fighting her way through the hubbub, Wilson looked for Mr. Browning, knowing he must have heard by now and would surely be rushing to his wife's side. They met on the Ponte Trinità, she seeing and calling out to him first. He crossed the bridge and seized her by the shoulders, shouting above the noise, "My wife? Does she know? Does she know?" Wilson could only nod her head and turn with him to go back.

In the cool of the entrance hall of the Casa Guidi Mr. Browning paused and asked, "How did she hear? In what manner was the news brought to her?"

"I told her, sir, coming as I did from the market where the news was fresh and thinking . . ."

"Yes, yes, Wilson, but how did she seem?"

"Angry, sir."

"Thank God for that." And then he was off up the stairs with Wilson, panting behind, trying to fathom the significance of his relief. Why should he thank God for anger? Only, she supposed, because it gave evidence of spirit and life—he had not wanted to hear his wife was prostrate with shock. But by the time they both reached her bedroom it was clear that, whatever her first reaction, Mrs. Browning was now in a world of her own. She neither spoke nor moved. Hovering in the doorway, Wilson heard Mr. Browning plead with her to say something to him and then she listened while he tried to make out a case for the French Emperor, to argue this might not be the betrayal it seemed, and that all hope might not be lost. His voice, low and urgent, went on and on but there was never an answer. Slowly, Wilson returned to her own house, awed by such suffering. It made no sense to her, but then it never had. She remembered the bride of one year, alight with the happiness of those early celebrations when the Grand Duke had granted the first liberties, and thought how strange it was for an Englishwoman to be so mad with joy. Now she was mad with grief. It was as though her father had died again, as though she had been injured to her soul.

Throughout the next three weeks Wilson was banned from the Casa Guidi. When she might have been at her most useful, since she was so much more skilled in nursing than Annunciata, she was not allowed near Mrs. Browning. She had given the instruction herself, saying she could not bear to see the person who had been the instrument through whom she had heard such infamous news. Mr. Browning was apologetic. "You know her, Wilson," he said wearily, "she is not as other people, and you have far too much sense to take this personally." But Wilson found she did not have too much sense. Far from it. She did not feel in the least sensible but rather resentful on her own account. Could she help the news? Had she not thought of her mistress first? Had not concern been her prime motive in going at once to Mrs. Browning? When she heard how a new doctor had been called in, all the familiar names having left Florence previously, thinking it was to be plunged into war, she felt indignant—why was *she* not called in, she who knew more about Mrs. Browning's illnesses than any other person? She raged to Ferdinando about this Dr. Grisanowsky, and even the assurance that he was a friend of Miss Blagden's did not make him more acceptable in her eyes. There was talk of the doctor saying his patient might have suffered a heart attack—"Nonsense," said Wilson—and then that her lungs were seized up—"They always have been," fumed Wilson. There was even mention that recovery might be impossible. "They do not know her, who say that," said Wilson. "They will see—in time, when she is over this, she will mend."

Within a month Wilson saw with her own eyes that she had been right. In a letter to Minnie, who seemed the natural recipient of the account she wished to give, she described how

—when first she was taken ill Minnie, which I expect you have heard of from Miss Arabel, who I dare say was given a terrible fright as were we all, many despaired of her life but I did not and I am pleased to say my faith was justified. We came here to Siena, where I have been before, though to a different house, to visit my husband who accompanied the Brownings last month, the doctor having ordered Mrs. Browning to be taken out of this city or he would not answer for the consequences. The villa is very beautiful and large and it has been possible for myself and my baby and my husband to stay together which is a very great privilege and one I did not look to have extended to me. I tell you, Minnie, I have fallen from favor of late and through no fault of my own, whereas my husband and son rest high in Mrs. Browning's estimation. The truth is, she does not seem to wish to see me and will think of every excuse to keep me out of her presence. I did not therefore expect to be invited here and was resigned to being by myself yet again and sure my spirits would once more be lowered. This not being the case I have benefited much from the peace and quiet and from the fresh air. But Minnie I ought to have suspected there was more to this kindness than appeared and so there is. Are you acquainted if only by repute with a Mr. Landor who is a poet? He is an old man who Mr. Browning met in the burning streets of Florence last month half out of his wits and with nowhere to go his wife having *thrown him out* for what reason I do not know. Mr. Browning out of the kindness of his heart and because Mr. Landor I believe was once his champion when no one thought anything of him brought the old gentleman to Siena and prevailed upon Mr. Story his friend to take him in. He was afraid to keep him in his own house because the old fellow rants and raves upon occasion and might distress Mrs. Browning. But now there is the pressing problem of what to do with Mr. Landor who seems incapable of acting for himself. The Storys leave for Rome at the end of this month and cannot take him with them. The Brownings have no room in the Casa Guidi should they ever be willing to shelter him and in any case intend to follow the Storys for another winter in Rome (entailing another in Florence alone for me). Now they have brought forward a plan which is that they should lend me sufficient money to rent another house in which Mr. Landor is to have the first floor, comprising three rooms, a book closet, and a terrace, and I am to reside on the ground floor and care for him receiving £30 a year for my trouble. That is a great deal of money Minnie which I do not need to tell you and would without doubt enable me to bring over my firstborn at long last. The house I now rent could be let again and in all I might find myself with a handsome income. This prospect is pleasing to me but I have seen Mr. Landor and confess myself alarmed. He is large Minnie and loud and not altogether sensible often and I would have no other man in the house to manage him if need be. His wife who I am told still resides up at Fiesole has been heard to call her husband "the old Brute" and when a wife speaks thus I am more of a mind to listen than not. But it is hard to resist this plan put before me and indeed it ought to be tried since I have no other resource. I have given up begging to be taken back into service since it is plain Annunciata is preferred. She of course is in a hurry to return to Rome where she left a sweetheart and has offered to do the ironing there to save on laundry expenses so great is her anxiety to be taken. As to my husband, he does what he is told as ever and I have faced the truth long ago that the Brownings are more important to him than I am. But he has been very loving this summer and much cast down by the failure of the Italian cause and I will not grudge him a livelier time of it in Rome. Next year Minnie I will be forty and hardly able to believe it but I am resolved to make great changes with the help of a hard winter's work. I have seen at long last that I need to be free of my beloved mistress and even as I write that word it is hollow for how can I love one who no longer has the least regard for me? Is it always thus, Minnie? You have had a long life of service and time to look back on it and if I did not know how your arthritis troubles you and with what difficulty you pen your kind notes I would ask you to help me in this. Is everything I did for Miss Elizabeth worthless and am I foolish to expect more of her? It seems to me often that her husband is kinder and more thoughtful. I have not seen her *alone* face to face all the time we have been here and when I do see her in company she is wont to turn from me. Who would have thought it would come to this? Think of me, Minnie, as I think of you.

Putting her pen down, Wilson sighed. Thinking of Minnie was to think of days long ago when she had been at the center of things.

Now, unless she could rescue herself, she had not even a place on the outside of Mrs. Browning's life, and what troubled her most was that she cared. What she must teach herself to do was to stop caring, learn to stand up for herself.

CHAPTER TWENTY-SEVEN

WILSON LIKED this other house. Taken by Mr. Browning to view it—though since it had already been rented her approval was of no importance—she was at once charmed. It was a small house, directly behind the church of Santa Maria del Carmine, and a good deal less gloomy than the other next to the Casa Guidi. Though it was much less grand, it reminded her of what her mistress had called "the doll's house," that little house they had rented for six months in the winter of '48 in the Piazza Pitti. She could see its possibilities straight away, something she had never seen in those gloomy other chambers. But that was not all: Mr. Browning said Mr. Landor's rooms were all to be painted, carpeted and furnished and that he thought her own quarters might at least be painted if she contributed only a little to the cost. Wilson hesitated over how little "little" would be but, when she heard the sum, could not resist agreeing since it was so very small. The painters being on the premises, and the landlord seeing the advantage, the job was done cheaply. (Ferdinando said he expected the profit on Mr. Landor's rooms was so enormous it covered the cost of the rest more than double.)

Wilson bore the departure of the Brownings and her husband stoically this time. She was determined to make a go of this new house, in which she felt so much more cheerful, and understood fully how much depended on Mr. Landor's tractability. She must see that he was comfortable and cared for so that with contentment would come peace. To help her, she had a new maid, Teresa, older and more confident than Maria, who had left to be a nursemaid. Wilson left Teresa in no doubt as to her main function in the house: keeping the old gentleman happy. His every whim was to be catered for, however strange, and he must be put first at all times. This was more difficult than it sounded since he did not keep either regular or normal hours. He was capable of wanting nothing all day, of sending every meal away and not allowing Teresa in, even to make up his fire or turn down his bed, and then, around midnight, calling for his breakfast and complaining he was cold because the fire had gone out. It would have driven every other landlady to distraction but Wilson was determined not to be bested.

When he roared for food at midnight, she attended to him herself. She went to him, wearing her dress over her shift, and said, "Now, Mr. Landor, sir, what is this, at this hour, sir?"

"This is hunger, woman, this is starvation!" he shouted. "This is a disgrace and I won't have it and I *will* have my coffee and rolls and eggs and I *will* have a good fire or I leave tomorrow and to hell with you."

"It is midnight, sir . . ."

"I don't give a damn what time it is. My stomach says it is hungry and that's the only time I know. You're idle, the lot of you."

"Idle I am not, sir, but at midnight *my* stomach says it is asleep and if it must be wakened it needs warning."

"Then warning it is given—ten minutes and no more, mind. Quick with you, be off and see to it."

Furious, Wilson went down into the freezing kitchen, where the well-banked-up fire had not quite died down, and poked it vigorously until it began to burn up. The kettle sang quite quickly and meanwhile the stove, never entirely allowed to go out in the winter, had coughed into life. She warmed yesterday's bread and cooked three eggs and laid a tray and took the lot upstairs, meaning to return with coals for Mr. Landor's fire as soon as he was placated with the food. He was asleep. She put the tray down noisily, made sure the coffee with its strong smell was under his nose, even lit a lamp, but to no avail. He snored, deeply asleep. Standing over him, she saw how very old he must be, with the skin of his face and neck pleated in heavy folds of wrinkles and his wild hair quite sparse and white, and only her respect for his years prevented her from shaking him. Instead, she covered him with a blanket and put a cushion behind his head and blew out both lamp and candle.

In the morning he was without any memory of the night before. When she heard movement above—there was no shouting—Wilson went up and knocked on the door and was told, in the most mild of voices, to come in. Mr. Landor was standing scratching himself, and none too particular about where. The tray remained untouched. He seemed bewildered, shuffled about his room yawning and stretching, and only after several minutes of this focused on Wilson at all.

"You are not my wife," he said, startled. "In the name of God you aren't. Who the devil are you?"

"I am Signora Romagnoli," Wilson said calmly, "and I am your landlady whom you called in the middle of the night to give you food and there it is."

"Well, it is cold and I do not want it. But I am very glad you are not my wife, for she is a bitch." He rubbed his eyes hard, like some truculent baby. "I am tired and my throat is dry. What time is it?"

"Ten in the morning."

"What morning?"

"January 7, sir."

"What year?"

"Eighteen-sixty."

"What place?"

"Florence."

"What am I doing here?"

"Mr. Browning brought you, sir."

"Mr. Browning? Mr. Browning? What was he doing with me? What business do I have with him? The world has gone mad."

Gradually, Wilson learned how to deal with the old man. The roars in the night, it turned out, could safely be ignored. Once this was understood, it became part of the pattern and both Wilson and Teresa and even the landlord's son, who slept in the garret, all sighed at the disturbance, then turned over and went back to sleep. A few more yells and crashings about and Mr. Landor invariably wrapped himself in a quilt and fell asleep. But no daytime cry could be left to die out—it must be investigated immediately or the rage was tremendous. Only let there be a five-minute delay and pots would be thrown, furniture overturned and the servant arriving, whether Teresa or Wilson herself, threatened with clenched fist. So the moment the shout was heard, one of them would rush and then try to provide what was wanted on the instant. The real problems arose when that something was unobtainable. It was impossible to explain that strawberries were not available and nor was a copy of *The Times.* In such cases, it was best to say one would go directly and to rush out of the room and hope the substitute finally brought would convince him this was what had been asked for. That was all that was necessary and to proffer whatever it was, saying with great emphasis, "Here is what you asked for, sir." Often, he would say thank you, and take it, or look puzzled, but always take it. The fatal approach was to falter and say that whatever he had asked for could not be found—then the violence was terrifying.

Wilson, writing to Mr. Browning to report how his self-imposed charge fared, expressed the opinion that

—he is not exactly mad, sir, begging your pardon, as unable to remember himself. He is ever confused and his confusion makes him angry and I cannot see that it can be helped though it is hard to endure. Were he among familiars it might help him but as it is he cannot place himself here and it is pitiful to see how lost he is. He does not go abroad much which is as well since he has little sense of direction and has twice been found many miles from home wandering the streets. I cannot prevent him going forth, but am ever relieved when he has returned. As to the poetry, sir, I do not think there is much done in that direction though paper aplenty is screwed up and thrown on the floor.

Wilson found it hard to believe Mr. Landor had ever written poetry, that he had ever been judged a great poet, but Miss Blagden, who had moved into the Casa Guidi for the winter, swore that he had been much admired and gave her a whole list of his published works. "He is not *like* a poet," Wilson said, sniffing, "and I have lived with two of them."

"You mean poets may not have tempers, do you not?" Miss Blagden said with a smile. "Is that it?"

"No, ma'am, though temper he has and . . ."

"Oh, he is famous for it and I believe sent down from Oxford for it. He is very old, you know, Wilson. Eighty-five, I think."

"It is on account of his age I restrain myself, ma'am. But it is not his temper makes him unlike any poet I have ever known so much as his, well, as his coarseness in general. He has no love of beauty that I can see. I cannot think what his poetry would be like."

"It is dramatic stuff, I believe, though I confess not to have read any. He has had an unhappy life, when all is said and done, unhappy in the personal department. It is fortunate for him that Mr. Browning has rescued him. Dear Robert, such affecting tenderness."

"He is a kind man, certainly."

Something in the way this was said clearly caught Miss Blagden's attention. Wilson saw she was scrutinized inquiringly and blushed. "A very kind man and always good to me," she said with more emphasis. It would not do to have Miss Blagden imagine she bore any grudge.

Nor did she, against him. In fact, as the winter wore on, she felt grateful rather than otherwise. Her savings mounted and she was confident that, come the summer, she would be able to afford a journey to England. This time, with some need to be cautious and not show her hand too soon, she said nothing to Ellen who she judged would most likely have forgotten she had sworn to come and get Oreste herself. Forgotten, or decided it had been idle talk, a vow impossible to realize. So all winter Wilson wrote only of Pilade and of Mr. Landor, innocent gossipy letters which would most likely bore

Ellen but not alarm her. Meanwhile, the moment there was a hint of spring in the air, she began to lay her plans. Not for nothing had she made all those journeys with her employers—she now showed herself to have a familiarity with timetables quite out of the ordinary and was able to spot at once where a connection could be made. The Brownings and Ferdinando would be back in June so it would be best to go at once, when it would be more likely that her absence would be looked on leniently. And she would provide a substitute for the two weeks she reckoned it would take her, an English maid called Phoebe Crabbe with whom she had become friendly. Phoebe was her own age, near forty, and had been left behind in Wilson's old house when her employers went home because she was ill with flu and unable to travel. Wilson had nursed her and taken care of her and Phoebe was only too willing to show her gratitude. It was all planned.

Afterward, Wilson could not forgive herself for endangering these beautifully laid plans. It horrified her to think how foolish she had been and she could only excuse herself on the grounds that she had suffered some kind of fit. That was what it was, a fit, during which something in her burst and she lost control of herself—or perhaps it had had something to do with the terrible heat. Once upon a time, she had been able to withstand Florentine summers better than any Englishwoman she knew but of late they had begun to tire her, to make her feel that in everything she did she was pushing a large boulder up a hill. It was her age, she supposed, and nothing could be done about it. But that late June day, soon after the Brownings and Ferdinando returned from Rome, she felt more than exhausted. She felt as though she were suffocating in the heat, as though it were stopping her nostrils, sealing her mouth, and when she tried to breathe it forced itself down into her stomach and made her heave. Twice that morning, before even the heat was at its worst, she had to lie down and mop her face with a cold wet cloth and when she took the cloth from her skin it seemed to steam. She had been woken up at one in the morning by Mr. Landor and again at four, and both times he had been abusive, calling her "a bitch as fat and stupid" as his wife. When his dinner arrived from the *trattoria*—he had told her long ago he preferred their food to hers, which suited her perfectly well—it was eight minutes late. She took it up the stairs herself, adding another two minutes to the delay because she had to pause and rest halfway up. She was scarlet in the face and perspiring profusely by the time she entered the old gentleman's room. The moment she did so he was on her, grabbing her by the arm, so that the tray shook violently in her slippery hands, trying to drag her to the clock as he screamed, "Look! Look! Is *that* the hour I ordered my dinner? Is that how a gentleman should be treated?"

"The *trattoria* sent it late, sir," Wilson gasped, putting the tray down as carefully as she could manage, longing to escape from the room.

"Sent it late!" he roared. "And why was it not made plain by you —by *you*—the consequences of such slackness, eh? Are you the landlady? Are you? Is it you who collects my money week after week? And for what? To bring my dinner late, far past the hour, you disgusting, ugly fool?"

The snarl on his face, twisted horribly with contempt, was terrifying to behold but worse was the way he wiped the saliva away from his slobbering mouth with his sleeve and seemed to cast it toward her. She began to back out of the room, trying to focus on a picture hanging behind the old man on the wall above the mantelpiece, a weird dark picture in which an angel of vengeance flew across a purple sky lit by flashes of lightning, sword in hand, and below a man with blood streaming from his neck prayed for mercy. But Mr. Landor advanced upon her, step by step, and because she could no longer bear to look at him and because his distorted face seemed to merge with the angel's she turned to dash for the door. A crash behind her made her turn and she saw the enraged old man had hurled his soup dish at the far wall where it hit the pretty paper and ran in thin trickles down onto the pale gray carpet. Oh, I will never get it clean! ran through her mind, but already there was worse to witness, for a plate of spinach was already spattered on the tiles of the fireplace and a bowl of zucchini sailed out of the window. But what brought her to the point of retaliation was the sight of his hands mauling a plate of sliced mutton, digging his fingers into the pieces of meat and snatching them up and trying to screw them up like pieces of paper and hurl them at the bookcase. She could not stand it another minute. Something snapped inside her and she found herself grabbing the mutton and wresting the plate, with what was left of the uncut joint still on it, and running with it from his crazed presence. He followed her, howling and swearing, so that Teresa, who had come out of the kitchen at the tremendous noise, cowered against the door and put up her arms to protect herself from what she believed would be an attack. Wilson pushed her back into the room, the mutton skidding from the plate as she did so, and locked it behind her, then dragged a chest in front. Panting, she waited, but the madman never paused, seeming to hurtle out into the street still cursing and yelling. Then there was silence and she sat down on the chest, weeping and shaking.

Of course, as she had guessed, he went into the Casa Guidi, to complain to the Brownings. An hour later she was sent for and went as she was, still in the apron spotted with bits of meat and potato where they had clung to her as she fought for them. Her hair was untidy and her face still on fire and she knew she presented a distraught sight. To her relief, Mr. Landor was not present. "Now, Wilson," Mr. Browning began, looking grave and weary, "what is this we hear of you ill-treating your guest, our friend?"

"Ill-treating? Oh, sir, do you look at me and say you see someone who has been doing the ill-treating?" And she promptly burst into tears, throwing her soiled apron over her head to hide her humiliation. She felt Mr. Browning's arm around her and the gentlest of pressures as he pushed her into a seat. He waited. Her tears dried and she pulled her apron away, ashamed and miserable. "You do not know, sir, the provocation. What I must endure from Mr. Landor, night and day. There are many can tell you what I suffer at his hands though I serve him as best I can. Never have I been so reviled, never, and I have taken it all, knowing him to be old and alone, and I . . ."

"You have done very well, Wilson, and we all know it," Mrs. Browning said.

"We did not pretend it would be easy," Mr. Browning murmured, "which is why you are recompensed so handsomely, Wilson."

"Money cannot soften some things," Wilson said, "and you cannot begin to imagine the insults, the nature of the insults, as though I were a woman of the *streets* . . ." and she began to weep again.

"He can be violent, I admit," Mr. Browning said, "but he is not himself when he launches into these diatribes and you must remember that, Wilson."

"Sir, even when he is not angry you do not know his habits, how filthy he can be and expect me——"

"Wilson, I do not think you need enumerate Mr. Landor's faults, and I repeat, we know he is difficult, but in a man of his years, with his temperament, and cast out by his wife——"

"She was wise, sir."

"That is not for you to judge, Wilson."

"No, sir."

"Now let us come to the point: are you willing to overlook this— this regrettable incident and try again?"

She was silent a moment, thinking of Oreste and her journey to England and the future of her family and how it rested largely at the moment on Mr. Landor's £30 a year. "I have no choice, sir. I am bound to keep him or be much the worse off."

"Then try, dear," Mrs. Browning urged, "not to get in a temper to match his, rise above the poor old gentleman's tantrums and meet his ravings with dignity."

"I will try," Wilson said stiffly, barely able to get the words out.

"He has agreed to act as though nothing had happened," Mr. Browning said. It angered her that he appeared to think this amounted to a great concession.

"Oh yes," she said, very quietly, "he is expert at that, sir. But the evidence of what did happen will be all around us, the wallpaper being ruined where the soup dripped down it and the carpet, I should think, impossible to clean."

"It will be paid for," Mr. Browning said, and again she was angry. She did not care what money was given for repairs. Tired, she got to her feet and made to leave.

When she got to the top of the staircase and Mr. Browning had gone back inside his apartment, she suddenly felt so ill she had to sit down on the stone step and compose herself before going on. Head in her hands, she tried to pull herself together. For the sake of Oreste, she must be cool and calm and take matters into her own hands instead of waiting so feebly for fate to help her. She ought, there and then, while with the Brownings, to have chosen that moment to outline her plan and ask for their cooperation. What, after all, could they do with Mr. Landor should she turn him out? *She* could get other boarders, *he* would never, with his reputation, be taken in by any other landlady in Florence no matter what was paid. Slowly, she began to climb the stairs again, resolved to return and put her case. Hesitantly, she pushed open the door, which stood ajar to let in what air there was, and entered the hall. They would still be in the little sitting room. Ferdinando was out, she knew, and so were Pen and Annunciata if the total silence was any indication. As she lifted her hand to knock on the open door to signal her return, she heard Mrs. Browning's light, high voice say, "I am tired of her, Robert, truly I am. It is nothing but trouble, nothing but *her* problems when we have enough of our own."

"That is hardly fair, Ba."

"Of course it is not fair, but it is true. I do not even like to see her, it makes me uncomfortable and I wish her gone, as quickly as possible."

"People in trouble *are* uncomfortable, but it is hardly their choice."

"She lays it at our door, I am sure, and yet it is not our fault she is in difficulties."

"It is partly our fault—we prevailed upon her to take Landor."

"I did not mean that. It is her whole situation—she is so mournful and silently accusing and sometimes, Robert, I think her as mad as Landor with all this nonsense she makes of the Bible from time to time. I am really very tired of her."

"That is a little hard . . ."

"Then I am a little hard. For example, what of Siena? Are we to cart her with us there next month?"

"We can hardly leave Landor here with her—think what might happen, on days like today, were we not here to be a calming influence!"

"Both might murder the other and have done with it."

"Ba! You are savage beyond reason."

"There is no reason in it, I am most unreasonable and know it."

"But not proud of being so, I hope?"

"I hear the rebuke, Robert. No, not proud, ashamed, but unable to suppress the wicked thought. What *of* Siena?"

"We must take Landor, and if he goes, Wilson must go to look after him, for we cannot and the Storys cannot be imposed upon again. There is no other solution."

"Not if one is good, as you are."

Then there was silence. Numb, Wilson turned once more and crept out, all in a run, all the way back to her own home. Pilade came stumbling out to greet her and she clung to him, crushing him to her and stroking his hair and crooning to him. More than any other comfort, his delighted kisses in return soothed her and eventually she was able to put him down and go into the kitchen to speak to Teresa about the day's duties. But Teresa was not there. The kitchen girl, standing scraping carrots at the table, looked frightened and said Teresa had gone—and gone, she had said, for good. Wilson could not believe it but it was true. Her younger brother was sent by Teresa later in the day to say she would not be returning to a house where a dangerous lunatic lived and no one could expect her to—she would rather forfeit that week's wages than wait long enough to give notice. And then, on top of such bad news, came another message, a letter from Phoebe saying she could not after all repay Wilson's kindness by standing in for her because she had this very day been ordered back to England and arrangements she had no part in had been made. The world, thought Wilson that night, was crumbling around her no matter how hard she tried.

A month later, this was how Mrs. Browning described her own world. She lay in the garden of the Villa Alberti near Siena with Wilson shelling peas at her feet and Pilade picking grasses and admiring each one extravagantly. "The world is crumbling around me, Wilson," she said, the words so faint only a finely attuned ear could have heard them. In her hand she held the letter from England that had come that morning and Wilson knew what it contained: news of Miss Henrietta, of Mrs. Surtees Cook, who was mortally ill with cancer of the womb. Her husband's letter had reached them as soon as they arrived in their summer resting place and had plunged them all into abject misery. To Wilson, it had seemed all of a piece, all part of her own unhappiness, of that weary feeling that nothing mattered, nothing, no amount of effort could alter what was to happen. All there was left to do was to stumble on, dutifully following the tracks on the ground as they appeared. She had given up all hope of ever bringing Oreste over. Day after day she did what was expected of her and there was so little fire left in her that, when Mr. Landor emptied a jug of red wine over a white damask tablecloth and kicked in her direction a cushion which split and sent feathers flying everywhere, she said not a word. She cleaned up the room, did not even hear his curses, and thought how nothing could affect her any longer.

But Miss Henrietta's illness did. Minnie had written to her, a short and agonizing note, penned with obvious difficulty, and she had replied at length, describing her

—horror, Minnie, to hear of these floodings and most of all of the terrible pain which made my own insides contract in sympathy. I imagine it to be like the worst kind of monthly cramp and the most fierce of labor pains but perhaps it is even worse. Her sister thinks of this pain all day and night and says it is the worst part and I think it is, worse even than how it is to end. I must tell you Minnie that things have not been good between my old beloved mistress and me which it is not fitting that I should now go into but this blow has brought us closer together in our love and concern for Miss Henrietta. Who would have thought it would be her, Minnie? Always the strong one, never ailing like her sisters, and so happy with her three little children. It does not bear thinking about and yet we think of it all day long in this pretty place, not noticing the sun and flowers. Mrs. Browning likes to have me with her now, no other person will do, and we talk of the old days and Miss Henrietta slipping off to Regent's Park to walk with Mr. Surtees Cook and the squeezes she loved to hold in

Wimpole Street when her father was away. Do you remember the jellies you made for her, Minnie? There is no one else can remember except you Wilson Mrs. Browning says to me not even Robert, and it is true.

It was impossible to convey to Minnie or anyone else how this new closeness lifted her misery in a way nothing else could have done and yet Wilson herself marked how curious it was that *she* should feel forgiven when there was nothing to forgive. Without her wishing it to be so, it seemed in the nature of things for her always to seek favor and her mistress to bestow it. Always, maid or matron, she was the supplicant and her standing varied with her usefulness. Now, she was more than useful, she was necessary, and because she was necessary her faults faded into insignificance. She was called upon, day after day, to sustain Mrs. Browning in her awful anxiety and she did it willingly, dragging out from the furthermost corners of her memory evidence of Miss Henrietta's strength and fortitude together with examples of women of whom she had heard who had survived this disease. She held out hope and it was taken eagerly and when with each letter the hope waned she was ready to support Mrs. Browning's own faith that death was but an extension of life and not to be feared.

All she could not share was Mrs. Browning's other intense fever, her other passion. Here, she took a step back and called on Ferdinando to discuss Garibaldi and his Red Shirts and the promises of Cavour—they were names to her and nothing more. She had not the least interest in the fortunes of Italy, did not care that once more liberty and unity were the watchwords, and it astonished her that Mrs. Browning could seem as anxious about war as she did about her sister's health. Listening to her and Ferdinando discussing the latest onslaught—Piedmontese troops were said to be sweeping south throughout the summer—Wilson could hardly believe the enthusiasm displayed. What did it matter who ruled whom? What difference did it make, if you were a woman? She watched Pilade run around laughing and trying to catch butterflies and heard Pen shrieking in the distance as he urged his pony to a faster trot and she knew she did not care a jot for Garibaldi or Cavour or any other Italian hero. Her concerns were here, in front of her, concerns that were domestic and intimate and not to be spoken of in the same breath as supposedly greater events. She did not think them greater, failed entirely to see why she should. Mrs. Browning, Ferdinando swore, was more like a man than a woman and an Italian man at that. He adored her for it and when Wilson chose to murmur against her interest, saying she could not see how it could be real, he was angry and said she was narrow and selfish, like most women.

Mrs. Browning said much the same to her, observing how she did not join in when Garibaldi's victories were being discussed nor did she rejoice.

"You have no interest in these great events, Wilson," she said, a statement rather than a question.

"No, ma'am, and I do not see why I should."

"Well, dear, there are good reasons. You are married to an Italian, you live in Italy, what happens here is of great importance to your future."

"My future, ma'am? I cannot see how this war can affect my future. My life is set to go on as it always has and no war can change it that I can see."

"Then you are a trifle shortsighted and do not see the general for the particular. The future of your children will be very much affected by who rules their country."

"Of my child, ma'am."

"Your child? No, your children. Your two sons."

"Only one is here. The other never will be. I must think of him as English and belonging to my sister."

"Wilson! You shock me. You cannot abandon Oreste thus—come, it is a moment of despondency, that is all, say it is."

"No, ma'am, it is accepting the truth. I have tried to bring him to me and failed and now I cannot hope any longer. He is four years old and will not remember me."

"Four years is very little in a lifetime, dear."

"Four years is very long in his, ma'am."

"And his father, what does Ferdinando say to this?"

"He pays, he sends his wages, it is enough."

Mrs. Browning was quiet for the rest of that day. Wilson saw she was being watched, closely studied, and dropped her eyes to concentrate on the jacket she was making for Pen. He came rushing across the garden while she sewed and she called out to him to come and try the sleeves. He could hardly stand still for the two minutes it took to slip them over his blouse and he shouted at her to be quick, that Ferdinando was waiting to take him rabbit shooting. When he had darted off, his mother sighed and said, "He grows quicker than ever." Wilson could not stop herself saying, "But you see him grow. I try to see Oreste, or used to before I gave up the torture, but all I see is a baby, fat and dimpled. . . ." Mrs. Browning moved restlessly, cleared her throat, said nothing in reply, but then what could be said? Yet a week or so later she surprised Wilson by returning to this topic again, beginning, "Wilson, you remember the Ogilvys?"

"But of course, ma'am, how could I forget? And Jeannie, I remember Jeannie well and wrote to her for a while, but she was not much of a correspondent."

"They are at their home in Scotland, but Mrs. Ogilvy writes that Gigia, their Italian maid whom they took back with them, is returning to Florence next month."

"Indeed, ma'am," said Wilson politely, not seeing this had anything to do with her.

"I have written to Mrs. Ogilvy and inquired of her if Gigia might, for a consideration, and everything being arranged for her, if she might accept a traveling companion."

Wilson looked up, bewildered. Mrs. Browning's voice was heavy with a significance she could not rightly interpret. "A *young* traveling companion. Do you take my meaning, dear?"

"No, ma'am."

"Oreste. Gigia is prepared to escort Oreste and even to collect him from your sister's and take him to Liverpool from where she sails for Leghorn by way of Marseilles. What do you say, Wilson?"

She said nothing. She sat in the garden, half paralyzed, unable to take in this information. Her heart began to pound and Mrs. Browning, smiling in front of her, seemed to swirl before her eyes. She was speaking again, describing how Ferdinando would need to go to

Leghorn to conduct Gigia and Oreste home, and how she, Wilson, must write the clearest possible instructions to her sister Ellen, leaving no room for mistakes. All this she heard, even understood, but still she was speechless. Tears came more readily than thanks. She stood up, holding her hands to her face, laughing and weeping at the same time, gasping for breath, feeling her heart and only finally throwing her arms up in joy. Then she ran to find Ferdinando to tell him and they embraced and it was he who said, "She is an angel!" of Mrs. Browning and Wilson realized she had expressed not a word of gratitude. Back she stumbled, Ferdinando with her, and before a smiling mistress they both fell to their knees and thanked her. "It is an answer to a prayer I had stopped praying," Wilson said, "and you, not God, have answered it." This appalled Mrs. Browning, who said at once that it was God using her as an instrument and that Wilson should have had more faith. Humbly, Wilson agreed.

She wrote straightway to Ellen, though not without considerable difficulty. She did not trust Ellen, knew she must show some cunning and somehow invoke the name of law to frighten Ellen into co-operating. All the emphasis, she felt, must be on this coming as an order which could not be disobeyed and yet put in such a way as not to be offensive. So she began with praise:

—the more I think on it Ellen the more beholden I am to you for how you have cared for Oreste and the more fortunate the child for having you. He has known no want either materially or of a mother's love for you have supplied both abundantly and he will be reminded of this all his life you can be sure. But now Ellen the time I have long awaited has come and I write to tell you that an Italian maidservant by name of Gigia who is traveling home to Florence having been in Scotland with a family who are friends of the Brownings is to come to you to collect Oreste and take him to Liverpool where she will be joined by Mr. Ogilvy and from whence they will sail for Italy. She will arrive on September 1 and depart on the 2nd and I trust you will make her welcome as I know all our mother's daughters would. You need send nothing with the child Ellen as he will need quite different clothes here and when I have seen and measured him I will make them myself.

Send him only with enough for the journey and such toys he shows an exceptional fondness for you having mentioned he will not be parted from the train William carved. And do not let him think he is to be parted from you forever Ellen for this would not be the truth. If you will not come to us I am resolved to bring Oreste to you by and by so you may see how he progresses which I hope will be as well as when he was under your care. Write Ellen and by express even telegram for which I will pay in order that I might have the relief of knowing you have understood and all is clear.

No relief came. Worried, Wilson confided in Mrs. Browning that she feared Ellen might not have received her letter, the posts being so very variable, and was instructed to write again and have it sent with a reply paid, a system she was assured was possible if expensive. Still no acknowledgment was made and it grew near the time when Gigia would be setting out on her journey. Over and over Mrs. Browning emphasized what a deal of trouble the Ogilvys were being put to on her behalf, by allowing their maid to do what she was going to do, and Wilson knew it was true.

"You have written very *plain*, I hope?" Mrs. Browning asked severely. "There was no room for doubt in your words, Wilson, nothing left to query?"

"Oh no, ma'am, I could not have been plainer as to everything."

But all the same Mr. Browning thought it wise that she should send to the Ogilvys a letter for Gigia to carry in which both she and Ferdinando formally requested the return of their young son and gave her power to remove him from the care of his aunt and conduct him to Italy. This was even read by a legal advocate, before whom Wilson and her husband signed the letter. It was a solemn moment. The language of the letter itself made her shiver—the "we hereby, being the parents of one Oreste Romagnoli," seemed so important and the ending, though it only gave the date of the document and names of the witnesses, truly portentous.

Then it was all done and the waiting began. Wilson made her own little calendar on a sheet of brown wrapping paper and wrote the numbers of each day large so that Pilade might learn them. Each evening the child was given a piece of chalk and shown how to cross the days off, which he did with great satisfaction. On the day Oreste and Gigia were due to sail with Mr. Ogilvy from Liverpool Wilson had drawn a ship which excited Pilade more than anything else. His mother held him on her knee and explained for the hundredth time how big the ship would be and how many oceans it would cross and what his big brother would see from it. They had one likeness of Oreste, sent at Christmas when Wilson had requested it should be taken, and this was removed from its frame and put at the end of the chart. Nearer and nearer the squares came to the picture until there were only four left and Ferdinando made himself ready for the journey to Leghorn, where he would take over Gigia and Oreste from Mr. Ogilvy, who continued to Rome, and see one to Florence and the other to Siena.

The night before her husband was to leave, Wilson could not sleep. It was all unbelievable. Her own intense excitement had given way to a hollow feeling in her stomach and she had been quite unable to eat for several days. She felt frightened and strange as she thought of greeting her firstborn, who would not know her and might recoil with horror and cry for Ellen. If he had any lingering memories, which was almost impossible to credit, they would not match what he now encountered. She had aged in four years, lost whatever attraction she had ever had, and it made her miserable to realize this son would not remember her without gray hair. When had her hair gone gray? She could not recall. These days, when she occasionally took over from Annunciata and brushed Mrs. Browning's hair, she marveled that a woman so much older than herself should still have such black, black hair with only a very few silver threads in it (which she was instructed to pull out). And if Oreste would not recognize, and might be afraid of, her, what of his father? Ferdinando had aged, too, was no longer as vigorous nor did he walk so tall and straight. Forgetting his father's darkness, his swarthiness, Oreste might cower and scream. But then she scolded herself—who was better with children, even foreign children, whose language he did not speak, than Ferdinando? Nobody.

They all turned out to watch him go, Pen clamoring to accompany him so that he might be the first to embrace and welcome Lily's baby.

"He is no longer a baby," Wilson told him, holding his hand for comfort, "he will think himself a big boy."

"Bigger than me?"

"No, for you are twice his age."

"Will he like me, Lily?"

"He will like you and he will need you for you, speak English and he speaks no Italian, and not even his brother will be able to speak to him at first."

"Poor little boy. I will love him, Lily, like this," and Pen gave her a strangling hug so that she gasped and laughed and begged to be released.

Ferdinando was already on his horse, which he was to ride as far as the station. She flew to give him last words of advice, all of them unnecessary. "Be gentle," she said, "be patient. He may be ill from the voyage, he may be homesick for the only home he has known, he may be . . ."

"He may be happy to see his father!" Ferdinando shouted. "He is my son and blood will tell. Now let me go." And off he galloped, with her watching until he was a speck on the horizon.

A whole day to Leghorn and a night spent there and then the last but one square on the chart was reached. Guiding Pilade's chubby hand, Wilson's own trembled. Had the ship docked safely? Had Ferdinando greeted his son? Were they already the best of friends? Had Oreste already learned some Italian? At least Ferdinando now knew a great deal of English, whatever she had said to Pen to make him feel important. Again, she did not sleep and for once was glad when Mr. Landor called out, cursing the heat and wanting cold, *cold* water at once—even seeing to the old man's wants was preferable to lying awake worrying. In the morning she made up a cot for Oreste, placing on the pillow a small felt rabbit Pilade had once loved. In a strange place, who knew how this four-year-old might suffer? Something soft to cuddle in the night if he was bewildered might be a comfort. She wandered around all morning, unable to sit still, wondering what Oreste might like to eat. Fruit, surely, though there had not been much fruit on Ellen's table, and bread, all children liked bread, familiar and comforting, but then Italian bread, baked with oil, was not English bread and she began to panic at the idea of his rejecting it and going hungry. Then cake, the soft lemony Madeira cake Pilade and Pen loved, she could bake that and sprinkle it with sugar and tempt him with that.

The day dragged on, full of such random thoughts. By late afternoon she thought she might be ill. Her spine was so tense, her shoulders so rigid, that she ached all over and that empty and gnawing pain in her stomach seemed to increase in severity as dusk approached and the hour when son and husband would return grew closer. She vomited but had nothing except bile to bring up, a sweat thickened on her forehead which no amount of wiping away would banish. She knew little moans of anguish were escaping her, whimperings such as a dog might give. She walked out of the cottage where she and Pilade were lodged in charge of Mr. Landor and along the road to Siena so that she might see them approach before anyone. Pilade was asleep, leaving her arms free for the precious embrace she longed for. On she walked, quarter of a mile, half a mile, watching the sun begin to set and knowing that when it touched the horizon she might see the horse coming and Ferdinando waving and maybe, if he was not slumped asleep in the saddle in front of his father, maybe another small hand too. The moment that red ball began to flatten, she sat on a rock and strained to see along the flat road, along the plain leading to Siena, and sure enough she saw a black dot which grew larger and became a single horse and then she stood up and began to run toward it, waving and shouting. A few yards on and she saw there was no answering wave and she faltered, uncertain if this was Ferdinando or some other lone horseman before whom she would make a fool of herself, but the closer he came the more sure she was that this was her husband and then she chided herself for thinking he had hands free to wave when one was needed for the reins and the other to hold the child. She stopped, her hand to her heart, and smiled and resolved to wait and be calm. The horse was almost upon her and she shut her eyes, the better to see when it had reined to a halt. All in a flurry of dust it came toward her and then she heard Ferdinando shout her name and the neighing of the horse as it was pulled in and she trembled as she opened her eyes and looked up.

Even before she registered that there was no child, she saw his anger. His usually placid, cheerful features were contorted with rage and she stood dumb while he poured out a stream of abuse upon Ellen and upon her and upon the Wilson family and upon the English and upon everyone and everything he could think of. He swung off the horse and stood in front of her, tired and dirty from traveling, and all she heard was a sound like the crashing of waves on pebbles and she put her hands over her ears and swayed in pain at the roadside. She had no idea afterward how she got to the Villa Alberti where Ferdinando took her to break the news and tell the tale of his fruitless trip. Did she ride? Did she walk? Was she carried? All she knew was that she came to lie on a garden bench and it was dark and the stars overhead were piercingly bright. She did not cry, or rage like Ferdinando, nor was she much interested in apportioning blame. Oreste was not here. Beside that, nothing mattered. Ferdinando was still vowing to the Brownings, angry themselves, that he would not send another *scudo* to England and calling heaven to witness that he had been cheated and betrayed, but she lay there impervious. Everything was at an end —the hope, the joy, the new happiness that had been in her. All life had become a series of promises unfulfilled. She thought she would lie there forever, let others do to her what they wished. She was finished with planning, with striving, with looking forward. When Mrs. Browning spoke to her out of the darkness, saying, "Come, Wilson, come, dear, you must not give way," she thought, Why not, why *not* give way?

CHAPTER TWENTY-EIGHT

Ellen's letter arrived the following week, by which time life could be said, by all but the most observant, to have returned to normal. For twenty-four hours Ferdinando's rage had continued and been listened to most sympathetically by the Brownings. He had repeated, over and over again, what Gigia had said, of her humiliation before Ellen Wilson, of how she had not even seen Oreste. Mrs. Browning had declared it was all too bad, too dreadful an imposition to have been responsible for, and that she would not be able to look the Ogilvys in the eye ever again after causing them such vexation. She had hinted darkly that Wilson herself must be to blame, that she must have been weak, must not have written plain enough and as she had been instructed. Then everyone had sighed and tutted and the thing began to be forgotten in the continuing concern for Henrietta.

Wilson allowed it to be forgotten. She took no part in the exclaiming and protesting and analyzing nor would she indulge in speculation as to what had really happened or as to why the letter of authority had not been used against Ellen. Hearing her own firmness doubted, she felt the beginnings of anger but quickly suppressed it.

There was no use in being angry with Mrs. Browning or Ellen or anyone else. It was all done with and had ended how things always seemed to end for her. She went about her normal business without speaking, unless it was impossible not to reply to some query. She was glad Ferdinando was in the Brownings' villa and she was with Mr. Landor and Pilade in another. There was no comfort to be found in her husband's arms and in fact comfort was something he did not offer, being much too preoccupied with his own sense of injured pride. When he said again and again no more of his wages would go to Ellen for his son's upkeep she concurred, did not challenge the underlying assumption that Oreste was no longer his responsibility. She felt numb and tired and surprised herself by managing to sleep deeply and well.

But she knew Ellen would write and that the letter would be in the nature of both a declaration and a justification. It would be hard to bear and she dreaded such a letter because it might disturb her wonderful composure. Mrs. Browning handed her Ellen's missive as though it were hardly fit to handle and she took it with equal reluctance. "Unless there is any quite remarkable news your sister has to tell," Mrs. Browning said, "I would rather not hear what she has to say since I imagine it is a tissue of lies, of excuses and complaints." Wilson did not reply. Why should it be imagined *she* would enjoy such lies? Even to open the letter was a burden and she waited until she was alone and hidden from view to do so. Her eyes scanned the first page quickly, taking in the expected account of how Ellen had looked after Oreste as her own, but when she came to the reasons why he had not been handed over to Gigia, Wilson slowed down and even repeated the words to herself. There was no doubting her sister's passion as she struggled to express her resentment, writing:

—on my life Lily I declare I want only what is best for the child and would not be Cruel to him nor the cause of Cruelty and what you asked was Cruel the child knowing no Italian and being Fearful of leaving me the only Mother he has known and who he loves as his own. And the girl who came for him was Young and Insolent and spoke to me as if I were some common washerwoman who must do as she was told which is not in my nature nor never was. If you were to come yourself Lily or the child's Father I could not stand in your way whatever my feelings which are strong, but to hand over my Precious little one to a Young and Foreign girl who spoke his only language poorly that I could not do and send him with her on a dangerous voyage most frightening to him. You will say I ought to have informed you I would not part with the boy in such circumstances as you had taken trouble to describe but until I saw the girl I was not sure in my own mind what to do and only made it up when confronted with her and not taking to her at all. You will be angry I know and accuse me of all manner of evil things but one thing you cannot accuse me of Lily is not caring for your son upon whose life I swear I love him truly and want only what is best for him. I cried after the girl had gone and he seeing my distress and I explaining I feared your anger he put his arms around my neck and comforted me and said he was sure his real mother could not but love her sister and believe she had acted for the best.

Wilson smiled thinly at that bit. She did not believe a word of it and despised Ellen for concocting such a sentimental and silly scene. A four-year-old child say that? Never. The likelihood was that Oreste knew nothing about anything, and no one in Italy was ever spoken of. Ellen was sure now that she had him for her own and most likely thought it a fair return for her investment of time and trouble. She would not even bother to argue the rights and wrongs of what had occurred since it would be futile. Her desire was never to see or speak to Ellen again but of course she could not allow herself such a luxurious vengeance. It was important for Oreste's sake to keep good relations and so with a good deal of lip biting and general effort of control she finally wrote to her sister in most moderate terms, expressing surprise, confessing intense distress, but apportioning no blame. She did not mention that no more money would be sent—let Ellen discover that when the monthly money orders did not arrive in the punctual way they always had done. It would be in the nature of a test for her: if, as she claimed, she looked after her nephew as her own, then she would not query the lack of financial support; if she asked for it, then it would be easier to force her to part with the boy. There were dangers in this silence—Wilson well understood that the steady remittance of funds for the care of Oreste constituted a claim on him over and above that of natural parentage—but she thought them worth risking. As Oreste grew he would become more expensive to keep and Ellen might not find his maintenance so easy.

The effort of being diplomatic left her depressed once more and miserable. It struck her how much of her life had been spent dissembling. To her mistress it was understandable that she should never speak absolutely freely but it was intolerable that she could not do so to the last remaining member of her family, or even to her husband. Twice Ferdinando had come down to spend the night with her and twice she had refused him without offering any adequate reason. He did not understand that she felt so shriveled and drained, and all thought of sexual relations was abhorrent to her—she was not a fit partner, and shrank from his attentions with loathing. He went off bewildered and hurt and she knew it was quite likely he would seek solace elsewhere. Let him. She found she hardly cared and when Mr. Browning, with some evidence of concern for her, said that he feared they must take Ferdinando to Rome almost as soon as they all returned to Florence in October, she simply nodded. "I expected it, sir," she said, "with Mrs. Browning's health as it is."

"Will you keep Mr. Landor, Wilson?"

"Certainly, sir. He is quite used to me now and even accords me some respect."

She knew everyone watched her carefully, not knowing how to interpret her steady dutifulness, not crediting that it would last. She had never been less communicative either in speech or in manner and it was remarked on by Mrs. Browning with curiosity. "You have done well, Wilson," she said on the last day in Siena. Wilson inclined her head but did not comment though she took care not to appear sullen. "You have got over your distress and disappointment most admirably, dear." Again, Wilson merely nodded. "Will you manage the winter alone?"

"Indeed, ma'am. As I have managed others."

"You grow quite professional as a landlady. I hear on all sides of the excellence of your establishment."

Wilson knew she was being patronized if not mocked outright, but no trace of expression crossed her face and it gave her satisfaction that she knew it did not.

"Pilade is a fine child," Mrs. Browning said next, and her eyes filled with tears. "He is not in the least like any of Henrietta's children, but when I see him laugh and run he makes me think of them, being nearer the little one's age than my Penini. Oh, Wilson, what will become of them?"

"They have a father, ma'am," Wilson said, gently enough but nevertheless detached from Mrs. Browning's distress, "and each other and will not come to want."

"But the greatest want of all is of a mother when one is a child— no other will do."

Stoically, Wilson finished the packing she had offered to help with. There was no point in calling Mrs. Browning's attention to the deeper implications of her statement—she would only take it ill. Her coughing had started again and soon tears mingled with wheezing and she was in a sorry state by the time her husband came back to say the carriage was ready. "Now, Ba! What is this!" he exclaimed. "How can you travel so distraught? We must wait until you compose yourself. What brought this on, Wilson?"

"Thinking of Miss Henrietta's children, sir, and them being soon perhaps in want of a true mother."

Mr. Browning sighed and put his arms around his wife's heaving shoulders and drew her to him. Presently, as Wilson watched, quite impassive, Mrs. Browning stopped weeping and her breath came easier. In another hour she was ready to go, carried to the carriage by her husband. Watching him with his burden, Wilson reflected it was as though he cradled a shadow in his arms. His wife lay there so limp, so insubstantial, her black hair hanging down like the tail of a whipped animal and one white hand clutching his sleeve as though it were her only hold on life. Tremors of feeling flickered through Wilson as she took in the scene. All was not dead in her. Her love for her mistress refused to die completely however hard she rejected it. Turning to go back to her own house to oversee her own arrangements for departure, she realized how little good the summer had done Mrs. Browning. There had been no transformation, as so often there had been, but instead a marked decline in her powers. Her husband spoke of a winter in Rome working miracles but why should it when a summer in Siena had failed? She shivered, even though it was hot, and fancied death and disaster lurked everywhere these days. Nothing and no one was safe, least of all Mrs. Browning, and as she reflected on this a sense of futility overwhelmed her.

It remained with her throughout the month the Brownings spent in Florence, before going to Rome, and nothing seemed to lift it. Bulletins of Miss Henrietta's condition were regular reminders that death was indeed in the midst of life but did not help to make her value her own any more. Nothing Mr. Landor could do could touch her any longer—she could endure rages, witness violence and not flicker an eyelid. Paradoxically, as though realizing his power to upset her had gone, the old gentleman became more docile. She knew his ways and had adapted to them and this seemed to give him a satisfaction which quietened him. Mr. Browning, before he left for the south, complimented her on her handling of his friend. "You are as skillful as you were with my wife, Wilson," he remarked. "You would soothe a wild animal in the end." She showed no pleasure in the compliment, discomfiting him. "Not," he went on hastily, "that I liken my wife to Mr. Landor or to a wild animal, but she had similar need of kindness and nursing expertise." Still Wilson neither smiled nor nodded, but stood with her hands clasped in front of her, as though waiting. "So, Wilson," Mr. Browning said, shifting uncomfortably, "you have done well and I am grateful. I trust you find the arrangement satisfactory? That you are agreeable it should continue?"

"Yes, sir."

And that was how they parted. This time, Wilson did not go out in the street to wave goodbye nor did she weep. Ferdinando spent the night before departure with her but he might as well not have done. She brought Pilade into their bed and refused to send him out and the night was passed in mutual recriminations. Ferdinando's were the stronger. He said she had become like a stone and tempted him to treat her as one and hurl her away. He accused her of blaming him for his failure to return with Oreste when, if anyone was to blame other than her sister Ellen, it was she herself. Finally, he swore and said she was a bad wife and if another woman of greater warmth came his way no one could accuse him of adultery in taking her. Wilson let him rant and clutched Pilade to her. Toward dawn, she said to his sleeping back that he loved his employers more than he loved her and if he had been half the man he thought himself, he would have left them rather than abandon her. As he snored, she told him Florence was full of jobs for the likes of him and by no means all were living-in. It was his choice, she said, to cleave to the Brownings and he was a hypocrite to say otherwise. She said it all, knowing perfectly well none of it was heard, and then she slept a little. When she woke, her husband had gone and outside she could hear horses in the street. The carriage would have left by now. She had not time to dress and make her way to the Casa Guidi. This realization, instead of distressing her, made her feel relieved. There was no guilt in the way she snuggled down under the coverlet, only a welcome sense of freedom. She was free of Ferdinando, toward whom her feelings had not so much changed as vanished, and of Mrs. Browning, who still troubled her so.

She had bid her old mistress farewell the day before. Looking at her, swathed in shawls though the room was too warm and the day itself not cold, Wilson had once more felt those twinges of alarm which she resented. There was such suffering in the huge dark eyes, such a tremble about the pinched mouth, that all her instincts were to rush forward and abase herself and beg to be allowed to offer comfort. But she had not done so. She had said she hoped Rome would prove beneficial and the journey not too arduous. She had spoken stiffly, knowing she did, and she had seen how this wounded. It was hard to stand her ground but she had done so, not wishing to be reclaimed by old emotions. Only toward Pen had she let her guard slip and that was because he himself claimed her as his own, rushing into his mother's bedroom and hurling himself into Wilson's arms. "Oh, Lily, darling," he cried, "I wish you and Pilade could come to Rome. Won't you come, my Lily?" He was a great lad now, though still slight and not above average height for eleven years, but he had not changed toward her in the least and his adoration of Pilade was touching. She had no doubt of the genuine affection he had for her and knew she would be a fool not to acknowledge it. "I will miss you, Penini," she said to him, giving him a hug in return, "and I will kiss Pilade for you every day." They embraced one last time and then he was off, rushing to Ferdinando to help him carry down what he claimed were his "very most precious" things. "He loves you dearly, Wilson," Mrs. Browning murmured. "And shows it always," Wilson replied, "even though he is no longer a child." "Of course he is a child!" came the quick response, so sharp that a coughing fit inevitably followed. "He is as far from being a man as he is from being a baby."

There the interview had ended, Wilson leaving with another wish for good health, a wish she could not believe would be granted. Lying in bed, Pilade still asleep in her arms, she remembered the journeys she had made with the Brownings and the pleasure the intimacy of the carriage had given her. Now, if she were seated in her old place, wedged between the window and Penini, with his mother opposite encircled in her husband's arms, or, if the men rode alongside or traveled on the outside of the carriage, sitting with her mistress while Pen and Flush lay on the other seat—now she would feel stifled, trapped, longing to get out. What had brought this change about she hardly knew, but whatever the cause she did not regret the consequence. It was a miserable business pining for those who had gone and she thought back with something close to horror of the unhappiness she had endured while wishing herself elsewhere. Better to be in Florence, alone, independent, not subjected to sudden swings of mood, than be with people who she felt no longer valued her, whatever they said. She had her own life and in it no one bothered her. All Mr. Landor and the other lodgers cared about was that their rooms should be kept clean and their food brought on time, and she was expert at both. They did not want to be bothered with her joys and despairs and she did not want to be bothered with theirs. Pilade was the only one to whom she showed her true self and at three years of age this was no burden to him.

She no longer wrote to Ferdinando or to anyone else except Ellen and these were dutiful inquiries after Oreste's health with reports of her own and Pilade's. The desire to draw Ellen into her own life, to involve her in her worries, had left her. Ellen wanted none of it so let her dictate her terms. Every day she went to the Casa Guidi and collected any letters for the Brownings to redirect them to Rome but she no longer envied the recipients their voluminous correspondence. But even that, she could not help noticing, had diminished—so many people were dead. No more letters for many a year now from Miss Mitford, none from Miss Trepsack, none from Mrs. Jameson, who had always been so kind to her. All dead. And now none from Miss Henrietta, whose untidy hand she knew so well. Instead, Miss Arabel wrote, in her neat, tidy script, and Mr. Surtees Cook. Picking up his letters made her hesitate. She wanted very much to know what news there was, though she feared it would be bad. Before the Brownings left Florence she had inquired of Mr. Browning how things stood and had been told very ill, but that this must be kept from his wife until she was in the warm south and better able to stand the inevitable end of it all. "Do not fail," Mr. Browning had said, "to send on any letters from Somerset with all speed." So she sent them on immediately, longing to know what they contained and never finding out, but supposing that so long as they did keep coming the worst could not yet have happened. When, in the last days of November, a telegram arrived she knew what it must contain and trembled as she held it in her hand. It had been delivered as she paid her daily visit to the Casa Guidi or otherwise would have languished at the post office, returned as unclaimed. It struck her as peculiar that Mr. Browning should not have given Mr. Surtees Cook his Rome address, for this telegram could not be relayed south in under another twenty-four hours and perhaps more. Taking it back to the post office herself and explaining the circumstances, she met with every kind of difficulty about the redirection and was compelled to pay out of her own pocket to have it seen to. She did this willingly, but wondered at Mr. Browning's unusual lack of forethought.

It had all, of course, been a mistake—instructions as to the Rome address had been given to George Barrett and not properly passed on. Mr. Browning wrote to thank her for her diligence and in doing so confirmed what she had been certain of, that Miss Henrietta had died. He said his wife was struck down, was inconsolable "in the old way." Going about her daily routine, Wilson was dry-eyed, as she knew Mrs. Browning would be for a while yet. No one was spared. The rich, the good, the pretty, the blessed all shared the same fate as the poor, the bad, the ugly, the deprived. Nothing anyone did could make any difference in the end. She could see Miss Henrietta yet in her mind's eye, so young and lovely, laughing up into the face of her adoring Captain Cook. Such gaiety she had had, such an enthusiasm for life. And now this cruel end, just when she was happiest. Wilson could not bear to imagine the horror of such a death. Minnie had written to her about how terrible it had been, how Captain Cook had brought his wife up to see a specialist who had examined her and said at once there was nothing to be done, there was no operation possible, and he must take his wife home to die. Wilson thought of that home in Somerset and thought of Henrietta walking in the lovely garden, doubled up, so Minnie wrote, with pain. Everything had been tried but to no avail—the suffering had been agony, not even deadened with morphine. Wilson's own insides contracted at the thought and she raged against the injustice of such a thing. She could not remember the age of the youngest child—was he one, or two, or even three by now? But the eldest was younger than Pen and the girl no more than five, she was sure. What kind of leave-taking had that been, such a mother dying and leaving three young children? And Surtees Cook himself, as loving as ever Mr. Browning was to her mistress. It was monstrous, dreadful. Resentment gathered in her in a hard knot but still the tears would not come.

Her own life had to go on. She cooked, she cleaned, she shopped, she walked Pilade, she saw to her lodgers—day after day she did the same things at the same time, and instead of being driven half mad with boredom, insane with frustration, she found herself strangely at peace. And her savings mounted steadily. She spent little and, even caring for her lodgers generously, she did not need half the income she found she earned. It would, she saw, be perfectly possible for her and Pilade to go to England the following year if someone could be found to run her boardinghouse for the time it would take. But this realization, which only the year before had excited her, merely pleased her. She made no more plans. When the time was ripe, if it was ever ripe, she would go and if not she would stay. She had given up all idea of exercising any power over fate. It was not just her station in life which precluded choice but life itself and she felt foolish not to have realized this long ago.

Mr. Landor, for all his selfishness, for all the fact that he was old and self-absorbed, felt the change in her. He scowled at her, as ever, but looked at her longer from under his shaggy white brows and one day soon after Christmas was moved again to comment how unlike his wife she was, the highest of compliments. She knew better than to reply. But in tucking a cover over the old man's knees, for there was snow on the ground outside and in spite of a roaring fire the room was not as warm as he was used to, she felt her hand patted and then he said, "Peace and good will, peace and good will, that is the secret after all." He gave a great sigh and if she had not known him better she might have thought, as he slumped forward, that he had expired on the spot. But it was only one of those sleeps into which he was ever more likely to fall during the day and she knew he would waken, roaring, in an hour or so. She banked up the fire and took a look around the room before she closed the door. There were so many possessions in it, brought from his old home in Fiesole by Mr. Browning to make the old gentleman feel as familiar as possible, that it was difficult to move about. Every piece of furniture, every object had associations, according to Mr. Browning. Some of them were valuable. There were ornaments worth many guineas and pictures, however weird they seemed to her, which she had been told were of great artistic merit. Occasionally Mr. Landor would accuse her of stealing from him when he had mislaid a silver spoon or could not find a precious paper knife, but she had always treated these accusations with the contempt they deserved. She had none of the fears of the normal servant that her honesty might ever be in doubt and her absolute conviction of her own integrity had finally communicated itself to the old man and been conceded by him.

She wrote a short monthly letter to Rome, merely reporting on

Mr. Landor's condition and saying all was well in the Casa Guidi. In reply she always received an acknowledgment but rarely more unless Penini wrote. To her surprise, he wrote to her more that winter than at any time before and she was touched to find him attempting more than the sweet but stilted compositions he had managed previously. They were so free in expression, she wondered if they had been read at all by his parents but presumed they could hardly have escaped their eye. She heard that

—Papa is grown stout and has need of bigger trousers but Mama cries he is more handsome than ever and so do I. I have little time my Lily to write because I am put to Latin with the Abbé which is sore hard work and gives me the headache. I would that you were with us to hear me play the piano which I do every day and Papa declares I make good progress. I have begun to Fence which is a man's game and I am to have my uncle Sette's foil when next we go to England which may be in the summer. I hope you will come with us Lily and Pilade too and we will have fun.

There was as much chance of that as flying to the moon but Wilson was grateful for Pen's long memory. He never forgot how it had once been, never seemed to regard her in any other way but as the person who had cared for him and loved him without reservation. Every time she saw him again after an absence she stood aside humbly, expecting him at last to have reached the age when she was an embarrassment, expecting him to shuffle his feet and color and do no more than extend a cool hand, and she would have held none of this against him. But so far this had never happened—always, it was straight into her arms, no matter who was present, and all the hugs and kisses in the world most fervently given.

She wrote back to him careful little letters to which no one could object, fearing to display too much emotion in case it called attention to the boy's overregard for her, but she managed all the same to make her affection felt, telling him:

—Pilade looks for you everywhere and will not believe I have not hidden you in a box. He has no one to play ball with and tosses his ball against the wall in a most despondent fashion. He thanks you for the toy soldiers you left behind for him but wishes The General was here to organize them in fighting order. You are very kind to have thought of him and when I gave him your kiss he gave me a hundred in return to pass on to you believing I could and indeed I wish he was correct in his supposition.

That was as far as she felt she could go, though it was harmless enough. She had seen the children in other families break away entirely from the too zealous claims of an old nurse and when the time came, as it surely must, she wished to protect herself from the pain which rejection could cause. Of all the nurses she had known, only Minnie Robinson had remained loved and revered and even now, when she was old and pensioned off, Miss Arabel visited her faithfully and turned to her in complete trust for advice and comfort. She could not be to Pen as Minnie was to Miss Arabel since there was a mother in between but she had a great desire to see her former charge treat her as freely when he reached manhood. Of course, being a boy made it the more difficult, it would not be as easy, but it had begun to seem to her not impossible to keep in touch with Pen wherever he was.

As for England, she heard enough to doubt that there would ever be another trip there for the Brownings, or at least for Mrs. Browning. Ferdinando surprised her by having someone write a letter for him toward the end of March which made it plain that Mrs. Browning had fared no better in Rome than in Siena and was very ill. He wrote not to tell her this or to send her any kind of greeting but because he wanted her to do something for him. It seemed he had left in the Casa Guidi a gun of which he was fond, taking only his hunting rifle in case he had the chance to go into the country to shoot rabbits. Now his hunting rifle had lost a piece from its firing mechanism and he had been unable to replace it. He requested her to parcel up most carefully in an oiled cloth his other gun and have it sent to him. She was at first incensed at the idea—as if she had no more to do than pack up guns, as if it were an easy matter to send such an object at all, as if she existed only for his convenience—and then amused. Rabbits, indeed.

She was not fooled for an instant or so cut off from news that she had not heard that war was in the air again. Ferdinando was far too old, but only mention the cause and he would be into his old daydreams, seeing himself at the head of a column moving relentlessly on the Austrians. She wrote to him quite sharply, not caring who read her letter, that

—it is impossible for me to *post* a gun as you ought to know you foolish man for what would the post office officials think were I to turn up with a gun to send? And do not think such an object can be disguised for that is manifest nonsense as you have only to try to discover. But Miss Blagden, whom I met by chance yesterday, is going to Rome and when I told her the absurdity of your request she volunteered to carry your ridiculous weapon saying she had always had a fancy to be a gunrunner and that it would be a tale to tell her friends and astonish them. So you will have Miss Blagden to thank and now I suppose that since I am useless to you I will not hear from you again which will not grieve me if that is all I am good for.

That was spiteful and unnecessary but she did not score it out. Not a word had she received from Pilade's father as to his son's welfare all this long time and if she had given him cause, as he might argue, to abandon her she had given him no such leave to forget his child. No reply came. Miss Blagden duly took the wretched gun and it was she who was kind enough to write on delivering it:

—I found your husband very well, Wilson, and as expected by you much agitated over the rumors that another concerted effort is to be made to free and unite his country which subject I may say engages the minds and hearts of his employers hardly less. Mrs. Browning, who looks weak and I believe has hardly moved from her room all winter, though she has ventured on a carriage trip or two since spring arrived, is excited by the promise Cavour has made to bring some statesmanship into this affair and hopes much from him. Your heart would go out to her, Wilson, if you were to see how she struggles to be her old self but is exhausted after a mere ten minutes of conversation, and then she is obliged to fall back and take no more part in it though wishing to do so. I dare not ask directly what is the precise matter but I see in Mr. Browning's eyes an anxiety deeper than usual and he confessed to me the other day that he fears there may be water on the lung. She will not hear of it and tells him the summer will restore her to her full strength, a story you have heard before and will not believe any more than I do. She asked after you and was pleased when I told her how well your business was doing and that you seemed in good spirits since she said she had been anxious for you.

Wilson read that several times—"anxious for you." Why? When? And if so, some manifestation of this concern would have been welcome. Anxious, more likely, that she would become a nuisance again, would let Mr. Landor down or cause trouble over Ferdinando being taken away. All that Mrs. Browning required of her, surely, was that she should be docile and self-contained and grateful.

But then, as Miss Blagden said, she was ill and depressed after her sister's death. Has all charity, all true compassion, left me? Wilson wondered. She seemed to *feel* so much less, neither joy nor sorrow moving her extravagantly. The child of one of her lodgers died in her house in April of an undiagnosed heart complaint—the tiny thing's heart simply stopped as it lay in its cot—and though she was sorry for it and sympathetic to the last degree she was aware that inside herself she shrugged and felt none of the horror and distress such an event would once have caused her. Nor could she decide whether this was a blessing or not. It was a relief not to weep and toss sleepless at night after such tragedies but her own indifference shocked and troubled her. Had she become hard? Had life buffeted her so that now she was impervious to all storms? But then, if that were so, why did it not make her happy? She felt, in her new severity (for want of a better word), only half alive; she knew she wanted the old enthusiasms and passions and expectations to course through her and arouse her. To be so accepting of whatever came her way was to be comfortable but also to be dead.

It often occurred to her that she might never leave Florence again even when she had the money and means to do so. She could not decide if this was something she cared about or not. Once she had thought of herself as so English that, however happy she was abroad and even if married to an Italian, she would always one day gravitate home. Now she was not sure. She could no longer identify her own Englishness—it was lost under the thick veneer of assumed Italian ways and manners. Mrs. Browning had teased her only that summer for becoming more Italian than English and there was some truth in it. Italy had made her lazy, and it was this indolence in herself, in her mind as well as her body, which astonished her. She could sit for hours in the sun these days, content to watch Pilade play, doing nothing whatsoever. She could put all but the most essential tasks off until the next day, or the next, and did it all the time. Little by little everything that was most English about her had been eroded and all she had left of it was her honesty, her natural courtesy and a slight reserve she could not entirely eliminate. She found it unsurprising that her lodgers, with the exception of Mr. Landor, assumed she was Italian, especially if their own command of the Italian language was weak.

When she heard them talking of home in her house it was as though it were a foreign country. Who were these actors and actresses of whom they spoke? What had happened to Macready and Mrs. Kemble? What were these acts of Parliament they spoke of, to do with factories and labor? And this Women's Movement, which so many of the ladies whispered about, what did it mean? At least the Queen was still on the throne and nothing changed there, even though she was long a widow. She heard, too, that wages had begun to climb and that a lady's maid, such as she had been, commanded what seemed an astronomical salary—thirty guineas a year in London in some houses, twice what she had ever earned. But prices were higher too. Several guests had difficulty hiding the fact that they found her charges cheap (though they were not cheap by Italian standards). One gentleman even said to her that, were she to run such a boardinghouse in England and charge what she charged in Florence, she would be besieged. So she knew that in the few years since she had last been in England great changes had begun to take place, from some of which she might clearly benefit. She was the one who was standing still, frozen in every way into herself.

The arrival of the Brownings and her husband in Florence at the beginning of June was the beginning of what she felt to be a softening of her self and she was glad to find the hard crust she felt encasing her crack and dissolve. It was the shock of seeing Mrs. Browning to whom she went, a little reluctantly, on June 6, a little after midday. Nothing Isa Blagden had said had prepared her for the fright. She was used to her old mistress's pallor, to the skeleton thinness, to the heavy, bruised-looking eyes but, walking into her bedroom on the beautiful summer's morning and looking toward the bed, she was stopped in her progress and forced to control the exclamation of horror that rose to her lips. Here was a face, buried in its cloud of hair, which looked more like a mask than a living thing, a mask such as might be worn on All Souls' Eve to scare the children, all thickly white with painted black sockets for eyes and a mouth so crudely gashed it was but a slit. It was dreadful to see and all the more frightening for the misery of the expression which no attempt at smiling could lift. "Oh, ma'am!" Wilson said, and covered her mouth with her hand to try to hide her distress. "That is a fine welcome," Mrs. Browning murmured. "I am a little drowsy, that is all, a little tired with the journey, though I feel better than I thought I would. How are you, Wilson? And Pilade? And Mr. Landor?"

"All well, ma'am."

"And have you had a quiet winter?"

"Not so quiet. We had guests over Christmas, the house full, and three stayed until Easter which—oh, ma'am!" She came to a full stop, quite overcome, quite unable to continue such a pedestrian account. Her heart beat in a way she had not been conscious of it beating for many a month and she felt near to tears. Timidly, she went close to the bed and when the invalid stretched out her hand she took it gratefully and sat beside her. The hand was hot, the skin dry, and the slender fingers lay in her palm like splinters of fine porcelain—she was afraid to squeeze them for fear they might snap. But now Mrs. Browning was cheerful, talking at once, though with long pauses for breath, of politics and how much she hoped from Cavour. "I learned much from Ferdinando's friends in Rome," she said. "Oh, we had a regular revolutionary den, Wilson, I assure you, our house was a hotbed of intrigue and your husband in the thick of it."

"I am sure. It is all he thinks of."

"It is very nearly all I think of, the hope in it, the glory to come . . . if I live to see it."

"Live? Of course you will live. Why, when the summer . . ."

"Wilson, I saw your look just now, dear. There is no use in telling me I shall soon be running up mountains. I know what I am become and so do you."

"I had not seen you for over six months, ma'am, it was merely surprise that you have lost a little color. . . ."

Mrs. Browning began to laugh but the laugh brought on a coughing fit and, when Wilson rushed to her aid and raised her higher on the pillow, her face took on an ugly blue tinge, which she had never seen before. Mr. Browning, coming in at that very moment, ran to his wife's side and all but hauled her out of the bed in order to get her upright—in a moment, the convulsion was over and she sank back quite exhausted and drained. Down from one corner of her mouth Wilson was alarmed to see a thin trickle of dark red blood. She looked at Mr. Browning, startled, and he drew a clean handkerchief from his pocket and wiped the blood away tenderly, saying, "She tells me it is nothing, nothing she has not had before."

"Never *dark* blood, sir," Wilson murmured, very low.

"It is gone now. It is never much."

They both stood looking down at the poor sufferer, neither speaking. Gradually her expression relaxed and soon they saw she was genuinely asleep. Together, they left the room.

Mr. Browning, she saw, was as robust as his wife was pitifully weak. He strode about the drawing room restlessly, occasionally hitting the back of a chair with his hand, and she saw how pent up were his energies. Finally he came to a stop in front of the fireplace and, turning to face her, said, almost accusingly, "*You* know her, Wilson. What am I to do?"

"Well, sir, I fear there is nothing you can do except what is done already, which is to keep Mrs. Browning calm and quiet and endeavor to feed her nourishing food to give her back some strength."

"That is the precise problem it has always been. How can I feed her nourishing food when she will eat nothing? I have sat with her for hours spooning broth into her and a tedious business it is to make sure any of it goes down. *You* know, Wilson, you *know*, you cannot have forgotten how it is."

"Certainly I cannot. But I remember too that it was always unwise to fuss too much over what was taken, for then she becomes anxious herself and her throat seizes up and nothing can go down . . . oh, sir, she seems very ill."

"It is nothing to how it has been. I feared in Rome I detected a great change for the worse, but she has stood the journey well, better than might have been expected, and now, if all remains serene, we may see her build up again."

But everything did not remain serene. Unaware of the news which had spread swiftly throughout the city, Wilson returned to the Casa Guidi late in the evening, not really thinking to see Mrs. Browning again but wishing to inquire after her and to take a knead cake she had made specially. It would not be eaten—she had not the faintest illusion of that—but it would be looked on and smiled over and would bring back happy memories and it was all she could think of to signify her reborn affection. So she hurried through the streets, hot and dusty, the still warm knead cake covered with a cloth, and she was aware of a certain agitation in the people passing her, without catching anything said. Concentrating on keeping her gift level and unsquashed, she climbed the Casa Guidi stairs carefully, glad when she reached the last bend. But as she did so she thought she heard a thin, piercing sound, like the wail of a child who has just wakened up and found himself alone. She stopped, listening. It could not be Pen, whose voice these days in all its guises was strong and most unchild-like. Nor could it be a cat, for there had never been a cat in the Casa Guidi. It came again, a most piteous keening sound, and she hurried on, her thoughts turning to the highly strung Annunciata, who might be mourning yet another lost Roman lover. The door was propped open, to catch what air there was, and she entered hesitantly, her gift thrust out in front of her. There was no sign of either Ferdinando or Annunciata in the kitchen so she was bold enough to tiptoe toward the drawing room where she hesitated again and peered around the door. The room was empty, but she could hear Mr. Browning's voice from the bedroom and was now certain that was where the cry was coming from. It could only be from Mrs. Browning. Fearing a tragedy of epic proportions—her mind leaped at once to Penini and then to Miss Arabel—she knocked on the open door and Mr. Browning came through from the other room, so haggard and drawn in contrast to his morning self that once more she was convinced something dreadful had happened.

To her, it was nothing dreadful after all, but she was compelled to keep silent and pay lip service at least to the general despair, for fear she would be outlawed otherwise. Cavour was dead, that was all. Cavour, only fifty years of age, the great statesman Italy had needed for so long. This was the death that had reduced Mrs. Browning to a grief more overt and terrible than she had ever shown before and all around her there were faces nearly as stricken and voices almost as crazed. There was nothing Wilson could say or do. It did not make sense to her. Miss Henrietta's death had seemed so much more terrible and yet when she ventured to say this she was met with blank looks. Putting her knead cake down in the kitchen, she went back to her own home through the streets where already black crepe banners were being hung from every window. God knew what effect this would have on Mrs. Browning, but as she went to bed that night she had no feelings of optimism left and already there yawned ahead a great void.

CHAPTER TWENTY-NINE

IN THE DAYS that followed Cavour's death Wilson came near to wishing he had never lived in the first place. All she heard, in the street, in the market, and most of all in the Casa Guidi, was the name Cavour until she was sick of it. Such a fuss, such a song and dance, making her feel that those worries she had entertained of having nothing English left in her were after all misplaced—she suddenly felt very English indeed in her disdain for the extravagance of this public mourning. Ferdinando was distraught, weeping openly and going so near to tearing his hair in fact as well as metaphorically that she could hardly credit it. "And you a grown man!" she exclaimed scornfully. He tried to explain to her the dreadful significance of this great man's untimely death but she had no interest in the explanation. Of far more concern to her was Mrs. Browning's condition.

She visited her every day, drawn irresistibly to the sick woman's bedroom and finding some comfort in seeming to be welcomed. Annunciata was not good with an invalid, being still too young and energetic to take kindly to tiptoeing and ministering calmly to someone suffering. Watching her, Wilson saw at once that as well as a certain ineptitude the girl had a dislike of illness itself. Every time she had to deal with a handkerchief soaked in phlegm she could hardly contain her disgust, and in a patient as sensitive to every nuance of voice and expression as Mrs. Browning such revulsion was hurtful. Then the girl, though doubtless with the best intention in the world, was so determined to be cheerful it jarred on the nerves. She would come in singing and beaming, sure this was the way to make her mistress feel better and having no conception of how offensive this heartiness was. There was nothing Mrs. Browning liked better than someone young and vivacious about her when she was well but when she was ill it was anathema to her. So she was glad to see Wilson, so quiet and calm, and Annunciata was equally pleased. When it was suggested she might take the afternoons off, with Wilson offering to be there each day from two to four, she accepted the idea gratefully, and everyone was satisfied.

Wilson took sewing with her, remembering how soothing Mrs. Browning had always found the sight of her stitching, the ins and outs of the needle she plied seeming to have a hypnotic effect. She settled herself near enough to the bed to be able at once to deal with any coughing fits, or the results of them, but not so near that her presence would be oppressive. The room was stifling hot, since outside the June temperature had soared to near 90 degrees in the shade, and almost dark because the shutters were closed against the glare, but she could see well enough. She hardly moved and did not speak unless spoken to but there was no constraint in her bearing. Instead, she felt curiously contented sitting there, as though all time was suspended and with it everything that plagued her. She looked forward to her time in the sickroom and was sorry to leave its peace. Sometimes she was not needed because Miss Blagden had come and then she felt bereft and did not know what to do with herself. On impulse, she wrote to Lizzie Treherne one afternoon, not knowing why she should think of doing so when she had not penned a line to Lizzie in three years and had received nothing from her but only feeling the need to try to express and communicate something of what she felt to someone who had once cared as much about the poor suffering invalid. Once she had begun she found it difficult to stop, telling Lizzie:

—there is an attraction about old friends which dies hard Lizzie and makes me wish to see you again. I have no one I can call a friend as you were my friend and think back with astonishment to my early days in Florence when I never seemed to want for a companion and was famous for having made my own way in what society was available to me. But now I would be hard put to name a single woman of my acquaintance, English or Italian, with whom I pass more than the time of day. Such is the lot of women I fear, marriage and motherhood taking them away from their own sex if they have not family and friends from far back to hand. Now you may say Lizzie that my husband is my friend and ought to suffice in that respect but without embarrassment I tell you that in my case at least that is not so. Ferdinando is a good man but if I ever thought we shared the same interests and tastes upon which friendship thrives then I was blinded by love. I am blind no longer. All my husband thinks of is his country and the state of the movement toward unity. He is hardly more interested in his son than that and it grieves me sorely. The truth is Lizzie we have grown apart and I fear the fault if fault there is lies in me. He may still be the same man I married but I am not the same woman nor would I wish to be. Why, as I sit beside our old mistress who as I have just related is languid with her old complaint and think back to Wimpole Street I cannot believe I was ever as naive and trusting as history shows me to have been. Think of my ambition then Lizzie and what I was intent on making myself! Think how happy I vowed I should be with a husband and children to love! I could laugh if not more inclined to weep over those fond hopes. Now this sounds bitter Lizzie and you may shake your head in sorrow at my ingratitude when I seem to have been so blessed but believe me when I say this is no petty complaint against fate that I make. I am not satisfied with what I have become nor with how I have conducted myself and that is all there is to it yet if you were to ask me what I would have done otherwise I could hardly tell you.

Nor had she been able to tell Mrs. Browning who, one afternoon, when she seemed rather better than she had been and was sitting up in a chair propped with pillows, looked at the sewing Wilson was doing and asked if she were not content with her little boy Pilade, for whom she was making the blouse.

"Content, ma'am? In what way?"

"To have him, Wilson. To be a mother, to have a home and family as once you longed for."

"It is not quite what I longed for, I am not exactly content with it or with myself."

"Yourself?"

"What I have become."

"And what have you become that dissatisfies you?"

"Dull, in myself. I go through each day in a dream, thinking, Is this all there is, work and very little else?"

"Wilson, you shock me!"

"I shock myself."

"Pilade is such a fine boy, with all his future ahead of him . . ."

"And I with all mine behind."

There had been a long pause while Mrs. Browning stared at her, her expression a strange mixture of curiosity and bewilderment. Then she coughed and took awhile to recover so that it was full half an hour, long after Wilson thought the subject forgotten, before she ventured, "You disturb me, dear, with this dullness of yours. It half terrifies me to find you regarding your life so little, if you mean what you seem to say. After all, you have made something of yourself, more than many a lady's maid does, and have an interesting life when all is said and done, living as you do in Florence in these exciting times."

"The times are not exciting to me. That is the trouble—I find nothing exciting."

"And I am all excitement, or was, until this illness. There lies the difference between us and I cannot help but wonder why."

"You have your work, ma'am."

"Precious little of it, these days."

"And your husband."

"Ah yes, my husband. But you have your husband."

"Sometimes, and I hardly care when I do, for that part of me is dead, I think."

"Love is dead?"

"If love it was, something is dead in any case."

"You are very frank, dear."

"You taught me to be frank, ma'am."

"Did I?"

"You did, as you taught me to hope and expect miracles with confidence and believe in myself."

"What a lot you lay at my door. I had never credited myself with such power, it is quite alarming. Was I cruel to impress all this upon you if, as you say, I did?"

"I did not think so at the time."

"But you do now?"

"I feel I have failed, that is all."

Another pause, for a sustained bout of coughing this time, made Wilson regret she had ever responded as she had. She urged the invalid not to speak, to stay quite still and let her thoughts turn to some pleasant and soporific subject without delay. To help them do so she began to describe the new lodger who had arrived at her house the day before, but she had only begun on her account when she was interrupted and the previous conversation continued.

"I cannot bear to think," Mrs. Browning said, her voice very weak, "that you judge yourself a failure and I am to blame."

"Oh, not to blame, ma'am, never to blame. Now I am all confused, I did not intend to say anything about blame. What I said was mere idle talk to amuse you."

"It was no such thing. Do not sweep it aside so. Half our lives we spend on inconsequential chatter and since I no longer have anything as generous as half of mine left I want no more of it. I respect your confession, Wilson, and am honored it was made to me."

"Do not upset yourself, ma'am, that is what I fear."

"I am not upset. I am interested and will not have my interest turned aside. And concerned, dear, I am concerned as a friend and as a woman. It occurs to me there is something in what you say for all women of our age."

"Oh no, ma'am, not for you and those like you. You are quite content and happy with your lot."

"Only because of Robert and Pen who, as you yourself say, are not for you matched in your Ferdinando and Pilade."

"I love Pilade."

"But he does not, on your own admission, make you feel less dull, he does not, it seems, give you a joy that lightens your whole being and makes sense of your existence."

"No."

"Then that is how I am different and how others are more akin to you. If I did not have Robert and Pen where would I be? Dull, like you."

"You would have your poetry."

"But how happy, at this age, would that have kept me? We cannot know, but I suspect now that I should have been a sad creature, fit for very little."

There was a silence, full of awkwardness. Wilson felt uncomfortable and disturbed. She had not intended their chat to take this direction and found it hard to remember how it had. As ever, she was bested by Mrs. Browning and never ended up saying what she meant. Nor could she understand why she had begun to speak as she had done. For the last fifteen years, it seemed, she had been forever blurting out thoughts best kept to herself, forever striving to make of her relationship with her mistress what she had ample evidence could not be made of it. Again and again she had been disappointed, hurt, even humiliated and still she had not learned her lesson. She sighed, and then, as Mrs. Browning looked up at her, tried to explain the sigh with a reference to an aching back. Pen's coming in at that moment successfully excused her from further explanation. First he went to his mother and kissed her and then he came to Wilson and kissed her too, hardly less enthusiastically but a good deal more energetically. Then he stood looking at his mother, his stare level and appraising.

How he had grown, and not just grown but changed beyond all imagination. . . . Wilson had to remind herself of his age, twelve years and three months, before she could account for the transformation. He was no longer slim and girlish nor ever would be again. She saw that his shape was that of Mr. Septimus, Mr. George and Mr. Octavius, which was to say broad in the shoulder and tending toward the heavy. He had none of the Barrett height, though, being no more than average for his age, and she fancied he might not grow much taller than his father, who was only five foot six or thereabouts. But what was most unexpected of all was the masculinity of him already, even before the years of real bodily change ahead. Did his mother see it? she wondered. Did she see that the long hair now looked absurd around the newly filled-out face, suddenly square and strong? Did she notice how the muscular legs were at a variance with the satin pantaloons and that the hands protruding from the lace cuffs were covered in cuts, which came from a determined indulgence in sport? It was impossible to tell. She treated him exactly the same, as her baby, her precious darling, her little one who could do no wrong. And he was as loving and demonstrative as ever, which was a relief to witness. There was no sign of any growing embarrassment, no turning aside of the head to avoid kisses. But all the same she knew Pen's life was now very much outside his mother's sphere and that he functioned in it as a different animal. His fencing, his riding, his love of company, especially female company, were all more important to him than the love of literature which was the mainspring of her life and which she had tried to nurture in him. Yet there was no breach between them—the bond seemed as close as ever.

"Mama, are you better?" the boy asked gravely.

"Indeed I am, Penini, a little better every day."

"*Is* Mama a little better every day, Lily?"

"She has told you she is, Pen, and so she must be."

"But what do *you* say, Lily?"

"It hardly matters what I say. . . ."

"Oh, indeed it does, Lily, because you are wise and you can judge as she cannot. Is that not so, Mama?"

"I suppose it must be," said his mother, smiling slightly.

"Is Mama better, Lily?"

"A little."

"There you are," his mother said, "my very own opinion endorsed. Are you happy now?"

"Not happy, Mama, not until you are truly well."

Her eyes, Wilson saw, filled with tears but Pen had turned aside to pick a grape from the bedside table and by the time he turned back his mother had her grief under control. He fed her the grape and then said he must be off to practice his music or Papa would be displeased.

It was very near time for Wilson to go. She began gathering up her sewing and folding it to put in her bag.

"Wilson," Mrs. Browning said, "what date is it?"

"June 19, ma'am."

"June 19. Nearly Midsummer's Day. I always think of England on that day, of the green and the soft rain. I shall never see it again and never thought I cared until now."

Wilson kept silent. She knew she must not burst into emphatic assurances that this was nonsense.

"Midsummer's Day," Mrs. Browning repeated, drowsily, "and I have been ill some two weeks. Well, we must see an improvement soon, I expect, if just to satisfy Penini. Robert talks of doctors but I will have no more of them. Wilson, if he takes counsel with you, you must tell him all over again that you have seen it before and it is the old trouble."

"But it is not precisely," Wilson murmured.

"What extra is there?"

"Not extra, ma'am, but something missing."

"Missing? Good heavens, how can that be? I thought to have the usual full complement—cough, headache, languor, weakness, a pain at times in my side—now which is missing of my old adversaries, pray?"

"The will, ma'am," Wilson said, very softly.

"Oh, now come, dear, you romance. I have as much will as I ever had, too much of it, some might say. It is will which has kept me going and sometimes precious little else. Explain yourself, Wilson, or stand corrected."

Wilson hesitated but was not put off. "I see it in your eyes, ma'am. There is a—a blankness there which was not there before." The word she had wished to use was "deadness" but she had not been able to get it out.

"It is the morphine," Mrs. Browning said, "it makes me feel far away."

Wilson did not argue. Perhaps it was even true. Certainly, she had noticed the doses of morphine were more frequent and stronger. But she knew a drug-induced vacancy and this was not it. She said goodbye for the day, but the invalid seemed already to have drifted off to sleep.

The next day she did not go to the Casa Guidi in the afternoon, since Miss Blagden had called and said she would be there, but went instead in the evening merely to inquire if there had been any change. Even at eight o'clock it was still fiercely hot, one of those cauldron days when the thought of the greenery and rain Mrs. Browning had mentioned seemed utterly desirable. Doubtless Mr. Browning would endeavor to remove his wife to Siena or Bagni di Lucca as soon as she was fit to travel but Wilson thought it unlikely she would be invited to make up the party. This was as well. She had not the energy to pack up and go, even for Pilade's sake, and her house, most unusually for the time of year, was full. Arriving exhausted at the Casa Guidi, she ducked into its shady entrance hall and was bracing herself for the climb up the stairs when Miss Blagden came down them. She seemed to rush the last few steps and clutched Wilson's arm in a most agitated fashion. "Oh, Wilson dear," she gasped, "it was not at all my fault—she would have the window open and would sit near it and there was nothing I could do and now there is a soreness in the throat and Robert is anxious."

"A soreness in the throat need be nothing, Miss Blagden," Wilson said reassuringly. "Why, it may be a mere dryness we are all feeling today. So Mrs. Browning was out of bed today, was sitting up?"

"Yes, Robert insisted and carried her to the chair when I arrived."

"Well then, that is a good sign, that she was able to endure it."

"I do not know that she was. It was her husband who could no longer endure the wretchedness of seeing her in bed day after day."

"But it is better for her chest to be in a chair."

"So she was told. Oh, I hope this sore throat is nothing or I shall feel to blame."

Wilson did not, after all, go up to the Brownings' apartment, knowing she would learn nothing Miss Blagden had not already told her, but when she went along the next afternoon as usual, hating the dustiness of the hot streets, she was prepared to find the invalid not better but worse—as indeed she was. A cough had developed in the night and it was not of that intermittent sort to which they were all used, nor did it come in sudden fits, but was instead an almost permanent hacking, rasping affair which seemed to tear the sufferer's poor wasted frame to pieces. Mr. Browning was distraught. He seized on Wilson as soon as she came and hurried her into the bedroom where Annunciata, smiling vacantly, was halfheartedly rubbing Mrs. Browning's back with one hand and holding a cloth in the other. Wilson moved swiftly. The invalid was all lopsided on the pillows, which were bunched up ineffectively somewhere in the region of her heaving shoulders and quite useless as a support. Nor were the pillows themselves much good, being huge, soft things. Whipping the sheet off, Wilson dragged the bolster into an upright position and then got Mr. Browning to lift his wife so that this leaning post ran the whole length of her back. She could not keep herself upright but by forcing her backward at a very slight angle they were able to maintain an almost perpendicular position. After only a few seconds the coughing quietened in severity, though it did not stop. Then Wilson took the water reposing on the table and was able to slip a little of it, teaspoon by teaspoon, through the cracked and swollen lips.

"Thank God," Mr. Browning said, and sank down on a chair, his head in his hands.

She stayed long after her usual time and left reluctantly, feeling frightened and even more frightened of showing it. Mr. Browning had also stayed in the room all afternoon, his eyes never leaving his wife's face. Nobody had spoken. Mrs. Browning, who could not be asleep because of the coughing, nevertheless seemed not fully conscious. Her breathing was very heavy and Wilson thought, constantly bending over her to wipe her forehead, that there was a foul smell coming from her mouth. When she finally left, Mr. Browning followed her out.

"I shall send for the doctor tomorrow if this has not lifted. You would agree, Wilson?"

"Yes, sir, though what he will be able to do in such a case I do not know."

"Nevertheless, we ought to have a medical opinion. You will come again?"

"Of course, sir. Indeed, were you to need me, I would stay, if it would not cause offense to Annunciata."

"Offense does not come into it," Mr. Browning replied rather irritably, "but there is no need, I shall sit up myself."

Wilson heard from Ferdinando, who came at six in the morning to tell her, what had happened. The doctor had been sent for at one o'clock when another terrifying bout of coughing had made up Mr. Browning's mind. The doctor had applied a poultice to the invalid's chest and sat her feet in a mustard bath. By dawn, anxiously watched by her husband, the doctor and Annunciata, a great deal of phlegm had been expelled and the coughing had once more subsided into its customary pattern. But the verdict was that in all likelihood an abscess was on the congested right lung and might very well burst with fatal consequences, if not dispersed, which would be no easy matter. Ferdinando wept as he relayed all this, but Wilson ignored him. She spoke to her maid, a much more reliable girl than she had ever had before, and instructed her in the care of Pilade and the running of the house, saying she would engage reinforcements at once because she feared she was needed elsewhere and would not be at home much for a while. Then she packed a small bag and kissed Pilade and, returning with Ferdinando, announced to Mr. Browning that she would stay and help Annunciata until the crisis was over.

To her surprise, Mr. Browning appeared cheerful enough. "It is an abscess, Wilson," he announced confidently, "and we need wonder no more at this excessive weakness or as to why the coughing is so very troubling. I knew there was something in particular wrong. Did I not say so? Did I not wish a doctor to examine my wife and diagnose the precise problem?"

"You did, sir."

"It explains everything, do you see? How can Ba recover if this wretched abscess is clogging up her lung? It is not to be expected."

He seemed dangerously optimistic all of a sudden, but when she went in to the invalid herself, with whom Mr. Browning left her for a short while, there was not the same relief. Wilson, trying to make the bed a little more comfortable, thought its occupant looked worse rather than better. Her eyes, ever the clearest indication of her true state of health, were black and opaque-looking, without light or recognition. "Who is it?" she murmured as though she could not indeed see.

"Wilson, ma'am. Come to make you as easy as I can."

"Ah, Wilson."

She tried to smile, but the pathetic wavering of the mouth was too much for her. Gently, Wilson took a cloth and squeezed it in the cold water lying in the washbowl and with infinite tenderness passed it over the sick woman's brow. Her hand went up to hold it there and then fell back, too weak to keep the position. For half an hour Wilson methodically cooled down all the exposed parts of the invalid's body but felt it was a losing battle—her skin was so very hot and dry. Occasionally Mrs. Browning's eyes would close and she would seem to drift away and then, when once more she opened them, the expression in them would seem even more hopeless. "Doctors," she murmured once, "they know nothing, nothing. And he has the wrong lung, it is the left that is infected, not the right, it is the left. Do you remember, Crow dear, it is the left?"

"I am not Crow, ma'am," Wilson said very quietly, "I am Wilson. But I remember I was told it was the left when you were very ill in the days before I came to you."

"Oh, Wilson, is it? How times change."

Then she seemed to fall properly asleep and Wilson was left to look at her and feel very strange indeed. She did not know why being mistaken for Crow should have the curious effect of making her feel insubstantial, as though she might at any moment float away. It was an understandable confusion, one that had arisen many times in the old days, and the likely consequence of heavier and heavier doses of opium. But she felt that day as though it canceled her out, as though everything that had happened to her since she left Newcastle had no reality. She crouched at the bedside in that stifling room, kept as ever in almost total darkness when the sun was at its most fierce outside, and closed her eyes half the time, beginning to feel dizzy with the heat and the tension and her acute awareness that her mistress was very ill. She felt that she was on the edge of hallucination herself and that if she were to give herself over to the drowsiness which threatened to overcome her she could once more be in Mother's arms and walk with Fanny by the river, threading daisies. Again and again she jerked herself upright and pressed her knuckles to her eyes and only when they came away damp did she realize she appeared to be weeping. Furtively, she wiped away the tears that would keep falling, though she persisted in her surprise that she was crying and felt she was wiping them away from someone else's face. There was an ache at the base of her throat but she could not connect it with these tears and wondered if she was about to start a cold.

When Mr. Browning came to relieve her, he assumed she had been crying over his wife and was a little irritated. "Now come, Wilson," he whispered, "we want no tears, that is not the way."

"No, sir."

"It is a touching sight, I grant you, but the news is good, remember."

"Yes, sir." It was too much trouble to tell him she had not been distressed on account of his wife but for some other reason she could not divine. And this feeling of utter sadness persisted throughout the day whether she was in the Casa Guidi or not, until she came to regard the sickroom as a welcome refuge, the only place where her misery had a proper home. Even when the invalid seemed to be making progress, there was still the same atmosphere of suspended time, of being cocooned from all outer pressures, and she longed to stay there. Leaving the room each day, she was almost afraid to step into the comparative glare of the other rooms and even more afraid of speaking to other people—she longed for any questions to be of such simplicity that a nod or shake of the head would suffice in reply. She did not want to share her peculiar grief with anyone and looked on in disgust as Ferdinando and Annunciata conducted themselves in true Italian fashion.

On Friday, June 28, when she arrived at Casa Guidi—for she was not after all staying at night, though she had begged to take the night watch which Mr. Browning claimed for himself—Mrs. Browning was still in bed. The habit had been, for the last three days, that she should once more be put in a chair and that chair should be taken into the drawing room to give her a change of air. Wilson had not liked this, though obliged to concede it was beneficial. In the drawing room there was no intimacy. Mrs. Browning slumped in her chair, hating it, and though the vast room was cooler and altogether more comfortable to sit in, Wilson felt happy only when at last the time came to put her mistress back to bed. Then, both of them sighed with contentment and were glad of it. But that Friday Mr. Browning was entertaining Mr. Lytton and had agreed it would be more convenient altogether if his wife remained in bed, which she had never had any desire to leave in any case. Wilson was pleased, though she did not of course show it, and went through to the bedroom almost eager to enter its womblike darkness, to let its peculiar peace envelop her.

But, in fact, Mrs. Browning was disposed to be livelier than she had been all week and there was as a consequence a different and less soporific air in the room. Somehow disappointed, though chiding herself privately for being so, Wilson also took in that the shutters were not quite firmly closed and the curtains were half open. There was enough light to see everything plainly and quite to destroy the illusion of being anywhere but in a bedroom. She did not remark on it but said instead, "How much brighter you look this morning, ma'am. It is a pleasure to see."

"Brighter? Oh, I am hardly bright, only less dead for not being dragged into the drawing room. I think I could rest here forever and may very well do so." But she smiled, and it was a real smile and lightened the shadows in the poor sunken cheeks. The bones, Wilson noted, now stood out alarmingly, the skull plain to see beneath the skin, but then a diet of spoonfuls of milk and even smaller sips of broth for the past month was hardly likely to have put flesh upon the body. Quietly, efficiently, Wilson smoothed the bedclothes and plumped up the pillows and did all the usual number of little things which were part of her routine and all the time she felt bereft, as though something she treasured had suddenly been taken from her. Perhaps Mrs. Browning felt it too, she thought, for she murmured that the curtains being opened was not her idea nor did she wish the shutters to be other than shut, but "Robert will have it that it is healthier thus and will aid this recovery of mine he is so determined on." Once Wilson had finished her tasks and had settled down in her usual place, she repeated, "Recovery. A strange word, Wilson, do you not think? *Recuperare,* to recuperate. But then what is regained, do you think? Control of one's senses, of consciousness. To make one's way back, but to where, and can it be done? And why do it when in the end it *cannot* be done, when the day will arrive when it is impossible. What would you wish to recover, dear?"

The voice was low, as usual, and thin and a little hoarse, but Wilson was as impressed as ever by the strength of the mind which had thought all this, which deliberated in such a way even in the middle of such illness. She remembered how nervous it had once made her to be made to respond to such inquiries and then, gradually, how she relished it and learned to take part. So now she repeated "Recover" herself and then thought awhile before answering with the honesty expected of her, "Why, you, ma'am, I should like to recover you." Slowly, the head turned and into the lackluster eyes came the faintest flicker of curiosity. "Me? You mean you would like to recover my health for me, dear?"

"No, ma'am, though that too, it goes without saying, but I meant rather the feeling, ma'am, which I believe to have been between us, the understanding, if I was not wrong."

The eyes closed but Wilson could tell from the way the hands plucked at the bedcover that her mistress was not asleep and from the crease in the forehead that she reflected still on the topic. Great energy was needed in her condition to say anything at all, and she was merely, in the long pause, husbanding her resources. Where once the interchanges would have rattled along, they now cost such effort, every word had to count for more and Wilson felt guilty at provoking any other response at all. "Perhaps, ma'am," she said, "you ought not to talk or upset yourself."

"If talk now upsets me I am done for," Mrs. Browning said. "No, I must talk, dear, and I wish to. It is touching, what you say, and I see the truth in it. There was an understanding, a sympathy, between us. I valued it. I shrink from believing, as I suppose I must, that I sacrificed it in anything I said or did or in how I may have behaved toward you.

These things happen. I wish they had not. You were very dear to me, Wilson."

The long speech, longer than she had managed for many a day, exhausted her. Stricken, Wilson seized her hand and held it and said, "Oh, ma'am, forgive me. It is I who was at fault. And if you held me dear I hold you dearer to this very day and want only to be close to you and with you." There was no reply, but her own hand was squeezed, the very feel of the fingers thrilled her. They sat hand in hand, all the rest of the hour Mr. Browning was with Mr. Lytton, and when it was time for Wilson to go her mistress opened her eyes wide and said, "We will talk more, dear, tomorrow, we will talk of ourselves and what we mean to each other." All the rest of that day she felt an uncontrollable excitement at the prospect of going over what had come between herself and her mistress, of trying to fathom what had created the coolness between them and then dispelling it and "recovering" the past happiness. She could settle to nothing, walked feverishly and foolishly, considering the broiling heat, around Florence, longing for the sun to set and the darkness to descend and the new day to come. By nine in the evening she could no longer stand to be away from the Casa Guidi and was compelled to go there once more and brave the stairs merely to inquire if Mrs. Browning had settled for the night comfortably. To her joy, she was invited in, Mr. Browning boasting his wife was not even asleep but livelier than she had been for a month. He wanted Wilson to see her so she could agree a corner had been turned, and when she entered the bedroom, where the doctor was finishing the twice daily visit he had made for the past two weeks, she was so looking forward to the next day that she was determined to see an improvement which would make their heart-to-heart certain. "Oh yes, sir," she said confidently, "Mrs. Browning looks better, and so late in the evening too." Pen caught her on her way out, after she had bid a good night hardly worth making when tomorrow was so near, and asked her, "Is Mama really better, Lily?" and she hugged him close and had no difficulty assuring him that yes, she was.

She did not sleep the entire night and toward dawn gave up all pretense. She went out into the tiny courtyard at the back of her house, taking care not to waken Mr. Landor with any noise, and stood looking up at the stars and the thin crescent of new moon. There was nothing refreshing in the thick, humid air but she felt exhilarated, and paced about restlessly. She watched the sky eagerly, straining to see the stars disappear, willing them to, and the moon to wane and the far horizon above the rooftops to lighten. Even then, it would be hours before she could decently go to the Casa Guidi and retreat into that dim, still bedroom where she was to bare her heart and be received once more into her mistress's own. The stone of the house against her back was warm, even though it was night. As she came to lean against it, its roughness scratched her spine. She liked the sensation and moved against the wall like a cat. All the heavy dullness in her had vanished and she felt alert, ready to walk for miles or climb mountains or sail the seven seas. She smiled at the absurdity of her thoughts and went inside, thinking she ought at least to lie down for another hour and try to compose herself.

The smile was still on her face when she heard a loud knocking on the outer door and her name being called. Quite unworried, not in the least concerned, since her mind was elsewhere, she drew the bolt and opened the heavy door to reveal Ferdinando in a dreadful state of incoherence. He clutched her to him and for once her body did not resist but allowed itself to be enveloped by his. She felt, with her arms around him, as though she was supporting him and she waited in some bewilderment but with no apprehension to hear what she was sure would be the inevitable story of some Italian patriot who had died, or some battle lost. Her husband seemed quite unable to talk— the sobbing and hiccuping were frightful to hear and he stumbled as she led him into the kitchen and half thrust him into a chair. "Now come, come, Ferdinando," she said soothingly, "it cannot be so bad you must make yourself ill." This only produced more tears and he put his arms on the table and buried his head in them under the weight of his grief. Patiently, she poured a glass of wine for him— whatever the hour, her husband could usually be revived with a glass of wine—but no amount of coaxing would make him drink it. He seemed quite destroyed and in spite of her lack of interest in the affairs of Italy she found herself growing curious as to the precise cause of all this flamboyant distress. Doubtless Mrs. Browning would be similarly affected, which would be very bad for her and would put back her recovery yet again, and at this realization she began to grow anxious, seeing that her tête-à-tête would be threatened. "Come, Ferdinando," she said, "this has gone on long enough. It is time to tell me what has happened, else there is no use in your being here."

She saw him shudder and make a great effort and he lifted his head and stared at her with eyes full of an anguish so apparent, she was shocked. Filled with a compassion for him that took her by surprise, she stroked his shoulder and wondered if all tenderness for him was after all gone. He was a good man, a kind man, and he did not deserve to be landed with a wife who showed no more regard for him than a stone. Perhaps for a long time now she had not been herself, had been in some way ill, and if she could be restored to her former state of mind she would find that Ferdinando once more would mean something to her. "Come," she said, squeezing his arm, "come, tell me." He closed his eyes and groaned, then pushed his great fists into them and a mumble came out of his mouth, which she could not at first decipher but the more she asked him to repeat it the less distinct it became. All she caught were the words "mistress" and "asleep." Slowly, she took her hand away and clasped it in her other one. Calmly, still not filled with any real foreboding, she repeated, "Your mistress is asleep? Well, it is not yet morning, it is good that she sleeps." And then he let out one more word in a great bellow— "Forever!" he cried. "Forever! Forever! She is dead, dead!" and he began beating his fists on the table and weeping loudly all over again.

She did not move or speak for almost a full hour. Dawn came, the first rays of sun sneaked through the shutters into the room, the first noises of people rising began, and still she sat at the table, a faint frown on her face. Now it was Ferdinando who was doing the pleading. His awful news once out, he had begun to explain in a torrent of words and gestures she seemed to ignore. At half past three Mr. Browning had woken him and told him to send the porter for the doctor because his wife was hallucinating. But he had gone himself and, to save time, he had charged through the streets of Florence and knocked up the doctor and brought him back himself. When they reached the Casa Guidi Annunciata met them at the door of the apartment and one look at her face had told them all—*"Quest'anima benedetta é passata!"* Annunciata had said. "Her blessed soul has passed to another world." He had seen her himself, he had gone in with the doctor and seen her at peace, her face that of a young girl's, and then, pausing only to make sure Penini still slept, he had come to tell his wife and take her to the Casa Guidi with him. His weeping at last in control, he urged her to rouse herself and come with him because they would both be needed that day in the house of mourning.

He was all action now and she was his puppet, allowing herself to be dressed and her hair roughly pinned up. She heard him rouse the new maid and give her instructions and she let herself be led away though her legs were uncertain things, moving of their own volition. He pushed her from behind up the stairs of the Casa Guidi and when they reached the apartment he all but carried her in. She felt she would choke as she was half dragged to the bedroom and put a hand to her throat, feeling the tightness there. Mr. Browning was there with Penini, both of them quite still and silent. Penini turned when he heard them enter but Mr. Browning did not move. As Ferdinando had described, his mistress looked young and beautiful. There was nothing hideous about her corpse, nothing that might terrify Penini—she did indeed simply look asleep. Her hair had been brushed and looked still alive and it was hard not to imagine the thick black eyelashes did not tremble a little. Ferdinando backed out of the room almost at once and Annunciata, who had been hovering at the door, went too, but Wilson became part of the tableau. She took her place beside Penini and when his arm went around her waist she put her own around his. They stayed in this worshiping attitude until suddenly Mr. Browning rose and said, "We must leave her. There are things to be done." He led the way out and Wilson had no option but to follow him and his son. She knew what the things were that needed to be done and could not bear to think of a strange hand doing them but nor could she answer for her own composure if she were to offer to do them herself.

It was not until they were in the drawing room and the woman who was to lay out Mrs. Browning had entered the bedroom, watched by Penini's curious eyes, that Wilson realized no one wept. Ferdinando and Annunciata could be heard in their quarters sobbing together, but in the drawing room not a tear fell. Mr. Browning was ashen-faced and exhausted-looking, but he was dry-eyed and held his head high. Penini looked bemused but his lovely face was not stained with grief and his eyes, though troubled, were clear. The two of them stood by the window, where, though the curtains were drawn, there was a narrow gap through which they could look into the street. Wilson saw Penini slip his hand into his father's where it was clasped firmly. They were bearing up admirably, for the moment. She waited, without the will to make the decision to go. It seemed wrong to say anything at all and in any case she had no words to offer. But while the woman was still busy in the bedroom Mr. Browning turned and sat down heavily and Penini was pulled down with him, leaving only her standing.

"Sit down, Wilson," he said softly, "sit down, I beg you." She sat, stiffly, on the very edge of a chair. "Well," he sighed, "it is all over. There was nothing that could be done, nothing."

Wilson said nothing, never taking her eyes off Mr. Browning's face.

"Papa," Penini said, "is Mama in heaven now? Is she there yet?"

"Yes, my son. And she will pray for us."

"Will we hear her?"

"No, Penini, we will not, but because we love her she will never really leave us."

"I loved her," Wilson suddenly said, coloring at the way she blurted this out. Penini left his father's side and came over to her, not running as he usually did, but walking the short distance slowly and purposefully. He took both her hands and said in tones that would have been comical if the circumstances had not been so sad, "And Mama loved you, Lily, you can be sure, and now I will love you for her, see if I don't."

The day was long. People came and went without Wilson having much idea who they were or why they had any business there. She stayed with Penini while his father went to arrange the funeral service, the heat being so fierce there could be no delay in burial. Miss Blagden arrived, trembling and red-eyed, and it was decided Mr. Browning and Penini would go to stay with her up at Bellosguardo for the moment. Wilson said she would remain to watch over the body, with Ferdinando and Annunciata in residence to support her. She could hardly wait for them to go. So far from fearing to sit all night with the corpse, she longed for the opportunity. It was twenty hours since she had heard the news and yet still not a tear had left her eye. She felt very weak and tired as she settled herself beside the bed, with only one candle lit, but also suddenly relaxed. There was no one now to watch her, no one whose own feelings had to be respected. There was just herself and her dead mistress. Ferdinando and Annunciata would no longer come into the room, scared that spirits might hover near the body, scared of death itself, but she had no such fears. That body was no more her mistress than the coffin which would receive it. It was a poor reminder, and that was all. But, in knowing this, Wilson also knew her mistress was still there in the very air of the room, in the belongings within it, in the books and papers everywhere in evidence. She hoped that during the night something would communicate itself to her and she sat, expectant, all her senses finely tuned and receptive to the slightest nuance. She watched the shadows the candle made, smelled the wax melting, picked up the faintest vibrations of the thin muslin curtains moving in the welcome breeze and catching on the lock of the shutters. About two in the morning, though she only guessed at the time, she took a turn around the room to ease her aching back and when she sat down again she sensed a change in the atmosphere. Unable to divine what it was, she willed herself to be open to whatever was happening. She breathed deeply and steadily, as Mother had once done, and closed her eyes and lifted her head. Any moment a hand might stroke her cheek or a whisper be made in her ear and she must not flinch. But neither touch nor sound came and presently the moment had gone. Then she wept, convinced she had failed, that an attempt had been made to reach her and she had let it go. She wept and wept until dawn and when there were no tears left she fell asleep with her head drooping onto the same pillow as the dead woman's. When she woke, she felt the cold, cold cheek against hers and moved away, repelled. It was, as Mr. Browning had said, over, all over.

CHAPTER THIRTY

ONE WEEK LATER Wilson felt moved to pick up a pen and hunt out some paper and ink. It was so long since she had written any kind of real, lengthy letter that she felt the pen awkward in her hand and could not get the nib to write smoothly, wasting two good sheets in the effort. The ink seemed too thick and the paper too rough and she became irritated with her own incompetence, but then at last she got into the way of it and once she had done so, once the rhythm of writing had been established, she felt a return of the old pleasure such correspondence had once given her and wondered that she could ever have given it up. She was able to confide in the writing paper in a way she had been unable to do ever since her mistress's death and it was the greatest possible relief to her. Down it all went, the shock of the death itself, the terrible numbness that had followed it, the aching sense of loss which nothing could fill and now, in the last day or so, the fear that her life had no meaning anymore and never had had ever since she had properly left her mistress's service. To Lizzie Treherne, the only one of her own status, who even now would remember the pull Mrs. Browning exerted, she chose to write:

—how cruel it was Lizzie to be even then that very day on the brink of a new understanding after those years of bitterness on my part which I cannot now think of without torment. I look back Lizzie and I cannot forgive myself for my resentment nor for seeking from her what she could not give. I think I worshiped her for too long to regard her as any kind of ordinary mortal and had come to believe she would always be as devoted to me as I to her. I made no allowance for how I had changed and become a trouble to her and held it against her that she was not willing to put me first in which I was woefully wrong. The seeds of these, my expectations, lay in those early years Lizzie, before we left Wimpole Street, when she made something of me until I came to believe I was *special* and then in the flight to Italy when without meaning to I laid at her door a debt and expected it paid in full. I had quite forgotten by then I was but a lady's maid and had come to see myself as her *friend*, to be treated as such. There is no such thing in this world Lizzie nor will there ever be, alas. Those who serve can never hope to breach the gap between themselves and those who are served and I ought to have remembered it. And yet there was something between us which was over and above the maid-and-mistress position and that is what I must cling to. What shall I call it, Lizzie? A sympathy, it was, a feeling, which at times crossed the barrier. There was a tenderness until her marriage which I treasured and even after it there were times when only I would do. Now all that has gone and I never expect to enjoy such a thing again. What I shall do with myself I do not know. Mr. Browning and Penini leave here at the end of this month—oh, Lizzie, so brave they have been! You would not have thought they could endure the pain of the funeral as they did, both so dignified and composed though their hearts broke. I cannot describe to you what the service was like for I hardly heard a word being transported in time to that other church where she married and in my dream noting nothing of this latest somber occasion. At the graveside I stood back as befitted my station and in truth did not wish to see the coffin go down or the earth fall on top of it. The streets were lined with mourners on the way there, all Florence seeming to know who passed and to weep. Mr. Browning and Penini stay at Miss Blagden's and make their preparations for departure. I have not seen much of them, not wishing to intrude on their grief, but I have heard Mr. Browning's composure broke down after the funeral and that he wept on Miss Blagden's shoulder many an hour saying he wanted she who had gone. Penini is all of a sudden a man and when I saw him I saw him with his mother's eyes and felt her sadness. The golden curls have gone and the silk and satin clothes, and before my eyes I saw a plainly dressed right masculine youth, proud of his masculinity. But he was not too proud to kiss me and behave toward me as he has always done and I saw that still inside himself he is the same and a credit to his mother's teaching. Mr. Browning has arranged everything for Mr. Landor's care and I have undertaken to watch over him as before and to inform Mr. Browning of any change. It is true the old gentleman's presence keeps me in Florence but then where would I go? Ferdinando stays too. He did not wish to leave his country again to live in France or England and Mr. Browning seemed content to let him go, not having any house as yet which he would need a servant for. He lives here with me for the present but must shift for himself before long since I have grown used to being husbandless and no longer have a taste for it. This will sound cruel, Lizzie, and I daresay it is and he the father of my children, but I cannot be what I am not and I no longer feel a wife. Mr. Landor is nearly ninety years of age and frail now, and quieter with it, and I will bide my time until his end comes which cannot be long, then I have a mind to return to England to the dear North and see if I have enough Englishness in me to make a life there. But this is a hazy notion and one I have entertained before in a romantic way and it may not come to pass. I am growing old and less able to uproot myself and yet I do not feel since my dear mistress left me that I can rest here. Mr. Browning is said to declare he will never return and that Florence with its memories is unbearable to him and I have a mind to agree. I see her everywhere Lizzie and sometimes I am sure it is not my imagination, but her very self. Yesterday as I crossed the Piazza San Felice I fancied I saw my mistress as she was eleven years ago when she was at her strongest after the birth of Penini and able to walk about wherever she wished. She smiled at me and looked so pretty and happy my heart almost broke and then she was gone and I was left shivering in the hot sun. And then today when to aid Mr. Browning I packed her clothes, Annunciata not wishing to handle a dead woman's garments, I thought I heard her laugh next door in the drawing room, and when I went to look I caught a glimpse of her in her white wrapper as she vanished onto the balcony. If this is a haunting Lizzie then I can only say it brings me comfort and that I am not afraid and would wish to be haunted thus every hour of the day and night. But I fear that in time it would drive me mad with the longing to go back into the past and that my nerves would not stand it and I would be wise to leave this place where she is for she will never leave it. Mr. Browning said to me I was to choose something of his wife's for myself not as a remembrance for he knew I needed no aid to my memory, but rather as a keepsake if I understood the difference which I do. I deliberated long over it at first thinking I might choose a shawl so that in wrapping it around me I might wrap something of her but the moment I came to pick up her clothes I could not keep hold of them they being too strongly affecting. I chose the best of these articles and on Mr. Browning's instructions had them boxed up to send to Miss Arabel. I could not of course have my pick of her jewelry which is precious and all of which goes by rights to Miss Arabel except for her wedding ring which her husband keeps to himself and a few other trinkets which he wishes to give to Penini in the hope that one day they will go to his wife. I fancied I might request a small oval hand mirror the same which I used to hand to her every day and upon the handle of which our two hands would meet in the exchange and it is a pretty thing with a frame of worked silver. But then again to look at my face in it would only cause me pain and I turned instead to a cup and saucer of pink and white china which was part of a set bought the week I started in service in Wimpole Street and out of which she drank her coffee. I felt in holding it I would have something of her in a comfortable way and besides I have always admired it. But there again it is very delicate and I would not dare to use it and it might be broken by Pilade. This left her books and her writing things and I knew every book to be valuable to Mr. Browning who would not expect me to choose such a thing and might be pained if I did and so Lizzie with some trepidation that I went too far I asked if I might have her little inkstand, one of several she used. Mr. Browning seemed surprised and seeing his surprise I was quick to say I had overreached myself and he must forget what I had requested, but he said I must have it and it was an excellent keepsake and that he was impressed I had thought to choose it. So now I write to you Lizzie out of her inkstand and it gives me great pride and pleasure. It is of a dark wood with a handle to carry it by and two square holes for the inkwells which are of crystal and have caps on hinges. There are two grooves for pens and a drawer to pull out and use for letters. The whole is not above twelve inches in length and eight in width and two or three in height and it is not heavy. Mr. Browning says it is one she bought herself or so she told him in Malvern when she was a girl and kept with her all her life though she had several others in prettier wood. It is a little chipped at the corners and the knob is missing on the drawer and there are several scratches made he says by Flush on the wood but it is solid and not likely to come to any harm. I like to touch it as I write and in the feel of the wood I have some comfort. Write to me Lizzie if only a line that I might know you are alive and well and have received this sad news.

As soon as she had finished this immensely long letter Wilson wished to start on another but could think of no one but Ellen to whom she might write. Minnie Robinson was dead. The black-edged card, telling her of this other death, had arrived while she was still struggling to accept Mrs. Browning's, and she had been shocked later to remember how little grief she had felt. She would have liked to write differently to Minnie but had no desire to share her sorrow with Ellen, to whom it was likely to be meaningless. It struck her as little short of tragic that no matter how hard she thought over her friends and acquaintances there was no one other than Lizzie to whom she could write the intimate kind of letter she had in mind. What, she wondered, did this tell her about herself, about her life? Friendless, she was friendless, and almost without family. Penini meant more to her, now his mother was dead, than any other human being except for her sons and soon he would leave her and another link would be broken. He was aware of this too and spoke of it with feeling.

"We are going to France, Lily," he told her, sitting holding her hand while Pilade sat on his knee and looked up admiringly at him. "But I am to have my pony, Papa says."

"Well, that is a comfort," Wilson said, "and it will be cooler in France, I daresay." It was a pointless thing to say but she knew she must part from him without emotion or she would burden him still further and increase his suffering. "Are you to go to the seaside?"

"I believe so. And Aunt Sarianna and Nonno will come with us."

"Well then, that will be company."

There was silence. Pilade kissed Pen and broke into a little song, which Pen joined in. They handclapped the beat and Wilson smiled at their enjoyment. Suddenly, Pen crushed Pilade to him and she saw there were tears in his eyes. It was hard to know what to say or do. Quietly, she got up and found some sewing.

"What will happen to you, Lily?" Pen said, his voice husky but the tears under control.

"Why, nothing, Penini. Everything will go on as before, as it always has done. Have no fears for me."

"Then I shall come back and see you, if Papa will bring me, and if not I shall come back when I am a man to see you, Lily."

"And what a fine man you will be, such as your mother would be proud of."

The minute she had said this, she felt it had been a mistake to mention his dead mother and was about to cover up, with some inquiry as to which part of France he and his father were going to, when he said, "What would Mama have been proud of, Lily? Tell me."

Wilson shifted uneasily. "There now," she said, "of you, of what you are and will become."

"But what? What will I become?"

"Who knows? A fine young man, honest and true, that is what I meant, and kind and good, as your mama was."

"And as you are, Lily."

"Oh, not me, Penini, I am not good."

"Are you bad then, Lily?"

"No, no, but I am of the common kind, there are many of me, and your mama was very special, some say a genius."

"You are special too, Lily, and I know none other like you."

"But you do not see me clearly, you are only a boy and I was your nurse."

He smiled at her, an odd little smile, half mocking, half sad, as though he knew a secret but would not confess it. His face was strange to look at these days, with an unsettled look, unsettled in feature as well as expression. The very skin of it was changing, the silky smoothness giving way to a duller finish with here and there the small blemishes of early adolescence. And his eyes, which had once seemed huge, now seemed to have shrunk and no longer dominated his face. It struck her that the next time she saw him, if she ever saw him again, she might not recognize him, that this half-formed man might change into an adult quite different from his boyhood self, the self that still lingered there.

"I will never forget you, Lily," he was saying, most solemnly. "Never. Will you forget me?"

"Never, never. You are written on my heart." It came out of her with such ease, she had no time to be embarrassed at her own fulsomeness. Once she had said it, she liked the sound of those words so much that she repeated them. "You are written on my heart, as your mama is."

"Did you love Mama, Lily?"

"I did. I loved her dearly. She was my life." Again, she had found herself uttering phrases which did not feel her own and yet which pleased her. The words were trite and she would have laughed at them coming from another, but her emotion transformed them.

But Penini was frowning. "Your life, Lily? Then is your life with Mama? Is your life over?" He looked troubled, almost panic-stricken, and she hastened to reassure him.

"No, no," she said, "it was but an expression, a feeling, to show what your dear mama meant to me."

"I have heard Papa say it, to Isa, and she said he must not think in such a way."

"And she is right. Your papa is still in the prime of his life and it is nowhere near over."

"Isa said to him he showed little faith in himself. She said Mama would be sorrowful to hear such words."

"She would, she would."

"And Papa said it was a momentary lapse and he had much to do in this life yet." Penini paused, his account of this conversation between his father and Isa Blagden up to now delivered in a monotone. His voice changed, became more tremulous, as he asked, "Will Papa ever be happy again, Lily, do you think? Can he be happy without Mama?"

"Why, of course, my love, as can you, as can we all, as we must be, for what use is it to bury ourselves in unhappiness? Think how it would grieve your mama, to know she left on earth those she loved who could no longer smile or sing because she had gone ahead to heaven."

To her relief, she saw him nod, and then sigh, and then, because too long ignored, Pilade claimed his attention by throwing a ball at him and they began a game which soon brought shouts and laughter from him. He *was* young, only twelve after all, and by nature a happy boy. Not for long would his desire to enjoy himself be suppressed. However deep the wound left by his adored mama's death, he would recover, whereas for his father the way ahead was more painful, less certain to lead to contentment. Already, the hurtful rumors had started and she had heard them herself. People, ignorant people, whom she despised, people were saying Miss Blagden was more than a friend to Mr. Browning and that they would not be surprised if within a year and a day there was a marriage. Fools. She had dealt contemptuously with that canard. And then they said, these same malicious people, that Mrs. Browning's death was a blessing in its way to her husband, who had long ago tired of her invalidism. That was worse than foolish, it was *wicked,* and she had said so. Who else knew except her? Who else had watched their love grow and flourish and endure? No one, no one had the certain knowledge she had and she would never betray it. No one would get from her any tales of disharmony because there had been none. Ferdinando might mutter that there had been disputes she had not witnessed these past four years and Annunciata might nod her head significantly and indicate she knew a few secrets Wilson was not party to, but both of them were misguided. It was not a matter of knowing of this disagreement or that but of knowing *them*, and know them she did.

Mr. Browning said as much before he departed from Florence.

"Well, Wilson, we have had a long attachment," he said. "How many years was it that you were in our service? Ten? Twelve?"

"Two when Mrs. Browning was Miss Barrett, sir, and eleven after her marriage if you count only the actual years of employment."

"Which we never did, for you rendered often more than service after Annunciata took your place."

"I tried to, sir."

"At any rate, now it is at an end."

"Yes, sir."

"I will be truthful, Wilson. I do not expect to return to Florence, it is too painful to me, much too painful."

"I understand, sir."

"I think you do, I think you do."

She saw his face constrict and was afraid he would weep, but he controlled himself and the moment passed. He looked thinner, grayer, less fit than usual, and instead of the pacing about which had accompanied all their interviews in the past he sat on Miss Blagden's sofa, quite still, his shoulders drooping. How terrible it was, she reflected miserably, not to be able to offer any adequate sympathy, not to have some word or gesture which might express her compassion. She could have taken Mrs. Browning in her arms, whatever the difference in their station, upon an occasion like this, but such a thing was impossible with Mr. Browning, with men.

"I will write," he was saying, "and have arranged with the bank for money to be paid for Mr. Landor."

"Do not worry about Mr. Landor, sir, I shall not desert him."

"I know you will not. You are far from being a deserter," and he smiled, a little wanly. "Will you stay in Florence, Wilson, when there is no longer a Mr. Landor?"

"I cannot say. There is nothing for me here, but what is there in England?"

"What is there for any of us in England? I ask myself that and do not know the answer. We must all do the best we can." He rubbed his hands together and slowly stood up. "Shall we shake hands on it, Wilson, on the future, whatever it brings?"

So they shook hands and she thought how the firmness of his grip belied the exhaustion of his appearance. There was a vitality and strength in it which made her see this man would recover as surely as his son, even if he had more from which to recover. She wondered, as she made her way home, what would become of him, whether he would go on to become the great poet his wife had known him to be, but which, as yet, the world did not seem to recognize. And as to marriage, she was not so sure as she had been. He was a vigorous man, a healthy man, a man not yet fifty, and the urges of the flesh might be fierce. But then she knew him to be a tender man, a sensitive man, and his love to have been very great. She felt bowed down with his grief and sense of loss and trudged through the hatefully hot streets, tense with his despair. How agonizing to be left alone, as he was left, left to suffer so. But then, as she entered her house and sank down onto a chair in the dark recesses of the kitchen, she began to feel a curious sense of disquiet. What was she doing, weeping for Mr. Browning? Why distress herself with his distress? It was what she had always done, taken upon herself the troubles of the Brownings as though they were hers and drowned herself in pity for them. But who did the same for her? Not Mrs. Browning, nor her husband, not ever. Even as the first edge of this realization sliced through her mind she felt guilty, as though she had no right to the thought, as though she might be chastised and found out. It was an unworthy thought, surely, a resentful, selfish one, suggesting she held it against her former employers that they did not value her as she valued them. Half fearfully, she pondered over whether it were true and, if it were, whether it was fair. Was she entitled to feel cheated that she had never received what she had gladly given? She was a servant, they had been her master and mistress. Was it not outrageous to have expected any evenness of sympathy? People would say it was, that she had got above herself and must suffer accordingly, that she had no right to feel disappointed.

But it should not go on. Sitting there, alone, knowing that at this very moment Mr. Browning and Penini were boarding the train to leave Florence, to leave her behind very likely forever, she saw that it could not. It had to end somewhere and here and now was as good a place as any. She had tried before to escape from the trap in which her own adoration and loyalty had caught her and she had failed. Now she had a new chance. The trap had been sprung. Mrs. Browning was dead. Mr. Browning and Penini had gone. It was up to her to walk free of all of them.

She rose uneasily from her chair. It was time for Mr. Landor's lunch to arrive from the *trattoria* and she still made a practice of being the one to carry it in to him. She hovered near the door and when the boy appeared bearing the tray with its dish of fragrant chicken she took it and walked up the stairs. She had never resented bearing trays or many another task rejected by ladies' maids, who considered that sort of thing too menial, and she had always been liked for it. How I like to be liked, she thought, how I crave approval. It even pleased her that Mr. Landor now positively liked her and could manage a smile most days instead of throwing a dish at her head. He was sitting near the window today, peering out as though expecting someone, but there was no likelihood of visitors.

"There you are, sir," she called, "chicken, your favorite dish, and as hot as you like it, judging from the steam."

"Browning has gone," Mr. Landor said dejectedly, "he has left Florence."

"I know he has, and he said farewell to you." She went close to him and thought how frail he had become, skin and bone where once he had been so powerful. "But you must not worry, sir, you will be well cared for."

"That does not concern me," he said irritably. "It is the company I want, the company of a good mind, and where now shall I find that?"

"There are other minds in Florence, I believe," said Wilson, a little dryly.

"Well, I do not know them and none are like Browning's and that little wife of his." He paused and then looked up at Wilson, rather afraid. "She is dead, is she not?"

"Yes, sir, this last month past."

"Ah, the pity of it, the pity, and myself so ready to go in her place." The tears streamed down his face, but noiselessly. Wilson let them continue, knowing how little it took these days for them to fall.

"It was God's will, sir," she said, "and we must all bear up. Now come, eat your chicken." She removed the cover and to encourage him took a forkful and put the fork in his hand. Dismally, he stuck it in his mouth and made some attempt to chew and swallow, but once he had disposed of the mouthful he returned again to the subject of Mrs. Browning's death.

"You were her servant, were you not, from Wimpole Street days?"

"I was, sir. I went to her in April 1844 and was in her service in one way or another up to her death." It was not quite true but she wanted it to be.

"And was she a genius?"

"That is something I know nothing of, sir, but people who knew about poetry praised her highly."

"And did you?"

"Sir?"

"Praise her highly—do I not speak clearly enough? Are you deaf?" It was a flash of the old Landor and Wilson smiled to see it, noticing the chicken was now being devoured hungrily and with speed.

"Of course, sir. She was a good woman."

"What in heaven's name is a good woman? I have never met such a creature in my life. Women are pretty or talented or kind or gentle if they are not altogether horrible, but as for *good*, it is a nonsense."

"You go too deep for me, sir. I only know Mrs. Browning was never mean or wicked or cruel and to me that is good, what I mean by good."

"Then I expect you were blind."

"How would that be?"

"Servants are. Sometimes it suits their purpose to be so but mostly they cannot see what is at the end of their noses. They are too afraid of giving offense and losing their place. Never trust a servant's opinion of a master or mistress, and yet there is the irony, you see, for they are likely to know most, they have seen and heard what others have not. But they are all either idolizers or cheats so no good comes of it and I hate the idolizers most."

He was in fine fettle by now, waving his fork around and raising his voice and altogether enjoying himself as he pontificated to his audience of one. Wilson knew he did not really know to whom he addressed himself and that it did not matter. She left him still eating heartily and went back down the stairs to make ready for Pilade to be brought back from his outing with his father. But as she sat in the shade of the doorway looking out into the street, Mr. Landor's words, however absurd she had thought them at the time, nagged at her. Had she seen what was at the end of her nose? Had she recognized Mrs. Browning's faults and marked them well? Hardly. For a brief period she had been aware the lady was not perfect in relation to her, but whom had she blamed for that? Herself, mostly. And even now, thinking like that seemed too terrible to continue, too blasphemous to contemplate. Did this make her an idolizer? It must. Mrs. Browning had been her idol and she wished her to stay that way. What good could come of destroying her idol when she was dead? The last thing she wanted to do was examine the reality of her idolatry and discover she had wasted the best part of her life on it.

It was tiring to be thinking back and forth in this foolish way. She wished she did not think at all. That was the best way in life for a servant, not to think, to work, to obey and never, ever, to question why. And she must stop referring to herself as a servant. She was not a servant. She had not rightly been in service for the last four years. She ran a business, and ran it with moderate success. She was beholden to no one. As the proprietor of a boardinghouse she might be a working woman but she was *not* a servant. How strange, then, that this gave her so little pleasure that the joys of independence, or a sort of independence, seemed muted. Perhaps, if things had been otherwise between herself and Ferdinando, they would have meant more to her. She saw him now, coming down the street holding Pilade's hand. His farewell to Mr. Browning and Pen had been far, far more emotional than her own—oh, the sobbing, the evidence of a broken heart! She had thought he might at the last minute throw himself in front of the train bearing his beloved employer away. He looked utterly downcast, was not replying to his little son, who she could see was chattering away. Here was a man not disposed to ponder any Landor-like statements on the nature of service, a man quite unworried by the slur of being a blind worshiper. Ferdinando questioned nothing, was only miserable because he was now deserted. She could feel, as he came closer, the hardness gathering in her.

"They have gone," Ferdinando said as he came in, and he spread his arms wide in that gesture of helplessness she knew so well and had come to despise.

"Then that is over," she said sharply, "and we must get on with our lives, which I for one will be glad to do."

"What life is there?" her husband said with such deep gloom that if she had not been so irritated by it she would have laughed out loud.

"Plenty," she said, "unless you are quite without spirit."

"I am without anything," and there was another melodramatic gesture of despair.

"Oh, what nonsense," she snapped. "I should be ashamed to say such a thing and so ought you. Tomorrow you must go in search of a new situation. You have Mr. Browning's references safe? Well then, a king himself would employ you with such evidence of virtue. You will soon have another hero in your life to keep you happy and it will be Mr. this and Mr. that and you will hardly notice the change."

He looked at her in such bewilderment that she had to turn aside and busy herself washing Pilade's hands to hide her sense of shame. She did not know what made her speak to her husband so viciously when he had done so little to deserve it, but so often now she could not help herself. "There is some food in the kitchen," she said, her back still to him. "You may help yourself if you will." If he touched her, she would shrug him off but mercifully the lure of the proffered food distracted him. "I have new lodgers today," she said, "and must see their rooms are ready. Come, Pilade, it is siesta time." She left hurriedly with the child and put him on his bed and lay down herself. Ferdinando, who could sleep anywhere, in any circumstances, would slump in the kitchen but in case he sought her out she bolted the door.

A fine thing, to bolt one's door against one's husband in the middle of the day, and she chided herself for it. But the door stayed bolted.

She did not expect to sleep, so tormented was her poor mind with these doubts and accusations as to Mrs. Browning's perfection and her part in it, but she slept deeply until there was a persistent tapping at her door. Drowsily, she raised herself up and, leaving the still sleeping Pilade on the bed, she opened the door to the kitchen girl, who had come to say the new lodgers had arrived and wished to see her and were waiting downstairs. Hurriedly, Wilson washed her face and tidied her hair and wondered how late it was.

The new lodgers sat stiffly in the little sitting room, a man and a woman, both middle-aged, both dressed in black. They appeared hot and flustered but then to travel any distance at all in the heat of an Italian July and at the hottest part of the day was to invite suffering. She saw at once that they were at the end of their tether and said, "Welcome to this house, sir, madam, and please allow me to offer you some iced tea, which will be brought directly." Their faces relaxed instantly—it never failed. She kept a store of tea specially for English visitors, who were always charmed and reassured that they had come to the right place. Knowing better than to make conversation, Wilson poured the tea into glasses and, decorating each glass with the thinnest slice of freshly cut lemon and a tiny sprig of mint, which she grew in her own yard, she offered the weary travelers the drinks. The man drank thirstily, with no pretense of refinement, and the woman more slowly but still with more gusto than elegance. Then Wilson led them to their rooms on the first floor at the back (at the front were Mr. Landor's, which she explained as she showed them in). These rooms were hardly splendid but they were cool and immaculately clean. Wilson waited for the woman to draw her finger surreptitiously over the surface of the dressing table or peep at the sheets while pretending to rest—she had seen it done countless times and relished it, knowing no fault could possibly be found. But neither man nor woman made any attempt at examining their quarters, merely expressing themselves pleased, and said they would rest at once.

Back in her own kitchen, where she was used at that time of afternoon to begin supervising preparations for supper, Wilson found herself wondering about the new people. A Mr. and Miss Hargreave, brother and sister, come to her through Miss Blagden, as so many of her guests did. She could tell from their accent they were from the Northeast of England and when a little time had gone by and it would not feel too familiar she had promised herself the pleasure of discussing that part of the country with them. They were bound to know Newcastle and possibly the Graham-Clarkes and the northern branch of the Barrett family, and perhaps even Fenham where she had been born. But even without this connection, they intrigued her. It was the wrong time of year for such visitors and they did not have the air of being here for pleasure. She wished she had inquired of Miss Blagden who these Hargreaves were but now, with Miss Blagden departed with the Brownings, it was too late. There was something familiar about the woman but she could not imagine what. She had never known anyone called Hargreave, surely, neither in England nor during her years in Italy. The interest this couple kindled in her made her look to the next few days with less loathing— she would not quite be marking time but have this small voyage of discovery to make, a voyage having nothing to do, she thought, with the Brownings.

But in the event, it had. By the following week she had realized why she had appeared to know Miss Hargreave. It was nothing to do with the Northeast: Miss Hargreave and her brother, though not so regularly, had attended the Regent Street chapel where she had gone all those Sundays while she lived in Wimpole Street. They had never of course spoken, or sat next to each other, but many a time, according to Miss Hargreave, they had passed each other in the aisle. It was she who revealed this without any questioning from Wilson, who would never have been so impertinent. And she was shy about it. "I do believe, Signora Romagnoli," she ventured one morning at breakfast, "that we are not entirely strangers to each other."

"Why, madam, I had exactly the same thought myself," said Wilson, quite delighted to be so drawn into a conversation, "and I thought that since there were indications you and your brother were from the Northeast of England, where I am from, that I must somehow have seen you, perhaps visiting a house where I was in service?"

"Ah no," Miss Hargreave said, smiling. "Not in the Northeast, though you are right, we come from Scarborough. No, it was in London, in the Regent Street chapel."

Wilson's astonishment was genuine. "And you noted *me* there, madam?" she asked. "How can that be? I was a shy servant girl and quite unnoticeable, I am sure, even more than I am today."

"But I knew whose maid you were," Miss Hargreave said, blushing deeply. "Miss Elizabeth Barrett's." She spoke the name reverently and cast down her eyes. "I am devoted to her poetry," she whispered, "and to everything to do with her."

Wilson contemplated the woman before her with a mixture of exasperation—it was annoying to have such a prosaic solution to the mystery—and pity. She had seen this kind of admiration before and many was the time her mistress had made fun of the likes of Miss Hargreave. Mostly such ladies had written to her, letters Wilson remembered of quite embarrassing flattery, but occasionally they had turned up at the house, seeming to find no shame in begging to pay their respects to Miss Barrett. Always, they had been turned away and often she had had to do the turning. Perhaps she had even seen this Miss Hargreave off but, if so, she could not recall the occasion. She would not bother asking how it had been known she was Miss Barrett's maid—these adoring disciples had their ways and means and she knew it was quite likely she had been watched pushing her mistress in the park and then trailed from the house to the chapel in the vain hope that by being near her they would be nearer to their heroine.

"Well," she said, "I was never more surprised in my life, but I admit you were by no means the only one who doted on Mrs. Browning."

"And now—now she has been taken!" Miss Hargreave declared with a passion that startled Wilson. She did not approve of such a display, it was quite inappropriate, and frowned when she saw tears in her lodger's eyes.

"Yes," she said, stiffly, "Mrs. Browning is dead."

At the word "dead," Miss Hargreave covered her mouth with her handkerchief to stifle her sobs. Wilson was about to say something,

something she was afraid would come out sharp and unsympathetic, when Mr. Hargreave, who had breakfasted earlier and gone for a walk, came into the room. Seeing his sister in tears, he said, "Now, come, Victoria, you promised there would be no weeping, you promised most faithfully. If you are to get yourself in a state of hysterics we will pack and go immediately."

"I am sorry, Charles, only it was Signora Romagnoli saying she was—saying a word I cannot abide."

Mr. Hargreave raised his eyebrows inquiringly and Wilson said, not at all apologetically, "I merely confirmed Mrs. Browning was dead, sir, which everyone has known for a month."

There was another anguished cry at the same word, which Wilson had used quite deliberately, and Mr. Hargreave said angrily, "Victoria! You have been warned—we shall pack our bags and go if this continues and there will be no visit to the Casa Guidi or to the cemetery."

So that was their game. Wilson supposed she should have guessed it would begin soon, that ladies such as Miss Hargreave would come on a pilgrimage to Florence and visit the grave of their heroine to pay their last respects, but she had been unprepared. What they got out of it she could not imagine, but when Miss Hargreave came back from her visit to the Casa Guidi, which was not yet occupied after Mr. Browning had vacated it and where an obliging porter, palm crossed with silver, no doubt, had allowed her in, she appeared transfigured.

"Oh, to have stood in the room where she wrote *Aurora Leigh!*" she exclaimed. "Oh, Signora Romagnoli, you cannot guess at the ecstasy!"

"No, I cannot," said Wilson dryly.

"And to be in the room where she gave birth to her son—it was heaven, it was bliss!"

"It was a long day, a long night," Wilson said, her mind of its own accord conjuring up images from that time.

"You were *so* blessed," Miss Hargreave said, "to be with her, to be at her side, to *touch* her . . ."

"Oh yes," Wilson said, "I touched her. I washed and dressed her and soothed her brow many a time. She always said none had my touch."

"*So* privileged!" Miss Hargreave gushed.

"Privileged?"

"To have been her maid—I would have died for the honor."

All that day Wilson went about her work bemused by Miss Hargreave's attitude. It ought, she felt, to mean something but quite what she had not decided. There she had been, coming to the conclusion that the best part of her life had been wasted serving the interests of a woman who had never really appreciated her finer points, a woman who had pulled back from true friendship with her maid, while being proud to think she offered it, and now along came this rather silly but undoubtedly sincere woman to tell her that on the contrary she had been privileged and honored above all others. Which was the truth? And was it of any consequence? It was only when Miss Hargreave came back from the Protestant cemetery that she began to think she knew the answer. The young woman was in tears, naturally, but her brother, permanently discomfited by his sister's sentimentality, was kinder than usual since now he really could pack his bags and instruct his sister to do the same—his job was over and tomorrow they would return to Scarborough. Wilson made them tea and he left to begin organizing their departure.

"There was only a mound," Miss Hargreave whispered, "such a *little* mound, and nothing other to mark the spot."

"There will be a fine memorial in time," Wilson assured her. "Mr. Browning took a deal of trouble over it and the artist is commissioned."

"Not even a flower laid there," Miss Hargreave said, "but I placed some white roses at her side."

"They will shrivel in a few hours in this heat," Wilson said, "and that is why there were none there."

Miss Hargreave seemed a mite offended and said, "I do not care if my roses do not survive. They are there for the moment and were to express my sorrow and my admiration." She paused, dried her eyes, took a sip of tea and went on, "You appear untouched by this tragedy, Signora Romagnoli. I wonder at your calmness. Had I been her maid I would have been quite distraught for months after, I am sure, and wishing to throw myself into that grave with her I loved."

"Well then, madam, you would not, like me, have had two children to think of, perhaps, and as to throwing myself into my mistress's grave, the very idea would be repugnant to her, I assure you. She knew what grief was, true grief, and she knew the strength of life and went with it as long as she could, as I will. And now, madam, I think your brother is in haste to be gone and if you like I will help you make ready."

Miss Hargreave looked stricken and seized Wilson's hand. "Oh, forgive me," she said, "I did not think, I spoke stupidly, and I see I have angered and hurt you. Can we not be friends after all?"

Wilson watched the Hargreaves go, an hour or two later, with a curious sensation of there being a bond between her and that emotional woman. She felt she would see her again though they had nothing in common except Mrs. Browning. Miss Hargreave had been most insistent she should take her address in Scarborough and had said that should she ever return to the Northeast she must be sure to look her up. When Wilson, for the form of the thing, had demurred and pointed out the impossibility in England of such socializing between their different classes, Miss Hargreave had impressed her with the vehemence of her reissued invitation. It was all a little odd but the genuineness of feeling was there. She had inquired most kindly of Wilson's personal circumstances and, hearing the tale of Oreste, which had not been told now for some time to a new person, she had been interested and concerned. She had reason to go to East Retford the following month and would, she vowed, call on Ellen and then write to Wilson. The thought of such a letter filled her with so much hope and joy that she all but kissed Miss Hargreave on both cheeks.

That was all that anyone needed in life, Mrs. Browning had often said, a little hope, a little joy. For too long, Wilson reflected as she put Pilade to bed, I have looked backward, fearing to look forward, but it can and must be done. Her life was far from over. She would have Oreste brought out and would endeavor to make for herself a new world in which the center was not Mrs. Browning. Never again would she tie her life to another person in quite that way but would seek to stand on her own more truly than had ever been possible. And perhaps, after all, it was her mistress's teaching, in ways too subtle and complex for her to analyze, that had in the end given her the insight to see both what she had once made of herself and what she must now seek to make of herself. Her days as a lady's maid, which even when they were actually over she had refused to accept as finished, had died with her lady. Now she could be herself and not poison what was left of her life with regrets and resentments. The yoke was lifted, and what she had been required to do and be, under it, should have no relevance to her future. She was a lady's maid no longer.

AFTERWORD

Fᴀᴄᴛ ᴀɴᴅ ꜰɪᴄᴛɪᴏɴ have been threaded so closely in this novel that it might help to know exactly how much of it is based on truth. Elizabeth Wilson was a real person, born in 1820 in or near Newcastle upon Tyne, and she did indeed travel to London in April 1844 to become Elizabeth Barrett's maid. She had a mother and sisters who are known to have lived in or near Sheffield and one of those sisters, Ellen, did live in Carol Gate, East Retford, after Wilson went to live in Italy. It is true that Wilson went to Ellen's for the birth of her first son, Oreste, and that when she rejoined her husband and the Brownings a year later she left her child with Ellen. The details about Pilade's birth and Wilson's new occupation as boardinghouse keeper in Florence are true, as is her relationship with Walter Savage Landor. All the information comes from Elizabeth Barrett Browning's letters. There are no surviving letters from, or to, Wilson, although they are known to have been written. Wilson's two youngest sisters, May and Fanny, are inventions, although she is known to have had other sisters. The circumstances of Ellen's marriage are also imaginary.

Wilson's life after 1861 changed dramatically again, just as it had done in 1846. Oreste finally joined her in Florence in the summer of 1862, but in 1864, after Landor died, Wilson, most surprisingly, returned to England, to Scarborough, where she set up a lodging house. Her husband Ferdinando does not seem to have joined her and I have been unable to establish whether she took her two sons with her. In any case, she was soon back in Italy, destitute, after the Scarborough venture ended in disaster. Robert Browning, for old times' sake, made her an allowance of £10 a year, though making it clear that he felt no obligation to do so.

It was Pen Browning who became her savior. In 1887, when he was thirty-eight, Pen married an American heiress. They bought the Palazzo Rezzonico in Venice which Pen restored and furnished. This became the home not only of Wilson but of her husband Ferdinando, who had turned up in Venice working as a cook for an American family. Ferdinando died in 1893 but Wilson survived to move with Pen to Asolo after his wife left him. Here the two of them lived, devoted to each other, until Wilson's death in 1902 (Pen died ten years later). Wilson was remembered as recently as the 1950s by people in Asolo who had seen her wandering over the countryside, talking to herself. What she talked about—presumably all that had happened to her since 1861—might someday be the subject matter for a sequel to this novel.

ABOUT THE AUTHOR

Born in Carlisle, England, in 1938, Margaret Forster has published fourteen previous novels and is the author of four biographies, including the award-winning *Elizabeth Barrett Browning*. She lives in London and is married to writer and journalist Hunter Davies.